His
Wife
Leaves
Him

His
Wife
Leaves
Him

———

STEPHEN DIXON

FANTAGRAPHICS BOOKS

Someone knocks on his classroom door. "Come in," he says. It's his department secretary. "Excuse me for interrupting your class, but you have an urgent phone call." "My wife?" "No, a man." "He say what it was?" and she says no. "Let's take a ten-minute break now," he tells the class. "You've heard; I got what's supposed to be an urgent phone call, so if I'm not back in twenty minutes, let's say, or make it thirty, next week's writing assignment and the readings from *Short Shorts* will be posted on my office door." "Where's your office again?" a student says, and he says "This building, room four-forty." "Does that mean we won't be critiquing my story today?" another student says. "Because last week we also never got around to it," and he says "I don't know; please, let me go," and he leaves with the secretary. "The caller didn't even hint what it could be?" he says, as they walk to the department's office. "Maybe he meant 'important' instead of 'urgent,' and it's good news; an award or nomination of some sort for my last book. Well, one can always dream, right?" and she says "No hint; nothing. He just said to get you." It's someone from a local hospital; his wife had a stroke while riding an exercise bicycle at a health club and was taken by ambulance to Emergency and is now in ICU. "Took us a while to find out who she was, since nobody at the club knew which locker her belongings were in, and then to reach you, since she's unable to speak." "Oh, geez; she only joined that all-women's club last week. Before, she was in mine. I'll be right over." She's hooked up to tubes and monitors and something to help her breathing, seems to be awake. "Darling...sweetheart," he says when he first sees her.

"I'm here; you look fine; you're going to be okay," and takes her hand, but she doesn't give any sign she knows he's there. He sits by her bed for as long as they let him—fifteen minutes an hour for about ten hours a day; sleeps on a recliner by her bed for a few nights after she's moved into a regular room. She gets stronger and more alert, goes through several weeks of in-patient rehabilitation, and comes home. She's paralyzed on one side of her body but gets back most of her speech. "Look at me," she says. "Four months since my stroke. I still can't do a thing for myself or anyone else. I can't hold anything without dropping it. I try to walk with a walker, I get three feet before I feel I'll fall." "Look, that was some blow you took. It takes time, sweetie, time, and you have to admit you're a hell of a lot better than you were a month or two ago. And from when you were discharged? —We won't even mention what you were like when you first went in. I couldn't have hoped for anything so quick. But back to normal? The doctors say what?—a year, year and a half from the time you had the stroke—but I'm sure, the way you're going, it'll be much sooner." "I'm sorry I'm such a burden on you," and he says "What are you talking about? I'm happy to do whatever I can for you. Really, it's a privilege to help you, my darling." "Oh, I know it's not—how could it be?" And he says "Have I ever complained once? You know me. I can be impatient and I get frustrated easily, but I've never been angry at you concerning your condition or that it's taxing me in any way or keeping me from my work. What can I do to make you believe me, get on my knees?" and he does and hikes up her skirt and kisses her kneecaps, and she laughs and says "All right, stop, I believe you; I just needed a bit of convincing. Thank you." So he can teach and hold office hours and do other things like write at home and shop and go to the Y to swim and work out a few times a week, he has caregivers looking after her every weekday afternoon. Weekends, if one of their daughters doesn't come down from New York, he takes care of her all day himself. Sometimes it's hard—getting her started in the morning, lifting her out of bed or into a chair, her incontinence a couple of times a day, cleaning up when she spills some drink or food or knocks a mug or plate off the table—and he thinks, "God, not again; I don't know how I can do this anymore, but what's the alternative?" or looks at her and thinks "Come on, you're a smart woman, so show some brains. If you know you're not going to be able to hold something, have me do it for you." Or "If you know you're about to shit or piss, tell me, so I can get you on the toilet or a bedpan under you, because you just make things worse," but never says anything or makes any kind of face that shows how he really feels. All he says is something like "That's okay, that's okay, don't worry about it; this is what paper towels and those latex gloves are for. Complete recovery takes time, as I've said, but you're definitely getting there. Each day there's a little improvement, I mean it." "I wish I could see it." It takes a few more months for her to work herself up to walking from their bedroom to the living room with just a walker, and a couple more months, about the same distance with just a cane. "You see?" he says, "what did I tell you? Although the truth is, which I didn't want to say a while back because I didn't want to discourage you, I never in a million years thought you'd progress this fast," and she says "I actually do now feel things are finally getting better for me. I can't wait till I no longer need anyone's assistance, and then can walk without the cane." He always walks beside her in case she starts falling, which she sometimes does, and he always catches her. She also doesn't drop or spill things as much, and goes for days without being incontinent and weeks without an accident. When she does have one, she says things like "Oh, dear, look at the trouble I'm causing you; I'm so sorry," and inside he's seething, thinking of all things he hates doing most—piss, he can handle—but this; it's so goddamn messy and time-consuming. But after one accident, he says "Damn you, can't you give some warning when it's about to happen and then hold it in till I can get you over the potty?" and she starts crying and he says "Don't; stop it; just let me get the job done. And I didn't mean it. I'll never say anything like that again." "But you'd think it," and he says "No, I wouldn't. It just came out, as if it wasn't even me saying it. It had nothing to do with my being on my best behavior and suddenly losing control. I know you're not responsible for what happened and you want to make things as easy for me as possible, and for a few seconds I was a total putz. Please forgive me." "Okay, though I wouldn't blame you for thinking it. Just hearing it is what makes me feel so bad." She has another stroke, same side, a few months later, shortly after she began walking around the house with a cane without him having to stay beside her, but this one a lot worse. She recovers much more slowly than she did after the first stroke, goes through months of physical and occupational and speech therapy, first when she's in the hospital and then as an out-patient, but she still can't walk a step with a walker, even with his help, and spends most of the day in a wheelchair. "Try pushing it yourself," he says, six months after she comes home—he wanted to say it sooner but held back— and she says "I can't. I can barely feel the wheels when I try to grip them. I have no strength left for anything, and my speech is still so terrible that I'm not even sure you understand a word I say." "Oh, I understand; I'm hearing everything you say clearly, and I'm not being sarcastic. But just try, once, pushing." "I have. Lots, when you weren't looking. Maybe I need to exercise my arms and hands more, but I don't have the strength for that either." She's depressed almost constantly. Getting up: "What am I getting out of bed for?" Eating: "What's the use of food? Just means more time on the toilet and all the problems that go along with that." Working on her voice-activated computer: "I used to be a thinker, and now I can't think straight. And there's no project I once wanted to do that I'll ever be able to finish." Talking to their daughters or her friends on the phone: "Tell them I'm busy or sleeping or too tired to talk. I just have no desire for petty talk or conversation." Sex: "No feeling: no interest. I know, though, how much of a deprivation it is for you." Going out for lunch or what he calls "a walk": "Why should I let myself be the object of other people's stares and pity?" Listening to books on tape: "I can't keep up with the story or lecture anymore." Watching a DVD movie at home: "They used to be enjoyable when I was healthy and had some hope of recovery. Now everything I do and see tells me how sick and feeble I am and that I'm only going to be worse." When he says "Come on, give me a smile, will ya?" she says "Would you be smiling if you were me, even one on demand?" "Sure, because, you know, it doesn't help either of us if you're always bitching about your condition and how weak you are and moping around all day with your all-suffering down-in-the-dumps face. I'm sorry: that was mean." She's already crying, and he says "Okay, okay, I said I'm sorry and I meant it. It was stupid of me." "Oh, you apologize and you apologize and you apologize, but don't once more tell me you didn't mean what you said. As I've already told you: I'm a drag and a drudge and you should get rid of me," and he says "And then what would I do with myself? Can't live without you, so shove that thought right out of your head." "I don't believe you. But for now, just to make myself feel a little bit better and to show you I don't think of myself as utterly hopeless, I'll accept it not as a lie." He bends down—she's in her wheelchair—and hugs her and kisses the top of her head. She hugs him back around the waist and says "Thanks. I feel better but I'm not going to smile, even if what I just said could be construed as funny. But you really would be better off if I were gone and you were free to take up with another woman, one who wasn't in a wheelchair." "What did I tell you? I don't want anyone else. And if anything, God forbid, did happen to you where you got much worse, there's no chance I'd hook up with someone else. So get healthy, you hear?" She can do less and less for herself over the next year. He has to feed her most of the time, hold the mug or straw to her mouth so she can drink, catheterize her four to five times a day because she has no control over her bladder and gets lots of urinary tract infections, turn her over on her side and back several times a night, force her out of bed at ten to ten-thirty in the morning, or else she'd sleep till noon or one. "Gwendolyn. *Gwen*. Come on, get up, open your eyes, you're losing the entire day." Don't say anything to make her feel bad, he keeps telling himself. Don't make things even worse for her. "I mean, you can do what you want, but I'd think you'd want to get up now, am I right?" She opens her eyes, looks at her watch on her wrist and says "But what am I doing? I can't see these little numbers, even with my glasses. What time is it?" "Past ten," and she says "Let me sleep another hour. I got to bed late." "You got to bed around eleven, which is when you normally start conking out," and she says "Please, twenty minutes longer. And give me a very tiny piece of Ambien so I can sleep, because I hardly got a wink in last night." He usually says "No, I gave you more than enough last night, and since you snored half the night, you obviously got plenty of sleep. You get more Ambien, you'll sleep till the afternoon." She sometimes says "Don't be such a dictator," and he says "I'm not. I'm just doing what I think's the right thing for you. I don't want you to waste your life away in bed. And I know what you're going to say. Okay, twenty minutes; no more," and he leaves the room, reads or goes to his typewriter in the dining room, comes back half an hour later and changes her, exercises her legs and feet, swings her around and sits her up so her legs hang over the side of the bed and massages her shoulders and back and neck. Every other week or so—doesn't want to do it more or else she'll think he's only massaging her for this— while she's sitting up in bed and he's massaging her, he drops his pants or takes his penis out of his fly and says "If you can, could you play with it while I work on you? I can use a little pleasure too." She tries to, while he rubs her breasts under her nightshirt or continues massaging her, but she usually can't grab hold of it, even after he wraps her hand around it, or she pulls it a little and then her hand slips off and she tries getting it back on or he does it for her. "It's good exercise for your hands too," he says, "right?" and she smiles and he kisses her head or bends her head back and kisses her lips and says "Anyway, for the time you were able to do it, it felt good." Then he raises his pants or puts his penis back in his fly and massages her some more so she knows he did it as much as on the days he didn't get her to play with him, and lifts her onto the wheeled commode and unlocks it and gets her into the bathroom. Once, after struggling to get her from the commode into the wheelchair, he says "I hate saying it but it seems to be getting increasingly hard for me to lift you. Maybe you've gotten a little heavier the last year, although you don't look like you have…in fact, I bet you've even lost a few pounds. Or else it's the dead weight of your body that's making transferring you so hard…that you're not helping me because you can't." "Use the Hoyer lift like the caregivers do," and he says "And then what? I'm to spend ten to fifteen minutes getting you in and out of the lift sling seven to ten times a day? Who's got time for it? And also, just turning you over in bed at night isn't getting any easier either. Let's face it, all that's becoming harder for me because I'm getting weaker with age, no matter how much I work out at the Y, and I'm scared to think what it's going to lead to. Dropping you on the floor, which is all we need, for how would I get you back up?" "The lift, if only you'd stop being so stubborn and learn how to use it," and he says "You'll teach me at the time, if anything like that does happen. But I'm worried, I can tell you, and you'll also probably get hurt in the fall, and then there'll be more to do and further complications. Oh, God, everything is going from bad to worse, when things are supposed to let up a little as I get older. I'm not supposed to have so many responsibilities. What a freaking mess to look forward to." "Then put me in a nursing home and be done with it," and he says "I don't want to, would never want to, and besides, though this isn't the reason I wouldn't want to, we can't afford it. We can afford twenty hours of caregivers a week, and the rest has to be left up to me. That's all right, I don't mind, and you'd be miserable in a nursing home, thoroughly depressed and bored, and deteriorate quickly rather than getting better or just staying the same as you are now." "Please, you know I'm getting worse by the day," and he says "You're not; don't say it. If you were, do you think I'd be so, I don't know, calm about it?" and she says "Yes, as an act. But you give yourself away enough for me know what you really think." "What I really think is that you're getting better, and I selfishly say thank goodness to that, for in a few years I'll be the one who's sick and weak and you'll be fully recovered and will have to take care of me," and she says "What B.S." "Look at her, my wife of almost twenty-five years; she called me a bullshit artist. Believe me, I would never fool you, baby; never." "I pass." About a month later, after he gets her into bed, she looks like she's going to start crying, and he says "What's wrong now? I was a little rough with you getting you on the bed?" and she says "No, you were fine; it's just that there's no sense to any of this." "What do you mean?" and she says "Will you stop saying you don't understand? What the hell do you think I'm referring to?" "Don't yell at me. Not after all I do for you. Look, life isn't so great for me either. I'm not comparing our situations, but there's a lot of work for me to do and, in case you don't know it, it gets frustrating and hard and a little tedious for me too." "I'm sorry. You're right. And I won't disturb you anymore tonight. Please turn off my light and cover your shade. I want to go to sleep." "Oh, boy, are you angry at me for what I said," and she says "Not true. I'm only angry at my body. Please, the light." A few weeks later, after he gets her ready for sleep and is about to get in bed himself, she says "Don't get angry—please—but I'm afraid I need changing." "What, ten minutes after I catheterized you? You're just imagining it: you've done that before. Or you don't want me to get any rest in bed, right?" And she says "Will you check?" He feels inside her diaper and says "Jesus, how did that happen? You're so wet, I'll have to change the towel and pads under you too." "Could be you didn't catheterize me long enough; sometimes you're too much in a rush to get it over with," and he says "I kept the catheter in till I saw a bubble go backwards in the tube. That's always been the sign you're done. What do I have to do from now on, catheterize you twice a night, one after the other? I've done enough tonight; I just want to get in bed and read." "I'm sorry. If I could avoid this, I would," and he says "Try harder to avoid it. Think; think. If you feel it coming, say so, goddamnit, and I'll get you on the commode without you soaking the bed. I should really just let you lie there in your piss…I really should." She starts crying. "Oh, there you go again," he says. "Great, great." He turns around, slaps his hand on the dresser and yells "Stop crying: stop it. Things are goddamn miserable enough." She continues crying. Without looking at her, he says "I need a minute to myself, but don't worry, I'll eventually take care of you," and goes into the kitchen and drinks a glass of water and feels like throwing the glass into the sink but puts it down and bangs the top of the washing machine with his fist and yells "God-all-fucking-mighty, what am I going to do with you? I wish you'd die, already, die, already, and leave me in fucking peace." Then he thinks "Oh, no. I hope she didn't hear me; it's the worst thing I've ever said." He stays there, looks out the window at the carport, has another glass of water and rinses the glass and puts it in the dish rack, turns the radio on to classical music and thinks "Ah, what the fuck's the use?" and turns it off in about ten seconds and thinks "She still needs to be changed, so get it done and go to sleep," and goes back and says "Okay, I'm here. A few minutes was all I needed. Tried listening to music to change my dumpy mood, but who the hell wants to listen to music." She says "What you said out there—what you shouted—that is how you feel, isn't it?" "What'd I say? I stubbed my toe in the kitchen on the door frame. That's what happens when I think I can run around barefoot from one room to the other in the dark. So I said out loud—maybe yelled—'Goddamnit,' and other stuff, that's all." She says "You hoped that I die. Don't try to get out of it. 'Die, already,' you said, 'die.' You could only have meant me." "I never used the word 'die.' You're hearing things. Besides, what makes you think you can hear clearly from this room to the kitchen? If I remember correctly, and this isn't completely exact, I yelled 'Goddamnit, you stupid fool,' meaning myself; that I'm the fool. For banging my toe. But really the whole foot. It still hurts." "You're lying. You're fed up with helping me, and who can blame you? You've done it longer than should be expected from anyone. Or else it's become too much work for you because I've gotten much worse. But you should have told me calmly, not the sickening way you did, and then we could have worked something out to get other arrangements for me. I would have understood." "No, you're wrong," and she says "Please change me and the towel before I pee some more and you get even angrier at me and maybe hit me instead of whatever you hit in the kitchen." "I'd never do that to you; please don't think there's even a remote possibility of it. And try to believe I was only yelling at myself over the pain in my foot that nearly killed me. You know what the hell a stubbed toe's like." She looks away and shuts her eyes and he says "Oh, well, you're never going to believe me tonight, but it's the truth, I swear." She still doesn't look at him. "Okay," and he changes her, gets the wet pads and towel out from under her and puts clean ones down, says "Which side you want?" and she points and he turns her on her side so she's facing her end of the bed, covers her, says "Are you comfortable?" she doesn't answer, "Is there anything more you want me to do?" with her eyes shut she shakes her head, he turns off their night table lights, dumps the wet pads and towel into the washing machine and thinks should he do a wash? Are there enough clothes in it for one now? Nah, save it for the morning, when there'll probably be more wet pads and towels, and the noise might keep her up, and washes his hands in the kitchen and gets into bed. "Why don't you sleep in one of the girls' rooms tonight?" she says. "I don't want to be in the same bed with someone who hates me and wants me dead." "You're being silly and a touch melodramatic, Gwen. I never in my life said or thought such a thing. I'm here to help you. I'd never say what you're accusing me of because I'd never feel it even in my worst anger to you, which, by the way, I was to you a little before—angry—but nowhere near to the extent you said." "Do what you want, then. But don't try to touch me, and sleep as far from me as you can." "Without falling off the bed, you mean. —Okay, no time for jokes. Anyway, now you're really being punitive, keeping me from doing what I love most, snuggling up and holding you from behind in bed. But okay. Goodnight." Doesn't say anything or look at him. He gets on his back and thinks What the hell does he do now?

Stupid idiot. If he had to say it, to get out some anger, why so loud? Now she'll be like this for a couple of days no matter how much he apologizes. She heard. He only made it worse by trying to make her think she didn't. Of course he doesn't want her to die. She can't believe he does. "Maybe I should sleep in one of the other rooms," he says. "I want to do what you want. I don't want my sleeping near you to make you feel even worse." Waits for a response. None. "You asleep or just ignoring me?" Nothing. "Say something, will ya? You're not giving me a chance. Isn't it possible— isn't it—that you might've misheard? —Listen, if you don't say anything I'm going to assume you're asleep and my presence here is no longer bothering you." Just her breathing. She might be asleep. Good sign, if she is, that she wasn't so disturbed by what he said that it kept her up. "I'd love for you to say, though I know you're not going to, that you're so unhappy, and not necessarily because of what you think I said, that you want me to hold you. And it's not, you understand, that I want you to be unhappy just so I can hold and console you, by…okay. I better drop it. I'm getting myself in deeper, I think. I just have to hope I didn't make you feel even lousier by what I just said. Put it down to my being dopey." She hear him? By now he's almost sure not. He yawns, thinks Good, he thought dozing off would be more difficult, shuts his eyes and is soon asleep. Wakes up about three hours later to turn her over on her other side, then around three hours later to the side she fell asleep on, then around two hours later on her back, which is what he does every night and at around the same time intervals, give or take an hour. From what he could make out in the dark, her eyes stayed shut all three times. It's now six-thirty and he tries to sleep some more, can't, dresses, does some stretching exercises in the living room, gets the newspapers from the driveway and reads one while he has coffee. Looks in on her at eight, just in case, although it's early for her, she's awake and wants to get up. She's still sleeping on her back. Usually she snores a lot in that position, but he hasn't heard any. He goes for a run—a short one, as he doesn't like leaving her alone, asleep or awake, more than fifteen minutes—showers and shaves in the hallway bathroom, and a little after nine, right after he listens to the news headlines on the radio, he goes in to wake her, or else she might complain he let her sleep too long. What he doesn't need, he thinks, is for her to get angry at him over something else, especially when she just might wake up feeling much better toward him. She's surprised him a few times by doing that; mad as hell at him when she went to sleep and pleasant to him in the morning, where he didn't think he even had to apologize to her for what he'd said the previous night. One of those times she even grabbed his penis in bed and pulled on it awhile without him having to ask her to. Then she got tired and stopped. "That was so nice," he said. "I wish you had continued and there was more of that, not that I'm not satisfied with what I got," and kissed her—tongue in mouth, the works, and she kissing him that way also for about a minute. Then he put her hand back on his penis, but she said "I can't. No feeling left in that hand anymore, and the other one's useless." Anyway, best behavior today, okay? From now on, all days. Even to the point of being oversolicitous to her, because he has to take care of her better and wants to convince her that his bad moments and irrational outbursts are behind him. He just has to make a stronger effort, and keep to it, to make sure they are. Now he doesn't know if he should wake her. Eyes shut, face peaceful, covers the way he arranged them when he turned her onto her back: top of the top sheet folded evenly over the quilt. "Gwen? Gwen, it's me, the terrible husband. Only kidding. It's past nine o'clock. Not a lot past, but I thought you might want to get up. You usually do around this time. If you want to sleep or rest in bed another fifteen minutes or so—anything you want—that's all right with me too. I've got about fifteen minutes of things to do in the kitchen and then I'll come back. Gwen?" One eye flutters for a moment but otherwise she doesn't move. She normally would by now after that amount of his talking. At least open her eyes to little slits and maybe mutter something or nod or shake her head. "Are you asleep or falling back to sleep? Does that mean you didn't sleep that well last night, although you seemed to have. I turned you over four times at night, more times than I usually do, and you didn't seem to have wakened once." Doesn't give any sign she heard him. "I'll let you sleep, then, half-hour at the most, because we both have to get started sometime," and leaves the room, but a few steps past the door, thinks "No, something's wrong; she's too still and unresponsive," and goes back and says louder "Gwen? Gwen?" and nudges her and then shakes her shoulder, moves her head from side to side on the pillow, puts his ear to her nostrils and throat and chest and then parts her lips and listens there. Knew she was breathing but wanted to see if there were any strange sounds. None; she's breathing quietly and her heartbeat seems regular. But it might be another stroke, he thinks. This is how it was the second time; came into the room, couldn't wake her up. Pulls her legs, pinches her cheeks and forearm, pushes back her fingers and toes, says "Gwen. Gwendolyn. Sweetheart. You have to get up." Calls 911 and says he thinks his wife has had her third stoke. "Anyway, she isn't responding." While he waits for them to come, he kneels beside the bed and holds her hand and stares at her, hoping to see some reaction, then stands and puts his cheek to hers and says "I never meant any harm to you last night, I never did. I blew my top, but it was only out of frustration, all the work I do, one thing after the other, so exhaustion too. But I was such a fool. Please wake up, my darling, please," and kisses her cheeks and then her eyelids and lips. They're warm. That could be good. Straightens up, holds her hand and looks at her and thinks wouldn't it be wonderful if her eyes popped open, or just slowly opened, but more to slits, and she smiled at him and said "I don't hold anything against you. And I'm sorry if I frightened you. I was very tired and couldn't even find the energy to open my eyes and speak," and he said "I was so worried. I thought you had another stroke. I called 911. I'm not going to call them off. I want them to check you over, make sure you're okay. That is, if you don't mind. Oh, God, how could I have acted the way I did to you last night." "Don't again," he'd hope she'd say. The emergency medical people ring the doorbell and he lets them in. He leads them to the back, tries to stay out of their way, thinks he didn't hear a siren before they came. Maybe the absence of one's a good sign too. By what he said on the phone, they didn't think it that serious. No, there must be another reason for no siren. That there was one but they turned it off when they got to his quiet street because they no longer needed it. They work on her for about ten minutes, say she's in a coma and they're taking her to Emergency. He says "I'll go with you, if it's all right. If not, I'll follow." He thinks, as they wheel her out on a gurney, that if she dies he'll never tell anyone what he said to her last night. That he took out of her whatever it was that was keeping her going. That he killed her, really. He holds her hand in the ambulance taking them to the hospital and says to the paramedic sitting next to him "If she doesn't come out of this, then I killed her by telling her last night, when she was awake in bed, that she'd become too much for me and I hoped she'd die." The woman says "Don't worry, that wouldn't do it, and she's going to be just fine." "You think so?" and she says "Sure; I've been at this a long time." "She's suffered another major stroke," a doctor tells him in the hospital, "and because of her already weakened condition, I have to warn you—" and he says "Her chances of surviving are only so-so," and the doctor says "Around there." He calls his daughters, stays the night in the visitor's lounge. She's in a shared room in ICU and they won't let him be with her after eleven o'clock. "Even for a minute?" and the head nurse says "I'm sure she wants you there. It's the other patient who might be disturbed by your back-and-forths." Next afternoon he's feeling nauseated because he hasn't eaten anything since he got to the hospital, and says to his daughters "I gotta get something in my stomach; I'm starving. I'll be right back."

He runs to the elevator, gets off it and runs to the cafeteria, gets a sandwich, unwraps it and wolfs half of it down while waiting on line to pay for it, thinks maybe he should get a coffee too, he's tired, and goes over to the urns, thinks no, he hasn't time and he'll have to walk slowly with it or it'll spill, and runs back to the ICU with the rest of the sandwich, hurrying down the stairs instead of taking the elevator. His daughters are standing outside her room and the younger one says—the older one bursts out crying—"Daddy, Mommy died." "Oh, this goddamn fucking sandwich," he says, and throws it down the hall, and says "What am I doing? Why am I such a jerk?" and goes after it and picks up all the pieces and the plastic wrap the sandwich was in and looks around for a trash can, doesn't see one in the hall, goes into the men's room a few feet away and dumps everything in the can there. He washes his hands and goes back to his daughters, both are crying now, and says "I'm sorry, for everything," and hugs the younger one from behind while she's hugging her sister. When did she get so tall, he thinks, for he used to tower over her and they're now about the same height? Two doctors come out of the room, or they seem like doctors to him, white lab coats, stethoscopes around their necks. One walks over to them and says "Mr. Samuels? Dr. Bender. Because of the shock of the news, I'm not sure how much of what Dr. Kahn and I said was absorbed by your daughters before, so I'd like to also provide you with a few details of your wife's death and what efforts were made to try and save her," and he says "They're smart, they understand everything, much better than me, so they'll fill me in. Thank you for all your efforts," and the doctor says "Our condolences, then, in your deep sorrow," and goes down the hall with the other doctor, reading something on a clipboard he's holding. "I don't want to know," he tells his daughters, "and I'd forget whatever he said. She died of a stroke; they said her chances were slim; she was very weak to begin with; that's all that's important." "Maybe someday," Maureen, his younger daughter says, and he says "No, no day; never tell me. And I'm sure I'd immediately forget what you said too. Don't ask me why—I don't know myself—but I'm inured, and always have been, to those kind of facts and terminology, so you needn't bother." Just then a nurse comes over and says "Your wife and mother's to be moved to a private room so you all can be alone with her," and he says "My wife and mother?" and Rosalind, his older daughter, says "Daddy." "No, I really didn't know," he says. "Excuse me." Soon after, a body's wheeled out of the room and past them, completely covered by sheets. "That her?" he says to the nurse steering the gurney, and she nods. They follow the gurney to a single room at the end of the hall. The two nurses and aide who brought her into the room stay there, door shut, for about fifteen minutes, probably to clean her up, brush her hair, put a fresh hospital gown on her, make her look better than she did when she died, he thinks. Or maybe they did all that in the other room. If they brushed her hair, what brush did they use, since she didn't come in with one. He'd like to have that brush. He'd put it in his dresser drawer, the top one, where he keeps his socks and handkerchiefs and underwear. Stick it in a ziplock bag first. Take it out every now and then, touch the hairs still there, maybe smell the bristles. The nurses and aide come out, the aide pulling the gurney behind him, and they go in and he shuts the door. People can still see inside through the large window in the door, but it'll be quieter this way. Rosalind's holding his hand—when did she take it? He thinks—and he says "My sweetheart, no slight, but let's do this individually," and slips his hand from hers and then thinks What did he mean? And she could have only been holding his hand to help him. Did he hurt her? He doesn't want to look at her and see if he did, and it'd be too confusing to her if he now took her hand. He'll try to explain it later to her. He looks around the room, out the window to the trees across the road, at the television set on a platform suspended from the ceiling, at a poster across from her bed showing the sequence of smiling and frowning and grimacing faces of pain, then at Gwen. She's on her back on a regular hospital bed, sheet folded over her shoulders the way he did the covers yesterday morning after he got her on her back, her head on a pillow. She looks like a corpse, he thinks. The bedrail closest to the door is raised all the way, the other's down. Must be for a reason, other than the nurses and aide forgetting, why both rails aren't one way or the other. But what's he thinking about that for? His daughters kiss her forehead and say things to her he can't hear. He goes around to the other side of the bed so they all won't be crowded at one side and looks at her and says "This is so, so… something. It's hard to see her like this," he says, without looking up at his daughters, "Not only my eyes, because of the water, but just hard, difficult to take. One day she's alive—not well, but wide awake and talking and even for a few minutes, cheerful. I forget what it was. Some joke I made. I wish I could remember it. And the next day, or day after the next—I'm losing track—she's like this, dead. I've had enough. I've said goodbye. That's what they shooed us in here for, right? Said it yesterday. I knew she was going to die. No clear-cut reason. There was a change in her. And it's not that she was suddenly dramatically worse. I just had a feeling. Okay, I'll kiss her forehead." He kisses it, looks at his daughters and says "Please permit me; I can't do this anymore. I'm also confused. I've never felt worse," and leaves the room and shuts the door and cries outside it. Hands over his eyes, deep sobs, for a minute, even less, and then wipes his face with his handkerchief, swallows hard because his throat aches and neck feels tight, and waits for his daughters. He looks down at the floor. If he had a book with him, one he was interested in, he'd read it, but he didn't take one when he left the house. Maybe the first time in fifty years he left the house without a book he was reading or planned to start. Oh, there had to be other times, and he's not talking about activities like jogging or grocery shopping, but even there he usually has a book with him in case he has to wait on a long checkout line. And he didn't take one when she was rushed to the hospital after her second stroke. Like this time, he just never thought of it, or he thought it the wrong thing to do, looking for a book for later on while the emergency medical team was working on her. But he even had one at his parents' funerals. Maybe even two if he was near the end of one, but books small enough to fit into his jacket pockets. Would he really read now? Well, he thinks he would. He hates hanging around with nothing to do and looking up and seeing people looking at him. Some of the patients and their visitors and most of the staff on the floor must know his wife just died. "Please," he says to himself, "nobody come over and say how sorry you are for my loss." His daughters come out ten minutes after he did. Ten, fifteen: about. "You kids okay?" he says, and Rosalind hunches her shoulders, Maureen shakes her head, both are wiping their eyes. "But you're done now?" and Rosalind nods. "I really had a stupid thought while waiting for you. I wanted to have a book to read to pass the time." "I apologize we took so long," Rosalind says. "No, it's not that; please don't think it. It was just, I'm saying, such an odd thought to have so soon after Mommy died. Where'd it come from? I don't know. I even thought of the book I wanted to read and why. Of course I never thought of taking it when I left in the ambulance with her. The biography of a writer I like. I'd go right to the pages—my favorite part in all biographies of writers—where we're approximately the same age, if the writer's lived as long as I have at the time I'm reading the book, and if he hasn't, then to the last years of his life. I like to see how he conducted himself then and where he was in his work and getting it published and the reception to it or if he stopped writing for a while after so many years at it or just gave up. Or, like Melville, switched mostly to poetry, although he did write that last short novel that was found after he died—I can't remember the title. My mind's a blank. I know it rhymes with mud." "You're being facetious," Rosalind says; "trying to cheer us up." "No, I'm serious; I wouldn't say anything light now. And the writer I wanted to read about lived well into his eighties. Parkinson's. Died of pneumonia. Anyway, crazy, those thoughts at such a bad time, huh?" and Rosalind says "I don't think so. I've had some weird ones today too." "Same with me," Maureen says. "Thanks," he says. "That reassures me, for you girls are anything but…well, something. You're commonsensible and sane. I guess we should tell them we're done with the room. We'll all go?" They head for the nurse's station, but a man comes up to them and says "Mr. Samuels? And I assume these are your daughters," and gives his name and says he's an administrator for the hospital. "And of course my condolences for your terrible loss, and from the entire hospital," and his daughters thank him. "I know it's so soon after, but we have to think about what you want done with Mrs. Samuels' body. Do you have a funeral home to contact? If you don't we can provide you with a list of reputable ones: nondenominational, religious, whatever you prefer." "Not necessary," he says. "She specifically asked me, though I've no documents to prove it—not that I'd think I'd need them—that she be given to science," when she'd told him a couple of times the last two years that if she dies before him, and it's almost certain she will, she said, she wants to be cremated and a box of her ashes buried in their garden under the star magnolia tree where the boxes of her parents are. "No monument; no marker; just that," she said. "If you can't or won't do it, ask the girls to." Rosalind says "Didn't Mommy want to be cremated? That's what she told me. And her ashes buried near the ashes of Grandma Gita and Grandpa under… what's that white-flowering tree in the garden by the circular driveway called?" "Star magnolia?" he says. "That's it. The flowers come up early and sometimes stay around for only a week. But that's what she told me. I quickly cut her off and changed the subject because I didn't want to think of her dead and her ashes and all that, but I remember." "Did she say that to you too?" he asks Maureen. "It seems familiar," she says, "but I can't say for sure." "It's something you don't forget," Rosalind says, and Maureen says "I think it was you who told me she said it." "When did Mommy say this to you?" he says to Rosalind, and she says "A while back. I believe it was right after her first stroke. She was feeling very vulnerable then and she also said she didn't think she'd live that long, another thing I didn't want to hear. Poor Mommy." "She was wrong, though, wasn't she? She didn't live long enough, that's for sure, and 'poor Mommy' is right, but she lasted much longer than she thought she would and her last two years weren't entirely morbid and empty. In fact, we had plenty of good times together. Anyway, that's what I meant when I asked when did she say that. She might have expressed an interest in being cremated at one time. But the last year or so she told me numerous times—I don't know why so many, for it wasn't as if I wasn't going to do what she said—that she wanted her body, for whatever good it'll do organ recipients and research scientists, and she was dubious it'd do any good to either, donated to science." "So," the man says, "unless there's any disagreement on this, I think your father should have the last word. But we have to move fast. Several of her organs need to be removed within hours and frozen or put on ice or they can't effectively be transplanted." "Okay with you girls?" he says, and Maureen says "If that's what Mommy said she wanted, it's all right with me," and Rosalind says "I have a bit of a problem with there being nothing left of her to cremate and bury, which means nothing in the garden for me to go to when I want to be close to her like that, but I'll go along with the two of you." "We could arrange something to be picked up by a funeral home and delivered to a crematory," the man says, and he says "Let's leave it as it is. It's sort of against what she wanted—which was, all of her donated—and it also sounds too gruesome. I wouldn't be able to get it out of my head, knowing the ashes of a cut-up part of her were down there. I'm sorry, girls, if I'm being too graphic here, but that's how I feel." He goes with the man to an office to sign release papers. Leaving the office, he thinks Should he go back to the room and see her alone a last time? No, they've probably wheeled her away by now and he'll never be able to find her, and the kids are waiting. Now she's really gone, he thinks when he leaves the hospital with his daughters. "What do we do now?" Maureen says; she's holding on to Rosalind's arm as if if she didn't, she'd fall. "Are you okay?" he says, and she says "I'll live." "Are you angry at me for some reason?" and she says "Why would I be angry at you?" "Just, your tone. I was mistaken. Well, as awful as this might sound to you both, we still have to eat. I know I'm so hungry I feel sick again. We'll go to a quiet restaurant, if we can find one, and talk about Mommy and what a horrible two days it's been, or just not say anything." Rosalind says "It was all so cut-and-dried—whatever that dumb expression is…settled, final, so soon after she died, in like two hours. And now there's no more of her, or will be, and she's gone forever, and it upsets me. I couldn't eat." "I was thinking the same thing about the swiftness of it," he says, "but what could we do? That's how hospitals operate. Let's go home, then, and find something, or I'll get some prepared foods for us at Graul's and whoever wants to eat with me, can. But I know I need to be with you girls today and I'd think you'd want to be with me." "We do," Rosalind says, "and I might have something." Lying, lying, that's all he can do and what he's best at, he thinks, driving them home. He should have done what Gwen wanted, but couldn't. He'd look out at the garden or walk along the driveway and see the spot her ashes were put and think of what he yelled out about her that night and how sad and demoralized she must have felt and what her face must have looked like hearing it. All because he couldn't keep his big stupid mouth shut. She'd be alive now if he had, he's almost sure of it. "Anyway," he thinks, "I'll never be sure if what I said didn't kill her." His daughters want to have a memorial for her, invite relatives and friends here and in New York. "It's too much to ask of people," he says to Rosalind on the phone, "to come that far, if they're in New York. And if we don't invite them and they get wind of the memorial, they'll feel left out." "We'll leave it up to them," she says, "but her friends and some of her former colleagues in Baltimore will want to come." "Besides, Mommy didn't want a memorial, funeral, anything like that." "She said so?" and he says "Not recently, but one time. The subject of cremation came up, but not depressingly. This was, of course, long before she said she wanted to be donated to science—maybe even before her first stroke. I joked 'Dump my ashes into a storm drain during a heavy storm, or down a toilet and then keep flushing till they're all gone.' And she said something like 'Mine you can scatter around the garden as fertilizer, but first find out if it's good or bad for the plants. If it's bad,' she said, 'then just leave the ashes at the crematorium for them to throw out.'" "She said that? It doesn't sound like her." "I said she said something like it. I forget her exact words, but the ones I used were close, or at least the idea of what she said is there." "Probably like you, she was joking. Mommy could be very funny." "Nope, she was serious but only might have said it in a jocular way. I remember then saying something to her like 'Really, what do you want done with your ashes if it ever has to come to that?' and she said 'Just what I said.' Strange conversation to have but we had it." "Okay, but we're not talking about a funeral or burial, Daddy, or what she wanted done with her body after she died—we covered all that when we left her at the hospital. What Maureen and I want is a memorial for her, something simple and tasteful where people speak about her and perhaps Maureen and I can read some of her poems, and then refreshments after at the house, if that's all right with you." "You didn't let me finish," he says. "Or let's say, I wasn't finished. After your mother said that about her ashes, or her cremains, I think they call them, she said she also wouldn't want there to be any kind of memorial for her either. 'Nothing programmed or ritualistic,' she said, 'where people have to come together over me. If they want to do that,' she said, 'they can do it in a natural and less formal setting and where their feelings and thoughts about me come out spontaneously.' Those were almost her exact words—maybe exactly what she said. No, that would be impossible. But I remember saying 'I don't know why you're asking me this. Because I'm so many years older than you and don't take as good a care of myself as you'—so this would have to have been before her first stroke—'I'm sure to be the first one to go, much as I'd hate,' I said, 'leaving you and the kids.' Then, like you, sweetie, I said 'Let's stop talking about this. It's too damn depressing and macabre!'" "Maureen and I sort of anticipated how you'd take to the memorial idea," she says, "so we've already decided to have one, with or without you. I'm sorry, Daddy." "It'll have to be without me, then. I love you girls and respect what you're doing and see the value in it for you and everybody who'd want to attend, but I don't want to go against your mother's wishes and what she specifically asked me not to do." "Then we'll rent out a private room in a restaurant for the memorial and refreshments, which could be done informally," and he says "No, that'll be too expensive. Hiring out a room in a restaurant? Hiring out any place. And the high cost of restaurant food and booze, for they won't let you cater it from the outside or bring in your own food and beverages. Okay, I'll come and you can use the house and I'll pay for all the food and such if you take care of cleaning up after. Nah, I'll use Dolores, the woman who cleans the house every other week; I'm sure she'll be free on a weekend. You just arrange the memorial and buy all the stuff you need and tell me what it costs and then see to your guests. One thing, though: don't expect me to say anything at it, please." While a few of Gwen's friends reminisce good-humoredly about her at the memorial in his living room and his daughters talk about her and read some of her shorter poems, he remembers how terribly he treated her, not just that last night with what he shouted out, but for months, maybe a year, before she died. At the table, when she dropped a fork with food on it and then her spoon, he said "Can't you hold a simple eating utensil anymore? Look at all the crap you spilled on the table and floor, and on your clothes," and he slapped some food off her lap. "I can't keep getting on my knees and cleaning up after you." "I'm sorry, I can't help it," she said. "My hands aren't working." "Well, get them to work," and she said "Wouldn't I love to." "So what does that mean, I have to feed you from now on?" and she said "For the time being, I'm afraid you'll have to if you don't want to keep cleaning up the mess I've made." "But I do enough. This, that and the other thing, and then something else. You've got me coming and going all day. But I especially don't want to get into the habit of feeding you because you've given up and expect me to do everything for you and you don't concentrate on doing the easier little things like sticking your fork into a piece of sliced-up meat or even signing you name. Concentrate harder and you'll be able to control your hands better," and she said "That's ridiculous, contrary to everything you know about my condition. All right, I won't eat," and she pushed her plate away. He said "Forget it; you always win. Have I said this before? Even if I have a dozen times, I'll say it again: 'The tyranny of the sick.' Here, let me help you," and he got some spinach and chicken salad on a tablespoon and shoved it into her mouth. She said "Too hard; you hurt me, and you'll break my teeth," and he said "Sorry, didn't mean to," and fed her that meal and most of the ones after that, and from then on usually had to stick her pills into her mouth and hold her special large-handled plastic mug to her lips so she could drink them down or just when she wanted something to drink. "Uh-oh," she said another time, and he looked up from the newspaper he was reading and saw she'd torn the temples off the eyeglasses she was trying to put on. "God, nothing's safe in your hands," he said. "Now I have to take you to the eyeglass place for new frames, and also the goddamn expense. Why didn't you break the lenses while you were at it?" and she said "I tried but it was too hard," and smiled. "Big fucking joke," he said, "big fucking joke," when he knew he should just smile back to make her feel better, and she said "You used to have such a good sense of humor. It helped us both in situations like this. I even remember my mother saying 'You married a real funny guy,' and that my own sense of humor had improved since knowing you. What happened? Where'd it go?" and he said "I don't find much that's funny anymore when it entails more work for me and time. Let's get the damn frame business over with, what do you say? If we leave in a few minutes, we can be there before six, when I think the place closes." "Good, because I'm lost without my glasses. But there are some preparations we have to do before I'm ready." "Preparations, always more preparations. Always more work; always more for me to do, till I have no time for myself. And these chores are never when the caregiver's here, or hardly ever." "That's not true," and he said "Yes, it is. It's almost as if you plan it that way so I can work my ass off for you. Oh, how did I get myself into this?" and she said "If you stop complaining and help me, we can be ready in half an hour and we'd make it in time. Though maybe you should call the place first. It could be a late night for them and we wouldn't have to rush and you to get all upset." "I don't want to call. I don't want to do anything. What I want is for you to stop making me do all these things." And she said "I'll try but there's no guarantee. In fact, the opposite might be the case." "What's that supposed to mean? Not only your coordination and dexterity, but get your head under control too." She shut her eyes, turned the wheelchair around and wheeled herself out of the room. "You can wheel yourself okay, when most times you say you can't, so why you telling me you're having such a tough time with your hands?" How could he have acted like that? How could he have? Getting her dressed—something like this happened a number of times—he'd say something like—she'd be in her wheelchair or on the commode—"Try to get your arm through the sleeve," and she'd say "I can't; it's stuck inside." And he'd say "Damn, can't you help me even a little with this?" and pull her hand hard at the other end of the sleeve and she'd wince from the pain and say "What are you trying to do, wrench my arm off? Go easy, will you?" Or he'd put her shirt over her head and jerk her head or neck forward so he could get the shirt all the way down in back, and she'd say "Don't pull me so hard; I'm in enough pain without you straining my neck." He'd say, he almost always said, "I'm sorry, I didn't mean to," when he knew sometimes he did because of something she'd said to him before or because he wanted to get these chores over with so he could get to or go back to his work. She'd yell from their bathroom—this also happened a number of times—"Martin, can you come here, please?" He'd usually yell back "Give me a few minutes; I'm right in the middle of something," and she'd usually say "I need you right away; please." He remembers one time going to the back, telling himself "What the fuck is wrong now? Always something," and seeing her plastic mug on the bathroom floor and juice or tea around it and her dress wet in front. "It fell out of my hands while I was drinking from it," she said. "I think you'll have to change my dress." "One thing at a time," he said. "First the floor, then you, or else my feet will get wet from your mess and track up the bedroom carpet when I walk on it." He took a towel off the shower rod and she said "Don't use a clean towel." He said "It's not clean; you used it yesterday," and she said "Then a 'good' towel. Use paper towels or a rag." "I'll use what I want to; I want to get this over with. What the hell you think we have a washing machine for?" and she said "Please hurry, then, and take care of me. I'm getting cold I got myself so wet." "Want to know something? It's what you deserve for being so clumsy." He thinks: "Did I really say that? I said it." "It's what you deserve for being so clumsy. Maybe next time you'll be more careful, though I'm not counting on it." And he wiped up the juice or tea on the floor, went into the kitchen with the towel and put it in the washer, came back and got her dress off and said "Let me get rid of this." "Is that what you did with the dirty towel? I'm cold. Get a dress on me first and then deal with the wash. You're only trying to punish me for the mess I made," and he said "I'm not. I don't know where to put the wet things." "In the sink here." He put the wet dress in the sink and got a clean dress on her, pulling her head forward to get it through the neck hole and tugging the dress down in back too hard and tearing it a little. "That was smart," she said. "How many dresses of mine do you want to ruin?" and he said "I'm sorry. It was an accident." He didn't act like that all the time, he thinks. Most of the time he wasn't rough and did what she asked without complaining, or not out loud. "Martin will you help me, please?" she said another time. He was working in the dining room and said "Damn, 'Will you help me, will you help me, will you help me?' I help you all the time. All right; coming." And he went into her study—he didn't think he said any of that loud enough for her to hear, except the "All right, coming," and said "So what's wrong?" She was using her computer's voice-recognition system and said "My computer froze. Could you press the reset button, please?" and he said "Sure," and did it, and she said, "Thanks. A kiss, a kiss," and he pulled her chair back and moved the microphone away from her mouth and kissed her and then wheeled her back in front of the computer. He left the room and thought her computer's just going to freeze again and she's going to ask him to reset it and this is what happens five to ten times a day when she's using it. "Get a new computer," he should tell her, "or stop using them." But this is the way he should treat all her requests: don't argue or look like he's cross or say he hasn't time. Do it quickly and without protest or sarcasm so she doesn't feel she's a burden on him. Remember that next time. Another time, she was in the wheelchair and said "Can you change me, please?" he said "You always need changing. Do you realize what it entails?" "Of course I do. It's a lot of work and I wish you didn't have to do it, but it needs to be done." "It entails getting you on the commode, taking your pad off without hurting your crotch, maybe cleaning the piss off the floor that leaked out of the pad before I could get it into the trash can, waiting around for about five minutes till you're done peeing and sometimes a lot longer, putting a new pad down on the wheelchair if the towel on the cushion isn't wet. If it is, changing the towel, and if you've soaked through the towel and the cushion cover's really wet, getting a clean cushion and putting the soiled cover into the washer. Then lifting you onto the new pad and getting it to fit around you and you set up in the chair. I forgot that I also have to take the legs off the chair before I get you on the commode, and after you're back in the chair, putting the legs back on and also your slippers, sandals or shoes, which, in all the hoisting and moving and setting you down, usually fall off." "Good, now I know," she said. "But no matter how much time and effort it takes you, why can't you help me without always trying to make me feel I've done something wrong?" "I do that? *Always*? Sorry. Okay, let's just get the darn thing done with. But, boy, you're really an expert at making me stop whatever I'm doing to attend to you and then making me feel guilty." The time he was transferring her from the commode to the wheelchair and the commode's front wheels weren't braked, which was his fault—it was his job to brake them—and one of them rolled over his foot and gashed the big toe. "Goddamnit," he yelled, "your stupid fucking commode." Yelling in front of strangers in an apartment building lobby when he couldn't fit the wheelchair she was in through the elevator door: "Why is there always a hassle with you?" Yelling and slapping the back of her wheelchair's headrest when their van's electronically controlled ramp wouldn't lower. Brushing her hair too hard a number of times when he was angry at her or because of something else. A couple of times she didn't give any indication he was hurting her or tell him to stop brushing so hard, and after he tied the hair-band around her ponytail and turned the commode around so he could transfer her to the wheelchair, saw she'd been crying. All of those really happen? Something like he remembered, and some very close to what happened and even a little worse, and there were a lot more. "Dad," Rosalind says at the end of the memorial, "are you sure you don't want to say something?" "No, everything seems to have been covered, and more eloquently than I ever could, so I've nothing to add. Besides, I'm a little overcome by what you and your sister and so many of the guests here have recounted about your mother, that I doubt I could say anything even if I wanted to. Thank you all for coming," he says without turning around to the fairly large group of people behind him; he only looked at Rosalind standing in front and who ran the memorial. "Now I think we should all have something to eat and drink, don't you, sweetheart?" "If no one else has anything to share with us about Mommy," she says, "sure." No one does, so she says "Then Maureen and I also thank you for coming to our mother's memorial and we now hope you'll help yourselves to refreshments in the dining room." He has a glass of wine, talks briefly to a few people, mostly thanking them for coming. To one couple he says "It meant a lot to my daughters that you were here." Then he thinks Maybe that was the wrong thing to say and the wrong tense to use. Is it "were"? Is it "are"? And "means" instead of "meant"? Maybe, he thinks, he should get out of here before he says something even worse. And save the drinking for when everyone's gone, and he puts the glass down and says "I meant, of course, I'm very glad you came too. Just, you know, the day's confused me, and I also haven't been in the greatest shape since my Gwen died. 'My Gwen.' I never before referred to her that way. But not to worry, though, not to worry—I didn't say it for that. For you to worry. I meant about my not being in the greatest shape. But you knew what I meant." "Oh, God," he thinks, "I'm losing it. Who knows what I'll say next. I knew I shouldn't be here. But then how would it have looked? I should have let them have it in a restaurant, paid for it all there too—room, booze, food, whatever it cost. Then they could have said "My father's not feeling well and couldn't be here." But then people would be worried. "Are you all right?" the woman of this couple says. "Oh, yeah. Excuse me, I have to speak to my daughters about something important. It's been nice talking to you. Again, thanks for coming." And he goes over to his daughters, pulls them aside and says he's become exhausted by it all, physically and emotionally, and if they don't mind, he's going to rest. "You can hold down the fort. I was never very good at it. Socializing? Not my forte. That was unplanned. I'm not making jokes today. Haven't found anything funny in a while, really, and who knows when I'll next say something funny. I'm all confused. That's what I was just telling whatever-their-names-are." "The Smits?" Maureen says. "Do I know them?" "She was a colleague of Mom's—also French lit, but the century before—and I remember they once came here for dinner, so you've probably been to their house too." "Oy, I'm really in a pickle. Don't even know people I know. I hope I didn't give it away when I spoke to them. All confused. And if I had pronounced 'forte' the way some people do incorrectly—the musical version—I wouldn't be standing here like a schmo commenting about it. You know, the fort line. But tell everyone to stay as long as they want and that they won't be disturbing me, if they ask. Incidentally, this was very nice—cathartic, in a way— and I'm glad you had it. See? Next time I say not to do something, also don't listen to me. Oh, gosh, that almost sounded like a joke. I suppose I'm trying to sound lighthearted so you don't worry about me. Don't. I'm okay." "You sure you are?" Maureen says. "Anything we can do for you?" "No. Hold down the fort. Keep things going as they are. It's great." His daughters look at each other. They think something's wrong with him, he thinks. Okay. "You both look mystified. Don't be. I swear, I'm all right. I know how to take care of myself, believe me. I took care of your mom. Now I'm going to take care of myself. I'm going to retire at the end of this academic year—I've recently decided this—and rest, read, work out more, maybe travel. No, I could never travel alone. Did it as a college student and then later in my late twenties when I went by bus and train through France, and was always so lonely. Just what I need right now, right? Though maybe to the shore one day to sit on a rock and look at the ocean or to some state park where there's a mountain to look out at, but that should do it. But why am I making these stupid plans? It's too early. It's all come so fast. I don't mean Mommy's illness, but just two weeks since she passed away." "It's been more than a month, Daddy," Rosalind says. "A month, then. Really. I can hardly believe it. Went by so fast when you'd think it'd be achingly slow. What was I doing the last month, that I didn't notice? Walking around in a fog, sleeping a great deal, listening to a lot of lugubrious Bach, no doubt drinking more than usual and dozing off from it. That'll kill time. I'm not sure I'm using that expression right. And gardening, seeing to your mother's garden, something I didn't like doing when she was well, but got into the groove once it was obvious she couldn't do it herself. Making it nice and neat the way she instructed me to, as if I could still wheel her around outside so she could admire her garden and fruit trees. I can't tell you how sad it made me to push her wheelchair from behind and only see the back of her head but sense her smile. Though here I am telling you. I'm making you sad, aren't I?" and Rosalind says "No, you can tell us anything. It's good you get it out." "Is that what I'm doing? I'll probably let the garden go, though. I don't see myself continuing at the same pace, and I've no desire to keep it in the same condition as a monument to her. No monuments. I'll snip here, there; that's all, so it doesn't entirely grow over and the property loses value. Maybe sell the house if you girls don't want to assume ownership of it, and give you most of the money from it minus the capital-gains taxes, or whatever they're called." "If you retire," Maureen says, "you'll need all the money you can to live on, and where would you move to? I'd hope back to New York so we could see you more. But don't make any important decisions for at least a year, I've been told to tell you." "Who told you?" "People. Guests here." "How come they didn't tell me? Anyway, we'll see. As for retirement, I should've done it sooner so I could've helped out your mother more. And I don't need much—in fact, I like living on a little—and your mother made me promise to be generous with you girls. I've my retirement income and Social Security benefits and your mother and I have some savings and investments, which I'll split in half with you or just take a third, and I seem to make a little each year off my writing, and the house is paid off. There's also your mother's retirement money, not much but which you kids will get all of. Maybe I'll buy a small apartment somewhere, although I'm afraid, much as I'd love to see you more, not in New York. I was born and grew up there and went to school, college, my earliest jobs there—and then back to it for twelve more years; did everything there. Met your mother and lived with her in her apartment for a while, before we married there.

We conceived you kids there, and then with Rosalind moved down here, though kept our apartment there for years, but that city now gives me the jitters. And I like the easiness of life here and no trouble in finding a parking spot and the tree and flower smells and sounds of the owl." "What owl?" Rosalind says. "The neighborhood one out on a tree somewhere near, or else his hoots travel as if he is, which he does almost every night. Neither of you have heard him?" and they shake their heads. "You're young; you've few regrets and done little that's wrong, so you sleep soundly. Nah, that's too pat. Your mother and I just happened to sleep badly the last two years, she worse than I. She used to nudge me in the dark—last time was about a week before her last stroke—and say 'Do you hear the owl?' She was so happy with it. I'd say 'You woke me for that? Yes, I heard. Now try to sleep,' and I'd get half an Ambien out of the container on the dresser and drop it into her mouth, only because she asked me to—I wasn't drugging her so I could sleep—but it usually didn't start working for a couple of hours. But I'm making plans again, aren't I? And geese. You don't get geese flying north or south overhead, depending which season, and their collective honks. You and your people are right," he says to Maureen; "too soon. And if I get a simple one-bedroom condo, I think is what I'm thinking about and which'd be all I could afford, no owl or geese and probably no flower and tree smells, either, so that's out. I'll come up with something. Just so long as you kids get a hefty share. I doubt I can stay here with all my memories of her in it. And that expression 'passed away'—what I used before? Another one I never say. 'Died' is 'died.' Not 'she passed away, he did, they all passed away' or 'on.' On what? I never understood that wording, or maybe just not today. You can understand why. But, excuse me, I'm going to nap. Make all the noise you want, it won't disturb me. I'm that tired, and sleep'll clear my spaghetti head." "Spaghetti head?" Maureen says. "I don't know," he says, "it just came to me. Isn't spaghetti disordered and mixed up and roils around in water before it's cooked? But I'll be all right—I can see by your faces you don't think so. Really, I'm fine. Say my goodbyes and thank anyone who asks. I didn't see any relatives, mine or your mother's, but I'm sure some were here." He kisses their cheeks, goes into the bedroom and bolts the door. "Sure we can't help you with anything, Daddy?" was the last thing one of them said. When he's not looking at them, he often can't tell which one's speaking. Especially on the phone: their voices are that much alike. He thinks that's why they always identify themselves when they call, because he made the mistake so many times. "Hi, Daddy, it's Rosalind" or "Maureen." What an odd thing, he thinks, looking at it; bolt on a bedroom door. It was there when they bought the house and he never thought to take it off. The previous owners, or the original ones before them, probably feared burglars would break into the house after they'd gone to bed and get into the bedroom if the door wasn't bolted. For that—he's had similar thoughts, though would never have gone so far as to get a bolt or latch on the door—he has a thick stick the size of a baseball bat underneath his side of the bed, which has been there for about ten years. The cleaning lady, after she vacuums under the bed, always puts it back in the same place and has never said anything to him about it. Would he use it? He would. Imagined himself several times grabbing the stick, if he thought he heard burglars in the house, and sneaking into the hallway naked with it—if the kids were home, he'd quickly put on undershorts—and jumping out at them and smashing down on their heads and hands till they couldn't get up and their hands couldn't hold anything and then calling the police, or yelling for Gwen to. He also has a shorter stick in the van lying alongside the driver's door, but only since the day after the Towers were hit. Gwen was in the back bathroom that morning, the radio on, when she yelled "Martin, come in here, something terrible's happened; turn on the TV." He only used the bolt when he and Gwen were about to make love or a little after they'd started and the kids were home and it was daytime and he didn't want them barging into the room. It'd be awful if one of them found them coupled, or worse. Gwen never wanted him to use the bolt. Kids will try the door, she said, find it locked and imagine much weirder things going on in there than they are. "We just have to make sure they know to knock and wait for permission to enter before opening the door." Sometimes he quietly bolted the door—well, he always did it quietly, so the kids wouldn't hear it, but he's talking about the times he didn't want Gwen to know what he was up to—when he thought if she was still in bed or washing up in the john, that he could get her to make love. He could, about half those times, and a lot of times she said something like "I was hoping you'd ask," though more often she said "I'm really too busy right now" or "not in the mood." But if he wants to that much, she added a number of times, and doesn't expect but the minimum of help and participation from her and can be reasonably quick, okay. Actually, once, Maureen, or was it Rosalind?—anyway, one of them, when she was around nine or ten, came in without warning them while he was underneath Gwen and had forgotten to use the bolt, and darted out of the room and slammed the door. He didn't see or hear anything, not even the door slamming; Gwen did. She later spoke to their daughter, saying something like "About this morning, when you came into our room when Mommy and Daddy were in bed without any covers on them? What you happened upon accidentally is an altogether voluntary physical act that adult couples occasionally do. It's natural and healthy and normal in a marriage, and I'm not going to give you a phony-baloney explanation as to what you saw, for that would only confuse you more." Gwen said to him "She looked at me as if I were crazy, and said 'What are you talking about, Mommy? I wasn't in your room this morning, or all day, so I couldn't have seen anything you say.' I said 'Okay, maybe I was mistaken. I was still pretty sleepy when I thought I saw you in there, so I could have dreamt up the whole thing,' and let it go at that. Did I say the right thing at the end?" and he said "I guess so," and she said "With that dreaming-up-the-whole-thing excuse, she'd know it was a lie and think I was now trying to cover up something that I did feel was bad. Listen, we have to impress upon them more forcefully that we don't bolt doors in this house but also that no one in the family can come into anyone's room like that either. If the door's closed, knock; knock; everyone has to knock." He lies on his side of the bed. The cat scratches the door. He knows what will happen if he opens it. Cat will swagger in, wait till he gets back on the bed, then jump onto it and first want his head petted and then snuggle up to him. For a few days after his brother died—after his mother too the cat stayed by his side on the bed, which made him feel better or at least comforted him somewhat. Since Gwen died, cat's stayed mostly on one or the other of the kids' beds or on the rocker on the porch, when before he almost always spent the night on either side of the foot of their bed. Cat resumes scratching the door. Should he let him in? No, and just have to hope he won't start whining, which will bring back the kids. "Not now, Sleek. Go away. I want to be alone." Cat continues scratching. "I said *gegen weg*. Or whatever it is in German. But why am I speaking German to you? Just stop hounding me. 'Hounding me.' What a joke. Just go; vamoose. 'Moose.' Another unattended joke. That one also. Oh, God, I give up. Scratch all the hell you want." Cat stops scratching and slumps to the floor against the door, where he'll wait awhile for him to open it and then go somewhere else in the house and come back sometime later and probably scratch or tap at the door again. Maybe he's hungry and wants him to feed him. But he doesn't get his dinner till five or six, and last time he looked there was plenty in both food bowls, as if the cat had barely touched what he'd laid out for him this morning. Or it might be he's thirsty. But if his water dish was empty or turned over—one of the guests, getting something in the kitchen, might have stepped on or kicked it—he'd go to the other bathroom and spread himself out on the toilet seat, or if the seat was up, balance himself on the rim of the toilet bowl, and drink from that, if the last person to use the toilet had flushed it. And if it's that he wants to go out, he'd go to the kitchen or porch and scratch either of those doors or make the mewling sound he only makes when he wants to relieve himself outside and which his daughters are familiar with, and one of them would open the door for him. But he's quiet now, so maybe he's already left the hallway or is sleeping by the door. He shuts his eyes. He tried a couple of times since Gwen died to rest or nap in the middle of the bed, place he thought would be the most comfortable. But he felt—it's a large bed, queen-size—too far from the edge. He likes to be in reach of his night table, where there's always a pen and pad and where his watch and glasses and handkerchief, or sheet of paper towel, usually are. Also the night table light. He doesn't like to have to roll over or stretch for it to turn it on or off. He takes off his glasses, folds them up and puts them on the night table. He used to slip them into their case when he lay down for a nap or sleep, but lost it long ago. He's been meaning to buy one next time he's in a drugstore, but whenever he gets to one, he always forgets. He even stuck a note up on the refrigerator door: "Martin, you numskull: get eyeglasses case before you break your glasses again," but the note fell off, or whatever happened to it, and disappeared a few months ago and he never replaced it. "Why are you so down on your-self?" Gwen said after she'd read the note. "You're not a numskull." Maybe she was the one who took it off, but she couldn't have reached it from her wheelchair. She could have asked one of her caregivers to do it for her and not told him. Gwen's glasses in their case are on a bookshelf in her study; he moved them there from her night table soon after she died so they'd be out of the bedroom and he wouldn't have to see them every day, but he doesn't want to take the glasses out just for the case. He thinks he'll give the glasses away with most of her things the kids won't want, like what's left of her medical equipment and supplies and he doesn't know what else—some of her books, especially the scholarly ones and all those, except the dictionar-ies, in Italian and French; hair dryer, package of razors never opened and another of emery boards, things like that; costume jewelry, clothes, unsealed bottle of perfume, and her computer and portable phone—to some organi-zation like Purple Heart. Sure, Purple Heart, that's the one they always called for a donation pickup if it didn't call them first to say its truck would be in their area on such and such a date. His watch he never put on today, which is unusual for him, he thinks, and is still where he left it on the night table last night, and he has a handkerchief in his pants pocket. He takes it out, blows his nose into it, folds over the wet part, and drops it on top of the watch. And he once, maybe a week after Gwen died, tried sleeping on her side of the bed. He thought that because she was much lighter than he—about fifty pounds, and after her first stroke, sixty to sixty-five—the mattress might not have as much of a depression on her side as it does on his, but he found it uncomfortable, or some other word, lying there. Like the eyeglasses case: just because it had been her side and all that's attached to that. He'll probably never even take the glasses out of their case. Doesn't want to see them again and picture them on her face. As for her side of the bed: making love with her there (they never seemed to do it on his side or in the middle of the bed or not after her first stroke); turning her over and changing or straightening her pad; massaging her shoulders when he got her on her stomach; exercising her legs and feet every morning and night when she was on her back, and catheterizing her periodically or whenever she couldn't pee on her own and was risking getting a urinary tract infection. Leaning over her, after he got her set for sleep, and kissing her, if she wasn't angry at him or hurt by something he said that day, and saying "Sleep well" or "Sweet dreams" and "Goodnight." Then he'd kiss her and shut off her night table light. But all on her side of the bed, he's saying. Though some of those—turning her over away from him to massage her shoulders or change the towel underneath her or straighten her pad—a little to the middle of the bed. Anyway, tried resting every which way that one time on her side of the bed, but nothing worked. They have the kind of mattress—but how does he say it now? He has the kind of mattress that isn't supposed to be turned over. Though they were advised by the saleswoman when they bought it to turn it a hundred-eighty degrees around every three to four months so no one side of it gets unevenly depressed. He never did it because he either didn't want to mess up the bed and have to remake it or he didn't feel like doing it on the days he thought of it or Gwen asked him to do it or he felt he didn't have the strength at that moment to move a big heavy mattress around by himself, and after they had the new mattress set for a year or so—which would be about nine months after her first stroke— because he didn't want her lying in the depression his body had made. So he did do some nice unasked-for things for her now and then. Of course he did, several a day. Just, they were heavily outweighed by the many instances of his rage and other awful behavior to her since a little after she got sick, and which made her look at him sometimes as if she hated him. "What I do this time?" he'd say. "Whatever it is, I'm sorry." She usually just kept looking at him. "All right, I know what I did," he'd say. "You don't have to look at

me as if I'm the worst shit on earth, and I'll try not to let it happen again."
"That's what you always say," she said a number of times. "Your words aren't
to be trusted anymore. It'd be absurd (ridiculous, idiotic) of me to believe
you can change." "Believe, believe, because the last thing I want is to hurt
you," and he tried to hug her a few of those times and she pushed him away
or she let him but never hugged him back. He sometimes thought right
after: She'll get over it and he will try not to act like that again. He just has
to work on it: see it coming and stop it fast. Do that a couple of times
straight and he should have the problem licked. That time they bought the
mattress set. A good day for them. They went together—she drove—tested
several mattresses in the store: he did it quickly: on and off in about ten
seconds and without lying back on the beds: he thought he'd look silly. She
lay back on each mattress she tested, turned over on her side, then on her
other side, then on her back with her arms out, shut her eyes, looked like
she was sleeping, even made snoring sounds once as a joke, causing the
saleswoman and him to laugh, and finally, with one mattress, said while
lying on her back with her hands behind her head: "I like this one; firm but
not hard, and within our price range. What about you?" And he said "You
choose, because they all seemed the same to me." "No, they're each a little
different: soft, firm, rock hard, so I want you to feel as good with the one we
buy as I do. Try this one again, but this time lie on it," and he said "I don't
have to; I know it's good on your say-so. And I never have trouble sleeping
on anything, soft, hard or lumpy, so if this is the mattress you want, let's get
the woman to write up a ticket and we'll get out of here." "You're so easy to
please," and he said "Thank you. But you know me: I hate shopping for
anything but food," when he should have said "No, I can be a horror." But
he was much less of one then, right? It was her illness that did something to
him and he got worse and worse. He became so goddamn…ah, it's old
news. He has to stop thinking about it. He has to stop thinking about it.
After, they had lunch at a Mexican fast-food restaurant next door and then
lattes and a biscotti between them—little bits of chocolate and walnut in it,
his latte with skim milk, hers with soy—at a coffee place in the same shopping center. Only drinks sold in the restaurant were sweetened iced tea and
soda. "We ought to do this more often," she said when they were back in the
car, she at the wheel again, he reading a book in his lap, "Go out for lunch
or just coffee, take a break from work at home." "Deal," he said, and went
back to his book. Someone knocks on the door. "Yes?" he says, and one of
his daughters says "It's me, Daddy. Just seeing how you're doing." And he
says "I'm fine, I'm fine, everything's fine. I'm going to take a nap." "I didn't

wake you from one, did I?" and he says—it's Maureen, he's almost sure—
"No, I've just been resting. We'll go out for dinner tonight after the house
is cleaned up, okay?" and she says "Good, we have no plans. Would it be all
right if we invite three of our friends along? I don't know if you noticed, but
they came to the memorial—drove down together from New York this
morning—and I don't think it'd be right to just leave them like that."
"Sure," he says, "invite anyone you want, and our treat. Very nice of them
to come so far for it. They can even sleep over if you two don't mind dou-
bling up and you bring out the futon. Are they all girls? You'll work it out.
But we'll eat Chinese, to keep the cost down, when before I thought we'd go
to Petit Louis—okay?" and she says "Of course. I'll tell them of your
sleepover offer, but I think they want to get back tonight so they can be at
work tomorrow." "Maybe, then, you want to drive back with them—I'll be
okay alone," and she says "We planned on staying two more days—that is,
if you don't mind us to," and he says "What are you, kidding? I'm thrilled
that you're staying." "And if you're still napping by six, can I wake you so
they can start off around eight?" "Sure, wake me, but I'll be up. And forget
the Chinese. What do I care about the expense? We'll all go to Petit Louis.
Make a reservation for six-thirty," and she says "Let's stick with Chinese. It'll
be quicker and Petit Louis is where we went most to celebrate our birthdays
and New Year's Eve once and your wedding anniversary a few times, even
the twentieth, I remember. It's too loaded. Have a good nap, Daddy."
"Yeah." Did he turn off the phone ringer? Thinks he did. Doesn't want to be
jarred out of a nap. The twentieth. That's when they had their best meal
there. Told them to order what they want, don't worry about the cost, it's a
special anniversary, by all rights they should be at a more opulent place but
this will do, and he got a good bottle of wine, not the least expensive French
red on the wine list, which is what he always did, though the least expensive
of the various categories of red they have there are always good. She had filet
mignon, said she feels like she wants a very rich piece of beef. "Strange,
huh?" But she's been a good girl, she said, with no red meat for several years,
and what harm is one small portion of meat going to do her? And he, what'd
he have? Oh, something with scallops and a plate of pâtés and crab soup to
start with and a crème brûlée, when he usually had the croque monsieur or
slice of quiche or some other less expensive dish, even on his birthday, and
took a little from the appetizers and desserts the others had. So he has two
hours. Enough time to rest, and he assumes everyone but his daughters and
their three New York friends will be gone when he gets up. Suppose someone needs to use the bathroom here because the other one's occupied? Just

don't answer. Does he want to be with their friends? Not much. Actually, not at all, but what's he to do? Wants to make his kids happy. Does he want them around for two more days? Rather be alone, doing anything he wants, not worrying about having enough food in the house and getting them dinner and what time to sit down for it and so on. Drinking as much as he wants and falling asleep sloshed if that's what it ends up being. But he has to do what they want and not anything to make them worry about him. He does, they might think of staying longer or urge him to speak to someone like a psychotherapist, something he definitely doesn't want to do. All right, he knows he's depressed, but whatever his problem, it'll go away. He just wants to sit in his armchair in the living room and put on whatever music he wants, or not put any on, no music and none of theirs from their rooms or the TV or DVD going. Just silence except for things like the washer or dryer running in the kitchen or the cat's tapping toenails on the wood floor as he crosses the room, and fix himself a drink and read the *Times* at eight or nine at night (the *Sun* he reads in the morning) and then who knows what? Eat a carrot and celery stalk and that's all for dinner except maybe a piece of cheese on toast, masturbate in that chair, but better and less messy in bed. Sit with no undershorts on under his regular shorts or just in a bathrobe, but nobody walking through the room or sitting on the couch near his chair and saying "You okay? Need anything? Do you know what tomorrow's weather will be like? Have you ever read" such and such book or author? "Is there anything you want to talk about, Daddy, that you may be holding back?" And disturbing his concentration or redirecting his attention or startling him, because he fell asleep in the chair. But why even think about it? He can't change it. Any mail today? What's with him? It's Sunday, and even if there was, and there always is—not one delivery day in their thirteen or so years here (he always had to ask Gwen how long they've lived here or what year they moved in) except maybe in the first week or two, has there not been some kind of mail, and today there'd be mail from yesterday and the day before—not interested in it. Since she died, he's only gone to their mailbox every three to four days, other than to stick something in, for a medical insurance check that might have been delivered and the bills that have to be paid. A large bird, maybe a crow or hawk—no, too graceful and fast for a crow—swoops past the picture window opposite the bed and then back again, if it's the same bird, and it could even be a bluejay, and disappears. Loves this about the house: the woods around it and the birds and, a few times, one or two deer. "Martin, Martin," she shouted once from her study, last time either of them saw deer by the house, and by the time he ran there, thinking something was wrong with her, they were gone. "You didn't see them." "Yes, I did. Three." "Baloney. You just wanted to alarm me. Otherwise, you would've shouted 'Martin; deer!' What a faker." "No, I'm not. You're just sorry you missed them." "Faker, faker." "I swear." Did he then kiss her? Might have. Wouldn't have wanted her to think he was being serious with that faker business in even the slightest way. She was so excited by the deer. Why didn't he say "Ah, you lucky stiff." Not "stiff." "You lucky" what then? "Doll." Leaning up against the left side of the window is a 9-by-12-inch framed photo of her holding Rosalind in the air when she was…October: June; eight months, both smiling at the camera, Rosalind pulling on Gwen's hair but apparently not hurting her, or maybe she's tolerating the pain for the shot. Asked her about it a year or two ago and she said it was too far back to remember—only he pretends to remember exact wordings and actions from years before—and with her mind now in such sad shape, doubly impossible to. "I don't even remember who took the picture." "I know but I'm not saying." He really say that? Something like it, he thinks. "Ask me something from today or even yesterday," she said, "though even there I'm only good for remembering half the things that happened." What a beauty she was, he thinks, looking at the photo from the bed, though with his glasses off—where'd he put them? Always has to know. Looks at his night table and sees them—he really can't see it that well, though knows from before how beautiful she is in it, and such gorgeous hair. He's looked at it he doesn't know how many times; can hardly avoid seeing it in this room except when he's getting ready for bed or is doing his stretching or barbell exercises and pulls the drapes closed, covering the photo, but this is the first time he's thought of getting rid of it. It's been in the same spot for years since one of the eyelet screws in back came out and the frame fell off the bedroom wall and the glass broke. Gwen said a few months ago—came out of nowhere, or that's how he saw it—she had her back to it—that if he likes the photo on the window ledge so much— "I don't like how I look in it, though I'll admit I look immeasurably better than I do today, with my sunken cheeks and frozen face." "Oh, come off it," he said; "you're still a knockout," and she said "Sure, enough to be first runner-up in the Mrs. America Stroke Victim pageant. Anyway, you should get a new frame for it, if for nothing else but to preserve the great shot of Rosalind," something he thought of doing lots of times but never did. For what would it have taken? One of the four times a year or so he goes to Target to buy toilet paper and paper towels and such in bulk, he could have bought an inexpensive frame. Maybe Rosalind will want to take it. Why wouldn't she? It's a terrific photo of Gwen and her. So then why doesn't he want to keep it? Doesn't want to be reminded of Gwen ten times a day. So put it in a drawer. It'll tear. Then on the top shelf of one of the closets. There are things of his he's put up there that he hasn't looked at in years and probably will never need, including unfinished and old unpublished manuscripts, so he should get rid of them. Also things Gwen asked him to put up there because she couldn't reach any of the top shelves, before and after her first stroke—what should he do with those? Just start clearing out the place, get rid of everything he'll never and he doesn't think the kids will ever use, without even asking them. And maybe Rosalind doesn't want to be reminded so much of Gwen either, though for different reasons than his. She'll break down every time she looks at the photo, or not that much, but enough times to warrant not taking it. He wants to get up to turn the photo around so he doesn't see it or put it away someplace, but feels too tired to. That pleasant ache in his fingertips that till now only seemed to come when he forced himself to stay awake to type some more. Was the photographer of that photo at the memorial? A good friend of Gwen's from college, or good friend then, who came down from Princeton to take a few hundred photos for one she'd include in a photography book she was putting together of just literary mothers with their daughters, but he doesn't think it was ever published. Gwen would have bought a copy, even if she was given one by the publisher or photographer—she bought almost all the books by writers and scholars she knew, even the prolific ones and even when he told her not to because she knew neither of them would ever read it and the scholarly ones didn't come cheap—and shown it to him. Or maybe she did get it and showed it to him and he forgot. Maybe he'll give all the photos he has with Gwen in them to the kids and they can do with them what they want. Only one he'll keep is a small one in a plastic sleeve, or whatever it's called, in the wallet compartment with his credit and health insurance cards and driver's license and so on and which he only sees when he takes the bunch of them out when he's looking for one. Gwen once said, after he laid all the cards and IDs out on a table to go through them for the one he wanted, "You have a stacked deck. I'll raise you mine." He laughed but wasn't then and isn't now sure what she meant, unless—just thought of this—he heard "mine" when she said "nine." In other words…in other words, what? Nothing. She was simply commenting that they looked like a deck of playing cards, and because they did, she used card game and betting terms— "stacked," "raise you," and, for no special reason he can see, the number nine. Or maybe he's missing something and the number is significant and he should think about it more. Some other time. Photograph of her in his wallet was taken by another photographer friend of hers at an art gallery opening they were at a few weeks after they started seriously going together. In other words, not long after they first made love. Here's something odd. She claimed he didn't tell her he loved her till about a year after they met, although, she said, she knew he did by the way he looked at and acted toward her and made love. He said once "You've said that before and it can't be true—it's absolutely not like me to hold back like that," and she said "Believe me, my dearie, it's not something I'd make up, and it always stuck with me." And she? Said she loved him about a month after they met. A weekend morning, bright out, she just woke up, it seemed, he'd been reading awhile in bed beside her—her apartment was on the seventh floor, faced the Hudson, and didn't have curtains or shades. When she was sick—the flu, a virus—and wanted the bedroom dark so she could rest or sleep, she had him stretch a blanket across both windows and fasten the ends to the old curtain-rod brackets up there. But that time, she just looked at him, head still on the pillow, smiled, said it, and started crying a little. Must have seemed a bit strange to her that he didn't, instead of saying "What're you crying for? It's all right. I'm glad about it," say flat out he loved her too, since by then, she later told him, she knew he did. She said that what he used to say that first year—in bed, on the phone, at a restaurant once, etcetera—whenever she told him she loved him, and she didn't say it more than a few times, were things like "Same here" or "Me too" or "I feel the same about you," but never "I love you" or "And I love you" or "I love you too." Her eyes, in the wallet photograph, are looking off to the right, as if someone or a particular art work had caught her attention. She has on a white turtleneck, an opened suede jacket or coat (to fit the photo into the plastic sleeve he cut off the lower part just above her breasts), a shoulder bag strap's over her left shoulder, and her long hair's rolled up and knotted or tied or whatever it is in back but where it stays above her neck, and is still very blond. "A beautiful Jewish natural blond," he said to her around this time; "what more could I ever want? And, oh boy, would my father have been happy. 'Finally,' he would have said—and not because you're a real blond; in fact, that might've made him suspicious—'finally, one of my boys does the right thing.'" Photograph's been in the same plastic sleeve in a series of wallets for the past twenty-five years. Before that it was in a billfold she gave him as a Christmas gift the year after they met and which he never used—wanted to; because she gave it to him, but had no pocket to put it in his clothes except a sport jacket he wore once or twice a year—and kept in a dresser drawer for about two years before giving it to Goodwill in New York when he took his teaching job in Baltimore. "I don't know why," she said, "but I thought you'd like to move up to a billfold. I promise, that's the last time I'll try to change you." He's feeling even tireder now, so maybe a good time for a nap. Also feels cold. One of his daughters turns on the central air conditioning or fan because of all the people in the house? Doesn't hear any air blowing through the room's register, but that goes on and off, depending on what temperature was set. Tries to just lie there without a blanket, but now he's feeling chilled. Doesn't want to get under the covers. That'd be too much like sleep, and he'd never wake up. Gets up, turns the frame around on the window ledge—now she'll be looking at what she wants to, he thinks, but oh, so hard on himself, so hard, but he deserves it—and gets a cotton blanket off a chair—same one he used to put over her when she napped in bed or in the wheelchair—and gets back on the bed and covers himself with it. Puts the satin border or hem or edge—he always had trouble with the right words for certain things and would go to her for them—to his nose. Doesn't smell of her and he didn't think it would. But she was practically odorless, even when she hadn't had a shower, which means he hadn't given her one, in days, and also her hair, without a shampoo for a week, never seemed to smell, and her mouth, if she didn't brush her teeth that day, and if she ate a food that usually gave one bad breath, then he did too, so he didn't smell it. Cunt, too—he doesn't remember ever detecting an odor there, but that she probably took care of before they made love. But she couldn't have all the time. They'd be waking up, or he'd nudge her in her sleep or fondle her till she awoke, or he'd interrupt her working in her study and say "I don't mean to bother you, but like to take a break?" or "like a change of scenery?" and often they'd go straight to the bed without stopping in the bathroom. Gets a hard-on. Well, what's he expect? Their sex was always good before she had her first stroke, and after that he just took it when he could. Only time she had some aroma about her was when she had him spray her one perfume on her left wrist, she'd always stick out the left wrist, which she'd then rub on her neck or somewhere. Then she'd ask him, or she'd ask him before the perfume, for one of her necklaces and for him to put it on her, and they'd go. Last times for that were about a year ago, when they went to a concert or play or opening party for his department or dinner at some couple's house. It was always a couple's. But maybe he's wrong about the blanket. Smells it. This time, takes a deep whiff. Smells like a cotton blanket that hasn't been washed in a while. Tomorrow, if he remembers—anyway, one of these days soon—he'll stick it in the washer, and after he dries it, put it away for Purple Heart. And the perfume. Spray bottle's not even half finished and she's been using it for about ten years. Cost a lot—she had him buy it for her birthday—and he knows it's still good. That will also go in one of the boxes for Purple Heart along with her socks and bras and scarves that are in the same drawer with the necklaces and perfume. First he'll ask the kids if they want any of it—the necklaces he'll just give them— and if they don't, out all the rest of it goes. He won't offer them the bras. She was a lot larger there than them, though they have her round rear end and long torso and sort of short strong legs, although hers, the last year or so, became atrophied. But he likes the feel of only this thin cotton blanket over him for a nap. So he might have to keep it, for where would he buy a new one, and when? Hates malls. He'll deal with it all later. So many things to. Of course, he could always ask the kids, as long as they're here, to go to the mall to buy him the same kind of blanket, though different design. But bank stuff, investments, safe deposit box, titles to the house and van and just about everything else—income taxes, home and car insurance—all in both their names and which he hasn't done anything about yet. Feels himself drifting. Did he turn the phone off? Thinks so. Yes, definitely remembers—sees his finger switching the on-and-off button to the left. And his wallet. When he's home he always keeps it on the right side of the top drawer of the table linen chest in the dining room so he always knows where it is. All right. Nobody's going into that drawer, and if someone did, for some reason—can't think of one now. Looking for a napkin?—he wouldn't go through the wallet or take it. Was his brother here today? No, my goodness, what's he talking about?—he really must be out of it. Died four years ago—five, in March. He'll never get over it. Photographer's a much celebrated writer and just a few years older than him. Photographer's husband, he means. Makes a bundle off his work and readings and commencement addresses, he's read, and has been doing so for more than forty years, and he's a serious writer, though not one he likes. Well, who does he, of living writers? Used to see him—his counter on the main floor faced the Third Avenue entrance—when he worked in the men's pajama shop at Bloomingdale's: Burberry raincoat—collar up—floppy hat. He must have used the store to get from Third to Lex, probably when it was snowing or raining, or it was just a more interesting route than the long boring streets on either side of the store. Only time he met him was in front of the Whitney, when the photographer—Hilda—yelled out to Gwen. The women talked. He held Rosalind in a baby sling on his chest. Writer didn't want to talk to him. Looked every which way but at him. Might have known he was a writer, he thought then, and was afraid he'd hit him for a future blurb. But he wouldn't have. He'd never do that. Wanted to tell him about Bloomingdale's. Though he was envious of his early success and all that brought. His mother would have taken the memorial badly, if she was able to come down. Well, if she had wanted to, he would have driven to New York to get her and then, after a few days, if she was strong enough, put her on the train back. If he couldn't, what would he have done, driven her? She loved Gwen, thought of her as her daughter. Used to tell him on the phone "You always be good to her, or you'll hear it from me." "Why," he once said—oh, God, when they were both alive and Gwen thriving—"she say anything to you?" "No, she's too good a wife to; just I know you always had a temper." His dog Joan. What happened to her? Fifty, sixty years ago—sixty-one: just disappeared. She had to have been stolen or hit by a car and dumped in an ashcan, because she never would have run away. She loved him. He never feared she'd get lost or not come home when he let her out on the street to make, which he did that day. People sometimes said they saw her sniffing around blocks away—they recognized her by the limp in her right front leg—but she always found her way back and then would wait in his building's vestibule till he or his mother came out to get her. What a loss. Woman at the memorial he hasn't seen in a long time. Forgets if she was originally his friend or Gwen's, and now can't even think of her name, Hilda? No, that's so-and-so. Rhea? Rhoda? Rosetta? Something like that, though not necessarily where it starts with an "R," but what's the difference? He'll never see her again. He'll come out and everyone but his daughters and their friends will be gone. And he won't be able to go out for dinner, even something as simple as Chinese. Not tonight. There's also the car bicycle rack he's been wanting to get rid of for years. He's sure Purple Heart will take that that too. Plus her wheelchair and overbed table and things like that, though maybe those he'll give to the same stroke victims loan closet Gwen gave a number of things to—collapsible cane, walker, four-wheel rollator—when, as she said, she grew out of them. Hears ringing. Doorbell? No, he wouldn't be able to hear it with his door shut and from way back here. Must be a cell phone with a real phone ring, right outside his room. Listens for someone answering it but doesn't hear anything but people's garbled voices from farther inside. Sounds like a cocktail party. Good, let everyone have fun. Gwen wanted to get one of those phones but he said it'd always be falling out of her hands and breaking, so one more complication and expense to deal with, was the way he put it. But he should have, early on, gone to the phone store with her for one that she could operate and then taken her to lunch at a nearby restaurant.

He should have said "Hang the expense. And it shouldn't be that much, It can be on the same plan Rosalind and Maureen share." Why was he always saying no? Anyway, the kids went to the phone store with her and got her one. Wasn't there something she bought and wanted him to plant her last few weeks and he didn't? A rose bush? Two? Probably dead by now, if he did want to do it. He also should have said "Good idea, for both of us, the cell phone, in case an emergency on the road and things like that, and you can talk free to the kids all day if you want." Blanket's slipped down below his shoulders, and he pulls it up and then over his ears. Way Gwen liked to sleep after her first stroke, both on her side and back. She'd wake him at night and ask him to pull the covers up over her ears or she couldn't sleep.

Their phone's ringing. He's at his work table and thinks No, can't be the phone; wouldn't be able to hear it from back here, especially with the bedroom door closed. But don't they have one on the dresser? Looks. Two of them, side by side, portable and regular phone, both ringing at the same time. He yells to the door "Please—Gwen, someone, answer the phone. I'm right in the middle of a critical sentence and I'll lose it if I get up, and I can't stretch to the dresser from my chair." But they can't hear him if they're at the front of the house, and phones are still ringing. Damn, he thinks, lost it, and gets up and opens the door and yells "Will someone please stop the ringing? It's killing my ears," and covers his ears with his hands. "Help me. If it's the door that's doing the ringing, and it's for me, tell whoever's there I'm not home till I finish the sentence I started. Hello? Can anyone hear me? Then please answer." Answering machine comes on—the automated voice says to leave a message—and he listens to see who the caller is. "It's Rosalind, Daddy. I know you hate answering the phone, but please pick up. It's very important." He lunges for the phone, presses all the buttons on the answering machine so it won't record, and says, "Rosalind, where are you? I thought you were here." "I'm in New York, with Mommy." "What do you mean you're with Mommy? She's resting in bed here," and he turns around to the bed and she's not there. "Well, maybe that was yesterday. But where are you with Mommy?" "That's what I'm calling about. Mommy had to be rushed to the hospital again. Could you come right away? You have her living will and medical insurance cards, and they need them here before they can check her in." …Gwen nudges him in bed and says "Martin, wake up, I have something terrible to tell you. Rosalind called tonight and said Maureen was killed." "You call that something terrible?" he says. "There isn't a word for it. But if there was, 'terrible's' surely not the one. But it didn't happen and you must've just dreamt it, because if it were true, I would've found out the same time as you. You would've screamed and dropped the phone and I would've picked it up and Rosalind would've told me. Why do you like scaring me like this? Over and over again. It isn't funny; it's reckless. Grow up." She puts her hands over her face and starts crying. "Okay," he says, "I shouldn't have been so harsh. You don't deserve it. You had a bad dream that seemed real and you believed it. I apologize." She's still crying. He takes her hands away from her face. Her nails have dug into her skin so deep that they pierced it, and blood's running down her face. He looks for something to wipe it with, can't find anything, so wipes it with his shirt sleeves. "It's true, then, isn't it," he says. "How could you have not told me it before? You're not crying because you're ashamed of what you did, but because Maureen was killed. Oh, my gosh, what am I to do? What are we? What are you? I'm sorry, sorry, sorry for everything I said." …An alarm clock goes off. He's resting on the bed. Since when do we have an alarm clock? I want to get up, I get up; my body's the alarm. One of the kids here with one? He looks at his work table where the ringing's coming from. It's the phone, always disturbing me, waking me, getting me up. He gets off the bed and disconnects the phone from the outlet in the wall. I'm never again going to use a phone, he thinks. "Never again," he says to the phone, "you hear? What, you now have nothing to say?" He puts the portable handset to his ear. Maureen's voice is very low. "What's that?" he says. "Speak louder. I can't hear you because I disconnected the phone." "I was saying," she says louder, "that Mommy once told me that finding out in a dream that some-one very close to you is dead is a good omen." "When did she say that? And what's it related to that you're telling me it now?" "When after she died. She came to me in a dream." …Lots of people are in his bedroom. Maybe fifty or sixty, he thinks, and all very well dressed. He's in bed, pulls the covers off and sits up and says "What are you people doing here? This is a private room." No one looks at him. They keep drinking and laughing and talking to one another and taking canapés off two trays a waiter's holding out. One woman's banging on the bathroom door. "Will you please finish in there?" she says. "I have to make and the other bathroom has a line to it that extends outside." This has to be a dream, he thinks. For one thing, the bedroom's twice the size of the one he and Gwen sleep in, though all the furnishings look like theirs and are in the same places as in their bedroom. For another, he's in a suit, and he doesn't own a suit. And who lies down in a bed in a suit and tie, and under the covers? People in dreams do. The suit's a dark brown tweed, exactly like the last one he owned. That one got too small for him, or he got too big for it, and he gave it to Goodwill, who left a note in his mailbox that day saying they were junking the suit because it was so threadbare. What'd they do when they picked it up, open the plastic bag it was in with some other clothes and inspect each item to see if they were good enough to sell? He has that note somewhere, and looks in his night table drawer for it and then in his wallet. He bought that suit for his wedding twenty-five years ago. Gwen had insisted he get one. "I won't have you saying your vows in a sport jacket or rugby shirt. That's how I met you but not how I'll marry you. And I swear, this'll be my last request of you, except for things like opening doors for me if my hands are full and other normal things a husband does for his wife, and vice versa, like helping me move a couch out of the house or reach a cupboard that's up too high. You'd do all that for me, wouldn't you?" "Of course," he said, "what a question." So how'd he end up in his old suit if it was taken away? He looks around the room. It's even more crowded now—there must be a hundred people in it—and where's Gwen? She was lying here beside him, on top of the covers while he was underneath, her dress pulled up, his pants pulled down but his jacket and tie still on, after he told her in the living room "Let's ditch this crew and go to bed. After all, it's the traditional ritual to fulfill on such a day, and I've been waiting for this for a long time. Sharpening my pen, so to speak." She seemed asleep in bed, eyes stayed closed, didn't say anything, even when he put his hand between her legs, and now she's gone. A man, standing by his side of the bed, leans over him. "Congratulations," the man says, holding up a glass of champagne and slugging it down. "Good champagne. Good taste. You have good taste. You know how to throw a party and pick a woman and what to wear and serve and what to not. We're all indebted. Three cheers, everybody, right?" he says to the crowd, refilling his glass from a bottle of champagne he's holding—Piper something; good stuff. How can I afford it? he thinks. No one looks at the man. They continue talking and laughing and drinking and refilling their glasses from bottles of champagne they're all holding—Piper something again. God, this is really going to set me back, he thinks. But again, where's Gwen? She was here; suddenly she's gone. She's the one he misses most. He'd feel a lot more comfortable if she were here. Not necessarily on the bed—he actually wouldn't like that, in front of all these people, and he's not talking about consummating the marriage—but in the room. He'd love to see her drinking champagne and laughing and toasting—no, she's not a toaster—and talking to people and having a good time. …He goes into a hospital room. The bed's empty and the mattress is rolled up. He asks a nurse holding a pile of linens "Where's my wife?" "Who's she?" "Gwendolyn Samuels, though she also goes by her maiden name, Gwen." "What room she in?" "This one." "Sorry," she says, "but we recently renovated and just now opened this room and it's never been used in its present life. Its first patient's on her way up and I have to prepare the bed before she gets here." "That must be my wife, then." Two aides down the hallway are wheeling a gurney toward the room. A patient's on it. He sees the feet first, sticking out from the sheet; the socks, with moons in various phases and stars on them, aren't Gwen's. He looks at the face of the patient as the gurney's pulled past him into the room. Isn't Gwen. "Where's my wife, then?" he asks one of the aides. "Excuse me, sir. You're not permitted in this room if you're not in some way related to the patient." "I am, I'm her husband—not this woman's but Gwendolyn Samuels', who's also known as Gwen. Can you tell me how and where to find her? I keep getting lost looking for her. And I feel lost without her and especially not knowing where she is." …They're at the dining room table, about to eat dinner, when Gwen says "I know you went to a lot of trouble making this food but I don't feel well. I feel cold. Please take my temperature." "You're all right," he says. "You're all right, but let me check." He feels her forehead; it's cold. He holds both her hands and they're cold. He says "Excuse me, I have to do this, it has nothing to do with sex," and puts his hand down her blouse and presses it flat on her chest. It's cold. She says "What are you finding? And he says "Let me feel your thighs. They're always a good test if you have temperature or your body's cold." He pulls up her dress and feels her thighs. They're cold. "You're a little colder than usual. But just a little." "Please take my temperature." "I'm sure it'll be for nothing, but okay. Anything for you." He gets a thermometer out of the breakfront behind him, puts it in her mouth and holds it there. "Don't move," he says. "The reading will be inaccurate if you do, and probably to your disfavor." The thermometer's a digital and rings. He takes it out of her mouth and reads it. It says 90.6. "What is it," she says, "below normal?" "Just a bit. Ninety-six-point-one. That's not so bad. Enough to make your body feel a little cold and you to think something's wrong, but not low enough to call a doctor or rush you to the hospital, right?" "A doctor once told me," she says, "that normal is ninety-six-point-eight to ninety-eight-point-six. Funny how those numbers almost mirror each other. Anyway, as you said, no cause for alarm, thank goodness. Let's eat. Let's even open a good bottle of wine. I feel I've recovered from a very serious illness, for some reason." "Red or white? Oh, let's go with red. I've more of those." I should rush her to the hospital, he thinks. But it's been a long day and I'm already sleepy from the two martinis I've had and there's always a long wait in Emergency before they take you and it's an awful place to be, with people sometimes with gunshot and knife wounds and bleeding and groaning and vomiting, and she'll be all right. I'll put a sweater on her and wrap her in a blanket while she sits at the table, and she'll be fine. …They're sitting downstairs at a concert. It looks like Carnegie Hall but it could also be the Meyerhoff in Baltimore, he thinks. One moment it looks like one, and then like the other. And they've great seats, he thinks, right in the middle of the orchestra. He paid for balcony seats but they somehow ended up down here. He whispers into her ear "We really lucked out with this one." She whispers back "I know. I hate to see this tune end." "It's no tune. It's the *Ninth*, the last, a complete symphony if there ever was one, and then some, with five movements, eighty-six minutes, an orchestra of a hundred, a chorus of a thousand, an audience of millions, and it isn't finished yet. So sit tight. You got your wish. There's more than twenty minutes to go. We've time, plenty of time, to enjoy it." "That's good," she whispers. "And you know so much about music." "Just this one. It's all from the program notes." "Shh," someone says behind him. "I was whispering," he says to the woman. "Shh, shh," she says, finger over her lips. "But it's all right," he whispers; "she's my wife. And I told you, I was just—" "Daddy…Daddy, you up?" Rosalind says through the bedroom door, or maybe she's in the room. He keeps his eyes shut, pretends to be asleep. Doesn't want to talk to anyone now, even them. And if it's time to go out for dinner, he doesn't want to. It's not just their friends; he's tired and not hungry. "He's sleeping," Rosalind says, "so let's not wake him. I'll leave a note we went without him because we wanted him to rest." "Should I turn on Mom's light?" Maureen says. "It's so dark." "No, I'm sure he'll sleep till morning. He could use it. C'mon, let's go, before it gets too late for them." The door closes. "We should bring some food back for him," Maureen says. "I was thinking that too. What are his favorite dishes?" No food, he thinks. Don't waste your money. Ah, but they'll eat it for lunch tomorrow. But what was he doing? He should have answered them. If he didn't want to go, he should have said so. Now it's too late. They're probably out of the house, or about to be, and he doesn't want to stop them—they don't have much time—and also doesn't want them thinking he was faking sleep. He also could have asked them to make sure his phone ringer's off. And told them to use the credit card they share, because he wants to pay for everything while they're here, even for their friends. The cat's meowing from somewhere in the house. The sounds are too far away to know if he wants to be fed or let out. He hopes they fed him. A recent incident with Gwen comes back to him. For no reason that he can see: just popped in. They were lying in bed. It was around 6 a.m. He'd just put her on her back, pulled the covers over her, got in bed. There was a little daylight in the room. He usually kissed her lips or forehead after he got back in bed. He put his face over hers and saw she looked distressed. He said "What's wrong?" and she said she's having trouble breathing. He got scared—her internist had told him to look out for any sudden changes in her—and touched her body in various places to see if she was cold. She wasn't—she felt normal—but he got an erection when he touched her thigh. He took her hand and squeezed it around his penis and kept it there—her bad hand, because that was the side he was lying next to—and she said "What are you doing?" and he said "You're not interested?" and she said "I told you, I'm having trouble breathing, so I don't want you on me." "I don't have to get on you," and she said "Please, not now, nor"—he especially remembers the "nor"—"do I know when. I'm very uncomfortable." "Of course; I'm sorry. Anything I can do for you?" and she took her hand out from under his and off his penis and said "No, it's happened before; I just never said anything. If it's like the last times, it'll go away." "I'm sorry I can't help you," and she said "Same for me to you." He kissed her forehead, probably pulled the covers up over her ears, and went back to sleep. …"Martin, Martin, come here, I need to speak to you." It's Gwen. He gets out of bed and leaves the house. He's wearing only a pajama top and slippers. He doesn't own slippers or pajamas, he thinks, so they must be hers. Strange how they fit him perfectly; he's so much bigger than she and his feet five sizes larger and much wider. It's dark out. No moon or stars. He goes into the woods where he thinks her voice came from. Hears an owl in one of the trees. Maybe it was the owl who made sounds like Gwen calling him, and she's still in bed. He didn't feel around in bed for her and the room was so dark he couldn't see. She's lying on the ground, in a dress, shirt and jacket, but nothing on her feet. She'll get cold, he thinks, and cut her feet up bad. "The kids," she says. "What?" "They're in grave danger. Help them." "What danger? They're fine. I just saw them, or spoke to them on the phone, at least, just about an hour ago, and they were chipper and healthy. It's you who don't look well, from what I can see of you. You don't sound well, either. Your voice is so weak." He gets on one knee and lifts her head off the ground. Drool's running out of her mouth and he wipes it with his sleeve. "Your hair's dirty. You usually have such beautiful, youthful hair. Are you hurt? Did you fall?" She just stares at him. Then her eyes close. "Okay, I will," he says. "I'll help them. First this, though." and kisses her lips. They're cold. But he keeps his lips on hers and after a few seconds they feel warm. Her eyes open and look around before settling on him. She's okay, he thinks. "Can you talk?" She nods. "You scared me for a moment," he says. "Because why did you think the kids were in danger?" "They took them from me. Everything was nice and I was protecting them and they suddenly disappeared." "Who? When? How? Where? Oh, Jesus, this is like a play by Shakespeare, where the lead character's a journalist, or at least a Shakespearean play, but one I can't fathom or hear." …He tries the kitchen door. It's locked. He inserts his house key into the lock. The doorknob turns but the door won't open. He rings the doorbell. Rings it several times before Gwen comes out of the study and walks to the door. "Oh, you're walking without a cane," he says. "I'm so glad." "What do you want?" she says through the glass in the door. He can't hear her and thinks maybe she's just moving her lips to the words. He says "I want to get in." "I told you, we're through, finished, done with…it's over, so get lost." "'Get lost'? Is that what I heard, reading your lips? I'm surprised at you. You never spoke to me so crudely before." She goes back into her study and shuts the door. He rings the doorbell. Then pounds on the door with his fist till he puts a dent in it. He keeps pounding on the dent but can't make it any larger. He thought if he could get a hole large enough in the door, he'd stick his hand through and find the new key on the hook by the door, where he's sure she put it. He'd break the glass in the door to get the key, but he thinks she was barefoot or just in socks and he doesn't want her coming out and cutting her feet. He yells "You're wrong. Let me in. It's not fair." He grabs the doorknob and shakes it as hard as he can, thinking it'll fall off and he'll then be able to push the door open. When he does, he's really going to have a talking with her, he thinks. Nothing abusive; he just wants to work things out with her so he can live in the house again and eventually as man and wife. He misses her, he thinks. "I miss you," he yells. …They're in bed. There's a little daylight in the room, so it must be around six a.m. He feels around his night table for his watch but it's not there. It probably fell to the floor, he thinks. He leans over the bed and feels around the floor, but can't find the watch. Oh, what's the difference what time it is, he thinks; it's too early to get up, and he lies back on the bed. She's on her side, her back to him. He must have recently turned her over to that side because he knows he put her on her other side, facing him, when he got her set for sleep. She's so quiet, he wonders if she's breathing. No, of course she's breathing, he thinks, but what he means is he wonders if she's having any trouble breathing. Just before he turned off his night table light and fell asleep, she complained about feeling a bit ill and cold. He pulls her nightshirt up and puts his ear to her back and hears her heartbeat. He counts to the beat "One-two, one-two, button your shoe, button your shoe," which is a normal heartbeat, he thinks, so she must be feeling better. Good, that's all that matters. He pulls her shirt up higher and strokes her shoulder. Her skin is so smooth: another sign of health. He once said to her "Your skin's so smooth"—he forgets what part of her body he felt then; he thinks, her backside—and she said "Just like everybody's, where you're feeling." "No, take my word," he said, "yours is especially smooth, and all over, not just here." "You're only saying that because you want something from me, like my body." "Not really," he said, "although if you gave me it, I wouldn't mind." He wonders why he's thinking of this incident now. Anyway, he started to make love to her and he forgets if she said to stop. He gets an erection. Now he knows why he started thinking of the incident. He massages her exposed shoulder with one hand. She doesn't say to stop. That's a good sign too, for making love, he thinks, if she's awake. If she wasn't interested in his touching her and she was awake, she'd say so to stop him before he gets too aroused. She'd say "Please take your hand away"—always "please"—"it's keeping me from sleep." Or she'd say "I'm not feeling well, so please don't try and make love with me." He's nude; he always goes to bed nude. She always sleeps in a nightshirt and pad. He presses his penis into the crack in her pad between her buttocks; she doesn't say anything. Either she's asleep or it's another good sign, he thinks. He strokes her legs and buttocks and puts his other hand down her shirt and feels her breast. She doesn't say anything. All to the good, he thinks, all to the good. He unbuttons the pad straps in back, pulls that part away, feels for her cunt, holds it open with his fingers and puts his penis in. He can usually stay inside her for a minute, maybe two at the most, before it shrivels a little and slips out. He should have gone to the bathroom first, he thinks, got lubricant there and put it on him and jerked himself awhile and then got back in bed and, after wiping some more lubricant in her, stuck his penis in. This time he squeezes his penis at the end of the shaft to keep it hard, but by doing that he can't move back and forth in her. Then she starts moving back and forth. She has to be awake, he thinks, or else started dreaming of having sex when he put his penis in. It feels so good, what she's doing, he thinks. He thinks he's going to come in her for the first time in a couple of years or more. Is she asleep? Don't ask her. If he speaks, or even grunts, she might wake up, if she's asleep, and get angry at him for having sex with her while she's sleeping and tell him to stop. She continues to move back and forth, just a little each way but enough to keep him excited. He continues to squeeze his penis and feels he's about to come. He hopes he does before she wakes up or tells him to stop or says she's too weak or sleepy to move back and forth anymore or before his dream ends, because he suddenly thinks he's dreaming all this. …He has to take the train to get back home. It's late; past midnight, he thinks, and he also thinks he's had this dream, in various ways, before. It's always late at night; the subway station's never recognizable; he always gets on the wrong train or finds himself waiting on the wrong platform and when the train comes he sees it's not his. Or else he doesn't have a subway token and the token booth has a line of about twenty people on it, or he can't find the token in his pocket and the right train is pulling in but he won't be able to go through the turnstile to get on it in time. But maybe the platform this time is the right one, he thinks. He asks a man standing next to him "Does the BGE stop here?" "No," the man says, "just the opposite." "Where does the train on this platform go, because maybe I can take it and make a connection to the BGE at some station later on?" "It goes to the outer boroughs," the man says, "—landfills, sod farms, cemeteries, places like those. Any of them where you want to go?" "No, I want to get to the city and I need the BGE." "For that one you have to go to the upper platform upstairs and wait for it there." "This always happens to me," he says. "And if I miss my train, and it's due around now," looking at a clock, "that's the last one till morning. Why do I always take the last train home? Why don't I give myself more wiggle room? Then, if I get on the wrong platform and miss my train, I can go to the right platform and catch the next one." A train pulls in, doors open and the man gets on. The doors start closing and he holds one of them open and says to the man "You sure this isn't the BGE? I didn't notice any letters at the front of it when it came in, but it looks just like the BGE, and I've been fooled before. I once let a train leave that was the right one and the last one that night." "Please let the door close," the man says, and a woman sitting next to him says "Yeah, let it shut—you're holding us up." He lets go of the door and the train goes. Above him is a sign with an arrow on it and the words "To upper platform, BGE, SUP, EBD." He hears a train coming in upstairs and runs in the direction the arrow points to. This can't be the way, he thinks. When I came downstairs I came from an altogether different direction. I'm just going to get myself more lost. He sees someone with a railroadman's cap on and goes up to him. "Sir, excuse me, I need help." …He goes into his mother's apartment. Place smells wonderful; she must be baking something. He hears his brother Carl talking loudly from inside the apartment but can't make out what he's saying, except for "Yes, get the rope; yes, get the boat; yes, get the tree." Great, he thinks. Carl must have just got back from a trip he started out on long ago. He hasn't seen him for years and it's so nice to hear his voice again. He hurries into the kitchen. Carl's on the phone there, looks up at him and nods but doesn't smile; his face actually doesn't seem happy to see him. Is he angry at me for some reason? he thinks. What'd I do? Why, after so many years, isn't he glad to see me too? "I told you, didn't I?" Carl says on the phone. "So why do you pretend I didn't and force me to tell you again? 'Boat, ship, tree. Rope, ship, tree.'" His mother's pulling out of the oven a large baking sheet of mandelbrot. She smiles at him and says "You'll stay awhile and have some of these with fresh coffee I'll make. They're best when still warm but not hot, although, if I can say so…no, I won't say it." "No, do." "I don't want to sound boastful, but they're always very good. At least your father and I think so." "So do I and everyone else." His father and Gwen are sitting at the kitchen table across from each other, both in bathrobes; placemats and silverware and folded napkins in front of them but no plates or food or beverages. They look very old, or sick and old, he thinks, Gwen as much as his father, who must be fifty years older than she. He starts calculating: 1895; 1947; so more than fifty. Sixty. Seventy. Their faces are beet red and scarred and have the texture of cracked untreated leather, he thinks, as if they'd been burned and were still healing. They stare at him as if they want to say something but can't. "Gwen?" he says. "Dad? It's so good to see you, and Mom and Carl too, though he seems angry at me for some reason. Do you know why?" Carl puts his hand over the receiver and says "Will you be quiet for a second? This is an important call. A lot's riding on it for all of us, and I can't hear my own voice," and shakes his head at him. "You see?" he whispers to his father and Gwen. "For the life of me, what'd I do to deserve such treatment? Maybe one of you can answer it. For Carl and I were always very close, despite our age difference, or close once I reached twenty and he thirty, and it's now as if he wants to punish me." …He's lying in a bathtub filled with water, smoking a cigar and listening to a late Beethoven string quartet on the radio—he's not sure which one but thinks it could be the thirtieth. He's had surgery for a new face, hair transplants to give him a full head of dark hair, cut off ties with everyone he knew in the past, has a new name and IDs and works at a menial job in a small town where no one has any social contact with him or knows who he was. The police and FBI are looking for him. They think he did something he didn't. He'll only turn himself in when things are safe and normal for him again. If he's caught now he thinks he'll be quickly tried and sentenced to life imprisonment with no time off for good behavior or chance for parole. The doorbell rings. He's expecting no one—he never expects anyone—so let it ring till doomsday, for all he cares. Now there's knocking on the door. Probably someone who came to the wrong apartment and is looking for someone else. Well, knock, knock till your knuckles fall off, he thinks, but I'm too comfortable here to leave. Knocking becomes louder and more insistent and his real name's shouted out. "Martin Samuels; Martin Samuels; for crying out loud, open up!" Must be the police, he thinks. Face it, you're caught, and he gets out of the tub and walks naked and wet to the door. I should put on something, he thinks. And dry the floor before I open the door. At least get a bathrobe to hold up in front of yourself. It could be extremely embarrassing appearing this way. But really, what's the difference? If it's a woman cop, she's seen everything. A man, he's seen everything too. But don't open up for nothing. He looks through the door's peephole; maybe the person on the other side's gone or naked too. What would he do then? If it's a man, he wouldn't open up. A woman, if she's not old or very unattractive or tough looking, he might. He doesn't see anyone through the peephole, so he covers his genitals with one hand and opens the door. It wasn't locked, he thinks. Someone could have walked in and killed him in that tub. He looks down the hall. The elevator door's closing. "Did you come for me?" he yells. "Is there something you wanted to leave me?" The door of another apartment opens. He backs into his apartment and tries to lock the door. It won't lock. Damnit, he thinks, why is every freaking thing not working? Now I'll have to get an all-night locksmith or stay by the door till morning. He looks for a phonebook. ...Someone seems to be calling out to him. "Yes," he says, "that one of you kids?" "Both," Maureen says. "We didn't want to wake you, but you were talking in your sleep, and from what you were saying we thought you'd want to wake up." "Where are you? I can't see you." "By your bed; on Mommy's side. Want us to turn on a light?" "No, it'll hurt my eyes and I want to nap some more." "Maybe you should get up, Daddy," Rosalind says. "If you nap too long, you'll never get a good night's sleep." "Not yet, thanks. But what was I saying in my sleep?" "The exact words were 'Your mother is a ghost.' That's why we at first thought you were talking to us. But you kept repeating it—the last time almost shouted it." "Sorry if I frightened you. But you sure it wasn't 'brother' and not 'mother' I was saying? Uncle Carl's the one who's been haunting my dreams lately, especially today." "No, 'mother.' It could be you dreamed of your brother but it came out as 'mother' when you talked in your sleep." "By the way, Daddy," Maureen says, "we brought some goodies for you from Cafe Zen, things you like. It's still warm, the stuff that's supposed to be, so we'll leave it out for you. We're going out again. There's a good group playing only one night here and we don't want to miss them, but wanted to get the food to you first. Will that be all right?" "Sure. Have fun. You get your friends off on the train okay?" "They came down by car." "Car. Good. I'll get the food later. No appetite now. In fact, put all of it in the fridge. I'll have it tomorrow. Or you can, or when you come home tonight." "See you in the morning, Dad," Rosalind says. "I'd kiss your forehead goodnight but I don't think I'd find it in the dark. Sleep well. Love you." "You too," he says; "you both." They leave the room. "Turn the lights on outside, okay?" he yells. Carport and kitchen door." "Will do," one of them says. He can smell the Chinese food from here. Makes him hungry and he'd like to have some of it, right from the containers, but doesn't feel he has the energy to get up for anything but the cat saying he wants to poop outside. Minute later the kitchen door's slammed shut. Hopes they remembered to lock it. Should he turn on his light and read a little to get back to sleep? Wants to start from the beginning the reminiscences of Dostoevsky's widow, book on his night table the last two months and before that for fourteen years in the bookcase in Gwen's study and before that on one of their bookshelves in their first house. Seemed easy reading and interesting, when he skimmed it a few weeks ago. Really has no mind or inclination or desire—that's the word: desire—to read anything else. Shuts his eyes. Cat's asking for something from another room but it's too late. …He's giving what he's calling his last public reading in half an hour and looks for the book he's going to read from. It's not where it was, on his night table. "Gwen, where's my new novel? I can't find it and it's the only copy I have." She turns over in bed, grabs a book off her night table and says "Where it always was, right in front of your face," and hands it to him. "Were you reading it?" and she says "Why, in God's name, would I do that? It's yours." "Wait a minute," he says, looking at the book, "the title's *L'Escaliers de la Mort*. What is this, the French translation of my book? I don't remember getting it or even any French publisher saying they were going to publish it." He looks for the author's name on the cover and inside and on the back, but there is none. "Who wrote this? It couldn't be by a phantom. Anyway, this all you could find?" "All. My nightstand's now bare." "But it isn't my novel and I don't understand French that well and it'd be *absurde* for me to read it to an English-speaking audience composed mostly of college kids. You trying to get back at me for something?" and she says "I'm not." "Then 'even with me for something,' but if I don't turn up my book, I'm stuck." Next moment he's leading an entourage to a reading he's giving at Radio City Music Hall. The guard at the door to the auditorium says to them "Sorry, no room inside. House is packed and there isn't even space for standing." "But I'm one of the readers," he says, "the last." "You got your ticket?" He gives the man two tickets, says "Sorry" to the people who came with him, none of whom he recognizes, and takes Gwen's hand and opens the door. The man jumps in front of them and says "I can only let one of you in." "We go in together," he says, "or not at all. Think what kind of reading it'd be without the last reader. It could go on forever or till the lights went." "You got a point," the man says, and steps out of their way and they go in. The theater's dark. A movie's playing. Every seat seems taken and people are standing and sitting in the aisles all the way to the back. A few people look at them when they come in but everyone else is staring at the screen. The movie sound is bad and the print is grainy and out of focus. He looks at Gwen. She shrugs and says "It's ominous, I know." Next moment he's in a taxi with Gwen, heading to a reading he's giving. "You have the stuff I'm going to read tonight?" he says to her. "No, don't you?" "But I gave it to you at home; several manuscripts in an interoffice envelope," and she says "The heck you did. You're just trying to blame me again for something you forgot to do. Grow up, already, will you?" "Okay," he says, "I'll try. Watch." He raps on the glass partition separating them from the driver and says through the grille "Sir, even if I know we're short of time, would you please drive back to the house you picked us up at? The clothes I put on for the event we're going to are all wrong and I have to change." "Can do," the driver says, but he doesn't turn around at the next intersection. "Sir," he says, "you missed the turn. Will you please make it at the next cross street?" "Will do," the driver says, but passes the next cross street and continues straight ahead. "I'm sorry, I can't be mature about this," he says to Gwen, and slams the partition with his hand and shouts at the driver "Damn you, when I say turn, I mean turn, turn, turn." ...Gwen says in bed "Martin, help me; I can't see. My eyes. There's nothing there. Everything's black." "That's because it's night," he says, "there are no stars or moon out, the curtains are closed and your eyes are probably shut. Are they?" "Yes." "Then open them." "You're right," she says; "now I can see. Thank you. Although the room's still very dark." "I told you; it's late, or early. Want me to switch on your light?" "Just tell me the time so I can be sure what you say is so." "You have to begin to trust me," he says, "but okay." He fingers around for his watch on his night table, presses the button on it to light the watch face, sees it's quarter past four; four-seventeen, to be exact. "It's three-thirty," he says. "That's in the evening, or morning. You'll be all right. Go back to sleep." She doesn't say anything. "You already asleep?" Nothing. "You must be." He moves closer to her, one each of their knees and shoulders touch. "Want me to get your breast out? Nothing sexual in that suggestion, I want you to know. Just, usually when you're lying on your side in bed, you lie partly on your breast and ask me to pull it out. It's not something I mind doing. In fact, of all the things you ask me to do for you at night, this is the one I like doing most. Does that sound infantile? I hope not." She doesn't say anything. "Last time. Gwen?" Nothing. "Good, I'm glad, you're sleeping peacefully. But I want to help you with your breast so you're not bothered by it later on. I'm sure it can be uncomfortable." He reaches over her, grabs her right breast, pulls it out from underneath her and continues to hold it. Then he rubs the nipple. "Don't," she says. "I want to sleep." …He wakes up. He tries to remember a dream he just had, which seemed important. Gwen was driving a car, a convertible, but with the top up. It was snowing and a thin layer of it covered the ground. It almost looked like it was painted on, he thinks. He doesn't ever remember snow in one of his dreams. He doesn't recall it ever raining in a dream either, but he's sure it has. It was a light snow, the flakes quite large and falling slowly. What else? She was steering the wheel with her left hand, waving to him with her right. Then, as she drove past, she blew a kiss to him. He was standing at the corner of a city sidewalk, waiting for the light to change. There were no other cars or pedestrians. When she got to the next street, she made a U-turn and pulled up beside him, the engine still running. Her window slid down and she started speaking to him. He thinks she first said "Hi, how are you?" and then something like "I'm about to say the most important thing I've ever said to you and I don't want you to forget it." Then she said it, but he can't remember what it was. Maybe if he shut his eyes and thought even harder, he'll remember. He does that but nothing comes. Damn, he thinks; probably the best thing in all his dreams so far and he loses it. Holds out his arm and presses the button on his watch. Little past two, he sees. But why's he even wearing the watch? He's not leaving his room tonight except, maybe, to get a glass of water in the kitchen from the filtered-water tap. Takes his watch off and places it face-up on his night table. And his clothes. He'll sleep better without them, and even better if he gets under the covers. Sits up, undresses, throws the clothes onto a nearby chair, gets under the covers on his side of the bed, shuts his eyes and tries to remember what she said. …He's getting out of a cab in front of his mother's building. He's with his sister and sees Gwen standing in the street, her hands holding a book a few inches from her face and reading. "Look, there's Gwen," he says to his sister. "I don't see her," his sister says. "You never met her, so you wouldn't recognize her, but the person there reading in the street." "Where? I still don't see her." "*There, there*," he says, pointing. "She's so close we almost could touch her." Gwen doesn't look up; just keeps reading. "Oh, Gwen, what am I going to do without you?" he says. A car comes down the street, almost hits her, but she doesn't move or look away from her book. "What're you reading that's so engrossing?" he says. "Because that's just what you need, a book so good that it takes your life from you. But really, is this any time and place to be a bookworm? Put it down, look around, next car might clip ya." She continues to read. "Gwendolyn, my precious doll, listen to me for once. You're not a pigeon, though even they occasionally get run over. So you gotta move. For the last time, you have to. Come just a few feet closer to me and I promise you'll be safe." She stays where she is, reading. "You were never pigheaded," he says, "so I don't understand what you're doing. Anyway, all I can say is that's one thing you never were." ...He's waiting for a bus at a bus shelter. One comes and he steps into the street but doesn't signal it and it goes past. Three more come, one after the other, all of them his bus, but he lets these pass too. A fifth bus comes and he sees Gwen seated at a window on his side of the street and looking straight ahead. He yells "Jesus, Gwen, wait, stop!" and runs after it." ...He pushes Gwen outside in her wheelchair. It's cold, he thinks Below freezing, and looks like it might snow. He's in a winter jacket, muffler and watchcap, but she's only wearing indoor clothes and slippers without socks. Her eyes are closed and she's slumped to one side. "Gwen, you awake?" he says. "No? Okay." She'll freeze to death out here the way she's dressed, he thinks, and locks the wheels of her chair and goes inside. He lights the burner under the tea kettle and looks outside. She still seems to be sleeping. She'll come in when she wants to, he thinks, and gets the can of coffee out of the freezer. ...Gwen's lying in an aluminum rowboat that he's pulling with one hand through a party. She's on her back, her head on a seat cushion. "I hate dragging you around like this," he says, "but I have to find that woman," and she says "That's all right; I've time." He's looking for a tall thin beautiful blond woman. He met her once, he forgets where, and they seemed to have hit it off and she said to look for her at this party. He pulls the boat through another room, this one even more crowded than the last. People are gabbing, drinking, several of them smoking cigarettes. "Don't they know those things are bad for you," he says, "and the sidestream smoke bad for anybody you're near?" "Live and let live," Gwen says, smiling at him and adjusting the cushion so her head's right in the middle of it. "I'm glad you're finally happy again," he says. "I am. This is fun. Though it must be difficult for you, dragging me from room to room in this, without any water under it." "No, you're light." He drags the boat into another room, the most crowded yet. Must be the formal room, he thinks: men dressed in suits and ties and most of them smoking cigars and the few women in it dressed in long black dresses and lots of jewelry. The men seem to be mostly Indians and Pakistanis—anyway, from that part of the world: Southeast Asia, if that's where those countries are. "She's not here either," he says to Gwen. "You can't see from down there, but take my word." "So let's give up on her and get something to eat," she says. Then he sees a woman across the room waving an empty champagne flute at him. It's the beautiful tall blond, and she starts over to them. "You see, I'm right, she is here," he says to Gwen, but she's no longer in the boat. In her place, where she was lying, is a celery about five feet long, the top leaves resting on the pillow where her head was. "How can that be?" he says to the woman. "Not only is my wife gone, when it would've been impossible for her to get out of the boat herself and if anyone helped her I would've seen them, but she's been replaced by a monstrosity. She must've thought you and I wanted to be alone together," and the woman says "Why on earth would she ever think that? And celery's supposed to be good for the blood. I think we should stick around till she comes back." "All night? Even if the party ends?" and she says "Longer, if it has to come to that. Don't be a bad example of your own behavior." "What do you mean? Seriously, and I'm not trying to sound naïve, what do you?" ...Gwen's on a bed in a hospital room, feeding and excreting and breathing tubes in her. She's on her back, looks uncomfortable, and he thinks getting food from outside for her will boost her spirits. "I'll be back soon," he says. "I'm going to get you a big surprise." She stares at him and moves her mouth. "Don't try to speak. It's no good for you. Don't even move your eyes. And whatever you do, keep your mitts off the tubes, especially the ventilator one in your mouth." She nods. "Not even your head," he says. "Nothing. No movement. Stay absolutely still, you hear? Although don't indicate you do or don't. Goodbye, sweetheart," and he kisses her forehead. She smiles. "What did I just tell you? No expressions, either." He leaves the room. He's on the street and heads for the Triple-X Theatre a few doors down from the hospital. Three tough-looking policemen are standing in front of the theater, one of them, it seems, telling a joke and the other two laughing. He has to pass them to get to the lobby and thinks they're going to ask where he's going, but they ignore him. He goes through the lobby, pushes a curtain aside and enters the theater. It's faintly lit and there are no people in the audience or exotic dancers on the stage, just a man with a broom sweeping it up. Pity, he thinks. He wouldn't have minded a little dancing and simulated sex thrown in with the food. Any kind of sex, really, but only women. He goes up to what seems like a refreshment stand at the back of the theater and asks the man behind it "Do you sell Indian food?" "On both counts, you're right," the man says. "We sell and it's Indian." "My wife likes it and is in the hospital, some say on her death bed, others—well, I won't say what they say, and I want to give her a lift. What do you have today that's special?" The man says "I'm not a full-blooded Indian myself but I am for the first time making chicken breasts," and he says "That sounds good; I'll have one to go." "You have to have two if I'm to go through all the trouble of killing a chicken and making it." "Two, then, which doesn't seem unreasonable." "Come with me." They go to the front of the theater—the sweeper's gone but there's an old man in dark sunglasses sitting in the middle of the first row and staring at the empty stage, or maybe his eyes are closed—and climb the steps to the right. The man points to a door partially hidden by a stage curtain and says "You can pick up the food in there." "Nice to meet you," and he opens the door and goes inside. It's the interior of an Indian palace overlooking a great expanse of water. In fact, he thinks, it must be an enormous sea or one of the oceans. There are no boats or anything else on it and no people on the sandy beach. The palace has very gaudy furniture and a marble staircase and chandeliers hanging from the ceiling about thirty feet up with lots of bright candles in them, some of them flickering and about to go out. If one of the chandeliers falls and nobody catches it, he thinks, or even a single candle, this place could be a firetrap. He smells food with Indian spices in it but there's no booth or window around to get it from. "Is anybody here?" he yells. "Such a vast space and nobody to populate it? How do you do your cleaning, then, because this room is spotless. Anyway, I got to get back to my wife in the hospital up the street, so if you have my take-out ready, let me know. Hello? Hello?" ...It's night and he's walking on a dark cobblestone street with his sister. Looks like old Europe, he thinks, but how'd they get here? His sister seems to be around thirteen, when he thought she died several days shy of her tenth birthday. Well, it's obvious she didn't die, or people can come back. She's holding his hand and says "Martin, I have to make. Do you know where I can, because I have to go badly." "There's a toilet," he says, pointing to a door in a brick wall with a handicapped sign on it. "I'll use it after you, even if I'm not handicapped." She goes in and he waits outside. A man tries the doorknob, it's locked, and he says to him "My younger sister's in there. She shouldn't be long, but there's a line. She's number one. I'm number two. And you're three." "Fine," the man says, "anything you say, sir." Nice guy and polite and very reasonable, he thinks, the way people should always be. His sister comes out, the toilet's still flushing, and the man darts to the door. "Hey, wait, you agreed to the line. And I have to go as much as anybody." The man rolls up his sleeves and says "Ya wanna make something out of it? Because you're lying, buddy; big, big lying. You were three and I was two, so you're after me." "What a bunch of junk that is," he says, "but okay. You're a lot bigger and younger than I and I'm not anyone to physically fight over anything. Those days, and I don't only credit the change to my increasing frailty, are long past." "Fine," the man says, "anything you say," and goes into the toilet, which is still flushing. "That, my dear," he says to his sister, "is a classic example of flagrant untruthfulness and bullying," and she says "I wouldn't know. I wasn't around to hear it." …He's lying on a bed with a woman he was once engaged to. They're fully clothed and kissing. Then he says "Whew, need some air," and separates his face from hers, "You know, unlike me you're remarkably pre-served for someone who's almost seventy," and she says "I don't know if that's something someone wants to hear, but I'll be honest with you. I take nothing to make me look this way. It's all natural, even the adolescent acne and blond hair." Though her legs are much heavier than they were, he thinks, her thighs especially, and she was a professional ballet dancer. Best not to comment on them. "So," she says, "if you're done looking, we ought to get hopping." She sits up, slips off her jeans and socks and is naked from the waist down. "I can't," he says. "My wife. It's crazy, because since you broke off our engagement forty-five years ago, I've dreamt of making love with you numerous times and in a few of those dreams I even got in you but never ejaculated. Came close, but the dreams always ended before. It was so frustrating, because it felt like the real thing we were doing. Sometimes I'd be on top, sometimes the bottom. And now, when it's possible, top or bottom or even sideways if I wanted to, I'm sure, or like two dogs, it's impossible for me to." "Oh, come on," she says. "Sure you can." She unzips his fly and sticks her hand in and searches around for his penis. "Don't," he says. "I said I can't, and I can't." …He wakes up and thinks Just like always when he's making love with her in a dream, except this time it was he who stopped it from completing, and it ended long before where he usually gets. Why couldn't he have done what she wanted, stuck it in at least, moved around a bit, taken it as far as it would go? Maybe he would have come. She looked just like she did when he last saw her some thirty years ago, and her thighs were slim and strong again once she took off her jeans, and what did she mean about acne? In real life she might have had a few scars, but her face was perfectly smooth in the dream. If she hadn't broken off the engagement he might still be married to her, if she hasn't died, and their kids would probably be in their forties. Strange to think. But what a body she had. Best of any woman he knew. Grabs his penis. Surprise, no hard-on, not even the start of one. Jerks it for about a minute, rubs the tip against the top sheet, then pulls the covers off and gets on his back and jerks it some more, but it stays limp. Give it up, he thinks, and sex again with anybody?—forget it—and gets on his side and pulls the covers up over his shoulder and holds his penis and shuts his eyes. …His older daughter yells through the bedroom door "Dad, Mom needs you." "Where is she?" he says, and she says "On the hospital bed in my old bedroom." He goes there. She's not there. He goes through the house looking for her, yells down to the basement "Gwen, you there?" Opens the kitchen door and yells outside "Gwen, Gwen, you out there?" Runs to the mailbox and back, walks around the house, goes into his daughter's room—she's lying in bed, listening to music and reading a book—and says "You sure Mommy wanted me?" She says "She said so, but maybe she no longer does." …Gwen holds up a big square rubber eraser and says "How much do you think I can get for this?" "One dollar, tops," he says. "Could you sell it for me, then? I haven't the energy to and we can use the *gelt*." "'*Gelt*'? You? I never heard you use a Yiddish word in your life. That's my father's word and expression—'We can use the *gelt*'; 'Make a lot of *gelt*'—not yours. And what're you talking about our needing a dollar? We've plenty of money, or enough, if we don't hang on too long, for the rest of our lives." "Maybe you have—you're self-supporting—but not me. Sell it and put the money you get into a triple-A safe account in my name, with the kids as beneficiaries." …He's in the driver's seat of a car, she's in the passenger seat, but the steering wheel and foot pedals are in front of her and she's driving. "We must be in jolly England," he says. "No," she says, "in jolly U.S." "I'm saying 'England' in the sense that the ignition and controls are on the wrong side of an American car and you're driving much too fast." "No, the right side, and I'm in fact not driving fast enough," and the car speeds up. Then it swerves sharply to the right and almost goes over an embankment and he yells "Gwen, what're you doing—you want to kill us? You almost drove off the shoulder into a ditch." The car continues to swerve left and right on the narrow shoulder. He grabs the wheel with his right hand and steers the car back onto the two-lane road, slows it down by stepping on the brake pedal, then feels guilty he yelled at her again. "I'm sorry," he says. She starts crying. "I'm sorry, I'm sorry, I said I'm sorry. Oh, damn, here, take the freaking wheel already," and she says "I eventually will, but do you have to be so mean about it?" "No, I don't; I'm sorry," and she takes the wheel and drives at the posted speed and doesn't veer off the road. "Good, that's the way to go. I'm so ashamed, though; really. I could've corrected you more gently and less physically. But you'll forgive me like all the other times, won't you?" and she says "I don't see how I can." …They're walking beside a stream in the woods, he pushing Gwen in her wheelchair and their older daughter behind them. Gwen says "She's not holding on to either of us. You won't let her get too near the water, will you?" and he says "Oh, she's all right." "She's not all right; she's not even two. She can wander off and fall into the stream and drown in a foot of water." "Believe me," he says, "she has the common sense and good judgment of someone two or three times her age. She'll know not to get too close to the water, and if she does get very close, she'll know not to fall." "People fall even when they do know not to," and he says "Look, how else is she going to become self-sufficient and independent of us but by dealing with things, even potential catastrophes, on her own? But don't worry; I'm looking out for her." "Then look out for her now," she yells. Their daughter's standing by the edge of the stream, bends over to reach something in the water, and falls in. Gwen screams, tries to get up out of the wheelchair and the chair starts to fall over. He catches the chair just before it hits the ground and gets it upright with her in it and with his other hand grabs his daughter out of the water and sets her on her feet. "Look at that," he says. "Saved you both and at the same time. What husband-father you know could have done what I did?" Gwen, stroking their daughter's hair, says "Neither would have happened if you had listened to me. But, oh no; you had to be stubborn and contrary, just like you've always been. You'll never change. You're like a heroism-obsessed firefighter who starts forest fires so he can save people when he puts them out. You're too dangerous to live with. Once we get home I'm calling a lawyer to start proceedings for a divorce." "You can't do that. It's the last thing I want. And think of the kids." "We only have one," she says, and he says "But we're going to have two." …Gwen's in a hospital bed in his sister's old bedroom. His mother's standing beside her, holding her hand through the bed rail while dabbing her forehead and cheeks with a washrag. He's sitting in an armchair in the room, reading a magazine, when the phone rings on the side table next to him. He answers it. It's his doctor. "Jake," the man says, "I've very bad news for you. Your report came back from the lab. It's just what I thought. You have cancer and you have to be operated on right away to eradicate it." "Thank you," and he hangs up the phone. His

mother's old and somewhat feeble, he thinks, and he doesn't see how he can
leave Gwen alone with her for so long. He says to them "That was my
doctor. He called me Jake, for some reason, but I know he knew he was
talking to me. Must've been a slip of the tongue. 'Jake' means okay, and I'm
not. He says I have the most serious cancer a man my age can get and I have
to have surgery today or I'll be dead by next week. I don't know what to do.
Leave or stay. Abandon you both for a while to try to save my own skin or
continue to help Mom with Gwen and die in a week. Tell me, what should
I do?" Gwen hunches her shoulders and gives a look as if she doesn't know
what he should do. His mother says "Do what's right for yourself; that's
always the best way. That's what I'm doing with your lovely bride. If I didn't
look after her day and night I know it'd upset me so much that I'd get
mortally sick and be dead very soon." "Gwen," he says, "please say something. Don't leave me guessing what you think." She hunches her shoulders
again and gives a look as if she knows what she wants to say but doesn't want
to say it to him. "Then whisper to Mom what you're thinking and she can
tell me." She shakes her head. "You're no help," he says to her, "you're no
help," and he starts crying uncontrollably. "Oh, my poor boy," his mother
says, patting his shoulder. There, there, everything will work out. You'll
come to the right decision for yourself without any help from either of us
and feel much better in the end." He shakes his head and wants to say "No,
it won't," but he's too choked up to speak. ...Someone's knocking on his
bedroom door. "Yes?" he says, but the knocking continues. It's coming from
some other part of the house, he thinks. He gets off the bed and goes into
the kitchen. A policeman's behind the screened storm door, his fist just
about to knock again. Big guy, maybe six-four, and muscular, with a fat
neck, and looks very serious. He backs up a few feet when he sees Martin
and puts his hand on his holster. He's suspicious of me, he thinks, or maybe
I got it wrong. It's bad news, though, that's for sure, either for me or about
someone I know. Maybe one of my daughters, or both together, died in a
car crash or got sick all of a sudden and was rushed to a hospital. No, if it
were a death, there'd be two policemen. But that's only when two soldiers
show up at a door to tell someone their son or another close relative died in
the war. "Yes, officer," he says, opening the door, "what can I do for you?" Is
this fourteen-oh-seven Hazelton?" "No, thank goodness. I mean, that what
you've come for isn't related to me. I was thinking the worst for my family
again. House you want's farther up this driveway." "Are you sure you're not
fourteen-oh-seven? We got a call from a lady at that address that her husband's being very rough with her, might even have threatened her life, but

before we could get her name, the phone was slammed down and nobody would pick up when we called." "I didn't know she had a husband. Anyway, people often come to our house when they want hers. Pizza deliverymen and UPS drivers and the like. Maybe because we have no name or house number on our mailbox and they think the first house they come to on this driveway is hers. But I swear to you, nothing but harmony between me and my wife." "May I talk to her?" and he says "She's out. You can look around the house, though," and the policeman says "No, that's all right," and gets back in his car and drives up the hill. He goes back inside the house. "Gwen, you'll never believe what just happened," he says, walking into her study, where she's working at her computer. "A cop was at the door and said you called them to complain I was roughing you up and possibly threatening your life. He asked to see you but I told him you weren't here. Good thing he didn't take me up on my invitation to inspect the house. I could've been charged with giving false information, maybe handcuffed and thrown into the back of his car. But he must've believed me when I said there was nothing but good feelings between us and the last thing I'd do is harm you in any way, shape or form. Yes, we've had our spats, I said, but worked them out almost right away. Like my parents used to say about their marriage, I told him, we never went to bed angry at each other, which meant we always got a good night's sleep, unless we were sick with or worried about something. One thing I find puzzling is why he knocked on the door when he could have used the bell. The bell is much more civilized." She raises her shoulders and turns back to the computer and resumes typing. "So what're you working on these days?" he says. She continues typing. "All right, I'll go." …They're watching a movie on the DVD player. She's in a wheelchair and he's lying on the bed and feeling sleepy. "What film is this?" he says, yawning, and she says "*Marie Antoinette*." The old one or the new one?" and she says "neither of those but one of the two or three in-between. 1938." "That would make me two. Did I order it or did you?" and she says "You never order anything online because you don't know how to." "Also," he says, "because I can hardly stand seeing anything on the TV screen for even a single minute and most movies are pure *dreck*. Violent, vulgar, stupid, sophomoric—" "All right," she says, "all right." "So I figure, why bother renting a movie at a video store or even asking you to order one online that probably neither of us will like. In addition—" and she says "Shh, let me watch. It's not as if I have to find worthless everything you do or that you can convince me to." "Me? Your hubby? You got the wrong body, lady. Because why would I—" and she puts her finger over her lips and looks sternly at him and then turns back to the movie. Marie's berating some foppish-looking man over a necklace he wants to be paid for and she claims she never bought, when the picture disappears and the screen starts flashing horizontal lines and then goes dark and next the room's lights go on and off a few times and then stay off. He jumps off the bed and looks out the window. The whole neighborhood's dark. "Oh, my goodness," she says, "I'm frightened. Hold me," and he says "Glad to, but stay there—it might take me some time," and feels his way over to her by touching the dresser and bed and then her chair, and runs his hands up her legs and arms and hugs her around the head. "My sweetheart," he says, "this is so awful. I'm very frightened too. I don't want—this outage has convinced me of it—to live anymore." "Don't say that," she says, "because where will that leave me?" Just then the generator starts up and the lights in the room go on and the movie resumes. "Thank God," she says. "But shut the movie off and send it back. I don't want to watch any more of it. It's a familiar story with gorgeous sets but acted quite poorly and it's all going to end badly for Louie and Marie." …She's in bed under the covers, he's sitting in a chair beside her holding her hand; they're watching *Marie Antoinette* on their DVD player. "Do you know if this is the new one or the old?" he says, and she says "I'm too sleepy to care." "Did I order it or did you?" and she says "All I know is it wouldn't have been my first choice," and clasps her hands together on her chest and shuts her eyes. "Don't fall asleep," he says. "I don't want to watch the movie alone. And you speak French, so I need you to translate it for me." "The movie's in English, made in America," and he says "I haven't understood a word anyone's said." "Then turn it off, because I'm not interested," and he says "Glad to," and presses the power button on the TV. All the lights in the room go off but the movie stays on. He gets up and looks out the window. "We seem to be the only ones who've lost power," he says. "Martin, Martin, help me. I'm scared, I feel this is the beginning of everything going." "Glad to," he says, and lies down beside her and kisses her forehead and eyes and puts his hand under the covers and feels between her legs. "Now everything seems a little better," she says, "but I won't be able to sleep with the movie on. It's going to end brutally, with their heads sliced off or the sounds of them rolling on the ground, which is just as bad. Take me to another room for the night." He stands up, puts his arms under her back and legs and lifts her and carries her into their older daughter's room. …"I'm going out for a walk," he yells from the kitchen, and Gwen says from somewhere in the house "I didn't hear you; what's that you said?" "I'll see you later," he says, and leaves the house. He walks for a few seconds on the road by his house and then feels a sharp pain in his right temple, thinks Oh, no, it's happening, what I for a long time dreaded, and collapses to the ground. I'm dead, he thinks. Probably a stroke, or shot an embolism, as my mother used to say. I got off easy, though. Pain for just a second and no lingering death. He's now sitting on a tree limb about ten feet up, looking at his body on the ground. So this must be what I looked like when I was asleep, he thinks. I always wanted to know. Of course I could've had Gwen or one of my old girlfriends take a photo of me while I was asleep, but I never till now thought of doing that. Gwen. What it's going to do to her. No preparation for my death, which she'll find out about pretty quickly. Our house is right over there. I can see the roof through the trees. I want to cry about the spot I've put her in, but can't. He feels his eyes. Nothing, he thinks, and I also don't feel any tears welling up. I guess when you go you stay dry. No pissing, spitting, sweating, tears. A jogger stops about twenty feet away, approaches his body cautiously. "God almighty," she says. She gets on her knees and puts her ear to his chest and mouth. "Poor guy," she says. "Not a sound." She tries dragging him off the road by his arms, probably so no cars will run him over, but it's obvious he's too heavy for her. And dead weight, of course, he thinks. A car stops; then several: a line of cars and a school bus. One of his kids on it? What's he thinking? They're grown up and out of the house. "Turn that thing around," someone shouts at the bus driver. "There's a dead body here." Their cat crosses the footbridge from their house and licks his hand and then settles down beside him, its head resting on his chest. People get out of their cars, some on cell phones. Then sirens: an emergency medical truck. Four women run out of it with equipment, some they carry, some they roll, and hook up lines and tubes to him. "I know the man," the jogger says; "I just realized it. He's sort of an institution around here. Writer of some note and a very popular college teacher too. I read a front page article on him just last week. Because of it, I wanted to stop by his house and meet him and shake his hand for continuing to do what he does, although I never read a word of him, and now it's too late. This always happens to me. I get a great idea to do something, and by the time I'm prepared to act on it, the possibility of it fizzles. His name's Kyle Faulkner. He said in the article it's a difficult name for a writer to have. Readers will always think of the shorter Faulkner, make unfortunate comparisons, though it didn't seem to hurt him that much. As far as this neighborhood's concerned, he's famous." "His name's Martin Samuels," a man says. "Where'd you ever get 'Faulkner'? And 'writer of some note'? Maybe 'one note,' because his work's surely not to everyone's liking. Too granquilogent and pompastic, or whatever the damn words are. I happened to have read a little of his work, or, rather, listened to him read a sample of his newest novel on a podcast connected to that article, so I'm in a position to say." "I plan to listen to it," she says, "and I will, but up till now I haven't found the time." Then he sees two policemen at his kitchen door, one of them knocking on it. He's sitting on the patio table there. Normally, it'd topple over if he sat on it, he thinks. The policeman knocks again, but harder. "Ring the bell," he says to him; "the knocking will only alarm her." Gwen wheels her wheelchair around from her computer. "Open the door," she says; "it's unlocked." He sees her saying this from the opened kitchen window. The policemen go in and one of them says "I'm afraid we've come with extraordinarily bad news for you, Mrs. Samuels. If you are Mrs. Samuels." "I know what it is," she says. "I sensed it but didn't want to believe it, even before I heard the sirens. My husband died of a stroke while jogging, didn't he?" "Walking," the policeman says, "though you got half of it right. I don't know how I know about the walking part, since no one saw him fall, but I do. A jogger did find him." "Walking," she says. "So that's what he was shouting out to me before he left the house. I thought he said 'I'm going out for a talk,'" and she lowers her head till her chin touches her chest, shuts her eyes and starts crying. "I don't know what I'm going to do now," she says. "You mean after we leave?" a policeman says. "We'd want you to come outside and identify the body first." "I mean I don't see how it'll be possible to live without him. He was my main help. I used to say to him 'Nobody but us could ever realize what we endure.'" "Now I understand," the policeman says. "May I?" and he gets behind the wheelchair—the other policeman's holding open the door—and pushes her outside. He gets off the table and follows them. …He's walking along a busy city street and talking to himself. "I don't know what the hell I'm doing. I'm engaged to a woman who looks somewhat like a man and whom I don't especially like. She's really quite unpleasant, not just to me but to everyone, and overly assertive and too domineering, and not at all my physical type. She's unattractive. Well, people can be unattractive—I'm unattractive, though I didn't always used to be—so that alone wouldn't stop me from falling in love with someone. But she does nothing to make herself even a bit more attractive. She wears blood-red nail polish and her hair's always a mess and her clothes are all wrong for her. And she has too much hair on her face. She should get most of it removed. Gwen used to have a little blonde mustache and a few hairs sprouting out of her chin, and she went to an electrologist to get rid of them about once every six weeks. We used to drive there together and after the treatment, have lunch at the same place every time. Great sandwiches and salads and soups and moderately priced. We never tired of the place. Great coffee and the service was efficient and quick. Even the water: fresh and cold and with no ice in it, which is how we first asked for it and we didn't have to tell them that a second time, and with a lemon wedge fixed to the rim of the glass. The owners soon knew us by name and greeted us warmly every time we came in and asked about our daughters. Why did we have to break up and divorce? I should've fought to keep the marriage going. Not doing that was the worst mistake of my life. I could kill myself for not acting better to her the last two years of our marriage. Idiot! Idiot!" People on the street look at him as he talks to himself. He yells to a bunch of them "Go on, look, what do I care? Things couldn't be worse for me, so what does it matter what you think? I screwed up my life and am continuing to do so, royally, royally. Ah, the hell with you all." He continues walking and talking to himself. "I should've promised her that I'll be a much better husband and friend to her. 'I've always been a good father, haven't I,' I should've said, 'so what makes you think I can't be a good husband again to you too? Just give me time, but you have to trust me. It'll be worth it to you if you do, I swear. I won't blow up at you again.' I should've said, 'I promise. I won't be mean, short and impatient to you, get angry at you over nothing, talk under my breath against you, ever. I'll be sweet and kind and good-natured and sympathetic and everything like that to you,' I should've said, 'if only you'll not divorce me. I'll be a much more agreeable person all around, you'll see, and it'll be real, not put on. I know how despicably I've behaved to you in the past,' I should've said, 'and I plan to change all that and be nothing but good and helpful to you from now on.' Those are some of the things I should've said. What in God's name stopped me? How did our marriage get so bad that we separated and then divorced and I ended up with this woman I don't want to marry but have promised to? Where did I even meet her? She just appeared, and next thing I knew I was living with her, and then engaged, with the wedding set for next month." Just then he sees Gwen driving down the street in a cream-colored sports car. Her wheelchair's folded up in the back seat, its wheels sticking up and spinning. He goes into the street and waves his arms at her and yells "Gwen, Gwen, stop." She pulls over to about a foot from the curb—he has to jump back onto the sidewalk or be hit by the car—and says "You. I thought I'd seen the last of you. Why did you flag me down? What are you doing in this city? Are you stalking me? Why did I ever stop for you, the last person on earth I'd want to meet?" "Gwen, you got to listen to me. I'm doing something really stupid. I'm marrying someone who'll assure my constant unhappiness for the rest of my life. She's all wrong for me, intellectually, morally, socially, physically. Even her clothes are ugly, her hair's always unkempt, and she's a tyrant and she doesn't like kids. She had to have forced me into getting engaged to her, though I don't remember that, because I never would have agreed to it voluntarily. Maybe she has something on me that if she reveals it would ruin my life, but I have to get out of it. Only you can help. Please take me back. I want us to remarry. May I get in the car?" "Let me think about it," she says, smiling. "Does that smile mean yes? About letting me in the car? Remarrying me? Both?" "I'm not sure," she says. "You're not sure if that's what your smile meant?" "I don't like you jilting another woman for me," she says. "It'll be the last time for that, I swear. You're the only one I want to be with, and I'll stick by you forever. No matter how sick you might become, I'll be there for you, regardless of how hard it gets. Please give me one more chance." "Then, yes," she says, "get in. She unlocks the door with a button on her side and he reaches for the door handle. Before he can open the door, she guns the motor and drives off. "Wait," he says, "wait." He resumes walking and talking to himself. The street, which was almost deserted a few seconds ago, is crowded again. "It was so close. If only I'd got in the car before she drove off. I would've sat beside her and said what a great driver she is and how beautiful she looks and what a lovely dress she has on and how happy I am to be sitting next to her and that I'll never, ever be anything but good, sweet, kind and patient to her again. 'You've seen the last of your Mr. Bad Guy, I swear on a stack of Bibles to you,' I would've said. Then I would've asked her to park in an out-of-the-way spot and when she did I would've kissed her eyelids and fingertips and felt her thighs and breasts and then kissed her lips and said I loved her—'I love you'—and have never stopped loving her since I first met her, not even once. 'I am so happy now,' I would've said, 'I could cry.'" …She's lying in bed on her back, doesn't seem to be breathing. "Gwen? Gwen?" he says. He listens through her dress for a heartbeat, feels her temples and wrists for a pulse. Nothing. But she's smiling, or looks like she is, but didn't he read somewhere that it might, soon after someone dies, have something to do with the accumulated gas inside? He pushes up her dress, shirt and bra and puts his ear to her chest. Nothing. He thought maybe all those clothes were concealing her heartbeat. He feels her chest for a heartbeat, then strokes her breasts, then kisses her nipples and thinks Why not; it's not impossible. Nobody's around and nobody will be coming around. Just once. If it turns out to be too difficult or disgusting, he'll stop. He pulls off her panties, raises her legs up into a crab position, gets the lubricant tube out of her night table, squeezes lubricant on his fingers and smears it on her vagina. He unzips his fly. No, he thinks, do it the way you always do it, and keeping your pants and undershorts on will make it more difficult to get inside her. He takes off his shirt and pants and shorts, her knees have folded in so he spreads them apart again, gets on top of her and sticks his penis in. He comes very quickly. About as fast as he ever did, he thinks, or since he was in his twenties. He can't even remember feeling anything now. Anyway, he wouldn't have wanted it to go on much longer. He gets off the bed, wipes her vagina with his undershorts, puts her panties back on, pulls down her bra, shirt and dress. She still seems to be smiling. He puts his ear to her nose and mouth. Nothing. Maybe it is gas, he thinks, and puts his ear to her stomach but doesn't hear anything in there. He puts his clothes back on and dials 911. "Reason for calling?" a woman says. "I've just done something terrible," he says, "maybe worse than that, but definitely something most people would find disgusting. I made love to my wife after she died a natural death, probably from a stroke." "So you're reporting a death and the deceased is there with you now?" "Yes." "Give me her name and address where you are and then I want you to wait there," and he gives them though doesn't think the house number's right. "But you're certain she's dead? You a physician?" "No." "Then I can get someone on the phone to give you instructions how to help her if she's showing even the slightest signs of life. Just listening and feeling for her breath and pulse doesn't tell you everything." "She's dead, I'm sure." "An emergency medical team has already been dispatched and should be there in five minutes." "There's no rush," he says, "although it's true I'd like to get this over with soon as I can," and he hangs up. The phone rings right after. It's the same woman, he's sure, though he has no idea what for. Let it ring, he thinks; I've told her everything. ...He wakes up. What was that all about? he thinks. Well, it's been awhile and he's a bit horny, or thinks he was when he fell asleep. Could he actually do what he did in the dream? Forget it. No, could he? If she were in bed right now and just died or within the last hour or so, maybe less, and nobody was around and there was no possibility of anyone interrupting him, he might. He could. One last time. He thinks so. Probably, yes. And then do everything he did: wipe, re-dress her, etcetera, call 911. ...They're in a cabin in Alaska or somewhere far north. He looks out the window. Snow all around—fifteen-to-twenty-foot drifts in some places and pine trees, or some kind of evergreen, that might be a hundred feet tall—but no other cabins and no roads. The cabin's next to a body of water that isn't frozen. Looks like an ocean or huge lake or could even be a very wide river whose opposite bank is too far away to see. Doesn't understand sea ice and currents and the warming effects of the Gulf Stream, if it is an ocean, and things like that, so won't try to explain why there isn't even a little ice on the water. You'd think, though, he thinks…but forget it. He hears a motorboat come close to the cabin, stop for a few seconds, and then putter off. "I think our lunch has come," he says to Gwen, who's at the dining table typing out a new poem on a small manual typewriter. "Good," she says, without looking up; "I haven't eaten since breakfast and I'm starving. Why do they send it over to us so late? Artists have to eat to create." "Oh, I'm an artist? You could've fooled me. But not eating doesn't seem to have stopped you. Look at you: scribbling away like there's no tomorrow, while I have nothing to say." He goes outside on the deck that surrounds the cabin and walks to the end of their pier. Should've put a coat and cap on, he thinks, but for some reason, though the temperature must be ten below zero, he feels warm. Dry cold, it must be, but again, he doesn't know and he's never heard of the term "dry cold," so he shouldn't try to explain. And while he's at it, what's sea ice? Does it have anything to do with permafrost, which is big up here but he also doesn't know what it is. Gwen would know, he thinks. She knows everything. A wicker basket, which the motorboat operator always puts their mail and lunch pails in, only has a note. "We thought you'd like this puppy," he reads. "Kind of a cute guy, isn't he? Hope all's still well with you both. The staff." But there's no puppy. Then he sees, about thirty feet away, an enormous polar bear drinking from the lake or river or whatever it is. That's what they think's a puppy? he thinks. Only animal around, so must be it. He goes inside the cabin. Gwen's sealed up an envelope and is putting stamps on it. Poem she was working on, he thinks, off to a magazine in tomorrow's mail and he hopes a quick acceptance. She could use it. "So you finished it?" he says, and she says "Two of them, and both quite long. It's been a very creative day." "Well, your creativity might have to stop, even though there doesn't seem any stopping you, because our lunch wasn't dropped off. But the boat did leave us a puppy and a nice note. I don't think they meant for us to kill and cook the puppy, though. Things haven't got that bad." "A puppy," she says. "I've always wanted one." "But you got to see it. Not your typical small dog. Color and size of a white polar bear. Maybe all polar bears are white from birth, but I don't know of any polar bear puppy this big. Eight feet long at least. I think I once knew the name of this breed. You must know it." She looks out the window and says "Oh, it's so cute. I want to keep it." "We can't," he says. "It'll feed itself from what it catches in the water—that won't be a problem—but it's too big to bring inside." "We won't have to," she says. "Look at that thick coat. It'll stay warm outside no matter how cold it gets, and it'll be great protection against anyone who might want to harm us. One look at this huge puppy dog—and just imagine how big it'll be when it's fully grown—and they'll run away. When we leave here we have to take it with us." "There's no room for it in our house. Our neighbors would be frightened of it. It'd have the local dogs barking all day and night, keeping everyone awake. And suppose it gets loose, because what hidden-fence system could keep it contained? Just think what it'd then do to our garbage cans and everyone else's. The mailman won't come within fifty feet of our mailbox once he sees the dog. Besides, how would we transport it to our home? It can't fit in the car. I say no and that's what it's going to be, no." "You're such a despot. You always have to have your own way. You never think what I might like," and she goes into the other room in the cabin— their bedroom—and slams the door. "Meanwhile," he yells, "what are we going to do about lunch? The boat's gone. There's no way of communicating with them because this stupid place doesn't believe *artists* should have phones in their cabins. We'll have to wait till dinner for food, and I'm famished myself and could also use a thermos of strong black coffee. Or maybe I missed something in the basket. Do you hear me, Gwen? I think I might've missed some food in the basket and am going outside to check." She doesn't say anything. "Boy, when you're mad, you really stay mad. How long you going to hold that grudge?" No answer. "Okay, I get the message," and he goes outside and looks in the basket. There are two jars of jam and a knife to spread it with, and underneath a cloth napkin, two warm rolls. The puppy, though, he thinks…where'd it go? He looks around sees it standing waist-deep in the water. It leans its head back, holds a large thrashing fish above its mouth and then drops it in and swallows it whole. …They're in their van traveling north. He's driving, Gwen's in the seat beside him, and Rosalind's sitting behind them. "Did you know," Rosalind says, "—Daddy, are you listening to me?" and he says yes. "Mommy, can you hear me?" and he says "Shh, she's asleep; don't wake her." "Then did you know, Daddy, that the very road we're on, the Merritt Parkway, was originally built—I believe, more than eighty years ago, and this was a new concept in road-building— so people in the city could take leisurely weekend drives in the country and admire the scenery on the road? In other words—and I learned all this, strangely enough, in a college lit course—the road was not just to be used utilitarianly to get from one place to another in the most direct route possi- ble and in the shortest period of time, but to—" "What's that?" he says, and she says "I was saying—" and he says "No, that loud cracking sound outside. What is it? Grief, I bet I ran over something that's going to mess up the car's undercarriage, or something important's fallen off the car. I just know the goddamn trip's now ruined," and he looks back through the rear window and sees a tree coming down on a car about fifty feet behind him. "Oh, my gosh," he yells, and Rosalind says "I know; I saw. It missed us by a second and a half." "Three to five seconds, I'd say, but what luck. 'Luck' that it didn't fall on us and we weren't killed. The poor people in the car, though." And he sees in the rearview mirror the tree on top of the car's squashed roof. "Gwen," he says, "Gwen," and shakes her arm. "Wake up, wake up. You're not going to believe this close call we just had." "Shouldn't we stop?' Rosalind says, and he says "Stop for what? What could we possibly do?" "Help them. I mean, there's nobody on the road behind us; we could simply turn around." "You want to actually look in that car?" "What are you guys talking about?" Gwen says, and he says "Look behind you; you can still see it. A tree. We were the last to get through. First I heard the cracking sound of it splitting in two, I assume, and then falling. Or just splitting off from its base; I didn't hear it fall. No whoosh sound; anything like that. Not even a crash. Maybe all the brush on the tree softened the sound of it hitting the ground. But I knew something was wrong. I thought it was our car, the underside of it, but the tree landed on the one right behind us. Rosalind says we missed getting hit by a second and a half. It was so tall, it fell across the entire road. The cars behind it will be stuck there for two hours at least till the car's pulled out of the way and tree's cut up and removed. That's because—well, you can see for yourself—the barriers in the median strip, so they can't turn around and go back. It's just going to fill and fill with cars till the last exit we passed. I can't believe we were so lucky, not only not getting hit but not getting stuck. I can't believe it. It's just so hard to believe." "I think we should call 911," Gwen says, and he says "Do we have a cell phone?" "You know we don't, but we could get off this road and call from the nearest service station." "By that time—by even now, probably—a few hundred people in cars backed up behind the tree, and others going the opposite way who drove past it, have called from their cell phones. Really, let's just go on and pretend it never happened. Or not pretend, so much, but not constantly talk about it. I'm upset, and talking about it is upsetting me more." "Me too, in a way," Rosalind says. "It's only now sinking in." "I suppose it's a good thing I was asleep," Gwen says. She puts her hand over his on the steering wheel. "Don't let it upset you so much that it affects your driving." "I'll try not to," he says, "but I think the damage has been done.

I'll just stay in the right lane for the time being and drive slow." …He pulls into their driveway. Several cars are parked on it and the kitchen door's wide open and the storm door's been taken off and set to the side. Something's wrong, he thinks. Gwen. But no ambulance or cop car or anything like that, so he's probably mistaken. Or the kids. Something could have happened to one of them, or even both, in the city they live in together, and the people in the house are consoling Gwen. But the storm door. Another bad sign? Taken off to get a gurney through, so it was Gwen. He gets out of the car and rushes into the house. Their daughters and Gwen's father and her best friend from New York are in the kitchen along with some older women he doesn't remember ever seeing. "It's Gwen," her friend says, taking his hand and rubbing the knuckles. "Be brave, Martin. Be strong. *Courage*; *ayez courage*. She's already been taken away. You were out so long, we made all the arrangements ourselves. We were waiting here to tell you." "Daddy," one of his daughters says behind him. …There seems to be a war going on. Their house and all the surrounding ones have been destroyed by explosives. Gwen's running down the street with Rosalind in her arms. She seems to be around six months old. But it can't be her, he thinks, since Gwen and Maureen and he went to her college graduation exercises a few weeks ago. Has to be somebody else's kid who looks exactly like Rosalind did at that age. But why would Gwen be running down the street with her? She's also got on Rosalind's favorite pajamas then—the ones with dancing bears and toads on them—and is waving and smiling at him and she seems to be saying "Daddy, Daddy" to him. "Gwen, wait up," he yells, running after them. "I apologize for being late. Forgive me, already, will ya? But I'm here now, aren't I, so tell me why you're running with this strange kid and what happened." She turns around, holds the child above her head and says "I've no place to go now, no place to go. That's the situation in a nutshell, I'm afraid, and you're lost." Is there a way of getting out of this? he thinks. He's done it before. Come on, come on: out! …He wakes up. What to make of it? he thinks. The "lost" part he thinks he gets, but the rest is confusing and disturbing. He doesn't want to think about it or even remember it. Good thing these damn things disappear so fast on their own. He looks at the window. It's still dark out, probably isn't even near six yet, he thinks. Go to sleep, even if you're not tired. In other words, try to, and he shuts his eyes. …He's outside the house, digging a hole for another rose bush Gwen bought, when there's an explosion. He looks up and sees their roof collapsing. Oh, shit, no, he thinks, another invasion. "Enough, I want peace, for freaking sakes," he yells. Then bombs or mortar shells or something like that, he thinks—could even be bazooka rockets, though you never hear about them anymore—explode around the house, a little shrapnel cutting into his arm, but he's not bleeding. His neighbors' houses seem untouched, though the explosives are going off around them too and all their tall trees have been destroyed by them. He hears helicopters. What sounds like ten to twenty of them, flying close together? He looks at the sky but just sees a V-shaped formation of geese or ducks flying in his direction. Then he hears them when they're directly overhead: ducks. Gwen runs out of their house carrying Maureen, who's just an infant. If he'd known they were inside he would have gone in to get them, he thinks, no matter how dangerous it was. How come he didn't think they might be in there? Stupid of him, stupid. The kitchen and dining room windows shatter and flames come out. "Help me," Gwen shouts, running down the street with Maureen in her arms. "Someone, anyone, save me." He throws down the shovel, kicks the rose bush and says "That's it for you, buddy," and runs after her and yells "Gwen, I'm here, I'll help you, but stop. I'm not as fast as you, even when you're carrying Maureen, and I can't run anymore. My knees. But don't worry, sweetheart, we'll find a way out." "No," she says, still running, "there's no place for me to go." "There is, I'm sure of it, and this time I'm not going to let you down. And where's Rosalind? She still inside? Don't tell me I made another mistake." She keeps running and then disappears around the curve of the street. "My God, no," he screams, and runs toward the house, then walks as fast as he can, as both his knees buckle. ...He's in their guest bathroom, scrubbing his nails with a nailbrush. "They're not clean enough," he says, "I have to scrub them more." He puts more soap on the brush and scrubs his fingers and nails and rinses them under the faucet. "They're still dirty," he says. "I'm not cleaning them hard enough, and I've only done the right hand, not the left." He squirts liquid soap on his hands this time and scrubs both sides of them with the brush and then the fingers and nails. "Scrub harder," he says, "even harder. Your hands are still dirty; your fingers and nails still filthy. Even your wrists could use a bit of cleaning. You can't touch other people with your hands unless they're absolutely clean, so if you have to, scrub till they hurt." He rubs the bar of soap into the bristles of the brush and scrubs his wrists and then the hands and fingers and nails much harder than he did before. He scrubs the right hand so hard that he cuts several of his knuckles. He holds the hand under the faucet to wash the blood away. "Blood, too, is dirty," he says, "so I have to start over. And now the brush is dirty too, so clean that first." He cleans the entire brush with the bar of soap, rinses it, then rinses the soap and scrubs all of his hands again. "That should do it, he thinks, "but it hasn't. The wrists and brush are now clean but I have to scrub every part of my hands some more." He squirts liquid soap into his palm and runs the brush bristles in it. …Gwen and he are walking past a bookstore. He stops, holds her by her elbow and says "Want to look in the window?" "You know, this is as good a time and place as any to tell you something I've been holding back on for too long." "What's that?" he says, and she says "Well, to be quick about it, you smell. Not you personally—as a person, I'm saying—but your body." "Good? Bad? How do I smell?" and she says "Very bad." "That's funny," he says, "because you once—okay, this was quite a number of years ago—said I smelled like toast, which I took to be good. But how can you say I smell very bad? I shampoo what little hair I have, twice a week. I take a shower almost every day—maybe three days out of four, so every day that I need to and some days when I don't. I change my clothes—socks and undershorts and whatever shirt I might be wearing, usually a T—daily. And I smell my sneakers and moccasins and shoes every day before I put them on to make sure they have no odor. If they do, even the slightest, I put deodorizing powder in." "I'm telling you, you smell so bad I can't even stand to be near you," and she walks away. He watches her cross the street, hail a cab and get in it. He raises an arm, pulls back the short sleeve of his T-shirt and smells his underarm. "What's she talking about?" he says. "I don't smell anything." He looks in the bookstore window. Nothing of mine in there, he thinks. Why don't they have anything of mine? …He's driving home and thinks his family's not going to believe what he went through today. "First, a flat," he'll say. "Then, when I'm fixing it, a woman backs up into my rear and busts both my taillights. While I'm waiting to get the tire fixed, I slip on a strip of black ice and cut my hands and scrape my knees. Of course, my pants tore, but that hardly counts, although I felt stupid walking around all day with holes in them. Later, some guy screams the worst obscenities at me because he said I wanted to steal his parking space. I gave up the space to him, though I'd gotten to it first, because I didn't want him coming back after I parked and breaking off my windshield wipers. So I drove around for half an hour looking for a spot, before I gave up and decided to put the car in a lot. But they were all filled except for one that charged forty dollars, and only in cash, while all the others would've been twenty, check, cash or card. Then, around one, I go out for lunch and forget to get my credit card back at the restaurant. When I go back there, they say they don't have it. I said 'C'mon, I last used it here,' but all right, and from their phone I call Chase Visa to cancel the card. Only good thing to come out of the day is that no one had run up a number of illegal charges on the card in the forty or so minutes since I lost it. And because so many of our monthly bills are automatically deducted from that card, I'll have my work cut out for me once I get the new one. Then, returning to work, I get a stomachache so bad, and probably from that lunch, that I had to sit on a bench outside for around fifteen minutes till I felt good enough to resume walking. Just before I'm leaving school, my department chair calls me into her office and says I'm doing, as she put it, based on the complaints of some of my students, a rather lackluster job teaching this semester, that my student evaluations for the last semester were pretty poor too, and that there's a good chance my contract won't be renewed for next year. What I'm getting at—and I left out a few things: losing several stamped envelopes I was about to drop in the mailbox; forgetting to show up for an important faculty committee I'm on; misplacing my school keys, so having to call Security to let me into my office; jamming the photocopy machine and the department's administrative assistant giving me hell about it—is that it's been one of the worst days of my life. Nothing tragic or crushing or that I couldn't deal with; just one thing after the next; one thing after the next. Even when I tried calling home to talk to Mommy about it—I felt I had to speak to someone the line was constantly busy." He gets out of the car and goes inside the house. "Hello, I'm home, everybody," he shouts. Maureen comes into the kitchen. She looks despondent, starts crying. "What's wrong?" he says. Then Rosalind comes into the kitchen and starts crying. "Both of you? What the heck's the matter? —Gwen," he shouts. "What's happened? The kids can't speak. — Where's your mother?" he asks them. "She's not answering either. She out?" …Gwen and he are at the Baltimore airport, sitting at a table in a snack bar. Behind her, through a floor-to-ceiling window, he sees a huge jet taking off. She's saying something, and he gestures for her to wait till the plane's gone: he can't make out anything she's saying. Then it's quiet and she says "I hate to be cut off in midsentence," and he says "I was only trying to let you know I couldn't hear you over the noise and that whatever you were saying was being wasted. Now, what were you trying to tell me?" and she says "That you shouldn't have driven me here. I could have taken a cab. And that after you did drive me here, you shouldn't have parked. But if you had to park, you shouldn't have come into the terminal with me. This only prolongs what I know is misery for you." "Misery? Being with you? Hardly. I'd buy a ticket and get on the same plane with you if you let me. Sit next to you, if the seat was available, just to have six more hours with you. If the seat was taken, I'd ask the person sitting in it to switch seats with me. If the person didn't want to, I don't know what I'd do. Do you really have to go?" "Don't ask silly questions." "You'd be much happier with us, you know." "With the kids, yes, I'd be happy;" she says; "very happy. But, in case you forgot, I'm married to someone else now, I love the big lug, and, unfortunately for me and the kids, he got a very good job in California, so I had to move out there with him. Maybe one day we'll come back. He understands I don't want to be separated from the kids too long." "Listen, move back with me now," he says. "You're the only woman I've ever really loved. Without you, I'm finished for the rest of my life." "Not so; you'll find someone." "No one," he says; "I've tried. It doesn't work with anyone but you. Nothing even came close." "Here, I've got a couple of minutes left; I'll find someone for you. —Miss," she says to a waitress walking by and who looks almost exactly like Gwen did twenty years ago "are you taken?" "If you mean am I busy, no. You'd like me to get you something? Refill on your coffees? Your check?" "I meant, are you attached to anyone in what we'll call a romantic way?" "Yeah," the waitress says. "I live with a guy I like and we'll probably get married in a year." "You see?" he says to Gwen. "No matter what anyone tries to do for me, it never works, it'll never work, and I don't want it to. All I want is to be with you." "Darn," she says, looking at her watch. "Time for me to go to the boarding area and fly home." She stands, grabs her bags, says "Don't walk me, and this time do what I say. Besides, they won't let you past Security." She puts her cheek out, he kisses it and she leaves. "You forgot to pay for your coffee," he says. "Only kidding. I'll take care of it and leave a good tip. Look at that: you leave, I leave." She doesn't turn around, keeps walking. "Please look back at me and wave," he says. She doesn't, just keeps walking, "All right, keep walking," he yells. "It's supposed to be healthy for you, I read. But don't ever come back, you hear? Don't even think to. It's too tough on me. I can't take it. Don't even come to the East Coast, because I just might bump into you. Florida, Maine, and every place in between: just stay away. You want to see the kids, I'll fly them out to you and take care of the costs." …The doorbell rings. He's upstairs in his parents' apartment and his mother says "Martin, could you get it? I'm all tied up." He goes downstairs and opens the door. Their postman, who says "Man, have you ever become the hot ticket. So much recognition from the outside. Just look at all these letters for you, from everywhere, and a package sent express from France." "Nothing for the rest of my family?" and the man says "Not today." He takes the mail into the kitchen and opens the package. It's a small tin of cookies. No return address on the wrapping or note or card who it came from. His father's sitting at the kitchen table in the blue-and-white striped

terry cloth bathrobe he wore for more than forty years. He's having breakfast and cleans all the pulp out of half a grapefruit with a tablespoon till the
inside of the rind is white and smooth, then holds it over his face and
squeezes whatever juice he can get out of it into his mouth. "Save the yellow
part of the rind for the garbage," he says. His father looks at him as if
puzzled by the remark. "I was ribbing you. It seemed like you wanted to eat
all of it. Don't; you'll get sick. Look, cookies someone sent me, I think a
secret admirer. Like one?" He gives him one of the five cookies in the tin.
His father dunks the cookie into his coffee and nibbles it. "Good, huh?
They're supposed to be the best. From France, from someone I don't know
the name of but who obviously thinks well of me. Unless they're laced with
poison. Just ribbing you again." His father continues dunking and nibbling.
"Mom," he says, "want a cookie?" She's pulling a baking sheet of mandelbrot out of the oven. "I'd be delighted," she says, "if you took one of mine."
"You'd be delighted if I took one of your cookies, or delighted to take one
of mine?" "Both; neither. Why do you have to complicate everything? Try
not to be so clever. In the long run, it hurts." "Hurts me? You? Hurts who?
And in the short run, does it also hurt, but less so?" and she says "See what
I mean?" "You asking if I do or don't? Okay, I'll knock it off." "Besides," she
says, "my mandelbrot's still so hot it'll burn your tongue if you try to eat it,
and I can't grab one of your cookies with these oven mitts on." He puts one
of his cookies into her mouth and holds it there till she bites off half.
"Good, huh?" and she says "As you can see, I'm swallowing." "They're from
France, where you expect the best and get it, though nobody makes mandelbrot like you." He turns to his sister, who must have just sat down at the
table across from his father, and says "Have a cookie? They're from France,
sent anonymously by someone who I suspect has a fairly high regard for
me." She's dunking a tea bag into a mug of steaming water and doesn't look
at him. "Come on, what do I have to do, hand-feed you? I will, because I
know that if you don't eat one you'll be missing out on something important. Tiny tins like this don't come to our household every day. Okay, you
forced me," and he holds a cookie up to her lips and then jabs them with it.
She keeps her mouth closed, and he says "You're right; that was a little too
aggressive of me," and puts the cookie in front of her on the table. She
nudges it off the table with her index finger. "What're you doing?" he yells.
"There are only two left," and he tries to catch the cookie with his foot, but
it bounces off it and breaks into hundreds of crumbs on the floor. "Must be
made of cornbread," he says. She's drinking her tea now and still doesn't
look at him. "She must be mad at me over something," he says to his

mother, "though I've no idea what." …He's walking along Amsterdam Avenue, when he suddenly darts into a funeral home. A man standing by the inner door says "You can't come in here in shorts. Show respect. If you're here to attend a funeral, we have a number of gray flannel trousers in different shades and most sizes, if you don't mind trying them on in the cloakroom. And a yarmulke. You'll need to wear a yarmulke. That we can also provide," and takes one out of his jacket pocket and gives it to him, "I'm not here for a funeral," he says. "I came to pick out a coffin for myself." "Downstairs," the man says. "You can take the elevator or walk." "Just one flight, right? I've been here before for my parents and sister. I'll walk." Then he's in the basement and pushes open a door that says "caskets" on it. Two men are applying makeup to the neck and face of a young female corpse. "Pardon me," he says. "I must've read the sign wrong." "It said 'staging area,'" one of the men says. "What did you think it meant? You get your kicks looking at dead naked women? Come closer and take a real look. We'll even part her legs for you so you can peek inside." He leaves and pushes open a door with no sign on it. "Here's a very nice one," a woman in the room says to him, grazing her hand over an opened casket with lots of hardware on it. "Hermetically sealed and exceptionally sturdy. Guaranteed to last a lifetime, we like to joke." "It looks like it was built for a Mob kingpin," he says. "Ten G's, am I close?" and she says "Twenty. It's a hundred-percent ebony, so like your top grand piano, it'll never lose its shine." "Let me see your cheapest coffin. I'm on to your selling stratagem, showing me your most expensive box first, and when I reject that, your next expensive, and so on down the line." "Follow me," and they go through several rooms of coffins till they come to the last one, with a single plywood coffin in the middle of it. "This will do the job," she says. "It won't last more than a few days, but by then, who cares, unless you have fears of being eaten alive underground. Another joke we occasionally use. Making light of death seems to relax the client. So when is the happy event?" and he says "You know, you're going to be mad at me for wasting your time, but I'm not quite sure why I'm even here. I'm going to be cremated when I die." "Good thing not before," she says. "Anyhow, office for that is on the third floor." "I'll take the elevator this time," he says. "I suddenly feel tired. Excuse me," and he reaches around her to press the elevator button. …Gwen and he are in a motel room. It's stuffy, almost airless, he thinks, and he tries opening the one window but it won't budge. He lets down the venetian blind and snaps it shut. "They don't even supply the room with a fan," he says, "and the shower only runs cold. What made us come here?" She's lying on the bed in only her pajama top, watching one of the movie channels on cable. He sits on the bed beside her and runs his hand along her thigh. "Not now," she says. "I want to watch this. I've seen it before, it's quite good, but the opening's terrifying. You won't want to watch it. You'll cover your eyes, and the scary sounds from it will make you want me to turn it off. You should go out. Run, swim, work out in the exercise room, or get yourself a coffee. But please don't disturb me when I'm doing something I like," and she takes his hand off her thigh, slaps it playfully, and turns back to the TV. "I'm sorry," he says. "I thought I was being affectionate." He grabs his bathing suit, leaves the room and goes down a dark hall, thinking he's heading for the indoor pool. The door at the end of the hall opens onto a food court of a mall. All the food stands are shuttered except for an old-fashioned soda fountain with about ten padded stools screwed into the floor. A soda jerk's behind the counter, dressed in a white linen jacket and cap soda jerks used to wear and who looks just like Jeff Chandler. Tall and broad-shouldered like him and same pepper-and-salt hair that starts low on his forehead. Maybe it is Jeff Chandler, he thinks. After his movie career ended, he might not have been able to find any other work but this. But he doesn't want a soda and the place doesn't seem to serve coffee or have anything to boil water for tea. He looks around, because he thought he heard a couple of shutters going up, and then back at the soda fountain. Gwen's sitting at the counter. "How'd you get here?" he says. "You were just in our room, less than half dressed. And what happened to the movie?" "You were right," she says. "I was? Well, whatever I was right about, good. Because that doesn't happen too often. Your saying it and my being right." "You're too hard on me. I've said it plenty; just you never want to hear it. And how'd I get here so fast? I flew." "Mind if I join you?" and she says "Need to ask? You're the one who brings in sixty percent of our household income, and besides, aren't you my spouse? You get first dibs." He sits beside her. Man sitting on his right turns his way and blows smoke in his face. "Did you have to?" he says, and the man says "What am I doing? I'm smoking. Since when is that a capital crime?" He says to the man who looks like Jeff Chandler "I'm not going to refer to you as 'soda jerk.' I find the term pejorative. I'm going to call you 'counterman.' So, Mr. Counterman, isn't there a city ordinance against smoking in public places that serve food?" "There is, but we don't observe it. Bad for business; keeps customers away. Look at all those other food joints here that have closed. We're the last holdout." He moves to the other side of Gwen and says "The counterman's the spitting image of Jeff Chandler." "Who's that?" she says, and he says "Oh, that's right; you were too young, maybe not even born. Famous movie actor when I was a kid. Used to play a lot of Indian warrior roles, and he always seemed to get gunned down by the cavalry in the end. He was Jewish, you know. You should move to the other side of me so you don't get the guy's sidestream smoke. That can kill you too." "I'm happy where I am." "What'll you have?" the counterman asks her, and she says "A lime rickey in one of those tall, chilled, smoked glasses, and lots of ice." "And you?" and he says "Plain seltzer, not flavored, and no ice or anything else in it, and in any kind of clean glass." "Before I bring you two anything, there's a large tab the lady's run up. Could you pay that first?" "How could she have run up anything?" he says. "She just got here." "Thirty-seven dollars and fifty-five cents," the counterman says menacingly. "Okay, okay. If you are who I think you are, I know what you've done and what you're capable of, so I'm not going to argue with you. And what the hell. Not a lot of money." He pulls out his wallet and opens it. His credit card's gone. "Oh, no." he says. "My worst fear." …He's working out on one of the strength machines at the Y, when Gwen comes in. He waves to her. She stops to look at him, doesn't smile or wave back, gets on an exercise bike and sets a book on a holder in front of her and starts pedaling while reading. What strange behavior for her, he thinks. She looks around at him while pedaling. He smiles and mouths "Hi, what's doing? And why didn't you say hello?" She faces forward again, pedals, looks back at him a couple more times, gets off the bike, wipes it down and comes over with the book under her arm and stares hard at his face. "It's you," she says. "I told myself when it happened that I'd never forget your face, but here I have. Good thing you kept making yourself obvious to me. Yeah, go on, smile and wave, you filthy bastard, but I'm getting the police. Everybody," she yells, "don't let this man leave here. He raped me more than a year ago and was never caught. I'm going to call the police now," and she leaves the room. She comes right back with a policeman and says "This is the man who jimmied my kitchen window to break into my apartment and forced himself on me in bed." "That's ridiculous," he says. "We live together; she's my wife," and she says "Since when?" "I'm afraid I'll have to take you in, sir," the policeman says, and motions him off the machine, grabs his arm and starts walking him out of the room. "Gwen," he says, "do you realize what you're doing and what's going to happen to me? Whatever your reason for joking around like this, it's gone too far." …He wakes up, shakes Gwen's shoulder from behind and says "Dostoevsky's dead." "Of course he is," she says. "1861." "1881. 1861 was when I think *Notes from the House of the Dead* was published and the American Civil War was in its second year. He wasn't in it. Never got to America and I don't think he ever wanted to. Baden-Baden; gambling; that's what he liked. I've been reading his second wife's reminiscences of their fourteen years together. His first wife died of TB. He also lost two children and a favorite brother. Jesus, what a life. A lot of what she writes about is his gentleness and thoughtfulness and empathy and compassion and his love for her and she for him. She worshiped him. Before I fell asleep I finished the part where Dostoevsky died. So he's dead. He's really dead. What an awful thing to consider. I doubt I'll be able to get back to sleep tonight." "Do you want to hold me from behind?" "Yes, that might help. Thank you." …"Rosalind, Daddy, Mommy's sick again," Maureen shouts. "Call 911." …Gwen and he have just made love. He gets off her. She says "I can't believe it." "Can't believe what?" he says. "That this is how we produced our two daughters and now they're both over twenty-one. A miracle; two miracles. And that we're still going at it after so long could be considered another miracle. How was our lovemaking, though?" "At the count of three," he says, "or just now?" "How would I know?" she says. …He's at a cemetery with his sister and Gwen. Some men are digging at his parents' gravesite. His father's coffin is lifted out of the grave by the men and pried open with crowbars and shovels. He looks in the coffin. His father, in a fetal position, looks the same after being buried for more than thirty years. Not even dirt on him, he thinks, and his clothes look as if they were just put on. "Okay," he says to the gravediggers. "I've seen what I came here to see. You can nail it up and let him down again." His sister says "No, you can't re-bury him. I swear I see some movement in his chest." "But look," he says, "his eyes are shut, his face is perfectly at peace and he hasn't eaten for close to thirty-five years. How can he be alive?" "If you ask that, why not ask how he could have a heart-beat? Because he has one. Don't deny it. You can see it as well as I." He looks closer at his father's chest. It's moving up and down, up and down. "That's not a heart beating," he says. "That's his lungs going in and out, in and out. Gwen," he says, turning around to her, "you know everything about every-thing. Tell us who's right." …He walks into a room, looks around for his wallet, and sees Gwen's head on a chair. "Oh, no," he says, and a man behind him says "If you cry, and I'm not saying 'cry out,' we'll cut off your head too." The man's dressed in black and has a watchman's cap pulled down over his face, with slits in it for his eyes. "Though we will spare your mother," the man says. "Because of her age and infirmities and that no one should think we're entirely disrespectful." "But my wife was infirm too. Three strokes in two years. She was on a respirator the last month of her life. How could you do this to her? She was so goddamn sweet and good-natured to everyone. Ah, kill me already, you bastards. What do I care, now that she's gone?" He pushes the man aside and goes into a bedroom to look for his wallet. An ex-girlfriend's tied to a chair, her mouth gagged. "She's next," the man says. "Then your wife again, then you." "Why? What is it with you guys that you can't let them live in peace? What'd either of them ever do that could be considered wrong, except once know me? Oh, Christ, what people never stop doing to each other." And he drops to his knees and bangs his forehead on the floor and keeps banging it till he passes out. …"This was the most important thing I could tell you," Gwen says to him. "But you were either too busy with your work or indifferent to my needs to pay attention, or you simply didn't bother to listen, even if you had to have seen how much it meant to me." "Not true," he says. "I just must've forgot. Tell me it again. Then repeat it three times, one after the other. That's how I'll remember." "I want to commit suicide." "I won't let you. And there's no way you'd be able to find the strength to do it alone. You need my help and I won't give it." "I can starve myself to death," and he says "Then I'll force-feed liquids and food down your gullet." "I'll clench my mouth shut to stop anything from coming in," and he says "I'll find some way to pry it apart. You're staying alive, by hook or crook. It'll be worth it to you, I promise. If anything, do it for me?" "Please," she says, "I beg you to help me kill myself, or at least not stop me." "By hook, by crook, by God, no. I'm keeping you alive and that's the last we'll talk of it." …He goes into work at a convenience store. The owner, who's Chinese, says "How many hours you planning to put in today?" and he says "As many as you want. I'm here for the duration." He gets behind the sales counter and rings up a pack of cigarettes. God, I didn't know they were so expensive, he thinks. And they end up killing you. That's ridiculous. Two boys run out of the store with sodas and candy bars they didn't pay for. "Stop, thieves," he yells. "Be right back," he says to another customer, who put a carton of milk and bag of doughnuts on the counter, and runs after the boys. He looks both ways on the street, but they're gone. Kids are so fast, he thinks. I used to be fast too. He goes back to the store and gets behind the counter and opens the bag to count the doughnuts. The owner comes over and says "You intentionally let those young punks get away. Do you realize what this petty thievery's costing me? Get your things and get the hell out of here." "But I need the job; something to do." "Too bad." He walks out of the store with a Chinese co-worker. "I'm seventy-one," he says. The co-worker pats his shoulder and says "Boring; boring." "My wife died this year." "That, too, is boring." …Gwen's sitting up in bed, drinking tea. He says to her "Your principal caregiver called and said she's been diagnosed with stage-three cancer and can't come work for you anymore." "The poor dear; such a fine lady and so good to me. How I'll miss her. She's all alone and doesn't have any money saved. Who'll take care of her when she starts falling, and now who'll take care of me?" "I will, although now full-time." "You? I want to laugh—with all my recent set-backs, I'd like to find something funny—so don't tempt me." "But I will take care of you, much more than I have, I promise. Till the rest of our lives together or whoever dies first." "Go away and let me grieve for her and myself. This has been quite a blow." "You'll see," he says, and takes her empty mug and leaves the room. …He's around eighteen and lying in the upper bunk of the bunk bed in what they call the boys' room. Gwen's sleeping in the lower bunk. He reaches under his pillow for his alarm clock and looks at it. It's one-thirty in the afternoon. How can that be? he thinks. The window shades are up and there's bright sunshine in the room and he's never slept past noon. "Damn," he says, "I was supposed to get up at eight for an important makeup test in history. Now I'll flunk the course. If I do, I won't be able to graduate this term and start college in September. That'll put me a half year behind—that is, if I pass the history test next fall. If I fail that one too, or even sleep through it again, I'll be a full year behind and maybe won't ever get into college because of all the times I failed and missed the test. All because this freaking alarm clock didn't go off," and he smashes it against the bunk rail and throws it to the floor. "Shh," Gwen says. "It's still early. Let me sleep." …He and Gwen and a couple of their friends are sitting in a theater watching what he'll call an acrobatic dance company on stage. The dancers are all young and very trim and wearing tight skimpy bottoms and nothing on top. Looking at the women's breasts should be somewhat exciting for him, he thinks, but for some reason it isn't. The entire troupe has turned itself into what looks like a wagon wheel—three of them as the rim and four as spokes. It moves around in circles, bumps into several objects and almost rolls off the stage into the orchestra pit, and then the spokes fall off and the rim breaks apart and the seven of them leap to their feet and hold hands and bow to the audience. There's lots of applause. "That was amazing," he says to Gwen. "What people, when they're working together harmoniously, are able to shape themselves into. They looked and acted just like an out-of-control wagon wheel. I bet, though, they've fallen off the stage a few times and had other accidents, especially when they were first trying out that routine, and got plenty of bruises." She points to the stage and he looks. Another dancer, or acrobat—he really doesn't know what to call them—steps out of a large black box four of the others carried onto the stage with exaggerated difficulty and set down. He's much bigger and older and heavier than the others and not even as muscular as any of the women. He kind of looks like me, he thinks. In fact, it is me. "Look, I'm part of the company," he says to Gwen. "About to dance or do acrobatics and make an utter fool of myself. But don't look too closely at my belly. I've a huge beer gut and it's much hairier than it normally is. To tell you the truth, I look disgusting and ridiculous, compared to the others, and I can't imagine what use I'd have for them up there." She puts her finger over her lips and turns to the stage. The tallest of the other men climbs up the front of him as if climbing a robe ladder and stands on his shoulders. Then another man climbs up him the same way and stands on that man's shoulder. Then two men grab an arm and leg each of one of the women and faster and faster swing her back and forth a few times and throw her onto the shoulders of the man on top. Then the tallest woman climbs up him and the two men and woman as if she's climbing a much longer rope ladder and stands on the shoulders of the woman. Then the shortest woman—she can't be more than five-one, and very slim but solid—climbs up him and the two men and women the same rope-ladder way and stands on the shoulders of the woman on top. Then this tower of performers—maybe that's what it's supposed to be, he thinks: the Leaning Tower of Pisa, or another famous tower but one he's unfamiliar with—sways from side to side and nearly falls over but rights itself just a few feet before it would have hit the ground. The tower's so tall that the head of the woman on top is obscured by the overhead of the proscenium. Then this woman dives into the outstretched arms of the two remaining men standing below. The next woman also dives into their arms, and the two men and women still on top of him jump off at the same time, land on their hands and immediately backflip to their feet. Then all eight performers bow and blow kisses to the audience. There's even more applause than before. "Now I know what my purpose was on stage," he says to Gwen, who's still applauding though everyone else has stopped. "It's that I'm sturdy enough to support a tower of people on my shoulders and keep it from crashing to the ground. How I did it, I don't know. But I did a good job, didn't I? …He opens his eyes. It's dark out; must be around 3 a.m., he thinks. Turns to Gwen in bed and says "You up? I just want to warn you. There's an unmistakable smell of death in the room. I recognize it from when my parents died. It has to be the cat. She's been sick and getting worse the last three days. I should've taken her back to the vet when you told me to. Now I'll be sorry the rest of my life." He turns on his light, gets out of bed and looks for the cat. She's not on the floor near the TV where she's been lying quietly for two days. He looks under the bed; not there either, and the dish of water and plate of kibble he set by her last night don't seem to have been touched. He puts on his bathrobe because his daughters might be home and goes around the house looking for the cat, saying "Here, little baby; here, little baby. Come to me, come to me," and finds her at her food bowl in the kitchen. "So, you all right?" he says. She keeps eating. "You're all right. Good." …He and his best friend are standing outside his apartment in the East Village. He has a party to go to and wants his friend to come along. "I'm sure the host won't mind if I bring you." "No can do," his friend says. "I have to be on call at the hospital early tomorrow and it's a twelve-hour shift. But I've got me a gut feeling you're gonna meet your future wife there. Have fun," and his friend goes down the entrance to the Astor Place subway station. He starts walking downtown to the party. He talks to himself as he walks: "Be honest now, you really don't want to go to the party. Instead of meeting your future wife or even a future bedmate, you'll stand by yourself all evening, have too much to eat and drink because you're so uncomfortable, and then tell the host what a great time you had and wonderful people you met, and the conversations—oh, they were the most stimulating and interesting you've had in a dog's age—and leave. Turn around. Go home or stop off at your favorite bar for a couple of ales, and then go home," and he turns around, turns around again and continues walking to the party. "Nice night," he says. "Well, at least something's good. Not warm or cold; just right. Sweater weather." He likes that: "Sweater weather. Sweat her, wet her." He goes through Chinatown, then Little Italy, thinks of stopping at an Italian pastry shop for a cannoli or almond macaroon horn, then says "Nah, you came this far, get there, and there'll be plenty of good food at the party, and why waste your appetite and money? No reason. You've a small appetite and little money. So go, go." His feet feel funny and he's stumbling. He looks down and sees the street's made of cobblestones. When did he step off the sidewalk, he thinks, and the street turn from asphalt to this? Can't remember. And there are no sidewalks anymore, just street right up to the buildings, and so narrow he doubts even a small car could pass through it. He goes under a stone arch that spans the entire street, and is now in this odd landscape of ruins, he'd call it—Italian, maybe old Roman, maybe Pompeiian. It looks like those paintings, or drawings, or whatever they are—prints, lithographs, if there's a difference between the two—God, there's so much he doesn't know about art and ancient Western civilizations, he thinks—by a seventeenth- or eighteenth- or nineteenth-century artist whose name he forgets. It's one word and starts with a P or T or maybe even a B—Bruneschi? Pinelli? Torichelli?—who did buildings like these: empty; gutted, even; with cracked and broken walls and no entrances or exits, or at least none he could ever find, and with mazes of hallways and dead-end staircases, some winding through roofs and going another story or two up. Unlike in those paintings or whatever they were—etchings, he now thinks—there are people on the street here, and outdoor markets and carts and stalls, most with fruits and vegetables or leather goods like wallets and bookmarks and eyeglass cases on them. Funny, he thinks, but in all the years he's lived in this city, which is most of his life, and he got around, he's never been in this neighborhood or even heard of it. Maybe if he knew its name. It's charming, though. Who needs to go to old parts of European cities if we have this here? All the streetlamps go on at once. It's gotten dark, while it was light when he said goodbye to his friend and started down here. He keeps walking, past more peddlers hawking their wares in Italian, or it could even be Latin—at his age, and with his education, he thinks, he should know the difference. He stops to look at two identical dilapidated Catholic churches side by side, with no airway in between. Both must still be working churches, he thinks. A bride and her maids of honor are going up the steps of one of them and a priest in a white smock and some kind of gold shawl around his neck is on the top step of the other, blessing an elderly couple, who are having trouble getting into a kneeling position. All the other buildings on both sides of the street seem uninhabited: no lights in any of the windows and nobody going in or out of them. The facades of several of them have been sandblasted or steam-cleaned—he thinks You're not allowed to sandblast buildings anymore in New York; something to do with releasing asbestos into the air—and have signs on them advertising "luxurious" floor-through apartments for rent and condos for sale. "Fresca piss," a man sitting behind a cart of iced fish says, and he says "No, thanks; I'll be out too long." He goes under another stone arch. The street sign on the corner of the first building to his left says Willis Street. That's the one the party's on, he thinks: number 22. He says to a woman "Excuse me, but which is Willis Street: the one we're on or the side street perpendicular to it?" "Perpendicular?" she says. "Perpendicular? Don't be perpendiculous. We both know you're talking the wrong angle and Willis is this street here." He hears what sounds like wooden wheels going over cobblestones; then sees coming out of the barely lit side street a man pushing a gurney. A woman in a hospital gown and sheet up to her waist is on it, securely strapped in. Must be terribly uncomfortable for her, he thinks, and even painful, especially if she had surgery and was just sewn up.

The gurney passes him and he runs after it to tell the man, for his patient's sake, to go on a less bumpy street. He gets in front of the gurney, blocking it. "What's the big idea?" the man says. The woman's eyes are closed. She doesn't seem uncomfortable. In fact, she appears quite peaceful, seems to be smiling, and looks exactly like Gwen. But it can't be her, he thinks; he hasn't met her yet. "I'm sorry," he says to the man; "I have the wrong party. Now that's funny, because according to my best friend, who's also an orderly, I'm on my way to the right party, one where I'm gonna meet my future wife." "Funny to some, maybe," the man says, "but to me it's no joke. Marriage is sacred and shouldn't be laughed at." "Hey, you don't have to tell me," and he steps aside and the man resumes pushing the gurney in the direction of the churches. They going there to get married? he thinks. Can't be; she's destined for me. He looks at the numbers of the buildings he passes on the even-numbered side of Willis Street and stops at 22. It's a long stoop and he runs up it. "Whew-wee, I took those steps as if I were a kid," he says. "I really feel healthy and strong, so I must look it too, which'll be a plus." The front door's unlocked and so is the vestibule's. Very trusting building, he thinks. Good sign; seems the opposite of ominous as far as the party's concerned. The ground floor's dingy, with dim lights and torn lobby furniture and an urn of ugly plastic flowers on a side table by the elevator and walls that are stained and need plastering and painting. And the smell: can't be anything but roach spray. Bad sign, he thinks, for who starts a romance in a slum building? He presses the elevator button. "Oh, crap," he says, "I forget the last name of the person giving the party and what her apartment number is or even what floor she's on. It could even be this one." He holds his breath and listens for party sounds from the three apartments on the floor, but doesn't hear anything but a steady dripping. There's a bad leak somewhere, he thinks. A woman enters the building and yells "Hold the elevator. Hold the elevator." It's Gwen, he thinks, though he doesn't know her name yet. She hurries down the hallway and says "Now what gave me the idea it was waiting for me?" and sticks her hand out to press the elevator button. "I've already rung for it," he says. "Been waiting for it I can't tell you how long. Judging by the condition of the building, it's probably broken." "It'll get here," she says. "I know this building. The elevator's old and takes its time but always comes." "You going to the Willis party?" "Do you mean the Tourelle party? On the top floor? Not that there couldn't be two going at once. This is a lively building." "Tourelle, that's right. Willis is the street we're on. And it has to be the top floor. Otherwise, I'd walk." The elevator comes, door opens, and he gestures with his hand for her to go in first.

"I don't know. Am I doing the right thing in riding alone in an elevator with you?" she says. "Because I'm not sure you were invited to the party or that you even belong in this building, although I do know you didn't follow me in." "I'm safe, believe me. I met our party host at an artist colony this summer. She was there for photography and I was there for something else. We were next-room neighbors and shared the same bathroom and bar of soap, but at different times. And four to five floors isn't a long ride on an elevator, no matter how slow it goes, unless it gets stuck." "Okay, you sold me," she says, and gets in the elevator, he follows her, and she presses the button for the fifth floor and the elevator starts rising. "Five's the top floor, right?" he says. "There's none higher in this building," she says, "and I know the party's not on the roof." "So the elevator doesn't go to the roof?" and she says "Do you know of any that do? Oh, I suppose there's one somewhere, but this isn't that anomaly." He wakes up. It's almost light out. Must be around seven, he thinks. The dripping's from the sink faucet in the bathroom and he gets up, turns it off, and gets back in bed. He did first meet Gwen at an elevator. But on the sixth floor of a much larger and better-kept building in SoHo, not far from the neighborhood or district or section or whatever's the right word for it where the last scenes of the dream would have been if it were a real place, but after they'd left the party separately.

He puts his hands under his head on the pillow and thinks about the first time they met. He left the party and saw her at the other end of this long hall. She was standing in front of the elevator, waiting for it to come. Then she must have heard him behind her. No, she definitely heard him. They talked about it sometime later. She said her first thought was that someone was about to grab or attack her, and that she's usually not so paranoid. That his feet stomped as he ran as if he were wearing combat boots. He wasn't running but hurrying now because he didn't want her to get in the elevator before he got there and the door to close. Though if the elevator had come he would have yelled "Hold the elevator," wouldn't he? She then might have pushed the "open" or "6" button to keep the door from closing—not an easy move to do, as you got to think fast and have quick coordination—or held the door open with her hand. Or maybe she would have let the door close. Intentionally, because she still might have felt he wanted to hurt her, or because she couldn't get to the right button in time. If that had happened, he thinks he would have run to the stairway and down the five flights. But by the time he would have reached the ground floor, she would have been out of the building. Would he have tried, if he had run out of the building and saw her on the street, to catch up with her? Doesn't think so. Wouldn't want to startle or scare her. But he could have just walked fast—that is, if she hadn't stopped in front of the building—and then slower when he got near her, and said something to start a conversation, like what? "Excuse me, but we were at the same party tonight. My name's Martin Samuels, I'm a friend of Pati's, and I hope I didn't just now startle or scare you in any way." Ah, why's he speculating on something that didn't happen? Because it's interesting, going through all the possibilities that could have happened and then zeroing in on what actually did. And what the hell else he's got to do now? And he likes the idea of, well…of, that he was going to meet and get to know her no matter what. What's he mean by that? That if all else flopped—if the elevator had closed with her in it and she wasn't on the street when he got there—he would have asked Pati if she knew the slim blond woman with the beautiful smile and her hair in a chignon, if that's what that is when it's knotted or rolled up at the back of the head. Or knew someone at the party who did—the person she came with— and if she could fix them up somehow or just give or get him the woman's phone number, if she isn't married or engaged. Or if married, not separated. And, of course, she wasn't married or even seeing anyone then. And Pati would have got him her number and he would have called, or asked Pati to call her first about him, and then called and arranged to meet her for coffee or a drink. Anyway, on the sixth floor, waiting for the elevator, she heard him and quickly turned around, looking a bit startled. He said something like—or he also could have asked Pati for the woman's name and address or whereabouts in the city she lived, if she knew, or just what borough, and he would have got her number out of the Manhattan phone book because it turned out she was the only person in it with her name. But he said something like—definitely the "leaver" part, though; that he definitely remembers, his first attempt at trying to be funny or clever with her—"Don't worry, it's just me, a fellow partygoer and now -leaver, and also a friend of the host. That is, if you are a friend of Pati's and weren't brought to the party by someone who is or who knows her in some other way—a colleague at her magazine, let's say." She said something like "No, I know Pati quite well." "That so?" he said. "May I ask from where?" and she said "Grad school. She was a few years ahead of me but we became friends." "I only met her this summer. At Yaddo—you know, the artist colony, or art colony, or whatever they call it." He said that to let her know right off he was an artist of some sort and serious enough at it to get into that place. He thought, maybe because he assumed she was interested in the arts, he thinks, she'd ask him what he does, and then, because he also must have assumed she was getting or had gotten a doctorate in some kind of literature at Columbia, like Pati, what he was working on up there and was it a productive stay and so on. Probably not the latter. But she just as easily could have assumed he was working on nonfiction. Pati had gone straight from getting her doctorate to working for *Partisan Review* and was at Yaddo the exact same time period he was—they even took the bus back together—writing a biography of an influential eighteenth-century French thinker whose name he forgets. Starts with a T, his first name. T-s, T-z, T-p—but it's not important. He never read anything the guy wrote, though Pati had loaned him a couple of his books at Yaddo and then at the party asked for them back. Such a stupid move, though, trying to impress Gwen fifteen seconds after he met her with that "leaver" remark and then the Yaddo business. Thierry, that's it. He should have thought at the time—maybe he did, but just couldn't stop himself— that she was very smart—she certainly looked it, and her voice, if he can put it this way, was very smart too—to see through his inept maneuvers. She might even have thought "What bullshit this guy's trying to hand me." Not "bullshit" but some other word. "Hokum"; "bullcrap"; "baloney." Can't think when she ever cursed, and he bets she also rarely did it in her head. Though once, when she was very sick, she cried out "Why the fuck did this have to happen to me? Excuse me; I'm sorry; I didn't mean to be vulgar. But I'm fed up with my illness; fed up." But about that first night, she later said—weeks later, maybe months, when they were seeing each other almost every day—that she knew—he'd asked—he'd made the Yaddo reference to impress her. He'd said something like "I thought so. And what a dummy I was, too, because it doesn't take much to get into Yaddo—a few publications and a couple of good references—and you probably knew that. It was so desperate, but it shows how eager I was to get you interested in me, at least to the point where you wouldn't brush me off when I asked, and I was intending to, if we could meet for coffee sometime or a drink. I'm just glad it didn't do any lasting harm. It didn't, did it? And she said—now he remembered: they were having dinner at her apartment; he'd brought food from Ozu, a restaurant he'd discovered and which became, more for dining there than takeout, one of her favorites for a couple of years—"What do you think?" "What about my 'leaver' remark from the same night?" and she said "'Leave her'? 'Leaver'? 'Lever' like the handle?" "As in 'fellow party-leaver,' one of the first things I said to you when we met at the elevator after leaving Pati's party. Also said just to impress you?" She said "I think I didn't understand what you meant with that leaver but didn't want to question you on it, so I let it go. Now I see what you were getting at—'partygoer, partyleaver.' I can be slow—and I'd say it's so-so to maybe a-little-more-than-that clever. At any rate, original. I'm not aware of anyone else who's used it. So you are, to the best of the little I know, a coiner." For a while after that, when he called her, he'd say "Hi, it's your coiner calling," or just "It's the coiner" or "your coiner" and once or twice "your coiner calling from a corner," till she stopped laughing at any line with "coiner" in it, so he stopped using it. Anyway, sixth floor, after he mentioned Yaddo and got no verbal response and he doesn't think any visual reaction to it either, "So, I assume that, like Pati, you went or still go to Columbia for your doctorate?" and she said yes. "Went? Go?" and she said "Went, although I'm still very much there." "So you're not completely done with it? Or you are—orals, dissertation, defense of it, if the orals and defense aren't the same thing," and she said "They're not, and I am done with them." "Literature, also, like Pati?" and she said "Same language but literature of a different century." "What are you doing with it? Or maybe I should say, why are you still at Columbia, if that's not too personal a question?" "I'm doing a post-doc and also teaching a humanities course as part of their Great Books program." "That should be interesting," he said. "And a feather in your cap and gown, I guess, and no doubt a terrific addition to your vita for a possible job there or somewhere else, though I'm not sure what a post-doc is." "It's short for post-doctorate," and he said "No, that my little pea brain figured out. But it's not another degree, is it?" and she said no. "So what were your thesis and dissertation on? And it is a dissertation for your Ph.D. and not a thesis, right?" and she said yes and gave the title of her thesis and he said "You're not going to believe this, though I don't see why not, but he's just about my favorite nineteenth-century fiction writer. Maybe favorite of any kind of writer and of all centuries and millennia, not counting whichever one Homer was in. though he only wrote, if we can call it that, two books, while your guy filled up volumes and everything I've read of his shines," and she said "You of course know he extended into the twentieth century, though not by much, but is considered primarily a nineteenth-century writer." "Right," he said, "the late great stuff," and gave a couple of the titles. "As the title suggests, I wrote about his long stays in France and his friendships with intellectuals there and all things French. He's not who I wrote about for my dissertation," and he said "Oh, and who's that?" and she said, and he said "This is amazing. He's one of my favorite contemporary writers, and I'm not just saying that." She smiled, not, it seemed, at what he said but as if that was to be the end of their conversation, and turned to face the elevator. "Tell me," he said, "and if I'm talking too much or you no longer want to talk, tell me that too, but have you been waiting long? I mean, more than the three minutes or so we've been standing here?" "Not that long." "So what should we think, the elevator's broken or stuck?" "It was working fine when I got to the party. I'd say it's not working and that if it doesn't come in the next minute we should think about walking downstairs. It's only five flights." "You walk," she said; "I don't mind waiting. And I'm sure it's being held up because someone's loading or unloading a lot of things off it and that it'll eventually come. Besides, I don't like those stairs." He said "Why, what's wrong with them?" and she said "They're unusually long and insufficiently lit and also a bit creepy. And the one time I walked down—not because the elevator didn't come—I couldn't get out on either the ground or second floor." "In that case, you're right, and I'm glad you warned me. But it'd seem locking those doors would be against some fire regulation." "I don't know if they were locked or, as someone explained to me, it had something to do with humidity and air pressure. But I thought the same thing about a fire regulation being violated and told Pati and she said it's happened to her too, more than once." "Someone ought to complain, then, in case there is a fire or something like that," and she said "Pati did, several times, she said, and the situation hadn't been corrected when I walked down the stairs, so you can see why I don't want to take the chance." "I'll be with you," and she said "No, thanks." "I was just kidding, of course," and she said "About what?" "Nothing. I thought I might've sounded pushy," and she said "I didn't think so. You were trying to be helpful. Thank you." The conversation went something like that. More he talked to her, more he knew he didn't want to leave her without getting her phone number and some assurance she'd meet him sometime for coffee or a drink. He still didn't know if she was married or engaged or had a steady boyfriend. She had gloves on now but at the party he got close enough to her to see she wore no ring on either hand. He remembers thinking at the elevator What a beautiful voice she has, clear and soft, and a lovely face and good figure. And she speaks so well, he thought, and is obviously very smart and seems gracious and he likes what she does: teaching and getting a Ph.D. in literature and at Columbia. They'd have lots to talk about if they started seeing each other. He was never a scholar but he did like to talk about books and writers and he often read literary criticism of novels and stories he'd recently finished but felt there was more to them than he got and wanted somebody else's take on them. He could reread her writer or read some of the work he hadn't read or she recommended and what she thought were the best translations of it, and later talk about it with her. He liked the way she smiled and laughed at the party—not loud, and the smile warm and genuine, and the intelligent look she had when she seemed to be in a serious conversation. She usually had a guy or two talking to her and one time three or four men surrounding her, each, it seemed, vying for her attention. That made him think that maybe there wasn't one particular guy in her life, but of course, he thought, it could be that her husband or boyfriend hadn't come to the party. She was the beauty there, that's for sure. He remembers when she came in—alone, took her coat and hat off in the foyer, probably her gloves too, and went in back with them and, he assumes, put them with most of the other coats and where his was too, on Pati's bed. When she came back out and waved to some people and went over to them, he said to himself something like "Jesus, what a doll." He practically stalked her at the party, losing sight of her only when he went to the bathroom or into another room for a drink. He was waiting for a chance to go up to her and introduce himself or say anything to her, just so long as they started talking, but she was always with someone, mostly men but sometimes a woman or two. She never noticed him staring at her because she never turned his way when he was. He wanted her to and then, he thought, he'd give an expression with his raised forehead and some other thing with his face that he was interested in her or had been wanting to talk to her but didn't want to barge in and could she free herself for a moment? How he was going to get any of that in with a look, he didn't know. But he thought he could—maybe just smile in a way that suggested he wanted to meet her—and she might even come over to him or at least gesture in some way—hand or face or some move with her head—for him to come over to her. Then she was gone. A man tapped his shoulder from behind, and he turned around. "Aren't you Donald Boykin?" the man said, and he said no and the man said "You look just like him; sorry." When he turned back to the spot he'd been watching her at, she'd disappeared. He looked for her in the room he could see from the one he was in, but she wasn't there. He went through the entire apartment looking for her. He'd made up his mind; he was going to go over to her even if she was with other people. He didn't know what he was going to say; something, though. Maybe make up a woman's name—Dorothy Becker—and ask her if she was this woman and then say "Sorry, haven't seen her in a long time and I used to know her fairly well and I thought she'd think I was ignoring her if I didn't say hello. And now that I think of it, you couldn't be her because her resemblance to you is from more than ten years ago when she was around your age. Stupid mistake on my part. But may I ask your name? Mine's…I was thinking of saying I almost forgot it, but that'd be such a dumb joke. Martin Samuels," and he'd stick his hand out to shake. If she was with someone, he'd ask that person's name and shake hands. If she was with two or more people, he'd just say hello to them. The joke part, only if she was alone. Or probably not the joke part; too silly, so he'd just give his name. He actually thought of this while he was looking for her. If she wasn't alone, he'd first apologize to her and whoever she was with for breaking into their conversation. He didn't know what he'd do after he asked her name and gave his. It could be embarrassing, being the stranger of the group and just staying there, but he'd take the chance. Maybe he'd say "Well, nice meeting you all," and walk away and try to catch her later if she was alone, now knowing her name and the introduction, of sorts, out of the way. Then he thought she might be in the hallway bathroom. When he passed it to look for her in Pati's bedroom, the door was closed and he could see through the crack at the bottom that a light was on inside. Although someone could have left it on after using the room. He didn't want to try the doorknob to see if it was locked. He didn't want to give the impression he was trying to get the person inside to finish sooner. He stood outside the bathroom. This almost had to be where she was, he thought. And if she was in there, this'd be a good opportunity to speak to her alone when she came out, but another woman came out. He said "Hi," went in and locked the door. He didn't want the woman to think he'd been waiting outside the bathroom for nothing. And as long as he was in here, he thought, he should pee. He was going to have to do it soon anyway, what with the three or four Bloody Marys and bottle of water he had, and then he really might have to go and both bathrooms might be occupied. He peed, then went through the apartment looking for her again. Nah, it's hopeless, he thought. He went into the bedroom for his coat. He didn't see any reason to stay, now that she was gone. He knew nobody at the party but Pati and she was always getting or taking away things or introducing people. Birdbrain, he thought. For that's what he should have done: got her to introduce him to that woman, but too late for that. He really hadn't met anyone on his own here because he spent most of his time trying to meet that woman. He started to look for Pati to say goodbye. Then he told himself he'd call her tomorrow or the next day—probably tomorrow—to thank her for inviting him and to ask about this woman he tried speaking to but she was always surrounded by other people, and left. They waited for the elevator for about five minutes, maybe more. No, had to be more. There were long stretches when neither of them spoke and she looked mostly at the elevator, he mostly at her, and every so often she turned to him and smiled a bit mechanically and then looked back at the door. One time he said something like "We should seriously think about using the stairs. I'm sure the door down there will open or just need a good shove." And she said "I told you: you go. I'll go back to the party and tell Pati the elevator's not working—yes, I concede; you were right all along," and he said "Maybe I wasn't." "Anyhow," she said, "she can call the super. But I'm not walking downstairs to get out of the building, at least not yet." "It's not that you're in any way apprehensive of me," and she said "Do you mean afraid of you? Of course not. You're a friend of Pati's, so why would I think that?" The surprising thing, he now thinks, was that they weren't joined by anyone else from the party or floor, which had about eight apartments to it and it wasn't late. The elevator came around then. He said "Like tie-ups on highways, no explanation when traffic finally gets moving," and she said "I know, but hurray." They got in the elevator and the door closed. "Think it's safe?" she said, and he said "I now bet it was just someone unloading a whole bunch of packages or furniture." "No," she said, "it took too long." "A huge piece of furniture could've got stuck in the elevator door or the person or persons kept the door open with something heavy while they carried some stuff into the apartment, and then got caught up in a phone call there," and she said "Please, let's get traffic moving." He was nearer the button panel and said "Which floor should I push for you?" She looked at him as if she found the line peculiar or she didn't quite know what it meant or something else but she didn't smile or laugh, and he said "Just trying to be funny. I don't know why I feel I always have to crack you up." She said why would he want to? and reached past him and pressed the button for the ground floor and the elevator started moving—and he said something like "Before you think I'm entirely ridiculous or nuts—I'm not, the second one, anyway—let me in as adroit a manner as I can manage under the circumstances tell you why." He said that what he was about to say must have been obvious to her at the party. He'd wanted to introduce himself to her since she got there but, and these were his exact words, "I didn't have the guts." Also, "and believe me, none of this is a line," she was always talking to someone or several people and looking as if she was having a good time and he didn't want to butt in. He must have made her uncomfortable, though, staring at her so much, and he apologized for that. They had to have been out of the elevator by now and might have been walking to the outside door. She said his staring, as he called it, wasn't obvious to her because she didn't remember seeing him at the party, and he said "Oh, you had to have, at least my shirt," and opened his coat. "You see, I didn't know it was going to be so formal an event." His shirt was a long-sleeved rugby type, blue and yellow stripes with a white opened-neck collar. "I thought it was going to be a small informal get-together of friends Pati made at Yaddo this summer. I thought that because the day we left there, that's what she said she was going to do this fall. I didn't see anybody from Yaddo there. But I didn't know she knew so many well-known painters and writers and high-powered critics and book editors and the like. I didn't get to meet any of them but overheard people saying they were there and a couple of them I recognized. In fact, I was talking briefly with some writer a few years younger than I, who cut me off and said 'Excuse me, so-and-so publishing bigshot just came in and I was told I should meet him.' What a schmuck." "He was only trying to push himself a little; that's not too bad. But what I find curious is that I still have no recollection of you at the party." He remembers she took a while buttoning her coat and wrapping her muffler or scarf around her neck and maybe even adjusting her gloves and cap before they went outside. "Oh, I was there, all right," he said. "I know, but what I'm saying," she said, or at least something like this, "is that I think I would have remembered you, as you said, from your shirt. I don't mean to make you feel uncomfortable, either. I certainly hope I'm not. Your shirt is just fine, and that it has long sleeves, even better for a late-fall party. But it does stand out in its own way and would have contrasted with all the jackets and ties and dress shirts. Were we ever in the same room together?" and he said "Oh, yeah. And by the way, you were very diplomatic just now and I don't at all feel uncomfortable in what you said. At first I felt a bit odd at the party in this shirt, but I quickly got over it. But I even got so close to you in a couple of rooms—I'm afraid to even admit this bit of snooping, but here goes; I've just about told you everything else except, maybe, how surprised and disappointed I was when I saw you were suddenly gone from the party—that I... where was I? That I was able to see—that's it—that you only half-finished your glass of red wine and left it on a coaster on a credenza and that you seemed to favor the smoked salmon and carrot sticks, but with no dip on them, of all the hors d'oeuvres and crudités on the food table. I also like carrot sticks, but with the dip. Anyway—" They had to be outside by now because he said something like "So, here we are. Which way you going? I live on the Upper West Side and was going to take the Broadway train." "So do I," she said, "— Upper Upper. But I'm taking the Lexington Avenue line to meet someone on the Upper East Side." "Someone important?" and she said "If you mean in my life, a good friend." "Which subway station, the one on Astor Place?" "There's a closer one near Prince. I know how to find it from here." "Would you mind if I walked you to the subway?" and she said "It isn't necessary and would take you too far out of your way. And the streets down here on weekends are always crowded at this time, so I feel perfectly safe going alone." "No, I'm sure you do. It's just I only suggested it because I've enjoyed talking to you and I'd like to—you must've known this was eventually coming—for us to meet again. And not meet accidentally, at a future Pati party, let's say, but intentionally. Willingly. Something. Prearranged. For coffee. Would that be okay with you? You can check with Pati first to see what she thinks of me. But she wouldn't have invited me to her party—the only acquaintance from Yaddo there, as far as I saw, though maybe the others couldn't make it—if she thought poorly of me. Oh, I don't know what I'm saying. I've killed it, haven't I?" "Why do you say that?" and he said "Because I'm just bumbling, bumbling." "Really, you're too tough on yourself. Sure, we can always meet for coffee one afternoon when I'm not teaching or busy with something else and you're also free." "Afternoons are good. Mornings too. I'm pretty much unemployed now except for my writing and what I make off of it, so I can meet anytime. It's easy, and I don't mind, breaking up my workday, because I can easily get back to it and usually with fresh ideas and better ways of saying what I was working on that I wouldn't've had if I just continued writing without that break. I don't know if that was clear, what I said, but I call them, these breaks, constructive interruptions. Anyway, I'm holding you up. So, great, we'll meet. How should we arrange it?" and she said "Call, since I won't know till I get home what my schedule's like the next few weeks other than for my classes and office hours." She gave her last name and the spelling of it and said he doesn't need her address to find her in the Manhattan phone book since she's the only Gwendolyn Liederman in it. "Nice to meet you, Martin. You go by Martin and not Marty, am I right?" "Always Martin. Kids called me Marty when I was young and I never liked it. I always pictured this tubby shlub, which I never was. Otherwise, I'm not so formal. Then I'll call you, Gwendolyn. 'Gwendolyn' and not 'Gwen'? They're both nice." "'Gwen' is fine," she said, "although I like Gwendolyn better. But either. Goodnight." She put her hand out, he shook it, and she started for the Prince Street station. "Sure you don't want someone to accompany you?" he said. And she stopped and turned around. "I absolutely don't mind going out of my way. It's not that cold and I like to walk and I've nothing to do now but go home. Oh, that must sound ridiculously pathetic. Or pathetically ridiculous. Neither is what I intended it to be. It's just that it's still so early." "Go back to the party, then," and he said "No, I've already said goodbye to Pati. It'd seem too peculiar, coming back, ringing up to be let in, putting my coat on the bed again, etcetera. I'm happy to go home. I've plenty to do." She nodded and resumed walking and he headed for the subway station on Canal Street. He looked back a short time later and she was gone. He remembers thinking she walks fast and disappeared as quickly as she did at the party. He hoped she wasn't hurrying to meet up with a boyfriend. Weekend night; it makes sense. But if she was, why would she agree to meet him? Maybe to get rid of him and when he calls she'll say she changed her mind and doesn't think it necessary to give a reason why. Or the reason is that she's seeing someone or she's too busy with her work to meet anybody now, even for coffee. Or she might have agreed to meet him because she likes to take a break herself and the boyfriend she can always see in the evening. It's all innocent, in other words, he thought, walking to the subway station: tantamount to nothing. She has no plans whatsoever in getting to know him better than as someone to meet once, and if she finds him interesting enough, maybe meet for coffee a second time, but just for talk. But he was so inarticulate and clownish with her, what could she have thought they could talk about? Her authors, for one thing, but she must know ten times as much about them than he does. He should have asked if she was presently seeing someone, he thought. Well, he sort of did, she skipped around it, and anything more on his part would have been prying. Later—a couple of months or so—he was thinking about the first time they met and said to her "If you were seeing some other guy when we first met, would you have agreed to meet me for coffee or even told me how to get your phone number?" "I doubt it," she said. "I knew you were interested in me and I wouldn't have wanted to lead you on. Of course, it all would have depended on how serious a relationship I was in." "As serious as the one you're in now?" and she said "Then, no." "Semi-serious?" and she said "Maybe. Or maybe it would have had to be several notches below 'semi.' A relationship that wasn't going anywhere or I was coming out of, with no chance of going back." "Can I ask why you did agree to meet me?" and she said "The usual reasons. I wasn't seeing anyone, hadn't in a while, and I found you attractive and pleasant and smart—" "Smart? You thought I was smart? I acted like a complete putz." "No, you didn't. Let's just say I saw past what you called that night your bumblingness." "I didn't say it that way exactly, but you were close. I'm surprised you remembered even that much of it." "I also liked your nervous approach. You weren't cocky or presumptuous or anything like that. But another thing that interested me was that you were a writer." "Writers turn you on, eh?" and she said "No. But writing about them and their work is a lot of what I do. So I think I was interested in talking to you about your work and what got you started at it and how you go about doing it and what keeps you at it, and so on. I didn't at the time have much of an opportunity to speak to a live writer." "I'm sorry," he said, "that was a stupid thing for me to say." "It wasn't one of your brightest remarks," she said, "especially because you knew the answer." "Okay, I won't make that mistake again, or I'll try not to."

So what happened next? he thinks. As he walked, he probably looked back for her a couple of times, even though he must have known she wouldn't be there. He was also probably thinking What a doll, what a doll. This has got to work out, it just has to. Got to the subway entrance and started down the stairs and then thought something like What's the big rush to get home? Walk till you get tired or bored with it and then take the subway or bus. Walked all the way home. Took him about two hours. Doesn't remember being cold. Remembers a full moon. No, why's he making that up? But he does think there was a brief fall of light snow and he looked up at it and thought how pretty it was and romantic. Probably also thought Wouldn't it be nice walking with her now in the snow? Starting from when he was around seventeen he'd wanted to hug a woman from behind while it snowed, burrow his head into hers, but just never had a chance to, and of course a woman he was in love with. Later, after they'd been seeing each other a few months and were walking along the park side of Riverside Drive in a much heavier snow, he got behind her and hugged her and nuzzled his nose into the back of her neck and she said "What are you doing?" and he said "What do you think?" And she said "We'll slip; let go. You want to kiss," she said after he let go of her, "that's different, though my lips are probably cold," and they kissed. First time for that during a snow? Doesn't think so. Could have got home quicker but stopped at a bar, sat at the counter and ordered a draft beer and asked the bartender if she had a Manhattan phone book. Remembers she was tall and striking-looking and young, around twenty-five, or looked young, and was built and moved around behind the counter like a dancer and had short blond hair almost the same color as Gwen's but not looking as real. He really remembers all that? And he means the hair color real. Yes. He still has a vivid picture of her and the bar but can't recall what streets it was between and avenue it was on. Somewhere between Houston and Eighth Streets, he thinks, in the middle of the block on the west side of the avenue. Good-looking and trimly built as she was, if he can put it that way, he had no interest in her and wouldn't have even if she had come on to him, which she never would have. First off, on her part, the age difference, and on his part, she came off as hard and tough, qualities, if that's the right word, he disliked. Maybe she was just acting hard and tough because she was a young attractive female bartender and felt she had to put up that kind of front with her male customers, especially the ones sitting at the counter. She also smoked, another thing that put him off, and ground out her cigarettes in an ashtray full of butts, but he might be imagining the last part of that. But most of the rest did happen, or close to it. He recounted to Gwen several times what he did that night after she left him. And one of those times he said something like "Of course, in telling you all this, I'm saying that I fell for you immediately—maybe even while stalking you at Pati's party—which is one more reason I had no interest in the beautiful bartender." "With me," she said, "I knew I liked you after our first two dates and thought that something could possibly develop between us. But falling for you took a much longer time." "How long?" and she said "I forget. Maybe weeks, once we started going together." "Why so, do you think?" And she said "Innate cautiousness. Self-preservation. Because of my early history, perhaps, of jumping in too fast and getting burned when the man's feelings for me went sour and flat. I'm not quite sure why, but that's the way I was since my senior year in college." "Well, we went to bed pretty quickly—third date, and first was just a short walk and cup of coffee, but in reverse order," and she said "That's something entirely different. I liked our foreplay, I got very much in the mood, and I felt you weren't the type to get too terribly hurt if I decided not to see you again or for a while." "Why would you decide that when we were really just starting out as a couple and had just slept together and, as I recall, it was pretty good lovemaking for both of us, and everything seemed to be working out fine?" and she said "Because I might have thought I'd reverted to my old self-destructive propensity of jumping in too fast and risking getting hurt and I needed time alone to think more about it. I know it makes no sense, especially the part about not seeing you again, and how I'm explaining it is only muddying matters, but for now that's the best I can come up with. If you want, ask me again some other time and I might have a clearer answer. Anyhow, my sweetie, things continue to go well with us, don't they? And I haven't just now troubled you unnecessarily, right?" and he said "I don't see how you can say I wouldn't be terribly hurt if you had broken up with me then or said you didn't want to see me for a while. I know what the last part means. In the past, whenever a woman said it I knew she was just giving me time to adjust to what was actually her cutting me off and that she had no intention of resuming anything with me. As for your question do things continue to go well with us, yes." He's also written a lot about their first meeting. Self-contained chapters of novels and parts of or complete short stories, changing it around some each time. In three or four of these pieces the party's in different kinds of buildings in SoHo and TriBeCa: a three-story brownstone, a tall modern apartment building, a warehouse or factory—he forgets which—that's been converted to six floor-through artist lofts, with a fancy women's shoestore occupying the entire ground floor. Other times he meets her in a theater lobby with a mutual friend, at a subway token booth where he tells her he forgot his wallet and could she loan him a token or money to buy one and he'll mail one back to her if she'll give him her address, at a rally for the Solidarity movement in front of the Polish consulate on the East Side, at a book signing in an academic bookstore on the Upper West Side, with the Gwen character the author of a biography of a not-very-well-known avant-garde twentieth-century Russian fiction writer. He came into the store to browse and look at the literary magazines and maybe buy one or a book if they weren't too expensive. A table was set up with Georgian wine and chilled Russian vodka and various pickled herrings and a small dish of caviar on a plate with little squares of black bread around it. The Gwen character—he thinks her name was Margo—was seated behind the signing table—no, it was Mona—with stacks of her book on it. A lot more copies were in two large cartons on the floor. Oh, boy, he thought, would he ever love to meet her. Beautiful face and smile, trim figure, nice-sized breasts, he liked the simple way she was dressed, and no doubt a big brain too. Also, the way she graciously and unhurriedly made conversation with each of the four people on line who wanted her to inscribe her book for them. "Take as much as you want," she said, when a woman said she's taking too much of her time; "I'm not going anywhere for the next hour and I'm truly enjoying our little chat. Thank you." He looked at her hands and saw she wore no engagement ring or wedding band—an action he used, he thinks, in every piece he wrote about their first meeting, and also in each she had long blond hair, sometimes hanging loose over her shoulders or in a ponytail, but mostly pinned or rolled up in back, with a big enough clump there that he knew it was long. So let's see, he thought, what could he do to meet her? Got it, and he grabbed her book out of one of the boxes and read the jacket copy and checked the price. Book was more than 400 pages and had lots of photographs and was published by a university press, so it was very expensive. Really worth buying it? Hopes so, but if his plan doesn't work out he could always, when she wasn't looking, and before he paid for it, slip it back into the box. He got on line with it. When his turn came—there was no one behind him—he said to her "Hi, how's it going—exhausted by all this yet?" and she said "No, and I'm fine, thanks." And then something like "I first want to say—and I'm going to buy your book, by the way—but how unusual it is for a bookstore, or maybe it was your publisher who sprung for it, to put out such a generous spread. Usually, and not that frequently these days—publishers and bookstores alike are cutting back—it's crudités without the more expensive veggies, and cheap white wine. But caviar, and all the appropriate accompaniments? They must really love you. For me, and here I'm talking about just once, it was pretzels and tortilla chips with no salsa or dip, and nothing to drink." "Well, I'd like to give this store and my publisher credit for this modest spread—it'd certainly look better for me— but I happen to be the sole provider of it. I thought it the least I could do for anyone who'd make a special trip or stop what he was doing in the store to hear me." "You read? I'm sorry, I didn't know, and I missed it." "You bet, I read. To standing room only, but that's because the store manager said she had just one chair to spare—I'm sitting on it—and nobody wanted to sit on a cold uncarpeted floor. Around six people attended the reading. I'm sure half of them were store employees told to put on their coats and look like customers so I wouldn't think the audience was too small. Believe me, I came with no illusions there'd be a crowd, and was simply doing what my publisher asked of me. But nothing will go to waste. I can always take home the unopened wine and recap the vodka bottle. As for the food, I perhaps overbought, but I love pickled herring of all sorts and it takes a while for it to spoil. I can't say the same for the caviar, though, if any's left, so you should go over there and have some now." "I will, and some of your vodka too, if you don't mind. But to change the subject, I also want to tell you how much I admire biography writing. It's got to be the most difficult and time-consuming form there is. All that research before you even get a word down, and the traveling you must've done in the Soviet Union. And no doubt dozens of interviews with people who knew him and going through archives and having to read twice, three times, maybe more, all of his fiction, and according to the flap copy, he was very prolific, in addition to the thousands of letters it says he wrote. The copy also says this is the first book-length bio and exegesis of him and his work in any language. That means you had to retrace his life and get all the facts and such yourself and couldn't crib some details, as a legitimate shortcut but in your own words and citing where all the references came from, from other scholars' books.

By the way, did this book come out of your Ph.D. thesis at Columbia, or was that on someone or something else? But I'm prying, which I usually don't do, and as one of the women before said, taking too much of your time. I also probably don't know what the heck I'm talking about as to what goes into writing biographies. So let me buy your book already before the store closes. But would you do me one favor, though? I don't know how you're going to take this—maybe you saw something like it coming long before—and if it's wrong of me or wildly misdirected, and not because of anything you said or did, and you feel offended or just put off by it in any way, I apologize. But could you, when you inscribe the book to me, if you'll still be willing to after what I'm about to say, put your phone number under your name?" She said "Now there's an approach I never heard. And I'm not offended. I in fact think it's funny. But I'd rather not have my phone number near my inscription or anywhere else in the book. I can just visualize it. You forgetting the book on a bus and some sleazy guy picking it up and calling me. No, that's carrying it too far. But all right, if you want to get in touch with me to have coffee together one afternoon, you know my name and I'm the only one with it in the Manhattan phone book. Now tell me yours, in case you do call, so I'll know who you are when you give it, and can I make the assumption you teach on the college level too?" "Nope. I just write what others teach, although nobody's ever taught my work, far as I know, or written about it except in a few small mostly negative book reviews." And he's said a number of times to Gwen and their daughters and a friend or two and once in a taped phone interview—right after the call he had misgivings he said it and called the interviewer to delete that part when she edited the tape for radio and she said she would but didn't—that his first meeting with Gwen was the single most important thing to happen to him. "Event" was the word he used in the interview. "How could it not be," he said, or something like it, "for look what it led to. The deepest most enduring love relationship in my life and the marriage and children I always wanted and at least a dozen fictional pieces and a whole novel and about half of another one based on that night. I even took a teaching job I didn't want and have held on to it for more than twenty years now so I could support a family and get good health insurance for them and send my daughters to college no matter how expensive and buy a house with lots of trees around it and no neighbors close by and do some traveling with my wife and spend summers in Maine in a nice rental cottage near the coast and have a good retirement plan and then when I'm retired, enough money put away to shell some of it out to my kids, and so on." But maybe he's saying—he means, what he's saying is that he might be getting some of what happened in that first meeting with Gwen mixed up or in with what he changed or took liberties with in the writing of it. He thinks he finally got that thought straight. Anyway, that can happen and has several times, especially with something he's written so much about. But where was he going before, regarding the bartender? Not so much her but the bar. He was excited at the possibility of seeing Gwen again, if just for a coffee and maybe a walk. That's what he thought as he headed home soon after he left her. He'd gone into the bar to look her up in the Manhattan phone book to see if she was really in it with the name she gave. If she wasn't in the book, what would he have done? Not think she intentionally misled him; she didn't seem the type for that. If she didn't want to give him her phone number, he would have thought, she'd have told him straight off that for one reason or another, or no reason given, she'd rather he didn't call her. He wouldn't have liked it. He probably would have thought at the time "Too bad, what a loss, first woman in a long time I'm really attracted to and think something could come of our seeing each other, but nothing I can do about it: she's not interested, so that's that." Or maybe he would have pressed her a little—sure, that's what he was like then—and said "Listen, what's the harm, just for a cup of coffee, and, if the weather's okay, maybe a short walk. Or forget the walk; just a coffee. Though maybe you don't want to meet because you're presently tied up with some guy and you don't want to lead me on. If that's the case, not that I have to tell you how to act, you should say so, although I still think it shouldn't stop us from meeting sometime for a longer conversation about your work and past studies and European literature in general, even, over coffee," or something like that. Also, if she wasn't in the bar's Manhattan phone book, he would have checked the cover of it for the period it was printed for. If it was even a year out of date, it might have meant she had an unlisted phone number then or had only recently got her apartment and didn't have a phone yet at the time the book was printed, or did have one but it was too late to get her listing in it. If it was an old book—last year's or later—and she wasn't in it, he thinks he would have gone to another bar farther uptown, ordered a beer and asked the bartender for the Manhattan phone book, if it's the current one, or looked for it at the pay phone there, if they had one, or just gone home and looked her up in his phone book. The phone company dropped off a stack of Manhattan phone books once a year in the vestibule of the brownstone he lived in then and he always picked one up and brought it to his apartment, so he was sure to have the current one. If she wasn't in any of the phone books he looked at, current or out of date, he would have called Pati the next day for the phone number, saying he met Gwen for the first time at the elevator after they both left the party, they seemed to hit it off, at least enough so that when he asked her if he could call her sometime to meet for coffee or lunch, she didn't so much give him her number as tell him how to get it in the Manhattan phone book, but he couldn't find it. He looked in several other Manhattan phone books and her number wasn't in them either. Would Pati have it? If she gave it to him right away—she might have said something like "Let me see if it's all right with Gwen first, even if I'm sure it will be, based on what you just said"—he would have called Gwen that day or the next and said it was Martin Samuels from the other night, Pati's friend from Yaddo. He couldn't find her name in the phone book where she said it'd be, so he got it from Pati, if that was okay. She still interested in having a coffee or something one day? If she is, then maybe they should just set a time and date. He also probably would have thought before he called Pati or went into another bar for a current Manhattan phone book or looked in the one he had at home, that maybe he got the spelling of her last name wrong. Then he would have looked up in the Manhattan phone book in the first bar, even if it was an old one, all the possible spellings of the name he could think of: Leaderman, Leiderman, Leederman, Lederman, even Liedermann and Leadermann and so on. But before he looked up any of those, he would have dialed Information from the pay phone in that bar and given the spelling of the last name he thought Gwen gave him and said he thinks it's under "Gwendolyn" but it could also be under "Gwen" or just the initial G instead of a first name and that the address, if it's listed, is an Upper West Side one, most likely around a Hundred-sixteenth Street between Amsterdam Avenue and Riverside Drive or even on Amsterdam or Riverside Drive—anyway, near Columbia University: a Hundred-tenth to a Hundred-twenty-fifth—and got her number that way. The bartender said there was a Manhattan phone book by the pay phone just past the entrance to the bar. He said he saw the phone when he came in but not the book, and she said the book's got to be there unless someone's stolen it again. "It's attached to the phone stand by a chain, but a flimsy one," he thinks she said. "Or it could be hiding in the little cubbyhole in the phone stand." He went to the entrance. Chain but no book. He actually hadn't seen the phone when he came in and doesn't know how he could have missed it, but didn't want to admit to the bartender he was so oblivious. Could be all he had his mind on was Gwen and getting into the bar and asking for a Manhattan phone book to see if she was listed in it, and if she was, to write her phone number down. Pen and folded-up sheet of paper he always had with him. But what does he do now, he thought, or something like it, go to another bar for a phone book? He also might have thought he should forget it for now—and dealing with the bartender, just from her harsh looks and voice, could turn out to be unpleasant—and pay up and leave the bar and go straight home and look in his phone book there. He really didn't want the beer he ordered—he'd already drunk plenty for the time being. When he gets home, especially if he walks all the way, he's sure, he may have thought, he'll want a beer or two or couple of vodka and grapefruit juice drinks, something he started drinking when he was a bartender two years before, though he told his manager and customers if they asked, that it was plain juice to keep his energy up and just to drink something, and drink them while he sits in his easy chair and reads a book or the *Times*. He only ordered the beer, with no intention of taking more than a few sips of it, so the bartender wouldn't think he came in just for the phone book. "Pain in the ass," he could imagine her thinking, "making me look for the fucking book and then put it back." He's still like this. If he's on a city street and he has to pee, which he's recently been having to do frequently, and goes into a bar to use its restroom, he always first orders a beer, if he doesn't have to pee real bad, and leaves most of it. If it's a coffee shop he goes into, he orders a coffee at the counter and drinks it after he pees. If he has to pee real bad for both those or all the stools at the counter are filled, then he goes straight to the restroom and usually leaves without ordering anything. Leaves fast, though, without looking at the person behind the counter. In other words, he never likes to use something in a bar or coffee shop or place like that, without buying something, but the cheapest drink they have, and when he does, he always leaves a tip, even if he only drinks a little of the coffee or beer. Part of that's because…because of what? Lost the thought. Not tired, either. He thinks something to do with…about how relieved he is to have peed. That he was able to find, he probably means, a restroom that was free. He went back to the bar in the bar, the counter, whatever it should be called here so it's clear what he went back to—suddenly he's having trouble not only remembering what he was saying but putting his thoughts into words—and sat on a stool at it. Other customers in the bar? Thinks so; doesn't remember, but can easily picture it. Bartender put his glass of draft beer in front of him—so she knew what she was doing, not drawing and putting it down before—and said something like "I was right, right? The phone book's in the cubbyhole or dangling on the chain," and he said something like "Chain's there, book's not, so it was probably stolen like you said. Look, I was once a bartender—not too long ago, either—and we always kept the Manhattan phone book under the bar's counter. In fact, four of the five boroughs' phone books. We didn't keep Staten Island's. I think we even had the Manhattan Yellow Pages, but all of them in case a customer wanted to look up a phone number or address." "Then you must've not had a pay phone in your bar," and he said "I think we did, in the three I worked at, and with the Manhattan phone book and Yellow Pages by it or resting on top of the phone. The books under the bar were mainly for the convenience of a customer who didn't want to get off his stool to look something up. If he wanted to make a call, though, he had to use the pay phone." She asked where he worked and he said "Main one was a restaurant-bar on West 57th between Seventh and Eighth Avenues. Lunch-hour drinkers, mostly, and sort of the runoff from the Coliseum trade shows, and also the after-work crowd starting around five for a couple of hours. Subway entrance was right there, and for a while, at happy hour, we had a buffet table with free hors d'oeuvres." "You must've made a bundle," she said, "getting regulars. Here, it's more than not customers I'll never see again, so I usually get stiffed. Okay, though you're making more work for me, so don't be next asking me for Brooklyn," and she went to the end of the bar, opened a cabinet under it and got out the Manhattan phone book and gave it to him. He checked, and it was the latest edition: 1978–79. He looked up Gwen's name in it and it was there as she said it'd be: the only Gwendolyn Liederman in the book, at 425 Riverside Drive. Way uptown, he thought. Past Columbia? It could be that enormous curve-shaped Columbia-owned faculty residence he'd been in once, a few blocks south of 125th. He forgets the building's number, if he ever knew it, since he was taken to this private piano recital by someone who was invited. The area didn't seem that safe, and it might worry him going there to pick her up or take her home, if it ever came to that. But she did it, though maybe during the day was safe and at night she always took a cab to her building, or called one from it, or got off at the 116th Street subway station on Broadway and then got a cab. Or the Riverside Drive bus—the number 5?—stopped right in front of her building and same with the downtown one across the street. But he remembered a way to figure out what street her building was at. For about two years when he was fourteen and fifteen, he was a delivery boy for a food market and catering service in the West Seventies. To help him make his deliveries, he had a street-location guide to find the cross-street a building was closest to for every avenue on the Upper West Side. He only delivered the smaller orders; the larger ones and anything to the East Side or any area that would have taken him a long time to get to, were delivered by truck. Central Park West and Riverside Drive were the two easiest avenues to use on the guide, and he still remembers how to do them now. For Riverside Drive, just lop off the last digit of the building number and add 72, the street the Drive started at, to what was left. For Central Park West, it was add 60. West End Avenue he remembers as being complicated to do, and he rarely delivered—maybe never—anything to Columbus and Amsterdam Avenues, since those two hadn't been gentrified yet, and the place he worked for was kind of fancy and expensive. He used the guide for Gwen's building number and came up with a hundred-four-teen. So it might be Columbia-owned, he thought, and if so, a better and more convenient location and probably a more attractive building too than the institutional-type one near a 125th. He wrote her name and phone number on the folded-up sheet of typing paper he took from one of his pants pockets—most likely one of the back ones, which was where he usu-ally kept it and still does, whenever he goes out; the pen, then and now, always in a side pocket so he doesn't sit on it. He thinks he finished his beer and thought something like Hot damn—well, maybe not that. Just: Oh, boy, she was leveling with him after all. Now, what he wouldn't give to have their first date, so to speak, and he could call it that because why else would she have given him her number if not to see him again, but to go well and then to start seeing each other regularly and for it to become serious between them and for them to start sleeping together exclusively, if he can put it that way—*nobody else*—and everything like that and for it to only get better and them closer and marriage, even, and for it to never end. It's about time, and he can visualize it; foresee it as a possibility; something. For everything about her; everything; he just knows. And with a name like Liederman, he remembers thinking—maybe not the "Gwendolyn" so much, and not from anything about her mannerisms and face and voice and way she spoke and what she said—she's probably Jewish, so even better. For all the women he got serious with and the three he lived with the past fifteen years, except one, Rhoda, whom he gradually didn't much care for but it took a while to finally stop seeing her because she kept calling and was so good in bed, were Gentile, and most had a kid or two—actually only one had two—and the relationships always soured or sputtered out. And she didn't seem to have a kid. In fact, it was obvious she didn't; it would have come out. Good, because he already told himself after his last bad breakup more than a year ago that if he did get involved with another woman, and he was beginning to doubt he ever would, he wanted it to be with someone who had no kids and was a nonobserving Jew, among all the other things he wanted her to be—smart, interesting, sexy, gentle, and so on. Pretty, genuine, slim, intellectual. Was that asking too much? Was it asking for the wrong things? No, he doesn't think so. The change could be good. And he wants to be happy with someone and have a relationship that's easy for a change and lasts and goes on and the rest of it, and she seems perfect for him—again, in the short time they spoke and long time he observed her at the party, everything about her, everything, so this has to work. It's got to, he means, got to. He put the folded-up sheet of paper into one of his pants pockets, paid up, gave an extra large tip for a single draft beer, said to the bartender, when she took the phone book off the bar to put it back in the cabinet, something like "Much thanks for the use of the book. You've no idea how important it was to me, which must sound silly to you but it's the truth," and left.

So what'd he do once he got home? And he did walk all the way, right? As he said: why it took him so long to get home. And it was late enough that he was able to get the early edition of the next day's *Times* at one of the kiosks on 72nd Street and Broadway, the only places in his neighborhood he could buy it at that hour, and read the headlines, which he always did unless his hands were full, as he walked up the three flights to his apartment. Once in, and maybe even before he took his coat off, he probably went straight to the bathroom to pee. He and his brother always had a notoriously weak bladder, they called it, inherited from their mother, they thought, if such a thing can be passed down to your kids—maybe it was just a smaller-than-normal bladder she passed down—who frequently raced through the apartment from the front door when she came in, dribbling piss along the way to the bathroom in back on the first floor. "Oh, I did it again," she sometimes said, coming out of the bathroom and pretending to be ashamed. "Awful, awful of me." Then, if someone hadn't already taken care of it—one of them or the housekeeper—wiping the urine off the breakfast room and kitchen floors with a rag. The dining room and foyer were carpeted, so little she could do about the urine there till she got them professionally cleaned, which she seemed to do every other year or so, along with the carpeted bedrooms and living room upstairs. Actually, he's sure he would have peed right before he left the bar as a precaution to having to pee before he got home. But even if he had because he drank the entire beer there and the drinking he did at the party, he might also have had to pee badly as he went up the stairs to his apartment, or even on the street as he approached his building, the urge getting worse the closer he got to his front door. And then struggling to hold it in—this happened a number of times and happens even more today—as he fumbled with his door keys in one hand, his other hand squeezing the head of his penis through the pants to keep from peeing. Not always succeeding, either, and a few times, part-way up the stairs or standing in front of his door, but never on the street, giving up and peeing in his pants till he completely relieved himself, later—as quickly as he could do it—cleaning up the mess he made on the stairs or landing. Now—the last two years or so—he pees a lot in his pants. Just short spurts till he reaches the toilet. He just can't hold it in as well as he used to, even normal pees. After he peed in the bathroom, he probably took off his clothes, which had to be smelly from all the cigarette smoke at the party. It seemed half the people there smoked, so her hair and clothes would have smelled of it too, something he never thought before. If they had somehow hit it off big that night—at the party, not at the elevator: that wouldn't have been possible unless they continued to talk outside, which they did, and then went someplace for coffee or a snack or drink instead of separating on the street. And ended up at her apartment and necked or slept together—that never would have happened with her the first night, the sleeping together, no matter how much she might have been attracted to him, though it has happened with two or three other women—he would have smelled the cigarette smoke on her, just as she would have smelled it on him, unless they showered before they started necking or got into bed and also washed or thoroughly wet their hair. So? Nothing. Just saying. And it's ridiculous what he's thinking. They never would have showered before they started necking. And they would have necked before they got into bed. And the shower, if they thought they should take one because they didn't like the smell of cigarette smoke on their bodies and in their hair, would have had to be taken separately. She said, the one time he suggested they shower together, that it was dangerous and unnecessary and unappealing for other reasons and not at all erotic. When she was much younger, she said, and against her better judgment, she once let a boyfriend convince her to do it, and it practically ruined what was up till then a very nice relationship. "The lucky bastard," he said, "just that he was able to shower with you and wash your front and scrub your back and whatever else went with it," and she said "You don't know what happened. We both slipped and it nearly killed us. He broke his nose, gashes in our heads, my front tooth went through my lip; everything." He then probably—this was what he always did when he was living alone and came home from a party or bar with his clothes reeking of cigarette smoke and he wasn't too sleepy or a little drunk—half-filled the bathroom sink with water and soaked his shirt and pants in it and wrung them out with his hands as much as he could and hung them up on hangers or off the shower curtain rod over the bathtub. That was how he washed all his clothes then. He never had his own washer or dryer till he and Gwen married and moved into a fully equipped apartment in Baltimore. Sometimes he rubbed soap on the clothes in the sink or put laundry detergent in with them and washed them by hand. That took a long time, though, rinsing and dunking the clothes in several sinkfuls of water to get the soap or detergent off, and it always seemed to make a mess on the floor. If he also washed his socks—and for them he always used soap and put a sock on each hand and rubbed them into each other—he hung them over the tub faucets after he soaked them and wrung them out. If he came home a little high or sleepy from a party or bar in smelly clothes or just didn't have the energy to soak or wring them out, he left them on a bedroom chair, maybe brushed his teeth, took two aspirins or an Alka- or Bromo-Seltzer or that Italian antacid drink an old girlfriend had introduced him to—Briosci; something; he liked the taste better than the others but it was a lot more expensive—and went to bed and soaked the clothes in the morning. The only things he washed in the Laundromat were linens and towels and sometimes clothing that was too dirty to wash by hand. He had two sets of sheets and pillowcases and changed them every other week unless he knew some woman was going to spend the night at his place. Sex was always better on fresh linens, he thought, and when she laid her head down he didn't want the pillow smelling of his hair. He'd originally bought the second set of linens so he wouldn't have to go to the Laundromat more than once a month. When he moved in with Gwen he pooled his linens with hers—they both had double beds and only slept on cotton sheets— and used her building's laundry room for washing everything. Before he soaked his clothes that night—and he's almost sure he did; the cigarette smoke smell took weeks to go away unless washed or soaked, and he came home sober and alert and full of energy—he took out of his pants pocket the piece of paper with her name and phone number on it and put it by the phone on his night table. Now that he thinks of it, if he did smell from cigarette smoke when he got home, he would have showered soon after he took off his clothes and taken them into the shower with him and dropped them in the tub and sprayed or soaked them there while he was showering and then, standing in the tub with the shower off, wrung them out and hung them from the shower curtain rod, maybe later on hangers. Then he probably put on the terrycloth bathrobe he had then. It had been his father's for god knows how many years and now his for six: wide blue and white vertical stripes and quite frayed. When he was alone in the apartment late at night he liked to lounge in it with nothing on underneath, the belt, what there was left of it, untied and his genitals exposed, which he'd play with from time to time, usually without looking at them. He probably read awhile in the Morris chair he bought used before he met Gwen—she'd had new cushions made for it while she was recovering from her first stroke—and finished that day's *Times* or started tomorrow's while sipping a couple glasses of wine or a grapefruit juice and vodka drink or two. Or read from one of the *Gulag Archipelago* books he was reading then. He read all three, one after the other, took him a few months. Gwen had asked the next time they met what Solzhenitsyn he was reading. He always brought a book with him to read when he was going someplace by subway or bus, and she only saw because of the way he was holding the book and then put it down on the drugstore's luncheonette counter, the author's photo: a full-face shot that took up the entire back of the cover. Did he intentionally keep her from seeing the front of the cover? No reason to, so doesn't think so. He had a different book with him the night he first met her. A paperback of contemporary German short stories, thin and small enough to fit in his coat pocket or squeeze into his back pants pocket. He didn't bring the Solzhenitsyn to read on the subway—which he would have wanted to—he always liked to finish a book or just stop reading it before he started another—because it was an expensive library copy and he felt he wouldn't know where to leave it once he got rid of his coat and he was also afraid of losing or forgetting it at the party and even of someone taking it. Why would he even bring a book along if he was going to meet her at a drugstore a few blocks from his building? Not to impress her, that's for sure. He thinks he thought their afternoon coffee date could end up with—at least this might have been what he hoped for—a long leisurely walk uptown along Riverside Drive on the park side, since it was a very mild day for December. Maybe even to the door or lobby of her building if they really got involved in their conversation and agreed to spend more time together than the hour or so they'd planned to, and then he'd take, because she lived forty blocks from him, a subway or bus home. "Agreed" to spend? What would be the right word there? Can't think of it. And why stop at her building's front door or lobby? If he walked her that far, he must have thought, he's almost sure she'd invite him to her apartment for tea or glass of wine or something, but nothing more. But what's he thinking? He couldn't have thought she'd walk that far with him. She made it clear in his first phone call to her when they arranged the meeting that she was especially busy with school work these weeks and didn't have that much time to spare. So they'd walk twenty blocks, he could have thought, or half that, and then she'd take the River-side Drive bus the rest of the way and he'd take the Broadway bus home. That couldn't have been it, either—still too far a distance and she didn't have the time, so he doesn't know what. Maybe he thought, before he left his apartment to meet her, that after they separated at the drugstore or the closest bus stop or subway station for her, he'd go to a coffee shop on Columbus Avenue near his building—there were one or two of them then—and get a double espresso or something and read there. He held the book up to show her the title on the front cover. She said she liked much of Solzhenitsyn's early novels and that collection of short stories and prose poems and especially the novella in it—*Matryona's House?…Home?… Hearth?* he thinks? What the hell's the name of it?—a lot more than his nonfiction other than the Nobel Prize speech. She got less than halfway through the first *Gulag*, never touched the next two, so was curious what there was about the book—maybe she was missing something in it that he could tell her—that made him go on to the others, so it must have been number three he took with him that day. One thing he knows he did that night after he got home…Wait, what'd he answer her? He thinks he said that Solzhenitsyn's descriptions of life in the gulag and how the prisoners got there and what they went through and did to survive and also the many accounts of those who slave-labored till they died were some of the most powerful and harrowing writing he's ever read, good as anything in any novel by any writer; *House of the Dead* included, and in such clear strong prose. At least that's what he remembers now of his reading of the three books almost thirty years ago, so probably some of that is what he told her, and no doubt a lot more if he was feeling talkative that first date, for he had only read them the last few months. Although he has to admit—and he may have told her this at the luncheonette counter if it was the third *Gulag* he held up for her—that *Gulag* Three was slower than the first two, maybe because it was beginning to read like more of the same. It could be, and he doesn't think reading them in order was necessary to understanding and appreciating the books more, though he could be wrong on that—he for-gets—that if he'd started with *Gulag* Two and then gone to Three, he would have found One the least interesting and not as powerful and Three more interesting, powerful and readable than he did. But he read them all, he's certain of that, and he thinks Three was the last thing he finished of his. A few years later—they were married by now, subletting a large beautiful apartment in Baltimore and she was nursing their first child. Morning, rocking chair, newspaper and books on an end table next to her, mug of coffee or tea on the floor by her feet so she wouldn't spill it on the baby; doesn't know how he remembers all this, but he does. Even what it was like outside: bright and cheery; he thinks it was early spring. Actually, she wasn't drinking even decaffeinated coffee then because she was nursing. Only caffeine-free herbal tea, and at dinner, instead of her usual glass of red wine, Guinness stout because she'd read or her obstetrician had said it helped produce more breast milk. And she said to him—he'd just entered the living room, on his way to school, he thinks, for office hours or to teach—a new Solzhenitsyn novel was reviewed in today's *Times*. She knows how much he admires that writer, so would he like her to get it for him? He said if it's new—said something like this, of course—it's probably very long and expensive because of its length and he's about had it with that guy's work. His last two novels, he thinks he went on, read and were written more like history than fiction, so he couldn't really get in to them. Good history, but not what he wants to read. Then he probably kissed her and the baby too. More than probably. Doesn't think he ever left the apartment, if he was going to be out awhile, without kissing her goodbye. Except maybe, and this rarely happened then, they'd had a disagreement that wasn't quite settled, or he, not because of anything she did, was in a foul mood. He remembers saying something like this around that time "We don't seem to have any major problems in our marriage. It's looking good. I hope it lasts." One thing he knows he did that night after he came home and maybe before he showered or soaked his smelly clothes or even took them off was look up her name in the Manhattan phone book, though it seemed the same one the bar had but in much better shape, and of course it was there. And *Matryona's Home* is the title of the novella, he's ninety-nine percent sure. Then he looked up his own name in the book for no better reason than he hadn't since he got it and one year, a couple of years before, the phone company made the mistake of not putting him in the book. At the time, the only way someone who didn't have the number could get it—well, if they knew a friend of his or how to reach his mother or something like that, they could—was by dialing 411. Then he checked the number of the page his name was on and went to the page she was on and got its number and thought something like the two of them—he and Gwen—are so far apart in this book. L and S, more than a thousand pages, he figured. And then— he thinks he did this—he subtracted his page number from hers; rather, hers from his, and got the exact number of pages that separated them.

A pointless thing to do, if he did it, but she was on his mind almost constantly when he got home. Then for no good reason he could explain to himself later, although he knows it's a dopey and absolutely ridiculous and even bordering-on-the-nuttiness move he remembers thinking then and thinks now, he tore out the page with his name on it and put it face down on hers. There, he thinks he thought or said, but definitely something like that, the pages with his and Gwen's listings are pressed together and everything that suggests or implies till he gets next year's Manhattan phone book from downstairs and throws this one out. Later, he thought—it was the same night—suppose things work out between them and she comes over here one day, or things work out between them enough for her to come over here one day and she asks to use the Manhattan phone book and he gives her it and she sees, because he'd forgotten how he'd left them and didn't pull his page out before he gave her the book, those two pages pressed together like that. It could happen. She'll think him peculiar, and he went back to the hallway coat closet where he kept the two phone books he had, the Manhattan and Yellow Pages, and took his page out and threw it away. Then he probably just drank and read and went to bed.

He had a strange dream that night. He had several dreams that night, not unusual for him, but this was the only one he woke up and remembered having that interested him enough to want to write it down. He always kept a piece of paper and a pen or two on his night table—still does—to write down things that came to him in his sleep or he thought of while lying in bed. If he used up that piece of paper or took it to his writing table to work off of, he replaced it with another one when he went to bed that night. The room was dark when he woke up from this dream. He thought about the dream awhile and then wrote the dream on the paper and probably got out of bed and had a glass of water and peed and went back to sleep. He read what was on the paper when he woke up in the morning and then a number of times the next few days—usually after he first got into bed, since the paper was still on the night table—and then thought this dream is worth saving. If he doesn't save it he'll lose the paper somehow—it always happens—and eventually forget what the dream was about. He kept a notebook in the top drawer of his night table—still does, in the same drawer of that night table but a different notebook from the one of that time. That one, he filled up and put someplace. It was the first notebook he ever filled up—took him around fifteen years—and he now doesn't know where it is. Doesn't matter. Well, he'd like to have it, but it really doesn't matter. Whatever he could take from it, he thinks he did, and he'll probably come across it sometime, not that it'll be of any use to him. He has a theory—nah, forget that. But it has to do with if something's lost, it'll emerge someday if it's important enough. He means in his mind, an idea or something he wants to add or take out or replace in a work he's working on and sometimes even in one he's finished but hasn't published. Or hasn't in book form. Anyway, he wrote that dream down in the notebook and got it out of the drawer a few times that week to read it. He did get rid of the piece of paper the dream was originally written on. Didn't think he needed it anymore now that the dream had been transferred to the notebook. He also read that dream once to Gwen a short time after they got married, all of which is why—the number of times he read it—he remembers the dream so well and doesn't need the notebook to remember it. How many times does he think he read it? A dozen or so, and he doesn't know why it took him so long to read it to Gwen or even tell her about the dream. Maybe he thought it'd alarm her in some way, or make him out to be somewhat odd, having that dream the first night they met. Or else he didn't think it'd be interesting to her—this could be possible—and then something came up that made the dream seem more important or applicable to their lives. The whole thing's a blank. His sister died of a rare kidney disease. Something with "neph" or "nephr" in it. Another of those words he can never remember when he wants to use it no matter how many times he's said it, or almost never remember. "Demagogue"—he got it now—but it almost always trips him up. "Demagogic," "demagoguery"—anything with "demagog" in it, the same. For about a year before she died she was confined to a wheelchair. "Confined"? Doesn't seem the right word for what she was. "Restricted to" would be even worse. At first she could get around in the chair by pushing the wheels herself. Then she didn't have the strength for it anymore and someone had to push her in the chair. He used to push her outside to Central Park. A few times across the park to the Metropolitan Museum. Someone said to him—maybe Gwen; he seems to picture it, but long before her first stroke—that it must have been difficult pushing her so far, all these dips and hills, up and down curbs. He said it wasn't, except for maybe crossing the bridle path in the park. The chair had wheels, for God's sake, and he was much younger and stronger then, and his sister was a lot lighter by the time she became bound—that's the word—to the wheelchair, down to sixty pounds from around eighty. She looked awful. Emaciated face, bony shoulders slumped forward, ankles swollen to almost twice their normal size, other things. It was before wheelchairs had seatbelts on them, so he had to tie a sheet around her waist so she wouldn't fall out if he hit a bad bump or crack in the sidewalk or navigated a curb poorly, yet she did once and cut her hands and forehead. Just like what happened to Gwen, but in the house, seatbelt buckled by him but obviously not well, and she broke her nose and had trouble breathing in her sleep from then on. Kept him up so much at times that he left the bed to sleep in another room. She said once "I patted your side of the bed early this morning but, sadly, you weren't there. I patted and patted in the dark in the hope I'd find you, till my arm couldn't reach any farther. I'm sorry I make so much noise." But the dream. He and his sister are walking down a dimly lit windowless hallway. This, just around eight hours after he first met Gwen and almost twenty years after his sister died. Low-wattage lights with dark shades on the walls. He says to his sister "My God, you're walking, when before you were stuck in your wheelchair and someone had to push you. An overnight cure or miracle must have taken place." She smiles at him but doesn't say anything. Like Gwen and his parents and his brother and his best friend Mischa, and his sister in other dreams—none of them said anything to him when he dreamt of them after they died. Actually, not so. His father did once, if it was his father; it certainly was his voice. And in one of the many dreams he had of Gwen last night and this morning, she could have said something to him and he forgot. But with his father in that dream of just a couple of weeks ago, he was sleeping alone in this bed when the voice said "Martin!" just as his father used to do when he didn't like how he was behaving or wanted him to do something for his mother or him right away or some household chore he'd been assigned to and his father thought he was avoiding or stalling. One, when he was a boy, he remembers hearing a number of times: "Martin! I'm surprised at you. Take the garbage out already. And this time line the pail with newspaper when you bring it back. For some reason only you know, you're always forgetting." He woke up, in the dream, though it seemed more like from it. He doesn't believe in spirits or ghosts, but the truth is he came closest to thinking one of those could be so after he had the dream. Anyway, he was lying in bed, in or out of the dream, and saw a gray amorphous—smoky would be the best word for it—figure, no definable feature or form and taller by about six inches than his short father was and with his father's rough voice, moving back in a slow curling motion to the corner between the picture window and closet and then come apart, the last bit of smoke disappearing where the head would have been. He stared at the spot he last saw the figure at and then sat up and turned on his night table light—he was now definitely out of the dream—and looked at the time—he'd already guessed it by a few minutes: three-fifteen—and lay back in bed with the light on, thinking about the dream and how real it was and what it might mean. His treatment of Gwen those last few weeks and especially the last night, that's for sure. What else could it mean? Oh, he could come up with something, but that one's probably it. His father was saying "Shame, to treat your wife, and so sick, that way. Where'd you ever learn such behavior? Certainly not from your mother or me." He could just hear him. And what would his mother say, if she knew? "*Oh, Martin.*" So his sister smiles at him, doesn't say anything, and they continue walking down what's turning out to be an endless dimly lit hallway, with no doors in the walls either. "What do you think will be the outcome of all this?" he says. She smiles and shakes her head in a way that says "Not to worry, dear brother; you're going to like what happens." They start walking up a long steep flight of stairs similar to ones he remembers in the London underground, or maybe it was the Metro in Paris, where he and Gwen, on a short visit there more than twenty-five years ago—and he'd been to Paris and ridden the Metro long before he met her—decided to walk up them rather than take the elevator or escalator. "You're right," she said, when he suggested the idea, "we could use the exercise. Too much good food." She also said, between her first and second strokes, or second and third, "I'm sorry we didn't live more in Paris. Now we can't chance it." He and his sister go around another landing and start walking up another long flight. At the top of the stairs is a fireproof door that looks like the one that opened onto the roof of the building he was living in when he first knew Gwen. "Ah, at last: fresh air and natural light," he says, and sees he's now talking to Gwen. "Miracle of miracles," he says, unbolting the door and pushing it open, "not only was my sister alive and walking but she's turned into you, when before you were paralyzed from the waist down." "That is something, isn't it," she says, "since the only time I've ever been sick in my life was with chicken pox: twice." They go outside and from the middle of the roof—"Don't go any farther," he says, taking her hand. "It's dangerous and I wouldn't let you go out there alone and we could fall off"—and look at the city all around them. "Tell me," he says, squeezing her fingers, "which—" and she says "Ouch, that hurts." "I'm sorry. I thought I was being gentle," and lets go of her hand. "But I was saying, out of all these buildings, if you had the choice, which one would you want to live in with me if you wouldn't want to live in the one we're standing on now?" and she says "I have a very nice apartment uptown, big enough for both of us and with a view that rivals this." The dream ended then and he woke up. He doesn't think he turned on the night table light—no, he had to have, but later, to write everything down. At first he just lay in bed in the dark thinking about the dream and what it might mean and how quickly she entered his dreamlife—that must mean something, he thought. Then he turned on the night table light—there was only one, on the same side of the bed he sleeps on now, the left. At least he thinks it's the left. He's always had trouble with that one. For facing the bed, it's the right. But it's got to be the left. Left side of the road, right side of the road. That doesn't work. Maybe it's just that he's a little more tired than usual right now, and the whole terrible day. Nah, the last is just an excuse. Tired, maybe. He once even asked Gwen, when he got confused again as to which side is which—it had to do with something he was writing—and she told him and he knew she was right—she didn't hesitate when she told him and she looked at him as if he were kidding—and he probably said something like "That's what I thought," but forgets which side she said was which. He also doesn't remember how they decided which sides of her bed they should sleep on after they made love the first time. It wasn't that after they were done and had uncoupled they stayed on the sides of the bed they ended up on. And he, probably with his weak bladder, no doubt got up to pee so he wouldn't have to an hour or two later. He thinks he remembers her saying she sleeps in the middle of the bed when she sleeps alone. And he thinks he remembers saying he sleeps on only one side of his bed, and it's a double bed like hers. She must have first said, when they were getting ready to go to sleep, "Which side of the bed would you like to sleep on?" Or he asked her which side of the bed would she like him to sleep on. Or it could be, when he got back from peeing and maybe washing his face and rinsing his mouth, that she was already on what he'll call the right side of the bed or on the right side close to the middle. But he doesn't recall that. He recalls one of them asking the question and his saying something like "Either side's okay with me. Though at home, because the night table's there, though I guess I could always move it to the other side—there's room—I sleep on what I think's the left," and pointed to that side. He doesn't remember her correcting him, so that time, unless she was just being polite or didn't think it important enough to correct him at the time or thought it the wrong time to—their first time in bed—he thought he knew. If she had had only one night table by her bed he would have known which side she preferred sleeping on when she slept with someone. But she had matching night tables on either side, with the same kind of lamp on them. One of these lamps—the other he broke when he was trying to put back the plug that had come out of the socket behind the bed and pulled the cord too hard and the lamp fell—is on the night table now. She bought a different lamp for her side, one for two bulbs, though it was his lamp he broke, and gave him hers. Next he took the piece of paper and a large hardcover book off the night table—probably one of the *Gulags*—and placed the book against his upraised thighs, flattened out the paper on it and wrote the dream down on both sides of the paper and also what he thought the dream might mean and other things about it—that he'd never met anyone who entered his dreamlife so quickly, for instance, and that must mean something, and so on. He filled up both sides of the paper, knew he could write even more about the dream, but this was enough for now, he thought, and he was getting sleepy. He turned the page over to the first side and wrote in printed letters in the little space not written on at the top of the page and underlined it: "This dream is significant. 3 a.m. or thereabouts, Nov. 21st, 1978. Do not destroy!!!" After he read the notes to Gwen—only what happened in the dream, nothing about what he thought it might mean and other things related to it—he asked what she made of it and also that he'd had it so soon after they met. "Literal interpretation, I suppose you want? Then nothing more than the obvious. The long hallway resembled the stairway in Pati's building. You know: the one I told you of that I didn't want to walk down. Drearily lighted, dank and scary, no windows, naturally, and in a way, no door at the end of it either, on the ground floor, since it was locked or stuck the one time I tried opening it. What I don't think I ever told you was that at the time I was petrified that I wouldn't be able to get out of any of the doors upstairs, once I got inside the stairway. I saw myself pounding on the door on Pati's floor till someone rescued me, and for a few moments I even thought I'd suffocate there. Real panic. So, substitute bottom of the stairs, in my real-world experience, to us walking up the last flight of stairs to the roof in your dream." "I don't understand," he said, and she said "The obvious, how could you not see what I'm saying? You? My guy who rarely lets anything get past him? Please, you have to be kidding. Dankness for freshness? Unknown for the known? Dark night without end, to daylight? Seemingly lost in that corridor, to finding one's way to release? Bleak prospect for hope, and so forth, but maybe I'm going too far with that one. With the last three, probably, and I said I'd stay literal. Although your dream did end hopefully, didn't it? For you: the two of us together, even holding hands for a while till you started crunching mine. Now what was that all about? Perhaps to show there's a little pain in every relationship, even at the beginning, no matter how promising and good it looks. And then, with that big sweep of the city, talking about where we should live in it and my saying why don't you move in with me. Another thing is how protective you were of me that night. In the real world, I mean—saying you'd accompany me down that horrible stairway, and later, that you'd walk me to my subway station or bus stop, I forget which." "Subway," he said. "Because you thought the streets might not be safe. And in the dream, warning me not to get too close to the edge of the roof—for all I know, the warning might have been about getting involved with you—and also sort of saying that if I did fall off, you'd go over with me. You weren't alluding there to falling for me if I fell for you, were you? No, it would have had to be the reverse, since you fell for me first. So, not only protectiveness and concern for me, but already, in the dream, sticking by me in the worst of circumstances—the literal interpretation—all of which you still are today. Even, on occasion, overprotective of me, as if you think I can't deal with certain things or, more to the point, look after myself in what to others might be stressful situations, and I need your help. And I'm not criticizing you, you understand. Better that attitude from you than indifference and neglect, and it's just your way. Incidentally, the roof-edge part of your dream is like a very short story you wrote before we met and was only published last year. What I'm saying is it could have snuck into your sleep and influenced that scene. The one—are you still with me?" and he was thinking something like Boy, her mouth's on a roll; he's never heard her go on like this, but said "Why? Sure; yes." "That has a man jumping out of a plane after his young daughter, who was sucked out of the door when it fell off. The father grabbing the girl in the air—you had it that he catches up with her because he falls faster, being three times heavier, but I don't think it works like that in real life—and holding her close to him and their flying together like that at the end, chatting normally and admiring the beautiful mountains and rivers and forest from so high up till they can find, he says, a safe place for a landing. It was about, I think, a father's feeling of invincibility regarding his child, something most mothers might not feel, but I could be wrong there. You know—and this is how I think you'll feel—that he can get his kid out of any perilous situation when they're that young. The same reason he'd run into a burning building to save his child even if, from a practical standpoint, there doesn't seem to be a chance in the world his rescue attempt will succeed, so instead of only the child dying—tragedy enough—they both do, something the father would probably want anyway if he couldn't save his kid. Or maybe, taking from the last thing I said—have we talked about this before?" and he said "All you said after you read it was that you liked it and that you had read something else of mine similar in plot, maybe too much so because some readers—not that I have many; you didn't say that; I did—might think I was repeating myself." "That wasn't nice of me, and I now can't remember what it reminded me of yours." "*Free-falling.*" "Still no bell rings. Not even the title. Anyway, your story also might have been about that the father knew, even before he jumped out of the plane after her, that they were both doomed, but he wanted to alleviate her fear as much as he could by not having her go down alone. Did I get close that time?" and he said "Both are good but the second's better. But at the end they're still flying as if it's a perfectly normal thing for humans to do, so I don't know. The flying part could be an after-death fantasy—I'm the last person to ask—but what else about my dream?" "Something to do with elevators. Riding down in one. I'd have to have the dream read to me again or read it myself, something I haven't the time now to do. I know the elevator didn't come for a while when we were waiting for it in Pati's building, which gave us time to start talking. Otherwise, we probably wouldn't have continued to talk on the street and exchanged names and my telling you how you can reach me, and so on. By the way, do you ever hear of men running into hopelessly burning buildings to save their mothers or wives?" and he said "It has to have happened; it's just not as dramatic or emotional a news story. As for wives running in to save their husbands—I'm sure many mothers have run in for their young sons—it probably almost never happens. They instinctively know, if the fire's really out of control, that they're not physically capable of carrying or dragging out what in all likelihood is a much heavier and larger man." She said "Now as to my coming into your dreamlife so fast that night—you asked that—I don't know what to say. Can I be a little immodest by saying I might have made a strong impression, maybe even more than that? But I'm only repeating what you've told me a number of times, just as I've told you I wasn't that immediately taken with you. Interested, curious, at least open to meeting you for coffee? Yes. You were so awkward but I thought gentle and civil and even gallant and possibly deep, funny and smart. That's right, I took all that in. As for your dream—and I really have to get back to my work, sweetheart—starting out with you walking with your sister in that hallway and ending with you going up the stairs to the roof with only me, and I assume I was on the same side of you as your sister had been, and entering and walking around it? I'm going over old ground, I think, but that was both... oh, shoot, I lost it. It'll come back, and when it does I bet you'll find it wasn't all that sharp." "Never," he said; "everything you say." "Sure. What else, though, but quickly? My suggesting in the dream you live with me in my apartment? And how would you have known it was large enough for two?

Maybe you were fantasizing a life with me that could go, for want of a better expression, all the way to the top. The roof's the acme of a building, no? So: meeting for coffee, next for a glass of wine or beer, couple of dinners out, later seriously dating, sleeping together, part of our first summer together vacating to someplace north of New York, professions of love, or that came long before. You know: 'You know I love you,' and 'And I love you.' 'But I said it first.' 'But I mean it as much.' Then the big kiss and long embrace and so on. You moving in. Summer after that first summer, traveling around France. Picasso, Matisse, Giacometti, Braque, Chagall, Miró, maybe a chateau. Marriage, children, years and years of me till you're sick of my wizening face and kick me out. Or, because it's my apartment originally—no, by then we'd be joint lessees and we would have gone through several residences, maybe even owned a house— Anyhow, you leave and take up with a woman twenty years younger than I, which would put her around thirty years younger than you. That's me now kidding, I hope; how come you didn't laugh?" He said something and she said "I don't know. My mother says I've become a lot funnier and my sense of humor has vastly improved, since knowing you," and he said "So you've said, and I agree, but then you know I would never disagree with your mother. Oy, what am I saying? Bad joke, not even close to one—mine, and no offense to your mother, whom you know I really like and admire—and only kidding with my failed jokes too. Your sense of humor and flair for comedy and also your wit, etcetera—whatever I'm trying to say—were always tops. And you have, and not just compared to me—I'm hopeless, can't even remember punch lines to jokes I've heard a dozen times—a great memory for the whole joke." "I just thought of something," she said. "In your dream did you have to unlock the roof door to get out? And he said "Wasn't that in what I read you? It was one of those sliding bolts, no lock, same as in the brownstone I lived in. Why do you ask?" and she said "I thought there could be some connections to the stairway's ground floor door in Pati's building when I tried it from the inside and it seemed locked. And no alarm went off when you unbolted and opened the door? Although I think that only happens on roof doors of buildings when someone tries to break in from the outside, though in a dream anything can be the reverse of the real. All I'm saying is that if an alarm had gone off it could have been of some relevance to me. Think of it. The first night. We've just met. Hardly spoke. But your fantasy life's been fired up. You're already dreaming of me, and in the closest sorts of ways. So something self-protective could be warning you 'Wait a minute, hold off, don't jump in so fast,' especially after you ended up so disappointed and hurt in what you told me were your last three relationships the past year. Not so much the long one with Diana—that one you said was already over, other than for you sleeping with her once or twice a month, when she broke it off completely with you—but the short one with Karyn and the quickie with whatever the third one's name was," and he said "Nadine, and no alarm, outside or in. If there had been one I think I also would have thought what you said. But it probably would have awakened me, as dream alarms do—ringing alarms, I mean—before we stepped onto the roof." "So I got carried away a little, but not solipsistically, I hope you don't think." "Once again: you? Never." "Sometimes I think you'd let me get away with or explain myself out of anything," and he said "Maybe anything but sleeping with someone else, which you've said, and I've said too, you'd never do." "Why would I?" and he said "Same here, so long as we're together, which seems we're going to be—I don't know how it can't be—for life, right?" and she said "I'm glad we got that cleared up and worked out, not that I was worrying. Holding hands was sweet. I'm talking about the dream. And squeezing my hand, in addition to how I originally saw it, I'd say it was you who got dreamily carried away with your ardor or some emotion—not ardor. What am I trying to say?" and he said "Beats me." "It could have been just your uneasiness that I'd leave you for good if you let go of my hand—translate that as my not agreeing, when you called, to meet you for even a first date—so you felt you had to clutch it to stop me from pulling it away, and squeezed too hard. Anything in that?" "Would you consider it as even a slight act of desertion if I said I don't think so?" "Whatever reason you did it, I forgive you for hurting me. And you did seem, from your account, to let go the second I showed pain, and were genuinely sorry. Just as you are in your waking life if you accidentally hurt me—stepping on my foot, that jar of olive oil you thought you'd tucked safely away in the cupboard, or even in sex when you go in too deep or poke around the wrong hole. I did like the line—I know, I said I had to go, and I do have to, so, much fun as this is, I'll finish up—'Which of these buildings would you like to live in an apartment with me'—what was it again: and he read it and she said "I liked it—the way it was worded, and also the rest of the line: 'if you don't want to live with me in the building we're standing on now?' Again, what was the exact wording? Though it's something I remembered even that much of it," and he read it and she said "Nice, uncomplicated, no trouble in understanding what it means. Oh! And then I'm really going. Your deepest wish, hence your sister turning into me as she went up the last flight of stairs to the roof, was that she hadn't got sick and had stayed as healthy, active and ambulatory as me," and he said "That makes sense."

Why'd he take so long to call her? A week, maybe a day or two more. Thought about calling her every day during that time. Three-four times a day. What's he talking about? Five-six times a days, some days more. Had his hand on or near the receiver lots of times while thinking about dialing her number. Picked up the receiver a few times to call her but put it down. After a couple of days of doing this he knew her number by heart. The number eventually also became his number when he gave up his apartment and moved in with her. He still knows it though they haven't lived in what he always called her apartment for years. 663-2668. Lots of sixes, so that could be why it was so easy to remember and it's stayed with him this long. They loved that cheap spacious rent-stabilized apartment overlooking the Hudson, but were evicted about fifteen years after they moved to Baltimore for not occupying it often enough. Some New York City law which a landlord can take advantage of if he wants. They didn't fight the eviction. Would have cost too much and they would have lost. He dialed the first part of her number several times but stopped and hung up. Or stopped and held the receiver awhile, thinking if he should go on with the dialing, before hanging up. At least twice he dialed her number and hung up after the first ring, and he thinks the second time after two rings. If this were happening today—if he'd only just met her and was thinking of calling her to arrange a date—he wouldn't let the phone ring even once before he hung up. She'd probably, living alone—in other words, all their personal circumstances would be the same but it'd be 2006 instead of 1978—have caller ID and she'd be able to call back and might say something like "Excuse me, I don't recognize your phone number and no name came up with it on my cell phone screen, but did you just dial me?" He'd heard her, from the next room, do that once after, he assumes, she looked at the cell phone screen and didn't recognize the number that had just called her. The only other time, though—at least while he was around—she didn't call back and said something like "Maybe that ring was a mistake, but if that person does want to reach me, he'll call again." With him, when he once called her from his office at school and had to hang up after the first ring when he suddenly realized he was late for a meeting with his department chair, she said "Hi. Did you just phone me for any reason and then decide it wasn't important enough and hang up? Whatever it was, I thought I'd use it as an excuse to chat with you, even if nothing new or interesting has happened to me or our sweet little baby since you left the house." Either she heard the phone ring those two times he dialed her number and then hung up, or she wasn't home or was in the bathroom with the door shut—she once said she always closed it when she was on the potty, even when she was home alone—or some other place in her apartment far from the phone—at the rear of the kitchen by the service entrance and pantry or putting the garbage out by the service elevator—and didn't hear the phone. The one phone she had was in the bedroom, at the opposite end of the apartment. Soon after he moved in he convinced her to have a phone extension installed on the kitchen wall so he wouldn't, if he was there, have to run to the bedroom to answer the phone. "I hate missing calls," he said, "and it could be good news." He never spoke to her about his hesitation in calling her. Hesitation? *Fear*. He was actually afraid of what he might lose, or not gain, so "fear" used loosely—anyway, if the conversation went badly on his part. If he sounded like an idiot, in other words. On her part, who cared, long as she agreed to meet him. No, that's not altogether true, but go on. It would have been different if he had felt sharp and confident and other things like that. But those seven to nine days or however long it was he didn't call her he felt weak, vulnerable, nervous, worse, every time he picked up the receiver or sat down on the bed next to the night table with the phone on it or even approached the phone to make the call. He doesn't know why he didn't tell her why he took so long to call her. Yes he does. At first he thought—very early on in their relationship—she'd think he was a bit silly and even immature having had those anxieties about calling her, especially for a guy who, judging by his looks and maybe his recounting certain experiences—when he got out of college and so on—was obviously, if he hadn't already told her his age, about ten years older than she. He also didn't want her to think he had had any doubts about calling and seeing her. But after a few weeks of knowing each other—meaning, once they really started going together—he thought she would have said in response to his what-took-him-so-long confession, something like "Why the worry? If I gave you my phone number or the way to get it, that had to mean I was willing to meet you, at least for a cup of coffee." But by this time he didn't see any point in telling her, or would tell her or speak about it only if the subject of what took him so long to call came up, and even then he might lie or skip around the truth. "I'm not ready yet," he thought after her phone rang once that first time, and he hung up. "I'm still not ready yet," he said out loud the next night or night or two after that, after her phone rang once or twice and he hung up. "What will make you ready?" he said. "Just feel ready. But so far the whole thing's making me crazy. Look at me. My stomach hurts. I'm sweating. I'm talking to myself. I'm still talking to myself. I've got to call her already, but I'm still not prepared for it. How do you get prepared? And you're just dragging it out, substituting 'prepared' for 'ready,' when you know they mean the same thing. Like I said: Get prepared. Be ready. You have her number, so call and relax and let her phone ring and don't hang up. *Do not hang up.* Even if she doesn't answer the phone, you were at least ready for her to." Wait a minute; didn't he talk to her a little about it? Not about how he got her number. It was a while later. Weeks, months. By now they were a couple, being with each other almost every night. Most days he'd work in his apartment, then around five or six or seven he'd walk uptown to her apartment, usually along Broadway, which was livelier and had more to see than Amsterdam and Columbus Avenues, or take the subway or bus. If it was raining hard or the sidewalks were icy, he always took the subway or bus. They were eating dinner in her apartment; duck, he remembers, which she cooked in a rotisserie her godmother had given her years before. She put down her fork, seemed deep in thought, then said something like "I was thinking. Maybe you don't remember this. By the way, meat wasn't undercooked? I'm relatively new at this kind of cooking, and have only used it once before because it makes such a mess." "No, it's good," he said, "just right, perfect. You did it like a real rotisserie pro, and I'll do all the cleaning up. You cooked, I'll clean." "It's okay, I don't mind. I hope you didn't think I was complaining. But clear this up for me. How did you get my phone number to call me the first time? I'm glad you got it, of course, but did I give it to you on the street or did you get it from Pati or some other way on your own?" "Oh, boy, your memory's getting to be as bad as mine. That could be what happens when you spend a lot of time with me." "I don't need that," she said, cross, stern; she'd never come even close to acting like that to him before. He said "Sorry, I didn't mean it as a slight. Truth is, I don't know how I meant it. It was a stupid remark, if it was said without my realizing why it was said and what I meant by it. My apologies, honestly. Please accept them. Damn, our first disagreement or whatever you want to call it—where I made you angry at me—and all my fault. But not important, right? I hope not. You gave me your last name and the spelling of it and told me to look for it in the Manhattan phone book—that you were unique. You didn't say that; I added it." "So that had to mean I was willing to meet you for coffee or something simple and short like that, and we'd see how things went from there. But why didn't I just give you my phone number rather than make you work for it? That wasn't right," and he said "I don't think either of us had a pen and there was nobody around at the time to borrow one from." "You, a writer," she said, "who as far as I can tell has never left your apartment or mine without a pen and something to write on—never even gone to the toilet for any extended length of time without a paper and pen," and he said "Maybe you were in a rush to get to wherever you were going—I know you once told me but I forget what that was—or wanted to put me through some serious test on my pursuance of…of…Jesus, why do I get hung up on big words and long rambling sentences; probably the phony in me. In a nutshell: maybe you wanted to see if I'd make even that little effort to try to contact you. No, that's not you. I don't know why. Another thing that's not important, do you agree?" Suddenly he has to pee. Can't wait, either. Gets up, squeezes his penis to keep from peeing, rushes into the bathroom and sits instead of stands because the seat was down and he's tired and he had a lot to drink tonight and most of it strong stuff and he feels a bit woozy, so thinks he might fall. Sitting down, he pisses a little on his thigh and the floor. This sudden urgency to pee is beginning to be a problem, he thinks. Something to do with his prostate? Worse? He once had prostatitis, more than thirty years ago, before he met Gwen. Only symptom was a few spurts of blood coming out of his penis one or two days, scaring him but there was no urgency to pee or anything different in his peeing, and he took some medicine for it a friend with the same condition had some extra of and it went away. He's not going to call his doctor about it. If it continues, he'll tell him at his next annual checkup. Or maybe he'll put that one off—it was scheduled months ago—till next year, and maybe he won't even go in for one then. He's sick of doctors. Now that's a funny expression. But he doesn't want to see any of them. Saw them enough with Gwen, and all they seem to do—he knows that's not all of it, but it seemed so with her—is put you through a slew of tests and medications and refer you to other doctors. Doesn't think they did much for her but tire her out more than she already was as he dragged her from one doctor's office and lab and imaging center to the next. Besides, this sudden urgency to pee could be from his drinking and maybe also, as sort of one thing setting off another, remembering Gwen mentioning the toilet in that business with his pen. It could also be his age, where he's increasingly losing control of his bladder, just as his father did when he reached seventy or so, with nothing to do about it except pee more frequently though without waiting till he feels the need to. Prophylactic pees, once every other hour and a couple of times where he'd have to get up at night, so he wouldn't have to run to the bathroom and wet his pants or his thighs and the floor. Or it actually could be his prostate, enlarged or inflamed or even cancerous, but the hell with it. Once you get to around his age, he's read in a few newspaper articles, that kind of cancer is very slow growing, and the treatments for it could end up doing more harm to the body than leaving it alone. He thinks he's got that right. Finished, no more drops or dribbling to come, he wipes his thigh and the bottom of his feet with wet toilet paper and then the part of the floor he peed on. Before throwing the paper into the toilet he checks the water for blood, is none, and goes back to bed. One thing he has to remember, he thinks, is not to become hypochondriacal. He's bound to get sick one day, that's a given, but for now he's fine, not to worry, let him just have a little healthy time to himself. But what's he going to do with his life from now on now that this whole thing is over and he's really alone? In the morning. What is it, he thinks, resting the back of his head on the bed's two softest pillows, that makes him want to sleep on his right side or at least start off in that position, rather than on his left side or his back? He never thought about this before? Thinks he has and that he even discussed it with Gwen, but forgets what he came up with. Oh, sure: the back's easy for him to explain. It's impossible for him to fall asleep that way. For thinking, okay. He'll even get on his back in bed—either of his sides is no good for this—in the afternoon, not to nap but when he has a problem with something he's writing and wants to work it out. He hasn't written more than a couple of pages since Gwen died, and these over and over again. But when she was alive he used to say to her—she'd usually be in her study, working at her computer—"I'm going to take a break and rest awhile, so try to answer the phone, all right? I'm turning it off in our bedroom." He'd take the paper out of the platen, cover the typewriter and put a paperweight or sea-polished stone he got off a beach in Maine or something heavy like that—the petrified wood his older daughter brought back for him from the Painted Desert—on the manuscript pages he was working on, and lie on the bed. The right side because, of course, that's the side she ninety-nine times out of a hundred went to sleep on. Like him, before he had to do it for her, she turned over to the left side sometime at night. It was much easier for him to fall asleep if he could hold her or press up to her from behind. Her left breast. Both breasts. Left buttock. His hand between her thighs. So there's his answer, no big deal, and he can't imagine having discussed it with her. At the most he might have said something like, when they were lying in bed once, "I love holding you like this when we go to sleep. Don't change it; stick with going to sleep on your right side." He remembers she did once say she preferred falling asleep on her right side not only because her face faced open space, making breathing easier, rather than him and more bed on the left side, but also because she knew he liked to hold her when he was going to sleep and because she liked him to. "Otherwise, falling asleep," she said,

"one's so alone." So it's obvious why, after twenty-seven-plus years of sleeping with her that way, why he still starts off on that side. And also…no, he
was going to say it's as if she's still there sometimes, but he never feels that.
Anyway, just a thought. But getting back to that first phone call, how do
you get prepared to make a call like that, he thought, when you've little
confidence you'll come out sounding okay and you very much want to see
this woman again? As he thought before: you don't prepare yourself; you
relax. You dial her number and wait for her to pick up and if she does, you
say hello and your name and maybe where she knows you or you know her
from and then jump right in talking about something you think will interest her. You might even say, not right away though, that old as you are, and
you don't want her to think you're ancient—"Well, you know I'm not"—
you still get a bit nervous and frazzled calling up a woman for the first time.
Not that you call that many; you're not saying that. In fact, to be perfectly
honest, you could say, you haven't called a woman for months, for a first
time or one you know for a while. No, maybe that'd be too honest, he
thought, and she'd think there was some hidden motive in his saying it.
That he was trying to seem like someone he isn't: right up-front, no hidden
motives, and so on. Oh, he doesn't know what. Instead he could say "Not
that I do it regularly, calling up women, I want you to know, or calling up
anyone. Phones were just never my best form of medium. I'm much better
talking directly, with no, whatever you want to call it, interconnecting
medium. There's that word medium again," he'd probably say if he said all
that, "confirming to you, I'm afraid, my difficulty in talking on the phone.
I wasn't always like that, I want you to know. As a teenager I was a regular
chatterbox on the phone with my friends and girls my age, infuriating my
father, I can tell you, as he was pretty tight with money. Or maybe he was
just being realistic, since you paid, I think, a dime a minute for a local call
then, after the forty or fifty free minutes a month the phone company gave
you." But he wouldn't even say that. Going into personal family history and
his youth too soon, and most of the other stuff he'd sound silly saying and
he'd get flustered trying to get out of it. Best: keep it simple and relatively
quick. You're relaxed, you're ready, you dial and if she doesn't pick up, you
call again an hour or two later, still relaxed and ready, and if she doesn't pick
up then or the next time you call that night, you call the next day, and so
on. But she has to pick up some time, unless she's away, and even if she is,
she'll come back, and when she does pick up, you say "Hi, how are you?"—
if she has been away, that'll be his excuse for not having called sooner: he
tried, her phone didn't answer, he suspected she was away and decided to

give it a few days—"it's Martin Samuels, fellow you met at Pati Brooks' party the other night, or should I say, in the hallway outside it, by the elevator." Or better: "Hello," or "Good evening"—no, too formal; just "Hello, it's Martin…Martin Samuels, guy you met the other night in the hallway outside Pati's party, both of us waiting for the elevator that didn't seem to want to come. Did we ever figure out what the delay was all about? Anyway, how have you been?" and maybe, with her help, since he's never been much good at initiating things to talk about on the phone, especially with someone he barely knows, the conversation will take off from there or just proceed naturally if maybe a bit awkwardly, but get better as it goes along. She might say something like "I've been doing okay, thanks, and you?" but the point is to get her to talk a little about herself and what she's been doing so then he could respond to it. A new movie or museum show she might have seen that he'd seen also and they could talk about it, or if he hadn't seen it—more chance of that with a movie, since he never goes to them alone—he could say "I've heard about it" or "read a review. Is it worth seeing?" Or he could try to come up with something else to get her to say what she's been doing lately, he thought. Teaching. "How's it going? I've never taught anything but junior high school for the Board of Ed for six years. Mostly per diem work, which wasn't too awful because you just come and go in different schools and rarely see the same surly and sleepy and sometimes sweet faces for more than two days in a row. But for a year and a half I was a permanent sub, teaching language arts to eighth graders, the worst and most dangerous job I ever had, and believe me, I know: I once drove a cab here when drivers were being robbed and bumped off regularly." If he did say that—maybe he wouldn't say the cab part—he'd just be trying to bring her in and keep the conversation going—she'd probably say something like "What made it so bad?" "Knots in my stomach going home every day, and weekends ruined thinking about going in to teach Monday. And twice, a knife, pulled on me in class, and I had to physically disarm the kids, leading to the mother of one boy complaining to the principal that I ripped the kid's sweater when I threw him to the floor and I'd have to pay for it. And one time I was going down the subway entrance after school and my least favorite student called me to look up and dropped a brick on my head. You probably saw the ugly scar my hair doesn't cover up anymore because of my receding hairline." He'd mention his growing baldness? Even in jest, why allude to it, possibly giving her more reason for turning him down? She already must think he's a lot older than her. He'd more likely just say "which left a long scar on my forehead you might have noticed. Not so bad.

My head's full of them, most of them much smaller and on the sides where they don't show, from when I was a very active but clumsy boy. I had that student suspended"—if she asked what happened to the kid, and if she didn't, he'd just tell her—"and feared for the wholeness of my head for the rest of the school year, especially when he was let back in school after two weeks though not in my class." She might ask why did he continue teaching if it was so bad? and he'd say "Money. At the time it was the best I could do and the long summer break gave me time to write. Not that I ever stopped while I was teaching, but did much less of it. But enough about me and my occupational hazards and adversities." That'd be a good line if he got the chance to use it and it didn't feel forced. "Tell me about your teaching. I want to know what it'd be like standing in front of a class without losing my voice every day shouting the umpteenth time for quiet, or not having to turn around every five seconds when I'm writing something on the black-board, to prevent another head-cracking object thrown at me." Then he could ask, if she didn't bring it up, what are some of the books she uses in class and then talk with her about one of them he might have read—chances are always fairly good for that—or say he hasn't read them all or maybe any of them, but one particularly he's wanted to read, or if he's read it, reread. "What's a good translation of it," he could say, "or maybe there's only one? Wouldn't I love to read even a semi-serious novel in the original foreign language. I've tried, in German and French, but couldn't get halfway through them without going to the bilingual dictionaries a million times, even with Simenon and Remarque." So, plenty of things to talk about. Her thesis and dissertation—what were they on? She could then say that would take too long to explain on the phone, and he could say "Then let's meet. I'd like to hear about your work and what you've written, and if you've done book reviews or published some of your scholarly work, maybe I could locate them. I'm always interested in the art work and critical writings and such that people I've just met do." He can be such a bullshit artist, he's thought lots of times. Maybe less so now but plenty then. But whenever he is he tries to do it in a way where he doesn't seem like one. Here, he'd just be trying to get over the early humps of his first call to her. Maybe, he thought, he should just say to her, without anything else about her teaching and writing and nothing about his, "I'm curious who some of the writers are that you teach, or did I say that the other night in front of Pati's building? Even if I did—it sounds like something I'd ask because I'm always looking for something new to read—we talked for so short a time, we couldn't have gone into it very much," and then see where the conversation goes from there. If he does refer to his teaching and writing—even if he told himself not to, he could find himself doing it—should he slip in how, in his one free period a day in those schools, he used to, with a fountain pen, edit and then rewrite repeatedly, and never without making a change or two every time he rewrote the page, a couple of pages of a short story he was working on at the time, while the rest of the teachers in the teachers' lounge were grading papers, writing lesson plans, napping, eating, smoking, talking, reading a newspaper, playing cards. It'd be a good anecdote, he thought, and again, without pushing it and if he could fit it into the conversation smoothly, give her an idea how committed he is to his writing. That he never leaves it home. In other words, if she asks what he means by that or he feels he needs to explain it or elaborate, that he always takes it with him, physically or in his head, so long as he has a copy of the original manuscript on his work table in his apartment in case the part he takes to school gets damaged to the point where he can't read it or lost. And when she does answer the phone and they talk and the conversation goes well or lags a little but sort of reaches a certain time limit for a first call and he says something like "With all your teaching and other activities, you must be quite busy and I've taken up a lot of your time, so I should come right out with it and ask if you'd like to meet for coffee or something one of these days—tomorrow or the next day or whenever you're free," what could be the worst thing that could happen? She says no. But no with an explanation that does something to his stomach. She's seeing somebody. Not only is she seeing somebody but it's somebody she feels quite strongly about. She's sorry she led him on. She probably wouldn't say that. At the time when she gave him her phone number—"You mean, how to get it," he'd say if she said that, and maybe say it a bit angrily, and she might say something like "Whatever way you got it—I wasn't completely aware how deep my feelings were for this man." She probably wouldn't say anything like that either. She'd probably think she doesn't need to explain. After all, they barely know each other, they only talked briefly, this is their first and probably their last phone call, so who is he to her? She's not even sure about his name. Is it Martin Samuels? Samuel Martin? Oh, she'd know his name all right, he thought, but as a joke to herself it could be what she'd think. Lots of people, when they first meet him and some awhile after, have called him Samuel or Sam. Instead, she might say, if that she is seeing somebody what's stopping her from meeting him for coffee and possibly also that she doesn't want to lead him on, "I don't think it's a good idea." If he said "Is it because you're seeing some-body that's stopping you from meeting me for coffee and also perhaps you might think you'd be leading me on?" she'd probably just say she'd prefer not going into it. Or just—after he asks her if she'd like to meet him for coffee one of these days or even a drink—she's sorry, she doesn't think so and she'd rather not go into why, but it was nice meeting him even so briefly, maybe she'll see him again at one of Pati's parties, and this time at the party and not after they leave it. "She gives so many of them," she could say, "and always one on her birthday, or has since I've known her, but where we have to promise not to bring a present." "Yeah," he'd say, "she already told me to set aside that date. An easy one to remember: Lincoln's birthday," and she might say "Darwin's too—Pati told me that." "Same here," he'd say. "That's the only reason I know and I'll probably always remember it." "Well," she'd probably then say, "goodbye," and hang up. Anyway, bad as he'd feel if she turned him down for coffee, or a drink at the West End, let's say, which is just up the street from where she lives, on Broadway, he can only find out what her answer will be by calling her. But if she told him how to get her number, which is the same thing, really, as giving it, then it had to mean she intended to meet him, other fellow or not, at least for coffee, and to continue what he thought, and she might have too, was a fairly good conversation for a first one, at the elevator, in it and on the street. They did talk in the elevator, didn't they? he thinks. More than just that business about pushing the floor button, or was that just in one of his dreams tonight? But the butterflies in his stomach, and they're flying around now like fighter planes, he remembers thinking and writing down someplace and coming upon sometime later and thinking "What was in my head at the time to want to write down such crap?" are telling him something. What? Something. But what? That he really doesn't want to blow this. He knows, he knows. So attractive and elegant and dignified, he meant to say, and seemingly good-natured and probably high-minded and obviously smart. He knows: whatever you do, don't blow it. For how many future chances will he get to meet a woman like this? And he wants the whole works with one: sex, love, marriage, children, and the chances of getting all that, let's face it, are fading. He's losing his looks and hair and back teeth and is only minimally successful in his writing after almost twenty years at it, and the prospects, though he is being published by small places and in one recent big place though at the bottom of its list, seem slim of ever living anything but skimpily off it. And he has very little money saved and only a small amount of royalties owed him and no job possibilities to speak of and it doesn't look good he'll ever have them: applied the last five years to he doesn't know how many English and writing departments, college and a few New York City private high schools to teach writing and, if he has to, a little contemporary fiction with it, and not one of them bit. Not one even asked him to be interviewed for the opening or wanted him, when he suggested it, to send his one and then two and then three published books. And a couple of them said, so many more must have thought, they'd never consider anyone who didn't have an advanced degree in literature or creative writing no matter how great a teacher and writer he may be, "and I'm not saying you are," one of them added, "though in all probability you could be. I'm unfamiliar with your books and have no idea what you're like in the classroom and was simply being hypothetical," and he doesn't know what other kind of work he can now do. Certainly not bartending or waiting on tables again or subbing in public junior high schools. So what would he be bringing to a relationship at forty-two? Though she might have found him halfway interesting and even physically appealing to a degree and maybe intelligent or whatever positive things she might have found him when they first met, on the phone with her, since he'll feel some pressure to perform and because of that will have a hard time trying to act naturally, she could easily think him dull or too self-absorbed, or self-conscious, or something, but fake. And just being nervous about calling her up and speaking to her and afraid of blowing it, he might say the wrong thing or a series of them and turn her off. Something dumb or trite or silly or truly stupid and then try to apologize or alibi his way out of it and get himself in even deeper. And would she agree to meet what she was beginning to believe was a silly or stupid man even once? Would he with a silly or stupid woman even once? he thought. He might. No, he wouldn't. He'd think nothing good could come of it. Going to bed with the woman that first date? After all, if she's silly or stupid or let's just say not very clever, she'd probably be more persuadable, so there'd be a better chance. That used to be enough, but not anymore. He feels too lousy about it after. That he's being totally dishonest, done something wrong, hurt the woman, convinced or tricked her into doing something she didn't want to or intuitively knew not to and now thinks less of herself, and so on. And she's a woman, this Gwendolyn is, who could probably get just about any available man she wanted, so he's saying if he acts like a sap on the phone, why would she want to meet up with him? Though maybe she's not as intolerant of people as he is, or so quick to pass judgment, is more like it, besides sensing his nervousness and making certain adjustments for that. After talking with people for a minute or so or a little longer, he often thinks he knows what they're like—silly, stupid, vapid, nothing to say, no original thoughts, uninterested in anything serious he is—and he sticks with that opinion. She, on the other hand, might think—she somehow seemed like this—that everyone's good for at least one conversation over coffee or a beer—well, maybe with her not the beer; but something he ought to try thinking himself, since he can be so rigid with people. That's not the word he wants, but he knows what he means. You can learn a lot about a person, and thus, people in general, that first and maybe only talk: hopes, goals, background, life history, so on, so on. Where the person's been, what the person's done, and everything that goes along with it, whatever he means by that. Maybe no conversation, or few, between two people can be so wide-ranged and packed tighter than the first one if it's long enough, hour or two, especially if they're eager to get in almost everything that interests them or think the other person will think interesting and makes them look good, something he doubts very much she'd do and he has to watch out for in himself if, and he should be so lucky, it ever comes to that. It'd be interesting, though, to find out what she really thinks about what he thought she might—that everyone's-good-for-at-least-one-or-two-hour-long-conversation, etcetera. For all he knows it could be close to what he guessed. And his hopes and goals and such, if they do meet and she asks? She's a part of them, that's for sure, but of course not what he so soon would want to express. Talk about scaring her off fast. He'd just be matter-of-fact, not give away anything as to what he's been thinking about her, talk seriously about his writing and where he wants it to go and that if some college, preferably here but almost anywhere in the States if that's all he can get, would give him a break and look at his list of publications and the New York State writing fellowship he's gotten and not just his lack of any postgraduate degree, he'd like to start teaching, for the income and time it'd give him to write, and other things in his life—"To be honest, eventually marriage, children. I'm already past forty, so you understand, but not to rush into anything, just to have these things." And after an hour or so and they've finished their coffee or she, tea, and maybe a refill—well, you don't usually get a refill of tea unless it's already in one of those small teapots that sometimes comes with the cup or mug—and start to leave—he'll pick up the check even if she insists he don't and she's had something, for him, expensive with her coffee or tea. He'll only have coffee and if she says something like "You're not having anything to eat?" he'll say "Not hungry, thanks," although he might be but knows once she orders a sandwich or some other food like that and he's intending to pick up the check, that he really can't afford more. Or maybe he'll do this—ask her if she'd like to meet him again—in front of the coffee shop, for that's what he thinks it'll be if she agrees to meet him a first time, someplace simple—and just pray, maybe even hold his breath; in other words, hope very hard she says that important second yes. She does, he thought, he thinks he'd begin to believe that maybe they'd started something, for why else would she agree to see him again? Would talking about his fairly prestigious writing fellowship be too much like boasting? Not if he says it in a way where it doesn't. For instance: The fellowship, and this only if the subject or it comes up or something closely related to it, enabled him for the first time in his life, and he's been writing for around twenty years, to do nothing but write for a year. More than a year. He managed to stretch the fellowship money to a year and a half before he had to look for work again. His most productive period too, though he won't say this to her, at least not yet, on the phone or if they meet, because that would really be boasting: forty-two short stories and a rewrite of a short novel, and most of those stories eventually got into one magazine or another and some of them into his first two story collections, while the novel is still making the rounds. Actually, he had another writing fellowship, but he doesn't know if he'd want to talk about it, again at least not yet, even if he had the chance. Certainly nothing to do with boasting. He got it years ago, an academic fellowship, and he had to uproot himself to California at some expense to take advantage of it and about a third of the fellowship money went to the tuition of the once-a-week graduate writing seminar he had to take and he felt the criticism he got in class from the other fellows and graduate student writers set his writing back a year. Just about all of them and one of his two teachers, though they referred to themselves as coaches, hated his work, and the other teacher or coach thought he showed some promise in the short story form but none in the novel and that he was going through the obligatory experimental phase almost every serious writer in his mid-twenties does who's been reading Faulkner, early Hemingway, Kafka, Borges and Joyce. Anyway, what he wants now, though, and he wishes he hadn't set himself up for such a big disappointment if he doesn't get it, he thought in his room about a week after they first met, sitting on his bed fully dressed, first week in December he thinks or last in November, for Pati's party was right around Thanksgiving, either day after or before, holding the receiver so long the dial tone went dead, determined not to stall anymore but to call her right now or sometime tonight and if she doesn't answer, he remembers thinking, not to wait around to call again but to go out for a short walk, maybe stop in someplace for a coffee or beer and call her from there or after he gets back home, is for her to say after they'd talked awhile about various things and he then asked her out some day for coffee—no beer: that could be the second date if the first went well—"Yes," or "Sure, that'd be nice," or "I don't see why not," or "Why not? What's a good day and time for you and we'll see if it jells with my own schedule? Let me get my appointment book," but something like one of those and they work out where and when. Just imagine, he thought, if it came out like that. After he hung up the phone he'd go "Whoopee," and make a fist and slam it through the air and maybe shout "Yeah, yeah; goddamn it, you dood it, you done dood it, you imbecile; it's working," and be all smiles and maybe have a shot of vodka from the bottle in the freezer or a glass of wine just to calm himself down and then go out to his neighborhood bar for a draft beer and hope his friend Manny was there—he usually was around this time; it had become his weekday nighttime hangout, first stool nearest the door if he could get it, under the shelf with the television on it and by the payphone, where he got and made calls—if when he reached her was the first time he dialed her and she answered and he hadn't already been out for a short walk. Oh, forget it for now, he told himself or might even have said out loud. He thinks he did. "You're still too nervous. You can call later if it's not too late. Or tomorrow. But definitely no later than tomorrow if you don't call tonight, around this time or late afternoon, the likeliest times, you'd think, other than early morning—and you don't want to call anytime in the morning; that'd seem like you were desperate to reach her—when she'd be home. But again, not too late if you call at night. No later than ten, maybe ten-thirty, but not a minute after that, and probably, because your watch might be slow, no later than a few minutes before. People get uneasy when they get calls later than that. You do, anyway—a little uneasy: your mother suddenly sick or hospitalized or worse, for instance?—and she might. You can see her hearing the phone ring and looking at her watch or a clock and wondering who could be calling this late and what could it be about. And later than ten-thirty, she might be preparing for sleep. Or she might be tired after a long day and want to get to bed and be in no mood to talk. She might even be in bed or soon going to be with some guy, a boyfriend or just some man she finds attractive and likes to sleep with. You hope not. Come on, what you really hope for is that you become that guy—the boyfriend, though you'd take the other for as long as you both wanted it and it could always lead to something deeper—and you never know. You can look at what you're giving off in a different way than you did before. You're actually still not a bad-looking guy and she never has to see that you're missing most of your back teeth, and you're built well, tall, not much blubber. Okay, you have lost a fair amount of hair and nothing you can do about that, certainly not comb it over.

But you've got brains and a sense of humor and you are a serious writer and published—there are plenty of serious writers your age who can't even say that, or not published in so many places—and it's happened with a couple of women as beautiful, or almost as beautiful as she. Give it time. Whatever you do—all this, of course, predicated on her agreeing to that first meeting—don't push it faster than it should go. You think you know what you're saying there. If all works out, it could end the way it did with the two other beauties, but better, and one of them—the other said she'd never marry you, when you raised the possibility; being married once was enough, she said, just as her one kid was all the children she wanted: that living together till either one of you lost interest in the other was as far as it could ever go—you were even engaged to, only time you were engaged, and came weeks or months away from marrying her, when she broke it off. Why? Some bullshit excuse that was nowhere near the truth. Their different religions and also that she didn't want to get tied down so young. She was how old? Twenty-five or twenty-four. Twenty-four, spring of '61, and you were a few months older. Maybe in the future, she said. Truth is, she didn't love you that much, nothing like the way you did her, and she didn't want to come out with it because she didn't want to hurt you. And when you grabbed her shoulders and shook her back and forth and screamed for her to give you the real reason she was breaking it off and admit she was getting rid of you for good, she told you to get your things together—she hadn't planned to ask you this soon, she said—and leave her apartment because she was afraid you were next going to hit her. 'I could, I could,' you said. But enough; no more talking to yourself out loud or at least not to go on so long with such chatter. Bad sign. Of what? Of the obvious." Anyway, it's not like he has a problem. He's not crazy, in other words. Talking to himself out loud isn't something he does regularly or has ever done, far as he can remember, at such length before. He was just horsing around, so what's the harm?—nobody was here to listen. And the butterflies—butterflies and horse, he thought; anything to make of that?—are gone. Went when he decided not to call her just yet and maybe not even till tomorrow. So maybe that's why he talked out loud to himself so long. To get his mind off the call he knows he's going to make. Something like that. He remembers slamming the receiver down fast after one or two rings the two times he dialed her entire number. So there'd be no chance she'd answer the phone and hear him putting the receiver down without saying anything. He thought she'd be alarmed or concerned in some way if she heard the slams. But he thinks he got the receiver down before she'd be able to pick up the phone. He just didn't want to get caught. Caught how? She wouldn't have known it was he slamming the receiver down. She might have guessed, though, maybe not the first time but the second—a wild guess, maybe something to do with the nervous and erratic way he thinks he acted with her by the elevator and then in it and later on the street and also that someone ringing and quickly hanging up twice in so short a time in one night, and the chances are pretty poor it could be two different callers, would seem less like an accident than only once would be—that it was he and wonder, if she was right, and it increasingly looks like she is, she might think, why he didn't stay on the phone. Butterflies in his stomach at speaking to her? she might think. She's so beautiful and desirable that it's probably happened, and she's aware of it, with other guys when they first called her for a date, he bets. If she asks, when he does finally call her, did he call her twice before or twice in a row last night and hang up after the first rings—it was just so unusual, she could say, and she thought, for some reason, it might have been him—he could say it wasn't, this is the first time he called, or he did call those times she said and he hopes he didn't upset her, and then give an excuse. Suddenly had to go to the bathroom and she might say "Twice?" and he could say "Yes, unbelievable as it might sound—and I don't have a health problem with it, by the way—twice." "Why didn't you call back after?" she might say, and he wouldn't know what to say to that, or not right away, so some other excuse. He's good at excuses, or usually. He's a good liar, is what he means. Probably has something to do with being a writer, or what helped him or steered him into being one. "I suddenly—just after your phone started ringing—got an idea for a story," he could say. "I'm a writer, you see—I don't know if I told you that night we met—fiction, only—so an idea for a story involving several phone conversations, though not one with you, and wanted to write it down before I lost it, and hung up. I figured I could always call you back later, but a good story idea, when I lose it I usually lose it for good. I hope you didn't mind, hearing the ringing cut off. And I was right. Wrote the idea down, then started on the first draft of the story right after—somehow got caught up in it—and I wrote the entire first draft in one sitting and it's a story I like and that stays with me, so after I finished the work I was working on—a short-short that took much longer that I thought—I started the first draft of the new one and will work on it till it's done." "I can understand your hanging up for that," she could say, "but why did you hang up a second time without waiting for me to answer?" "Did I say I hung up twice?" he could say. "I guess I did. Well, to be honest, and it wasn't something I thought quite right to talk about in our first phone call, but the first time I hung up—getting the story idea was the second—occurred when I all of a sudden had to go to the bathroom. I have no medical problem with it, you see. I just waited too long." "What's the story about," she could say, "other than involving several phone conversations?" He could say "Oh, I'm very bad at summarizing my plots—they always come out sounding idiotic and trite—but I'll give it a try. It's about a writer, pretending to be a customer, who phones several bookstores in town asking if they have his newly published book. Saying things like 'I think I have his name and the title right—anyway, it's supposed to be an exceptional novel.' Or 'I tried getting it at a bookstore closer to my home but it was all sold out,' etcetera. None of the seven or eight stores he calls carry his book or had planned to and most of them hadn't even heard of it. Maybe all of them hadn't heard but they just didn't want to admit it. His aim, or course, was to generate interest in the book and increase sales. What he finds out, though, is that his novel, far as interest and sales go, is pretty much a flop, which will hurt if not kill his chances of selling his next novel to the same publisher. Not to go on too long about this, most of the salespeople he speaks to on the phone say they can special-order the book for him and have it in the store, depending on its distributor, in a matter of days. To the first one he says something like—to the others he just says 'Don't bother' or 'No thanks'—'Yes,'—and all this will change a little to a lot in the final draft, since I do more than one of them and am always changing the text—'Yes, please order it for me—I wish the bookstore near me had suggested that—and I'll drop by in a few days to pick it up,' which he had no intention to. And this woman, or maybe it was a man—doesn't matter—asks for his name and phone number so she can call him when the book comes in, and he says 'Actually, I'm going to try some other stores to see if one of them has it, because I want to start on it right away,' and so on. You get the idea." He also thought in his apartment that night when he was debating with himself whether to call her now or put it off another day, maybe he's blowing this way out of proportion and she's really not right for him and same for him to her, so why bother? He was also worried—but didn't he go over this before? He's almost sure he did but forgets what it was he thought. Anyway: worried he'll sound like an idiot on the phone with her and he won't have anything to say, and he can't just come right out and say "Like to meet for coffee or a beer sometime this week?" without saying much of anything before. And he'll hem and haw and then probably apologize for hemming and hawing and maybe even admit he's a bit nervous speaking to her—now all that he's sure he went over before in his head. And she'll probably ask why, or she could, or she might not say anything but she'll certainly think it and already have formed a not very positive opinion of him and maybe think him, which he can be at times, a little goofy and juvenile and even somewhat dumb. By then, she might want to end the conversation, what little there likely is of it, because it was obviously going nowhere and she was getting tired of it and has things to do and it was getting late, and say—just come right out with it, since she has no interest in him so has nothing to lose—Did I really tell him how to get my phone number? she might think during or after the call—that she doesn't think it's a good idea their getting together, if that's what he called for, and she can't imagine, she could say, any other reason for his call, and it was nice speaking to him but she has to go now and then say goodbye and hang up, maybe not even waiting for him to say goodbye. No, she'd wait. And she wouldn't be so blunt. Way he reads her he's sure she's never rude and is usually very polite and would never slight or say anything that would hurt or anger him in any way, if she could help it, and she would know what would. But isn't most of how he imagines the phone conversation would be, going too far? First of all, surely he could talk and act on the phone much better than he's depicted himself here. Secondly…well, he forgets what that was. Anyway, he might be nervous or anxious on the phone with her, or maybe not, but he'd be able to control it where it doesn't show. Answer this, though: why'd you think she might not be right for you despite your wanting to call her so much? The possibility of your not being right for her you've already gone into, you think. Physically; intellectually, perhaps, and maybe even the age gap. Forget the "physically." You can see her—again, just something about her you quickly picked up—dating and even sleeping with, if she thought highly of the guy enough, homely, intelligent and artistic men. Scholars and talented poets. Architects who read, and the like. But the first question you asked? And there's those times when you're feeling worst about yourself and don't think you're right for any woman, but that always passes. Who doesn't have serious self-doubts? But answer the one about her not being right for you. I don't know. Yes, you do. I just can't this moment come up with an answer for it. Yes, you can; don't worm your way out of it. Her looks. Was she really all that good-looking? Oh, come on. First you think she's gorgeous and then you don't think she's that good looking? I didn't say she wasn't. I was just wondering if I saw right. I did have a little more than a little to drink that night. Also, my eyes are bad and my glasses are old and I need a new eye exam and lenses, so I could have mis-seen what I saw, for want of a better expression or word. "Mis-seen" isn't either, right? Stop it. She was pretty, very pretty, maybe beautiful, maybe even drop-dead gorgeous, besides being exceptionally pleasant, gentle and bright. Pleasant and gentle, yes, but that could just be good manners. But how can you tell about her being so bright, for you know I wouldn't want to go out, over a period of time, if it ever came to that, and same with sleeping with, with someone who wasn't, not necessarily "exceptionally," but very bright? The way she spoke, her look. The words she used, and other things: her voice. Maybe she's too smart for me, then. Did she seem that way? No. She just seemed smart, learned, quick, articulate, and probably very bright, and interested, from what I could make out—I forget what it was, but it was something—in some, maybe many— no, we didn't talk long enough for me to say "many"—of the same things as me. Literature. She teaches it, must have spent years at a very high level studying and writing about it. She has a Ph.D., said so at the elevator. But you know these academics. No, what? I never really got along with them, and for some reason the women more than the men. There was Eleanor, years ago. No Ph.D., just a master's in English literature, not that I'm knocking it with that "just." I barely made it out of college and never wanted to go further. Actually, not so. In '58, couple of months after I graduated college and exactly ten years before I met Eleanor and twenty before today—those ten-year intervals could be significant, although in '48 I was in seventh grade—I started an M.A. in American lit at Hunter and lasted all of three weeks. Walked out of a class in bibliography—one of my two courses—other was in pre- or post-colonial or -Columbian literature— remember, this was twenty years ago—still open to me because I registered so late. Left in the middle of the class, in fact, with the professor saying to me as I gathered up my books and stuff and headed for the door, "Yes?" and I saying "I'm sorry, this is just not for me. I was either naive or stupid enough to think that going for a master's in literature, we'd just read and talk about what we read, and after class, sometimes with the teacher, go out for coffee or beer and talk some more about our books and all sorts of things." No, I didn't say that, but wanted to. Also, what a pedant I thought he was and that I can't, because of the technical language of his trade, understand half of what he says. What he actually said to me was "Mr. Samuels, is it? Class hasn't been dismissed," but I just left the room without saying a word. But Eleanor—second woman I went with, although she was the first, whose thesis was on some aspect of Dickens' work. Windows, I think, and doors. "Oubliette." I never heard the word before and don't think I've seen it since. Good in bed, though she needed a lot of pot to get that way, but unattractively coarse and stingingly frank and aggressively self-serving and insufferably smug. Enough adverbs for you? I usually don't use them other than for "obviously" and if "probably" and "possibly" are adverbs. Boy, what she would have done with that. "Hey, buddy, let's get to it," she once said. "You only helped me get one orgasm, while I helped you get three." I didn't have three but couldn't convince her, so had to perform when I was spent. I told her this can lead to a heart attack and she said "Rubbish, you're too young." The second and third orgasms she referred to were continuations, separated by silence for a few seconds and then accompanied by the familiar noise, of the only one I had. But an example of her smugness? "Oh, you didn't know Dickens died before he was sixty? You must not have been paying attention in your high school English class." He did die that early? It'd seem with all those lengthy novels and book-length travel journals, he had to have lived well into his seventies and never put his pen down till he dropped. No, under sixty, but not by much. Funny, she mentioned high school, because that was the only time I liked Dickens. The abridged *Tale of Two Cities*. I memorized and used to declaim when I was alone and nobody could hear me the "It is a far, far better thing and place," etcetera, speech, from the ending. But as an adult, I didn't much care for Dickens. All those masterpieces I thought weren't. A good storyteller, if you like stories. Today I'd say MFM: made for movies. In those days, for reading tours. Written too quickly, with little re-examining and revising, and some of the most contrived situations and resolutions and initial encounters and final partings imaginable. Or that's my take on his work, but I could be wrong and he did write meticulously and go through multiple revisions, but to me it didn't come out that way. Two carriages going in opposite directions, each containing a member or members of the main cast, passing each other without recognizing the other at dawn, usually while crossing a moat. Maybe I'm exaggerating. Also, I don't know what funny names do to you, but they don't make me laugh. I once said some of this to Eleanor, and did she blow up. "You should be a quarter as good as Dickens," she said, "an eighth as good, even a sixteenth, in any page from all of his books, but with the literary conventions of your own century. Even if you adored his work you'd probably say otherwise, simply to rankle me. Anything I'm good at and devoted to, you put down." That true? No, I admired a lot of what she did, particularly how fast she read and got her ideas down, and went out of my way to praise her. Just when it comes to literature and what I like, I don't fool around. I break off a twig, chew one of its ends to a sharp point, dip it in ink and draw the line. What that means and where it came from, beats me. "Blood" for "ink" wouldn't make any more sense, or not to me at this moment, but it does sound more serious and dramatic. But I'm not much for the unconscious or accidental supplying some of my original ideas and thoughts, creative and otherwise. I think I meant something there that's connected to what came before it. What's the word for a mind that's going? It shouldn't be for a guy my age but sometimes it seems like it. Anyway, he never got along for very long with academic women—women who teach literature in college and have one or two advanced literature degrees—and he probably won't with this Gwendolyn or Gwen. Why? He's already spoken about some of her more positive qualities: pleasant demeanor, good looks and speech, soft voice and quiet smile, and she seems to have similar interests as he and an even disposition and a terrific mind. So, what's not to like? as his father used to say, though he was talking about other things: money and schemes to make it and getting things for free. She seemed a lot different than Eleanor and Diana, his other Dickens scholar. They were okay, he's not really complaining about them, and they certainly had a lot to put up with in him—he doesn't want to go into it but there were many things he did to them that were wrong—though they could be a bit stagy and stiff and too often cold and hard. It didn't seem she could be any of those, especially cold and hard, or if she could it'd be rare, short-lived and justified. How can he tell? He can't, little time he was with her. Then why's he saying it? Probably to give him more reason to call her or ward off reasons not to. Did he make any sense there? he thought. Does anything he say make any sense? He used to, almost all the time, but maybe he was mistaken. Maybe meeting her and wanting to call her so much and see her again has made him more unsure of himself than he typically is. What else? What else what? Her, about her. He liked the way she was dressed. Simply, good taste, muted colors. Small matter, but it does say something about why he was attracted to her. He likes his women—now that's funny; *his*—not to dress stylishly or ostentatiously or expensively, and nothing she wore seemed that way, or to wear something or have on some adornment that calls attention to herself and you think she only put it on because it does. Again, is he making himself clear? he thought. He knows what he wants to say but is having trouble saying it clearly in his head and he for sure would have even a worse problem if he had to say it out loud. It's late, or it's not so late, so maybe it's just been a long day, but it's something, so don't worry about it. But he doesn't want—a thought he knows he's already had tonight—to call her and have his words dribble out uncohesively. Incoherently. Unintelligibly. Un- or incomprehensibly. He's not joking with himself: suddenly he doesn't know. And right now if he had to decide on only one to use, because two or more if he said them to someone might seem like showing off, he couldn't. Couldn't decide. But to illustrate something he touched on before—clothes: Eleanor wore what to him were ridiculous hats and wool caps made in Guatemala and Morocco and Peru and enormous metal necklaces, maybe from the same places—she had family money and was a world traveler— that clinked when she bent over or walked. And Diana, who grew up "dirt poor," she said, "and made it all the way through grad school, unlike some of your previous girlfriends, entirely on my own," had a new hair style or cut every other month, it seemed, some of them he thought unflattering and made her intelligent face look a little silly. "What do you think?" she'd say. "You haven't said anything." "About what?" and she'd say "My hair; you noticed. So, out with it. Is it the disaster your face says?" and he'd have to hedge or lie. "I don't know what was wrong with the last one, and all these different stylings must come at considerable expense, but this one's nice too." Gwen had beautiful straight hair, worn simply. "Worn" the right word? Oh, there was another Dickens scholar. How could he have forgotten her? Also had her long blond hair up when he first saw her and he also wondering how far down her back it'd fall. Or he thinks he wondered that about Gwen at the party. Sharon's almost reached her waist. He likes long hair on women. All the things they can do with it. Loves it when he's on his back in bed and the woman's on top and leaning over him and her hair would cover his shoulders and head—this only happened with Sharon and Gwen—blocking out the light. And if not Dickens, then at least Victorian literature, and a Ph.D. also, so her studies, and possibly her teaching, had to include Dickens. California, Bay area, thirteen years ago. Got along with her just fine for about a year—in fact, as smooth a relationship as he ever had till then…never a disagreement between them till she broke up with him. Then he went berserk, smashed a glass on the floor, pounded the wall with his fists, called her a whore and a liar and a bitch who's just been leading him on or stringing him along but doing crap like that to him since they met, and even threatened to hit her. Saw her three to four times a week—usually she drove to his place because her husband, who she said had no trouble with her romance with him—"He's had his own sweeties, one he really flipped over, and he above all hates hypocrites"—worked at home. Then she wanted to have a child, and to be sure, for genetic reasons, who the father is—"It's very important medically, you know, and if he ever separated from me, for financial support"—and because she wanted to conceive soon as she could and then lead a normal family life—"I know I must sound like an utter bourgeois on this, but when it comes to my own child, out comes the hidden traditionalist in me"—she couldn't see him again except if he wanted to meet from time to time for coffee and just to talk and to see how big her up-till-now tiny belly can be. Before he went crazy that day, he said calmly "Divorce him and marry me and have a child. I'll never cheat on you, I've been wanting to get married for years and start a family, and you love me more than you do him." She said "No, I don't. What made you think that? You're a sweetheart, but you come in second. And for my marriage to end, my husband would have to divorce me. But he likes the way things are and doesn't mind adding marital fidelity and a baby or two to them. Besides, he's a successful writer, so has the means, while you'll be struggling for years." Met her at a health-food co-op in Berkeley. Diana he was fixed up with by a friend in New York. Eleanor he also met at a party in SoHo, but so far east it might be called something else. Sharon was behind him on the checkout line with three items in her hands: an unsliced loaf of millet bread, a can of inorganic garbanzo beans and a square chunk of tofu in a little plastic bag tied with a tab and almost filled to the top with water, like the kind one carries home a goldfish in from a pet store. Remembered how the bag always stunk from fish feces when he opened it. How'd he get the fish into the bowl without the feces? It was so long ago. When he was a kid. He gave them names. One was "Goldie." The fish kept quickly dying, never lasted more than a few days, so he must have done it several times before giving up on owning a fish. Probably emptied the bag out into a container of water first and then picked the fish up with his hand or a net and put it into the bowl. "If that's all you have," he said, "—even if you have more"—he was immediately attracted to her as he was to Gwen—"go in front of me. I've got a lot more than you." She said "No, thank you. I'm in no hurry. And what I have is hardly weighing me down." "Put everything on the counter then," and she said "The water could spill and I didn't bag the bread." "Of course," he said. "I should have realized that. I don't know what's making me so dense, but you're right," and he couldn't think of anything else to say and she looked away from him, so he turned to the front. Outside the store, he tied and retied his shoes, waiting for her. When she came out, same three items in her hands, he stood up and patted his pants pockets as if he were searching for his wallet or keys or just wanted to make sure they were there. Then he looked at her as if he had only just noticed her and said, "Oh, hi. Just thought I lost something, but as usual I didn't. Wait a minute. None of my business, but you going to carry that bread home or to somewhere, not in a bag?" She said "I have a bag for it in my bicycle but forgot to bring it in with me," and she unstrapped one of the saddle bags on a bike in a bike rack in front of the store, got a paper bag out of it and stuck the bread in. "So you slice it each time?" he said. "With a breadknife," she said. "The loaf always falls apart when I do it that way, even with a breadknife, which is why I get it sliced." "It stays fresher unsliced," she said, "and will stay even fresher if you put a few raisins in the bag." "Raisins?" and she said "Take my word. Try it." Then she put her three items into the saddle bag, the tofu wedged between the beans and bread and something else holding it straight—a rolled-up hand towel, it looked like—so it wouldn't move around and burst or spill. "Very ecological," he said. "I should do more of that. I try, in other ways—biking instead of driving if it isn't raining hard and the distance isn't too great and if there isn't an enormous steep hill along the way, since my bike's only got one speed, unlike yours—but I never thought to bring my own bags to a store. I'm afraid I've only used them for my garbage till now." "That's putting them to good use," she said. "You're being ecological by not buying garbage bags, which would probably be plastic." "I suppose. But what if I first used the bag to carry home goods from a store and then used it for my garbage?" "You could do that. Doubly useful. What an odd conversation this is." "Well, you get into things, you never know where you're going to go, but we'll get out. Unfortunately, I'm almost inherently discursive and digressive. My father, by the way—am I holding you up? I shouldn't say that, because I'm enjoying the conversation," and she said "I've got a few minutes." "My father was practicing ecology or environmentalism or whatever the right word for it is, long before most people, it seemed. But more out of thriftiness, which I'm sure came from his family being very poor when he was a kid, than saving the planet or preserving it a few years more than the global experts were giving it because of our planetary profligacy, I guess you can call it. As an example, and he's retired now and disabled and quite sick so he no longer does this, every day for lunch he took a sandwich to his office wrapped in the same wax paper he used for the entire work week. That is, if it didn't get too messy or tear, and by the way he wrapped the sandwich and refolded the paper after he used it, he made sure it wouldn't. He probably would have used it the following week too but had no place to keep it over the weekend. My mother I know wouldn't have allowed him to stash it in the refrigerator someplace because if anyone saw it, it would just seem too cheap, and if he kept it out for two days the paper would stink and parts of it maybe rot by the time he used it again Sunday night. Same routine with the paper lunch bag he carried the sandwich in, if it also didn't get too greasy or start to come apart. Folded the bag carefully along its natural seams after taking the wrapped sandwich and paper napkin and that day's whole fruit out of it—apple, orange, tangerine, etcetera. Napkins he used came from the dairy cafeteria he treated himself to lunch to about every third week, maybe also to restock his napkin supply. Would grab a couple of handfuls out of the dispenser and stuff them into his jacket and coat pockets. Where he kept them at home I don't know, but he took me to lunch there once or twice and I saw him do it and figured out that's where his never-ending supply of napkins came from." "Outside of the napkin part, she said, "it seems he knew what he was doing, reusing what other people indiscriminately throw away." "I guess, but I'm not certain, though I like your idea of looking at it in a good light. When I was growing up, though—even till about five or ten years ago—I saw it the way my mother did: that he was cheap. But to really exhaust the point and also to see this segment of my father's life, since it is sort of a story, to the end and then I'll stop, though I'll stop sooner if you want me to, he made the sandwich right after dinner, or right after he smoked his cigar after dinner—wouldn't allow anyone to do it for him—usually from a few slices of that meal's meat leftover. If it didn't look like there was going to be any meat left over, he saved a slice or two already on his plate and made the sandwich from that. What I'm getting to here is that if he only ate half the sandwich the next day, he brought the other half home with him, or whatever was left of it—even meat and bread scraps—in the same wax paper and bag he took the sandwich to work in and gave it to our dog, no doubt, in his mind, to save on the dog-food expense and, looking at it the way you do, to cut back on waste. He certainly didn't do it because he liked the dog. He called her 'public nuisance number one.' The only thing I can think of now working against taking the sandwich half and scraps home is that it gave the wax paper and lunch bag one less chance of surviving the entire week. After the dog died from something she ate—it wasn't from the sandwich but something she managed to claw out from behind the stove—I don't know what my father did if he didn't eat the second half of the sandwich, and there had to be times he didn't, since he never brought it home. Okay, that should do it, and did I go on? This is the classic tale of a stranger telling a stranger his family history and life story, but much more than she bargained for or ever wanted to hear." "No, I didn't mind," she said. "I kind of liked it. You're a funny guy. And I bet everything you said was intended to be funny, so a successful funny guy. So, not only amusing but interesting, your delivery and material, in a sort of time-capsule way. What was your dog's name?" "Penelope. I named it before I even heard of Homer. I must have got the name from a character in a comic book, which at the time was all I read for diversion. Anyway, enough of me. I'd like to shut up now. You might think that impossible, but I'm really not much of a talker and don't know how I got started rattling on so much. I'd much prefer hearing some of your life story and family history, but over coffee if you have a few spare minutes. More if you have more but a few if that's all you can spare. I'd also like to know what you meant by my delivery. But could we do that?" Please, please, he was thinking, and she said "I don't see why not. My bike's safe here even without a lock—the co-op manager once told me they never had a bike stolen—and what little food I have won't spoil. To save time, should we go to the snack bar they have here?" They went back inside, split a warmed-up buttered corn muffin and had herbal tea, his first. She ordered it for herself and he told the counterperson "I'll have one too," since the store had no regular coffee—not even in pound bags on the shelves—just grain coffee, which he didn't like. He thought he spoke more articulately and his mind was clearer and he said more intelligent and clever things when he drank caffeinated coffee with someone, at least when his was real coffee and black and strong. That was then; not today and not for years. Now he doesn't think it makes a difference, with or without. He's become somewhat inarticulate and often unintelligible, when he was almost never that way, and gets lost in what he's saying or breaks off his speech in the middle of a sentence because he forgets what point he was trying to make. There's a long word for it he always forgets. Starts with an A or O, he thinks, and when he finally remembers it, he forgets how to pronounce it. What happened to him to make him like that? Age; again, loss of confidence and resistance to doing anything new or to change. Not that so much or much of it at all, but just things repeating themselves. Page after page, section after section, novel after novel, and so on. Same job and same workers at work and same bed and same newspapers and same news and same things to eat and drink and clean up and same dawn. Wait, what's he missing? Gwen getting sick, that changed things, but ended up being the same day-to-day tasks taking care of her. Ah, why worry about it? He's not worrying, just thinking. But to get back. And why's he going on so long about Sharon? Could be because she reminds him of Gwen so much, more than any woman he's been close to. The quietness and education and intelligence and serenity and sense of humor and modesty and the way she smiled and spoke and her soft voice and the soft features and other soft things and that she always had a book with her and read a lot of poetry. Both also wrote poetry. Sharon, he later saw, published some of hers in literary magazines and may have even had a book or two of her poems published, while Gwen never sent hers out. "It's not that I fear rejection," she said, when he said if she doesn't want to do it, he'll send them out for her, he knows the market. "They just never seem ready." Maybe he can put together a collection of her poems, he thinks, with help from a poet friend of hers and the kids. Might take some doing, retrieving them from her computer, but the kids are probably whizzes at that. Also, how he met her. No, not even close, so why'd he think it? Gwen was by the elevator, after his eyeing her at the party for so long and she a few times catching him doing it, though she denied it. Sharon on the checkout line, when he looked around, as people waiting to be taken care of will do on lines, and saw her for the first time—she was looking around too and didn't for several seconds see him looking at her—and was instantly, he could say, as he was with Gwen when he first saw her, attracted to her. That didn't happen to him with many women, maybe just those two. And Terry, actress he saw almost every day for a couple of months—his first real girlfriend, really, meaning the first one he went with a while and also slept with—till she fell in love with an actor she was doing a love scene with in acting class. Her he also first met at a party—New Year's Eve, vast West End Avenue apartment, enormous tall paintings on the walls and smaller ones leaning up against the bookcases and chairs of elongated male and female nudes by the mother of the guy who gave the party, same day or day before Batista fled Cuba and Castro's forces were filtering into Havana for the final takeover of the island. He was elated at the news and then disgusted soon after when the revolutionaries, no doubt on Castro's orders, or maybe not, but anyway he didn't stop them and it went on for weeks, began lining up police and suspected Batista sympathizers and such against walls and shooting them. And Frieda, but should he really count her? He was sixteen, she fifteen, when he went with his friends to a dance at her all-girls' private high school on the Upper East Side and first saw her, dancing the Lindy, he thinks, with another girl in the gymnasium turned into a seedy nightclub. She looks like a model, he thought, so beautiful and slim and dressed so well and sophisticated looking. "Hands off," he told a couple of his friends who were also admiring her. "She's mine, or at least give me a clear shot at her before you horn in." She was the first girl he was in love with. It never came to anything, and he never told her how he felt but knew she knew by the way he acted toward her, other than for a number of dates, all but two of them on Sunday afternoons and a Jewish religious holiday during the week and one big long kiss at her apartment door at the end of their second and last evening date and a few French kisses in the Loew's 83rd Street movie theater. Just "Loew's 83rd" did they call it? He said on the phone weeks after she stopped going out with him "Didn't those kisses we did mean anything?" She said "I don't want to hurt you any more than I may have, but I'm new at it and was just practicing." He went over to her and said something like "Hi, I'm Martin and I wonder if I could have the next dance," and she said "I don't see why that couldn't be possible. Jessica." "Hi, Jessica." "It's actually Frieda, but I'd like it to be Jessica." They danced several dances in a row. He was surprised no other guy cut in on him, and told her so. She said "Oh, I'm a very unpopular girl," and he said "Tell me another one." She seemed to be having a good time with him—laughing and joking and whispering something in his ear he couldn't hear—and he found himself falling for her. She had a nice smell about her—carnation or something. It didn't seem like perfume or cologne—not as strong—so probably from soap. Wherever it came from, he thought, it was intoxicating, as they say. He imagined sitting in a movie theater, her head on his shoulder, and he was smelling that smell. When the Charleston was announced over the loudspeaker as the next dance, he said "Darn, I don't know how to do that one. But my aunt, who tried to teach me it, was one of the six original dancers in the George White's Scandals to introduce it to America." She said "You're making that up," and he said "I swear," and put his hand over his heart. "We can call my mother right now—it's her sister—and ask her," and she said "Okay, I believe you. It's not a man's dance anyway—you don't have the legs for it. It'd be like a man dancing the cancan. It's my favorite dance, though—I'm so glad it was brought back—so I'm going to dance it with my best girlfriend, if you'll excuse me." He said "In case my friends suddenly drag me out of here, can I have your phone number?"—she had her own phone, in her bedroom, something he'd never heard a girl her age having—and called the next night for a date and she said "Thursday's okay, but it'll have to be an early night; I don't want to be too tired for school Friday." They went to Radio City Music Hall. Took the Broadway bus down and then walked the two blocks to Sixth Avenue. But a cab back because he didn't want her to think him cheap. Weekday afternoons and all-day Saturdays he worked as a delivery boy for a catering service and was making enough money to pay for everything that night, even the candy at the theater's refreshment counter. "Should we go in for a snack someplace?" he said, after the movie, but she said it's getting a little late and she should get home. The movie was *Rhapsody*. The leads were Elizabeth Taylor and Vittorio Gassman and another young well-known actor at the time whose first name was John. She suggested they go to it. "So, what movie would you like to see?" he said when he picked her

up—they'd talked about going to one when he called her up for the date—
and she said "First things first—this is a family ritual," and she brought him
into the living room and introduced him to her parents and younger sister
and the live-in housekeeper. He didn't think he'd like the movie when she
described what it was about—a conservatory and music competitions—but
wanted to please her, and ended up loving the movie because of the music
in it. He'd never before heard any part of Mendelssohn's violin concerto and
Tchaikovsky's first piano concerto, he thinks it was, or maybe it was Rach-
maninoff's second—both were his favorites for a couple of years, the Rach-
maninoff a while longer—and a few days after he saw the movie with this
music, he bought long-playing records of them. He played them in his
bedroom so much that his father came to the door and said "Do you think
you can play something else, and lower?" "You ought to be happy I'm listening to this kind of music—I'm the only one of my friends who does," and
his father said "I am—we all are. This is a big change for you, but you're
busting our eardrums. Turn it down now." He was sure that buying the
records and listening to them so much had nothing to do with his feelings
for Frieda or anything else with her, other than that he probably never
would have seen the movie if it hadn't been for her and maybe not got
started listening to classical music so early. After their cab pulled up in front
of her apartment building and he pulled out his wallet, she said "Will you
at least let me pay for this ride? I do have money, you know." He said "No,
tonight everything's on me, not that I'm trying to give the impression I'm a
big sport. Can I see you to your door?" and she said "It's not necessary.
I know my way home from here." "Think we can go out again sometime?"
and she said "Call me and we'll see. You might change your mind by tomorrow and not think it such a wonderful idea," and she kissed her fingertip,
put it on the middle of his forehead and went to her building. So far, he
thought, as the doorman opened the door for her and said something and
tipped his cap, it seems to be going okay. What's with the finger on the
forehead, though? He'll wait a few days, or just two, at the most three, even
if he doesn't think he'll be able to hold out that long—he'll want to know—
before he calls her. Doesn't want to make her think he's too eager. But
maybe that's a good thing with her. She's different in almost every way, so
who can tell? He walked home, which was approximately—for how do you
measure it, he thought: Eighty-first to Seventy-fifth and three, no, two long
sidestreets and two medium-length ones and the much shorter one on
Seventy-fifth between Amsterdam Avenue and Broadway—fifteen blocks
away. Did Gwen, he thinks, when he first saw her at Pati's party, remind

him of Sharon? Doesn't think he thought of the resemblance and similarities till now, hard as that is to believe. Length and color and texture of their hair, though Sharon's a bit coarser. Was that because she shampooed less? She said shampooing your hair every day or every other day, as most women do, injures if not kills the hair follicles, so she did it no more than once a week and a lot of brushing. He forgets how often Gwen shampooed, but he doesn't think it was more than twice a week, and also lots of brushing. Blond eyelashes and eyebrows, where you had to look closely to see if they even had them. Sparse pubic hair, although it might have only seemed sparse because the color was so light. Lots of differences too, of course. Both liked to make love and usually let him do it when and how he wanted to. "Can I come in from behind?" "Sure," both would say, maybe in different ways, and get on their knees. "Could you be on top this time?" he'd say, and both, in different ways, would say they don't mind, and he'd get on his back. Both let him know early on in their relationship that anal intercourse wasn't something they'd ever let him do, so don't try. He asked Sharon why, "not that I ever thought of doing it with you or any other woman," and she said "Because that's where my shit comes out of. And no anus, no matter how meticulously it's wiped and washed, is ever entirely clean." He didn't ask Gwen what her objection to it was, but did say "Not to worry. I never did it that way and don't plan to. If you ever do find me approaching or touching or even penetrating that hole with my prick or finger or any other part of me, it's because the room's dark or I'm a little sloshed or very sleepy or both and I'm not conscious of what I'm doing, and it's a complete mistake." He now assumes her objection was for the same reasons as Sharon's, or it could be she let some guy do it to her once and it hurt. Actually, he now remembers Sharon saying once "Is this all I'm good for with you? I know it isn't, but sometimes I'm not sure. But I'm not here ten minutes and you already want to drag me to bed? If you are intent on doing it, and you know I always give in to you because I know you'll be miserable and petulant and other unfortunate behavior toward me, please be quick. In no way am I in the mood now and nothing's going to make me, so you can skip all the preliminaries." Maybe she didn't say all that. Of course, she didn't. He could never have remembered it from that far back, or even remembered it word for word if she'd said it two days ago, but she said something like it and he thinks she said it more than once. In fact, the first time she said it—this he particularly remembers because no one had ever referred to him in this way before—she spoke about what she called his "abject impetuousness," which is a real problem in their relationship, she said, but not fatal. She said she hates doing something she doesn't want to do, and hates herself for allowing him to get her to do it. Gwen, he still thinks, never said anything like that when the circumstances were similar. For instance, when he, all of a sudden and related to nothing that came before it, started fondling her. Usually both her breasts from behind and sometimes he'd sneak up on her and do this and a few times under her shirt and bra. Or he had that look that he very much wants to make love even if he knows it's the last thing on her mind, and he can't wait till later when it might be a better time for her. Or maybe he forgets. Almost thirty years together, she must have. If she did, he's sure she put it in a way that was milder or gentler or more lighthearted or good-natured, or whatever the word he wants but can't seem to come up with now, than the way Sharon said it. He even thinks he remembers Gwen saying, when he suddenly fondled her from behind, "What a goof you are." "Goof?" he thinks he said, and he thinks she said something like "Yes; goof; you. It's goofy, sneaking up and pouncing on me when I least expect it and frightening me, like some guy in his young twenties would do, not that I want you to stop the fondling part…just warn me," and he thinks he remembers her turning her head around to the right, while he was still behind her, so they could kiss. And what about when either of them wanted to make love and he was the one who wasn't in the mood for it or was involved in something else—writing, not reading—and didn't want to be disturbed? Can't remember Sharon ever doing that. That right? Thinks so. They either made love when he wanted to and she went along with it, not always happily, or when they were in bed, ready for sleep, had probably read awhile because each of them always took a book to bed—even when he just lies down to nap, though a little less so since Gwen died—and turned off their night table lights around the same time, though he usually read a few more minutes than she—didn't want to read any longer, even if he really wanted to, because she might be asleep when he turned off his light and she didn't like to be woken up to make love—and almost immediately turned to each other in the dark, if she wasn't already turned to him expecting what was to come next, and started touching and kissing and other things to each other. If she drove to his place—they both lived in the Bay Area but about an hour's drive from each other—she always stayed the night. With Gwen he was the one who took a book to bed. She once said she reads more than enough during the day—student papers and books and journals she reads for pleasure or class or research—and anyway she knows she can't read five lines in bed without her eyes closing and book dropping out of her hands. So she just got in bed, and if he was there she said "Goodnight, sweetheart," always "Goodnight, sweetheart" or "my love," and he gave her a little kiss, she shut her light off or, if she was facing him, he reached over her to shut off her light, and pulled the covers up over her shoulders. Then, when he was done reading, he'd shut off his light and maybe start making love to her, or lie for a while in bed thinking about other things—maybe the book he was reading—before he thought about making love, and she then would start making love to him. He knows he's contradicting himself here with some of the things he's saying about Sharon and Gwen, but that's because he's remembering things—he thinks it's because of this—he hasn't remembered before or not for many years. Back to Gwen, though: there were plenty of times—he'd guess a hundred or so—she came into the room he was working in—here or in their first house or in the apartments in New York and Baltimore they once had or the cottages in Maine they rented every summer for more than twenty-five years—1979 to the last summer— and would say "Like to take a break?" Or "Excuse me, I hope I'm not disturbing you, but would you like to take a break?" Doesn't think he ever refused, other than if he was sick, and then he probably said something like "You know me, I'm always up for it, but I'm just not feeling that well." But if he was feeling sick, would he be working? Depends how sick he felt. Or maybe he didn't ever refuse her, even when he wasn't feeling well, and he probably said something like—just to warn her—"Sure, or I'll try. It might cure whatever's ailing me." Not that but something else. "Maybe it'll make me feel better. If anything, making love with you would do the trick." A couple of times he remembers her saying, after she came into the room he was working in, "I know you weren't feeling well before. But do you think you feel well enough now to take a break?" Other comparisons and similarities? Sharon liked going down on him, Gwen not so much. Both of them, though, didn't much like his going down on them, something he loved doing, but usually put up with it. Fact is, he thinks Gwen only did it to him—other than the times he couldn't get or keep it up and she said "Maybe I can help"—when he pushed his penis near her face or swiveled his body around so his groin was near or over her face while he was going down on her and she felt it her duty or something to do it or just didn't want to deal with him if he made a fuss. But he wouldn't have made a fuss, so what's he talking about? He doesn't think he ever pushed either of them to do anything they didn't want to at the time. To Gwen, if he saw she didn't want to do it—she'd push his penis away—he would have said something like "I understand; maybe some other time." He remembers even once saying "But you aren't ruling it out forever, I hope," and she said no and he said "Thank goodness." Gwen had bigger breasts than Sharon, Sharon a narrower waist, slimmer tummy, thinner legs and smaller rear, more flat than Gwen's round, and they were about the same height though Gwen, he'd guess, was about ten pounds heavier. He just now remembers the time Gwen was in a hospital bed at home—she slept in one for around two months—and he was about to turn her over on her back and sit her up and help her into her wheelchair then, he thinks, and start the morning going. Instead, possibly because he'd been thinking of making love to her before he even went into her room or it had something to do, which it never had before or else he hadn't ever acted on it, with his exercising her legs and feet in bed and massaging her shoulders, he lowered the shades in his older daughter's room where the hospital bed had been set up—Rosalind was living away from home and her bed had been temporarily dismantled—and unzipped his pants and took his penis out of both flies and stuck it through the bed rail—doesn't know why he didn't lower the rail and drop his shorts and pants, maybe because he didn't want to give her the chance to say "What are you doing?" and pulled at it till it reached her mouth. She didn't object. She even smiled, as if she thought his doing it through the rail was funny or from her angle it just looked funny. He did say, when he got it by her mouth, "Is it all right?" and she nodded. She kissed it a few times and maybe—yes, definitely; it only happened once like this and he remembers it clearly—put her lips around it a short while and then said, still holding it, "Why don't you get in bed with me?" and he said "Wouldn't the marital bed be better?"—he actually used the word "marital," maybe the first and last time that way—"but we could do it here if you don't want to be transferred so much. I've never done it in a hospital bed, have you?" and she said "Don't be silly; come on, get in." He took off his clothes, put the other bed rail down, turned her all the way over on her side so there'd be room for him, got in bed and stroked her from behind and probably kissed her neck and shoulders and back, said "Think we need any gook?" and she said "No, I'm ready," and he lifted her right thigh a little—she was still a lot paralyzed on that side, which was why her doctor and physical therapist wanted her in a hospital bed: so her legs and back could be raised and lowered and she could be exercised better and there was less chance of her getting blood clots and bedsores—and stuck his penis in. After it was over for him he said "That was very nice; thank you," and she said "I just wish it had gone on longer. But since I wasn't expecting anything like this happening, I'm happy," and he kissed her back and she kissed the air. So, anything he left out? Both: long graceful necks, bluish green eyes, Gwen's with a bit of yellow in them, maybe just flecks; very pale skin that would burn under the sun, so they rarely exposed their faces to it without a brimmed or peaked cap on and a strong sun block for the other uncovered parts of their bodies that might burn, slender fingers that played Chopin and Schumann and Schubert and Brahms, and Gwen those short pieces by Satie: *Gymnopedies*, he thinks they're called, or close to that. He never heard Sharon play but she told him some of the pieces she'd learned or was practicing then and that if they were ever at a place where there was a decent piano and nobody else was around— it could even be her home, she said, which he never set foot in—she'd play for him. Gwen he heard hundreds of times before her first stroke. If she was playing an entire piece, not practicing one, he usually stopped whatever he was doing to listen till she was finished, even if he was working in another room, and later would sometimes say "I love to hear you play, something I know I've told you, but I mean it." She had a piano given to her by her grandfather when she was twelve and which they had moved from their New York apartment—they didn't move it to their Baltimore apartment because they still had the New York one then and would stay in it often—to their first house in Baltimore and from there to this one in the county. Before that it had gone from her parents' apartment in the Bronx to the one on West 78th Street and then to her own apartment on Riverside Drive. Actually, to two of them in the same building: She moved from the rear to the front. Gwen tried to get back to the piano after that stroke but got frustrated and disgusted with herself for playing so clumsily, she called it, because she was using two fewer fingers, and stopped. "My instrumental soulmate, dead," she said. "Not even Maureen plays it anymore after her last, what she thought disastrous recital so long ago. Oh, a run of tinkles every other Thursday when the cleaning woman wipes the keyboard down. You ought to take up the piano and give some life back to it. It might also calm you down." Sharon and he talked for a while that first day. While they talked, or while she was talking, he thought something like, as he did with Gwen the night they first met, "Jesus, she's beautiful and so refined and delicate and obviously smart. Can I pick that up in just a few minutes? You bet I can. My ideal woman; I've finally met her. Now if it can only work out." He looked at her left hand when it was on the table—did the same with Gwen from a distance at Pati's party—and there was no wedding band or any other kind of ring on it. One of the next times they met he said to her, holding the fingers of her left hand—so this had to be after they started sleeping together—"Been meaning to ask. How come no ring?" She said her engagement ring, which had been her husband's grandmother's and was a big gaudy diamond in a garish setting and always too big for her because her finger kept shrinking, so she was glad to be rid of it, she sold when they were down to their last nickel—"You know graduate-student couples." And the wedding band she lost in a washing machine at a Laundromat and never got it replaced, maybe the one thing her husband really minded about her. "'If I wear one,' he said, 'you should wear one too, even if we don't exactly adhere to our marriage vows.' But I like to have my fingers free, and without one it's easier to pick up guys like you." He also remembers the times—not as many times as she did it to him—he'd go into Gwen's study or wherever she was working and say—the kids had to be out or napping or not yet born—"Like to take a break?" She usually said "Sure," but if she felt she didn't have the time right then she always said—he doesn't recall her ever not using this expression—"I'd like to, but can I take a rain check?" Later, if he was still interested in making love or his interest, if he can call it that, had been renewed, he'd say to her—in her study or better if she was in the living room or kitchen or better yet if she had just lay down for a nap in their bedroom—no, if she had the odds are she would have said "I'm going to lie down for a nap. Care to join me?"—"Think I can take advantage now of that rain check I gave you?" and half the times, he'd say, she said something like "I don't see why not." He already remember this tonight? If he did, he forgets. But it's a nice memory and it's made him a little excited, which is okay, not that he's going to do anything about it. He'll save that for another day, when the kids aren't here and maybe with a magazine with nude women in it, if he'd have the guts to buy one. Doesn't see himself choosing one off a stand and going up to the salesperson—especially if it was a woman or there was somebody on line behind him, again especially if it was a woman—and paying for it, but he might have to. As far as playing with himself till completion, how many times would he say he's done it since he first went to bed with Gwen? Twenty? Thirty? And he thinks mostly when he was on tour for a few days to a week with a new book—only happened twice—and another time teaching at an out-of-town summer writers' conference for two weeks, something he hated doing but Maureen was on the way and they needed the extra money. Of course, also when he first started teaching down here and for two years she stayed in New York and taught—they weren't married then, or were, at the end, when she was already pregnant with Rosalind—but he used to train up to be with her for three days almost every week. And he did, he now remembers, spend at least one night at Sharon's when her husband was at a girlfriend's house and it was understood between them that when he did that Sharon could have her lover over, but what he's getting at here is did she play the piano for him? He thinks she just made dinner for them and they went to bed and he left before eight in the morning so he'd be gone—this was also the understanding between them—before her husband came home. "He's an early riser," she said, "and he likes to get at his desk before nine. That's one reason I haven't let you sleep here before. The other is, I never liked the idea of sharing his bed with you. Too peculiar, and I'd have to change the sheets twice." He asked Sharon that first day if she was a graduate student at Berkeley. "I mean, you look young enough to pass as an undergrad, but by the way you speak and the subject matter, I suspect you're not." "Was," she said. "I got my master's there." "Did you go further?" and she said "All the way." "What was your thesis on?" and she said "If you mean the dissertation for my doctorate, I'm still writing it. My master's thesis was on Boris Pasternak and cats." "Seriously?" and she said "Animals in Pasternak's poetry but mostly cats. I was lucky to get away with it. My thesis advisor was a young new hire who had a crush on me. I led him on a little till my thesis was approved." "Where'd you get the idea?" and she said "If you mean for my thesis topic, it was inspired by a visit my boyfriend and I made to Pasternak's dacha at Peredelkino." "So that's how you pronounce it," he said, "accent on the second syllable? You must speak Russian, then," and she said "Just Russian poetry. But you've heard of Peredelkino," and he said "Sure; I love Russian poetry. All poetry, but twentieth-century Russian poetry the most. No, that's not true. I love early twentieth-century French poetry better, or as much, and some post-World War I and II German poetry, particularly when it's written by a Czech or Romanian." "I won't ask who they are because I think I know. But not English poetry?" and he said "English, American, Whitman, Housman, Berryman, all the men, but I was talking about poetry in languages I don't fully understand or understand at all, and excuse me for that stupid joke about men. I really didn't mean it the way it could be interpreted. Could you recite a Pasternak poem for me? Any Russian poem. I'd love to hear one in the original. Pushkin. Mayakovsky. Ahkmatova and Mandelstam. They were good friends, no?" "I'm able to recite lots of them. I studied with a teacher of Russian poetry who had us memorize fifty Russian poems. She said it'd come in handy if for some reason we didn't have a book on us to read and were waiting a long time to go aboard something or for it to arrive. In other words, we'd have this whole anthology in our heads—but I don't want to. It'd draw attention, and Russian poetry can't be recited quietly." "Could you whisper the translation of one to me?" "Please, no more of that. I've already expressed my disinterest." "Tell me about your visit to Pasternak's dacha. You met him?" Wait a minute. If she got her master's from the Russian department, why would she then go for her doctorate in English literature? He must have it wrong. Is he thinking about some other woman he knew? No, he's sure he's not. It'll come back to him. That's it: she went to Stanford for her doctorate because her mentor at Berkeley switched to there and she wanted to stick with him and he helped get her a good financial arrangement, or was it U-Cal at Davis or one of the other U-Cals, and her connection to Dickens was his influence on the nineteenth-century Russian novel, or the reverse. It was so long ago. Forty years. She must be around sixty-five by now, if she's still alive. She developed a serious kidney disorder he learned from a mutual acquaintance of theirs, and something was also wrong with her blood. He thinks those are the two things. She had two children with her husband, got her Ph.D. and taught awhile, he doesn't know what or where or if it was a tenure-track appointment, and then had to cut back her teaching to two courses a year and then one because of her illness. He was told all this around twenty years ago, in a letter, and it was the last he heard about her. The mutual acquaintance died in a motorcycle accident a year or two later, his wife wrote him, or sent him without comment, as she must have done to a number of long-time acquaintances and friends who didn't live near them, a photocopy of his obituary in their local newspaper, and her husband was the only person he knew who knew Sharon. He can't recall the name of the guy or how he came to know him, though he knows it was in California. Sharon should have had his child. That's what he wanted then: for her to get pregnant by him and leave her husband and marry him. Of course it was a stupid idea. He had no money saved and just a temporary department-store salesman job and was making nothing from his writing. But she took him seriously and said—what did she say? she said for any of that to happen, Bill, his name was—her husband's—would have to leave her first and start a divorce, something he said he was never going to do. He liked things as they were, she said, and deep down, "in spite of our crazy errant marriage, I know he loves me more than a little and he knows I love him enough to stay with him. Surprisingly and perhaps unbecomingly traditional as this might sound to you, although I don't think it would if you were my husband and Bill were you, a vow is a vow and sacred to me, the one about till death do you part." This was when Sharon and he were still sleeping together and seeing each other about twice a week. "But tell me about your visit to Pasternak's dacha. You met him? He was still alive?" "He died in 1960," she said. "We were there in '61. We were both seniors at

Michigan State, part of a very select group of American college students studying Russian language and culture in Moscow for a month. It wasn't my idea to go to Peredelkino, it was my boyfriend's. He was also interested in Pasternak, but his prose. I was reluctant to even get off the train there. I thought it too pushy—too American—to just barge in like that, and pleaded with him to turn back right up till the time he knocked on the door." "What you were on must have been part of the rapprochement between the two countries, and when there were various cultural and people-to-people exchanges. I remember. I was a reporter in Washington in '59, when it all started." "Right. So, he sort of forced me—grabbed my hand and practically dragged me to the house—and I'm glad he did." But he's confused again. If she was a college senior in '61, then the earliest she could have got her master's at Berkeley was '62, so it's unlikely she could have been writing her dissertation in '65, isn't it? Doesn't it take at least three years to get through all the coursework, especially in literature? It took Gwen even longer than that before she started writing her dissertation. She got her B.A. in '68, her M.A. in '69, and he thinks she completed and defended her dissertation the year before they met in late '78, or maybe that same year but at the beginning of it. Maybe Sharon was only sketching it out while she was still doing her coursework, hadn't even got a word down, just ideas. Though maybe it is possible to finish the coursework in less than three years—it might depend on the program—and writing the dissertation could take, if you work on it day and night, a year or two, but not if you teach, as Gwen did, lower-level literature and humanities courses for two or three years after you finish your coursework and spend a year on fellowship doing research abroad. You'd think he'd know more about it, having taught at a university for twenty-five years, though mostly undergraduate writing courses, and being married to a Ph.D. Just, the subject never came up with Sharon, or not that he can remember, and up till now he thought he knew. As for Gwen taking so long to complete her Ph.D., she said it was pointless rushing through it. The dissertation, which she wanted to be a book for the common reader as well as academics, would suffer, and the prospects were slim there'd be a teaching job in New York or the surrounding area when she finished it, and New York was where she was determined to stay. Besides, she said, she had other things to do: writing essays and poetry and traveling and just lots of fun living. Of course, getting married and divorced when she was a grad student and having an abortion and the emotional toll that took slowed things down too. "My husband thought having a kid so early would bring our studies to a standstill and I just didn't think he'd be a good father."

But Sharon: "The old servant of Pasternak's opened the door," she said. "His two sons were there, Boris and Leonid, and they graciously asked us to come in. They served us tea and cookies. After a long conversation about art and music and literature, all connected to their father—are you really interested in this?" and he said "You bet. I love personal accounts and anecdotes about serious writers. Go on." "They invited us to stay for dinner, but we had to be back in our Moscow dorm by nine or we could be thrown out of the country the next day." She said she first got the idea for her thesis topic when Pasternak's old cat—his favorite—ripped one of her stockings with his paw and knocked her cookie off her plate. "They told me he wanted us to be talking only about him and his contribution to Pasternak's poetry. Later I learned the cat used to follow Pasternak when he visited his mistress in this same community, and was the principal muse to him, even more so than his mistress and wife." After about an hour, she stood up and said "This has been very nice and you've been patient in listening to my blather." "I told you," he said, "I love such blather. Like to meet again? I sure would, in other words. Can I call you sometime?" She said she was married, so it wouldn't be a good idea. "It would if you were interested in me," he said. "But you're married? I'm surprised that didn't come up." "It did, but you must have chosen not to listen, or you're not being entirely honest with me." "Honestly, I'm being honest, and we'd only meet for some more liter-ary talk," and she said "Oh, yeah. I'm sorry, but I really have to get home. My husband expects me and he worries. And he's doing the cooking tonight and I've got the tofu." "One big chunk will do for the two of you?" and she said "He's probably already diced and sliced the other ingredients that he'll cook with it, sort of a stew." "You both vegetarians?" and she said "Please," and they went outside, she put out her hand and he shook it and she got on her bike and he headed for his car. He forgets how they paid for the pastry they shared and coffees, or she, tea. And their names? Surely they must have given them. What a waste, he thought, watching her ride off, admiring her body from behind—her rear end looked plump on the bicycle seat, which it didn't when she stood—and which he would later tell her he thought, after they'd begun sleeping together: "Not of my time, a waste, but, because I was so quickly attracted to you, that you were married and wanted to stay faithful." "I did want to," she said. "I'd already had too many affairs since I got married. Not many by your standards, perhaps: just two, but one too many. The first was partly to try it out, because everyone, including my husband, was doing it. And by telling Bill I loved the man, which I didn't, to see how much I could hurt him after some real dirty things he did to me.

I found out I couldn't hurt him or make him the least bit jealous, so broke off the affair. No loss; my affairee was inept and dull and I didn't like his conversations. The second was also a dreadful stupid mistake, in a different way, but full of love and tears on my part, and lasted. My partner was sexy and exciting and intellectually energizing and metaphorically flicked his cigarette ashes on me. My first broken heart." Was the one-too-many her mentor, he thinks, and must have thought then, and the reasons she followed him to whatever university he switched to and why he helped her get such a good deal at it? She never told him who the two men were and how long the affairs lasted because, she said, when he asked, she wanted to keep that part of her life secret from everyone but her husband. "We even, in fact, wrote it into our marriage vows: to promptly tell the other the truth about everything seemingly important to the marriage we've done, no matter how bad." He next saw her on the main street of Palo Alto, which now makes him think that her mentor had switched to Stanford and that's where she got her doctorate. So maybe she had finished all her coursework by the time he met her, and maybe in two years, not that he ever heard of it, though that doesn't mean anything, and now only came to Stanford once a month or so to do whatever a doctoral candidate has to do for her department once she's done with her classwork—take her orals, attend a lecture by a prominent visiting professor in her field, meet with her dissertation advisor, and so on. Otherwise, he thinks he would have been with her more, since he lived in the next town over from Palo Alto. He knows that the deal she got at whatever university she got it from was over, where she didn't have to teach for her department for two or three years. Oh, he'll never remember it completely, no matter how hard he tries, so give up. It was in the afternoon, a beautiful spring day: bright sky, soft breezes, the air smelling of flowering fruit trees. He was on his way to pick up his typewriter at the typewriter repair shop on the street. Saw her walking, couldn't believe his luck, because he had thought about her a lot, and came up alongside her and said "Wow, this is a coincidence, bumping into you after just a few weeks," if that's how long it was—it was a short time, though, that he knows—"unless I've been following you. I haven't. Nice to see you again," and he put out his hand to shake but she didn't take it. She looked puzzled and he said "Martin Samuels" —if they had given their names the first time, and even if they hadn't— "from that Berkeley health food co-op? Tofu and herbal tea?" "It's not that I didn't recognize you and from where," she said. "It's what you said about following me. You make such odd remarks and bad jokes; forgive me if I'm being too frank." "No, I like it, and you're right, it was odd and my humor does tend to fall, from time to time, flat. Unfortunately, it seems a habit I can't seem to break, but I'll try. In order to change the subject and get the focus off me, can I ask how you've been? What are you doing on this side of the bay? You bike all the way? People do." "No, I came here as you'd expect me to: I drove." "So, another odd remark on my part, right?, though maybe not as bad." He doesn't remember if she said what she was doing in Palo Alto. "But I think my explanation why I keep saying these odd and sort of inane things is, one, I'm not odd but I can be inane and dumb. And two, I'm probably—I must be—and maybe here comes another of either of those that I'm going to regret but I'll say it anyway—nervous speaking to you. Yes, that's something I should've repressed. I had the time to; I caught myself before. But I'd already started it so thought it was too late to stop." "So, why?" and he said "Did I think it was too late to stop?" and she said "Better we drop the subject. You did explain yourself sufficiently, although I wouldn't worry about it if I were you. Your nervousness is kind of charming. I can't remember ever making a man nervous before with just my presence." "How else, then, could you have," he said, "if you don't mind my asking?" "When I crossed the street against the light, but with someone who didn't want to, and cars were coming. And when a man I didn't know was crossing the street against or with the light and I nearly ran into him with my bike." "So it seems only on the street," he said. "Look, I was on my way to pick up my typewriter at the repair shop there, but would you like to step in someplace for coffee?" and she said "Sure, I've time." "You don't think—no, I won't say it; I've cured myself for today." "I'd shoot for much longer than that, because you don't want to ruin what could be a good thing. For the time being—and please don't try to squeeze out of me what changed my mind—we'll avoid talking about him, okay?" "I live in Menlo Park," he said, "—very near here. Do you live in Berkeley?" "I thought you already knew I did." "Like to, instead of a coffee shop, have it in my small modest flat? I also have crackers and cheese and different kinds of teas." "Flat?" she said. "How cozy. Sure, I'd go for that too. Give me the address and directions—you can just tell me and I'll remember—and I'll drive there." "Think I should get my typewriter first? Don't want to stop the momentum, but why should I go back for it when it's right here, and I'm going to need it later?" She walked him to the typewriter store, then he gave her directions to his building, said he'd meet her out front and walked her to her car. "Volvo," he said. "All the latest safety features. It's the car I'd expect you to drive." "I know I'm breaking my interdiction about talking about him, but it was a decision, buying this car, my husband and I made together after considerable research. That's what married couples do. It's fun." They had tea and crackers. "I'm sorry, I'm very hungry," she said, "so I'm going to have to eat your last cracker, unless you want to split it." "I should've stopped for lunch food on the way here," he said, "but I didn't want to keep you waiting. I thought you'd leave." "I wouldn't have," she said. "If you were delayed I'd know it was for something you thought important and that was probably related to me. What we first should have done was go for a snack someplace. That's what I was about to do when you saw me on the street. The conversation we're having now we could have had anywhere." "I forgot, I've wine," he said, and poured them each a glass. After he finished his, he took her glass out of her hand—"This could be considered rude of me, taking your wine away without asking you," and she said "I've drunk enough and I know what you're about to do and it's okay." They kissed a few times. When he started to feel her up, she said "Some other time. I don't want to do everything in one or two days." "So you think something's started?" and she said "Yes, I think something's started." "I have no love life; do you, or not much?" and she said "I can see why you might think that about me but it isn't true. In any case, could you please get your lips over here? Make it one that lasts my entire drive home, and then I go. Unlike you, if this isn't an anomaly on your refrigerator's part—I took a peek inside—ours is always stocked with good food. Maybe one day you'll come by and I'll make you lunch." Then, about a year later, or maybe a few months earlier than that, she said…But he suddenly remembers something about her that he thought at the time characterized her a lot. It also relates to Gwen. They were making love and she was unusually tight down there, and he stopped—he was behind her—and said "This must be hurting you. I know it's a bit uncomfortable for me," and pulled out. "I don't think you're producing the required amount of vaginal juices, and I'm not saying it's your fault. I probably entered you too early." She said "Do you have any lubricant for it?" and he said "No, nothing." "Just spit in your hand and smear it around in me," and he said "I don't think I could. Not only unsanitary but I think too sloppy." "Then I will, if you want to get on with this," and she spit in her hand and put it inside her vagina and they resumed making love, he thinks with her now on her back. "See, it works," she said. Once with Gwen when they were making love—this was before her first stroke but after her menopause, or however you say it—she was also very tight and she said "I could use some of my K-Y jelly. Would you get it for me?" He said "You know, you can just spit in your hand and use it as a lubricant," and she said "What a thing to suggest. My own spit? Inside my cunt?"

and he said "Then I could spit in my hand and do it. It's not dirty, and I doubt you need much." "Even worse, somebody else's spit. Sweetie, I know you don't want to get out of bed—the room's so cold and the flannel sheets are so warm—but please get it and also put some on your penis," and he did and squeezed some more on his fingers and rubbed it around her vagina for longer than he needed to and they resumed making love. "Much better," she said. "Thank you." After her first stroke, when she had trouble using her hands and she started having frequent bladder infections, they always had specimen jars and a tube or two of surgical lubricant around—they still are on the bathroom shelf—in case he had to catheterize her to bring a urine sample to the lab or to empty her bladder. They always seemed to know when she had a new infection, sometimes just by the urine color or smell, and a visiting nurse had taught him the procedure. So then, about nine months after they met, or maybe it was a whole year, Sharon called and said "I know you don't expect me today, but I don't want to tell you what I have to tell you on the phone." He thought she's pregnant and she's sure the baby's his. She came over, they kissed at the door, and she said "You're not going to like this, or maybe you will. Who knows. After putting up with me so long, you might be relieved." "You're breaking up with me," and she said "It's a little scary, because it's not as if we're an old married couple—"and he said "How often I know what you're going to say. It wasn't hard this time. Your face and how you prefaced it." He knows he's gone in to this but this is a more accurate account of what he did and she said. "Bill and I have decided to have a baby—we've already begun working at it. And because we don't want there to be any uncertainty who the father is. And also for the sake of family harmony and marital fidelity, which he promised to observe if I do, and of course for the emotional and mental well-being of the child—" "'This is the last time we can meet, except, if you wish, sometime in the distant future for the occasional coffee and good conversation we've always had and to catch up on what we've been doing and me to tell you all the cute and funny and endearing things my baby's doing.' No chance. If we're breaking up, let's do it for good; that means starting right now." That's about when he got really angry. "You fucking bitch," he said, and other names. "Leading me on, dropping me off, kicking me in the ass, then a swift boot to my balls. Just get the hell out of here." Angry at her for the first time, he thinks. He doesn't think they ever once had a spat. He was always saying "Anything you want, fine by me." "What bullshit this is; what stupid things you've got me saying." Banging his hand against the wall, but an open hand, not his fist. That he did with Terry when she called off their engagement five years before—"I need more time, I feel I'm rushing in to this too quickly"—"No, no the whole thing's over; don't tell me"—and he broke two fingers. Doing all that. Tearing at his hair. Kicking over a chair. First she tried to calm him down. "My dear friend, I'm so sorry." "Friend? Friend? Well, nothing's wrong with that, I guess, you bitch." "All right," she said, "maybe that was the wrong word. But truly, if I had known you were going to act like such a crazy lout, I would have told you all this over the phone or in a letter." "You should've, you should've," he shouted. "For then I wouldn't have had to see your rotten face." She looked frightened—maybe it was the change in his face, that he now looked violent, or he'd raised his hand to her—he forgets—but she left. "Wait," he yelled, running after her into the building's hallway. Maybe that's when he said "Stop the production; let me be the father. I'll be a better one than Bill because I want it more and you're guaranteed I'll be faithful. Okay, I know why not. But you've forgotten whatever you kept here—a change of clothes, some books. And at least, if no kid, let me have one final fornication. I'll even put on a condom if you have one," but she had long been out of the building and was probably in her car and driving away, thinking what an asshole he turned out to be. That was the last time he saw or spoke to her. Several months later— Did any of the other third-floor tenants come out? Doesn't think so. But if one had, he would have been so embarrassed. That night he thought he should write her an apology for all the awful things he said and for frightening her, and he thinks he wrote a few drafts of one over the next couple of days but never sent it. Several months later—oh, he doesn't know how long; may have been a year or more—he got a letter from her. Or maybe it was a birth announcement—no, she wouldn't have done that—but something in a regular number 11 envelope, so another reason it couldn't have been a birth announcement: they come in their own envelopes. Her return address was the same. At the time he thought he knew what the letter would say and do to him and tore it up without opening it and dumped it in the paper bag he used for his garbage. Later, he was sorry he'd torn it up and went to look for the bag in the building's trash cans outside—he was going to put together the pieces—but it had already been picked up. He thought of calling her—if Bill answered, he'd immediately hang up—saying he got her letter and accidentally lost it before he could read it, or maybe he'll tell the truth—"I got anxious as to what might be in it and didn't want to get hurt or feel guilty all over again"—and would she mind very much telling him what it said, but knew it'd be the wrong thing to do. Something like this happened with Gwen the summer after they first met. She also said she has something to tell him he won't like. They'd just driven back from the cottage they rented in Maine for two months and were sitting in the car, double-parked, in front of his building. He thinks the car belonged to a friend of hers, who was in London doing research for his dissertation. He'd thought she'd driven him there to drop off his things—knapsack with clothes, typewriter, books, manuscripts and writing supplies—and then they'd go to her parents' apartment a few blocks from his—the doorman would watch the car while they brought up her parents' two cats, who'd spent the summer with them, and say hello and then go to her building and he'd help her in with her things and two cats and later they'd go out for dinner, or because they were tired from the nine-to-ten hour trip, get take-out and he'd stay the night at her place. He opened his car door and she said "Don't get out just yet." She told him she has a bad feeling about him and their relationship and wants to end it before he gets even more involved. "'Want to'? Meaning you haven't completely decided on it?" and she said "No, I've decided; completely." "Oh, boy. Can you give me specific reasons why? I know we've had a couple of bumps this summer, but that shouldn't be too unusual, since we never lived so close for so long, and I thought we worked them out," and she said "I already told you…the strongest reason yet: my gut." "So it's not someone else—the guy whose car this is?" and she said "You're not listening. I'm sorry. Nobody else. You've been my only lover the past nine months and the only man I was in love with till sometime this summer when I began to have my doubts about us, and now it has to stop." Years later, and he thinks he spoke about it again to her just a few years ago, he said "That time you dropped me for a while early in our romance—I like that; *romance*. You know, when we'd driven back from the Spengler Cottage and you left me at my door? What was the reason? I was always a little confused by it," and she said "What I told you that day in the car." "And that was…?" and she said "A very strong gut reaction that turned out to be wrong. Anyhow, it worked out for the better. I found out how much I missed you. It could be that for any relationship to last it needs a breakup that feels real. That sort of fits in with what Grace told me: to have a long good marriage it helps if you had a bad one before." "So where does that leave me?" and she said "You had serious relationships that lasted twice as long as my marriage to Richard. You were even engaged once and came within a hair of getting married, even if you only knew the woman for half a year." "Terry," he said, "and eight months total. She broke my heart twice. First time after two great months, when she suddenly dropped me for another guy, whom she married in a few weeks and divorced in a year.

And two years later, when we hooked up again, got engaged too fast and she broke it off after six months. Plus, I forgot, one night thrown in when I got off the ship from France and was on my way to California, three years after she broke off the engagement. So, eight months and a day. Because she didn't love me, to be perfectly honest, though she never said that. What she said the first time was she didn't expect me to be so hurt. What she said the second time was to make it easier for both of us we shouldn't see each other for a while and, yes, she probably is going to start seeing other men if she meets any she wants to. What did I know. I was a kid. *Do you* still love me?" That was the first time he said that to her, and then as a joke between them or some kind of ritual or annual verbal renewal of their love he would say the same thing at dinner on their wedding anniversary, even when the kids were with them, and they mostly were—"This is a serious joke between Mommy and me," he explained to them once about what he was going to say—and she said "You know I do, very much," and he said "I do to you too, very much, more than ever, if that's possible," and he kissed her and at the restaurants after he asked it and they gave almost the same answers each time, he would always take her hand nearest him and kiss it. They usually sat next to each other when they went out to eat with the kids or friends, and always the last two years so he could help feed her if she needed it or hold her glass to her lips or pick the food off her she might have spilled or had fallen off the fork he'd brought to her mouth. He acted calmly in the car. No anger, no words he didn't mean or would hurt. He could see there was no changing her mind by talking about it and he felt they were finished for good, that she didn't love him or even like him much anymore—she didn't say it; her face did and he wasn't going to ask it because he thought he knew what she'd say—and that would make him feel even worse—and he said something like "Well, if that's the way you want it, then that's how it has to be. Not the way I want it, that's for sure, but what can I do? Nothing. So know I'm not going to phone or write, or anything," and she said "I appreciate that." "Then, so long, then," and he choked up a little, his neck tightened, and he said "That's because"—pointing to his throat—"I'm going to miss you," and she said "Thank you." "Ah, what am I talking for? Words not only fail me but are useless." He started for his building, then slapped his forehead and said "Where am I going? My things." He went back to the car and she smiled and said "I was wondering. All of yours in the trunk?" and he said "Yeah." She gave him her keys, he opened the trunk, got his things onto the sidewalk and gave her back her keys. "Bye, cats," he said through the back window to the cats in the carriers on the seat.

"I'm going to miss you guys too. Oh, the key to your place," and he got it off his key ring and gave it to her. He started bringing his things into his building's vestibule, didn't look at her again or say goodbye, and she drove off. He wanted to look at the car going down the street and then thought *Why?* He got everything upstairs in two trips—as always, manuscripts and typewriter first. He thinks he also said, after she said "I appreciate that," "I'm not going to be a nuisance," and she said "Good." He didn't call or write her. Doesn't think he even thought to, and felt if she called or wrote him it'd be over some practical matter: money he might still owe her for the rent and utilities for the cottage, for instance, or car expenses coming back. All the things of his he had in her apartment he took to Maine with him and brought back in the car. She had nothing of hers in his. She didn't have a key to his apartment because she didn't come to it much and when she did he was either with her or there. But the first night he called. He thought, after wanting to call her for about a week, this is getting ridiculous, and so on. What's to be afraid of? And wait too long—well, this would never happen but something like it could—she won't know who he is and he'll have to go through the whole awkward scene of reminding her. Call, and if she agrees to meet, they'll meet and he'll see where it goes from there. He knows he'll want something to—to start with, another date, where he'd be a little more confident—but if nothing does he just has to accept it. Look, you're past forty, he told himself, and if they meet for coffee, or whatever they meet for, and she says she doesn't see the point of their meeting again, or however she puts it—tactfully, he's sure—and he feels he'd be wasting her time and inviting disappointment on his part to call again for a second date because it's obvious she doesn't want one and she isn't attracted to him or feels there's any chemistry between them and so on—that he isn't even interesting, she could think—he shouldn't get upset as he always does when this happens. Wouldn't it be nice, though, if she called him. Dream on, lover boy. Although women have—a few, and not for many years—when he didn't call them and even for a first date, but not women he wanted to see. Oh, yes: Terry. "You said you'd call. Change your mind? It's okay if you did; I won't shoot myself. And I'm not going to give the lamebrained excuse that I thought you might have lost my phone number," and he said "I swear to you. After what you said about reading my play? I practically had my finger in the telephone dial when you called." She said "You're an unconvincing liar, but that's okay too. Next time I see you I'm going to give you some basic acting exercises in it. We still on?" Why hadn't he called? He forgets—nervousness, possibly; maybe for the same reasons he didn't call

Gwen till that night—because she was certainly worth calling: smart and quick and natural and funny and already successful as an actress—good part in a Broadway hit—and a beauty too. With all that going for her, why'd she call him? He was also smart—not overbright, just smart—and considered good-looking and he still had all his hair. And maybe she found him interesting, or at least literary—he tried to get that across to her in the two or so hours he was with her the night they first met—and potentially compatible: he wanted to be a playwright then and had told her he'd written several absurdist, or unconventional was the word he used, short plays and was working on his first full-length one. She said "I want to be the first one to read it. Promise me that. I also might be able to get it a stage reading, which I bet would be a first for you." No reading. When she dropped him the first time after two months, his play still wasn't finished. When they hooked up again two years later, he was only writing fiction and didn't show his plays to anyone because he thought they all stunk. But there has to be a half-dozen Martin Samuels in the Manhattan phone book, he thought, and maybe another half-dozen M. Samuels, so he didn't think this Gwendolyn woman would even try. Does she even know he lives in Manhattan? She could call Pati for his phone number—Pati has it, or would know how to get it, since she called him to invite him to her party—but she wouldn't do that either. She just didn't seem the type to ask a friend for the phone number of a man she only met briefly at the friend's party or to call a man for a first date when he didn't call her for almost a week after he said he would, even if only for coffee one afternoon, but he could be wrong. No, he's not wrong. She had the look of someone who'd think if he's interested in me, and it seemed he was—why else would he want my phone number?—he'll call; if not, no big loss. But he could really use—oh, brother, could he, he thought—and be very agreeable to a new relationship that showed signs…well, signs of something. That could become steady and promising and deep and so on and lead to all sorts of good things, because the last three were busts. Actually, the first of the three, Diana, went on for a while—almost four years and was pretty good at the beginning—but then, a year and a half ago, she ended it and moved into her own apartment with her daughter. She was fooling around long before that with two or three other guys, even while they lived together for more than a year. She'd just stay out all night or come back to their apartment very late when she said she'd be home much sooner—always when her daughter was with her ex-husband for the weekend—and say she didn't want to talk about it, "so stop talking about it; it's my life, my business, maybe my mistake," so it wasn't as if he didn't know by then their relationship was going nowhere. And a few months before their sublet was up and they separated, she didn't let him have much sex either. He said once, after she said "I'm sorry, I'm too tired," and pushed his hand away, "I guess you get enough of a workout with your paramours." She said, "What a stupid dirty crack, but I'm going to answer it anyway. Yes, I suppose I do; yeah. Though I still, from time to time, like doing it with you. You're here, you haven't moved out, which I've suggested you do in spite of the hardship it'd be for me to pay the full rent, and you're a skillful lover when you're not rushing. So if I'm feeling hot to trot on my own stimulus or your hand suddenly feels good on my thigh, which it didn't just before, why not? You know me: when I feel like it I help myself to what others might push away, even sometimes when I'm filled up. Is that enough of an answer or do you want more?" "No, I'm satisfied. But you don't want to put out for me a little now? I'd wake up in a better mood," and she said "Goodnight, or does one of us have to sleep in the spare room?" Why didn't he move out when she gave him the opportunity to? The apartment was in the Village, a part of the city he always wanted to live in. And it was luxurious and spacious compared to what he was used to—he had his own writing room—and his share of the rent was less than what he paid for his last apartment. And she was pretty and intelligent and she and her daughter were for the most part easy to live with, and when they did make love it was very good. But the woman about a half year after her, Karyn—she was right; they never would have worked out. She was just a kid around ten years younger than Gwen, whom he met several months later—and different than he in so many ways. She didn't read fiction, for instance—said she never liked it. Always found the plots and characters shallow and absurd and the language and dialog windy and unreal. "Always?" he said. "Yes, always." "That's ridiculous, " he said, and she said "That's what you think. But what would really be ridiculous would be for me to read your work"—he's never encouraged anyone to—"because I know from the outset I won't like it and because I am the way I am I'd have to tell you." She loved biographies and other books about visual artists and art history, though she wasn't an artist or studying to be one or an art historian; she was about to enter her first year of law school. Great big beautiful body and sweet face and always a long ponytail. When she told him—they were having lunch at a restaurant near where she worked—that she's been seeing another guy—a med student—and it is getting serious, so she's going to have to stop seeing him—he started to cry. "Martin," she said, "what's wrong? You know yourself there was never anything between us. It was more lust than love—a lot more; there was no love—and who cries over that? You liked me in bed and I enjoyed you. So we were just sex partners, till something better and more fulfilling came along—and it has for me; I'm sorry—servicing each other's physical needs. Look, I gave you crabs this summer, you remember that? Sent you the medication for it at that art colony of yours, something you wouldn't have forgotten because it must have burnt the skin off you as it did to me. But my point is that if we were really serious, would I have been screwing the guy who gave it to me, who's not the one I'm seeing now, same time I was screwing you? Please, stop crying. They know me here; I come in a lot." He said, "You're wrong; I loved you," and she said "You're lying, just so you can get me in bed again. But you can't, and I don't believe your crying anymore. You never loved me and I never loved you. Once more, and if I have to, again after that, till it sinks in: we were pals with mutual interests, culturally and sexually, but that's all. And the age gap—two days shy of it being exactly twenty years—is enormous and insurmountable and would still be enormous twenty years from now." He said, "I know it. What the hell could I have been thinking?" "You wanted young meat; what else? Come on, let's go; I have to get back to my books." She signaled for the check, looked at it and said "Fifty-fifty again?" and put some money on the table. "I've included my share of the tip. Be as generous as I was, because you made quite a little scene here." He pushed the money back to her and said "No, I'll pay and you go." She got behind him, kissed the top of his head and left. He stayed seated. Didn't want to leave right away and possibly see her on the street as he walked back to his apartment. The waiter came over and said "Everything all right, sir?" and he said "Yes, thanks; I'll be going," and sat for another minute. Then he put the money for their lunch on the table, plus two dollars more of a tip than he'd normally give, and left. Never spoke to her again after that. Three years later—he was teaching in Baltimore and coming, during the teaching weeks, to New York for long weekends with Gwen—he bumped into Karyn's best friend on the uptown Broadway bus. He had visited his mother and was on his way back to Gwen's. He asked how the friend was and then she asked how he was and he said "Couldn't be better. I'm getting married in two months." "That's right," she said. "I heard about it from Karyn." "How'd she know? I'm not in touch with her and I haven't spoken to anybody who is." "I don't know, but she knew and she told me she couldn't be happier for you…that you no doubt met the woman of your dreams." Then she said "Karyn also got married, to an Italian count she sat next to on a plane going to Italy. She left law school after two years and is now living in Milan and

New York and trying to have a baby. The man's much older than her and wants to have a baby now before people think he's the kid's grandfather. But there seems to be an obstruction in both fallopian tubes that will need corrective surgery, and she says even that might not work." "I'm very sorry, really," he said. "We also want to have a kid right away, and because of my age I can empathize with her husband. Next time you speak to her, please give her my best." Why did he get so upset at the restaurant? He must have seemed like such an immature jerk to her. There was some affection between them—he liked her and doesn't know why she denied even that; maybe to make the break easier for them both—but never any love. He knew, as she said, it was only a relationship for the time being, so why the tears? It might have had something to do with being rejected repeatedly in so short a time and that this was happening when he was past forty. First Diana, though he knew that was coming. Then at Yaddo in August he fell for a married woman about five years younger than he. A beautiful intellectual and respected poet and very lovely person and she must have, he remembers telling another writer, the best body of any woman poet around. "It's good, it's very good," this older poet said, "and she's tall—must be five-ten in flats—and she carries her height well. But her body, splendid as it is, isn't the supreme. I know we're talking like two old lecherous idiots, although you started it so I'm not going to take any of the blame, but you'll have to find out for yourself whose body that is." They played Ping-Pong a lot in the colony's pool house, she usually barefoot and in a two-piece swimsuit and beating him with a terrific serve. She also, in the outdoor pool, tried teaching him how to swim more efficiently and with less splashing by cupping his hands and not raising his arms so high out of the water and taking a deep breath and dunking his head every other stroke. And she let him quickly kiss her a few times at a bar she drove them to and later in her car and then one long one that same night at her bedroom door, and he thought he was in, but she wouldn't sleep with him or even let him rub her rear end or touch her breast. "What's the point?" she said. "You're nice, interesting, etcetera, but nothing special to me. If I'm going to risk my marriage and earn the enmity and disrespect of my two boys by getting involved in an adulterous affair, I'd want it to be profound and inescapable and hair-raising and foredoomed. As for a single night? I don't do those things. So no more smooching; not even hand-holding. Let's just be friends. Deal?" They stayed friends after they left Yaddo, exchanged letters and their books for a while, had lunch twice when she came to New York to give or attend a poetry reading and take in some theater, all while he was seeing and then going to be married to Gwen. "An infatuation at first," he explained to Gwen, "but an untroubled harmless one. I've had a number of those, but never again. To think I could have been instrumental in busting up her marriage. What a selfish scumbag I was. To me, now, doing that is sacrilegious. Boy, have I changed since I met you. I love it." Then she got very sick—Robin; no, Roberta. She didn't say with what but did tell him in a brief letter that she was almost too weak to write any poetry now but very short poems and haikus. "From now on I'll have to keep my correspondence down to only my closest dearest friends." He called her a few weeks later to ask how she was doing and she said "Awful, dreadful, frightened, so no more phone calls either. Takes too much out of me and it's a struggle just to hold the receiver. If I come out of this, I'll let you know. Otherwise, my friend, this is the end." For a couple of years he wondered what became of her: if she survived, if she died. He didn't think it right just to call someone who might know her and ask. Then he had an idea and wrote the new director of Yaddo if she knew what had happened to Roberta. An assistant wrote back saying "The director told me to tell you that as far as she knew Ms. Snow was happy and healthy and busy writing poetry. She was when she was a colonist here last year." He just realized he could ask one of the kids to go online to see if they can find something about her, but some other time. The third, or fourth relationship, and it couldn't even be called that it went by so fast, was with a woman about four years older than Karyn. Nadine, sometime in October, last woman he slept with or even went out with before he met Gwen. Doesn't remember much about it and has no memory of her body other than that when she slipped off her shirt or he took it off for her she had no bra on and had big breasts, which surprised him because when she had her shirt on it seemed she had almost no breasts at all. Next morning he even wondered if he had come. She said he did, but she might have said that so he wouldn't try to make love again to come at least once in her—"Not spectacularly, and mine hardly reached seismic levels either, but I'm not complaining since you were so inebriated I was grateful you didn't throw up on me." "Oh, I couldn't have been that bad," and she said "Worse. Feel your side of the bed. Maybe it's dry now, but after we were done you lost control of your bladder for a few seconds and wet the sheet. You don't remember grabbing yourself and slipping on the floor? Also from the pee; I had to clean it up. Because this is only a single bed I didn't feel too comfortable all night sleeping so close to you." He was a writer in residence for a week at an Ohio university's creative writing department. He read the fiction of graduate students and upper-level undergraduate writing majors and in a private office had twenty-minute individual conferences with them about their work. There was a huge coffee urn and a hot water dispenser in the office and enough paper cups and tea bags and accessories to serve all the students each day, plus a large tray of doughnuts and sweet rolls. She was a first-year graduate student and by far the best writer he read. Cute, too, a word Gwen hated when he used it to describe an older person's looks. Frizzy red hair, wire-rimmed granny glasses, bright blue eyes she kept squinting and straining to see with, little pointy ears, freckles and snub nose. So her face he remembers a lot, and though her torso was long, he now thinks she had short thick muscular legs, but he could be imagining that. He was immediately taken with her when he escorted one student out of the room and said "Nadine Hanscom?"—he had a list of conferees for each afternoon and the times they were supposed to see him—and she got off the floor, where she'd been sitting, put her book into her knapsack, adjusted her glasses, which had fallen down her nose when she stood up, and came into the room. "Mind if I shut the door?" he said. "I've something to tell you I don't want the others to hear." She said "Shut it but don't lock it, please," and he said "Never thought to." She sat across the desk from him. He offered her the beverages and pastries. She said she only drinks uncaffeinated herbal tea and eats nothing with sugar, but she will take a cup of hot water with a lemon wedge in it, and helped herself. When she was settled he said "You say in your cover letter that these three stories are new and haven't been work-shopped or seen by a teacher," and she said "You're the first to read them." "Then tell me, and I'm going to be very hard on you now, how in God's name did you come to write so well? You're a budding literary genius, the next who-knows-what. I hope they gave you a full tuition waiver, sizable stipend and a teaching assistantship if not your own undergraduate fiction writing class, because you could have got in at the top of any graduate writing program in the country. That's my opinion, at least, not that I ever taught in any; I'm here strictly because of my three books and lots of published stories. But you, if you have a book-length work of fiction or are deep into one, could very likely have a book contract by the time you graduate. Wouldn't that make your department happy. You'd be a walking ad for it. Anyway, if I were your teacher I'd take a hands-off policy to your work. I'd say 'Don't even come to class if you don't want to. Just write, let me see it solely for the pleasure of reading it but not to steer it here and there or to critique it line by line.' From what you've shown me you're miles ahead of your peers, miles—well on your way," and he gave her back her stories. "I hope, with what I said, I haven't offended you or made you feel bad in any way," and she started to cry. "Good," he said, "I finally got a smile out of you. What's with you—why so serious? Jesus, I can't be telling you anything new, can I? Because you must get praise like this all the time." She said "Now and then my teachers and fellow grad students have said kind things about my work, but nothing like this; though more often they've ripped it apart." "The students I can understand—they're competitive and you're winning, making them question, when they come upon a natural, what the hell they're in it for. As for your teachers, they're either jealous of your talent—I kid you not—or have some misguided or misguiding notion about teaching writing. Or maybe their intentions are good and they're holding back in their praise because they don't want to take that drive to succeed out of you—you know, because you're already partly there—so early in your career. But to me it's ridiculous they wouldn't just say how good you are. You don't seem the type to let it affect you adversely. Have I gone overboard, based on reading only three of your stories? No. Don't tell them I said this—I might want to come back here—but just use them for helping you get a first-rate literary agent and book and magazine editors interested in your work and what magazines to send to, which should be the highest-paying serious ones first, and things like that. When a young writer's starting out, he has to be a bit selfish and aggressive. Wrong advice? Maybe. But if they can't or won't help you, get my address from your chairman—tell him I said it was okay— and write me and I'll give you some leads. I'd give you the name of my agent if I were able to get one." She said she was taken aback—actually used those words: "Really, Mr. Samuels, or should I call you 'Professor'?" and he said "Call me by my name, 'Martin,'" and she said "I couldn't do that so fast. Wasn't raised that way. But honestly, Mr. S.—that'll be my compromise for now—I'm taken aback by what you've said. I've never been this complimented on anything I've done, and as a result I'm thrilled…overwhelmed…I'm obviously at a loss for words—deeply appreciative at what a professional writer I respect said about my work." "You deserved it, every word of it, every word. So, it seems I've run out of things to say. Although I could go on in detail as to what I liked about your stories so much, which would prove to you I wasn't making all that stuff up to get out of reading them," and she said "That's all right; I couldn't take anymore. It'd stop me writing for a week." "We still have ten minutes left. Like a refill on your hot water and lemon? We could also cut the conference short. But that might make your friends in the hall suspicious I've nothing much to say in these conferences and that I'm getting paid for doing very little—or we could talk about other things. Let's do that." He asked her about her family, what her parents do, where she grew up, what college she went to, degree she got, how long she's been writing—"I doubt it can be more than twenty-five years, which is what I guess as your age"—she said he was right—and what writers she likes, "and don't say me." "The chairman had a published story of yours put in all the grad students' boxes. 'Violet,' from *On and On*. So we'd be familiar with at least one of your fictions, he said, and that if we wanted to read more there were many copies of the collection in the campus bookstore. I liked the story but I don't think it'll influence what I write. Maybe the collection will, though, which I intend to buy." "No, don't buy, don't read me, don't get influenced; go your own way. And what the heck did he choose that story for, out of all the ones I've published? It could be the worst story in the collection. Possibly the worst story of mine I let be published. But I still must have thought it had something or I would have torn it up. Ah, you never know. More advice from me is don't throw away the ones you think aren't up to your best. Sometimes your fiction is better than you think and it takes other people to tell you. That you might not like the work for personal reasons—it reminds you of some person or experience you want to forget. Though that might be another example of my not knowing what I'm saying. There was a previous one, wasn't there?" Around then he looked at his watch or a wall clock. "I guess we gotta end this," he said. "Our time's more than up. It's been fun, talking to you about things not entirely related to your writing. Getting to know somebody, in other words. It was a nice break." She got up and said "First of all, thank you for everything. Secondly, you probably won't want to do this. You've read plenty of our work the last two days and there're more to come. But there's a reading tonight of graduate poetry and fiction writers I've been asked to invite you to. It starts at seven, never lasts more than an hour and a half, and that's with an intermission and post-reading chatter, so if you have other things to do after, there should be time. And the readers always provide exotic snacks and foreign beer and good wine—that's part of the bylaws of the series. And your being there would be a real treat to all of us. An older adult. Oh my goodness! For we never get our teachers to come or any audience but undergraduates and ourselves. Say yes?" and he said "Sure, why not? And I've nothing doing tonight. After these conferences are over I was going to go for a run, shower, have a drink—I brought my own—and find some depressing place to have a depressing dinner alone at, most likely the school cafeteria, for they serve beer, right?" She met him at the reading. "Martin, Martin," she called, "over here," pointing to the seat next to hers she was saving for him. She'd come with another graduate student and introduced them. Charlie, or Jackie, his name was, said "This is an honor, sir. I'm a fan." "Oh nonsense," he said. "Nadine must have put you up to saying that." "Did not," she said. "In fact, listen to this. Before either of us even knew you'd been invited here for a week, I saw him reading one of your books." "A story in *The Paris Review*," Charlie, he'll settle on, said. "A story, then, but quite a coincidence." "Did you read the story too?" he said, and she said "I didn't, and I don't know why. I know I wanted to by what Charlie said about it, but he had to return it to the library, I think, which could be why I thought it was a book. What was the reason?" and Charlie said "I loaned the magazine to someone who wanted to read the Cheever interview in it, and it was my personal copy, not the library's, and I never got it back." "Well," he said, "one story can't turn anyone into a fan, unless it's 'The Dead.'" "I read another story of yours in another literary quarterly," Charlie said, "but I forget the magazine's name." "What was the story about?" and Charlie said "That I also forget. I know I liked it. I'm sure it'll come back to me by the time we have our conference Thursday." "Was it in a recent issue? *Antioch Review*? *Story Quarterly*?" "Neither. Like *The Paris Review*, it was from far back. I got it off the magazine table in the Writers' Room we have here, but I don't think I told Nadine about it. But it's still here if she wants to read it and nobody's stolen it yet." He didn't like any of the work read, but after each of the four readers finished, she turned to him with the look "So what did you think?" and he tightened his lips and nodded or smiled and gave a thumbs up. He had a beer or wine during the intermission and a couple of cheese on crackers and some grapes. After the reading several students came up to him and wanted him to sign the photocopies of his story the chairman had distributed and said things like "Thank you for coming. It's great you could be here." One said "I hope Nadine didn't have to threaten to break your arm to get you here," and he said "Not at all. Lots of talent here, which I knew there'd be from the manuscripts I've read so far. As for the poetry, I'm no expert but I thought it was terrific and clear—able to be understood, for my poor brain, first time around." He said to Nadine and Charlie "Can I buy you guys dinner and a beer someplace? I'm starved." She said "The refectory in this building is still open and has authentic Sicilian pizza and other delicious goodies and tap ale and beer." He still didn't know what she and Charlie were to each other. No touching or endearments or loving looks or coy side glances, so he guessed just friends, or else they had made some agreement before not to show anything like that. When they were at the dining hall table and Charlie had excused himself to go to the men's room or to make a phone call, he said to her

"Nice young man. Are you two serious?" and she said "Oh, God, no. I wouldn't be even if he didn't have a steady boyfriend. We share the rent and give close and sometimes ruthlessly honest readings of each other's works." "He's still a nice kid and clever and intelligent, so I bet he's a good writer, though I haven't read his stuff yet." "He's the best, and an ideal roommate. Super cook and housekeeper and bill-payer—all the things I'm weakest at—and he doesn't smoke and respects my privacy, and is there when I need him when I get frustrated or sad. We're like a very compatible married couple who don't sleep together, although he, and not because he's gay, is more the wife. You'll see. He's going to be a major writer of gay fiction. He holds nothing back." "I'm looking forward to reading him. Listen, can I be frank with you?" and she said "Gay fiction repulses you." "No." "You want us to go off together, to dance in the moonlight." "Close. Is there any way we can be alone? If you think this is inappropriate of me to ask, please say so." "Just tell Charlie you want to be alone with me and he'll leave." "I couldn't say that," and she said "Believe me, he'd love to see something happen between us. He's all for young writers having interesting and different experiences to write about, he's said. I don't write that way, but he does, and it hasn't seemed to hurt him. And he's having his lover sleep at our apartment tonight, so he'll probably want to get away soon anyway." Charlie came back and she said "Martin and I want to take a walk together and talk," and Charlie said "Fine, I was through here, but first let's scarf down the pizza and beer. James is waiting for me and I want to come to him half-stoned." They walked a little around campus—she showed him a lake—and talked about he doesn't know what—his life, hers, writing, writers, her writing program, books—and then he said to her "They've given me a room in one of the dorms for a week, but for guests of the university, so a bit spiffier than the ones for students, I'm told. Would you like to see it?" and she said "Does that mean you want to sleep with me? Or are you just bringing me there to show me how well the room's appointed in comparison to a typical dorm room?" and he said "I'm sorry; I'm being careful. I didn't know how else to put it. Yes." "All right. Just wanted to know what I'm in for. And it sure beats going home and hearing Charlie and James through the walls, discreet as they'd try to be, whooping it up for a couple of hours. And you seem like a gentle sane man, not a masher or intimidator or kinky loonybird like some of the male visitors to our program I've heard about." "Any names?" and she said "No, so you can count on complete tactfulness from me, unless I've gauged you wrong. But you know you're quite a few years old than I, but not preposterously older," and he said "I considered that as a reason for not asking but decided to go ahead with it anyway." "You look much younger than Charlie said you are, even with a receded hairline and your sideburns turning gray. You must be very healthy and exercise a lot and eat well—flat stomach, muscular arms, no lines or creases except in your forehead, which I romantically think all serious writers eventually have, because it comes from the deep thinking while they're writing. You'd be my oldest partner by about ten years. How about me? Will the age difference be the greatest you've had?" and he said "There was one not too long ago, who was around three years younger than you. This past summer, if you want to know, and my last before you. She dumped me." "Everybody gets dumped at least once. You? Someone who's forty-two and has an eye for women has probably been dumped a lot and also dumped a lot of women too. Knowing, though, there was someone younger than I with you makes me feel better about this, for some elusive reason. Was it another guy or just the age difference?" and he said "Both," and she said "No doubt he was a lot younger than you too. That must have hurt." "And look," he said, "I didn't choose that my last two women be so young. It just turned out that way. She came over to me at an art opening. And I came on to you today," and she said "I'm not saying anything. But we should get moving, Martin." "Can I have a little kiss to start off with? I hate asking but it'd seem a bit awkward or cold, going to my room without so much as holding hands or rubbing noses first," and she said "Let's wait till we get inside and the shades or blinds or whatever they have in that grand room are down. This campus is excessively monitored and patrolled, supposedly for our protection, so our innocent kiss might get reported. I'm doing this to benefit you more than me, in case you really do want to come back." "I like you," he said. "You're smart and beautiful and considerate and on your toes," and she said "Well, thank you, kind sir. I said a lot of nice things about you too," and they went to his room, he had a couple of drinks while she washed up, and they made love. Later in the morning he said "Despite my many mishaps last night, which I swear to you I was unaware of till now, but I'm glad you told me about them, may I see you again? I have three more days and I can even stay the weekend in a hotel, if they kick me out of this room on Saturday." She said "You can see me, but not for sleeping with. Once was enough." "Please, I promise to be on my best behavior, and no more drinking or just overdrinking, which I think is what did it to me last night." "The other thing," she said, "is that what little there was between us is over, and I think our friendship, or the potential for it, will also be over if you persist in wanting to screw me." "Look, just give me a chance to change.

I have to read manuscripts now, but later we can have dinner, you choose the restaurant; it'll be nice. Just so long as you don't rule anything out," and she said, "I'm reluctant to say this, but feel I have to, that you are, as you continually make clear, pathetic," and he said "Maybe I am; and maybe I'm an asshole too, if that's not what you meant. But that doesn't mean I have to always be pathetic, and what I did last night was the exception. I'm cured." She stared at him and shook her head as if he were even more pathetic than she'd thought, and he said "Okay, what I just said was stupid. I'm hungover; not the best of excuses, but I'm not thinking of talking or even listening right. But I'll be better. I'll get rid of the manuscripts. Don't tell your friends I'm doing it so fast. And then we'll meet before my conferences, and talk and everything is ruled out," and she said "No way. And don't phone me or try to meet up with me. I made a huge mistake yesterday and I apologize for my complicity in all of this and helping to bring out the worst in you. I know there's a better side to you, from what I encountered in your office and what everybody's said. Just, you're a little oversexed, which makes you do foolish things," and she rubbed his knuckles, faked a smile, said to herself "Did I leave anything? No," and left. What am I doing to myself? he thought, getting into bed pretty well loaded that night. No more very young women, that's for sure. You got the hots for one, jerk off. And why do I get so damn sad every time a woman says she doesn't want to see me or sleep with me anymore? This one. What were my feelings for her? She was bright and a terrific writer and outspoken and cute. Frizzy hair, button nose, those glasses and knapsack. And very independent and sharp. But was I in love? How could I be? Attracted to a lot I liked about her, that's all. And seventeen years younger? But when she's still in her mid-twenties? You got her in bed, that should have been enough, so why go out of your head after just one time with her? She was right; you were pathetic. Pathetic with Karyn too, that time crying. From now on, an older woman, one much closer in age to you, and don't jump into bed so fast. Never works. Well, he did with Diana—five or so hours after they met they were making love at his place—and that one went on for years. But give things like this time. And for a change, maybe one who's Jewish, since—no, he's not kidding, but not religious Jewish—since that might have been in past relationships—not with Nadine; never came up; doubts she even knew he was Jewish and it was all so quick—a problem too. The different backgrounds, culture, other things. Someone—he's talking about the future—who knows what he's referring to and doesn't have to have him explain it when he makes a Jewish joke or remark and wouldn't be put off if he exaggerates or overacts in a

Jewish manner or accent as Terry and a woman he lived briefly with in California and a couple of others he saw from time to time were. And maybe even a woman who was brought up in New York, which'd mean they'd be coming from, like the Jewishness, and sharing even more things that were the same. Also, no woman who already has a child, even if she's separated from her husband or divorced, but one still young enough to have kids. And a woman who's built something like Karyn and Nadine. Sure, the body of this woman probably has changed from when she was their age if she's five to ten years younger than he, but one with full breasts, a nice-sized rear, thick sturdy thighs, even chubby, but no small or thin body like Diana's and Eleanor's and the woman in California he lived with and he thinks Terry's, except for her chest, although she was so long ago he mostly forgets. He wants a big strong body that can take his. So let's see, he thought, what's he have so far? An attractive Jewish woman from New York who's childless but can still have children and who isn't more than ten years younger than he and is of course intelligent and cultured and personable and gracious and good and so on, and stacked. Two years later he got a letter from Nadine, forwarded from his old address in New York. It was shortly after he started teaching in Baltimore and when he and Gwen had been together for almost that entire time, other than for when she broke it off and they didn't see or speak to each other for a month or two. She used to say "two." He'd say it was even less than one. "Isn't it in your journal of that year?" he once said, and she said "To my great sorrow, since they had in them how and when we first met and, other than for that episode, our first wonderful year, I can't find '78 and '79." In her letter Nadine asked for a blurb for her first book, which was coming out in six months. "I hate asking this of you," she said. "I remember you telling my friend James and me—you practically spit out the words, you thought the blurb practice was such sham and bunk—that you never asked a fellow writer for a blurb in your life and you never will. That's all well and good if you happen to receive, as you did, quotable pre-publication reviews for your first book, but in time to be put on the back of the book's cover, something my editor doesn't want to chance. She says that blurbs from other writers and prominent personalities are essential for a first-time published novelist. So I plead with you to consider what I don't think is an unfair request from me, seeing how you were once so positive to my work. You helped me with that encouragement and praise more than you could ever know—I still walk on air when I recall our office conference—and my novel is short, really just a long novella, and clearly written and shouldn't take more than a few hours to read, and you may even like it.

Thank you in advance." He wrote back saying he still is against giving and receiving blurbs and he especially doesn't see how an enthusiastic endorsement from a nobody writer like himself could help a book. It might even hurt it. Readers of the jacket copy, when they look over the book in the bookstore, will think how good could this writer be if she had to go to the bottom of the blurb barrel to get one? If I were you I'd only seek out blurbs from writers and critics with big names and hefty stature. No 'prominent personalities,' though, which I assume doesn't mean famous writers who can't keep their mouths shut about anything and so whatever they say is suspect, but talk-show hosts and celebrities like that. They could only help sell rubbish to undiscriminating readers, which I'm sure your novel is anything but." She wrote back that she doesn't know any other writers but the teachers she had in her grad program and they're even less known than he. "Please reconsider. What will my publisher think if I can't get even one blurb? And in some ways I feel I deserve one from you. And if the book's a hit—stranger things have happened—you get your name and two of your book titles under your blurb. (P.S.: I didn't think of that; it's what my editor told me to tell you.)" He didn't answer her; didn't know what to say. Now he thinks it was lousy not to blurb her. He could have praised the book even if he didn't read or like it. She was generous to him—let him screw her when she probably didn't want to but knew he wanted to a lot—and she was really a terrific young person, while he acted like a pig, so what would have been the harm? His principles messed with? Come off it. He's given plenty of blurbs, starting from around two years after she asked him for one. So many in fact, for former students of his and writers or their editors or publicists who sent him requests out of the blue—maybe they thought he'd be an easy mark when they noticed how many he gave—that he stopped giving them because he couldn't come up with anything new to say and was repeating himself to the point where a blurb from him wasn't worth anything anymore. She sent him an inscribed copy of her book soon after it was published: "Just thanks." There were three blurbs on it from writers he'd never heard of, nor was he familiar with their book titles and literary awards. From the jacket copy and the forty or so pages he read and the rest he skipped through, her novel was about a fifteen-year-old Midwestern girl and her family and friends and wealthy suburb during a very hot and boring summer in the fifties. Then she's deflowered by a much older motorcyclist passing through, who's almost pistol-whipped to death by her father and the girl ends up being transferred out of her local public high school to an all-girls' boarding school on the East Coast. The novel seemed written more for sophisticated younger readers than adults. The plot, despite the closing fireworks, was uninteresting and a bit dreary, and the writing was only so-so—certainly nowhere near as exciting and adventurous and even original as it was in her short stories from two years before. He wrote back saying how much he liked the book and how well written it was—"You were right; I breezed right through it"—and wished her lots of success with it, which he said he's sure she'll have, and a few weeks later sent her an inscribed copy of his new story collection: "Best always and with continued admiration for your work." She didn't write back thanking him for it. Her book got a short review in the *New York Times* Sunday book section: "An auspicious debut." He never saw another review or mention of a book of hers or anything else she may have written or about her in the next twenty-five years or heard from her again. With her, too, he could have asked Gwen or one of his daughters to search her name online. He was curious but he supposes not that curious to find out anything new about her. Sometimes when he was in a bookstore he looked at the front fiction tables and then the shelves for a book of hers. The only one he saw, a few years ago, was her first novel without its cover in a used bookshop in Ellsworth, Maine. So those were the last four or five women he was in love or infatuated with or just slept with or wanted to before he met Gwen. Call her, he told himself the night he finally did call. What's to be afraid of: If it's not that, then what is holding you back? Went over that. So go over it again. That she won't want to meet you the first time you ask her to on the phone? That could be part of it, though he knows that's the way it can go. What are the other parts? Too many busts with women lately? Said it already: yes. Afraid of getting serious? A little. Deeply and mutually involved? That, too, but it's also what he wants most. Because the short time he was with her—he doesn't see how he could know all this, but feels very strongly he does—she seemed to have everything going for her that he liked and he's probably putting too much hope on something happening between them. So, longer he doesn't call, longer he keeps his hopes up, ridiculous as he knows that notion, or whatever you want to call it, is. But something could happen. Not setting you up for a letdown, but you've got to give it a chance. If nothing happens, or not the way you want it, don't fall to pieces again. You're through doing that. I'm not going to say it, but you're going to act like a man. So call, goddamnit, call. Pick up the phone. Get your finger set to dial. Don't waste your time looking for her number, it's in your head. If her phone's busy, try again. She doesn't answer, call back later. If she has an answering machine and it comes on, tell her who you are and you'll call again soon. And you will. But now call or you know, or it could quite possibly be so, you'll never do it and, boy, will you forever regret it or for a long time to come. Because you'll always think something could have happened with this woman of your dreams if you had only called. And what's the only way to find out? That's right, so call. He picked up the receiver. "I feel nervous," he said. Well, what's so wrong with that? "It's not too late?" Looks at his watch on the night table. No, time's just right: not too early, not too late. Now dial. You've come to the end of your stalling. And if you hang up while the phone's ringing or right after she picks up, I'll kill ya.

He gets up, turns on the night table light, goes to the bathroom, pees, drinks a full glass of water from the glass there and goes back to the bedroom, plumps up two pillows, smaller fluffier one on top of the other, gets on his back in bed and rests his head in the middle of them, reaches over to turn off the light. "So, Gwen, my little sweetie, what happened next?" he says. No, he thinks, better not talk out loud. Kids could hear and knock on his door and say was he calling them, or is anything wrong? So just in his head. "Gwen, my darling sweetheart," he says in his head, "let's do something we never did before and that's to have a conversation in my head. I'll speak, I'll keep quiet while you speak, and so on like that. You remember everything, so tell me what happened next." "You know what happened next," she says in his head, "if I'm sure I know what you're referring to. You called me, didn't hang up, let my phone ring, and I answered it." "But what did we say? I know you must've said 'Hello,' and I must've followed that with 'Hello,' but probably 'Hi, it's Martin, Martin Samuels, guy from the other night at Pati Brooks' party, but really more so at her elevator and then in front of her building.' But I forget what happened after—what we said— except with it probably ending with my saying 'Do you think we can meet sometime soon for a coffee or drink?' although with my probably saying right before that 'Well, it's been very nice talking to you,' and your saying something like 'Okay,' and we set a date, time and place. But the rest. Help me; I want to go over as much of it as I can. To sort of relive it. Our first night, or night we first met. Because of what it led to. More than twenty-seven years. Twenty-four of them married. You may have loved someone more than me—in fact, I'm almost sure you did, two guys, but I never asked; didn't want to put you in that spot—but you never loved anyone longer. So if not for that night, nothing. No kids. No life together, which might've been better for you. No thousands-of-times lovemaking. No Maine. No Breakwater Inn. No Hanna Anderson. No Georges Brassens.

No France in '81. No Riverside Drive apartment. No jogging nun running past. I'm saying all those noes for me. So no a lot. And also, long as I have your ear, or have you here—they're so much alike, but what of it, right?— tell me, and this'll be my only aside in this talk, and it feels like a real talk, doesn't it?, other than for my nonstop monolog just now…you still there? I wouldn't blame you if you weren't." "I'm here. The talk feels okay: real enough in its way." "So I was saying, my darling…asking, with that 'tell me' before, if you forgive me." "You're being so loving. The 'sweetheart'; the 'my darling.'" "Because I love you, why else? Do you still love me?" "Let me try to answer your tell-me question. There were, since my first stroke, so many things to forgive you for. Just as there were many things to thank you for." "Not 'so many'?" "Just many. Couldn't have been easy living with someone so sick and often so helpless, and with a fatal next stroke, coming anytime anywhere, especially after the second one, looming over me. And my face, when it froze on one side for a while and my mouth got twisted. You like beauty. Without seeming immodest, I'm sure my prettiness was one of the principal reasons you went for me, and I felt I'd become too ugly for you." "Not true. I never looked away from you. I kissed that twisted mouth." "Not how I remember it. You kissed other places on my face." "Other places on your body, maybe, but I definitely kissed your lips. To me, no place was off base." "I know I had a hard time looking at myself in the mirror when I brushed my teeth or hair. I looked like old Mrs. Behrlich, do you remember her? But when she was almost a hundred and after part of her face got dis- figured when she was mugged. I took you to see her twice. The last time when Rosalind was just a baby, since she was named after her." "I forget that though now I remember it." "But you could be sweet and I could be forgiving. I needed you. You kept me alive." "You're just saying that. By forgiveness, I was talking about that last night when I said such horrible things, one in particular. You heard. You know. I'm sorry. I miss you so much, something I should've thought of before that night: how I would. And I won't be hurt or sink into deeper grief and self-hatred if you say you don't forgive me. I'd deserve it. And what does it matter, right? I did what I so stupidly and viciously did and now I'm paying for it. I was out of my mind that night, not the first time but never so bad. Maybe I'd drunk too much, although neither is an excuse." "If it'd be any comfort to you, Martin, what you say you said to me didn't change anything. I was going to die soon—the 'loom- ing'—anyway. 'Imminent' is the word the doctor would have used if he'd thought it necessary to be truly honest with me. I'm not saying this to make you feel better. I knew I was doomed. We even spoke about it." "No we didn't. And you weren't. And despite what you say, and I don't mean to contradict you on this, you still don't want to hurt me and in fact you do want to make me feel better. That's nice. That's wonderful. You're a dream-boat and you always were. But I don't see how, or for a very long time, I can ever feel better about anything, not just myself. But I do see through your white lie. Don't ask me why you can't be more convincing at it, and I'm not criticizing you for that. But you try to be, because that's the way you are. Kind and generous. Gentle and gracious. This and that. Just about everyone said so in their condolence letters and notes. I didn't read them—I couldn't without falling to pieces—but the kids did, since the letters were to them too, and recounted a number of them to me. That you always wanted to make people feel good, no matter how sick or distressed you were. Your radiant smile. Your cheerful, warm disposition. Your attention to them and their lives. You lit up everything and everybody with your light, one said. Not original but nice and right. 'She had a special luminous presence'— there's that light again—'and an inborn poetic spirit,' another said. I like that one—and maybe it was 'incandescent'—and wish I could tell you who it was from. Another was 'A phenomenal composition of beauty and bril-liance'—not 'light' this time—'more than anyone I've known. But so relaxed with it,' he goes on. 'No show and never took advantage of her good looks and always played it down if someone mentioned it or remarked how smart she was.' I know I hurried your third stroke along with what I said that night. And don't tell me you didn't hear what I yelled in the kitchen. Neigh-bors must have heard. You must have thought I was saying it more for you than me. I don't remember the exact words, and though I'd hate doing it, I could give you a good paraphrase." "I heard them but also can't recall them exactly. They were unkind, that's for certain. But I think said out of pity for my condition—so it was simply the wrong thing to say—and fear over my imminent third stroke and probable death and your frustration at not being able to save me and concern or uneasiness, or something, that you'd have nobody to take care of and you'd be living alone." "You're doing it again. Your generosity is hurting me more than your honesty ever could. My dar-ling, my sweetheart, can't we finally have it out but in the gentlest and most loving of ways?" "Better, let's forget it for now, the time after that and maybe forever. Yes, forever. I'm beginning to get, much as you'd be surprised at this uncommon emotion in me, according to you, annoyed with this talk." "Annoyed or disgusted?" "Do you want me to get angry too? I've been that. You've seen and heard it and despise it when it's directed at you. *Please.*" "So what happened next?" "You called. I answered. You didn't hang up before or right after I said hello. If you had, I wouldn't have known it was you. After all, we'd just met. And there have been previous guys who called, I think just to hear my voice, but never said boo, I've no idea why." "Your voice. And your dazzling smile. Both how lovely they were, people also wrote in their letters and notes." "The truth is I barely thought of you since we parted in front of Pati's building. Once, maybe twice. First time, while I was walking, that night, to the subway or bus. Which did I take?" "I think you told me the subway." "While I was walking to either one on Lex, or whatever it becomes down there—" "Fourth Avenue and Astor Place?" "I thought if I saw a bus coming, I'd take that, even if it's slower than the subway to get to where I was going." "Where was that again?" "I believe a piano recital at someone's apartment, but my memory's also hazy on that." "Sounds right to me. But what also sounds right is your meeting somebody at an East Side art movie theater uptown." "But I wondered while walking, or maybe on the subway—although now I'm almost sure I took the bus: I picture it—if you would call me and what I'd say if you asked to see me." "You actually had doubts I'd call? It must have been obvious: I'd already fallen for you." "No you didn't. You couldn't have. Too soon. Anyway, you were attractive, but dressed kind of peculiarly for a pretty spiffy party." "I thought just three or four people from Yaddo, an informal dinner. Maybe take-out. I think I might have—I must have—brought a bottle of wine, and when I saw the kind of party it was, left it in the kitchen. It was a good thing I didn't wear jeans. I almost did." "You were also so nervous and acted a bit strangely when we first talked on the street, that I felt somewhat wary of you." "Right after we parted, as you put it, I thought much of that about myself too. Even the clothes. As to how I acted: I was nervous. We talked about this before. You had that effect on me. You were so beautiful; the smile; your voice. The way you spoke and put things. And your gentleness and kindness and humility and refinement." "Again, it was too soon, so I don't see how you could have made such assessments of my character." "Oh, no, I could tell. Plus something you gave off when I was looking at you at the party. And I was right, in all those things. I was also nervous when I first called. You know; but what did I say?" "You got on and said something like 'Hi, it's Martin—Martin Samuels from the other night? Pati's party?'" "Sounds like me. That 'Martin—Martin Samuels,' and so on." "'I remember you,' I said, and you said 'That's good. How are you?' And I probably said 'Fine, thank you, and you?' which is what I invariably said in response to that particular question. 'Fine,' you probably said, 'and I'm sorry I didn't call you sooner. I don't mean tonight "sooner," and it's not too late to call, is it? and now I do mean tonight,' and I said no. 'I'd intended to call several days sooner, but I was working on a manuscript I needed to finish and it took longer than I expected to get it in shape.' 'Oh,' I said, 'a manuscript? Are you an editor?' and you said 'Writer; fiction. Didn't I tell you the other night?' Or maybe you didn't say that, but we somehow got into what you were and had been working on. That your literary agent said she'd like you to write one positive relationship-affirming story for the interconnected collection you gave her, before she submitted it to a publisher. Something showing why the couple, Jen and Willie, stayed together so long. For all the other stories—this was for *Partings*—with minor exceptions, she said, gave more of a reason why they should have split up years before. They were periodically compatible and loving and sexy to each other but also lots of complaints, fights, several tirades, Jen sleeping with other men, and she threw a glass at him twice and three different times literally kicked him off the bed while he was sleeping or falling asleep, resulting in a broken toe once. So you wrote it and hand-delivered it to the agent and were so tired from all that work, you said, that you wanted to rest up a day or two more before you called me. 'Did she like it?' I asked, and you said you haven't heard from her yet but she's usually very quick." "You know that excuse for holding off calling you was pure baloney." "I know. You told me about a month after we started sleeping together." "I figured that was a good time. You were in my clutches; not on the bed but in life, so to speak. But that little lie sort of showed how nervous I was in calling you. And my fear, because I was so attracted to you and saw you, after a series of bad or wrong relationships, as my one big hope in finding a permanent love mate, that you'd refuse me if I asked you out." "You'd finished that story weeks before." "Two weeks before I met you. And the agent…I'm not coming up with her name—" "Danuta Ott. She was very bright and tall and nice. Married to a climatologist, lived in the Village on La Guardia Place. I think he taught at NYU. We went to a party she gave for her clients. Several big names were there—best sellers—and one, with a slab of meat in his mouth, made a pass at you." "Danuta liked the new story and was waiting to hear what the publisher thought of the entire collection." "I remember when it was accepted. That was a while after. It took so long. That night we had a celebratory dinner at a very fine restaurant, and you ordered a bottle of my favorite champagne. I think, over dessert, and when we shared a cognac or B and B, was the first time you told me you loved me." "No, days before. A couple of times in bed. Maybe I was just renewing it in a romantic setting. Was there a candle on the table?" "If you're being serious, how could I remember?" "But I think that night, in the cab coming home, you told me you loved me the first time. It took the champagne and scrumptious food and half an after-dinner drink to get it out of you." "Not true; it wouldn't. And I don't remember the first time I said I loved you. I do remember that when I did say it, you said 'You do? That's great!,' and I think you got teared up." "You had tuna, I had salmon. I said, when we were deliberating what to order, 'We could do better than two fish dishes.' But you insisted on your tuna, and the most promising thing I saw on the menu that wasn't way overpriced was the salmon. We shared, didn't we?" "We always did." "I remember the most delicious potato dish I ever had that came with your tuna and same with the watercress and couscous with my salmon. The appetizer, or appetizers, we had draws a blank. I think you said we don't need one because you had a late lunch and you don't eat much anyway, said more because you wanted to keep the bill down, but I ordered a radish, sheep ricotta, walnut and endive salad that came on two long kayak-shaped narrow plates. 'I assumed you wanted to share it,' the waiter said, 'but I'll bring it back to the kitchen to put on one plate if I was wrong.'" "You couldn't have remembered all that." "I did. Even that the radishes were sliced into paper-thin coins, but so thin that I didn't know what they were and thought they were some other vegetable not listed in the menu's description of the dish. Listen, it was a great evening; eventful, momentous, hence the extensive memory of it. Cab home? We never did that except if it was very late or raining torrentially or the last two months of your pregnancies." "Your holding-off excuse gave me plenty to mull over. It was interesting and educating, I thought, what some writers—un-well-known ones—have to go through to get a full-length manuscript published, something I knew I'd have to go through one day with an academic publisher once I got my dissertation into book form. I never did. Lost interest. Old stuff. Wanted to write essays on subjects in and out of my expertise and do a few translations of important neglected works. I was lucky I got as far as I did in teaching." "Because you were a terrific teacher. And original essays don't count? And translated novels and literary memoirs with riveting and beautifully written introductions aren't books?" "I'm sure to some, especially my former fellow grad students in the French department at Columbia, I'm considered a failure, after all the work I did to get a Ph.D. and nabbing a prestigious postdoc fellowship." "Never. I'm sure to most you were a light in a murky field by not going along with the kind of academic gibberish and theoretical drivel you would have needed to use to turn your dissertation into a publishable book for a university press." "My dissertation was already that. I thought you read it. I know I gave you a copy." " I started to and don't know what happened. I think I read the first story, after reading what you wrote about it—the one about the woman who ends up having something like multiple orgasms from the stars—and went on to read the rest of the collection, I liked the first so much, and probably forgot to go back to your manuscript. I still intend to." "Don't waste your time." "Maybe I could try to get it published by a commercial press—one of mine, for instance—by making it more plain-speaking and concise and deleting the footnotes and bibliography." "Don't you dare. It's an old dead work I'm not particularly proud of, other than for having completed it and typing out all two hundred and eighty-five pages, so leave it that way. Besides, with all the new biographical and historical material published since then—I really only put the finishing touches on it in '77, almost exactly a year before we met—it needs to be brought up-to-date, a task you're untrained for and wouldn't be able to do." "I could try. You could guide and teach me. I'd do anything for you." "Do you remember what you next said in your first phone call?" "Go change the subject on you." "Do you?" "'In less than ten minutes in your presence I was bowled over by you. Could you upright me? And I know we should go slow, but will you be mine?' No, I don't." "You said 'Enough about me and my dismal unpublishable work. I want to know about you.' I said '"Dismal" is for you to judge—I haven't read you, although I'm sure you're being overly harsh on yourself—but why "unpublishable"?' You said, 'I just know. It'll be repeatedly rejected, first by the mainstream publisher who brought out my last novel this past June.' 'Oh,' I said, 'what's that one called? I may be talking to someone whose book I've heard of.' You gave the title. *Leaving the Theater.* I said 'I'm unfamiliar with it, but it's conceivable I read a review of it or saw an ad.' You said 'No ads. The publisher believed in word-of-mouth advertising, but apparently no mouths, either. But it did get a good pasting in the daily *Times* in a review of three crime novels. It wasn't a crime novel but a novel partly about a possible crime. You never find out what happens to the woman—the narrator's live-in girlfriend—who disappears on page two or three. The mistake in designating what kind of novel it was,' you said, 'occurred because the publisher must have decided it would sell better if billed as a serious crime novel rather than as a regular serious novel. What idiots,' I remember you saying, 'and how was it possible the reviewer didn't pick up on what kind of novel it was? So he panned it for, among other reasons—he also thought it should have had numbered chapters rather than just paragraph breaks and many of the sentences were too long—for not abiding by the strictures and structure of a traditional crime novel. Well, of course,' you said, 'well, of course,' getting heated. And then you said 'Excuse me, I always get mad, when I'm not falling over laughing, when I think of that review.' I said 'Then why would you want to send your new book to that same publisher if they treated your last one so cynically?' And you said 'It isn't so easy finding one for my work, even with a good agent, so I sometimes—well, at least that once—have to take what I get and hope for the best. But it's true,' you said, 'this time if perchance my new work does get accepted, I'm going to insist, whoever the publisher is, big or small, or I think I'm going to insist—don't hold me to it—that it doesn't mislead the reader, but first the person who buys the books for the store, as to what genre the book belongs to—the modern genre—in the catalog and promotional material and publisher's salesman's spiel and jacket copy and word of mouth it tries to stir up. But again,' you said, 'enough about me and my work. What about you? What do you do? Literature?' I said 'Literature, but not like you. I'm an academic, overtrained for years to be one, and I fairly recently got my Ph.D. in it. I should have finished up three years ago but got stuck in Paris for all the good reasons and put off my writing of it.' You asked what my thesis for my Ph.D. was on and I corrected you and said thesis is for a master's, dissertation is for a doctorate, which is what I got. You asked what I do now and I said I'm presently on a postdoc and teaching two humanities courses on the college level. 'Here or outside the city?' you said, and I said 'Here.' 'But you don't want to say what university or college?' you said, and I said, 'What are you trying to say? I wasn't trying to hide it. Why would I? I just didn't say it. Columbia.' 'Ooh, fine school,' you said; 'quite a credit to you, teaching there.' You really seemed impressed, which I found funny, though I didn't reveal my amusement. Or maybe you only pretended to be impressed, to smooth things over after your 'you don't want to say' question. 'But a postdoc,' you said. 'What's that, other than that I assume it's some honor or award or bestowal of some kind you can only get after you got your doc?' and I told you. Then you asked and we talked awhile about the author and the work of his I wrote my dissertation on. Camus, his only story collection, which you said you read and loved maybe twenty years ago—'It's got to be one of the best collections ever,' or that's what you thought at the time though can't remember even one of the stories now— when Camus was all the rage, you said, and at the time when the book might have just come out in English and you think Camus was still alive and you were just starting out as a writer. I said 'Nineteen fifty-seven was when the Gallimard edition came out and a year later Knopf published the English translation.' You said 'Yes, it would have been around then,' though you didn't take yourself seriously as a writer till '60 or '61, when you wrote your first stories you thought were getting to be something. 'As you can see,' you said, 'three books, and maybe now a fourth, if I'm lucky, aren't much in nearly twenty years of writing, and it's not because I'm a slow writer or that my books are enormously long. All three and the new one are even quite thin. It's because I wasn't able to get a book published till three years ago, and the first two from the smallest of publishers after trying everybody, with and without an agent, for fifteen years.' Then you asked about the finished manuscript of Camus' that was in his briefcase thrown from the car that crashed or found in the mangled wreck. 'A sports car,' you said, 'right? Heading back to Paris, though he had a return train ticket in his pocket, from some chic vacation spot in the south. In fact, Gallimard himself at the wheel, or son of Gallimard senior.' I said I believed it was junior, but could be mistaken. And that manuscript, an autobiographical novel of his early days in Oran, has been published in France, or is to be published, and will no doubt be translated into English and brought out here. 'Sorry,' I said, 'that I can't provide more information on it. I have my scholarly lapses. I do know someone who read a reproduced typescript of it years ago and said it was very good, so you might, if you like his work that much, have a new Camus novel to look forward to. But I decided, a year before I even got my doctorate,' I said, 'to take a break from all things Camus except *Exile*, or as much as I could, after being immersed in almost every aspect of his work for eight long years. Many Ph.D. candidates grow to hate the writer they're writing about, but by then it's too late so they have to go on, sort of like continuing a bad marriage for the sake of the kids. It was my good luck— I didn't choose it for this—that his fiction oeuvre, which I concentrated on, wasn't huge, and all four books are relatively short, and one is really no more than a novella. Attending conferences and giving an occasional paper,' I said, 'if I was fortunate enough to be asked to, and writing reviews of books by other Camus specialists for academic and scholarly journals are things I have to do if I want to get a position in a university's French department, but one where I wouldn't have to teach the language, or not more than once a year.' The thing is, I didn't know if I believed you on the phone that first time—not that you read *Exile* but that you thought so highly of it. If you had, wouldn't you have remembered at least one or two of the stories, no matter how far back you read them, for there are only six in the collection and not one alike? You even, in that conversation or another, compared the stories to the best of Hemingway and Salinger and García Márquez." "It was true. I thought so then and think even more highly of them now. That

I forgot them could have been a memory quirk or my nervousness in talking about them to an expert and coming out sounding like an ill-informed and overconfident jerk. I've taught the collection, as you know, and with your help, to my graduate students and several of the stories to my undergrads, especially the workers' story and the one where the schoolmaster lets the Arab go." "'The Silent Men' and 'The Guest.' Lets him choose his own fate, among other reasons." "Balducci, like the store, right?" "The old gendarme who hands him over to Daru?" "If that's the schoolmaster, yes. I used to love it when you came to my class and gave a half-hour introduction to Camus and the book. The students also loved it, praised you to high heaven for weeks, and I learned something new each time you came." "I guess I was keeping up on my research. But what I thought on the phone was that you were saying how much you like the book—" "*Dubliners*. Babel's *Red Cavalry* stories. Really, in this century—I mean the last—it was right up there with the very best." "—so I'd think we'd have much to talk about if we went out." "Not so, believe me, and after speaking to you that first time on the phone, I didn't think, and didn't think you thought, there'd be a conversation problem. Want to hear what I also loved?" "Go ahead." "It might seem silly. Tell me if you think so. That you spoke French fluently and knew enough German and Italian, and also Russian and Polish from home, to get by in those if you had to. I thought early on—because what was missing; English?—that if we ever traveled to Europe, a fantasy of mine with women I was close with that was never realized till I met you, I'd have my own personal interpreter, making the trip so much easier and more enjoyable. That once we got there, because my French was less than spotty, I could just sit back and relax and let you do, which you said you didn't mind to, all the room reserving and travel arranging and restaurant ordering and bike renting and so on. And of course the fantasy was not to have an interpreter— that turned out to be a windfall—but to go to Paris and the Dordogne and Aix-en-Provence and Saint-Paul-de-Vence with a woman I loved and who loved me." "I understand that. You didn't need to explain." "It was a great trip, the one in '81, wasn't it? It was near the end of it that I knew deep down we were going to marry and never separate. That was a wonderful thing to find out, even if you didn't say it." "It was a very nice trip, except when you got so sick in Nice and your first crippling sciatica later on when we were driving to Chartres." "But I was with you." "You also said in that call that you'd love it for someone to write a thesis or dissertation or just a long paper on your work. Not for the recognition. That you'd be interested—it's still way too early for it, you said, three to four books and about seventy published stories, though you have a drawer or two of completed long and short manuscripts ready to be published—what an academic or budding scholar, and you of course didn't mean me, would make of it. 'I'm already the age,' you said, 'Camus was at the peak of his fame and had probably by then collected his Nobel Prize, though his getting it so young had to be the anomaly.' 'That would make you forty-four,' I said, and you said 'I hate saying it but I'm forty-two.' 'Why do you hate saying it?' I said, and you said 'I don't know, but I'd better get on with it, right? If I'm going to make a name for myself in literature, which I swear is not one of my priorities or goals. I'm not ambitious; I just want to write. Good God,' you then said, 'that's so self-serving to say. And didn't I already say something like that to you once? I meant nothing by it. Forget I said it.' And then, I think before I could say something like 'If you wish,' you said—and I found this curious, coming out so soon; after all, this was our first real talk— 'I didn't mean to give you my age this quickly, because you might think I'm too old a guy for you. Oh, damn,' you said, 'I shouldn't have said that either.' But I said 'I'm thirty-one. Close to thirty-two. A man forty-two, or even forty-four, and I'm speaking hypothetically here, isn't too old for me if he doesn't act a lot older than his age.' Then you said 'That leads me to a question.' 'Let me guess,' I said, and you said 'Okay,' and I said 'Only kidding. I have no idea why I said that. What?' 'And please understand,' you said, 'that I can be somewhat inarticulate on the phone. With someone, I'm saying, I'm not used to talking to and whom I'm hoping for a positive answer to my question—and by now you must be able to guess what I'm about to say—but do you think we can meet one afternoon or sometime for coffee and sit down and talk? Well, of course to sit down and of course it's for talk,' which I got a laugh out of and said 'I'd like that, sure,' or 'I don't see why not, and sitting down even better,' or something like that. Both certainly sound like me. I mean, I knew there was no harm to it." "So you sensed by the—I don't remember our ever going over this, but we probably did—from our brief conversation at the elevator, even briefer in it, and then on the street and now on the phone that I wasn't Mr. Masher or potentially dangerous in any way, like boring the pants off you for an hour, or what else?" "Nothing like that. I sensed you were serious and intelligent and candid and not glib or devious and had a sense of humor, and listened—this was important in my first or second impression; didn't constantly butt in—to what I had to say. And I've always met interesting people through literature, so what would an hour over coffee cost me? It could even be stimulating and get my mind going, talking about literary and other things

I haven't talked about or not for a while. If it went well, I thought, or
gravitated in that direction—and I wasn't seeing anyone steadily at the
time—we could do it again, maybe over lunch or dinner. If we didn't hit it
off—if in our first meeting we showed little to no potential for anything else
happening or developing...Just was of little interest to you or me, then
kaput and goodbye. Anyway, you said 'So what's the next step?—I guess a
date and time and where to meet.' You said you were available every day,
since at the time you were working at home. I asked where you lived. You
told me and I said 'That's perfect. This Wednesday, if the day's still good for
you, I have an appointment for an hour at two just a few blocks from you.
So what if we meet at the Ansonia coffee shop a little after three?' You said
'How much after would you need?' and I said ten to fifteen minutes. 'Let
me check my appointment book,' you said. 'Oops, I forgot I don't have one.
I keep all my appointments in my head, except medical and dental—those
I write down on a piece of paper on the refrigerator door—but it gives you
an indication just how busy my schedule is.' I said 'Why, you could still
have a good memory,' and you said 'It's good, all right; to some people, too
good. But I forget a lot too. Particularly something cooking on the stove.'
'I do that,' I said, and you said 'Then we have something in common other
than literature and living on the Upper West Side.' 'So,' I said, 'Wednesday,
quarter after three, we'll say? If I am detained, it'll only be a few minutes, so
don't run away.' Then I asked for your phone number in case something did
come up preventing me from meeting you. You said—I forget what you
said. Something like 'Oh, don't say that, but if it has to be, then I hope we
can meet some other day.' You gave me your number and said if I lose it,
know that you're one of about ten Martin Samuels in the Manhattan phone
book but the only one with the middle initial V. 'If you can believe it,' you
said, 'I'm not the only one on West 75th Street. I'm between Columbus and
the park and the other West 75th Street Martin Samuels, no middle initial,
so he's first in the phone book, is between West End Avenue and Broadway,
I think number two-fifty. So you'll recognize me?' you said, and I said 'I
don't see why there'd be a problem. You might even be wearing the same
navy blue duffel coat.' 'Was that what I was wearing?' you said. 'Well, it had
to be, since it was fairly cold that night, I think, and winter, and that's my
only coat, other than for a thin rain one. But good; you remembered. And
I was only trying to be funny with that "recognize me" line, don't ask me
why. A bit compulsive, wouldn't you say?' I said 'You spoke about that, in
almost the same words, if I remember, by the elevator in Pati's building, or
maybe while we were riding down in it, not that I'm accusing you of

repeating yourself. I don't mind. I like humor and I love to laugh. I think I told you that about myself too. At least you were trying, and in your next attempt at it you might hit the target square in the circle,' which I thought reasonably clever for a spontaneous remark—I swear I'd never used it or thought of it before—but you didn't laugh or even fake a chuckle or show any sign you got it. It's hard to believe it went by you, knowing your mind now. Maybe you thought it was trite and you were being polite or didn't want to risk spoiling anything for yourself with me. The last one would have been more like you," "I don't remember you saying it. But it was a good one and I would have said so if I'd heard it—it's been said of us both that we speak too low, especially on the phone—or laughed or given you some kind of ha-ha. Or it could be I sneezed the exact moment you said it and my ears—you know my sneezes—were still ringing from it a second or two after and I didn't hear you." "I don't remember any sneeze, but it's possible you drew away from the phone to do it. But near the end of our first phone talk, I said 'One more thing, and then I really have to go. Do you know the Ansonia Hotel, or maybe it's just apartments now, and that the entrance to the drugstore, closer to 74th Street, is on Broadway?' You said 'You bet,' or something. 'The Ansonia's one of my favorite buildings in the city. Did you know it's mentioned in Bellow's *Seize the Day*?' "No, I never read it,' I said. 'I've been meaning to. My mother liked it so much she read it twice, second time right after the first, but she likes all of Bellow.' 'It's a good book,' you said. 'Terrific dialog; one of those everything-happening-and-getting-resolved-in-a-single-day novels, or maybe it was over a weekend, and where there's a yapping dog named Scissors…Bellow's great with names. And a very affecting last few pages—but I probably shouldn't say what it is if you're going to read it,' and I said 'Go on; it won't be for a long time.' 'Where the narrator becomes emotionally overcome at a funeral for a man he doesn't know—he by chance was in a crowd of funeral-goers on the street and gets swept up by them into what I assume's the Riverside Memorial Chapel on Amsterdam and 76th Street…you must know of the place,' and I said 'All too well; my grandfather.' 'I'm sorry,' you said, and that you brought it up. Then you said 'But the book gets a little slow in places, so the length, or thereabouts, of *The Stranger*, a novella I loved except for the last part in prison. Like Camus, Bellow, skillful and smart as he is, can get too cerebral and philosophical for fiction, not a complaint other readers might have of them, like your mother, for instance. But a lot of readers,' you said, 'love that stuff and want to get intellectually charged up by the ideas and intelligent exchanges, in addition to liking the story and style. I think Bellow started out as an anthropologist, might even have gone on digs. But what I started out saying about the Ansonia—' and I cut you off and said 'Please be brief,' and you said 'I'll save it for later, if you like, or skip it altogether,' and I said 'No, finish.' You said 'He has his main character—Willie—looking at it from the Beacon Hotel diametrically across Broadway, though the Beacon has a different name, but I don't think the Ansonia does. And I read that from where he claims to see the Ansonia's ornate towers and turrets on the roof, you can't. Minor point, right?, so why did I bring it up? Incidentally, I used to deliver food orders to the Ansonia's guests, also the Beacon's but not as much, when I was a kid and worked for the C & L, a combination deli, bakery, restaurant, bar and catering service a block north of the Ansonia, same side of Broadway. It's where Fairway is now. Do you remember C & L?' and I said 'No; to me Fairway has always been there, and every year getting larger.' 'Have you ever been inside the Ansonia?' you said, and I said 'Yes. What I remember particularly is the beautiful marble spiral stairway—huge, and I think one at each end, and both went up to the top floor. I used to take piano lessons there. The building got terribly rundown, though, or was the last time I was in it. So, see you Wednesday, Martin,' and you said 'I talked too much, didn't I? Didn't know when to stop, something I don't normally do. I'm sorry,' and I said 'Don't be. It's only that I've got a ton of work to do. Goodbye,' and you said 'Bye' or 'Goodbye,' and I hung up." "That was it? Actually, a lot for a first phone conversation—any kind of conversation between two people—with many diverse subjects and not much idle chatter, I don't think. Except for my big blabbermouth, and thanks for filling in most of what we said. I'd say we hit it off. What about you?" "I don't remember thinking that. It was just a conversation, longer than most of mine on the phone and among the longest we ever had—you were usually fairly brief on the phone with me, businesslike sometimes, except when you were away for a few days and you became lovey-dovey— and often terse and occasionally abrupt. Anyway, one I wanted to end long before it did, because of all the things I still had to do that night." "So what happened and what did we talk about when we met at the drugstore?" "Please, sweetheart, give it a rest. I no longer like this routine or format or whatever you care to call it—it really has no name." "Headtalk." "Martin headtalk. But it's feeling forced and it's also become tiring for me. No more. Good day or goodnight, but I'm going." This was fun, he thinks. And comforting, interesting, other things. Best thing that's happened to him since she died. He means it's the one good thing that's happened to him since then. Did it really happen, though? He thinks it did and then he thinks it couldn't have; it's crazy. Crazy, how? He doesn't know? If he told someone he thinks it really might have happened, that he spoke with Gwen in his head, that they had a long conversation, a very long one, they might say he's crazy, see a doctor, but don't get worried, it's part of his grief; why do you think they call it pathological? If he told them how responsible he feels about her death, they might also say it's part of his grief. How? That he's trying to concoct a way to get over his guilt. He doesn't get that. Unresolved psychological issues, they might say, if he wants it explained medically. But it sounded like her: what she said and the way she said it, and also the way she acted to him was like Gwen would, and she didn't seem to be angry at him anymore. He'd like to believe it was real and he could talk to her almost anytime he wanted to. Try it. "Gwen," he says in his head, "was I really speaking to you before?" Listens. She doesn't answer. "To put it another way," he says in his head, "were we really speaking to each other and your part in it wasn't made up by me? After all, we lived a long time together and were very close—I think you'd agree with me on that. At least close most of the time, although I don't want to be putting words in your mouth that way too—so I'd know beforehand what you'd say a lot of times and how you'd say it. Just as you, if the conversation were to take place in your head, would know a lot of what I'd say before I said it and also the way I'd say it. That didn't come out clear. What it comes down to is that if you told me our talk actually did take place, I'd believe you, and not just because I want to so much. Why do I want to? The obvious. So tell me, what do you think about all of what I just said, except for the stuff that wasn't clear?" and he listens. She doesn't say anything. And there was nothing in his head while he was speaking in it, when before, when she spoke, and even while he was talking, he saw her face, sometimes just vaguely, and her mouth moving a little same time her words were coming out. Face from when? Recent. Between the time of her last two strokes, he thinks, so one side of her face—her right? her left? He's trying to remember; how could he forget it when it was such a short time ago?—slightly paralyzed, but not so much to make it difficult for her to speak or be understood. And photos wouldn't help, since she wouldn't let herself be photographed after her first stroke. "Don't," she said, when he tried to take a picture of her with the kids, "I look ugly." "No, you don't," he said. "You just won't look in the mirror anymore, so you don't know what a doll you still are." The kids would know if he doesn't remember by the time he asks them. What a question, though. "Which side was your mommy paralyzed on?" Anyway, she looked good in his head. Well, she was always a good-looking woman. Her stroke, except for the first few weeks after, and age—she was almost sixty when she died—didn't much change that. Beautiful skin. Few lines or wrinkles. Hair brushed back, either in a ponytail or over her shoulders—he couldn't see behind her—just a faint touch of gray, or the beginning of it: a few strands in the middle in front—high wide forehead exposed, not wearing her glasses. Where are the glasses now? Just one pair, only broke the frames once in the about fifteen years since she started wearing them, though had the lenses changed every other year or less because her eyes were always getting worse, while he broke the frames of his glasses a number of times, usually by sitting on or rolling over them. In their eyeglasses case on the second to top bookshelf in her study, all the way over to the right. Took them off her the night before she died. Put them in their case and left them on her night table. It was days later he put them on the bookshelf. One of the kids had said "What do we do with Mommy's glasses?" Doesn't know why to the extreme right. Plenty of room in front of the entire shelf. Why on the second to top shelf? It was on eye level and he'd know where they were when he wanted them. What will he eventually do with them? Keep the case because he was always losing his, but the glasses? Maybe keep them too because in the future—both kids wear glasses—one of them could use the frame. It was pretty expensive, not like his, but then she did in all those years only have two. "Gwen," he says in his head, "I was just remembering one of the times we got our eyeglasses together. You asked me if I thought your frame cost too much, and you were teaching then and I said 'It's your money too.' And then I think we had lunch out after, which we always did when we had the new lenses put in, but never when we got our eyes examined. Then, because of the drops the ophthalmologist put in our eyes to dilate them and which didn't wear off for hours, we just wanted to go home. Donna's. In the same retail complex as the optician's shop was in. Cross Keys. That's all. Just a nice memory popping up. Restaurant lunches, which I remember better than the dinners. How come? And please tell me if I am tiring or exasperating you or both beyond the point you can take with my chatter. Or you can, if you don't want to respond to that verbally, shake or nod your head to it, and whichever it is—the nod or shake, if I see it, and to either tiring or exasperating you or both—I'll go on or stop." Listens. Nothing, and no face in his head. "Not clear again?" he says in his head. "I wasn't? And maybe even a little bit stupid? Well, we both know how I can be both those. I proved it that night, didn't I? More than stupid. Lot more. Much worse. Despicable, almost unforgivable, it was so bad. I'm so sorry, Gwen, So sorry. But please, one more question, my darling, and you are my darling, you'll always be my darling, and then I'll let you go. Maybe till some other time, though I swear not today, or maybe I won't try this means of talking to you again, seeing how you didn't like it very much. Or just that it tires you. I only want to do what you want. It's a very important question, though, and the one I want to ask, probably the most. That one long conversation I'm almost sure we had in my head? Did it mean—does it, you're no longer angry at me or fed up with me or you no longer hate me, if that's what it was and I admit I deserved, and I'm forgiven?" Listens. Nothing. "That didn't come out well," he whispers. "I'm saying, my darling Gwen," he says in his head, "that last thing I said—not the whispering, if you heard it—didn't come out well. But you have to know how much I want to hear you say that…that I'm forgiven for what I said to you that night—said in the kitchen, but it was probably meant to be heard by you—and if it's possible, that you still love me. So please say something. I know I'm being pathetic. And the last thing I wanted was for it to come true, what I said in the kitchen. But all this has to show how important it is for me to hear you say both—'forgiven,' 'love'—so I know that last time, when you called me sweetheart, or just said 'sweetheart,' the only time you said it in my head, wasn't a fluke." Listens. Nothing. Too tired to? That could be it. And she's already said she's had enough of it, so why's he pushing her? "Gwen, is it that you're too tired to speak?" he says in his head. "And why'd I say 'Gwen'? Who else could I be talking to? But just say that, a single yes to my too-tired-to question, and we'll call it a night." Listens. Nothing. "Oh, Gwen," he says in his head, "please come back to me, please. If you can't, and I mean to my head to speak, then you can't or just might not want to, and it's wrong and dumb of me to try to pressure you to. So I'll catch you some other time, I hope, okay?" and he seems to see her laughing in his head—no sound comes out—though the image is unclear. "Good, you're back," he says in his head, "And laughing, if what I think I'm seeing, I'm seeing. That could be a good sign, right?— between us, I mean." Or who knows what her laughing, if she did, and it's gone now, was about. That he's such a fool, maybe, and never changes, though he thinks he does. That he's such a dreamer, thinking he can talk his way out of what he did. "Live with it," her laughing could have been saying. "As you said yourself: you deserve it." No, she could never be so mean. But she could be frank to him and was a number of times, not holding anything back, really disturbing and even hurting him sometimes and not caring that she did or ever apologizing for what she said or mollifying him in any way. After listening to it for about a minute, he'd usually say "Okay, I've had enough. I don't know how much you think I can take," and walk away, sometimes out of the house, while she was still criticizing him. Though he'd later—hours, that night in bed if she let him sleep in it with her, the next day—admire her for having said it, difficult as it was to hear, and tell her so: "Excuse me, I want to say something. What you said to me today (yesterday)? I know I must have said this before, but you were right on everything. I'm terribly sorry for what I said. Please forgive me or if you can, try to start to?" And he remembers her saying once or twice something like "So, I finally got through to you. Not that your saying I was right or how sorry you are is going to make my anger at you fly away. You were awful, as bad as I've ever seen you, and for a while I truly disliked you and wondered why I stay married to you, and it's going to take some time for me to feel good about you again." "A kiss?" he said one of those times, and she said "We're a long ways from that yet." "Then just a little one, on the cheek?" and she said "Even that." "So serioso," he said, "which you should be and I respect it, and I wasn't making a joke," and she said "I don't care either way." But stop thinking about it. Makes him feel even worse than he was. That what he said those times to set her off also made her scream hysterically at him a few times, even when the kids were in the house, and cry after. Long cries, where he'd want to comfort her but knew she'd say "Get away." The poor sweetheart. What she sometimes had to put up with with him. He had to put up with nothing. She was always great. Suddenly she's in his head crying and he says out loud "Please, dearest; please don't. Really, you should get out of there. It's doing us no good. You too upset and me too sad." She continues to cry, again without sounds, and then looks as if she's sobbing. "Oh, no," he says, "don't. What did I do?" He blinks hard and keeps blinking to make his mind go blank. When he opens his eyes wide, she's gone. Thinks: Maybe now's a good time to get up to pee. And then he also won't have to do it later when he's feeling sleepy in bed.

He gets out of bed, goes to the bathroom, pees, washes his hands. Feels his face. Should he shave now so he doesn't have to do it later? He thinks. No, too early. And he has to get out of that habit of getting so far ahead of himself: preparing tomorrow's salad today, and so on. He'd like to go to the kitchen for a glass of water from the sink's filter tap. His mouth's dry and he also hasn't drunk much water today. He'd read somewhere, but read elsewhere a while later where this notion was debunked—actually, both in the *Times*' Tuesday health section—that the average mature adult male should drink no less than eight glasses of water a day, but neither said what size glasses. He doesn't want to run into the kids, though. One of them might hear him going through the house and come out of her room and say "Anything wrong, Daddy?" or say through her door "That you, Daddy? Everything all right?" He turns on the bathroom light and washes with soap the sort of scummy bathroom glass and rinses it till it's clear. Plastic juice glass he took two of from Gwen's hospital room her last time there. Thought they'd be useful in a bathroom, so has one on the glass and toothbrush holder in the other bathroom too. Less chance than real glass of breaking on the floor or when it falls into the sink and a glass splinter, after he thought he picked or swept up all the pieces, later cutting his finger or foot. And the glass's height, when he thought of taking the first one, seemed perfect to fit under the medicine cabinet door when he opened it, and he was right— made it by an inch. He drinks a full glass of water, then another not as full to make up a little of what he didn't drink today, and goes back to bed, lies on his back, head centered again on two pillows, pulls the covers up to his neck and thinks: So what happened next? He bumped into her on the street the day after their phone conversation and she said "Hi, how are you, what a wonderful surprise. If you've time, think we can move up our coffee date now?" They met at the drugstore as planned. He remember anything they said when they met there? He pictures them talking. Mouths moving but no words he can make out. Sitting at the soda fountain counter. She's smiling, he's smiling. What a beautiful smile she has, he thinks he thought. Must have. She had, always had—photos of her around the house show this, every single one of them—a beautiful smile. Something to do with her lively eyes and shape of her face and high cheek bones and length of her mouth. As they talked, he might have thought Did she think he has a nice smile? People have said he does and his mother used to say he has a beautiful smile. Well, his mother. And he should have mentioned the certain way she opened her mouth when she smiled, which he can't right now put into words, and her bright white evenly aligned straight teeth, which also might have contributed to it, but with a bit of her upper gum exposed, something she tried to hide. "Smile" ends, he thinks, if he rearranged the letters, with a lie, not that that has anything to do with what he's thinking here. Just popped in. Has anyone ever thought it? He waited for her in front of the drugstore. Day was unusually mild for that time of the year. Temperature in the high forties, maybe mid-fifties. Pretty good for the first week of December. And because he was able to read comfortably outside, probably no wind. Walking weather, he thinks he thought. Also: he'll suggest it if she doesn't bring it up. He was a little nervous, wanted it to go well. From this date to the next one and so on. Just act natural, he might have thought. Don't act false, vain, boastful, pedantic, anything like that. Good conversation will come. She was definitely pretty, he thinks he thought, definitely pretty. He looked at her enough at the party to know. He isn't so bad-looking either, he might have thought, and up till about five or ten years ago he was considered good-looking, though that doesn't help him now. And he still has a good deal of his hair—around half of it, while his father was bald at thirty—and it hasn't started turning gray. And he's fairly tall for his age group and lean and well-built, just as she is—not so much tall; five-feet-four or -five; of average height—so they start out with that: one really good-looking woman and a not-bad-looking guy. There are of course other things and that's part of what this meeting's about: to find out. He knows she's intelligent and witty and clever, from what she said in their phone conversation. What did she say? Things, things; he forgets what in particular but knows he was impressed. And he hates the word chemistry when it's related to two people pairing, but he's got to say it: they'll see if there's any between them. There was for him, talking with her on the phone and some of what went on by the elevator and on the street—she certainly gave off something he was attracted to and liked—so what he'll really see is if it's still there. He got to the drugstore about five minutes to three and she got there about twenty minutes later. The wait was easy. He enjoyed the anxiety. Feelings he hadn't felt for a long time. Well, he had some of the same ones while he was thinking of calling her, but now she was on her way and would soon be here. His stomach; things rushing around or rolling over but doing something in his head. His chest, even. This could be it, he thinks he thought or something like it; this could be it. Pretty, bright, speaks well, teaches at Columbia, and so forth. Loves literature. Camus. And that she agreed to meet him. Must mean she isn't hitched. He was curious what she'd be wearing and if she'd be carrying a book and, if so, what it'd be. Probably something to do with her teaching, which she should be finishing soon. Maybe the last class of the semester is this week and then there's study period and exams if she gives them and term papers to read. And even if she'd be wearing a cap or hat and if her hair would be pinned up as it was at the party or in something like a ponytail or brushed straight back. Did she wear makeup? From what he recalls, not even lipstick or eye liner, which he likes: that she didn't. No embellishments. Natural face. Didn't know why he thought all this, but he thinks he did. He was very curious about her, that's all. At home before, he thought she might get to the drugstore earlier than she'd said and he didn't want her waiting for him, he can't remember why. Oh, yeah. Didn't want her getting impatient for him to come, which might put her in a bad mood, though she didn't seem that way. He thought she'd think: "He's not late; I'm early." He brought along the *Gulag* Two book he'd been reading, in case there'd be a long wait. And thought, standing in front of the drugstore, he thinks, why not let her see him reading a serious book when she came? Will she think it an affect? Easy appeal to a literary woman? No, because moment he sees her he'll snap the book shut, remembering the page he was on if he doesn't close it on his improvised bookmark. People have given him store-bought bookmarks—his mother especially—but he always loses them: they seem to drop out of the book, even ones that fasten on to the page. Anyways, scrap-paper ones he can write things on, such as a word from the book he's reading he wants to look up or something to do with the fiction he's currently writing or an idea for a new one. He could have brought a much smaller book, one that could fit into his jacket or back pants pocket. But he only reads one book at a time—taking a slim paperback to the party was different—and doesn't mind carrying a heavy one. He pictures himself reading, holding the book open with two hands, every now and then looking around for her. On the sidewalk both ways. Crossing Broadway. On the island in the middle of Broadway, waiting for the light to change or for there to be no cars coming so she can get across. Surely she remembered, he might have thought; she seemed like the last person to stand someone up. Now he was getting worried. She didn't think it worth it? But she'd have to know he'd call later, and then what would she say? He looked at his watch. Must have looked several times. What is he, nuts? It's not even ten after three. It's not even three-fifteen. She's two minutes late, if you could call it that and if his watch is accurate. She'll be here and if she isn't, she'll have a plausible excuse on the phone. "So what other day do you think we can make it?" he'd say. He pictures himself turning a page in the book and his eyes going to the top of the next one. "Hi," she said, or "Hello," startling him, smiling. He said "Hi" or "Hello" or something and no doubt smiled back and snapped the book shut without looking at the page number or moving the paper bookmark from wherever it was in the book to the new page he was on. She said something like "That must be quite engrossing, for you to get so lost in it." "Why," he might have said, "did you have to say 'hi' or 'hello' a few times before I looked up?" "Just once, but I did have to shake your shoulder to get your attention. Only kidding, Martin, although I didn't exactly sneak up on you." That he definitely remembers her saying. "What is it?—your hand's covering the title," and he held the book up. She's been wanting to read it, she said, "but starting—which one's this?…volume two—with the first volume. I've also been told if you read that one you don't have to read the others. That they become somewhat redundant, and volume three, even boring." "So far," he said, "Two's better than One—the personal stories more riveting and emotional. Reads more like fiction, in other words." "Still," she said, "I'll start with volume one and see if I want to read further." But because of the humanities courses she teaches, she said, she has little time for outside reading other than for books about what she's teaching. "Somehow I feel we've talked about this," and he said "I'm sorry; if we did, I forget," and she said "I could be wrong." He thinks that this differs from what he previously thought about taking the Solzhenitsyn to the Ansonia drugstore, but he forgets what that was. "One interesting thing," he remembers saying, "is that this is the first book I've read—actually, *Gulag* One—that I got a short story out of. For a while its working title was 'Gulag Four,' but then I didn't think I should keep it—I wanted the story to stand on its own." "May I ask a naïve question? 'Naïve' because one's probably not supposed to ask a writer this. But what's it about? Something to do with that period in Soviet history? From what you've said about your work—I think it was you—it doesn't seem you write historical fiction." By now they were probably in the drugstore. He pictures himself holding open the door for her and following her inside. "Is this okay with you," he remembers her saying, "sitting at the counter? If you want to sit at a table, we could always go elsewhere." "No, we're already here. And no other customers, so it's quiet and we can talk." At some point—outside or in; most likely in—he started telling her what his story was about. "A man, through some see-through ruse he should have seen through, is snared off a city street by two elderly women and held captive in an apartment—handcuffed, most of the time shackled and locked in a windowless cell of a room—for reasons never clear to him or adequately explained and which keep changing. I know. Sounds more Kafkaesque than Solzhenitsynian. But it becomes more Gulagy when his imprisonment, always just as they say they're about to release him, gets extended a few months or a year for made-up-at-the-moment reasons—he forgot to flush the toilet, for instance, or couldn't stop sneezing after they ordered him to. Anyway, that's something of what it's about, and they do eventually let him go." "Why did they keep him?" and he said "Same as why they abducted him: no reason. Just to play with him. Something like that, though nothing sexual." "What happens to the two women?" and he said "Nothing. They're sweet old ladies who couldn't possibly have done the harm to him he said. All the criminal evidence against them is gone and his cell's been turned into a library and now has windows and brilliant sunlight." "And you finished it?" and he said "Why? You don't think it's a good idea for a short story?" "I'd have to read it to determine that," and he said "It's out now and I'm keeping my fingers crossed—I could use a good sale." She asked where he sent it to and he told her and she said "You aim high. They must be tough to break in to," and he said "I've had two in the first one since '73 and about fifty rejections from the second since '64. Maybe stupid of me to keep sending to it, I guess, and maybe to the first one too, since they have a new editor there who doesn't seem to like my work. Calls it idiosyncratic. But long as I have a box of nine-by-twelve envelopes and stamps and a postage scale, why not? There are so few serious places that pay well, and you never know." "What if they both take it?" and he said "Chances of that happening on the same day—just the chance of either of them taking…well, I hate to sound shrewd and unscrupulous, but I'm a good liar when it comes to something like that, so it's a chance I'll take. Did I just say the wrong thing?" "You tell me. You know your business, but there is the moral question to consider. I was thinking of the editor's wasted reading efforts for the magazine you'd withdraw the story from if the other one took it. That is, if you didn't tell them you were multiply submitting it," and he said "I didn't." "I know I would never do it with an academic journal. I could lose my job and jeopardize any future teaching position I'd apply for and be forever blackballed by a journal that's probably pretty important in my field. You choose one to send to and stick with it till a yes or no decision's made." "You're right," he said. "I've thought of it before but it never hit me as hard as when you just said it. And I'm not kidding you on this—I must sound like I am, my choice of words and the rest of it, but I'm not—or saying it to get in good with you. I won't do it again, I think, or certainly not with a magazine that's previously published me and that I don't ever expect to place a story in again." When she didn't smile and in fact bit her bottom lip a little but didn't say anything to what he said: "No, you're really right; it's wrong. I won't do it from now on, period." "That's up to you." But she still didn't smile. He said "Please say you believe me and that you're not entirely dissatisfied with me." "Why would it matter?" and he said "It does. I don't want you to think I'm what I'm not." "All right, I'm not dissatisfied, as you said." "And you believe me?" and she said "I won't go that far," and smiled. He thinks this is how some of the conversation went that day. They talked about the woman who gave the party they met at. "She was the one who originally steered me to Camus." "And you can say if it wasn't for her I wouldn't be talking to you." Some of the books assigned to her humanities courses. "To me they're all still great to read, even the third or fourth time around in the space of two years. Of the six or so books she mentioned, he'd read two. "I won't lie to you that I read the others and then get them from the library and quickly read them so I won't get caught lying the next time we talk about them, if there is a next time and we do. I'm actually a bad liar in everything but my dealings with editors, and now that's stopped. Though don't tell me the other books your classes were assigned. I'm already chagrined, knowing you now know how unread I am. I mean, I'm always reading, and always have a book with me, and always serious literature, or what I think as such, but not the ancient classics." "Of the ones you haven't read, read *The Divine Comedy* first," she said. "Oh, I shouldn't be telling you what to read. Read what you like, but if you do read it, get what a couple of Dante scholars have told me is the best translation for each of them, and unlike what I said about the *Gulag* trio, try to read all three." He said "I loved the first two lines of the opening tercet of the first *terza rima* of *The Inferno*, if I got all that right. But then I could never get past—and I tried—the first ten pages, maybe the first five. One of the lesser translations, maybe? In other words, not my fault? I have read *Metamorphosis*, but the other one, several times." "They're spelled differently," she said, "but that's okay," and he said "Are they? Which one did I get right? Anyway, Homer, of course, both books twice and in the original Portuguese." "Boy, you sure keep them coming," and he said "You don't like it? I could always put in the plug," and she said "As I think I told you, I like jokes and punning and laughing and the like, and I know that's not the only side to you. Incidentally, my *Divine Comedy* pitch? Three in a row, or even in one season, no matter how good the translations, could be a bit much. They might be better read broken up, or the first two and then a break. It's not like Proust's *Remembrances*," and he said "Oh, God, I'm going to get in more trouble with you, but there's another one I couldn't stick with. At least they don't have to be translated," and she said "Do you reach French?" and he said "Not well," and she said "Then I'll have to think about your remark," and he thinks he said "Don't. It didn't come out at all the way I wanted it to, and if you think about it I'll just appear silly to you." She said "Don't worry. I'm so bad at being funny and making people laugh, I don't even try," and he said "I can't believe that," and she said "That's nice of you to say, but it's true." She was smiling and seemed pleased about something and looked over her teacup at him as she drank and he thinks it was around then he thought they might be hitting it off and that he no longer feels he's in over his head with her. Gwen later said—weeks, months; "It's even in my journal," which he's been unable to find; looked everywhere; not with the others, which he hasn't read any of but probably will one day; asked his

daughters and her two best friends if they knew where her '78 and '79
journals might be, the years he was most interested in because he still hadn't
moved in with her and he wanted to know what she thought of him and
their sex and being together and stuff like that early on but kept it a secret
in her journals; he even suspected, after her first stroke, she gave them to
one of the friends to hold so he wouldn't read them because there were some
things about him he wouldn't like—that she started thinking of him then in
a possible-mate-sort-of-way, and more than anything at the time because of
his sense of humor, honesty, way his mind works and that he makes her
laugh. He knows he likes her, he thought at the drugstore—a lot—and that
she's everything he thought she'd be, and pretty too and a nice body. Don't,
don't, don't, whatever you do, he thinks he told himself, seated on the stool
next to her, listening to her talk or watching her sip her tea, fuck it up. He
can do that and has with other women he was interested in, but he doesn't
think any of them came near to matching her. Maybe already too many
jokes, though don't get falsely serious. If this is working, do what you've
been doing; otherwise, you'll come out a fake. She asked if he does any kind
of work now but his writing. "What I'm saying," she said, "and maybe this
is too personal a question—" and he said "It isn't," and she said "How do
you know what I was going to ask?" and he said "It just seemed what was
coming next. I'm still living off an old small book advance and the hope of
a new one. Didn't I speak about this in our phone call?" and she said "If you
did, I'm sorry but that was a while ago and it isn't that I wasn't listening."
"Also the occasional sale of a short story to a literary magazine, which
doesn't amount to much but helps. My rent is fairly cheap and I'm on a
tight budget, which doesn't mean I can't spring for your tea and our English
muffin. Oh, yeah. I cashed in a few months ago a two-thousand-dollar
insurance policy my mother took out on me when I was ten. I could never
get her to explain why she did. I wasn't prematurely old or diagnosed with
a fatal illness and I didn't become the family breadwinner till I was twelve. I
remember salespeople of various kinds coming to the apartment and setting
their sample cases and paperwork on the dining table—Fuller Brush man,
Electrolux lady, someone for cosmetics, etcetera—so the insurance agent,
who came regularly, must have talked her into this unusual policy for such
a healthy kid. Thirty years later I benefitted from it. But if nothing comes
my way in a month or two, I'll have to go job hunting. This time for
something more lucrative than bookstore salesman, which I did last year for
six months till the store closed. Big Apple Books, on Columbus between
73rd and 74th?" and she shook her head. "I thought maybe you might have

gone there and it was my day off. Good literary bookshop. Just the owner and I, but she refused to sell bestsellers. Or something less mind-numbing than bartending, which I did the two years before last, and also less dangerous because of all the cigarette smoke blowing my way. You don't smoke, do you?" and she said no. "Neither do I and never have. You might think this is narrow-minded, and that I'm also limiting myself because of it, but I couldn't go out with a woman if I knew she smoked, even if she didn't smoke around me," and she said "I can understand. I don't like it either, but it's never stopped me from going out with a man or even getting serious with one. Cigars might, but I never dated a cigar smoker. My former husband took up the habit after we were married. He liked one about once a week, always in the evening when he was watching a sports event on TV, but you put up with such things in a marriage and he kept the door closed." "So you were married. How long?" and she said "Two years, though technically three, when we were both going for our Ph.D.s." "I never was. My guess, because of my age, you might have thought I had been," and she said "No, I didn't think of it." "Got close, in my early twenties. But the woman— she hated the word fiancée—even younger than I and already divorced, did the smart thing and disengaged us." "Any reason you want to give?" and he said "You?" and she said "Not really." "We were too compatible and having too much fun. I'm not kidding. It still mystifies me. We went to bed happy and had just got up and she said 'You're not going to like this, Martin…' She even denied we'd ever been engaged, though the wedding was tentatively scheduled to take place at her folks' house a short time before she called it and us off. I didn't argue with her—I was too angry and sad—and only have seen her once since, other than for the times I moved my things out of her apartment. That was at the Natural History Museum here, when she was with her two young sons and I was on my way to having a drink with a friend under the giant stuffed whale. We said hello and she introduced her kids to me and that was that. No, I saw her twice. The first time when I came back from Europe in '64. No, I actually saw her a number of times. But regarding a job, maybe you can advise me. Eventually, I'd like to teach fiction writing. Four books, we'll say, seventy to eighty published stories—maybe even a hundred. I've lost count…but that ought to qualify me for at least an adjunct position in some college in the area or a continuing ed program." She said "One would think so, and I wish I could help. I took creative writing courses in college, but I don't know how my instructors got their jobs. I guess you just apply. You do know that adjunct work at any level—even if you've been doing it at the same school for ten years and they've given you the grandiose title of Visiting Associate Professor—pays piss-poorly, as they say," and he might have said—he knows he concealed his surprise at her saying "piss-poorly"; she might not like him calling attention to it as if he thought she was above or beyond the expression or it didn't seem quite natural her using it and it in fact sounded a bit artificial—"It's a start, though. Which may, after only a year, give me the teaching credentials, plus my published work, and there'd likely be more by then, and availability and just that I've been writing without let-up for twenty years, for a contracted position someplace, or whatever it's called," and she said "Tenure track?" and he said "Yes, but there's another word I'm thinking of for an academic hiring agreement that isn't tenure track but could lead to it after a couple of years if they really like you and want to keep you on, but I'll take tenure if it's only that." She said "Non-adjunct positions are hard to get around here. Too many respected professional writers live in the city and academics with multiple degrees who can't get permanent English department appointments but can teach creative writing. But as you said, you never know. Though to be honest—and I'm not trying to discourage you— your age for an assistant professorship, which is what you'd ultimately want to go for, doesn't help you." "Too young?" and she said "That's right. If you had only started later," and he said "I tried, but the latest I could get my first book published was when I was forty. Hey, that was good." Did he mention that when they got to the counter but before they sat down she said "This okay for you?" Yes, he did. Meaning, sitting on stools at a counter rather than chairs at a table, which might make talk easier and not be so hard on their behinds? That too, sort of. And he wasn't just being accommodating. This he knows he didn't mention before. It was because they'd be sitting closer on stools and sharing the same small counter space between them and possibly even bumping knees. The last he just thought of now. He pictures them both smiling and maybe laughing at his "Hey, that was good" line. And continuing to talk and sip tea and drink coffee and share an English muffin and maybe be serious, though he thinks the talk about teaching writing and tenure was as serious as they got. No, there were other things. And the words he was looking for, he just now remembers, were "two-" or "three-year permanent appointments," something, he would have told her if he'd said them then, he'd of course take too because the salary for that position, he's heard, is just a little below an assistant professor's and the workload isn't more and you get the same university benefits, but he can't think what else they might have said. Books, probably. They were always talking about books, right from the beginning. Maybe even at the elevator when they first met. He thinks he went over this, but isn't sure. He was carrying one that night and he doesn't think it was hidden in a pocket and she must have seen it and could have asked about it. Books he read, she read, them both. But he doesn't think they ever read the same book at the same time, even for a while after one of her first two strokes, when she was reading—hearing?—*reading*—no, she used to say "listening to" books on tape. He knows some of that is familiar. Probably some more about her teaching and what she's planning to do once her two-year teaching fellowship ends. He knows he asked her where she just came from to get to the drugstore, since it's not in her neighborhood, "but I should mind my own business." She said "That's all right and this used to be my neighborhood. My parents still live on West 78th, but I didn't come from their place. The Esplanade Apartments on West End," and he said "For a therapy appointment? I'm sorry; I shouldn't have blurted that out," and she said "I don't mind," and yes, her therapist is there. How'd he know? He said "A couple of people I know go to therapists there, or did—maybe one of them to yours, but I don't know the therapists' names." "Mine's Lonya Silberblatt. She's also become a dear older friend and is an accomplished self-taught painter of Jewish themes, biblical to modern. I have a terrific one of hers of shtetl life. Do you know how to spell shtetl? It's a word that's always been a problem for me," and he said "Shtetl? Cousin of shtick; that's how I always get it," and he spelled them both. "I'm Jewish, you might have surmised," he thinks he said then—it was a good place for it—or maybe he said it on their next date, over beer at the bar they met at or the restaurant they finally settled on, but he knows he brought it up in one of their first two meetings. "Yes, I thought so," she said, if it was then the subject came up. "Not so much because of your looks or accent—definitely not your looks and if your speech has any identifiable characteristic, it's just a trace of New York. It's that you know how to spell shtetl and shtick, and your name." "Martin Samuels?" he said in an exaggerated Jewish accent. "So you think that's *Jewish*?" And then dropping the accent: "My guess is you're Jewish too. But what I should have said, rather than what I did, was 'And what religion are you?' Or 'religious persuasion' might be better, or better yet 'What religious belief or faith were you raised in or inculcated with and may have since rejected?' If even any of those are right. Also, definitely not your looks or the way you speak. There's no trace of Judaism or New York in your speech or any region, here or abroad, typifying you other than as a person with a very nice voice and very good diction. Also, only a little because of your name, but your surname only, since Gwendolyn's not your typical Jewish name.

You are, though, aren't you?" and she said "Why, is that a problem?" and he said "Quite the contrary. Both of us being Jewish?—but you are, right?" and she said yes. "I'd think that makes it easier talking about some things, like being Jewish. And no doubt more things to reference and connect with. Just as a Roman Catholic is probably better able to connect with another Roman Catholic—fish on Fridays, confessional stalls, ears tugged by angry nuns, and so on; blood and wafers, the pope. Does that make any sense, and I'm talking about two Roman Catholics who have both either stayed in the church or left, or do you think I'm being slightly ridiculous? Don't answer. I'm Jewish and I don't want to hear—no, that's enough." "What does being Jewish have to do with it?" and he said "Nothing; that's why I cut myself off." "Listen, Martin, I think we have to change the tone and direction of this conversation a little if we're to come to some understanding of one another," and he said "Uh-oh. I don't know if I'm going to like this," and she said "Please let me finish," and he said "Of course." He remembers having that sinking stomach feeling again—he was expecting the worst; she was about to kiss him off; something—and pictures them sitting on the stools and looking at each other but not smiling. "Long as we're on the subject of Jewishness," she said, "I want to explain something to you, but seriously, no jokes," and he said "Got you." So what she was about to say wasn't going to be as bad as he'd thought, he must have thought. And they did get serious, he thinks, more than he first remembered, at the drugstore or possibly one of the two places they went on their second date. Knows it wasn't in her apartment, which they went to for what she called a nightcap—"Like to come up for a nightcap?" she said in front of her building, after he walked her there from the restaurant. Nor the third time they got together, when he phoned her from the street around ten or eleven at night, after not calling for about a week, and asked if she wanted to meet at that bar again for a beer and she said "Now?" and he said "Too late?" and she said something like "If you don't think it'll take you too long, why don't you just come here?" She said that time "Though I'm by no means a religious or observant Jew—at most, I'll buy a box of egg matzos for Passover, though I'll continue to eat bread and rice over the holiday—my Jewish identity is very strong and important to me because of my family history. In fact, the reason I've never been seriously involved with Gentile men since high school, or really only one and not for long, is because I never felt they could understand my experience of growing up as the daughter of Holocaust survivors." "They lost a lot?" and she said "Everyone but my mother's father." "I'm sorry," he said, "so sorry. I can't imagine what it must have been like for them and no doubt still is," "Also, because I know how much it'd hurt them, I could never have married a Gentile, although if I had it couldn't have been as disastrous as the one I had to a Jewish man, but that's not my point. But have I made myself clear? I worry sometimes that I don't," and he said "Very much so. And I appreciate why you brought it up now," though at the time he wasn't sure why she did. He must not have caught everything she said, he thought. Her voice was soft and low, and it could have been that because of the seriousness of what she was saying, he didn't want to cut in and ask her to speak up. He knows he liked that she was telling him something so important and personal to her. She said "Last thing I wanted to do, with my Jewish identity talk, is put a damper on our little meeting" or "first real date. But when the matter of our religion came up and our feelings about it, I thought it too opportune a time for it not to come out. Now as for my name, Gwendolyn… it starts with the same initial as my paternal grandmother's, Guta—you know the Ashkenazic tradition regarding given names. But my parents thought—I was born almost two years to the day the war ended in Europe and conceived a month or two before they got here; not quite on the boat but almost—that they were protecting me in the future in case there was an American pogrom or even another Holocaust by giving me a Christian name." The serious Jewish stuff couldn't have been said at the drugstore or their walk after—too early—and certainly not the second time he was in her apartment. The first time there, maybe. More likely it took place on their first real date, as she always referred to it, and at the restaurant, which he thinks he remembers as being quiet because it was nearly empty, and not, because that's the way it always was when he was in it, the crowded noisy bar. She said "What about your family…when did they first get here?" and he said "All my grandparents came over in the major Jewish wave about fifty-five years before your parents did, if my calculations are correct. Settled on the Lower East Side like most of the others…worked there, kept kosher, had my parents, never learned much English, at least my father's folks, because they didn't have to—the perfect world: everybody spoke Yiddish. Not much really to tell. Nothing like what your parents went through, and all were buried before I was born." And she said "Oh, that must have been a very interesting time then and as hard for them as it was for my parents and grandfather, starting out new here," and he said "No, you're right. As for my origins? Conceived in an apartment in Flatbush, where my parents first lived, delivered in New York. Also an only child, although there was one before and after me, so that's how it turned out. But can I say something about my going out and so on with Gentile women?" and she said "That's an odd question and one never directed at me, but go ahead. Although I want you to know that some of my best women friends are Gentile," and he said "Did you just make that up?" and she nodded and smiled proudly and he said "Very funny," and she said "It wasn't that much, but thanks. To be fair, dozens must have coined it before me, but I never heard it and felt I had to say it. Again, too good an opportunity to pass up." "No, but I bet you were the first to say it, and I'll probably use the line several times in the future and then, after the laugh, give you credit for it. So, are you ready? A confession to parallel yours. Just about every woman I've gone with for any length of time since my last years in college has been Gentile, don't ask me why," and she said "Surely you know," and he said "I'm telling you, I don't. it wasn't that I had anything against women who were Jewish because they were so smart and tolerant and warm and kind, or that I was predisposed to women who weren't Jewish because they gave me a hard time and were *uber*-critical of me and after a while wanted to sleep with other guys. No, that didn't work. Gentile women just happened to be the ones I met, when I wasn't seeing anyone, and got involved with. Lived with three—only women I ever lived with—almost married one, wanted to marry a fourth but she was in too ugly and hopeless a marriage to want to give it up. Talk about disasters? Every last one of these relationships…involvements…love affairs…call them what you want: disasters, became one for me, and with a couple of them, though I should have known better, two and three times. She phones me; she drops by my apartment unexpectedly: she's waiting for me after work in my office building lobby: she sticks a note under my door, and I get sucked into it again. One was estranged—am I going on too much about this?" and she said "Finish." "Estranged from her mother, sister, brother, even her twelve-year-old daughter, not to say her ex-husband, all of whom I met and they seemed to be nice- and reasonable-enough people and her daughter a dear, so what act of idiocy made me think she wouldn't ultimately estrange herself from me? Did all of these not work out because I was Jewish, unreligious and nonobservant as I've been since my bar mitzvah? Maybe, or had to be, or more than a little. That's why I said before, which you might have taken umbrage with or simply didn't like, that I was glad you were Jewish. Fact is, for want of a better word this moment— maybe because I am so thrilled—I'm thrilled. I'm sitting and talking with a Jewish woman and having one heck of a good time and hope she is too. So that's what I wanted to say. 'Parallel,' I don't know, but nothing much, right?" and she said "I won't comment." "You can if you want." And she said "I don't want. Except to say that this is all quite interesting. I've never before been complimented just for being Jewish, and it's true, I don't think I like it." He said "While I was saying it I knew I was being excessive and I apologize for making you feel uncomfortable and hope it doesn't make you want to run out of here without me." And she said "Little chance of that. I don't go in for dramatics. But I am glad you're not religious. Though being a wee bit observant, like sitting down for the Passover Seder the first night and going through the ceremony quickly is all right, but I have a real hard time with yeshiva boys." He said "I was bar mitzvahed in an Orthodox synagogue—W.S.I.S., on West 76th, just a block from where we lived—and tutored for it by rabbinical students who wore tsitsis and peyes. Does that count against me?" and she said "Peyes, I know, but tsitsis?" and he told her. "I also come from a family where my father, on both nights, used to do the entire ceremony a lot less than quickly, but I used to love the four small glasses they allowed me of sweet wine." "I thought it was only three," she said, and he said "Not if you complete that part of the ceremony that's supposed to take place after the dinner. Anyway, I thought I'd get it all out in the open now," and she said "I think you're safe." How did they end up with an English muffin? The coffee and tea is easy. The counterman came over—they'd just sat down; he'd taken off his jacket and scarf and put them on the stool next to him; she kept her coat on, maybe because she was cold, he thought; as for remembering he had a scarf: he always wore one from around November first on—and asked what they would have, they said one coffee and one tea, and the man said "Anything to go with it?" It seemed from his expression and way he said it that if they were going to take up two stools for themselves and one for his clothes, even though there were no other customers at the counter, they should have more than a coffee and tea, and he said to her "Like to have a sandwich or bowl or cup of soup if they have them, or a pastry?" and she said "I'm not hungry, thanks," and he said "How about an English muffin?" and she seemed to pick up by the way he glanced at the counterman and then right back at her that they should have more than what they ordered, and she said "That'd be okay, if you'll split it with me," and he said "You like it toasted well done or just regular?" and she said "Since you'll be eating most of it, you choose," and he said to the man "Also one fairly well toasted English muffin, please. Butter on the side and…jam or jelly do you like?" he asked her and the man said "We only have jelly, those little packets," and he said "Honey would be good too," and she said to the man "I'll take the jelly, thanks." They ate and drank. She finished her half of the muffin and said "That was good, toasted that way." He had a second coffee, asked her if she wanted some more tea and she said

"One cup's enough for me if it's not herbal. I should have asked." "You can have an herbal tea if you want," he said, and she said "No, I'm fine." He later regretted the second coffee. When they were getting ready to leave he knew he'd have to pee soon because of the coffee and asked the counterman if there was a men's room here. The man said "Only for store personnel, but you can use the one off the Ansonia lobby," and directed him to the door at the back of the drugstore to get there. He knows he asked her sometime in the store "Are you cold?" and she said "Not at all; why?" and he said "I really meant, would you be cold if you didn't have your coat on?" and she said "When I'm in a place like this and there's no coat hook or rack, I usually like to leave it on. It's big and bulky and if I fold it up and put it on a stool as you did with yours, it would only fall off." He thinks he forgot to mention that when he first got to the drugstore and saw she wasn't waiting outside— he thought she might have got there early—he went inside to see if she was there. There was no one at the counter but the man behind it, reading a tabloid, probably the *Post*, since it was the afternoon. Only one customer in the store, in the greeting-card section, reading a card she was holding. On his way out to wait for her on the sidewalk, he said to the counterman—the counter went right up to the door—"Looking for someone. She's not here yet. I was actually supposed to meet her outside if it wasn't too cold. We'll be back," and the man said "That's all right," or something like that. Eight to ten stools, he thinks, and he also thinks the leather of the one he sat on, or fake leather, had a slit in it. "Maybe it is too hot with a coat on," she said, and took it off, folded it in two and got up, put it on her stool and sat on it. "No, this is uncomfortable," she said about a minute later, and put the coat back on. "I'll hold it for you, if you want," he said, and she said "Thanks, but this way is better, and I don't want to go through getting off the stool and taking it off again." During that time—when she was taking her coat off, folding it up and getting it on the stool and putting it back on her—he had several chances to look at her chest without her seeing him. It seems full, he thought. Not the most important thing, but he was curious. When they met for a beer on their next date and while she was hanging up her coat on the hook near their table before she sat down opposite him, he looked at her chest again and also caught a glimpse of it later: when she closed her eyes and sipped her beer and smiled. Her chest didn't seem as full as it did in the drugstore, maybe because she was wearing a dark-green loose-fitting Shetland sweater in the bar, while only a long-sleeved T-shirt, he'll call it, or maybe "polo shirt" because of the three buttons at the top, in the drugstore. When she turned to the right for something on the counter in the drugstore, he also got a good look at her nose. It wasn't large, so why'd he think it was? Even if it was, what of it? That alone would keep him from being interested in her? She's very pretty, he thought in the drugstore. Beautiful, he could say, and such a spiritual and intelligent face. Beautiful neck too; graceful. And that lovely soft voice. He could listen to it and listen to it and listen to it. He'd love to hear that voice in the dark in bed. A beautiful smile. Not one fake or unflattering expression. Beautiful lips and cheeks and teeth. And her hair: shiny and tidy and clean-looking, and sort of a reddish blond. He'd never seen eyes like hers. What color are they? he thought in the drugstore. Not entirely green, for they have yellow and blue in them, but a healthy yellow, if that makes any sense, and he thinks he saw gray. He thought of asking her in the drugstore what color would she say her eyes were, but too soon to ask and it might not be a question she'd like. He did ask her at the bar or more likely in the restaurant they went to after or even more likely on the sofa in her apartment after one of their first kisses and her face was still close to his but far enough away for him to stare at her eyes and the room was well lit. She said "First of all, please stop staring at me," and he did. "As to an answer, I'm going to be irritatingly capricious and vague. They're multi-changeable-colored. I've rarely seen this, but people tell me. They change with whatever light they're in. Daylight, sunlight, full-moon light, artificial light, fireplace light, flashlight, but they never turn red, except when I break a blood vessel there, and but they don't glow in the dark. As you can see, I don't like talking about them." "I'm sorry," and she said "Don't be; I didn't mean it as a rebuke. I just don't like talking about myself, if you understand me," and he said "Oh, I do. As for me, my eyes are an ordinary brown, no flecks of anything in them, not even hazel. You know, I'm not sure what color hazel actually is. Light brown?" and she said "That or yellowish brown, like the nut." "So it is like me. Only kidding. Anything for a laugh at my own expense, though honestly, I don't dislike myself." At the drugstore her hair was done up, if that's the expression, in a ponytail. At the bar it was parted in the middle and hung over the sides of her face and dropped a little on her shoulders. At the restaurant— she must have changed it in the ladies' room there or the one in the bar—it hung freely down her back. At the party her hair was bunched or knotted up in back but above her neck. He seems to remember a long white stick like an ivory chopstick through the bunched- or knotted-up clump, but maybe not. Probably, which she usually used when she had her hair like that, just a clip. At the drugstore she wore dark kneesocks that were pulled up under her skirt to her thighs. At the bar she wore pants. At the party she wore a skirt that came halfway down her calves and in her apartment the second time she wore the same pants, so he never got to look at any part of her legs uncovered, even when she crossed them for a short time on the stool, till they were in bed. They'd been necking in the living room awhile, went to the bedroom, sat on the bed and he said, holding her hands, "Funny question, but do you want to be undressed or should we both take off our own clothes? And she said "Undressed." He took off her slippers and socks and then her blouse and bra. They kissed during all this, little ones, big ones, and after he had her bra off he kissed her breasts and then started unfastening or unbuttoning or unzipping or whatever he did to start taking off her pants. "I'll do the rest," she said, and went into the bathroom, which was in the little hall between the bedroom and living room. He thinks he was in bed but without the covers over him when she got back, and she took off her bathrobe and that was the first time he saw her legs. Or he waited for her with all his clothes on except his shoes and socks, which he stuffed into his shoes, till she came back, and then put his shoes under the bed, went into the bathroom, took off the rest of his clothes, washed up and came out nude carrying his folded-up clothes and put them somewhere in the bedroom. The lamps on both sides of the bed were on. She was in bed under the covers, no top on, he could see, so he supposed no bottom on either or just underpants. She pulled the covers back to invite him in and that was when he first saw her legs. They were chunky and sturdy and strapping and strong, and the thighs looked soft. He loved legs like this, he might have thought. He sat beside her on the bed, leaned over her and closed his eyes and kissed the top of her thighs and then the inside of one, and she said "Not yet," and held her arms out for him. He lay beside her and she pulled the covers up over them. It was late, probably past twelve, and there was little heat on in the apartment and the room was cold. Anyway, one of those, he thinks the second, when he first saw her legs. Till they made love again when they awoke the next morning, he still hadn't seen her backside. They'd slept on their backs or with her pressed into him from behind. He'd felt it in the dark, though, his hand twisted around her or squeezed underneath her, and from those feels he knew it was full. Also, from what he'd earlier made out from quick looks at it under her coat and skirt and pants and bathrobe, he knew it had some shape to it, wasn't flat or small, which he was glad of. He liked a backside that bulged and he could clutch. She also seemed to be as gentle as any woman he'd gone with, he thought at one of those places: drugstore, bar, restaurant, first two times in her apartment, even while walking with her outside on those dates. A few years ago—before

her first stroke—he said to her—she was at the dining-room table correcting papers while eating a lunch she'd made, he'd come into the room from
their bedroom where he was working then—"Look what I found I wrote
about you on the inside of my thesaurus book cover," and he read to her—
he's memorized it since, he's read it so many times, coming upon it accidentally or opening the book on purpose: "'May 6th, 1999. I didn't choose you
for your beauty and sexuality, but more for your intelligence, kindness and
gentility.'" The rest of the conversation went something like this: "Did you
mean to say 'gentleness' instead of 'gentility'?" and he said "I wrote it as
'gentility,' but I meant both." "Very nice," she said, "but how do you know
it's about me? Does it say so?" "No, but who else could it be? Nineteen
ninety-nine. Twenty years after we met, and she said "You could have been
thinking of one of your old flames. You've told me they were all intelligent
and sexy and pretty and a couple of them were quite beautiful and sweet."
And he said "Sweet, I don't know. They were intelligent, in varying degrees,
but none as intelligent and learned as you. And sexy, some more than
others, but again, nothing compared to you, and I'm not just saying that.
But they were all, for the most part, or turned out to be, awful, or just to
me. You're the only one who's unfailingly been gentle and kind, and for all
our years together, I want to tell you, so for sure since May, 1999. I know
you can't say the same about me of the men you've known, in gentleness,
intelligence, refinement, maybe sexiness, and the rest of it, but that's okay
so long as I take the lead in artistry. We'll pass the last off as a joke, though
there's a little seriousness to it. What's more, you're the only women I've
loved and hankered for and everything else like that since I met you, or a
week or two after. And by far and more than that the one I've loved the most
of all the women I've known, and you don't have to respond to that with
some fanciful something about my own desirability and so on," and she said
"Okay, I won't. What you said, of course, is very nice to hear, and I believe
you," and indicated with her finger and then pointing to her lips that he
should come closer because she wanted to kiss him, and he lowered his head
to hers and they kissed. Then she said "I made enough chicken salad for
both of us, if you want some," and he said "Yeah, I'd love to sit down with
you, if I won't be disturbing your work." "Want something else to eat?" he
asked at the drugstore, when the counterman took their knife and plate,
and she said "Little I ate, I'm full." "Then like to walk it off a little? It's not
bad out, though I'll have to find a men's room first," and she said "That'd be
nice. We could head uptown, and then I'll catch a bus home along the way."
She took the check, he just now remembers, when the counterman held it

out to him. He said "No, please, let me," and reached for the check in her hand, and she said "I'd like to take care of it. It isn't often a check for two is so small that I can afford to pick it up." "Fine, if you let me pay for dinner out sometime, if we ever have one," and she said "We'll see." She paid up, he went to the men's room, they went outside. She left a generous tip on the counter, he noticed, much more than he would have. Did he mention that the opening in his coffee mug handle was so small that he could barely fit the tip of his forefinger through it? For some reason this intrigued him, or he thought it might make for funny conversation, so he brought it up with her just after the counterman poured him a refill. "Why didn't they make the opening larger? We can't blame everything on the Chinese. It was probably made there but the design for it could have been done here. Your finger could fit through it but mine almost got stuck. How would it look, my walking around with a coffee mug I couldn't get off my finger? Seriously, though, it'd also seem the mug would be easier to spill, with so little handle to hold on to. That could result in the drinker burning himself, especially when you get it hot and black, like I do," and she said "I haven't a clue." Outside, she said "Should we head up Broadway, Riverside Drive or the park? Not West End. It's the dullest avenue in New York. All bricks and stunted trees and awnings with pigeon droppings on them and sixteen-story apartment buildings on both sides of the street." He said "Any of the ones you said would do. Though the park might be a bit dangerous this time of the year. Fewer pedestrians, and it'll be getting dark soon," and she said "It's safe till the low nineties, but okay. Riverside Drive, on the park side. It has the prettiest views and I can get a number five bus on it, which stops in front of my building." "That's right," he said, "you live on the Drive. Do you see the river from your apartment, or have I asked that?" and she said "Most of it, like now, when the trees aren't leafy." "So you probably see stars and sunsets and barges and all sorts of lights on the river," and she said "All that plus enormous apartment buildings on the Palisades that make the ones on West End look small, and the sunrise reflections off their windows. What do you see from your place?" and he said "Oh, I have a huge terrace in the rear, so I get to see lots of other terraces and backyards and the backs of buildings, especially the one at the corner of Columbus and 75th—La Rochelle, it's called, though nobody calls it anything but its number, fifty-seven. Also, some sunsets, though not so far when the sun sinks into New Jersey and drowns, like it probably does from your window. Mine, I just see disappearing behind La Rochelle, and maybe twenty minutes later some nice colors in the sky." He pictures her looking pleased, talking to him as they walked. He's never been able to describe that look. Tried, verbally and on paper. But he knew by it when she really liked something. Maybe "pleased" or "satisfied" or "self-satisfied" is all it is. He would love to hold her as they walked, he thought. Hold her hand, he meant. Then to put his arm around her shoulders and draw her to him. Then stop to kiss. Nobody was around. Even if someone was. What would she do if he tried to kiss her? he thought as they walked. Don't try. Whatever you do, he thought, don't. But if he did try and she complied? And he's talking about a deep kiss, or something like it: eyes closed, lips pressed. That would be it. He'd be so happy. "Kiss me," he says in bed, in the dark, on his back, covers up to his neck, and shuts his eyes and puts his lips out for her. He actually once imagined—it wasn't too long ago—he felt something wet and soft on his lips when he did it. He knows it's crazy but at the moment he believed it and has tried the same thing a couple of times since. Anyway, he was really getting to like this gal, he thought as they walked. Or maybe he thought all that when he walked her to her building from the restaurant on their second date. Or maybe he didn't think it there, either, and is only thinking it now in bed. He doesn't think so but it's a possibility. He remembers, he forgets, he thinks something happened that didn't, he gets things mixed up. It was so long ago. Twenty-oh-six, end of seventy-eight. She mentioned her age—something about how it took her a few years longer to get her Ph.D. than it does most candidates in her field, and gave the reasons for it—marriage, travel, working as a guide in a USIA exhibit in Belgium and France for six months, divorce, getting over it—and he got concerned about their eleven-year age difference, though for eleven days a year, he later learned, it was ten. Again: they talked about the woman who gave the party they met at. He said "It was very nice of her to invite me to such an…well, I was going to say 'elegant,' but to some other word gathering," and she said "It was a pretty distinguished group of people, but why are you so surprised you were invited? I'm sure she liked you, and that you were a writer—she loves writers. And she might even have been a little taken with you—she also likes younger men. What she might not like is that we met after the party, even for coffee. Have you spoken to her since?" and he said no. "I don't like asking this, but could you tell me if there was anything between you two, just in case I need to know what to be prepared for with her?" and he said "I think I told you. We shared the same bathroom at Yaddo, but at different times, and had some lively breakfast conversation. So lively that people at the silent table whispered to us if we could tone it down. As for Pati being even a little taken with me—you said it, I didn't—I would have heard from her sooner, wouldn't you think? Because from what I've seen, she doesn't hold back," and she said "True." Talked about a well-known Russian poet, now American, who was there. "He and I were the only men without ties," he said, "though he did wear a dress shirt and crisply pressed slacks." "I had a long talk with him," she said. "He's a brilliant poet and essayist—he supposedly came close to getting a Nobel soon after he emigrated here—and he gave me his card," and he said "What's that mean…he has eyes for you?" and she said "It's possible." "Have you heard from him?" and she said "I think he wants me to call him. But he was a bit filled with himself. And he smokes too much and still has a wife in the Soviet Union and, according to Pati, a girlfriend or two here." "So you spoke to her about him?" and she said "No, she spoke to me about him. You seem to be cross-examining me, Martin," and he said "Well, I want to know what I'm up against. Poets always get the girls," and she said "That's utter nonsense." "Then the girls always get the poets," and she said "Nonsense too." "I'm sorry. Are we still friends?" and she said "We haven't known each other long enough to be friends." "Then putative friends," and she said "You'll have to translate for me." "I think I meant it as 'potential,' and got the word wrong," and she said "Don't let it bother you." About a well-known literary and cultural critic and his psychoanalyst wife. She'd first met the woman at one of Pati's parties. "Or possibly it was at some PEN event I was taken to. We've had coffee several times. I like her very much. She's exceptionally intelligent and articulate and knows as much about literature as her husband—more about foreign literature—and has a greater love for it. With him, it's often his business. No, that's too harsh. Erase that. Did you get to speak to them?" and he said "Wanted to, but I'm intrinsically shy, so didn't know how." "You could have asked Pati," and he said "I also didn't want to intrude." And lots of other writers. "Again, I didn't speak to many people," he said. "Mostly just noshed, sipped and watched, though that wasn't what I wanted. In fact, I talked almost to no one at any length—writer or otherwise. I was also too busy following you around, looking for an opportunity to introduce myself. Boy, were you popular. But there was a young novelist and his young short-story writer wife." "I know them," she said. "I was his sister's counselor at summer sleepaway camp. He and I became friends when we were both in graduate school at Columbia, he in writing. A bright talented couple." He said he's never heard of either of them and she said "They're just starting out. Although each had a story in *The New Yorker* the past year, his a novel excerpt made to read like a short story," and he said "I don't get the magazine. But good for them. That should get them on their way. I've been

rejected by that magazine so many times, I don't send to it anymore."
"Never give up. That's what Aiden, the novelist, told me," and he said "Nah,
I've got ten years on them, so I know when I'm licked." An artist who does
covers and other work for *The New Yorker*. "His stuff, of course, everybody
knows from posters and other reproductions made of it," he said. "He can
be a bit slick and self-imitative, but I really have no opinion. Pati, I saw, has
an original drawing of his in her bedroom, expensively framed and affec-
tionately inscribed with what I guess is his nickname, Izzie," and she said
"That's what he's called by his friends—from Isador, his middle name," and
he said "Makes sense, then. I didn't know his first two names, just their
initials." A Hungarian novelist and freedom rights activist in his own country, who probably will get a Nobel, she said, "for literature or peace." "Now
him I've read," he said, "—all two translations. He's almost the rarity of
rarities today, a great fiction writer, though there's every now and then
something not quite right in his writing or missing. But more times than
not he's powerful and original and hits all the buttons." "So, other than for
your qualifications about him, we finally agree on someone," and he said "It
could be because he's the only writer mentioned from the party so far whom
we've both read, other than for our Russian poet and American literary
critic, and those guys I've only read a little of—I also don't get *The New York
Review of Books*. Should I be ashamed?" "Far be it from me," she said,
"although it could never hurt to read more of them." "All in all, it was quite
a group," he said. "I've never been to a party with so many well-known
people in the arts and related professions in one room. Well, if I'm counting
right, four rooms." He brought up again the rugby shirt he wore to the
party. "At least it had long sleeves. My pants were all right: corduroys, not
jeans. But just so you know: I would've worn a different shirt. Not a dress
shirt. I don't have one, or the one I own is threadbare and I don't know why
I keep it. But a more dressy kind of shirt, one with buttons all the way down
the front and one solid color—navy blue—and not stripes. Would have
clashed a little with the beige pants, but it still would have been a better
choice. I don't know what I was saving it for. As I think I told you, I thought
it was going to be a small informal gathering." "You did tell me," she said.
"People from Yaddo this summer," and he said "I don't know how I got that
impression." He thinks she said "Your shirt was fine, or let's say I only
thought about it once at the party. Or did I? And out of all the men there—
all of them in jackets and most in ties—you're the one I'm walking with
now and just had coffee and tea and an English muffin with" or "dinner
with and before that a beer"—she actually had a Guinness Stout that came

in a bottle and which she drank from a special glass that either collected or dissipated the foam on top. He forgets what the glass, which had the Guinness logo on it, was supposed to do. He pictures her smiling at him as they walked and talked. He liked what she last said, if what she said about the English muffin was the last thing she said, and other things she said about them before. Made him think things were going pretty well between them. That she might be agreeable to seeing him again. For sure he's going to ask her if she'd like to meet again, he thought, or else say, when they were about to part, "I'll call." And maybe she'll eventually invite him up to her apartment for coffee or tea, or just to see it, or even for dinner. Or say something like "We should go out for dinner sometime," if this wasn't their first date and they weren't walking to her apartment building after having dinner in a restaurant. Did they split the check? He thinks they did. Or he paid and she took care of the tip. He now thinks that's how it went. And the dinners out after that? —not that they ate out that much early on. They were both short of money for a while and she liked cooking at home and trying out certain French and Italian dishes on him. Their next dinner out he thinks she paid and he took care of the tip. Then he paid and she took care of the tip, and so on. Or maybe he took care of both around two out of every three times. He seems to remember it that way and it sounds more realistic. Till he got the teaching job in Baltimore and from then on he paid the dinner check and tip. Even if it was a very expensive restaurant? He doesn't think they went to one till they were engaged. In fact, the first time they went to one together was to celebrate their engagement, and he took care of the check and tip. No, the first was when he sold his fourth book. Lunches, he remembers taking care of from the beginning, check and tip, even if he was only having coffee and she was having a complete meal. So what else could they have talked about during their walk from the drugstore? Her family a little, his. The Bronx, where she lived till she was around fourteen. Manhattan, now back on the same block he lived on till he was twenty-two, other than for the first nine months of his life in Brooklyn before his family moved. He once told her "I even know the name and number of the apartment building on Ocean Avenue across from—I have no memory of it, of course—Prospect Park. Two thirty-nine, and it was called Patricia Court, or maybe it was 'Patrician.' I thought I knew it. I'll have to ask my mother and hope she remembers. I know she told me our apartment was on the first floor in back and that there was a long awning in front above the entire entryway, with the building's name and number on it." Before her family moved to 78th Street, they lived on Knox Place near Mosholu Parkway, second to last subway stop on the D line, she said. "So many X's in my life," she once said and wrote something almost identical to it, but without the part about sex, that he found on a piece of paper sticking out of a book on her night table. What actually happened is that a short time after she told him about the X's, he got curious about the book because of its title—*Forgotten Yiddish*—opened it, saw she'd written on the paper being used as a bookmark, he supposed, and read it. "The Bronx, Knox Place, where I lived in it: Ruxton, where we live now; Aix-en-Provence, where I did so much of my doctoral research; my ex, Rex, and lots of sexy sex with you." He said, "Was 'Rex' Richard's nickname?" and she said "No, Ricky was. But it's what I called him when he was acting imperiously to me, which he did a lot of the last year of our marriage." She said, if this was their first date, she thinks she better be getting her bus, as she has a good deal of class work to do at home. They were outside for more than an hour. Walked very slowly as they talked. Got to 86th Street or somewhere around there, sat on a bench facing the river and park for about fifteen minutes. The bench was his idea and he probably asked her if it was too cold for her to sit and she might have said something like "Is it too cold for you? It isn't for me." He seems to remember a huge tanker making its way up the river. If he's right, then they probably talked about it because it was so unusual and the ship was so big. He knows it happened once during one of their walks along the park side of the Drive. The car traffic going north—it was past five o'clock by now—was probably heavy as it always was on weekdays around that time and for the next hour or more—drivers trying to avoid the even heavier traffic going north on the West Side Highway—and they might have talked about that too. How, when they started their walk, there was hardly any traffic going either way, the Drive was relatively quiet and the air fresher, with so little car fumes, and it was still light out. Shortly before they got up from the bench, he thinks they stared in front of themselves awhile and then looked at each other and smiled. That's what he pictures. He thinks it was around then when she said she better be getting her bus. He waited with her at the bus stop. She said he didn't have to, she'd be all right, and he said "Are you kidding? I'm not leaving you alone here; I don't care how long it takes the bus to come." She said "The schedule"—there was one on the bus stop pole—"says…let's see…they're supposed to come every seven minutes at this hour, but you know New York." He said "We should do this again—meet, one of these next few nights. But maybe for a glass of beer or wine this time, and early around five or six, if you like," and she said "That'd be fine with me. Why don't you call me and I'll see what my calendar's like. I know this weekend I'm busy. My parents, one night; a friend, the other. And Sunday I prepare for my class on Monday…a lot of reading, which I like to do the previous night." "Not even for just a wee small drink for half an hour on Sunday? I'll come up to your neighborhood, make it as convenient as possible for you," and she said "It wouldn't be worth the bother to you for just a half-hour, and besides, I have to stay focused." "How about if I call later tonight to see what you're doing next week," and she said "Best, once I get home, I don't think of anything but my work—there's that much. Being relatively new at teaching my own course, you can say I like coming to class overprepared." "But you do want to meet again, though, right? I mean if you don't, that's okay too," and she said "I thought I said so; yes. It was fun, this afternoon," and he said "I'd like to say 'likewise,' but that'd sound corny and it's not something I'd ever say. Tell me, what am I saying? God, this is going badly, isn't it? I must seem like a complete schlemiel to you," and she said "Why do you say that? There's my bus," he thinks she said around then, and he thought it had ended badly and now he doesn't know if she will agree to see him when he calls. He better give it a few days before he does call. Monday, to show he was in no rush. Oh, damn; strategies, he thought. He was feeling so good, so why couldn't he have shut up at the end when he should have? But maybe it's not that bad. What's so wrong in showing you're interested, so long as you don't show you're too interested too early on and maybe scare her off? More strategy, and what he thought after her bus left. He thinks it was the number five. No, he knows. They kept her apartment on Riverside Drive, till three years ago. When they were evicted because New York wasn't their permanent address and they lived in the apartment for less than six months a year. Some regulation for rent-stabilized apartments, which lots of landlords don't know about or take advantage of, but theirs did. With them out, he could fix the place up: new kitchen appliances and cabinets and toilet and paint job and sanding the floors and maybe new energy-saving windows—and get four times the rent they were paying and, under the table, because the apartment had such a great view, ten to twenty thousand in key money too. That's what they'd heard. Gwen was very upset over it. She loved New York and her father still lived there at the time, while his own mother had died six years before and he didn't much care for the City anymore. Too hectic and noisy and smelly and other things. He doesn't know when he'll next get there, even for just a day or two. They could have fought the eviction. She wanted to. The rent was affordable on their two salaries and she'd had the apartment since a few months before they met, and for about five years before that had lived in a smaller apartment in the back of the building with her first husband and then alone. But they were told by people who knew about things like this that they'd lose—the Real Estate Board or Commission or whatever it is almost always sides with the landlord—and they'd have to pay all court costs and about two thousand dollars in lawyer fees, theirs and the landlord's, if not more. He's repeating himself; he knows. The bus stopped. When he turned around he saw there was also now an elderly couple waiting for it, the man with a walker—he doesn't know how he hadn't heard the walker clanking on the sidewalk as the couple approached the bus stop—and the right front of the bus had to be lowered. He pictures putting out his hand and saying "So I'll see ya; this was fun," and she smiling and shaking his hand and saying goodbye and getting on the bus after the couple and standing in the aisle near the front—the bus was packed; he wonders if anyone gave up his seat to the elderly man; he knows he would have, or to the woman if someone had already given up his seat to the man—and taking a book out of her bag and waving it at him while with her other hand holding the pole above her head, as the bus pulled away. He waving back. After that, just about whenever he walked her to the subway or a bus stop, he'd kiss her goodbye and then blow a kiss to her as she went through the turnstile—he usually walked downstairs with her, didn't just leave her at the top—or her bus pulled away, and she'd always smile at him, as she didn't that first time on the bus, and often wave. "Unlike you, I'm not naturally demonstrative that way," she said once when he asked her "How come you never blow a kiss back to me? Not important, so long as you kiss me just before we go our separate ways," but she told him. And then said "If you really want me to do it every time we separate, I will," and he said "It's up to you. I like it but wouldn't want you to do anything that's unnatural for you," and she continued not doing it. This was after they first slept together and maybe a few days after that said they loved each other. No, it took more time. He remembers it as being morning, around seven or eight, her bedroom was very cold, he got another blanket out of the linen closet and spread it out over the bed, got back in bed with her and she opened her eyes, must have just got awake, and said "What's all the fuss about so early?" and he said "Keeping you warm, my dovey. You know I love you," and she said "And I love you," and they kissed. At least he thinks that was the first time they said it. He really now doesn't know. He's never been able to get that straight and when he asked her he thinks she said she didn't know. And he now thinks she must have thought that blowing kisses was silly but she didn't want to hurt his feelings by saying so. So what did he do after her bus left? Might have watched it disappear up Riverside Drive and, after a while, just its interior lights, and thought something like "She's on it," and pictured her standing and reading and grabbing the pole above her or the handle on the seat next to her when the bus was coming to a stop. Or thought again how lovely and smart and perfect for him she is, and what luck he's getting to know her. Luck that he'd gone to Yaddo when he did and his room and Pati's were next to each other and they became friends. And again, that business about don't screw it up. And that things hadn't gone as badly as he first thought they had. He can be clumsy in what he says sometimes, but she didn't seem like someone who'd make something of it. She must see by now he's a little awkward around her but having a good time. The conversation was good and that's what'd seem important to her, he'd think. Have they started seeing each other? he thinks he thought. Anyway, he could have. In a way, yes, but so small a way that it's too early to be certain of even that yet. There is going to be another date, that he's almost sure of. And if there's one or two after that, he thinks he's in. Next one could be for dinner or lunch or just drinks somewhere, but not for another coffee and tea unless she says that's what she'd prefer it to be. Actually, doesn't matter to him what it is, he might have thought, so long as they meet. He probably walked down Broadway, could have stopped in at Fairway for a few things, maybe also the liquor store on Columbus near his block for a bottle of vodka or the fancy wine shop on 72nd for a bottle of wine, and went home. It's possible he wrote some more and read for a while and then made himself a cheese sandwich, which he used to do around seven or eight just about every other night: rye toast or toasted rye bagel, tomato slices, lettuce, Dijon mustard, preferably an imported Swiss or French-like Swiss cheese and, if he wasn't going to meet anybody that evening, thin slice of what used to be called Bermuda onion. Called his friend Manny later on and said something like "Want to meet for a beer? I want to tell you about this woman I met at a party last week and saw for coffee today and whom I'll probably see again and I think I could really get to like." Knows he called Manny that night because Manny reminded him of it several times, even at his wedding. "Who's the first person you had to speak to about the future bride? Me. I take great pride in that and knew from the start you were lost." They met at Ruppert's. Doesn't know what it's called today. Something, he thinks, with "American" and "Café" in it, but that name could also have been changed since he last saw it. Or maybe it was still "O'Neal Bros." when Manny and he met there that night. Knows it still wasn't Kelly's Bar & Grill, which it had been for about fifty years when they first started going to it in '68. They sat or stood at the bar. The television above the bar was on, as it always seemed to be—usually, around this time and month, to a hockey or basketball game. Manny said "So who's this chickie you're so knocked over by that you had to drag me out into the cold to talk about her?" and he said "I didn't say I was knocked over. And come on, it's not that cold out and your place is the same three blocks from here as mine. Anyway, I'm just beginning to know her—it's only been a week and one phone call and coffee date—but I think there's potential there." "Potential to bed her?" and he said "Potential to have a good relationship." "What are her looks like?" and he said "She's good-looking. Very good-look-ing, I'd say, though you might not think so." "I don't know. We agree on some things. But specifics," which is what Manny liked to say. "Give me specifics," and he said "Long blond hair, but a real blond, and beautiful smile and skin and, I think, green eyes." "How can you tell her hair's not bleached?" and he said "It's just that when it isn't, it looks like it isn't. I've lived with a couple of real blonds. And she has a wonderful disposition, which is not looks, but helps. Soft, calm, as is her voice." "How old is she?" and he told him and Manny said "Lots of years between you two, but that's all right. She'll take care of you in your old age." "She's also very bright. I know this means a lot to you. Has a Ph.D. from Columbia in French lit-erature—her dissertation was on Camus. You like Camus. You've said *The Stranger* is one of your favorite books." "It's the only one I read of his and I don't know if I'd want to hear an expert on it. Too much like school," and he said "You'd want to hear her. She's clear, unpedantic, and that voice. She's now on a prestigious postdoctoral teaching fellowship and is teaching at Columbia for two years." "Is she Jewish like you?" and he said "If you mean is she a Jew but doesn't practice it, yes." "Does she have a big nose?" and he said "God, you can be such a putz sometimes." "Then I'm sorry, forget I said it; let's get down to more important things, her build. Does she have big tits?" and he said "Big, little, medium-sized: what's the difference?" "You saying you'd take little to Miss Flatchested over big?" and he said "I'm saying it wouldn't affect how I feel about her, just as the size and shape of her nose wouldn't." "So you didn't even look?" and he said "I looked—I checked them out, as you like to say—and they're pretty substantial, or seem to be, but so what?" "'Substantial,'" Manny said; "what a word for it. Well, that's better than her having nothing up there, isn't it? But listen. If things ever get hot and romancy between you two, then whatever you do, don't try to fix me up with one of her friends. I know they'll all be brainy like her and condescending to me and not interested in any of the things I am." "Deal," he said, "but let's see how far it goes with me first. I'll be honest with you. I'm really hoping." "Good, that's good; congratulations. At our age, what guy in his right mind, especially one who wants kids, as you've said you do, wouldn't want a woman eleven years younger than him as a permanent mate? Now do you take issue with that too?" and he said "No. It wasn't one of my original reasons for hoping, but there's something to what you say." "Should we drink to it?" and he said "Yeah, why not," and they clinked glasses, drank up, had another beer, talked about other things, he gave Manny his share of the tab and put a tip down on the bar and left and Manny stayed. "You're taken," Manny said. "Me, you never know when some honey's going to come in here and flash on me. Hard to imagine, but it's happened." On his way home he might have thought why in hell is he still friends with that guy? Ah, Manny's seen him through a lot, been a loyal and uncritical friend, and he can be very funny sometimes and cut through most bullshit and he often makes a lot of sense He doesn't think Gwen would like him, he also might have thought. Too vulgar.

He thinks the second date went something like the following. Anyway, he's gone over it plenty of times in his head and also written about it and they talked about it, each confirming what the other had to say or in some parts giving a slightly different version of it, so it'll be close. He called the next night and said "Hi, it's Martin, how are you doing?" and she said "Fine, thanks, and you?" and he said "Great, couldn't be better," and she said "That's good. Anything special happen to make you feel that way?" and he said "No, I just feel good; head, body, the works. I usually feel good. No, that's not true, but also the writing went well today, so that helped. I wrote the first draft of a new story, and one I like, which means I have something to work on that I want to tomorrow and don't have to worry I've nothing to write. Listen, I had a nice time with you yesterday; I hope you did too," and he gave her time to speak and she said "It was very pleasant." "Good. So I think we spoke about this. Would you like to meet again, maybe for a drink and, if you're up to it, dinner after, but at a different place?" and she said "Why at a different place?" and he said "Well, you know; first we can meet at a bar near you, if that's convenient; and then think about a restaurant, because a bar, I don't think, is where you'd like to eat," and she said, "I see. Sure," and they arranged to meet at six this Sunday at the West End, a short walk from her building, and then, if she doesn't still have a lot of preparing to do for her class the following day, have dinner somewhere else. Once they settled on when to meet, he got off the phone quickly. He'd run out of

things to say and ask her and she wasn't asking him anything either or vol-
unteering to talk about herself and what she did that day and so on and he
didn't want there to be just silence on the phone. She might think "What,
we've nothing to talk about already?" he thought. So he said "Terrific; the
West End. Six, day after tomorrow; I know where it is. And at a table, not
the oblong bar, if they still have it, which isn't conducive for talk," and she
said "Okay, see you then, Martin," and they said goodbye. He got to the bar
first, right at six, looked around, she wasn't there, sat at a two-table and
ordered a beer. Domestic? Foreign? Just get the cheapest draft, he thought.
Doubts he'll finish it, mainly because he doesn't want to have to pee soon
after, as he did with the coffee at the drugstore. She might think he has a
bladder problem or something and he also doesn't want her thinking about
his peeing so much. When he gets to the restaurant, if they go, that'll be
different, seem more natural. If she can't go to dinner, then he'll pee here,
just to empty his bladder for the ride home, which could take a half-hour or
more. She came a little after six—he was looking at his watch when she
suddenly appeared at his table—and said "Hello, Martin; am I late?" and he
said "Not at all," and stood up and put his hand out and they shook hands
and sat. "By the way, it wouldn't matter if you were late. I've brought a book
and ordered a beer, so I'm good for a long wait. Let me tell the waitress—
I see her—what you'll have," and she said "A Guinness Stout, please, but in
the bottle, not draft, and with a glass. Sometimes they bring it without
one." And he said "How do they expect you to drink it then? Straight from
the bottle, which can cause burps, or through a straw?" and she laughed and
said "That was funny—the image, drinking Guinness through a straw," and
he said "Thank you." He got up and went over to the waitress. Then he sat
down and said "I hope we can have dinner later," and she said, "I'm free.
I should have tried to call you about it in case you didn't think we'd have
dinner and wanted to make other plans," and he said "No, I was counting
on you. Didn't work out, I'd just go home and read." Their drinks came.
They talked about lots of things. She asked what book he brought with him
"for the long wait that never came," and he said "Also for the subway ride
up here and back—got to have something to read," and she said "I hope
meeting me here wasn't too much of an inconvenience for you," and he said
"That's nice of you; but it was easy." He forgets what book it was. Knows it
was small enough to fit into his not-too-large coat side pocket. An old
paperback. When they went for 95 cents. He can almost see it: cover torn,
pages dog-eared. He didn't want to take the Solzhenitsyn hardcover he'd
been reading at home, because then he'd have to put it on the table they sat

at or a nearby chair and carry it when they walked, and displaying such a big
serious book in front of her again seemed ostentatious. Chekhov stories, he
thinks. If it was, then they spoke about some of them or just Chekhov in
general, for she'd read for her thesis several of his stories he wrote in Nice
and later a large collection of them to see if there was a Camus connection
as there was for Camus in Dostoevsky's fiction. "There wasn't," she said one
time, "or none I could find, and after about fifty of his stories, I gave up. I'd
thought there might be a groundbreaking article in it for me. They were a
delight to read, so I don't look at the project as a waste of my time." No
doubt something more about her teaching than she told him in the drugstore, or was it on the phone in their first call? What college she went to and
what she majored in and more about her master's thesis, and he the same:
college, major, no graduate degree, and both of them born in New York, she
at Mother Cabrini in the Bronx—"I'm a Bronx baby," she said—he at New
York Hospital's Lying-In. Also their public high schools in the city: "Oh,
you went to an elite one," he said. "I did too, but flunked out in a year and
had to transfer." Jobs he's had, travels. Her marriage and divorce. "You said
you were never married," she said, "right?" after she spoke about her husband and a little about why they broke up. Not her two abortions. That
they spoke about weeks or months later. Second one ten years after the first.
Her husband said the baby would interfere with their doctoral studies and
teaching at Columbia. She didn't think so but went along with her husband.
"Besides, the marriage was already in deep trouble." The first with another
man. Actually, just a boy, she said. Both of them were seventeen. "Got
pregnant the same time I lost my virginity. He was quite a skillful lover for
someone so young." "You mean he helped you reach orgasm," and she said
"Several in one afternoon. So it wasn't, as they say, a total loss. Later, I'd pay.
Going to a quack in Philadelphia and hemorrhaging and getting kicked out
of his office with blood running down my legs. Lucky my boyfriend's older
brother was with us and drove us to a motel." Her parents. What parts of
Eastern Europe they were from. How they got to America. Her mother's
father was already living in New York, so he sponsored them. It's a long
story. The rest of her mother's family starved to death in the Łódź ghetto
and all of her father's family were murdered by the Nazis in Byelorussia. She
was born five months after her parents got here in '47. Conceived in Paris,
a stopping-off place for them, which she said could account for her love of
French language and culture. "I may be a Bronx baby, but before that I was
a French fetus. I love humor but can't make up or tell a joke. I think I've told
you that." In high school she wanted to be an actress and was the lead,

"because I showed modest early talent and had good diction and could remember the lines, in all the musicals and plays. In elementary school, I played Alice because of my long blond hair." She didn't want her parents spending their hard-earned savings on her expensive college, so for the most part she paid it all herself by working in school dorms and their cafeterias for four years." Her birthday. Eleven days before his. "So we're both Geminis," he said, and gave his birthday, "not that that or astrology, as a whole, is of any significance," and she said "I'm not so sure. We're talking here of stars and planets." They finished their drinks and he said "Like another Guinness?" and she said "No, thanks. Two would unglue me." "Does that mean no wine with dinner? Because I'm going to have another beer, if you don't mind, and at the restaurant order some wine," and she said "By then, on a full to medium-full stomach, I should be able to drink a glass of wine without later needing you to help me home. Please, have some more beer." He got his beer and said "I was just thinking. I'm eleven years minus eleven days older than you. Do you think that number means anything?" and she said "A numerical coincidence, but that's all. You might also happen to have eleven siblings in your family," and he said "Because of the way it ended up, like you, none. The two of us, one and one." About her living in the Bronx till she was around fourteen. It turned out that the high school he transferred to from Brooklyn Tech—"Transferred to illegally too; I didn't live in the district, but the high schools I would have been forced to go to in Manhattan were even worse"—was near where she lived. "Maybe I saw you once or twice when I walked from the subway to school or back. I thought you looked familiar," and she said "Come on." "All right, that was silly, but we must have crossed paths a couple of times after your family moved to the West Side. Both of us in the same neighborhood, you 78th, me 75th? At Fairway, for instance, which I've frequented a lot over the years, the cheese and olive departments particularly. I have to admit that if I saw you there and you looked older than eighteen—no, I'll be honest: sixteen—I would have stared a little or maybe just looked at you on the sly, so as not to alarm you. I'm saying, because of your looks," and she said "Please stop talking about it. It makes me feel self-conscious, and I hardly see the point of all this." "Again, that was stupid of me. I shouldn't have brought any of it up," and she said "Forget it. It was nothing." How did her mother's father—he asked—happen to leave his family in Poland and settle in New York? He wanted the entire family to come, but her grandmother said the Germans didn't harm the Jews in the first war, they won't hurt them in this one, and she also didn't want to leave her own mother and home. "My mother was studying in Russia at the time, which saved her." Her mother's mother was Rose. Her middle name is Rose. Soon after her grandfather learned his wife and two sons were dead, he married a woman named Rose. "Rose, Rose, Rose," he said. "A bouquet of Roses. It's a pretty name." She visits her second Grandmother Rose in Kew Gardens once a month. "She always makes a brisket of beef or roast chicken for me and a noodle kugel you can smell the sweetness of as you enter her apartment building, and sends me home with a shopping bag full of leftovers and other foods." "She sounds like my Aunt Esther, my father's sister, but she would travel from Flatbush to our apartment with these Jewish goodies. She died three days after my father, I wasn't allowed to the Orthodox funeral because, technically, I was still sitting shiva." "And your mother?" and he said "Bright and energetic and healthy and still interior decorating for a living." Her mother's a psycho-therapist, her father's a C.P.A. Some people see them in the same visit for therapy and taxes, her father in the dining room, which he's turned half of into his office, her mother in Gwen's old bedroom. Incidentally, she said, her father had been a lawyer in Minsk. But he felt because his English was so bad and nobody could understand his accent that he wouldn't succeed at law in New York, so he switched to the universal language of numbers, if she can put it that way. "No," he said; "nicely put. And the switchover must have been very difficult for him," and she said "After going through what he did in the war, he said, nothing was." She lived in Paris twice, once for a year. "Another possible place our paths might have crossed," he said. "I lived there for half a year in '64," and she said "Before my time." She married too young. Her ex-husband was even two years younger than she. But they got their Ph.D.s the same year at Columbia—his also in literature, but English—and attended the same graduation ceremony, but by then they were divorced for three years. He's remarried, has twin infants and an assistant professorship at a college in Nebraska. "Nebraska," he said. "It's a good job," she said. "Pays well, complete medical and dental coverage for the family, two-three course load"—he asked "What's that?"—"and his children will get half their tuition paid for by his school to whatever college they attend. Tenure-track jobs are short in literature and you have to grab what's offered, though I think I told you I'd never leave New York. That could easily condemn me to adjunct teaching and, if I hit it big, visiting assistant professorships for the rest of my academic life, but at least I get to keep my beautiful apartment." "Oh, I'm sure you'll do much better than that. You're so smart and no doubt very good in your field," and she said "And you're so full of compliments." "Too many?" he said. "I'm only saying what I believe. But all right, I'll try to exercise some self-control." She likes to cook. "I like to cook too," he said. "Maybe one day we can cook dinner together, or it could just be an elaborate lunch," and she said "I prefer cooking alone and taking all the credit and blame. What are some of the dishes you like to make?" and he said "Risotto with shitake or oyster mushrooms and artichoke hearts, lots of things with tofu, thick soups made with red lentils and various vegetables and Indian spices. But my favorite—you can call it my special specialty, since, as far as I know, I'm the one who devised it—is a meatless bratwurst with sauerkraut, baby Brussels sprouts—you can only get these frozen—and peas and corn and ground-up peanuts in a heated mustard sauce," and she said "It doesn't seem like something I'd like—the sauerkraut and sprouts—but the rest of it is okay." "What do you like to make," he said, "which I should have asked you before instead of going on about my own cooking?" and she said "That's all right. Right now? Mostly French dishes you wouldn't eat because they have some kind of meat in them. I'm sorry, but eating meat is more satisfying to me than its substitutes," and he said "I can understand. Every now and then I get a ferocious urge for a slice of roast beef." She's translated, and a few have been published, a lot of French and Italian postwar poetry. "Italian too?" he said. "I'd love to read them. It's been an unattainable goal of mine all my adult life to read and speak French fluently…what I went to Paris for in '64 and eventually to get a news job there. Would you send me some translations with the originals, if it's not too much of a bother?" and she said "They might take a while for me to find. I'm not the most organized person and I'm always forgetting to buy more file folders. I should just steal them from my department," and he said "No rush; whenever you can. And the Italian." She goes to Maine every summer for two to three months. Takes her and her parents' cats along. "They're one big happy Siamese family: mother, spoiled son and two sweet daughters." She rents a car for the summer. "That can get expensive," and she said because she takes their cats, her parents help out. "Where do you go, not that I know Maine?" and she said "A small coastal village, where every other summer person is a writer or professor or spouse or child of one—Brooklin with an 'i.'" She started renting this cottage three years ago to be close to where her doctoral advisor spends the summer with his family. It had no water or electricity or gas—it had been vacant for more than five years—so she had to have all that brought in. "I learned how to prime a pump to get the water going, which I've had to do twice first thing after getting there because the caretaker forgot to or was drunk." "How do you?" and she said "Please, you don't want to know," and he said "I'm a writer. I like being informed of obscure technical things I know nothing of so I can encumber my fiction with them," and she told him and he said "Very complicated; I'd have to have your help." He said "Two to three months in a cottage in the woods? Doesn't it get lonely sometimes?" and she said "I have dinner a lot at my advisor's house, my parents each come up separately for a week, and if I get lonely I invite other company," and he said "Then you're set." He said "Another thing I always wanted to do—" and she said "What was the other one?" and he said "Learn French…was to rent a cabin or cottage—you know, I'm suddenly not sure of the difference, if there is one," and she said "A cabin is more rustic and usually smaller and often doesn't have the basic amenities a cottage does." "Then just a cottage, but in Maine or Vermont for a month or two in the summer. A fantasy of mine since my early twenties. But I guess lack of money or that I was working summers at the time and that I've gone to Yaddo three of the last six Augusts, stopped me from doing it, and I also didn't know how to go about renting one." "I've spent summers in both," she said, "and I like Maine better. From my cottage I can see the ocean through the trees, or the bay of the ocean. It's only a thirty-second walk down to it from the back porch, and the cottage comes with its own secluded cove." "You're making my mouth water," and she said "Then one of these summers you should rent a place, while they're still affordable, in the same area I go to. I could give you the names of a couple of real estate agencies that specialize in summer rentals." Most of her time in Maine is spent writing essays and poetry and also some translating and preparing her fall courses. "Do you send your poetry out? Or should I say, has any of it been published?" and she said "So far I haven't had the courage. It's different with the translations, because I only pick works I love. By the way, I'm sure I'll find them and can send a few to you, but you'd have to give me your address." He wrote his name and address on a piece of paper he tore out of his memobook and gave it to her. "I'd like to give you one or even three of my books that have been pub-lished," and she said "Just one. You choose." He said "Let's start from the beginning, my first. Came out two years ago. Five stories, a hundred-twenty-eight pages, a cinch to read." She asked what the title was and then said "I'm afraid I haven't heard of it." He said "It didn't get around much and only a couple of reviews. Big pans. Both found it too scatological and one objected strongly to the couple in the longest story—they'd met in the hospital two days before—coupling in a chair in the room his father was dying in. I have your address but not the zip. Or maybe I'll just give you the book the next time we meet, if we do," and she said "We can do that. I'll save my poems for then too," and he said "No, send them, unless we're going to see each other in the next two days," and she said "I'll send them, then. Do I have your zip?" and looked at the piece of paper with his address on it and said "Yes, I do. Let me give you mine," and he wrote it down in his memobook. He said "May I ask you a personal question?" and she said "Depends. I don't think we should speak too personally so soon." "Then I won't." He was going to ask if she was presently seeing someone. They talked about something else. Then she said "All right. What was the personal question you wanted to ask? I have to confess; I'm curious," and he asked it and she said "I'll be honest with you, Martin," and he thought Oh, shit; here it comes. "There is an English architect whom I see whenever he passes through," and he said "And his name is David." "Why do you say that?" and he said "I don't know. I was once involved with a woman who began dating an English architect named David, so something in my stupid head assumed they were all named David." "He isn't. He's Evan," and he said "A good English name. How often do you see him?" and she said "Not very much, really. Every other month. Sometimes twice in two months," "So why isn't it more than that? Is he married?" and she said "No. I think it's because his London firm flies him here on business and it'd be expensive for him to fly here on his own. And that both of us are quite satisfied with the arrangement as it is," and he said "Do you ever go to London to see him?" and she said "Yes, once; it was fun. But I think we both knew things would never get that serious between us," and he said "Well, that's okay, then, not that I know what I mean. But it must be wonderful to go to London or Paris or a city like that to see someone. Anyway, thanks for answering me so frankly, and now we should probably drop the subject," and she said "Good idea." "What else do you like to do?" and she looked puzzled and he said "Do you like to go to plays, concerts, movies, opera, ballet?" and she said "All of them, when I have time, but opera the least. I like contemporary operas, though," and he said "Same with me. Chamber music?" and she said "More on LP's than in concert halls." "Friends? I'd think you'd have lots of them," and she said "I'm sure no more than most people." "Hate to sound like a loner, but I really only have three. Two men—a writer and a filmmaker—and a woman whom I've been close to as a friend for years. She's in publishing and we have lunch about every other week. She tries to fix me up," and she said "That's good," and he said "Not for me." She has two best friends. One lives in SoHo with her husband—both are artists—and the other's moved to California with her husband, but they talk all the time on the phone. The one in SoHo's been her best friend since their first day in college. "I was giving Melissa, my pet guinea pig, an outing on the campus green, and my future friend liter-ally tripped over us." "They let you keep pets in college?" and she said "Some of the girls brought their horses from as far away as Oklahoma and boarded them at the school's stables." He asked where'd she go for Thanksgiving and she said her parents don't celebrate it, as they don't Mother's and Father's Day, so she always goes to the SoHo couple's loft. "Where'd you?" "I took my mother out as I always do, usually with her sister. Not easy finding a restaurant that's open and serves something other than turkey and crab dishes and that isn't Chinese, all three of which my mother and aunt don't like." He asked if she knew other poets and she said "You say 'other' as if I'm one," and he said "Then just poets." She mentioned a few, two very well-known. "If you decide to send your own work out," he said, "all the names you gave should help get it to the best places," and she said "I'd rather not use anyone for that. If the time ever comes, I'll do all the submitting and coping. Who's your publisher?" and he said he's on his second and gave the name. "Oh-h, a very good house. Who's your editor there?" and he told her and she said "I know Fern. Sat next to her at a dinner party a few months back and then bumped into her on the street and we had coffee and talked some more. I like her and she's smart. She does all their poetry, so is someone else I'd never send to because that would be taking advantage of having sat in the right spot. Did they throw you a book party?" and he said Fern said they don't do that anymore except for writers who get huge advances and their books are potential blockbusters and they expect a party. "For writers like me: too costly and parties never pay off, as don't ads for the book. So I threw one myself. Made all the food and paid for the wine and booze and at the last moment, because it had started raining, ran out and bought a tarp and set it up over my large terrace. Otherwise, my apartment would have been too small for all the people I invited. Fern came with her husband and two kids. I also invited the publisher and executive editor—it was the wrong thing to do, Fern said; as if I was rubbing it in their noses that they didn't give me a party—and they both sent courteous regrets." Because she was an only child, she said, and her parents lost most to all of their families in the Holocaust, she got lots of attention and affection from them when she was growing up. "Same here," he said, "from my mother. My father was from the old school. He basically ignored me and wanted affection but didn't much care to give it, except for maybe pinching my cheeks and tweaking my nose and ruffling my hair, which I hated but couldn't get him to stop, especially in front of his friends." "This English architect," he said. "Is it approaching the time when he might be making his next professional visit to New York? Just wondering," and she said "I don't keep tabs on him, and we rarely speak on the phone when he's in London. But he usually lets me know a week or two before he arrives. In fact, that's the only time he calls me from there." "Gosh, you'd think he'd call more, but that's his business," and she said "I think it's a subject we should rule out of our conversation, Martin. Like your recent romantic connections to women, if you've had any," and he said "No, not of late, but I won't go in to it." He said "There's a nonpersonal question I've been meaning to ask you. You had tea at the drugstore. You don't drink coffee?" and she said "What a funny thing to ask. I love good coffee and I believe I already told you I had some with Fern. I just had enough of it for that day. But I never asked. Was the coffee there as dreadful as I once experienced and it looked? I should have warned you," and he said "I think you did ask and warn me, and I think I said it was awful." "Then why'd you have two cups?" and he said "Did I? I forget." "I'm almost sure, two. And after, you said that was the reason you needed to pee before we left," and he said "I always take that precaution, coffee or not, when I'm out for a while and think I'll be walking in the cold—you know how that stirs it up…something, the precaution, I think I told you about too." He asked where she went to elementary school—"Hunter, too?" and she said "Hunter was my next stop in my educational journey. PS," and she gave the number of the school in the Bronx. "We were very proud that Bess Myerson graduated from it—you know, the only Jewish Miss America?" He said he went to PS 87. "A character in one of Bernard Malamud's novels went there, but he didn't. He came from Brooklyn." "I think I've passed it. Between Amsterdam and Columbus?" and he said "The 87 I went to was torn down for the one you saw. We were very proud that it was a pre-Civil War building and reputed to be the oldest and most rundown grade school in Manhattan. When I first got my teacher's license I per-diem subbed in the new 87 a few times. My last two years of subbing I mostly did in IS 44, the next block over, till I couldn't take it anymore and quit in the middle of a class and never taught again." "What'd they do about your salary that day?" and he said "I told them to keep it, keep my entire week's pay; the kids who couldn't be disciplined were driving me crazy." Jobs she had, he had. She was a salesperson for Lord & Taylor, he at Bloomingdale's and, when he was in college, Macy's and Gimbel's during the Christmas season. Both worked in bookstores and waited on tables in restaurants and he also at Catskill Mountain resorts. He was a bartender and cab driver and newsman, she a group leader of a bike trip in Canada. "Me too," he said, "in Europe, but only half of it by bike."

Both were camp counselors. He was a technical writer in California, she a script reader for a film production company in New York. "When was that?" he said. "No, too early for you to have done any good for my second and third books, the two that were sent around as possible movies." She's never been to California. "I was heading there with my college boyfriend at the time and got as far as Nevada, when we had a terrible argument, decided we couldn't stand each other, and drove silently home for four days. I think the only words we spoke, depending on who was driving, were 'Like a pit stop?'" She had her appendix taken out when she was ten and was once so seriously ill with a bacterial infection that she nearly died. "Oh, no," he said. "I'm so sorry," and she said "Thank you." He's never really been sick. "I take that back. I had my gallbladder removed. Gallstones." "That can be painful," she said, "when they attack," and he said "It was. Worst in my life. I don't know how I could have forgotten it." How she's able to pay the rent for a one-bedroom apartment in an elevator and doorman building on Riverside Drive below a Hundred-sixteenth Street and with a river view? She was left some money by her godmother, her ex-husband invested it wisely in stocks that give a nice dividend each month, her parents help her out if she needs them to, she finished paying off her student loans two years ago, she occasionally does book reviews for *The Nation* and *New Leader*, which don't pay much but they bring in something, she private-tutors a couple of times a month, which pays very well, and her fellowship money is pretty good. "Is it Andrew Mellon the fellowship's named after, or Paul?" and she said "Who's Paul Mellon?" "Maybe it's 'Walter' I'm thinking of— the financier-philanthropist who helped found the National Gallery of Art in D.C. and gave it some of its most priceless art." "Andrew," and he said "Anyway, very impressive." "Not if you know I had a well-connected faculty advisor who backed me unstintingly. Without him it's unlikely I would have got a Mellon," and he said "I'm sure that's not true." Like him, she likes to doodle on the phone. "What do you like to doodle most?" and she said "Nothing specifically. Whatever comes out of the pencil or pen. Doodles are like dreams to me: I only see what I've doodled, and start interpreting it, after I hang up. And you? What do you doodle?" and he said "Cubes upon cubes. Pedestals upon pedestals with a Giacometti-like figure on top. And self-portraits, with eyeglasses, less hair than I have, so I'm partly doodling my father, and always in a dress shirt with the sleeves rolled up to the elbows, a pen in the shirt pocket, and a tie, though if I wear my one tie twice a year, it's a lot." He said "Hanukkah's coming up, has passed, or we're in the beginning, middle or end of it. Do you light candles for it? Obviously, I don't," and she said "My father always tells me when the first night is and gives me a box of menorah candies every year and sometimes a new menorah. It's not that he thinks I don't have one. It's because he knows how hard it is scraping off the wax from previous years. If what's holding you back from lighting candles is not having a menorah, you can have one of mine. They're piling up and I might be breaking some Jewish law if I throw them out. But to answer your question, I light candles two or three nights out of the eight and usually dispense with reciting the candle-lighting prayer off the box and I never leave the apartment when they're lit. The candles are so thin and unsturdy and often broken in the middle, that I'm afraid they'll fall." She said "What are you working on these days?" and he said "Didn't I tell you? Just another story. You? Besides school work—scholarly paper or poetry or maybe a book review?" "My ex-husband also writes poetry," she said. "He gets his in literary journals and last year he had a chapbook published by a small press, or maybe I told you. He's much more aggressive than I in sending it out and competitive about writing it. He once called my poems sentimental shit, when they weren't. He could get vicious when it came to poetry. He thought that's what made his work strong." "'Desultory,'" she said. "I forget what it means," and he told her. "Then I never knew what it meant. Or just assumed it was something else—'lazy,' for instance," and he said "I should have said 'random.' So pretentious of me," and she said "Not really. I like words like that. Not to use but to know them. Excuse me; I didn't mean you. And you can be my one-new-word-a-day man. I'll call you up at a designated time each day and you can give it. 'The word for Tuesday is...'" and she laughed. She said "After you finish your beer— I don't mean to rush you, but it must be fairly flat by now; it's long stopped bubbling. But we should think about dinner." He said "You don't smoke, do you? Oh, I asked you that, and I remember you didn't particularly agree with my reasons for not liking women who smoked, no matter how great they were in every other way," and she said "No, I didn't mind." They both had something to do with Hubert H. Humphrey. She, when she was a guide in a USIA exhibit in Lyon and he was vice president and stopped at her booth and they chatted awhile; he, when he was a reporter in Washington and Humphrey was a senator and he used to call him off the Senate floor to interview him for the two biggest radio stations in Minnesota. Talking about Maine again, he said three of the things she seemed to like most about it, other than the scenery and cooler and drier air, he unfortunately doesn't care for much: blueberries; sailing, because he gets seasick easily; and lobster, because he's a vegetarian and he hates the brutal way they're cooked.

She said "The last two I can understand, but how can you not like blueberries?" and he said "Because I've heard the sprayed ones never quite get rid of their spray and unsprayed ones have little dead worms in them because they're not sprayed." "Nonsense," she said. "I mostly eat the organic ones and I've never seen a worm. If I did, the one in a thousand blueberries, I'd just spit it out." "Well," he said, "I'm willing to give them a try." Her ex-husband, who also went to City College, graduated ten years after him. "It would have been eleven," he said, "but because I went to night school half the time—I worked full-time during the day—it took me five years instead of four." He asked "Do you sing? I say that because you have such a beautiful speaking voice," and she said "That's nice of you to say, but I have a perfectly terrible singing voice. When I do sing, it's only in a large group, such as Christmas caroling around Columbia, so my voice doesn't stand out. I do play unaccompanied pieces on the piano and take lessons from a world-class pianist. She says I'm not bad for a nonprofessional. She's Austrian, lives here permanently now, and should have won the Tchaikovsky competition in Moscow. But that year the Soviet authorities, to improve cultural relations between our two countries, or something, decided an American should get it." "Who was it?" and she told him and said "Oh, yeah, of course. And your teacher?" and she told him and he said "I have two of her Schubert recordings." She asked which ones and then said "What a coincidence; I have the same two. I bet we have lots of the same things like that, especially books. That's the way it was with my ex-husband when he was still my boyfriend and moved into my apartment. We must have had fifty of the same books, and he wasn't a French scholar and didn't even like French fiction and poetry of any era. Theory was okay." "Who could not like Camus?" and she said "There are essays of his I don't particularly admire," and he said "It's been a long time since I read any of them, but I think I recall feeling the same way. As for books, I don't have many. I either get them out of the library or give away or leave on the street most of the ones I buy. I have this thing about keeping my possessions to a minimum. Two plates, two forks, maybe three glasses, one change of linen. A bit nutty, huh? And I never reread. The only book—no, I've reread Kafka and the stories of Hemingway and Joyce and the Beckett biography, so I'll forget what I was going to say." "What book was it, though?" and he said "*Fathers and Sons*. And only because I first read it as a kid—it was around the house—and I thought it was a young boy's book. I got nothing out of it but I did read it through, and all I can remember from my second reading of it is someone getting out of a carriage. I don't think I ever spoke about this to anyone," and she said

"I feel honored. But now, really, Martin, we should find a place to have dinner. I'm very hungry. And I'll pay for our drinks," and he said "No, no, that's mine. I'm also taking care of dinner, wherever we end up eating." And she said "We'll see about that." He went to the men's room, paid up, helped her on with her coat, and they left. "Any special kind of food you want?" she said outside. "I think we can find something around here to satisfy your dietary restrictions. There's always this place"—they stopped in front of Moon Palace—"although the food's a bit of a throwback. Real old-time Chinese-American cuisine." "I'll take your word for it," he said. "And it's too brightly lit and they have only one table filled at peak dinner hour. Sad to see a restaurant doing so poorly, but not that sad to make me want to eat here." "Do you like Middle Eastern food?" she said. "Because there's always Amir's. No wine or beer, though, and you can't bring it in. And it's very small and they'd want you to eat up fast and leave so other customers can sit," and he said "They'd have plenty of what I can eat. But I can't have dinner without a glass of wine or beer, can you?" and she said "It's usually better with a good bottle of red, but sure." They walked down Broadway on the west side of the street. A couple of places looked okay except their menus outside didn't have a single nonmeat dish on them but different kinds of omelets. "I'd have one," he said—"that'd solve our problem. But I'm trying to keep my cholesterol low—my father's was very high—so I'm avoiding anything with eggs. I'm a real drag, aren't I?" and she said "Don't worry; we'll find something." "What I should do—seriously—is give up my prohibitions for a night and eat meat for the first time in years, or at least fish," and she said "No fish restaurants in this neighborhood. Although Tom's, across the street, always has one fish dish on the menu and a spaghetti in plain tomato sauce, and I think they have beer, but it's a diner." "Let's see what they got," and they crossed Broadway and looked at the menu on the window. "Maybe for lunch, if you're in a rush," he said, "but it doesn't even look like a good place for coffee. Sort of like the drugstore we went to, but with more things on the menu. No Indian restaurants?" and she said "Not that I'm aware of. There used to be Aki, a Japanese restaurant, on one of the side streets between Amsterdam and Morningside Drive, I think," and he said "Stop right there. I once ate at it—ate at it several times, the first time when I was in college—but once, a few hours later, this woman and I got violently sick from the food." "So we'll skip Aki, if it is still there, and too far a walk anyway. There is a Greek place up the block here—I forget its name, but its popular with Columbia students," and he said "I'm sorry; I never cared for Greek food," and she said "Dolmas?

Moussaka? Well, not if it's made with lamb. Unfortunately, this place isn't that good, so it wasn't the best suggestion, except that it was nearby. All the other possible restaurants are on the other side of Broadway, unless you want a slice of pizza." "You're beginning to think I'm acting peculiar about this," and she said "I'm not. That was a joke, not a gibe. I knew you wouldn't want a pizza slice at the pizzeria, and neither would I." They crossed Broadway and continued downtown. It was getting cold. It *was* cold, but he was only now feeling it, so she was probably cold too. They both had on gloves and mufflers and watch caps, hers made out of mohair and pulled down over her ears. Her hair came out of the cap on both sides and covered her cheeks. "It's gotten cold," he said. "I'm putting you through too much. Let's just go in someplace, I don't care where, so long as it has food and wine or beer." They were on a Hundred-ninth. "Big choice here: Cuban, Mexican or what's called continental," and he said "I don't know Cuban food and the Mexican will probably be noisy, because a certain boisterousness and loud music always seems to go with their restaurants. Sometimes it can be fun, but I'd prefer a quieter place so we can hear each other talking. Straus Park Cafe looks good. Attractive, fair number of older customers; seems subdued." He checked the menu outside, pointed to the cheese omelet on it and said "I'm going to have one. Comes with hash browns, which I love, and it's been about half a year since my last egg. See how quickly I make decisions?" and she said "Good," and they went inside. They talked. They ordered. They drank. She went to the restroom and came back with her hair in a ponytail. Maybe, he thought to keep it off her face when they walked. This way, that way; her hair always looked nice, he thought. They ate. She had liver and onions and a vegetable and salad. They both thought the bread was especially good. They laughed a lot. He felt comfortable with her. Felt she felt comfortable with him. She was cheerful, beautiful. Again, wonderful in every way. There wasn't anything he didn't like about her. Teeth, lips, nose. Her body was good. Her skin was the smoothest and clearest of any woman he's known. If there was only a better word for it than porcelain, he thought. He'll think of one but not use it on her. A word just for himself. Her nails weren't polished. He liked that. No makeup, it seemed; definitely no lipstick. They finished a bottle of wine. He had about two-thirds of it. "More wine," he said, "since we're still eating?" "How's your omelet?" and he said "Delicious. I don't recognize the cheese. Want some?" and she shook her head. "Salad? I'm afraid I already finished the fried eggplant," and he said "Is that what it was? No, thanks. Had plenty of salad for both breakfast and lunch. I love salad—yesterday's, dressed, particularly,

But no more wine?" and she said "Oh, I'm going to be in bad shape as it is, drinking so much. The Guinness, and then what I have, three glasses of wine?" and he said "Small glasses. But if you're not, I won't either. I've had enough," and she said "You can always get it by the glass," and he said "Nah, I'm fine. I'll drink water. But if you think you drank too much, know what to do? Two aspirins with a full glass of water before you go to bed. Then drink two or three more glasses of water during the night—you can keep a carafe by your bedside—and you'll be fine, no headache, no hangover." "It really works?" and he said "With me, almost every time. The only other helpful medical advice I have is for a nosebleed that won't stop." "I've had a couple of those," and he said "If there's a next time, roll a little piece of toilet paper into a wad—dampen it first. And any paper will do. And I know it must sound ridiculous, my talking about this, but something soft and absorbent like toilet paper's the best, and put it between your front teeth and upper lip, right in the middle." "Thank you, Dr. Samuel," and he said "'Samuels,'" but there's more. Keep it there for a minute or two, no longer because you don't want to stop the blood flowing to your head. I don't know if that's the reason, but it's something like that. Then take it out. Still bleeding, put it back, same two-minute time limit. That cure is infallible." "Where did you learn it?" and he said "I forget, but long ago. I've had a number of nosebleeds, and I've also used this procedure with other people, and it's worked every time." Sometime later, she said "Too bad you don't eat meat. They gave me too big a piece." "Just leave it," and she said "You must never have had a cat. I'm going to get it bagged for home. It's their favorite thing to eat, and here I have a nice piece without stinking up the kitchen cooking it. Could be why I ordered it, to make my cats happy." "I actually did have a cat once," he said, "on loan. It belonged to a woman friend, whom I lived with on and off till more than a year ago, first in her house in Rockland County and then downtown. When we broke up, she felt that the cat—well, it's a story. She thought she was allergic to it, it was by nature an outdoors cat, I had a large terrace with lots of plants, and the adjoining terrace apartment had a friendly female cat whom she thought would make an ideal mate for hers. But then she got lonely for her cat and wanted him back. That was fine with me. The cat—Posey—scratched and bit. But I almost lost him on the IND Seventy-second Street subway platform, returning him to her. He got out of his carrier because I didn't latch it well. Another story." "What did you do to catch him?" and he said "Me? Nothing. For a minute or so, till he heard the train coming and ran back into his carrier, I was scared as hell he was gone for good and I didn't know how I'd explain it to her. But we should go." He paid for the dinner. She said "That was very generous of you. But you have to know I would have been glad to go Dutch and still would like to, if you'd let me," and he said "I know. Thank you." Outside, he said "If it's too cold for you, I could get you a cab," and she said "No, my coat's really warm, and I like to walk after a dinner out. If you want to take a cab to your home, I'll be okay." He said "It is cold—I never seem to wear the right clothes—but I'd like to walk you to your building." "Because of the wind, get set for it being even colder when we head down to the river," and he said "It shouldn't last too long, so I'll survive." They didn't talk much while they walked. He thought because of the cold and that her muffler now covered her mouth. He did say—to break the silence—"What unusual weather," and she said "December; I guess what we should expect," and he said "But so early in the month?" and she said "I forget what the weather's like one year to the next." They started down the hill to the Drive at a Hundred-fourteenth Street. She put her arm through his and pushed her shoulder against his side and with her other hand held the bag with the liver, and they walked that way till they got to her building. "Well, again," he said, "this has been fun. We should do it another time," and she said "Like to come up for a nightcap? For you, not me, and it'll have to be a short visit; my work," and he said "I'd love to see—" and she said "Let's talk inside." They went through the revolving door into the lobby. She said "I'm sorry; what were you saying? The cold," and he said "That I'd like to see your apartment and meet your cats. Two?" and she said "Natalie and Dominique. They're probably asleep on a shelf in the linen closet, so they might not come out, even for their special treat," and she shook the bag. "Do they also like onions?' and she said "What do you mean?" and he said "Nothing," and she said "Ah, it just registered. I'll rinse the liver first and maybe heat it up. They don't like frozen liver." "You know," he said, looking down the long lobby to the back of the building, "I've never been to this building—it's enormous—but have been to the one we passed next door. A dreary New Year's Eve party a few years ago," and she said "That's too bad. I hope it didn't leave you with a bad feeling for this neighborhood." "And a lit Christmas tree. Looks nice," and she said "We have this tyrannical super who will only decorate it himself. No kids permitted near it, even when it's done. The candy canes look real but aren't and the wrapped empty boxes underneath are the same every year. But you're right and what I failed to give him credit for: it makes the place more cheerful." The front nightman was sitting behind an opened window in a small office with rows of tenant cubbyholes behind him and to his right three monitors showing another entrance to the building and the laundry room and a dim corridor in what looked like a basement. He was eating a noodle soup out of a large Thermos cup. Chicken, by its smell. "Good evening," and she said "Hi, Cal. This is my friend Martin," and he said "Nice to meet you, Cal… Calvin?" and Cal said "Cal. Something important from management for you, Gwendolyn." There was a notice in some of the cubbyholes—keys, too, in a few, and other things: a rolled-up *TLS* squeezed into one—and he gave her hers. "Goodnight," she said. "And don't go out if you can help it. It's bitter cold," and Cal said "I'll remember that." She pressed the elevator button and looked at the notice. "I don't know why he gave me this," she whispered. "It's for the D line, not mine," and he said "'Line' meaning bottom floor to top, all the D apartments?" "Yes. Lots of breaking through bathroom walls to locate a water pipe leak, but fortunately for me on the other side of the building, where I used to live. Maybe that's it. But I don't want to embarrass him by giving it back. I hope he didn't hear." Elevator door opened and they went in. "So," he was about to say, "we've gone down in an elevator and we're going up," but thought she'd think it stupid and just time filler, and what could she say to it: "That's right"? What did holding his arm and snuggling up to him on the street mean? he thought. No snuggle; just using him against the cold. And inviting him up? Nothing to that either. A thank-you for walking her home, and also to give him time to get warm again before he started back. It also showed—but the elevator opened on the seventh floor. She trusts him, that's all. Two apartments on this small landing and a fire door saying it led to two more: 7H and 7I. She unlocked 7J, turned on the hallway light, gave him a hanger from the coat closet opposite the front door, said "I suggest you put your scarf on the same hanger with your coat so you don't forget it," and he said "Good idea. I have a tendency toward amnesia whenever I leave a new place." "I didn't mean it like that," and he said "Neither did I. Excuse me." She hung up her coat, put her cap and muffler, or he now thinks it was a wool shawl, on the shelf above the coats. "Now, for your drink," she said, "come with me." She went into the kitchen—"Nice apartment," he said, going through the living room-dining room, "and quite a view"—set the bag down on the stove and said "Unfortunately, the beer is warm and not very good—a six-pack left by my subletter two summers ago. Does beer go bad?" and he said "Only it it's been opened and left around awhile, even if recapped." "I do have red wine, uncorked, which you can open if you like, and Israeli brandy from my father. I haven't tasted it, but he says it's terrific, though he thinks everything made in Israel is better than from anywhere else. He travels there once a year to see some old school friends from Warsaw, and always brings me back brandy and chocolates and table napkins and things. He says he's helping out their economy." "How nice to have a father who gives you brandy. Mine thought I was a *shiker*—I wasn't—and when he took my mom and I out to dinner, he didn't even like my having a single beer. I'll try the brandy." She got a nearly full bottle of brandy off a side shelf in the refrigerator. He wanted to ask why she kept it there, but then thought she might not like the question. For instance, her father might have told her to. She got a brandy snifter out of a kitchen cabinet, washed it—"I hate to say it but we some-times have little buggies here, clean as this building is and overfumigated"— dried it with a paper towel and gave it to him. "Pour as much as you want. I doubt the brandy's up to the glass—four of them were a wedding present from Tiffany's and this is the only one left—but it still might taste better in it. I'd even join you if I had some Benedictine." He sipped, said "It's quite good," when it was a bit sharp, and she heated up the liver, sliced it into tiny pieces and put the plate on the floor under the sink next to a bowl of water. "Ah, I'll give them fresh," and she changed the water. "Watch this, if it works." She made clicking sounds with her mouth and there were two heavy thumps from another room—had to be her cats jumping from some-where to the floor, for right away they ran into the kitchen and started eating. "Siamese," he said. "I love them," and she said "Well, you can either stay here and shower them with affection or make yourself comfortable in the living room. But I have to attend to something in the back. Excuse me." She went into the hallway that connected to the bathroom, he could see, and also to what was probably the bedroom, and shut the hallway door behind her. Going to use the toilet or something, he thought. Before she closed the door he also saw what was probably the opened linen closet the cats had jumped out of. He went back to the kitchen, finished what was in the glass, poured twice the amount he did the first time and put the bottle on the side shelf in the refrigerator. In the living room, he thought should he stand while he waits for her, sit? If he sits, where—the couch, which was really just a Hollywood bed with a corduroy spread over it and several large cushions against the wall? Morris chair, which was almost identical to the one he had in his apartment, but in much better shape? Not at the dining table, which was near the windows. That'd look ridiculous. She'd come out and see him sitting at the table with nothing on it but his glass, if he wasn't holding it. And if he sat there he would hold it or put something under the stem if he set it down. Table looks like an antique and he wouldn't want to mar its finish with a wet ring or even a drop of brandy on it. The view, he thought: river, moonlight on it, lights on the other side: it really is pretty. He thought he'd be able to see the George Washington Bridge from her windows, but he'd probably have to stick his head outside to do it. A crazy thought: say he were going to stay here awhile, where would he work? Not at this table, unless she has pads for it. And every time he wanted to write, he'd have to get them from wherever she keeps them—he guesses in the coat closet—and put them on? Otherwise, his typewriter could scratch the table, and just putting a place mat under it, the typewriter would slide around. The bedroom must be where she works, at a desk or table, for no sign of her working in this room. What he'd do is bring his typewriter table here—he only uses it now to hold house plants—and put it over the half-radiator under the kitchen window by the door. It's light and compact enough to carry on the subway or bus, and has wheels, so he'd be able to wheel it part of the way, particularly in the street. The work space would be small and crowded and the chair he'd use would be a little in the way of anyone going into or coming back from the kitchen, but he's worked in small and cramped spaces before and it's never interfered in his writing. And he's sure—let's say it came to this, he thought—he'd grab her hand every now and then when she was trying to squeeze past him in the chair, and kiss it. He drank some more, got the brandy in the glass down to where he first poured it, looked at the books in the narrow floor-to-ceiling built-in bookcases on either side of the living room windows. Mostly poetry and fiction, none French, and all in English. Her French books, in English and French, and probably her academic books and scholarly journals, must be in the bedroom on bookshelves there. He felt the radiator cover under the windows. Warm, not hot, and he sat on it. Feels good. Wondered when he should leave. Maybe not till she asks him to or gives a sign she'd like him to. She does neither, then in half an hour; make that the limit. "Excuse me, you still have work to do, so I think I should go." Something like that. So she knows he doesn't want to overstay. If she says he doesn't have to go yet, he won't. She might say for him to stay till he finishes his drink, and he will. Maybe he should get some more. No. Had enough, doesn't want to get sloppy in speech or have trouble getting out of a chair or walking, and he still has to get home. Heard the toilet flush. Few seconds after it stopped flushing—went on for a long time, as if it'd never stop, so it might need a new flushometer—the squeak of the sink faucet being turned on, same sound his makes in his bathroom. The sink must be against the wall separating the bathroom and living room, and she's probably washing her hands. Radiator's getting too hot for him no matter where he sits on it, and he got up. But he doesn't want to just stand there, pretending to be admiring her books, when she comes out, or the view from her windows, so he sat in the Morris chair, which was at an angle across from the couch, and put his glass on the glass top of the coffee table between them. Looked at the artwork on the walls. Had to twist around a little to see all of it. Liked them. Modern, mostly abstract, except for a realistic pencil drawing of Camus' face, it seemed. Wasn't sure what to make of the Brancusi-like foot-and-a-half-high marble sculpture on the coffee table—*Bird in Flight*? *Bird Taking Wing*?—which, if it isn't a Brancusi repro-duction, he thought, is a rip-off of his style. He picked it up carefully—all he needs, he thought, is to drop and break it, and on the coffee table?—oh, my God—and turned it over and looked at the bottom. Etched into it was "*A ma Gwendoline cherie.* Jean-Luc Bertrand, Paris, 23.10.74." Cherie. Dear? Was he a lover, friend? Anyway, four years ago. He put it back on the coffee table. She came out—"Sorry," she said—and sat at the end of the couch nearest the chair. "Think I should take the aspirins now? It'll also give me something to drink. I don't want you drinking alone. You okay, Martin?" and he said "Sure, why? Anything wrong?" "No; just asking." She went into the bathroom, same squeak from before but this time he heard water run-ning, came back with a glass of water. "Oh, I don't want to drink from the glass I rinse my mouth with. Using it for the aspirins is another thing," and she went into the kitchen, came back with a different glass of water, sat in the same place on the couch—"This is my third glassful; you said to drink a lot"—drank some more and they talked. Camus. The drawing. Who did it? He wouldn't know the artist, she said. And the other works? Most of them are by friends. Some she bought; some are gifts. And the sculpture? "Is it a real Brancusi?" and she said "If it were, I'd keep it behind Plexiglas in a vault and wouldn't be able to enjoy it," and he said "I didn't think so. I like it. A little bit of forgery, but it's good. Gift too?" and she nodded. "You're lucky to have so many good artist friends." Her work, his. The meal tonight. "I'd go back," she said. How she might have drunk too much beer and wine, "but I told you that; hence, the aspirins and drowning myself in water. Are you all right in the armchair? You seem to be squirming. At least you're not sneezing and tearing up from all the cat hair. It's their favorite place during the day." "I don't mind," he said. "And I don't seem to be allergic to any-thing. Where'd they go?" and she said "There's a shelf in the back of the kitchen that they usually stop off at before climbing into bed with me. I always have it set up with towels for them to lie on. Also, it's an uncomfort-able chair you've chosen, Martin. You should move to the couch." "To be honest, it is a bit uncomfortable, but it's a lot more comfortable than the

Morris chair I have at home. Do you mind?" and he got up, and she said "It was my suggestion," and he sat at the other end of the couch. "And that's right," she said; "it's called a Morris chair. I knew it was some name like that, but I thought 'Melvin.' Only kidding, but I really wasn't sure what name it was. A friend gave it to me with worn-down cushions. I meant to get the chair reupholstered, but so much for what I want to do and do. I shouldn't let anyone sit in it. I should put a rope across it, as they do in museums, and a sign on the seat that says 'Please do not sit.' Does yours also have an adjustable back?" and he said "I think they all do. It was designed and I think even first crafted by a nineteenth-century British poet," and she said "I know. Melvin Morris. Quite the Renaissance man." She's funny, he thought. But why'd he have to act like such a pedant? *Nineteenth-century. British poet. First crafted.* What bullshit. She dealt with it nicely, though. He wanted to move closer to her and take her hand. It'd be a start. Wanted to end up kissing her. For the pleasure of it and to get the first out of the way. Does it mean anything that she invited him up here and then to sit on the couch with her? he thought. Doesn't have to. Could be just what she said: that she wanted him to be warm before he headed home, and to get him out of an uncomfortable chair. Wasn't that uncomfortable to him but it might be to her and other guests. Anyway, what should he say to get some action going? "Do you mind if I move a little closer, and not because this part of the couch is uncomfortable?" "Mind if I move closer to you?" he said. "I feel so far away." "Sure, move closer," she said, "there's plenty of room," and he moved to about a foot from her. He was on her right. She put her glass on the coffee table; it didn't seem in anticipation of anything from him. He reached over for his brandy glass with his right hand and touched her right hand with his left. Did it intentionally, and immediately pulled it away. "Was my hand cold?" she said. "It feels cold," and he said "No, it was fine. Actually, I barely touched it, so I really couldn't tell. But funny you should bring it up, because it was something I was just wondering myself. If your hand could be cold from your glass. A thought that came out of nowhere." "Oh, come on," she said, "you didn't think it," and he said "I did, really; I don't know why. Here," and he sipped some brandy and put the glass back on the coffee table, "let me touch it once more." "Why?" she said, and he said "I don't know. To touch it. To make it warm." "So it *was* cold," and he said "No, it wasn't, or only a little, but I only touched it a second, so I'm not sure. Let me make the definitive test. I'll take your hand and tell you if it's as cold as you think. Of course, it might be warm now and get cold from my hand having held the cold brandy, but I don't think so." "We're being silly," and he said "You mean I'm being silly, and I know. But is it all right? Your hand?" and she said "If you like." He took her right hand in his and held it. "It's warm," he said. "Maybe it was cold before for some reason, but it's warm now." He put his left hand over his mouth like a megaphone and said "No cold hand, I have to report. And the other hand wouldn't be cold because you didn't hold the glass with it." He put his left hand under the hand he held. "You have small hands. I do too, for a man my height, but mine are small and fat, while yours are not small, I'm saying, for a woman, and thin. Normal." He took his left hand away, raised her hand to his face and kissed it. "I was about to say 'You're not going to kiss my hand,'" she said, "but you beat me to it." "Did you mind?" and she said "Uh-uh." "May I kiss it again?" and she said "No. Hands aren't very clean, even after you wash them. They should be scrubbed with a brush and I didn't do that." "But is it still all right to hold it?" and she said "Yes, you can hold it." "May I hold both?" and she said "If you want." He took her other hand with his left. Then they just stared at each other and he smiled and she did and he inched closer to her, still holding her hands, and kissed her forehead a few times and then her cheek once or twice, all with his eyes open—she closed hers every time he kissed her—and then he closed his eyes and kissed her lips. When they came apart, he was no longer holding her hands. It had happened without him knowing it. Maybe she'd pulled her hands out of his. Maybe she did it without knowing it. They stared at each other again and then smiled at the same time. He put his arms around her, and she put her right arm on top of his left and around his shoulder and then took it away—it must have been uncomfortable for her or she thought it'd be uncomfortable for him—and they kissed again, a much longer one. Her lips were soft, breath sweet, skin soft, hair falling over her cheek smelled sweet. While they were kissing a third time, he opened his eyes and saw hers were closed. She looked like she was sleeping. They kissed some more. She said once when they were separated but he was still holding her "That was nice," and he said "I know...I mean, it was." During their last kiss—there must have been five, six—he put his hand under her shirt in back and rubbed her waist and lower back and then moved his hand to the side and up and a little over in front till it covered the left cup of her bra. She said "Please don't," and straightened up and took his hand out and held it and said "Too fast. And it's getting late for me. And I don't feel right about it just yet," and he said "About me?" and she said "The fondling." "That's fine, there's always another day, and this has been so nice, I can't tell you how much. Being with you, the West End, dinner, having a brandy here; kissing, of course." She let go of his hand and pulled down her shirt." "The brandy was drinkable?" and he said "You bet. Not quite R.S.O.P., or whatever the initials are on the French brandy and Cognac bottles, but I'm hardly complaining. About anything, and it warmed me up for the outside." "Want to finish what's in your glass?" and he thought Should he? No, let it go so she'll think he can leave some behind, and said "Thanks; I've had enough." He stood up and said "I should get my coat." "Let me get it for you," she said, standing up. They went to the coat closet. She got his coat off its hanger and gave it to him and he put it on and buttoned up. "You should get a warmer coat," she said. "It's not even January," and he said "I should; one down to my knees and maybe with a fleece-lined hood. So—" and then "My muffler," and picked it up off the closet floor. "Sorry. I didn't put it there. And your cap?" and he said "In my pocket. So, I'll call you?" and she said "I'd like that." "One more kiss?" and she said "Just one, a little one. Then you have to go." They kissed, longer and deeper than a little one, but she let him. He should have just made it a quick little one, he thought; done what she'd asked. Well, it won't ruin anything. He stepped back and said "I want you to know I really, really enjoyed myself tonight. I'll even throw in another "really,'" and she said "Thank you." "Now I have to, though it's very difficult for me to, go," and he turned around and tried opening the door. There were two locks and he tried several times but couldn't get them unlocked at the same time. "It's tricky," she said, and unlocked and opened the door. "Bye," he said, and touched her shoulder. "You don't have gloves?" and he said "Did I leave them in the restaurant or bar, or did I even take them with me tonight?" "I don't remember them," and he said "I'm sure I left them home. If not, I have a duplicate pair, bought when I thought I'd lost the original one." "Also," she said, "thank you for not trying to push me into something. It wouldn't have worked but I'm glad you didn't try," and he said "No, I like the way the evening ended." "Goodnight. If you don't mind, I won't wait till the elevator comes. A breeze whooshes into the apartment from the broken window by the stairs there," and he said "Not at all. Go inside. Stay warm. I'll be fine." He rang for the elevator a few feet away and she closed the door. The elevator came. Two women were on it. "Good evening," he said, and one of the women said "Hello." "It's a nice night," he said, as the elevator descended. "Brisk and clear and not harsh." "Riverside Drive is always ten degrees colder than the rest of the West Side," one of the women said, and he said "Is it? Probably because of the wind and river." He stepped aside so the women could leave first. One of them said "Thank you," and they both went through the revolving door. He said "Goodnight, Cal" to the nightman behind the cubicle's window. Cal waved to him, and he went outside. I can't believe I'm so lucky, he thought, feeling his jacket pocket to make sure he still had his book with him. Again: hadn't gone to Yaddo, wouldn't have met Pati, wouldn't have met her. The girl of my dreams and a great kisser. He doesn't remember if he took the subway or the Broadway bus home. Knows he thought of waiting for the downtown bus across the Drive, but that might mean a long wait and it was very cold.

Now this is what he doesn't understand. Why did he wait so long to call her after their second date? After he first met her at the party, he can understand why he didn't call so fast. But he went over all that. Nervous about speaking to her. Didn't want to be rejected. Thought waiting a few days before calling would up his chances of meeting her than calling right away or even in two to three days. How many days was it? He knows. Around a week. But it was mostly just nerves and that he wasn't used to calling up someone for a date. But after the second date, when they had a good time together and the conversation flowed and so on and she invited him up and it seemed she was beginning to like him a little? They'd probably end up in bed next time they met or get pretty close to it, and then on the fourth date they would. Based on what happened at the end of their second date and something she said—he forgets what it was exactly but something like they shouldn't rush things too fast, which meant on their second date—he was almost sure of it. Would have been so simple. And he was no longer nervous about calling her. He'd call the next day or day after that, but no longer. She'd agree to see him, but for what? Maybe he'd suggest a movie and then a bite to eat and a drink after. She might say "A movie would be fine—I love movies—but something to eat and drink after, we'll see. Possibly just some nice place for tea. Anyway, I'd love to go to a movie with you." Does that sound like her? It sounds like her, and she'd say "I'm free," and mention the nights she was, and he'd say "I'm free every night this week and next, though let's not wait till next, so whatever day works best for you is okay with me." They'd meet, either at the movie theater or her apartment or in her building's lobby—no, why go to her building? He'd suggest they meet at the theater—he'd have, in preparation for this, the newspaper opened to the listings of movies playing. But that wouldn't be good for all week, maybe not even the next day, so they'd find out what movie to see and the times it's playing some other way. Maybe she'd say she'd like to see a certain movie, and he'd look in the newspaper to see where it's playing and call the theater for the time schedule on the evening they want to see it.

Then, after the movie, they'd have a drink or snack or both or tea and pastry in a nice place close to the theater and then he'd go with her to her building and in front of it or in the lobby or during the subway or bus ride or walk to her building she'd say something like "Care to come up again for a nightcap?" Or maybe not. Maybe she'd still have work to do that night for the next day or have to get up early the next day to teach. So they wouldn't go to bed together that night after the movie, or whatever they'd do on that date. But he'd make sure their next date would be on a Friday or Saturday night so she'd have no urgent work to do later on or a class to teach the next day. Maybe they'd go to a play this time or have dinner out again or he'd pick up Chinese or Indian food on his way to her place and some good beer and a decent wine, or maybe she'd want to make dinner for them in her apartment, and after one of those they'd make love. But he didn't call her for a week. Again, he doesn't know why. Thought about it a number of times and could never come up with an explanation that seemed right. He asked her about it sometime later—many months later. By now—actually, from a week or so after they first made love—they were seeing each other four to five times a week. He said "How come I waited so long to call you after our second date?" "Which one was that?" she said, and he said "When we had drinks at the West End and then dinner at the Strauss Cafe, I think it's called. I walked you home. It was very cold—unusually so for early or mid-December. *Early*, since I first met you at Pati's birthday party in late November—that night also turned out to be your parents' wedding anniversary—waited a week before I called you for our first date—that mostly had to do with nerves on my part—but I called you for our second date the next day. By the way, you had liver and onions and I had an omelet at the restaurant. Because it was so cold out, I wanted to share a soup with you, but you didn't want one. I think you thought it was too early in our knowing each other to share the same bowl—spoons I could have got two of—so I didn't order it. You invited me up for a nightcap, you called it— your father's brandy from Israel. I poured myself one. When you were in the bathroom I secretly poured myself another, a much larger shot—you didn't know that," and she said "Because you never told me, but it's not important. You like your liquor—I know that." "You mean all alcohol—wine, beer, aperitifs, and such—but never to excess. It's true, and it's not something I'm saying I like about myself, and I'm grateful you never made an issue of it, that there haven't been many evenings in my adult life that I haven't had a drink or two. We kissed, at the end of our second date, though didn't fondle. Then you sent me home—out into the cold—but said before I left that you were glad I didn't put any pressure on you to make love." "That I remember—the liver and onions and soup I don't—and I didn't think it was an act. I was impressed by the respect you showed my wishes and your self-control. And our third date?" and he said "That was the night we first made love." "After only three dates?" and he said "Two and a half, really. The first was just for coffee and tea and a short stroll, so I don't know if we should consider it a full date." "Consider it," she said. "Otherwise, I come off as being too easy." "Also, the third wasn't a date. I called from the street. It was late. Ten. More like eleven. I doubt I would have called you later than that. I think I had a couple of drinks in me, not that I needed them to want to call and be with you. You told me, after I asked if you'd like to meet at the West End for a quick beer, that if I can make it to your apartment fast, then come. If not, call again, but at a more reasonable hour. So maybe it was a little before twelve and I called you later than I thought I should," and she said "It seems like I never should have let you up. I don't know what was in my mind. Probably the same as was in yours. But why didn't you phone me earlier that night?" and he said "I was out, at a party—" and she said "You were at a party? I don't remember that either. Haven't we ever talked about this?" and he said "I guess we haven't. Or we did when I got to your place but it was a very quick conversation, you might have been tired, me too, and we both forgot it. How I got to the party's a bit complicated. My friend Manny had been invited and asked me to go with him. It was in the Twenties, Chelsea area, off Ninth Avenue. The couple who gave it lived in the entire three- or four-story brownstone and were giving a fundraiser for a new literary magazine that was going to, they said, pay major-magazine fees for fiction, poetry and articles. I don't know how Manny, not your biggest reader, got invited. Maybe one of the hosts or editors worked at the same company as he—Pfizer—and he thought I'd be interested because of the type of magazine and its fees, and he also didn't want to go alone." "What magazine was it?" and he said "No name yet, and it never got off the ground. I suppose the fundraiser was a bust—I know I didn't contribute any money—or the couple lost interest. But Manny seemed all right there. I was bored. The other guests were business people—lawyers, professionals, financial advisors, a college president...dull. So I left, started home—maybe now it was around eleven—but wanted some fresh air and exercise first, and after about half an hour into my walk uptown I thought of you—oh, I was probably thinking of you the whole walk—but why in hell I haven't called you, so, quite simply, I called. That's how I ended up at your place our first love night. Not a date, you see, or even a meeting, really. But a spur-of-the-moment something, or a whim or fancy, and I didn't want it to be one, that ended up being agreeable to both of us, it seemed, and everything after that turned out to be okay. Well, not everything—we had our big breakup—but almost." All but the end of that was a lie, and he never told her what really happened. Didn't think it smart to, even after they'd been married a few years and had kids and their marriage, for the most part, was solid. And he still doesn't know why he didn't call her sooner—two days after he last saw her, at the most three, but best the next day. "Said I'd call. Even if I didn't, you knew I'd call. Wanted to see you again. So here I am. You busy tonight or tomorrow night, and if not, the day after?" That's all he had to say. It wasn't that he was too busy to see her. All he was doing with his time was writing during the day and a little at night, but mostly reading at night, listening to music, seeing his mother at her apartment every other day around five for a drink, and sometimes around eight or nine meeting Manny for beers at O'Neal's. He could spend his time like that, without holding down a regular job, because he was still living off the advance for his last book and the sale of a story to *Harper's*, and was expecting—his agent said it was a sure thing, or maybe by now he already got it; he was never clear about the timing of this—an advance for his next book from the same publisher. Knows he was anxious. Probably about dating a woman he might end up really liking. So it was about getting involved again and all the problems that could possibly bring—the woman suddenly deciding she didn't want to see him again, etcetera, even after they'd slept together a number of times and said they were in love with each other, etcetera. He just doesn't know. Something, though, kept him back from calling her. Maybe the same reasons that took him so long—also a week—from calling her for their first date, when they met at the Ansonia drugstore. He forgets what those reasons were. He's remembered them and would again if he put his head to it, he thinks. Thought about her every day—he's saying, after their second date. Should he call her today? Should he call her tonight? What's stopping him from calling? If he does call and they meet, and he's certain they'll at least do that, there's a good chance he'll sleep with her that night. Sleeping with a beauty. That's what he wants, right? Or even better: sleeping with a beauty he really likes. What could be wrong with that? And she kissed so well. She's almost sure to make love well too. A foolish thought, if he thought it, and it's something at the time he thinks he would have. And it's been a while, he thought. Let's face it: he's been getting horny. But he wouldn't call her for a third date and the possibility of sleeping with her just because he's horny. He'd do it because he likes her and wants to be with her, and bed would seem, after what happened at the end of their last date, the natural and maybe inevitable place for them to end up. Oh, that's enough. By now it seems he'll never know what took him so long to call, and from the street, when he finally did, and so late. It's important to know? Now? No. Then give up on it. So what happened that night? In other words, what is it he never told her? He lied. No Manny that night. No party in Chelsea, and so on. He did go to a party at a couple's single-family brownstone there, but they already had a literary magazine, named after their P.O. box number—*Box 523* or something—and that was six to seven years before. A New Year's Day party. Lit Christmas tree that reached the ceiling. Champagne and a punch bowl and chafing dishes, with Sterno cans underneath, on a long mahogany table. A polished mahogany table. He was invited by a friend, not Manny, and stayed a few hours—there were several attractive women there, married and unmarried, but none of them, when he got to speak to them, interested in him. But that night, the one where he called Gwen from the street and she invited him to her apartment and about a half-hour after he got there they started to make love, he wanted to call her earlier but from home. Same old story. Told himself: tomorrow. Then: that's what you said last night and the night before. Why don't you call now? I don't know, he told himself. That's also what you said last night and the night before. Just take a walk. Clear your mind, think things out. Try to find out why you're not calling her when it's obvious you want to. But dress warmly, because it might be cold. So he took a walk downtown. Put a slim paperback in his back pants pocket first. Walked down Columbus Avenue to Lincoln Center, then down Broadway to Columbus Circle, all on the east side of the street because it was brighter and livelier. Then, for the same reasons, down Broadway on the west side of the street to 43rd or 44th. While he walked, doesn't think he thought much as to why he wasn't calling her. Usually doesn't think about something he specifically goes out for a walk to. Must have been around ten-thirty when he started back uptown, so a lot later than that when he finally did call her that night, since some of the Broadway shows were breaking. Stopped in what used to be called a cheap Irish bar for a Scotch on the rocks, or maybe it was an Irish whiskey. Then another, but he knows he didn't have a third. Didn't want to be tipsy so far from home, and he might not be able to get a cab if he thought he couldn't get home without one. He was feeling a little high when he left the bar. Probably because—two Scotches or whiskeys wouldn't have done it alone—he'd also had, though he'd walked off some of it, two vodka and grapefruit juice drinks at home to relax him enough to call Gwen from there. He'd walked a block or so north when he suddenly thought, and it did come to him like that—seemingly out of nowhere, though the drinking helped—why not go to a prostitute? Last one he went to was in San Francisco ten years ago. Got her phone number from a man he sat next to at a bar and started up a conversation with, and called her from a pay phone there and went to her the next day. Wanted to go to her that night but she said she was busy modeling for art classes. Tried kissing her while he was on top of her, but she wouldn't let him. "That you don't get even if you paid me extra." She was pretty and young and had a nice body, just like the man had said, but why would he want to kiss her? To make her seem less like a whore to him and more like his girlfriend? Or he thought kissing her while he was inside her would make the sex better. She also seemed fairly bright, by the words she used, and had a sense of humor—when he asked her name—it was probably a line she used a lot—she said "Kitty. That's not my real one, of course, but my nom de guerre"—that he had a fantasy about coming back weekly, but never did. He bought a copy of *Frig* magazine at a kiosk on Broadway, didn't know where to open it—not on the street with so many people passing—so he went into another bar, ordered a beer, went into a bathroom stall, sat on the toilet, pissed, and turned to the section of the magazine that listed and rated whorehouses in New York. He knew it'd be in there because he'd bought the magazine twice the past year, but for the full-page close-up photos of female genitalia, which he masturbated to a few times over a couple of weeks, and then tore up the magazine and threw it away. There was a highly rated house near where he was, between Ninth and Tenth Avenues, open till 1 a.m. "Clean, low-keyed, not pushy and, unusual for a house with budget prices, always ten to twelve eye-filling girls," it said, or something like it. A "shortie" cost fifteen dollars, "plus the expected $5 tip," which was cheaper than he thought it'd be. The prostitute ten years ago was ten dollars, and he thinks he gave her a two-dollar tip. Go ahead, he thought. If the neighborhood looks rough or the place is a dump and none of the women is anywhere near to being attractive, he'll leave without going with one, even if he paid his fifteen dollars at the door to get in. When he got about a block from the place, he thought You really going to a whorehouse, risking getting who knows what there? Why even think about it when you could be sleeping with Gwen the next week or so if everything goes all right with her? He doesn't want to wait. Besides, what's the guarantee anything will work out with her? Two dates, some big kisses, a good, he thought, rapport?…he's been wrong on that score plenty of times, and if the place he's going to does have ten to twelve women, he'd have a wide choice.

There's got to be at least one who's young and attractive and doesn't look cheap. And he'll make this the last time he'll go to a prostitute, and he'll wear a bag, which he's sure she'll have and even insist he put on. "Stardust"—that's what the place was called. It occupied an entire brownstone and had banners hanging from its third-floor windowsills that said "Girls! Girls! Girls!" A man was standing in front of the long stoop that led to the entrance, he assumed, handing out flyers to the place. What's he talking about? That was a whorehouse in the Diamond District he passed a number of times more than thirty years ago—usually when he was on his way to a photocopy shop on Madison—but never thought to go in. He knows exactly where it was: two brownstones up from the southeast corner of 47th Street and Sixth Avenue. He got to the street the Stardust was on and continued walking up Broadway. Going to whores, he thought, was something he did another time in his life. He just couldn't see himself choosing a woman from whatever number of them were there, no matter how good-looking she was, and if she was really young it might even be more depressing, and following her to her room, making small talk, maybe having to wash his genitals and putting on a bag and getting on top of her, maybe the tenth and last guy of the day, and sticking it in, though with his fat prick a couple of them have said he'd hurt them in that position so they'll have to get on top. Thinking about it, he gets an erection and starts playing with himself and then thinks No, what are you doing? and stops. He has to pee again but doesn't want to get out of bed. Oh, do it now, when you're not so tired, and he gets up, pees, washes his hands and gets back in bed. He dumped the copy of *Frig* into a city trashcan on the street when nobody was near enough to see him do it, reached Lincoln Center and wondered if he should cross to Columbus or continue up Broadway. Columbus would be shorter, but if he takes Broadway he could pick up an early edition of the *Times* at the newsstand on the corner of 72nd Street. Then he thought to call her. Again, thought just came. No, bad idea, he thought; it's too late. But he could pretend he didn't know how late it was. He could ask her out for a quick drink at the West End—say he'll meet her, in fact, in her lobby and walk her up there. His excuse for not calling her earlier tonight, if he feels he has to make one? He took a long walk—he was trying to come up with a story idea, since he finished a new story today and hates not to have something by his typewriter to work on the next day—a single opening line, even, that has the potential to grow into a story. That's the way he works, he could say, and he supposes is one of the reasons he's so prolific. But he must have started out in his walk later than he thought and also walked much longer than he thought. Did he come up with anything, if she asks? No, but he will. Later tonight. Even in a dream. Or tomorrow. If she sounds a bit put off that he called so late, especially after not calling for close to a week, he could say he's sorry and he'll call tomorrow at a more appropriate time, if it's still all right with her that he call. Oh, just call. No excuses or lies. He could ask her out for a drink, but she'll know the real reason why he called. What could be the worst she'll say—all this if she's home, of course, and he hopes she is, alone, and not out on a date: "Call me again at a more appropriate time?" He'd memorized her phone number by now, though it was also in the memobook he had on him. He checked the book to make sure he had the number right—he did—and dialed it from a pay phone by Lincoln Center and she said hello. He said "Hi, hello, it's Martin—Martin Samuels. How are you?" and she said "I'm all right, thank you. And you?" "Fine. Listen," he said, "maybe it's too late in the evening to call you—I know it is, and I'm sorry. I'm also very sorry I haven't called in the last few days. I wanted to, to talk to you and possibly see you, but things happened. It's a long dull story you don't want to hear. But I wondered, and I know there's only a small chance of this, if you'd like to meet at the West End, or I could come and get you, so you wouldn't have to walk to it alone, for a drink or hot chocolate or whatever they might have there that you might like?" "Do you mean now?" and he said "Yeah, didn't I say? Tonight. Now." "It is late. Maybe if you had called earlier I could have found the time." "Earlier than tonight, you mean?" and she said "Tonight would have been all right. But I'm saying, at an earlier hour." "Too bad I waited, then. And I hope I didn't wake you," and she said "No, you didn't wake me. It might be late for me to meet someone at a bar for even a quick drink"—"Yes, that's all I planned it to be, a quick drink and then I'd see you safely home"—"but it's still a little early for me to be asleep. I'm watching the end of a PBS nature program on gorillas, in fact." "Then maybe I'm holding you up and you want to get back to it," and she said "I've seen it before. It's a rerun; very interesting and unusually done. No dry narration telling us what we're seeing. Not a single word, right from the opening. Just the sounds of the gorillas and their activities and the nature around them—birds, wind, storms, a falling tree." "Sounds good," he said. "I don't have a TV—haven't much liked watching it for a long time—but what you're telling me is I might be missing something every now and then. Anyway, we can't meet. I don't know why I thought there was even a small possibility we could. At least you don't appear to be angry at me for calling this late. And I'm glad I didn't wait longer to call tonight, where I might have wakened you. I'm very prompt when it comes to appointments and meeting people but tend to lose track of time when I'm by myself." "I'm not angry at all. You could even say I'm pleased that you called. I'll admit I was somewhat puzzled why I didn't hear from you, but thought it was your own business. Look, let me think for a moment. Martin," and he said "Sure; take as long as you want," and she said "I didn't mean it quite that way. Where are you? Obviously, from the traffic noises, on the street, but whereabouts?" "Broadway and 83rd. I took a long walk, which might have contributed to making me lose my sense of time, to think over a number of serious technical problems in a story I've been writing." "You haven't had too much to drink, have you? You don't sound like it," and he said "I stopped in some place for a beer, but mostly to use its men's room, and finished less than a half the glass." "Then how about this possibility? You're not that far away from me where, if you want to come here, you can." "That'd be great," he said. "I'd love to see you." "I hate to sound demanding, but could you please be here in half an hour? It is getting late and I'd rather not be waiting around too long." "I can take a cab and be there in less than ten minutes. Lots of empty cabs passing every second," and she said "I don't know why I'm doing this. There's always another day. I guess I wouldn't mind seeing you too," and he said "Same with me, which you just said." "You know the address to give to the driver?" and he said "Four-twenty-five, corner of a Hundred-fifteenth. I even remember the floor you're on, though not the apartment number…not necessary. There are only two in the hallway. It's the one to the left when you get off the elevator." "The right," she said: "7J," and he said "I meant the right, and that your elevator's the one you see when you go through the building's revolving door." "You got it," she said. "I'll ring downstairs to the doorman to let you in the building and upstairs." "Same one from the other night; Cal?" and she said "I don't know who's on tonight. You do have a good memory, though. So I'll see you soon, Martin." "I'm on my way. Do you need anything? and she said "That'd just detain you, and I have everything I need. Good-bye," and he said "Good-bye," and she hung up. He thought about taking a cab and then thought subway's right here, 66th Street. It'll take him to the Columbia station in ten minutes, probably getting him to her place fast as a cab would, if he hustles once he gets out of the station, and for a lot less money. He took the subway. Train came in a few minutes and he got off at a Hundred-sixteenth. Ran south on Broadway for a block, then down Riverside Drive. Cal wasn't on. Another doorman, sitting in a leather chair by the door, reading a Russian newspaper, or some language in Cyrillic. "Good evening. Martin Samuels," he said. "7J said she'd call down to you beforehand that I was coming," and the man pointed to the elevator and said "Press seven button." In the elevator going up, he thought Should he kiss her when she opens the door? Certainly her cheek, if she offers it. But the lip kiss he should wait till she adjusts more to his being there. Okay, here goes, and the elevator opened. She was waiting at her front door when he got off. "Hi," she said, and he said "Hi," and they went inside. "I want you to know, I'm not psychic. I asked Boris to call me when you were coming up. I thought it'd be more hospitable greeting you at the door than letting you wait behind it." "I appreciate that. May I hang up my coat and put away my book?" and she said "What are you reading?" and he pulled it out of his back pants pocket and showed it to her. "No, I don't know it. You'll have to tell me about it, if you're enjoying it." He put the book and his cap on the shelf above the coats in the foyer closet and hung his muffler and coat on the same hanger. "Aren't you cold in so light a coat?" and he said "This isn't so light and it's not that bad out." Should he try for a little kiss now? Big, little, don't rush it, and holding off might even be the best move. She'd, he'd think, prefer him taking it slow, and besides, the conversation so far has been a bit stiff, nothing conducive for a kiss. She put her hand out for them to go into the living room, a gesture—the way she did it: sort of a sweep—he thought fairly formal. What's going on? She have a change of mind about him since they spoke on the phone and is going to ask him to leave soon? "Your cats," he said. "I'm beginning to think you don't have any," and she said. "You wouldn't think that if you had to change their litter box every other day. They've gone beddy-bye for the night. I hate to think it, but the poor dears are getting old." "Actually, I did see them the last time, didn't I?" "I don't know. Incidentally, I never asked if you worked out your literary problems in your walk," and he said "No, but I will. Sometimes it takes two walks." "A two-walk problem. Sounds formidable. Care for a drink? The beer selection hasn't improved, but I still have a good red wine and several teas, herbal and nonherbal. I can even make you a hot chocolate," and he said "That'd be nice, but would it be all right if I have another of that Israeli brandy? I really liked it," and she said "Help yourself. I think you know where everything is. Snifter in the refrigerator, brandy on the glasses shelf in the kitchen cupboard with the elephant-ear plants on top. Kidding. You can be so funny at times, I thought I should add my own joke. But please, take, I mean it," and he said "Take my brandy, please take my brandy." She said "I don't understand," and he said "You're not familiar with that old Henny Youngman line?" "Who's that?" and he said "A comedian; post-World War II. Very Jewish. A line about his wife. Also lots of quips about army life, or maybe that was Harvey Stone. I'm really dating myself here. And your joke was good and original," and she said "I don't know about 'good,' and it doesn't take much to be original. Just say what's never been said, no matter how dumb and non sequiturial. See? I just did it. Get your drink." It's going better now, he thought, and went into the kitchen. "Or maybe I should attend to it," she said from the living room. "Why am I suddenly being inhospitable?" "Stay there," he said. "I can take care of it. Want me to pour you some?" and she said "It's a little late for me to drink." "One short one won't hurt"—he didn't want to be the only one drinking and with booze on his breath—and she said "Oh, all right, but a thimbleful. Just put mine in a juice glass; you'll find it in the dish rack by the sink." "I can have mine in a juice glass too," and she said "Use the snifter. Your brandy will taste much better in it, and you can snift it. I'm having so little—more to be hospitable—it doesn't count." He got the snifter out of the cupboard—it seemed clean but he still rinsed it—and poured the brandy into the two glasses, inch for her, two inches for him. He drank half of his, poured another inch into his glass, put the bottle back on the side shelf of the refrigerator and brought the glasses into the living room. No TV around, he noticed, so it must be in the bedroom. She was sitting on the couch. "Maybe you're hungry," she said. "I should have asked. I have these delicious coconut macaroons." "Nah, I'm all right. Don't get up." "If you change your mind, they're in the cookie tin on top of the refrigerator. I also have chocolates from Mondell's, a candy shop up the block. People come from all over the city to buy them, some even send their chauffeurs. One's a famous actress, but I won't name names." "Why not?" and she said "The owner asked me not to. All right. Katharine Hepburn. Her particular favorite is called almond cluster. I think I have one of those left." "I'm not much for chocolates, but thanks." He gave her her glass—did it while he was standing so he wouldn't spill anything from either glass as he sat down—and sat beside her. "You gave me too much—you might have to finish mine—but cheers," and they clinked glasses and laughed at that. "What an odd couple," she said, "—a juice glass and a snifter. But we should drink. Otherwise, no cheers," and they drank. Talked. "So how have you been?" he started off with. "I know that sounds like a stupid question, but it has been a while." After she said "Good, fine, busy," he said "Me, it's been the same: write, write, write. Gets so dull." He asked and she told him what she's been working on the last few days. "Stuff that has to be done if I want to have a career." "You must work in your bedroom, because I see no evidence of a work space here," and she said "You're quite the quick observer. What else have you discovered about me?" "Nothing." They talked a little more. He forgets about what. He actually felt a little dizzy and there was a welling-up feeling—something—in his chest. It felt good but uncomfortable. By now he knows all he wanted to do was kiss her. Leaned over to. She said "I think we should put our glasses down or else they'll get crushed. They did, hers on the coffee table, his on the end table on his right. "So you know what I want to do?" and she said "You've given unmistakable signs." "Then it's all right?" and she said "Our glasses are down, and it was nice the last time." He leaned over to her again. She closed her eyes just before he did and they kissed. The first was long. There were others of all kinds: short, long, one with their mouths open, one where they touched tongues, lip kisses, cheek and neck kisses; for him forehead and then eyebrow kisses. "That feels funny," she said. "You don't like it? It's not something I have to do," and she said into his ear because their cheeks were touching "Martin, it's fine." They kissed some more on the lips. He put his hands under her shirt in back as he did the first night he was here, then up her left side and on the same cup of her bra. She let him leave his hand there and then let him move it around. He tried to get his hand under the cup, couldn't—something to do with the bra's supports or it was on too tight—so he started unhitching the straps in back while they kissed. She pulled her face away and said "Maybe we should just go to the bedroom." "I'd love to," and she said "Then let's, though let me shut off the lights in the kitchen first and make sure the front door's locked." She stood up, pulled her shirt down from the bottom and stuck her hand down her shirt in back to do something with the bra. "Done with your drink?" and he thought should he swig it down? Sip just a little? Leave it? Leave it, and he said "I've had enough." "Sure?" I don't mean to be hurrying you. I'm just being obsessive about cleaning up," and he said "Then let me take a last short sip. It's so good," and he sipped a little and gave her his glass—she already had hers—and she took them into the kitchen. She must have rinsed them—that was the sound he heard—and placed them upside down in the dish rack or on the glass holders on the side of it. She then switched off the kitchen lights and went to the front door and he heard the latch in the lock click and the door chain slide on. She came back and held out her hand to him. He took it, got up, made his way around the coffee table, still holding her hand, and they went into the bedroom.

This is one of his favorite memories of her. He'd just got off the elevator on her floor, was going to ring her doorbell. He had a key to her apartment, which she'd given him a few weeks before—two months after they started seeing each other—but it still didn't feel right using it if he knew she was home. She was playing the piano. Later, when he asked, she said it was the second Intermezzo for piano by Brahms. She had been taking lessons at the time from an Austrian piano teacher who'd also become a good friend of hers. The teacher played at their wedding in their apartment; the opening Preludes and Fugues of *The Well-Tempered Clavier*, before the ceremony began, and a late Haydn sonata during the reception. The Intermezzo was one of the pieces her teacher had given her to learn. Standing behind the door, he thought It's a beautiful piece and she's playing it beautifully. Lying in bed now, he hums the most memorable and tender part of it. He thought he'd hold off ringing the bell till she was finished. He didn't want to interrupt her and his listening to it. He'd wait a minute till after she stopped playing to make sure she was done. If she started again or another piece, he'd then ring the bell or quietly let himself in with the key. Probably the key. About a minute after she stopped playing, he rang the bell. She came to the door and said "Hiya, my darling," and he said "Hi, my wonderful pianist," and they kissed. "Have you been lurking behind my door listening to me play?" and he said "Just the last five minutes. I was entranced. I've never heard a piano piece played so exquisitely." "Nonsense," she said. "I'm only just learning it." "What can I tell you? I was very much moved by it," and she said "Maybe that comes from something that has nothing to do with my playing or the music. Which is not to say I don't very much appreciate what you said." "Do you think you could play it again for me? I'd love an interior hearing of it," and she said "Wish I could, but I've played it three times already this afternoon and I'm a little tired of it and also of playing. Can we just have tea?"

Another memory, also music. They're sitting in one of the front rows in the orchestra of the Meyerhoff Symphony Hall, but all the way to the left. He tried to get center seats but they were all sold. The Baltimore Symphony Orchestra is playing Respighi's *Pines of Rome*. "There's no other orchestral music I know of—maybe *Firebird*," he said when they were choosing which six concerts to go to in their subscription series, "that has as great a buildup and a more powerful ending, and I've always wanted to hear it performed live." "Anything you want," she said, "except Bruckner. I'm not familiar with it, either on record or the radio, though I have liked his *Fountains of Rome*. During the last few minutes of the piece, when the music is building to the climax, he moves his right hand as if he's conducting, and continues to, his motions getting increasingly more vigorous, till the end. Later, when it seems the entire audience around them is standing and applauding, he stays seated, grinning at her and crying a little, and says "Don't mind me. And stand if you want. But what do you think? Did you like it?" and she says "No, no, I'll sit with you, and I liked it a lot. I can see why one could get overcome by it." "I didn't embarrass you with my hand-waving?" and she says "Not whatsoever. You did a brilliant job of conducting. They never played better. Not a weak moment from any section in the orchestra. What I'd like to know, though, is how, in what I assume were the exact times they were supposed to come in, you got the birds to tweet."

Sibelius. He drives a poet and her husband to the train station after she gave a reading for his department. On the way home he turns on the Baltimore classical music station. It's playing a piece he's never heard before but which sounds like Sibelius. He parks, sits in the car in his carport till the piece is over so he can get the name of it. *Nightride and Sunrise.* Few days later he buys a CD of five Sibelius tone poems, listens to the whole CD that night and then just that one piece every night for around a week. He wants her to listen to it with him—not at dinner but in the living room where the CD player and speakers are—but she's always busy in her study researching and writing a paper for an academic conference in a month and also things to do with her teaching. Finally, he knocks on her study door and says "May I come in?" He tells her "Really, I want you to listen to that new CD I got. Just one piece on it; it's only fifteen minutes long. It's so moving and evocative of the sea and sky—you'll love it. And like the *Firebird Suite* and *Pines of Rome*, it has an incredible powerful ending." She says "I've heard it, I've heard it. You've played nothing else the past week." "But you heard it with your door shut. You're not getting the full impact of it. Come on; you're resisting too much. I'm going to have to insist," and he takes her hand. "You don't like it the first time, I'll never ask you to listen to it again." "All right," she says. "Looks like I can't stop you," and they go into the living room. He says "Sit in the Morris chair; you'll hear it best from there. Some wine?" and she says "Too early and I still have work to do, even after dinner." "Fire?" and she says "Too warm and too much of a bother." "Maybe I should shut off the lights. I know I listened to it twice that way, totally in the dark, and you really see the imagery Sibelius is trying to create," and she says "Sweetheart, just play it." The CD's already in the player from last night. He turns the system on, gets to the third track, turns off all the lights in the room and sits at the end of the couch near her chair. After it's over, *Finlandia* comes on. He turns on the floor lamp between them, turns off the CD player and says "So?" "It was lovely," she says. "Sea, sky, sun rising, waves breaking…well, I don't know if I'll go that far, but

I got, as you said, a full picture. Thanks for the experience of hearing it the way it should be heard. I love it when you get enthusiastic about something other than what you're writing. Now, work calls," and she gets up and kisses him. "One thing, though. Please don't play it again right away, or when I'm home for the next few days. It could lead to my hating such a beautiful piece of music," and she goes into her study and shuts the door.

She says "We know we're both very fertile—my abortions and your inseminating several girlfriends—so there's no doubt we're going to conceive. But the 'how' of it is something I've been looking in to. This article by a gynecologist I read says the best way is for me to get into the doggy position and for you to enter me from behind, penetrating as far as you can without hurting me when you're about to come. And after you come, for you to stay in me like that for as long as you can till you fall out. But to try not to fall out. Even if you feel your penis has become soft, keep it in till there's nothing you can do to stop it from leaving. That's what the article said, and that our chances are increased in all this by about triple. Tonight's as good a time to start as any. But to assure conception, we'll do it every night and we're not supposed to do it more than once a day, to keep your sperm count high, and ideally at twenty-four hour intervals." "Let's do it now, then," he says. "It's been more than twenty-four hours," and she says "Fine with me." They go into the bedroom, undress and she gets on the bed. "Shouldn't you take off your bra?" and she says "I didn't think it necessary, but okay." She takes off her bra and gets in the doggy position, rests her forehead on two pillows, and he gets on the bed. "Shouldn't we play around with each other a little first?" and she says "If I know you, you're already erect. Let's not let any of your precious sperm dribble out." He gets behind her and sticks his penis in. "Just remember, when you feel you're about to come—" and he says "I know." He comes and she says "Now stay in, as deep as you can get—you're not hurting me." He stays in for another minute, says "I think it's had it and is about to flop out," and she says "Let it do it on its own," and a few seconds later it does. "Now I'm supposed to stay in this position for another five minutes," and he says "Are you comfortable? I don't know how your head could be," and she says "I'm all right." He's sitting on the bed now and rubs her buttocks, then kisses them. "You have such a sweet tush," he says. "Sweet like 'taste'?" and he says "Like 'lovely, pleasing, adorable.'" "No, I don't. Be honest. I have a large tush," and he says "Sweet, too. I love your tush. I love everything about you. All this talk and my touching you is making me hot again. Can I try to stick it back in? There's only a fifty-fifty chance I'll be successful," and she says "No, that might mess things up." They get off the bed a few minutes later and dress. This was in New York. Their Riverside Drive apartment. When they were still using the bedroom for themselves. They were both on winter break. They were getting married in the apartment in a month. So it was around mid-December. They thought September or October would be a good time to have their first baby. Later in bed, after she turns off her light and they kiss goodnight, he says "So I guess we make love again tomorrow around seven," and she says "That's what the article said. As long as it's twenty-four hours after the last time. It couldn't have been very much fun for you, so technical and mechanical. At least you didn't have to wait for me to put in my diaphragm and you could come anytime you wanted to." "Not true," he says; "I enjoyed it. I've always liked that position. It's maybe the most excit- ing for me, although I wouldn't have minded a little more warming up. It's you whom it couldn't have been much fun for," and she says "The objective was more important than the pleasure. Once we know I'm pregnant, we'll go back to doing it any way we want." "And if you have your period?" and she says "If I do, and I tend to doubt that, we'll still do it any way we want for about a week and then go back to doggy."

It's three years later. Again, mid-December, Riverside Drive apart- ment, both on winter break. No, she's on break; he's on leave for a year because of a writing fellowship he got. She'll be on leave the following fall, when they plan to have their second child: not too soon after the first one, they think, and where the two kids will still be close in age. The Hollywood bed's now in the bedroom for Rosalind; the double bed in the living room for them. They wait till they normally go to bed, around eleven-thirty. She says "I'll get in the same position I did to conceive Rosalind. I think it worked with her the first time we did it. You remember the article I told you about then," and he says "Vaguely. By a dermatologist?" and she says "Always a joke. Always funny. Should we start? Don't want to make it too late." She gets undressed, sits on the bed and wraps part of the blanket around her. He checks to see that Rosalind's covered, shuts the bedroom door and the door to the living room, undresses and puts a record on. "Why music?" and he says "We won't if you don't want. But it's beautiful—maybe the most beautiful—and I think sexy. The Chaconne from the second partita. I probably would have put it on the first time with Rosalind, but we made love in the bedroom and the record player was here." No, we did it in the living room, on the bed Rosalind's now using, when it was in here. I suppose because it was early evening and we didn't want to mess up the double bed and the other bed was wide enough for the position we wanted to do it in," and he says "I could have sworn we did it in the bedroom on this double bed. But the music's all right?" and she says "Fine." She gets in the doggy position, pillows under her head, and he gets behind her. "You know what?" she says. "I think I'll need the lubricant. I'm too dry down there," and he says "I was hoping we wouldn't have to deal with that goop, but I'll get it," and goes into the bathroom for it, squeezes some on his fingers, applies it to her, wipes his hand with a paper towel, starts the Chaconne from the beginning—"It's only seventeen minutes long on this recording," he says. "Gidon Kremer; a terrific performance, though we'll probably be done by then, or maybe not." "Don't forget," she says, getting in the doggy position again. "Go deep when you're about to come, keep it in for as long as you can, and let it drop out on its own." "Got you," he says. He gets behind her and plays with himself a little. "What are you waiting for, sweetie?" and he says "For me to get a bit more excited. There, that should do it," and he sticks it in. After, and she's brushed and flossed her teeth and turned off the record player and all the lights and got back into bed, she says "So, we did everything right and the timing couldn't be better. And if depth and length of time you stayed in me are the final keys to success, then I think it's quite possible we have a winner," and he says "I hope so. Meet you here tomorrow around midnight?" and she says "You see? You do remember me telling you about that article."

The time he blew up at her for taking the wrong entrance onto the Massachusetts Turnpike. Everything was going well till then. They got an early start. So far, not too much traffic and no tie-ups. It was the middle of June and a beautiful mild day. They had two months before they had to be back in Baltimore to await the birth of their first baby and he had almost three months till the new semester began. They were going to stop overnight at a motel in Kennebunk, first time they'd be breaking up the trip. She thought that nine to ten hours on the road in one day would be too hard on her. He liked that they wouldn't be exhausted by the end of the trip and also wouldn't be getting to the cottage after dark when they'd still have a lot of things to do. They were going to have dinner at the Breakwater, which a friend recommended, and breakfast, also in Kennebunkport, at the Green Heron Inn, which a recent article in the travel section of the *Times* said was the best place for breakfast in Maine. She'd made reservations at both places, to make sure they wouldn't have to wait long for a table. He said he wouldn't mind the wait at The Breakwater—"I'll have a drink and we can watch the sunset from their porch"—but that he understood: it might tire her. Next day they'd stop at Farmer Jones' or Brown's shed along the Belfast road for pound-bags of cashews and roasted peanuts in their shells, and a quart of strawberries from a stand on the same road, if they were still in season. Then, about an hour later, lunch at a very simple café they liked on Main Street in Bucksport. He already knew what he'd get there—same thing he got last year: a haddock fishburger and cole slaw and onion rings. She hadn't decided what she'd get, when he asked. "I think last year you just got clam chowder and blueberry pie a la mode from the previous summer's blueberries and shared my onion rings." He was sleeping in the front passenger seat when she took the wrong entrance. They'd had lunch a half-hour before at a restaurant right off 84 in Holland or Tolland, Connecticut, same one they always stopped at for lunch and gas. She had a hamburger and he a cup of lentil soup, and they shared a garden salad. And coffee, always coffee, and she asked for hot water for the herbal teabag she brought in. Before he closed his eyes to nap, he said "If I do conk out, wake me when you pull into the first rest stop on the Pike—it'll be just two or three miles after you get on it—and I'll take over and you can nap." Once she got the ticket at the tollbooth, she said, she was confused as to which entrance to take—"The signs were unclear. They didn't say New Hampshire and Boston one way and Springfield and Albany the other, as I remember them. Just 'East' and 'West,' and I wasn't sure which direction I should go." "You must have missed the other set of signs that said Springfield and Boston," and she said "I could have. Maybe the tree branches were blocking them. That can happen up here. But by the time I realized that 'West' was the wrong direction, it was too late to correct it—I was boxed in by other cars and had to keep going." "Let me see the toll ticket," and she gave it to him and he said "Damnit; twenty-three miles to the next exit. That means forty-six miles to get back to where you made your mistake, plus getting off this road, paying the toll, getting a new ticket and getting back to going in the right direction. We're talking about losing more than an hour," and she said "it shouldn't take that long. Speed limit's sixty-five on the Pike." "Believe me," he said, "it'll take, altogether, at least an hour. I wanted to get to the motel by four so I could get our stuff into the room and the cats fed and settled, and still have time to go to Kennebunkport for a run on the beach and maybe a snack. But that whole plan has been screwed up. You screwed it up. If you were so confused at the tollbooth, why didn't you ask me which direction to take?" and she said "Because you were sleeping. I didn't want to wake you. You seemed tired this morning, when we had to get up so early, and also at the restaurant. That's why I was driving." "You were driving because we were sharing the driving. What a mistake that was," and she said

"Please don't be mean. I don't know how you can talk to me like this, especially when I'm carrying our child." "Oh, don't lay that one on me. You're pregnant with our future daughter and I'm not supposed to get angry at you for making a dumb, costly mistake," and she said "It was a simple mistake, resulting in the loss of an hour. Big deal. Instead of a run on the beach, which you can do tomorrow morning, you can take a shorter run around Kennebunk and maybe even have time for a snack. But why would you want a snack, other than the trail mix we brought with us, if we're going to Kennebunkport for dinner at 6:30?" and he said "I also wanted to have time to shower and have a drink in the room while I read the newspaper. Most of that's off," and she said "It doesn't have to be. You just make things shorter." He squeezed his eyes shut. She's right, of course, he thought, but now he doesn't have it in him to admit it and apologize. He kept his eyes shut. "You giving me the silent treatment because of my so-called dumb mistake?" "Yes," he said "and I don't want to talk about it. And right now that's all there is to talk about, so I'm going to stay silent, all right? Better for both of us, considering what could come out." She said "I've never seen you be so mean to me. You've been harsh and rude sometimes and angry, but never like this, saying things expressly to hurt me. So selfish. And so foolish. I feel like crying but I'm driving and I don't want my tears to affect my vision. I feel now, though, that I almost wish I wasn't carrying your baby. Three months to term. I can't believe you could be so insensitive and destructive. Good, let's not talk. And when I get us off this dismal road, you take over. I want to sit in back with the cats and try to sleep so I won't have to think how awful you've been." "Fine," he said, "I'll take over. But again, I don't want to talk about it anymore. Wake me up when you're approaching the next exit. I don't want you making another wrong driving move." "Drop dead," she said. "Go fuck yourself. You're disgusting to me; repulsive. Did that sink in?" and he said "Yes," put the toll ticket in the storage space in front of her and turned to his side window and shut his eyes. He thought: How stupid could you be? Even you didn't know how much. What do you say to make things better? Because you have to say something. He faced front and, eyes still shut, said "Sleep is stupid. We'll be at the turnaround exit in ten minutes. And look, if it helps any, you were absolutely right and I was absolutely wrong and I apologize for what I said," and she said "It doesn't help one bit. You're just saying that to get out of it. Typical of you: to quickly get past the harm you've done and I'm supposed to get past it too. But you're dead to me now and will be till I don't know when. No more talk. I mean it. Just leave me alone." They made it to the motel in plenty of time to get set up there and still go to the Kennebunkport beach for an hour. When he suggested it, she said "Last place I want to be with you," though at lunch she said she was thinking how nice it'd be to sit by the shore there and get some late afternoon sun and maybe walk out a ways on the long breakwater they have there. Now, she said she's going to stay in the room and read and maybe see what's on television. He said he'll take a short run around here and she said "What you end up doing doesn't interest me." "Okay, but are you hungry for something other than trail mix, or thirsty? I can get you a juice and snack while I'm out, or make you tea here—there's a coffeemaker, so I can heat up water in it for you," and she went into the bathroom with a book and locked the door. He drove to Kennebunkport, thought of getting her a lobster roll, which she loved, but knew she'd refuse it; ran barefoot on the beach a little, walked out about twenty feet on the breakwater, then thought he didn't feel like doing anything when she was so hurt and mad at him, and drove back to the motel. She didn't want to have dinner but he convinced her to—"For the baby," and she said "Yeah, a lot you showed you care." At the restaurant the only words she said to him were "No," when he said "Do you want a couple of my scallops? They're the best I've ever had and they gave me plenty," and "No" again, when he asked her if she wanted dessert; "Let's just go." That night she wouldn't let him hold her in bed from behind. "Please, Martin, don't touch me. And try to sleep as far away from me as you can. I appreciate, though, that you replaced their sheets with our cotton ones," and he said "Anything for you," but she didn't say anything after that. Next morning she dressed in the bathroom with the door closed and didn't want to go for breakfast. "I'm just not hungry." "You got to eat," and she said "I will later on at the rest stop. You go, if you want, but don't bring me back anything." "Boy, are you making me pay for my mistake," and she said "You deserve worse, believe me, if I only knew how to be as mean as you." She ordered a hamburger at a clam shack along the way. "Sure you don't want a lobster roll? It'll be your first of the summer," and she shook her head. He had a crab roll, and a fishburger for later, since he'd skipped breakfast too. "You know," he said, when they were sitting at a picnic table eating, "we didn't call the Green Heron to cancel our reservation," and she said "Interesting how concerned you are about others." "I'm concerned about you," and she pretended she didn't hear him. He drove the entire way from Kennebunk to the cottage they rented every summer in Brooklin. She sat in the back seat, her head on a bed pillow, mostly sleeping or looking like she was. She let him hold her from behind two nights after they got there, but said, when he started stroking her breasts, that she wasn't ready yet to let him make love to her and didn't know when she would be. "Sometime, of course, but not now for sure." They walked along the road to the point the next morning. He grabbed her hand and held it as they walked. "Did I ever tell you there used to be a sardine canning factory on the point?" and he said "No, you never did. Before you first started renting the cottage?" and she said "Long before." He picked a wildflower and said "Do you know what this is called?" and she said "There's a Maine wildflower book at the cottage, if you want to identify it." "I do. I'm going to look it up and all the others I find that I don't know. That'll be my non-writing project this summer," and tucked the flower carefully into his back pants pocket. "Maybe you should take two or three of them, in case the one you have falls apart in your pocket." "Good idea." Then he said "Will you let me kiss you? A little or big kiss?" and she said "Whichever you want. I'm okay with you now but will never forget what you did. Did you ever figure out why you acted to me like that?" and he said "No. Or I must have been temporarily crazy. But that doesn't answer it and is too facile an excuse. I guess I was too intent on getting to the motel in time because I wanted to take advantage of the beach. No, none of that explains it. Can't a person, for no fathomable reason, lose his head like that once?" "What frightens me is that it might not have been an isolated incident. But let's not get into an argument over it. That's all we need." "My kiss?…you said you were willing," and she let him—he thought it best to make it a quick light one—and he took her hand again and they continued their walk.

They crossed the Bay Bridge and were driving on Route 50, he thinks, to Washington College for a reading he was giving that night. The school was putting them up at an inn: he, Gwen and Rosalind, who was still nursing. Tallis's *Lamentations of Jeremiah*, he thinks it's called, was playing on the radio, or is it by another English composer of the same period—Byrd, maybe? The music was beautiful and he said to her "What a moment. Gorgeous music, infant sleeping peacefully after a long tantrum, sky lit up in several pastel colors by the setting sun." Then he heard geese overhead and said "Listen," and opened his window all the way and motioned for her to roll down hers and they heard the geese honking louder and then saw a flock of about a hundred of them flying in formation. "Oh, this is too much, too wonderful, all of this at once. I almost feel like waking the baby so she could hear and see this too." She said "It is wonderful, all of it. But the best part to me is that Rosalind's finally asleep, so please don't wake her," and they drove without talking and with the sky getting even more beautiful and the geese flying in the same direction as them. Then the geese flew off to the side and they couldn't see them anymore and only heard them faintly and then not at all. At almost the same moment, the music ended, and he turned the radio off. "That was truly something," he said. "It was," she said. "I don't think I'll ever forget it," and she put her hand over his on the steering wheel. "Better on my shoulder, so I can drive in absolute safety," and she put her hand on his shoulder and they drove like that most of the rest of the way.

Whenever they drove back to Baltimore from their apartment in New York, he got off at exit 7 on the New Jersey Turnpike, got on 295, and a few miles south on it pulled into a rest area run by the state. He'd get from the back a take-out container of basil rolls or sushi he'd bought at an Asian fusion restaurant before they left New York and give it to her with a couple of napkins. Then he'd go into the building and use the restroom and get a cappuccino or hazelnut-flavored coffee out of a vending machine there and sometimes either peanut butter crackers or a bag of salted peanuts from the candy machine. He'd sit in the car with her or, if it was a nice day, outside on a bench or at a picnic table and drink his coffee and eat about half his crackers or all the peanuts while she finished her sushi or basil rolls. Sometimes he'd get her both, but she'd only eat one at the rest area—usually the sushi because she was afraid it'd spoil—and save the other for home. Once or twice, after he told her they had them, she asked for an ice cream sandwich from another machine. He doesn't ever remember her coming into the building. And she never had anything to drink. She didn't want to have to pee so soon after, she explained. If the kids were with them, they'd get what snacks and drinks they wanted with the money he'd give them, or wait in the car till they got to the big rest stop in Delaware on 95, where they'd always get a plate of spaghetti and a garlic roll with it and iced tea and he'd get another coffee. At the New Jersey rest area, Gwen once said "This is the best part of the trip. Thank you for always thinking of getting me this food. Coffee smells good. Is it?" and he said "Not bad, coming from a machine. And certainly cheap enough, cappuccino for a buck." Then, about three years ago, they saw a sign a few miles after they got on 295, saying something like "Public rest area open, facilities permanently closed." "Do you think that means the building?' he said. And she said "Probably everything but the benches outside, if we're lucky." "Damn," he said. "No restrooms and vending machines and the end of our little traveling ritual. You could still eat your basil rolls there, which is what I got for you today, but it wouldn't be the same for my bladder." "Just get the container for me and I'll eat out of it while you drive." "It might be too sloppy," he said, "and it'll also mean stopping and getting it from the back. Let's wait till the Delaware rest stop. It's the nearest one to here, unless we want to get back on the turnpike, and I'll get gas and maybe something to eat and the kids can get their usual, and we can all pee, if I'm able to hold out that long. If I'm not, I don't know what." She said "How disappointing. I hate sounding pessimistic, but it's like bread in Baltimore. Just when we think we've found a good place to buy some, it closes."

He thinks it was at Alice Tully Hall. Anyway, Lincoln Center. They were at the first of a series of five Sunday afternoon concerts of the complete quartets and Grosse Fugue of Beethoven. It was May or June, they were both done teaching and he was back living with her in their apartment in New York. They sat high up in the balcony, which was all they could afford. He was looking around before the concert began and saw someone he knew. "What do you know," he said, "Adam Nadelwitz—the bearded guy there," pointing to a man two rows down and about ten seats over to the right. "He handled my work for a couple of years. First-rate rep as an agent and a really nice guy. So nice, that he didn't have the heart to tell me my work was unsalable—afraid, if you can believe someone thought this of me, of hurting my feelings—so I had to ask for it back myself. I want you to meet him." They went over to him at intermission—Adam stayed in his seat, was reading the program—and he said "Adam, hi; Marty Samuels," and Adam said "Why hello there," and they shook hands. "My wife Gwendolyn Liederman," and Adam said "Nice to meet you, Gwendolyn," and they shook hands. "So how are you? How's Ellie?" and he said to Gwen "His wife represented my one Y.A. novel and also had no luck in selling it. Well, not much to sell. I went to some great parties they gave at their apartment for their writers—Adam handled the adult fiction and Ellie the juvenile." Adam said "You'll have to forgive me, Martin, I thought you knew. I don't know why I assumed all my former clients did. But my dear wife died a little more than a year ago," and gave the date in March. Then he seemed about to cry, said "Excuse me," and covered his eyes with his program and then wiped them with a handkerchief. "I'm so sorry, Adam," he said, and Adam said "As am I for making you uncomfortable by springing the news. I thought I was finished with falling apart and making a terrible scene when I meet someone who knew Ellie but didn't know she had died. It was of something rare to do with one of her organs, if you were about to ask. Very quick. I won't go into it. Please excuse me, you two. I have to go to the restroom. If I don't see you after the concert, Martin, we should get together someday, although I know it's difficult for you to, living down South.

You see, I've kept up with you." "We still keep our apartment here. Gwen hasn't moved down yet but will in August, when we'll be waiting out the birth of our first child." "I thought so," Adam said to Gwen, "not that you're showing much. This is wonderful, just wonderful. Good luck to you both," and he went up the steps to the exit. "Damnit," he said when they got back to their seats, "I wish I had known about Ellie before I so smilingly approached him. And I called myself 'Marty.' I don't know why; I never do. Was there a memorial for her and I wasn't told? I would've gone, if I were in New York. They were very close, personally and professionally. Had no children. He was very open about it. Said they'd tried for years and she wanted to adopt and he didn't. So it must have been a combination of you being visibly pregnant and that we seemed so obviously happy, that upset him so much." And she said "I'm sure his reaction to seeing you for the first time since she died would have been the same, especially when he had to tell you she was dead. I can't imagine such a loss," and he said "Neither can I, and I don't want to." Adam didn't come back to his seat. They looked for him at the next concert and the one after that. "It's possible he only had a ticket for the first concert," she said, "or is sitting downstairs," and he said "Maybe, but I bet he bought for all five. And like us, the same seat, which was empty the last time till someone, probably from higher up in the balcony, took it during intermission, and all the seats in that row are taken today, which could mean he gave his ticket away. Nah, when we weren't talking about why publishers weren't taking my work, we talked about music. He was as much a lover of it as I, and Beethoven was his favorite."

They were in Aix-en-Provence, had just attended an organ concert in an old church, were walking out of the church when he saw what looked like notices, a couple with drawings of hearts on them, pinned to a message board on the wall. "What are these?" he asked her, and she said "Banns— public notices of the couples announcing their engagements." "What a nice idea. Let's post one," and she said "You can't, unless you're going to get married." "Let's get married, then: here, in Aix," and she said "Are you crazy?" "Why? Linda and Lewis will be here in two days. So before we all drive up to Paris together, they can be our witnesses as well as best man and maid of honor." "You're really talking foolish, Martin. If we ever did marry, I'd want my parents to be there and I'd think you'd want your mother and a number of our friends there too. But the point is, if I'm to take you seriously, that I'm not ready to marry you," and he said "Too bad—but think of it, though. Married in this sweet-smelling ancient city, birth and burial place of Cézanne and I think just the birthplace of Milhaud. A quiet simple ceremony. A delicious dinner that night of just the four of us, with the best wine and champagne and maybe an accordionist to play a few traditional Provençal tunes. Chartres and Paris and various chateau towns along the way for our honeymoon. And then flying home as new bride and groom and, if you want, a wedding reception we'll give in our apartment for family and friends. And you say you eventually want children, so we could even arrange your being pregnant before we get back. I wish we didn't have to pass up this opportunity," and she said "We have to. Sweet an idea as it is, it's ridiculous." "When can I propose to you then, where you'd most likely say yes?" and she said "We'll talk about it in four to five months. If we're still a compatible couple and we feel about each other the way we do now, it's possible I'll accept. But, you know, you might change your mind by then," and he said "Never. You're the only girl for me."

It was their second summer together. They were driving back from Maine, on the Belfast road to Augusta. She was driving and he was trying to pick up either the Bangor or Portland public radio stations, when a dog ran out on the road and she hit it. The dog flew over the right side of the car and landed on the shoulder. She pulled over, was crying, saying "Oh, my God, I killed a dog. I didn't mean it. I was driving carefully, but it jumped out on me," and he said "I know; it wasn't your fault; take it easy." He unfastened their seatbelts, put his arms out and she went into them and he hugged her. "It'll be all right. Don't think you're responsible. The dog's probably done this with cars a number of times and this was the only time it was hit. But we have to deal with it. You're too upset, so you stay here. I really don't want to look at it, but I'll go see how it is. Though at the speed we were going— and it wasn't excessive—and hitting it front on—I'm sure it's dead." Other cars had stopped on both sides of the road. There were already a few people around the dog when he got out of the car. "I saw it all," a woman said. "You're not to blame for it. It's its owner for letting it roam free like that." A girl of about fourteen sat beside the dog, rested its head on her lap and petted it and felt its nose and chest and said "It's not breathing, poor thing." "My friend was at the wheel," he said to the woman. "She was driving well below the speed limit. She'd be out here now but she's too upset over it." "I can imagine," a man said. "I saw it too, but from the other way. The dumb dog just zoomed in front of your car as if he wanted to kill himself. I'll vouch for your friend too, when the trooper comes." "How will we get one?" and the man said "I'll turn around and call from the convenience store no more than a mile from here. But you see, if you kill an animal on the road—even a deer but not something like a skunk or fox or raccoon—you got to stay

with it till an official report's made." "Will that take long?" and the man
said "It could. Not a top priority for a trooper to attend to, especially during
vacation season. I hope you don't have someplace you have to get to right
away." Then the dog stirred. "It's alive," someone shouted. Raised itself on
its front legs and then stood on all fours, wobbly at first and then straight,
and ran into the woods. "Well, what do you know," the man said. "Here we
were about to conduct funeral services for it, and it scoots away. Smart fella.
Didn't want to be buried alive." "Did it look okay?" he said, and the man
said "I didn't see wounds or blood. I'd say you and your friend are off the
hook. I know I feel good about it, and nobody has to wait around." "Thank
you all," he said. "You've been very kind." They went back to their cars. He
checked the car they'd rented to see if there was any damage. There was
some shit on the front bumper, but no dents or anything. He told himself
he'd wipe it off the next time they stop for gas or to pee, if it didn't fall off
first. He got in the driver's seat. She'd moved to the passenger seat. "Did
you see?" he said, and she said "I saw. I've never been so relieved in my life.
The dog must have been in shock. Did it seem all right when it ran away?"
and he said "A bit slower, which is to be expected after such an accident, but
everything else looked okay. Resilient little cuss. Gave us quite a scare and
could have kept us here for hours." "You were wonderful," she said, and he
said "Thank you," and she took his hand and kissed it.

New Year's Eve. They had three parties to go to. The first was at her
parents' apartment in the West Seventies. "They give it every year," she said,
"and it'll be nice for you to first meet them in a festive setting." The second
was at the SoHo loft of her best friend and her friend's husband, both artists. "There'll be lots of music and fine wine and champagne. Vincent, and
I know you'll want to say it's an appropriate name for him because of what
I'm about to tell you, is a wine maven of the most extravagant sort. He has
a wine cellar in their building with more than two thousand bottles, and the
best of them will be out tonight." The third, a few blocks from her apartment, he was invited to yesterday by the host whom he'd bumped into on
Broadway. She was once married to a very old friend of his. "I don't really
see the point of our going to her party," she said, "as you're not friendly with
her anymore and you haven't seen her in years. But since you're going to two
of mine, I can go to one of yours, but can we make it short?" "If we feel
we're over-partied by then," he said, "or just over-champagned and over-
kissed, we can even skip it." Going up the elevator to her parents', she said
"We'll stay no more than an hour, have some kippers and herring and lox to
minimize the effects of too much to drink later on—the Russians swear by

the pickled and smoked fish antidote—and then head downtown." One woman there—a research scientist; in fact, they were all, woman and men, professionals—said to him "May I steal you for a while to question you as to who you are? So far, you're an unknown quantity, and we're all curious about you." She led him to the kitchen and asked where he was raised and educated and were his parents born here and what does he do for a living and what are some of the titles of his books and in what magazines may she find his stories. "I belong to a good library, and when it doesn't have what I want, there's an excellent bookstore in my neighborhood. This is a reading crowd we have here, all very intelligent and high-minded about literature, so if you're a serious author, I think we can sell some of your books." He said he only had three titles and they're short ones and easy to remember, and gave them. "Now I'd like to ask you a personal question," she said. "What are your intentions to Gwendolyn? You have to understand, we are all former refugees, almost all of us Holocaust survivors, met in New York City after the war, and are like family to one another to replace the ones we lost, and Gwendolyn is like our own child." "We've only known each other a month," he said, "though for the last week and a half have seen each other almost every day. So I'd say I like her a lot and enjoy her company, and that what I find particularly appealing about her is her gentleness and intelligence and warmth," and she said "Does it go deeper than that? I can say that for most of us here, outside of our own, she is our favorite child, so we would be greatly upset if any hurt was done to her." "You don't have to worry. Women usually end up hurting me, which I'd think is better than the reverse. But you should speak to her and see what she thinks," and she said "I plan to, but not tonight. So, my opinion, after speaking to you, is that you are a pleasant, serious and honest person, with a good sense of humor, so I can only hope that something long lasting materializes between the two of you. As you might know, and if not, will surely learn, her one marriage was a catastrophe." That night he met her best friend and her husband for the first time too. As with her parents at their crowded party, he didn't get to talk to them much. "Another time," her father had said. The food, wine and champagne were very good. But the music was too loud and the living room where the dancing took place too dark and the cigarette and cigar and pot smoke were stifling and smelling up his clothes and probably his hair and the strobe lights hurt his eyes. After an hour, he said to her "Do you think we could go?" and explained why. "If you want to stay longer and dance with someone—music's too fast for me and I'd look silly dancing dances I don't know, and there seem to be a couple of guys who want to dance some more with you—I'll stay in the kitchen and nurse a glass or two of wine. You were right; it's really good stuff—everything they served." "No, I'm ready to go. Four times on the dance floor are enough for me. Do you want to go to your friend's party?" and he said "We don't have to if you don't want. We could go to a nice bar around here, order champagne and toast the new year in there." "That'd be depressing. Let's go to your friend's, and it's close to home. New Year's isn't important to me." "Except for whom you're with," and she said "I like being with you tonight, but who I'm with on New Year's Eve isn't that important too." It was a small party. Maybe eight people. They sat on chairs or the floor in the living room—there was no couch—and talked about the middle school in the Bronx they all seemed to teach at and how angry and tough so many of the students were and incompetent the administrators. Food was a few leftover pastries, and the only things to drink were hard cider and cheap wine. "Don't go into the kitchen," someone warned. A while before, someone from the SRO building that faced the women's kitchen shot a bullet through the window. "Fortunately, everyone was in the living room at the time," the woman said. They found the slug in the wall—"From a .22, a gun expert here said, which is why it only made a tiny hole in the window, with little cracks around it." "I don't know how you can live here after that," Gwen said, and the woman said "At the rent I'm paying, I can't afford not to." "Did you call the police?" and she said "I was advised it'd be an exercise in futility. For what are they going to do—go through every room facing my window? There must be a hundred." "Wouldn't they be able to tell which window it came from by the trajectory of the bullet?" and the woman said "You've been watching too many TV shows," and Gwen said "I don't watch any." "Maybe you're right," she said. "But I'll just keep my kitchen shade down for a few weeks and the kitchen dark when I'm not in it, and hope the shooter moves out—the turnover in these flophouses is very high." Soon after, Gwen got him alone and said "Please let's leave. This place gives me the willies, and I don't want to have my first kiss of the new year here. I'm also afraid one of the guests—the one with the Hebro; he's been eyeing me—is going to use the New Year's excuse to kiss me." "What time is it?" she said on the street, and he said "Three minutes till twelve." Just then they heard horns blowing and cars honking and people shouting "Happy New Year," and he said "I guess my watch is a little slow." She took her hand out of his and said "Well?" and he kissed her. When they got back to her apartment, he said "Not a great evening, except for meeting your parents and friends, however brief, but New Year's Eves never were." "I had a good time, other than for the bullet through the window and, I'm hesitant to say, your friend and her friends," and he said "And I very much enjoyed being with you. I can't imagine what kind of evening it would have been without you. I probably would have gone to that last debacle and left after half an hour, claiming I had some other place to go to or didn't feel well, and gone home and opened a good bottle of wine, or let's say one of my two bottles of wine, and read the newspaper. But I couldn't have gone to that party if I didn't know you. I was only in the Columbia neighborhood, where I bumped into her and we got to talking and she invited me to her party, because of you. So I just would have visited my mother around eight, instead of six, which I did, and had two or three drinks, instead of one, from the bottle of Jack Daniels I brought her, and then gone home too early to buy the next day's *Times*. While you, you might have met a new fellow at your friends' party. Some of them were handsome and spiffily dressed and quite polished looking, and good dancers and more your age than I am, and New Year's Eve parties tend to bring out the mating instinct in unattached people," and she said "There could always be that chance—I think I've met half my boyfriends and also my future husband at parties—but I doubt I would have gone if I didn't have a date. It's not a good night to be a single woman riding the subway." "You could have taken a cab," and she said "I could have, but who's to say I would have been able to get one coming home." "Did any other men call you to go out tonight?" and she said "To be perfectly honest, yes, two—men I've been close to—but I said I was taken." "That's nice to hear—the last part. But you wouldn't have even gone to your parents' party?" and she said "For an hour…for that one I could take the bus. They'd be disappointed if I didn't come, and I love all their friends. After, I would have taken the bus or a cab home long before midnight, when they'd still be available." "Incidentally," he said, "did one of the women there—I think her name was Riva, or Eva—talk to you about me?" and she said "Riva Pinska…yes, and I know she talked to you about me. We don't have to tell each other what we told her. I hope you liked her and didn't think her questions were too nosy. As she must have told you, as with my parents they all lost most to all of their families in the war, so they're extremely protective of me." "I told her I would never kick you down a flight of stairs. No, that's a bad joke. First of the year, and a lulu. I'm sorry. I don't know where it came from. No, I wanted to tell her I think I'm falling for you, but didn't think she should be the first to hear that," and she said "A good recovery from a rather strange gaffe. Now, do you want a nightcap—I don't—or should we just wash up and go to bed? I'm very tired." "But what else do you have to say?" and she said "I'm thinking about it."

The first time she saw him cry. They were eating dinner in her apartment. A particularly sad part of a Corelli concerto grosso was playing on the record player. It was still light out and the windows were open and they were both in short-sleeved T-shirts. So it was late spring or early fall, around or a couple of months more than a half year after they met, when the phone rang. She answered it, and said "It's for you—Pearl Morton," and he said "Pearl? Rob Heimarck's old girlfriend? Uh-oh; bad news," and he took the phone and said "Hi, Pearl. How are you?" and she said "Not good. And I'm sorry for disturbing you at your friend's place. I originally wanted to get you at home. You're not listed?" and he said "No, I'm listed," and she said "Well, I couldn't find it. Roberto had an address book on a chair by his bed, it had an old number of yours—must have been from when you were still living with your mother, because that's who I spoke to and she gave me this number and your apartment's but said chances were you'd be here. As you probably guessed by now—" and he said "He died?" and she said "Had a heart attack in bed when he was trying to call someone, probably for help. The phone was off the hook when they found him and the address book was open to the letter G. But that doesn't mean anything. The pages may have turned themselves. You know he had diabetes," and he said "I knew he was sick with something but I didn't know with what." "I'm surprised," she said. "It wasn't as if he kept it a secret, and you two were once pretty close. Had it for twenty years. Gave himself an insulin shot twice a day, or did when I was living with him. Lately, because he was getting so weak, he had a visiting nurse or a friend do it for him. The diabetes is what gave him the heart attack." "I'm sorry, Pearl. Very sorry. I know what you meant to him and what he meant to you," and she said "Yeah, well, I thought you should know. Happened three days ago. His body's been given to science, as was his wish and because he knew he had no money to be cremated, and his ashes will be scattered around Mt. Tamalpais, which is what he really wanted. But there will be a memorial, and I'll let you know. He liked you, you know—your fortitude and your work," and he said "Thanks for telling me that, and of course, same goes from me to him." "That's not what Roberto told me, and it sort of hurt him. But okay, he's dead, so we won't go into it. Will you be able to say something at the memorial? I'm lining up people now. I figured, you being a writer for so many years, you'd be able to scratch a minute or two out and read it." "I'll try. As you might not know, non-fiction doesn't come easy to me," and she said "So lie, what the hell. Now I've got to make some other calls," and she said goodbye. He sat back at the table. "You heard," he said. "Roberto was a good friend of mine. Met him summer of '61 at a writers' conference we went to at Wagner College. Saul Bellow was the fiction teacher. Then, the late sixties, we stopped meeting as often, I forget why. I think it was more on my part than his. I know he lived so slovenly that I hated going to his apartment because I thought I'd come home with cockroaches in my clothes. I actually used to shake out my coat after I left his place. Later on I only met him for coffee or beer once, at the most, twice a year, and for the last few years, not at all. But we should finish dinner." He picked up his knife and fork, started crying, and put them down. She took his hand and put it to her cheek. "I don't know why I'm crying. I never would have thought I would. The music's not helping, meaning, it's helping," and he got up and shut it off, and sat back down. "He was such a nice guy and always a big booster of my work. One time, I remember, he came over to my apartment when I lived on East 88th Street. I told him I was going to send my new novel to New Directions or Grove Press—anyway, one of them near where he lived in the Village—and he said 'Don't trust the mail with your manuscript,' and volunteered to drop it off there instead. Next day he calls and says he started reading my novel on the subway, couldn't put it down, read it till four in the morning, could he have another day to finish it? He calls the next day and says he finished it that afternoon and made the delivery. 'It's fantastic,' he says. 'They have to take it, and that's what I told the receptionist I gave it to,' and went on and on with his praise. I should have done the same thing with him, after I read a story of his in a magazine, and then his only published novel, which he gave me, rather than being stingy with my praise and a bit nitpicky. That could have been what stopped us from meeting as much. That he thought I didn't like his work. And he'd be right—he wasn't a good writer, at times he was even a lousy writer, but I never said anything close to that. Was I jealous that he got a book out before me? Not with the book he got out, but I got to admit I was a little sore. So maybe the falling-out was mostly my fault. But too late to smooth things over and make amends. And what a way to go. In bed, trying to phone someone for help, Pearl said. A very decent guy and a much better friend than I was, and I'll miss him, even though I didn't see him for so many years," and he started crying again. And the first time he saw her cry? At the same table. He'd finished wiping his eyes with his handkerchief or table napkin and saw her crying. "What are you crying about?" he said, and she said "You. I hate seeing you sad." "C'mere," he said, and he moved his chair closer to hers without getting up from it and hugged her and she hugged him. Then he started crying again and she started crying again. So also the first time they cried together.

It makes him think of another time he said something that made her cry. Maureen, no more than four at the time, ran into the room and said "Mommy, Mommy, don't cry. What's wrong? Does something hurt?" and Gwen stopped crying and said "No, it's nothing, my darling." "It's something," Maureen said. "People don't cry for nothing. Is it something Daddy said?" and Gwen shook her head. "I was angry," he said, "and said something I shouldn't have," and Maureen said "You have to say you're sorry to her." "I'm sorry, Gwen," he said. "I was wrong," and she nodded. "Don't make Mommy cry again, Daddy. Listen to me. Don't get angry anymore," and he said "You're right, I won't," and looked at Gwen and started shaking his head and then laughing at what Maureen had said, and she smiled and mouthed "I know." "Good," Maureen said. "Now I can go away," and she left the room. "God, that kid is great," he said. "Both of them. Two great kids. And I got off easy," and he made a move to try to kiss or just hold her, but she opened and turned the pages of the book she was reading a minute before she began crying.

He doesn't know why but he suddenly thinks of her Cuisinart, which she had even before they first met. One of only three food appliances they used, the others being a toaster and coffeemaker. Of course a stove and refrigerator, but he means the ones that sit on a kitchen countertop. Maine, that's it. They used to send it there every summer by UPS, and at the end of their stay send it back the same way, at first to her New York apartment and then to their Baltimore apartment and next to their house in Baltimore and finally to this one in Ruxton. It's a big Cuisinart, so no room for it in the car and later in a succession of vans, what with his two manual typewriters, which he didn't trust sending up, and her electric typewriter and then her computer and printer. And her two cats to one carrier and her parents' two cats in theirs. And their manuscripts and some writing supplies to start off with before the UPS boxes arrived. Also, for a while, a kid's stroller and whatever that infant carrier's called that he used to carry the kids in on his back. And a case of good wine. Wouldn't send that up and didn't think he could by law. Would have taken two if he had the room. And a suitcase and boat bag or two of clothes and some of her mother's things for when she came up, since she didn't like to carry too much on the plane, and necessary books. Dictionary, thesaurus, French and Italian dictionaries and scholarly works she was writing. Cat supplies: litter box and ten-pound bag of kitty litter for the overnight motel stay in Kennebunk and then Kennebunkport and for the house in Maine. Cotton linen for the motel—Gwen had trouble sleeping on polyester pillowcases and sheets. Blankets and quilts and pillows and other things, like a four-cup coffeemaker, which they didn't send up by UPS but often sent back. Plus they needed room in the car for three to four shopping bags of food and other goods, which they'd buy at the Bucksport Shop 'n Save thirty or so miles from their destination, for their first night and morning in the Brooklin cottage they rented for seven summers and the Sedgwick farmhouse for close to twenty. Gwen taught him how to use the Cuisinart. Which blade did what, and so on, but he only used the sharp metal one for things like hummus and pesto and chopped salad and smoothies and to puree soups. They had about four toasters and maybe as many coffeemakers in the time they had this one Cuisinart. The toasters and coffeemakers were cheap and always broke down in a few years, while the Cuisinart never stopped working or needed fixing. About a year ago she said "Do you think we should get the Cuisinart serviced before we send it up to Maine again?" and he said "Why, it's not running well?" "No, it's just that we've had it for so long, altogether for more than thirty years," and he said "We'll see; we've plenty of time. It must have been a big investment for you when you bought it," and she said "It was. I didn't think I could afford it at the time. I was just a graduate student, barely getting by. But it's proven to be worth every cent I spent on it. But what do you think if we bought a much smaller one for Maine—the one we have was the only model they sold then—and leave it at the farmhouse every summer? If it's not there when we come up the next summer, and I don't see why it wouldn't be, at least we'd know it didn't cost much—Cuisinarts of all kinds are much cheaper than they used to be. And think how much we'd save by not shipping it back and forth every summer, especially so because UPS rates have gone way up." He said "Good idea—we don't need one so big up there—and the box you originally bought it in is on its last legs. We can buy it at Wal-Mart in Trenton on our way to Acadia Park. Might as well get it at the cheapest place possible, and while there we'll buy a couple of reams of copy paper for your printer and my typewriter. That way we'll also be creating a little extra space in the van by not bringing all that paper up with us." "You think we need that much paper?" and he said "There hasn't been a summer that I remember, except two of them when you were still using your typewriter and we had to cut our vacation short to get back early to have our babies, when we haven't gone through as much as that. I alone use a ream and half."

They were sitting in the balcony of a Broadway theater, waiting for the curtain to go up. Or maybe the curtain was up when they took their seats or there was no curtain, and they were waiting for the houselights to dim and the actors to come on stage. Pinter's *Betrayal*, and he thinks it was the St. James Theater. That's what pops into his head. "Look," he said, "two available seats in the first row of the orchestra. I know they're not going to be taken. It's getting too late to and they're the last seats to sell because they're all the way over to the right. Let's grab them before somebody else does." "No, I couldn't do that," she said. "It wouldn't be right and I'd be too embarrassed if we were caught," and he said "It's done every day, at the opera and here, and we'll see and hear the actors better and enjoy the play more. And there won't be any embarrassment. If we're stopped, I'll do all of the explaining, and we'll just go back upstairs or find two other available seats down there that I can't see from here." "Suppose the real ticketholders are late and want their seats while the play's going?" and he said "Slight chance, and they're two end seats, so easy to leave. Come on, follow me," and took her hand and led her out of the row and balcony and down a flight of stairs, maybe two, and down the right aisle of the orchestra, not letting go of her till they sat in the seats, she the second one in, he on the aisle. Nobody stopped them. And an usher up the aisle even wanted to give him a playbill, but he showed her the one he already had. The actors came on stage but didn't speak for a while. He doesn't think there was an intermission. He could tell by glancing at her every now and then how engrossed she was in the play. After it was over and they were standing by their raised seats to let some people farther in get by them—he's not sure why they didn't move out to the aisle to make passing them easier—he said "That was terrific. Play, performances and from where we saw it from. So much better than the balcony. I bet it'd be like seeing a somewhat different play from up there, and all the lines and facial expressions you'd lose. But I'm always giving my opinion first. What'd you think?" and she said "The same; I loved it. And I haven't sat so close to the stage since I was a little girl and saw *Peter Pan*. Here, you could see the spit flying. And it was exciting what we did, taking these seats. I never would have done it if it wasn't for you. I don't even think I ever thought of doing it before. Good thing you held on to me. My heart was racing when we came down the aisle and I thought for sure we'd be caught, so I doubt I could ever do it again," and he said "Sure you will, if you stick with me and we get another chance to, and you saw how nothing happened. Maybe sometime when we have enough money to spare we'll buy our own orchestra seats to a play we really want to go to, though the way Broadway ticket prices keep rising, I don't know if we'll ever be able to. Maybe for your birthday or mine, if we're in town, or our wedding anniversary—then, we're always here on winter break," and she said "That'd be nice. Exciting as it was, I'd rather buy them, and every so often we can splurge."

They were out for a walk. It was Sunday, around five, getting dark, and when they still lived in the Baltimore apartment on West 39th Street. Rosalind was in a sling on his chest. He was holding her head up with one hand and holding Gwen's hand with the other. They passed a neighborhood Chinese restaurant on the way back—The Poison Dragon, he started calling it after the incident, when its real name was The Golden Dragon—and he said "Like to get takeout tonight? We've never had any from this place and we should try it," and she said "I already have dinner prepared—salmon and a quinoa dish and you said you'd make a salad." "Then just soup. We'll have it when we get home. It'll warm us up. But not egg drop or hot and sour. Something different." They went into the restaurant and ordered a large container of the "neptune house soup," with scallops and shrimp and rice noodles and black mushrooms and baby corn. About a half-hour after they ate the soup—maybe fifteen minutes: he knows it was an unusually short time—he got stomach cramps and felt nauseated and he said "Oh, no, shrimp again," because he'd got sick like this twice before from bad shrimp, and she said "You too? Cramps? Nausea? It has to be the soup. I'm so glad we didn't give Rosalind any. Both of us have to induce vomiting before it's completely digested." "You mean to stick your finger down your throat?" and she said "It's briefly uncomfortable and disgusting, but it can save days of being sick." "I can't do it. Never could. I don't know what it is, but something stops me, even though I know it's for my own good." "Well, I'm certainly going to do it. One of us has to stay well to take care of the other and Rosalind," and she went into the kitchen bathroom and he heard her throwing up. He waited a minute and said through the bathroom door "Gwen. I'm really not feeling well, so I'm going to lie down," and she said "I'm sorry, my sweetie. I only wish you had done what I did. I'm already feeling better." "Just so you don't think I'm a complete chicken, I did try to in our bathroom, gagged a little but nothing came up," and she said "Maybe you didn't go down far enough. Try again. It's always worked for me," and he said "I'm just going to have to hope it doesn't get worse than it is." "Well," she said, "yell for me if you need anything. I'm going to wash up, change Rosalind and get her set for the night, and then treat myself to a very weak tea." He rested on their bed, tried to fall asleep but couldn't, had to rush to the bathroom several times to vomit or because of the runs. She came in every half-hour or so, felt his head, said "No temperature, but I wouldn't have expected any," asked how he was and he said "Much worse," or just looked at him and said nothing and left. Then she came in and turned on the TV to the public television station. A promo was on for a *Masterpiece Theatre* series starting next Sunday. He said "What are you doing?" and she said "It's the final episode of the James Herriot program—the English vet. I know you don't like it, but I've been looking forward to it all week." "But I'm sick; very sick. Been doing nothing but vomiting and shitting diarrhea the last two hours. The TV noises and flickering—just the voices—will make me feel even worse. I need quiet and rest," and she said "I hate saying this, but if you had done what I first suggested you do, you wouldn't be feeling this bad. Now it's too late, and I don't think I'm asking too much. An hour, that's all." "There'll probably be a rerun of it sometime this week. Isn't that what they normally do with a series?" and she said "I checked the monthly program guide. If it were on this coming week I wouldn't have come to watch it now, but it isn't scheduled again. I'll keep the sound low and you could turn over so you don't see the screen. But what you should do is go into the guest room and try to sleep there." "I like our bed," he said. "I feel better on it and in this room," and she said "Listen, Martin, I'm sorry you're so sick. But you have to give me a little too. This is the only television I've watched since the previous episode last Sunday. If we had another television set in one of the other rooms, I'd watch it there. But we don't, and now the program's starting. So, my poor little sweetheart, I'm afraid I'll have to watch it here. Now please let me." "Okay," he said, "go ahead. But I have to say I've never seen you act this way to me before. You've never shown such inconsiderateness, such…well, you know, lack of sympathy…everything," and she said "Oh, if you want to call what I am asking for here that, which I don't think I'm being, then I've shown it. Maybe you just didn't pick up on it before." "No, you're wrong," he said. "I won't forget this, Gwen, I won't." Then he felt sharp pains in his stomach again and got up and rushed to the bathroom. The television volume was much lower when he came back. He got into bed, lay with his back to her and the set and stayed in that position and said nothing to her till the next morning. When she came to bed she said things like "Want me to sleep in another room? Are you feeling any better? Can I get you anything? Do anything for you? I'm sure you'll be much better in the morning. I certainly hope so. All right. Goodnight, dear."

The time he slapped her hand. This was long into their marriage. She was sick with a stomach flu and he was spoonfeeding her soup from a bowl. They were at the dining-room table. The kids couldn't have been in the house or else they would have come when they heard him yell and her crying. He held the spoon to her mouth and her hand jerked up and knocked the spoon to the floor, some of the soup splattering his face. "Damn you," he yelled, and slapped her hand. Then: "Oh, shit, I didn't mean to do that. I swear I didn't." She looked at him as if she was about to cry. Then she cried. Some of the soup had got on her neck and he wiped it away with the cloth napkin on her lap and then wiped his face. "Do you want me to wipe your neck with a damp towel?" he said, and she shook her head and continued crying. "I'm really sorry, Gwen. I've never done anything like that to you before. With Maureen, once, when she was around two and got out of her stroller and I caught her just as she stepped into the street, and I slapped her hand and told her what she'd been slapped for so she'd know not to do that again. I regretted slapping her that one time. I've told you. I should have made my point in a nonphysical way. But this with you is much worse. Please say you forgive me. I don't know where it came from. For sure not some up-till-now hidden animosity to you that even I didn't know was there, and I promise it'll never happen again." She stopped crying and wiped her eyes with her napkin. He picked up the spoon, went into the kitchen and washed it, and came back to the table. She pointed to the floor. There were a few drops of soup on it—he thought that was what she meant. He went through his side pants pocket for a paper towel—there was usually one there; wasn't any, and he wiped the drops up with his handkerchief. He held up the spoon and said "Here, let me get you some more soup. It's light, more like a broth—it has a little miso in it; brown rice miso, the kind you like—and you need liquids in you and nourishment." She shook her head and looked away from him. He put the spoon back on the table. "I understand," he said. "You're angry at me now, and for good reason. I can't tell you enough how sorry I am. And that I did it when you were still so weak and feeling so lousy. I'm so ashamed, Gwen. But you'll forgive me sometime for it. Isn't there something I can do for you?" She pointed to the spoon. "You want me to resume feeding you," and she shook her head. "You want to feed yourself?" and she said "Let me, but I can't reach the spoon." He gave her the spoon, moved the bowl closer to her, straightened out the place mat under it and said "Excuse me, I'm sure you don't want me sitting here, so I should probably leave you alone for the time being. If you want something, just yell for me." He got up. She put the spoon into the bowl, brought it to her mouth, swallowed the soup and put the spoon in the bowl for some more. "It must mean you're getting better," he said. He went into the kitchen and got himself a glass of water and drank it. "Like me to put on some water for tea for you?" he said. She didn't say anything or look at him. "I'll be in the living room," he said, "reading."

Here's one that's come back a lot of times. He doesn't know why, but it just stuck. They're in the minivan. Left Belfast about a half-hour before and were heading south on Route 1 toward Bath and 95, which they'd take to the Kennebunkport exit. They'd spend the night at an inn there and next day drive to their apartment in New York and the day after that to Baltimore. He was driving, she was in the passenger seat next to him. The kids and cats were in the back. They'd stopped in Belfast for sandwiches and toasted bagels at the food co-op there, and rain forest crunch coffee for him—he always got it when they stopped there; no other place seemed to have it—and carrot juice for her and other kinds of juices for the kids. The van's windows were open. He doesn't think the radio was on. They were passing a long lake on the right. It was beautiful sunny day, temperature in the mid-seventies, the air dry. People were driving and jumping off floats in the lake and others farther out were kayaking and canoeing. Lots of people on a sand beach and there was laughing and squealing from the kids in the water and he thinks he even heard splashing. It was a happy lake; that's what he thought. And no motorboat noises—not even in the distance—so those boats were probably banned on that lake. It was Saturday. They always left Maine for home on a Saturday. That way, they could drive into New York on Sunday, when traffic would be lighter in the city and there'd be far fewer trucks on the road and it was easier finding a parking spot on their block, or at least it always seemed like that. If they left New York around ten or eleven Monday morning and took the George Washington Bridge, traffic would also be lighter all the way to Baltimore. They never traveled on the Labor Day weekend. Too much traffic, and most times the kids started school the week before. Anyway, they were driving past the lake, whose name he looked up on a road map but now doesn't remember, and he had that "happy" thought and he looked at her and smiled and felt good about himself and her and everything. She turned to look at him, as if she'd seen from the side he was looking at her or just sensed it, and smiled and seemed happy and content too. This is a good moment for us, he thought. He'll no doubt forget it, but it's good to have it now. Then he faced front and concentrated on his driving. He looked at her again soon after they were past the lake. China Lake, was it? No, that's the one going the other way from Belfast to Augusta. She was looking at him, smiling the way she did before. Did she look away after he'd looked back at the road? he thought. Probably. He just didn't see her continuing to look and smile at him after he'd stopped looking and smiling at her. No matter. She's feeling good about me, he thought, and I'm feeling good about her, but especially good.

It's going to be a nice stopover in Kennebunkport. They'll go to the beach. He and the kids will run around on it and jump in and out of the water and she'll read. Maybe they'll all walk out to the end of the breakwater together. When they get back to their rooms, they'll shower one at a time and wash the sand off their feet. He'll have a couple of vodka on the rocks before dinner while he reads yesterday's *Times*. She'll have a cup of tea. They'll go to a good restaurant within walking distance of the inn. He'll order a bottle of wine and drink most of it. He'll say to her when they're having dessert "This has been a great day, one of the best, and it isn't over yet, and I continue to love you more and more each day." She'll say to the kids "Same with me to your father. And although I believe him, I think he's had a little too much to drink." Later at night, after the kids are asleep in the other bed, they'll quietly make love.

Didn't he go through this one before? They were driving back from Meyerhoff Symphony Hall. Seems familiar. She was at the wheel and he was in the passenger seat. That part's different. Usually he drives. But he had a large vodka martini in the lobby during intermission, so she insisted she drive. "But I said I'm okay," and she said "Listen to me, Martin," and he said "Whenever you call me by my name, when it's not something like 'Martin, phone call for you,' I know I'm not going to change your mind. Okay, and I do this most grudgingly," and he gave her his keys. This took place as they walked to the garage. They didn't speak again till they pulled onto 83 and she said "So, what did you think?" and he said "Oh, we're talking? Think about what?" "Did you enjoy yourself tonight? Any particular piece and how it was played? Did you get any good ideas during the concert for the work you're working on? Did you at least get a good snooze in during part of it or wish you were home reading and drinking or getting ready for bed, but anyplace but in the Meyerhoff? In other words—" and he said "You want the honest truth or just the truth?" "Are you still upset with me for taking away your driving privileges for the evening? All I thought at the time was how dumb it would be to get into an accident or near miss that could have been easily avoided by my driving us home," and he said "No, you were anxious—probably thought about the kids—so you were right. And the truth? Not about my ability to drink, I mean drive—that was intentional—with one watered-down drink in me, but the concert? The Mahler was bombastic and the Mozart schmaltzy. As for the Elgar. Well, enough with that guy already. He wrote one terrific piece, but I've heard it so many times on radio, I'm sick of it." "So you didn't like anything of anything? You've said you like the slow movements of all the Mahler symphonies and Mozart and Beethoven piano concertos. That's why I got us tickets for this concert, even though it wasn't part of our subscription series," and he said "Oh, what do I know? You play, I just listen," and she said "You know a lot about classical music, much more than me, and you've heard a lot more too. I think your anger's coming less from my dragging you to a concert you might not have wanted to go to than from my, you thought, indirectly criticizing your drinking. Next time I'll invite a friend to come with me, instead of having to put up with your puerile crap." "Wait. 'Puerile.' Where's my dictionary so I can look it up." "You're still sounding immature. But I loved the concert. I don't think I've loved one more. The Mahler, almost every part of it, though he's never been one of my favorites as he has been one of yours. The Elgar, even if I've heard it on radio dozens of times, always moves me. And the Mozart, and not just the slow movement, which I thought to be pure heaven. It transported me to a place in my head I've never been to before. And you knew I loved the playing of all three compositions—you could tell by my expression during and after each piece and what I told you at intermission about two of them—but you still couldn't help trying to ruin it for me as fast as you could. You can be a bastard, do you know that?" and started crying. "Are you crying?" and she said "You know I am. Not bawling, just crying. So why ask such a stupid question?" "You're that angry at me?" and she said "You know I am. Why ask such a stupid second question, as if there was any doubt about it?" "You know," he said, "we've played this scene before. Except I was driving, if I remember—no, I had to be, because I almost always drove when we went someplace together—but it was in the first minivan we had and you were in the seat I'm in now. I was angry at you for something you said—you were probably right, but anyway, I was angry—and you asked me if I was angry and I said 'What an inane' or even 'stupid question; you can see how angry I am.' And then you said 'Well, I'm sorry for making you angry and ruining your good time. I apologize.' and you took my hand off the wheel to kiss it and I pulled it away and said 'I need two hands to drive.' Are you still angry at me, Gwen? I'm apologizing," and she said "Are you still angry at me?" and he said "No," and she said "Neither am I." "And actually, I was lying before," he said. "I did enjoy the concert, especially the Mozart, which I didn't think schmaltzy at all. Also, most of the Mahler, the adagio particularly. And as far as the Elgar goes, I've never heard it played live and it was quite stirring. I'm going to have to read the program notes to learn again what he meant by that title. I did only say I didn't like them because I wanted to ruin, as you said, your post-concert euphoria for taking away my car keys and implying I can't hold my liquor, which sometimes I can't, at least not enough to drive. Truth is, I was a little high at the end of the concert from that one drink, probably because I hadn't had anything to eat tonight but the sandwich we split in the lobby before the concert began and a single olive. And I don't want you to go to the next unsubscribed concert with a friend. I want you to go with me, although you can bring along a friend. Next time we're there—in fact, all the next times—I won't even drink a beer during intermission. If I do have a martini or beer there, it'll be with more food in me than half a sandwich and a whole olive and before the first half of the concert begins. Finally, and I'm not making this stuff up, whenever you don't think I'm fit to drive because of how much I had to drink that night—even just one martini—or how little I had to eat before or while I drank, I'll go along with it without taking it as some sort of rebuke, for that's how fair-minded I think you are and how much I respect your judgment. So what do you say? Everything okay with us again?" and she said "Everything's settled. And you can kiss my hand, Martin, but make it quick because I'm driving," and she held out her right hand and he kissed it.

On the windowsill across from his work table is a three-by-five-inch Plexiglas frame with a photo of Gwen giving Rosalind her first bath. He doesn't have to get out of bed and turn on the light to see what's in the photo. He's looked at it so many times he's practically memorized it. Sometimes when he's at the table he's taken the frame off the sill and stared at the photo for a minute or so. A number of times he's looked at it through the magnifying glass he also keeps on the sill, to see if there was anything he might have missed in it. There wasn't, the last two times, though he's still trying to identify one object on the ledge behind her: an orange blob the size of a baseball. He once showed her the photo and asked if she knew what the blob was and she said that was a long time ago and it doesn't look like anything she remembers using in the bath or shower. He just thought of something. Maybe it's a sponge to drip water over Rosalind's head after Gwen washed it. He also once asked her if she minded his keeping the photo in such a visible place and she said "Why would I? My breasts are discreetly concealed and my genitals and pubic hair are underwater. And who sees it but you and the kids and the cleaning woman every other week, and if a plumber has to go through the room to get to our bathroom, I'd want you to put it facedown. Besides, it's as much a photo of Rosalind as it is of me, isn't it?" and he said "No. I mean, it's a sweet domestic scene of mother and child, but it's my favorite of you. Although there is one of you I like as much. You're at an outdoor cafe in Deauville with your boyfriend Hendrick, three years before we met. Your hand's covering his, he's got his other arm around your shoulder, you're both giddy with happiness, so it's not one I'd want to see every day unless I snipped him out of it, which'd ruin the part with you." She looks beautiful in the bath photo, but there are others where she's as if not more beautiful. Maybe he likes it so much because she also looks so happy in it, sitting in the tub and holding a calm-looking Rosalind halfway out of the water. It could also be something to do with her being nude, the only one he has of her that she let him keep. He did once have a full-frontal nude Polaroid of her when she was seven months pregnant with Rosalind, taken behind the cottage in Maine they rented, but she found it about ten years later when she was looking for photos for a family album she was putting together and tore it up. "It wasn't only my ugly bloated belly and what seemed like pubic hair crawling up to my navel, but my fat face and thighs and cantaloupian breasts," and he said "It wasn't that bad and you looked so *shtark* and radiant in it. I used to pull out that photo several times a year to look at it and now it can't be replaced." Her back's a few inches from the curved end of the tub. Her long blond hair, brown in the photo because it's wet, hangs over her left shoulder into the water in a single thick strand she made with her hands. The ledge is at the same level as the top of the tub and has a number of things on it besides what he's almost sure now is a sponge. Five bottles of shampoo and conditioner, a small bottle of Johnson's baby shampoo, a bar of red soap in a plastic soap container, the bottom part fitted into the top; two hairbrushes, one, he thinks, for taking knots out of wet hair. Two identical tubes of something, one squeezed a lot more than the other. In fact, the second one looks unused and he has no idea what the tubes were for. A baby's comb, a washrag glove, he'll call it, that they bought two of—one for each of them—on their first trip to France together in June '81. In the recessed soap dish in the tile wall above the tub, a bar of Ivory soap, which he always used—it's still the only soap he uses—when he showered in the tub. The red one was Gwen's, bought in a health-food store. A bath toy—a book with a plastic cover and pages—floated behind Rosalind in the tub. At the bottom right corner of the photo: part of a folded-up gray towel leaning against the rim of the tub, probably on a clean bathmat. How he came to take the photo. They were in the bathroom. The heat in the apartment had been turned up and the bathroom door closed to make the room even warmer. He was holding Rosalind, who was naked. Gwen took off her bathrobe and hung it on the door hook, felt the water with her hand, got into the tub—he'd filled it to about six inches from the top and dropped the plastic book in—and dunked her head in the water. "To make Baby less afraid of the water," she said when she came up, and then wrung her hair and shaped it into a strand. "All right; I'm ready for Baby's first bath and shampoo," and she held her arms out and he handed her Rosalind. Then he got the idea to take a few photos. "Be right back," he said, got the camera off the fireplace mantel in the living room, where they always kept it so they'd always know where it was, came back, got the camera set for shooting, held it up to them and said "Okay? A little smile?" She said "I've no clothes on; what are you doing?" and he said "Nobody but us will see it and this is a major event in her life." "Just one, then, but I don't want the flash going off in her eyes." She splashed the water with her feet, said "Look, Rosalind, look." Rosalind looked down at the splashing or maybe at the book floating past because of the splashing, and Gwen said "Take it now," and he took three quick pictures with the flash but only this one came out.

She dropped him off at his building. He's previously thought of this tonight. They'd spent the entire day driving back from Maine. He got his things out of the car and she said "I have to tell you something. You're not going to like it, or maybe not." "You want to end our relationship," and she said "That's right." "It was the argument I had with your mother," and she said "That contributed to it, but it wasn't only that. It's just not working out. And I don't see it working out. No, I definitely don't." "Okay," he said, "I'm not going to argue with you. I think it could work out and I'll be sad for a few days that I won't be seeing you anymore, but I'll be okay. So long, Gwen," and he picked up his typewriter in its case and a knapsack and a shopping bag with his things and went into his building. She called, he's almost sure now, around two months later. "Hello," he said, and she said "Hi." "Oh, Gwen, what a surprise. How are you?" and she said "I'm doing well; and you?" "Good." "How's your teaching going?" and he said "Well, you know, it's continuing ed, so not real teaching like yours. They're all adults, most of them around my age or ten to twenty years older, though there is a couple in their mid-twenties. They come in together, leave together, but sit at opposite ends of the room during class. Nice people, all. Intelligent, mostly woman, and a few are pretty good writers but not yet of fiction. I also try to do a short story a week from an anthology of contemporary European writers I had them buy, but I don't lead the class discussion well and I have little to say about these stories, so I might stop assigning them," and she said "But it's a good idea, getting them to analyze and comment on fiction by accomplished writers. And it's a break from just talking about their own work," and he said "That was my intention, but it isn't working. 'The Adulterous Woman' was one of the stories we read. That was the only one I had a lot to talk about, no doubt because you and I once discussed it and I remembered what you had to say. But then I started in about how at the end she seems to be fornicating with the firmament and getting a release from it, and they all thought I was nuts. I'm not a literature teacher. I'm a literature reader, and only for my own enjoyment and to pass the time in a quiet, simple way. And after I read something, even if I liked it a lot, I forget it and go on to the next. I've even taken to reading criticism, if I can find it, on the stories we read, but it hasn't helped. I think I'm doing a little better by them with their own writing, though, and I have lively literary conversations over coffee with some of them after class, primarily the ones who don't have to go back to work. But if teaching's the career I'm to fall back on for the rest of my writing life, I'm in trouble. But how are your classes going?" "Very well, thank you. Easier than last year, but same heavy load." "And your parents?" and she said "They're fine. Thank you for asking." "Your mother still angry at me?" and she said "She never was. She saw it as a minor spat too and half her fault. And I hope your mother's doing well," and he said "She's fine too, thanks. I'll tell her you asked." "Listen, Martin, you must be wondering why I called," and he said "I thought maybe just to see how I'm doing; catch up on stuff and things like that. It's been a while. I've been curious about you too." "That's part of it. I also wanted to know if you'd like to meet for coffee, so we can have a more extensive talk," and he said "Sounds good to me." "Then I suppose the next step is to arrange it. What's a good time and day for you and where would you like to meet? Your neighborhood, mine, somewhere in between?" and he said "Any place convenient for you. I teach at noon Mondays and Wednesdays on 42nd Street off Sixth—they've taken over five floors of an office building there—so we should probably avoid those days unless you teach a full load on Tuesday, Thursday and Friday." "This Tuesday would be all right. For coffee? A drink?" and he said "Coffee would be best. If I have a glass of wine or beer, I'll have two, and I want to keep my head clear." "You know, another possibility is my apartment. I can make Turkish coffee and also provide cookies from Mondell's." "I'd feel funny," he said, "saying hello to one of the doormen I knew. Better a nice unfrenetic coffeehouse. What about the Hungarian Pastry shop? I love that place," and she said "So do I. I remember you did most of the galleys for your last book there. Okay. This Tuesday, at three? and he said "Perfect. I'll be through rereading my students' manuscripts for Wednesday and also done with my own writing for the day." "So I'll see you then," and he said "Tuesday, three, Hungarian Pastry shop. I look forward to it," and she said "Thanks. So do I. Bye-bye,

Martin," and he said "Good-bye," and she hung up. "Oh, God, oh, God," he said, after he put the receiver down, "this is wonderful."

He got a call. Late afternoon, January 10th, 1983, their first wedding anniversary. He was in their New York apartment with Rosalind. They were planning to go out for dinner that night with another couple in their building, who also got married on this day but a few years before them. Gwen's mother was going to come over at six to babysit. He forgets what restaurant he made a reservation for—he wanted it to be the one Gwen and he had gone to on their first dinner date—but she didn't think it good enough for a wedding anniversary and said that the other couple wouldn't think it good enough either. He knows it was in the neighborhood so they could rush home in case her mother needed them. It was the first time they were going to leave Rosalind alone with anyone. The first time they actually did leave her was about a half year later with the college-age daughter of a French couple they'd become friends with in Baltimore. The caller identified himself—Tiffany's, Security, last name was Duff—and asked if he was speaking to Martin Samuels. "Yes, why?" and the man said "And you're the husband of, her driver's license says, Gwendolyn Liederman, four-two-five Riverside Drive, New York City?" "That's correct. What is it? Anything wrong? She okay?" "She's all right. No injury happened to her. I'll put her on the phone after I inform you she's being detained in our security office here till a police van takes her downtown to be booked for the charge of shoplifting. Tiffany's—" and he said "Are you kidding me?" "Tiffany's, I'll have you know, prosecutes all shoplifters no matter how small the intended theft." "But this is absolutely crazy. You've arrested the most honest person alive. Shoplifting? For what?" and the man said "If you mean the item, a handbag, or shoulder bag. A small leather bag hanging on her shoulder by a strap, which we caught her leaving the store with in her possession without having paid for it." "But you've made a mistake. She was probably trying it on, seeing how it looked, decided against it, and absentmindedly left the store with it still on her shoulder. Look, whatever the damn thing's worth, I'll pay for it over the phone with my credit card, not because she might want the bag but to get her out of this jam." "I can't do that. Maybe you didn't hear me, sir. Tiffany's prosecutes all shoplifters, and your wife left the store with a stolen item in her possession," and he said "And I explained to you. She'd never in a million years take something that wasn't hers. Come on, let her go. She's got a four-month-old baby at home. The kid's got to be fed. That means mother's milk. And today's our first wedding anniversary. One year. I know it's ridiculous, but it's so. We were going to go out to

celebrate tonight. Her mother's on her way over here now to babysit for us."
"Your wife should have thought of all that before. But nothing you say, sir,
will change the situation for her. The police van's already been called."
"Then call it off," and the man said "I'm sorry, Mr. Samuels. I can't do that
either." "Please put my wife on," and the man said "You've got one minute,"
and to Gwen: "Make it quick, Mrs. Samuels." Gwen got on. "I'm so sorry,
my darling, I must have thought I put that bag back. But I suddenly realized
how late it was and that I had to get home to feed Rosalind, so I just ran out
of the store. If this takes long, you know where my expressed milk is in the
refrigerator. If you run out of that or she'll only drink a little of it, use the
formula, but make sure she's not flat on her back while she drinks it. How
is she?" and he said "Chattery, playful, not interested in being put down for
a nap." "It was such a dumb mistake on my part. I heard you trying to
convince Mr. Duff to let me go, but it seems an exercise in futility. Against
company policy. That old fall-back-on. Call off dinner with the Skolnicks.
Don't tell them why yet. Just say we think Rosalind's coming down with
something and we'll do it another time. And call my mother and tell her not
to come and to stay by the phone in case I need her. She might have to bail
me out with cash. Mr. Duff wants me to end the call. Some paperwork still
to do for the paddy wagon. That's what it is. Imagine, me in one. But we'll get
a lawyer and it'll all eventually be straightened out." "I should get the phone
number where you are and address and phone number of the police station
you're going to," and she said "I'll give you Mr. Duff for that. Am I ready for
this? I better be. But don't worry about me. I'm in relatively good spirits,
and Mr. Duff and his associates have been very courteous. He even offered
to get me a sandwich and soda from the Tiffany commissary if I got hungry.
Bye-bye, sweetheart. Kiss Rosalind for me," and she gave Duff the phone.
She got back around four in the morning. He had dozed off on the couch—
Rosalind was in her crib in the bedroom—and jumped up when he heard a
key being inserted in the lock and opened the door for her. "Oh, so good to
have you home," and hugged her. "My mother says to say hello," and he said
"Thanks. Are you hungry?" and she said "I'm sleepy." "So show me your
new shoulder bag," and she said "You don't mind if I don't laugh?" and she
laughed. "How's it been with Rosalind?" and he said "Great. We had lots of
fun. So tell me, how was it?" and she said "Let me wash up first. The toilet
facilities there were filthy and communal, with no privacy or soap. I had to
pee in front of a dozen women. For bowel movements they led you to a tiny
W.C., where they left you alone but they had to flush it." "Probably so you
wouldn't just use it to pee in privacy," and she said "No, that makes no sense.

They'd know that lots of times, when you think you need to defecate, nothing comes out," and he said "Then I don't know." She undressed, put all her clothes into the laundry hamper and went into the bathroom. He followed her. "Please let me pee in peace?" and he left the room and shut the door. She showered, water-picked, no doubt flossed and brushed her teeth, and came out in her bathrobe and said "I should have a large glass of water." He said "I'll get it," and she said "No, I'm fine. They didn't torture me there. They had a water cooler, but no cups, and I was reluctant to drink from it. Miss Priss. Who knew?" She was the first one picked up by the police wagon and had a nice chat with the officer in back. "He said he was a big reader too, particularly *Moby-Dick* multiple times and everything about Melville and it. I had to confess I never could get past the part just before they first board the ship. I asked him if the wagon ever got unruly—that I was a little afraid. He said 'In all my times doing this, never a rumble or even a hint of back talk. Maybe they think I've some influence at the station, so they stay on their best behavior. Be very careful, though, once you're in lock up. Don't go to sleep or show your wallet.'" They gradually picked up more people: prostitutes, male and female, a three-card monte dealer and a man who peed in front of a movie theater. "'I had to go,' he said. 'New York ought to have more public toilets, especially in crowded Midtown. What did they expect me to do, buy a movie ticket just to piss?' A few of them in the back knew each other from previous rides, and this guy was a repeater." She was fingerprinted, more paperwork, put in a holding cell with the women from her van and others who were already there. "Most of them said to me 'What are you doing here, honey? You look like you belong in a church or leading a choir.' One of the prostitutes said she could help me make good money on the street, if I ever wanted to give up teaching or use it as a sideline or cover. That I've the right face and body and hair for it. 'What do you do to get it that color?' a couple of the women asked. When I told them it was real and that my being arrested was a mistake, you can guess the reaction I got. Lots of eye-rolling and 'Sure, baby's.' I've never been in a situation before where absolutely nobody believed me. They did say I did one smart thing for myself and that was to bring a big book with me to read, because it was going to be a long night for me. 'We'll be out of here in a few hours,' one prostitute said. 'You, because your crime's not victimless, could see two to three days.' The woman said she was once a lawyer, and that's when I didn't believe her. But I'm very tired. I'll tell you more tomorrow. I have a bunch of quotes and detailed notes written on the title and dedication and copyright pages of the book I never got to read."

When they were turning the couch into a bed, he said "Okay, the truth now—" and she said "I know what you're about to say, and I swear, it was an accident. I'm surprised at you for having even a shred of doubt." "I didn't at first," he said. "But then I thought, with the bag hanging off your shoulder and you by the door, that you might have done it for the excitement for the first time in your life of getting away with something like that. Then, when you were home, you'd send the store the money and also the sales tax for it, anonymously and in cash, of course, and maybe ten extra bucks just to play it safe." She said "It was an attractive bag but too expensive and really too small for what I wanted it for. But I've never stolen anything in my life and never will. You know me. If a waitress doesn't list some item that should have been on my check or a store clerk makes a mistake on the bill in my favor, I always correct them. It was something my parents drilled into me and I've always believed. You know, though, it'll cost us to get the charges dropped, and if they're not, then expunged. My father already consulted with two lawyer friends, but told them the information was for a tax client of his. As an experience, I'd say it was almost worth what I went through. It *was* exciting. The paddy wagon and petty criminals I was thrown in with in it and then the holding cell, a world I was aware existed but had never come near to experiencing. Have you ever been in a holding cell?" and he said "If I had, you wouldn't have heard about it by now? I did once see one when I went to the 20th Precinct on 83rd or 84th Street, years before I met you, to report my license plates had been stolen. There it was, for everyone to see, very small, though, maybe big enough for three men to stand in—nothing the size you say yours was—with one skinny hysterical man inside shouting 'Let me out,' and the policeman recording my license plate theft saying 'Shut up!'" "Well, I met some interesting people, none of them hysterical, some of them quite articulate and bright and all of them very nice. One even brushed my hair."

Free range chicken jokes. They usually made them up on long car trips between Baltimore and New York and New York and Maine. He thinks the first time was when she said, just after they crossed the bridge from Portsmouth into Maine, that what she wants to do soon as they get settled in the house is go to Sunset Acres Farm in North Brooksville for goat cheese and a free range chicken. "I've been longing to roast one for a while and theirs are the plumpest and freshest." One of the kids said "What's a free range chicken?" and she told her. That's when he, out of nowhere, it seemed, came up with the first of about a hundred free range chicken jokes they made between them, or, as he once put it, "laid." He said to Maureen, he thinks it was, "That's not all you should know about free range chickens. Did you know that free range chickens love opera? And do you know what their favorite opera is?" and she said "I don't know opera," and he said to Gwen "You?" and she said "No." He said "*La Bohen*." "Oh, that's terrible," she said, and he said "So do one better, though I didn't think it so bad. The free range chicken joke world is rich with bohential." "Now I get it," Maureen said, and Gwen said "That one's better. All right. What's a free range chicken's favorite musical?" and he said "I don't know," and she said "Maureen? Rosalind?" and Maureen said "We don't know either," and she said "*Bye Bye Birdie*." He said "That's a joke? It has to relate more to free range chickens, or just chickens, like my 'La Bohen.' Because what do you mean, a free range chicken flying away? Chickens might flap up and down a few feet, but they don't fly." "I could have just meant saying goodbye to one, it's off to the oven. You can be so hard to please sometimes. But I have another one. What's a free range chicken's favorite opera in German?" and he ran through his mind operas by Wagner, Richard and Johann Strauss, Berg, Gluck, *Fidelio*, the German ones by Mozart, couldn't come up with one, tried thinking of other German composers, finally said "It's taking my attention away from my driving. What is a free range chicken's favorite German opera?" and she said "*The Three Henny Opera*." "Now you got it," he said. "I was going to say *The Chickolate Soldier*, by Oscar Straus, which my father took me to when I was around eight, but that was an operetta and nowhere near as good a choice as yours." It went like that. They might have made a few more that first time. Favorite actor: Gregory Peck. Favorite actress: he forgets what that one was, but one of them came up with someone. He thinks he said, after her opera jokes—he knows he said it sometime, and if he said it then, then probably prefaced it with "As long as we're on music"—"What's a free range chicken's favorite orchestral composition?" and she said "I don't know," and he said "*The Eggmont Overture*." "That's good," she said: "Clever; erudite," and Maureen or Rosalind said "I never heard of it." He said "Beethoven, but not as famous as the *Leonore Overtures*." One time he said, again in the van and probably while he was driving—he used them to pass the time if they hadn't spoken for a while and there was nothing worth listening to on the radio—"You know what? We've never done a literary free range chicken joke," and she said "That should be easy for us, but I can't immediately think of one." "So we'll assume I've asked one about its favorite novel," he said, "And you've given up and my answer is *The Egg and I*." "Who's it by?" and she said "Betsy or Betty MacDonald. In the forties. American. It was a popular work. And along those same lines, what's a free range chicken's favorite movie?" and she said "*Bye Bye Birdie*," and he said "I thought we disqualified that one. *The Egg and I*. Also in the Forties. I think with Fred McMurray and Irene Dunne. God, how come I've stored these things? I never saw the picture." Another time—one of them was driving—she said "I have a good one," and he said "Free range chicken joke?" and she said "Uh-huh," and he said "So let's hear it." "What's a free range chicken's least favorite song?" and he said "Ah, we're changing the format around a little; good. I don't know. What?" and she said "'Home in the Range.'" "Now you're cooking," he said, "and I didn't mean that to be a pun. It just came out." "I've another," and he said "You're really rolling. What?" and she said "What's a free range chicken's favorite play by Shakespeare?" "*Henry the Fourth*?" and she said "That's too easy and not very funny." "*Henry the Fourth, Part Two*?" and she said no. "*Henry the Fifth*?" and she said "From now on, no more 'Henry' answers in free range chicken jokes." "Then what is its favorite Shakespeare play?" and she said "*Omelet*," and he said "Your best yet. Maybe the best from either of us. Can't be beat. Oh, I did it again. And I have one related to that. What's a free range chicken's favorite Shakespearean food when it's not an omelet?" and she said "I won't even try," and he said "Try, because mine's not too good," and she said "I can't; my last two wore me out," and he said "Eggs Benedict," and she said "It wasn't that bad." Another time she said "What's an unkosher free range chicken?" and he thought Eggs? Hens? Pullets? Capons? Poultry? Chickens? Chickies? Chicks? and said "Chickse," and she said "Right." "I have one close to that. What's an inebriated free range chicken called?" and she said "Tell me," and he said "A chicker." "I don't get it," and he said "*Shikker*. Drunkard," and she said "I never heard the word," and he said "You must have." Another time, he was driving, and she said "Martin?" and he looked at her and she was smiling and he said "Free range chicken?" and she said "What do you call one who's crossed the road?" and he said "A busy road?" and she said yes, and he said "A dead free range chicken?" "Quick. Another. When is a free range chicken not free?" and he said "When it doesn't cross the road? When it's living in North Korea? I don't know. Probably has nothing to do with incarceration. When?" and she said "I don't know either. I thought you might. We'll think of something." "How about when it's in the range? On it, trussed, ready to be put in?" and she said "I think we should give up. Did I already ask what's a free range chicken's favorite nightshade vegetable?" and he said "You did." "Skin inflammation? Not favorite but just is?" and he said "After the eggplant one, and because the possibilities are pretty thin, I'd have to say eggzema." "Then a free range chicken who's also a petty thief? As you can see, I've been thinking about these when we weren't doing them," and he said "Peckpocket?" "Favorite brandy? No, skip that. Favorite gum?" This went on for years. Less often on her part after her first stroke because she had trouble getting out what she wanted to say. He doesn't think they did them anyplace but in the minivan. Just once, when he was in bed recovering from an appendectomy and the painkiller wasn't working and she tried to take his mind off the pain and he said "Sweetheart, I'm sorry, but you might be making it worse. To change around an old nonfree-range-chicken joke a little, it's not only when I laugh that it hurts." But what's he getting at with this? She once said, after they exchanged a few free range chicken jokes or one of them was on a roll: "I hope you never tire of doing this, because I love our recurring routine. It's something just between us, not that we couldn't bring other people in, but I wouldn't want to. It's also as if we're two other people when we do them," and he said "I think I know what you mean. But there have been so many and some really good ones, usually yours, like 'omelet' and 'notherclucker' and 'chickanery,' that we ought to write the best ones down." "No, that'd ruin it. We'd start making them up for posterity rather than just for a good time," and he said "I don't think so. We'd be saving them for our old age—at least mine, since it'll come long before yours—when we might not be as quick and funny and could use a little humor, but I'll go along with anything you say."

He wrote only one letter to her, about a month after she broke up with him the first time they came back from Maine, but never sent it or told her about it. It read something like this: "Dear Gwendolyn," it began. Not sure why he didn't say "Gwen," which is what he always called her. Maybe to sound somewhat formal and indifferent. If so, his tone was a guise. He cared a lot about how she'd receive the letter and would have been upset if she didn't answer it the way he hoped, or just not answered it. Next: something like "I hope this letter finds you in good spirits and health." Again: formal, distant, reserved; all fake. "I'm fine, working hard at my writing, and my two classes at NYU's continuing ed program seem to be going well. I got off to a shaky and incoherent start—chalk that up to nervousness and inexperience, or nervousness because of my inexperience. But my confidence picked up once I began reading their fictions four times instead of first two and then three, so that now I almost give the impression I know what I'm doing. It became embarrassing missing not only the finer points of their stories and novel excerpts but the most obvious ones too. The classes and preparations for them take a lot of my time and the job doesn't pay well—

comes out to a hundred dollars a week for two classes of two-hour sessions with a ten-minute break for each. Not quite enough to get by on, though I'm not complaining; I'm glad to have found work. The students, of all adult ages—a few of them write almost exclusively about their grandchildren and married kids—seem to appreciate my input and like me personally. There are even laughs. To help out on the grammatical and punctuational end (never my strong suit) of my detailed typewritten critiques—some of them longer than their fictions—I rely on *The Gregg Reference Manual.* Are you familiar with it? Much simpler and easier to find things in it than *The Chicago Manual of Style,* which I also bought, and more helpful than Strunk and White's thin outdated book. Anyway, sorry to get into all of that. I don't know why I did. I don't typically run on. The main reason I'm writing you is to say I've been thinking that if you ever want to meet for coffee, though the unlikelihood of that happening should by all intents and purposes dissuade me from even suggesting it, let me know. I can't speak for you, but I'd welcome a nice chat, not to try to smooth things out between us but to see that things have turned out all right. I know I've adjusted completely to our splitting up, think you were right to want to do so, so no need to worry about that. I'd also, of course, love to hear what you've been up to. If you'd prefer to drop me a line rather than make a call, that'd be fine too. Whatever you wish. And if I don't hear from you, I'd understand that too. So, all the best to you, and my apologies for this overlong letter." He signed it "Martin," put the letter in an envelope, addressed, stamped and sealed it, kept it on his dresser a few days and then thought Does he really want to send it? Not only is it a dumb and phony letter, but what's the use? If she wanted to see him, she'd have written or called. That's how she is. She's certainly not waiting for him to initiate it. He put the letter in his top dresser drawer—wasn't sure why he didn't just throw it out. Came upon it a week later—it had somehow worked its way under a stack of handkerchiefs—when he was looking for a pair of socks; he was down to two—and said out loud as he shook it in the air "You never answered; I thought at least a brief polite note," and tore it up. For a couple of weeks after she broke up with him he wrote poems about her almost every day. He wrote ten, got them copied and thought of sending them to her, then thought she'd only get angry at him and think he'd become a bit twisted—some of them were sexually graphic and a few were hard on her—so he stored them away in his file cabinet of abandoned and unfinished manuscripts. About a year after they got married—he was teaching and she was mainly taking care of Rosalind and translating at home—she asked if he'd mind looking over a long modern French love poem she translated. He read it several times, said "It's great; doesn't need anything, far as I can tell. It's clear, sexy, full of feeling, and I loved it. You know, I don't think I ever told you this, but shortly after you broke up with me that time I wrote a series of poems about you that I called my 'G-Poems.' 'G-1,' 'G-2,' and so on, till 'G-10.' At first I thought of sending them to you, or even dropping them off with your doorman. But parts can be quite harsh, which is maybe understandable, maybe not, though they do show how much I was in love with you. I'd let you see them now, if I could find them and you had the time. I think our marriage is on safe-enough grounds to withstand an unfavorable reading of them. Remember, I'm not a poet, which I believe is a line right out of one of the poems, 'G-4.' That one's my favorite because it's the funniest and least self-pitying of a pretty terrible bunch." "Then just give me that one to read," and he said "Nah, let's get everything out. You have anything you've written about me that's scornful or supercritical and worse? and she said "I've never written about you. Maybe in a couple of years. That's how I write." He got the poems, said "I don't want to be in hearing distance of you, knowing how much you're going to hate the poems," and took Rosalind for a stroll in her baby carriage. Came back an hour later and said "So?" and she said "They weren't as bad as you pretended they'd be, but they're not very good either. To be honest— can I say this?" and he said "Sure," and she said "They're heartfelt and clever every so often, but too hastily written and as a group kind of slight. I thought 'He's a better writer than this.'" "Well, I asked, so I got. But what do you think your reaction would have been if I had sent them when I wrote them?" and she said "I would have thought 'I can't read these now and I don't want to put them away for later,' so I would have thrown them out. I was already feeling sad about what I knew I must be causing you, so reading them—after all, it's poetry—would have made me feel sadder. Are you thinking of working on them to try and make them publishable? Of course, these were written more than three years ago, so maybe you're a better poet today." "I had no intention to. I know they're lousy and unsalvageable, so that wasn't why I gave them to you—for close criticism and to see if you'd mind them being published. In fact, I'm going to reduce by ten pages the amount of literary junk I carry around with me," and he shoved the poems into the wastebasket under her desk. "Do you have copies?" and he said "Just one set, but I have no idea where it is and I don't care if it's lost." "Maybe you should empty the basket. It's already overfull and one of your poems just fell out," and he said "Let me change Rosalind first." "I'll do it," and he said "No, I should have done it right after I got back. She's wet."

"Then I'll empty the basket. Last chance to rescue your poems, Martin," and he said "Go." Doesn't remember much of what he wrote in those poems except for "G-4." That one he thought at the time he wrote it was the best poem he'd ever done. He made several copies of it and did try to get it published for a year or two before he showed it to her—*The New Yorker*, *Salmagundi*, *Paris Review*—but had no luck. Doesn't even think he got a response. He probably still has it around somewhere, maybe in a couple of places, but it starts off with something like "I can't write poetry but if I could I'd write a poem to you." A bit flat, but clear. And a few lines later—the poem's about twenty-five lines long—something close to "Poems have been known to express the ineffaceable, I mean the untraceable, I'm saying the inexpressible and ineffable, and that's what I'd like to try to express to you." And near the end, something very much like "It would be nice to be a poet and write words down like 'I love you like a red red nose,' and know the person you're writing to, which would be you, would know that in those seemingly insipid words would be the heart's deepest feelings and senti- ments." And ends "But I'm no poet and could never be, so I have to settle for prose that matter-of-factly says inexactly how I musically feel about you: My love is in boom again, tra-la, tra-la." The last, except for a missing or added word or two, is a direct quote from the poem and the part—maybe of the entire "G-Poems," though too late to find out if that's still so—he liked best of all. In this same period after they broke up he thought of call- ing her. When she answered, he'd say "Oh, my God; Gwen; what a surprise. I'm sorry, I wasn't calling you. You're not going to believe this but I was calling a fellow teacher-writer at NYU, Harold Axelrod. You both have the same three numbers for a prefix, 6-6-3, and I must have—this had to be it; some automatic reflex—dialed your number instead. But as long as I got you, how are you?" and after she said how she was, or whatever she said, and probably she'd ask about him—how teaching's going; his mother, per- haps—he'd say "Well, even if this call was by accident, would you like to meet for coffee one of these days?" Some months before they got married, or maybe it was on their two-day honeymoon at an inn with the word "Rock" or "Rocks" in its name. No, it was during their first trip to France together—on the train from Paris to Nice, he remembers, when he said "I have a confession to make, but with an ulterior motive in mind," and told her about the "accidental" phone call he never made to her and was curious if she would have fallen for it. "There actually was a guy named Harold Axelrod teaching poetry at NYU at the same time and on the same floor as me and he lived in your Columbia neighborhood and had a 6-6-3 prefix and I felt we were becoming friends. But after a couple of months he got a much better-paying teaching job at Middlebury and I think moved there, but I never saw him again. Called him, but his line had been disconnected." She said she wouldn't have believed his call was an accident, as good an actor as he could be, and it also would have been too early in their breakup to meet. "You were smart not to make that call. I knew you were a fabricator sometimes, but now I would have thought you were a schemer, which I think would have been too much of a realization for me to ever hook up with you again." He remembers they were eating their packed lunch on two of those pulled-out trays they had in the train compartment, and drinking bottled water.

For around three years now almost every time he leans over the cutting board in the kitchen and cuts up lettuce and other vegetables for a salad for that afternoon or night, he gets the same picture in his head. He mentioned it to Gwen once and she said she didn't know what to make of it other than it being a good memory and of course the association of lunch in the picture and food he's preparing, and salad more go with summer than any other season. Some six months ago she came into the kitchen while he was cutting up vegetables for a salad and said "Still getting that picture you told me about?" and he said "Same one, just a minute before you asked me about it. Weird, isn't it. Keeps replaying and replaying." The picture he gets is of them in Maine, five or six years ago, on the patio of Goose Cove Lodge a few miles out of Stonington, having lunch with Robin and Vincent, her best friend and her husband. And Vincent, holding up his wine glass, saying "This is just delightful; perfect. Beautiful day, wonderful company, delicious wine and food, absolutely magnificent setting, gorgeous view of the bay, heavenly smell of balsam or pine or both, and if we stayed around longer, no doubt a spectacular sunset. But let's not talk of what's not here. There's more than enough that is. I can see why you come to Maine every summer. Who needs to go to Europe? Or the Hamptons or Vineyard? It's all right here and then some. Thank you, dear friends, for allowing us to share it with you for a week. I am honestly and I hope convincingly moved," and they clinked glasses—he, his coffee mug, as it was too early in the day for him to have wine and he had to drive them all back to the farmhouse—and drank, he just pretending to. He looked over at Gwen. She had that proud smile of hers again, as if saying to him "You see? You see?" and said to Vincent "What you said is what I, perhaps a little more than Martin, have always believed. What place could be better?" and he said "What are you talking about, sweetheart? I've always loved this part of Maine and want to come back to it with you forever." "I said 'perhaps a little more,' but all right, I concede," and Vincent said "I thought they'd never stop arguing. But good; peace at last."

Maureen was spinning herself around the kitchen, to make herself dizzy, she later told them, when she lost her balance and slammed face-first into the refrigerator. "Oh, no," she cried out, "my tooth; I lost my front tooth," and started bawling. Gwen and he were still at the table. He remembers saying just a few seconds before "Don't run around so, Maureen. Let your food digest a little." He jumped up from his chair—Gwen put her hands over her eyes and stayed seated—and got on the floor beside Maureen and said "Wait; don't panic; let me look at it. Maybe it only feels as if it's come out," and she opened her mouth and blood dripped out and he saw that half of one of her top front teeth was gone. "I'm so sorry, my darling, so sorry," and pulled the dishtowel out from the refrigerator handle and put it to her mouth and with his other arm held her close to him and now both were crying. "I know how terrible this is for you," he said, "but we're going to make it all right," and she said "Why are you lying? It's my second front tooth, my permanent. I'll be ugly all my life," and took the towel from him and ran into her room and slammed the door. He ran after her and said through the door "Maureen, do you need any help?… Are you taking care of the bleeding?…Let me speak to Mommy." "It's her permanent one, she says," he said to Gwen, showing her the half broken part of the tooth he found on the floor," and she said "Don't you remember? Both front teeth fell out almost on the same day and she had this huge cute gap for months. Let's see what I can do." She called the emergency number of the kids' dentist, left a message with the answering service. Called some of her friends with children and one said the same thing had happened to her son, but with a bat, and at around the same age. If the half that Martin found on the floor can't be cemented back because the break was below the nerve ending, she explained, then the rest of the tooth will have to be filed down so a temporary tooth can replace it. Then, when her mouth's fully developed, she'll get a permanent tooth. Both will look and can be used like a real tooth and won't discolor. They knocked on Maureen's door, said they have some good news about her tooth. She let them in and they told her and she said "Then that's what I'm going to do, even if it hurts a lot, if they can't cement the tooth together. I want to look normal. You understand, Mommy," and Gwen said "Daddy does too. When Dr. Dworkin calls I'll tell him I need an appointment for you tomorrow. I'm sure he'll make room for you when I say how urgent it is." "But no tooth fairy this time because

I don't want this tooth put under my pillow. Okay, Daddy?" and he said "If you see me as the go-between to the tooth fairy rather than my being the tooth fairy himself, then okay: I'll speak to him." "Or her," she said. Gwen later said to him "What a reaction you gave when she had the accident. You immediately knew what the loss of that tooth meant to her. My empathy is so much quieter and slower than yours and I think in the end less responsive. Sometimes I think I'm emotionally cold to you and the kids, while the three of you tumble into tears if I'm hurt or very sad, or you respond close to that. What's wrong with me?" He put his arms around her neck and said "You? Nothing's wrong. And all I did was hold and try to comfort her for the moment, and as you saw, really didn't do much good. I didn't have the right words or just my holding her wasn't enough. While you were probably thinking of ways to make things better, and you did," and she said "Now you're trying to comfort me." "No, it's true. Your phone calls. I wouldn't have thought to make them, not even to Dworkin, at least tonight. I would have just continued to feel awful about how miserable she was, while you used your big beautiful brain and saved the day. Once more, we're a good team. Together we handled both aspects of a sad situation."

They were at Dick's Cafe or "Restaurant" or "Diner" on Water Street, he thinks it is, the one that runs perpendicular to Main Street, right off the bridge, in Ellsworth. Or maybe it was only called "Dick's," which is all they used to refer to it as, with no what-it-is after the name. Rosalind, at the time, was almost two. And why's he bringing up all this? Well, he'll see. They were having lunch there, as they had a number of times the last few years, when Dick, the owner and cook, came over and introduced himself and said to him "Don't take this wrongly, but whenever I see you walk in here I think 'Mr. Fishburger,' because that's what you always order," and he said "I like it, think about it long before I get here, and the cole slaw that comes with it." And to Gwen "And when I see you I think 'Mademoiselle Quiche,' because that's what you always seem to order," and she said "I've had other things. Lobster roll. Crab meat roll. And once a hamburger when my obstetrician told me to eat more food with blood." "Then I apologize, but I know I'm not wrong with him. As for your daughter, so far she's 'Little Miss Grilled Cheese,' and because last year you brought in your own food for her. But I want her to try something new," and from behind his back he brought out a fork with two French fries on it, and Gwen said "Thank you, but we don't think she's old enough for things like frankfurters or fries. She has such a darling small mouth, she might choke." "Trust me. I've had young daughters. She won't. And I know a thing or two about a special gentle Heimlich maneuver for kiddies if she does." Gwen looked at him and he gave an expression "I don't know what to do; you decide," and Dick said "It won't kill her," and held the fork in front of Rosalind's hand and she took the fries off and ate one and then the other and said "It's good. I didn't spit it out." "You see how she did it too," Dick said. "One at a time; didn't stuff her mouth. Smart girl. Her first French fry. I feel privileged to be the cause of it." Next time they came in that summer Dick waved to them from behind the grill. "I should have something different than a fishburger," he said, "but I don't want to," and she said "Then don't." "Maybe I won't ask for mustard this time." Dick came over after they'd been served and said "I've a new treat for my little pal," and brought out from behind his back a milk shake with a straw in it. "It's very kind of you," he said, "but we don't think she's ready for it—no ice cream or extreme sweets," and Dick said "Where'd you come up with that? French vanilla. From Hancock Dairy. She'll love it and it'll go down like water," and held the glass up to Rosalind's mouth and she sipped through the straw and then said "Me," and took the glass in her hands—"Watch it!" both of them said and started to get up—and finished most of it. "There you go," Dick said. "And I don't mean to boast about your child, but she knew straight away what to do." "Her first drinking vessel with no handles, Gwen said. "Her first straw too." They next came in the following summer and Dick said from behind the grill "Welcome back, Samuelses, and congratulations." He later came over to them with one hand behind his back, they talked about how their winters had been, then he said "What surprise you have for her now?" pointing to Dick's hidden hand, and Dick said "Don't worry. Nothing for the new one," and produced a small dish of something they didn't recognize. "Finnan haddie," Dick said. "It's got to be a first for her and it's one of the house specialties. I make it myself. Doesn't come from a supplier." "Now that," he said, "I have to put my foot down on. Too salty," and Dick said "Not salty. It's smoked. From wood. No chemicals," and held some of it out on a spoon to Rosalind. "You folks going to give me a green light?" and Gwen said "Half of that." He dumped most of it back in the dish, Rosalind ate what was left, spit it out and said "No good." "Another first," Dick said, wiping Rosalind's chin with a napkin, "but not one to brag about." So? So times when they always had a good time, isn't that it? And when they ordered—he thinks this happened every time—Gwen asked Ruby—Dick's daughter and their waitress on the side of the restaurant they always tried to sit on because it had windows and there were open tables and not confining booths—to save a slice of whatever was the seasonal pie on the blackboard: raspberry, blueberry, strawberry-rhubarb, and if they stayed into early September because both of them were on leave and the kids were still young enough to start school late, peach.

Not much to this one. Good times and feelings again, maybe, but he suddenly thinks of something else. Whenever he had trouble getting or keeping an erection when they made love or one that was full, he'd say "We should probably forget it for now" or "take a rain check, as you like to say," and she'd say "Maybe I can do something," or "Let me see what I can do" or "if I can help," and what she did—it took no more than a minute once they got settled—always worked. That's all there is to it? "Thanks," he said a few times, and once: "I'd do the same for you with your erectile tissue, but you never said you needed it," and she said "I don't like it done as much as you, and it never seemed crucial." He finds he's holding his penis, jiggles it a little, nothing happens and he lets go. Does he think he'll ever make love with another woman? With Gwen it was more than every other day, two hundred to two hundred fifty times a year for around twenty-seven years. Never even kissed another woman romantically in that time and she said same for her with a man. "I've had fantasies," and she said "So have I, but what of them?" "Masturbated maybe twenty times since I've known you," he said, "and most of them when we were split up that first year or I was out of town doing a reading and you were home," and she said "I don't think I've done it once since we met, not even when we were split up, and I didn't have another man then." But the memory he started. It was with her parents. Had to do with food. Whenever he and she and the kids drove to their New York apartment from Baltimore or came back to it after their long stay in Maine, her parents would come by that night around seven, even if it was raining hard or there was a light snow, with food from Zabar's. Always shrimp salad, which he didn't eat because he'd got stomach poisoning three times from shrimp, but Maureen and Gwen and her parents loved. And Nova, kippered salmon or smoked sable (they seemed to alternate), creamed pickled herring, two gefilte fish balls with a small container each of white and beet horseradish, potato knish and half of a rotisseried chicken, which he had to warm up in the oven—hated that in the summer because of the heat it generated—because her parents had bought all this that morning to avoid the store's crowds and nobody liked the chicken or knish cold. "Chicken's too much," he used to say, "and we already have potato salad so don't need the knish," and her father would say "Freeze what we don't eat and take it back with you to Baltimore." Cole slaw, potato salad, bagels, a sliced Jewish rye, a whole apple strudel or chocolate babka, which he'd freeze most of—by then they were all full—and throw out the next time they came to New York. As he said, they were all glad to see one another and had a good time. Around nine, her parents would say they should go—her mother had a patient coming early tomorrow morning, her father had several tax extensions to look over tonight, the "children," as they called them, have to get to sleep soon, "and both of you must be tired from the long drive in." He'd call the private car service that brought them there—it was an easy number to remember because it ended with 6-6-6-6," get nervous they wouldn't make it downstairs in time—the dispatcher always said "Two to three minutes; the driver's just a few blocks away"—and go with them to the car, hold an umbrella over them one at a time if it was raining or their arms at the elbow if it was snowing and kiss them both on the cheek and help them into the car. Just before he shut the door, her mother would say to him "I kiss you, my darling." One time, after the car had left, Rosalind, who'd come downstairs with them, said "Why'd Nona say that about kissing? She did kiss you, and he said "She meant it another way. That I'm a good son-in-law." Once, when he got back to the apartment, Gwen said "You're very nice to my parents," and he said "Because I love them, but that's not the only reason why."

He thinks they were discussing grammar. One of them said "Not me." Then one of them said "Which is it? 'Not me' or 'Not I'?" Then she said she saw the play. "What play?" and she said "Beckett's *Not I*, and another short play of his with it. *Footfalls*, I think, or *Where There* or something. "At Lincoln Center?" he said. "The Vivian Beaumont? Summer of '77? I wanted to see it, particularly *Not I*, very much. More than any play for years. I wouldn't have cared what play was playing with it. I went to the box office, even though I knew the cheapest ticket would be expensive, but they were sold out for the entire run. I didn't have much money then, but would have paid anything for a ticket. I even twice hung around the theater lobby before the performance began to see if anyone had a spare ticket to sell, but nobody did." "I went with my mother," she said. "She ordered the tickets weeks before." "I couldn't order anything. No credit card then. Lucky. That you got to see it and to have a mother who'd buy tickets for you and who'd want to go to a Beckett play. My mother would never buy the tickets. It's not that she's cheap; she's not. She'd just never think to. And if I bought tickets for her, she'd only go because she'd want me to have company or she'd think her going would please me." "To tell you the truth, both plays were a little wearisome but well done. My mother hated the first one—you know how she is with movies, sometimes within minutes if she doesn't like them—and left halfway through it and never came back." "Wouldn't have been wearisome or anything but wonderful for me, especially if that was where we first met. Was it a matinee you saw?" and she said yes. "That's what I would have wanted to go to too and those days I went down to the theater for spare tickets were all afternoons. I never liked going alone to movies or the theater at night. But, hey, suppose we had? In the lobby during intermission, for instance. There was one, wasn't there?" "An intermission?" she said. "Of course. Two plays, different scenery, spare as it was. For *Not I*, a giant screen showing a woman's mouth moving throughout the play till near the end when it abruptly closes." "No, it never stops moving or talking till the house lights up." "So you've seen it?" she said. "I read it and it had to end the way I read it did, since he was a stickler about the play following his stage directions. But I thought they might have done something unusual with the two plays because it was Beckett and ran them intermissionless, with only a brief blackout or lowered and raised curtain." "No curtains at the Beaumont," she said. "Theater in the round. You remember *Arcadia* and *Six Degrees* etcetera, plays my mother bought us tickets for. She did that lots of times when we came to New York. The Beaumont was convenient to their apartment and we could drop the kids off with her, which she loved, and walk down to it and have a good time. But what were you saying?" "I'd go over to you in the lobby during intermission, as I wanted to at the party when we first met." "It was at the elevator where we met, just after we left the party separately." "I know," he said. "I followed you there." "You did?" "I've told you that," he said. "I've kept nothing back. You were gorgeous and looked so bright. It was my last chance. But since your mother left during the first play and wasn't waiting for you in the lobby…was she? If she was, the fantasy I'm concocting is going to have to change." "She went home. She whispered she was going to just before she left her seat." "So you'd be alone in the lobby during intermission and the chances of you bumping into someone you know there would be very slim. I'd notice you, be immediately attracted to you, and see you were standing alone. So would other men, so I'd have to move fast. Oh, I forgot. Did you leave your seat during intermission? If it was only to go to the ladies' room, I'd come up with something to make us meet. Both of us leaving—not going into—our restrooms at the same time. But this fantasy has to stick to the facts." "I don't have the restroom problem you do, going to it every two to three hours to pee. I went to the lobby just to walk around and perhaps there'd be something interesting to see there or a cool nonalcoholic drink to drink. Lemonade. I think they had good lemonade." "Did you get one? If you did,

I'd have to include it." "I don't think so." "So I'd go over to you and I know almost exactly what I would have said. 'Hi. Enjoying the play?' Or rather 'Enjoy the first play?' But 'enjoy' is so stuffy. 'Did you like?' No doubt something trite or inane to get me started. Then, ice broken I could even say 'What did you think of it?' Then we'd talk about the play, Beckett. You'd maybe say you found the play a bit wearisome. If you did, I'd say I liked it, which I'm sure I would have. If you didn't say anything about the play being wearisome, I'd still say I liked it. 'Been looking forward to seeing it for weeks. And a ticket wasn't easy to get.' I'd probably also say, if I didn't think I was being too windy, how much I like his short plays, including the radio ones. *All That Fall.* Others. More than his longer works, plays and prose, and I like a lot of his poetry too. 'Cascando,' especially. That great passage 'terrified again of not loving...of loving and not you...of being loved and not by you...' and so on. 'I can recite very little poetry by heart,' I'd say, 'but I read that one so many times, and the language is so simple, I remember it...that part, I mean, and a little more.' Then the bells to get back to our seats would ring and I'd say 'Like to meet for coffee after?' And so convenient your mother went home, but I would have invited you both for coffee if she had come back to the theater to have a snack with you after the performance. That would have been a year and a half before we met. Think what we both would have been spared if we'd got together then. Me, not two but three quick bad relationships, which made me more and more disillusioned about myself when each of the women—two, actually—broke up with me, and the third—she was married, so it was ridiculous—didn't want to have anything romantic to do with me. And you, a pointless relationship with a man you didn't love but for some reason kept seeing whenever he flew into town and called." "Not pointless. He was interesting, very smart, witty, fun to be with, treated me well and was a good lover. He fit my needs and limitations perfectly at the time, and I used to phone him too." "Glad to hear it, for your sake. One thing. We probably would have married sooner and had babies sooner too." "I don't think so. You needed a decent-paying job first, and that didn't come till September, 1980, or we'll say, July 1st, since that's when your academic year began. But if we had got married and had a baby sooner, that would have meant no Rosalind. Though I'm sure the one we had sooner, daughter or son, would have been as wonderful. And Maureen, three years later, since that's the time spread we chose to have our children, would have been our Rosalind, but then we wouldn't have had our Maureen." "We could have had a third. I would have loved it." "We almost did," she said, "if I hadn't miscarried. But now you're going to say I wouldn't have miscarried, because the third would have been our Maureen. Don't. It's gotten too morbid and complicated for me." "I would have gone to Maine with you later that summer and also the whole summer of '78, instead of your sometime-lover English architect for a week. But I'm wondering if you would have been interested in a forty-one-year-old man when you had only recently turned thirty, rather than the forty-two-and-a-half-year-old man a year and a half later when you were thirty-one and a half." "Forty-one would have been cutting it close then, but I guess all right, and you rarely looked or acted your age except when you were working." "What else do you think we would have done together if we had hit it off that summer of '77?" "It's all down in my journals. More plays, parties, poetry readings, dinners, lectures, symposiums, maybe a weekend at Mohonk Lodge, and of course lots of movies. And since I wasn't in any kind of serious relationship at the time, I probably would have agreed to having coffee with you and later started seeing you." "And your needs and limitations?" "I might have changed them for you," she said. "You had many of the same positive qualities as my English friend, and in addition you were Jewish, a writer, and lived in New York." "And I would have quietly flipped over you that first day when we had coffee after the plays, and I'm sure we would have continued it till today." "Why not?" she said. "It's only a year and a half more. But you know, if we didn't begin anything then—" "If you didn't want to have coffee with me after the plays, or anything more to do with me after we did have coffee—" "We would have had another opportunity to become more acquainted at Pati's party a year and a half later. But this time, since we'd spoken to each other once before at the theater and maybe even had coffee together after the plays, we would have started talking inside the apartment and not at the elevator after we'd separately left the party. That would have been where I gave you my phone number, or how to get it, and not on the street in front of her building." "And if we did start seeing each other after the plays and got serious, I wouldn't have gone to Yaddo '78, where I met Pati; Maine would have been my Yaddo. I would only have known her through you and come to her party as your boyfriend." "Seventy-seven and '78 in Maine with you," she said. "I could have gone for that. Also as a distraction and breather from the three-hundred-page dissertation I was still working on those summers. I also would have tried to enlist you as a second reader of it, less for ideas than for looking out for possible mistakes and simplifying my language in places." "Just as you, in a way, would have been a nice distraction from the stories I was writing then. But by the summer of '78 they wouldn't have been the same stories I ended up writing, because by then I'm sure I would have already been writing about you. I wouldn't have let you see them so quickly, though. Not because you'd be in them or that I also couldn't use help in catching mistakes. It's just I never liked anyone reading my work before it was published but literary agents and magazine and book editors. Although I had nothing against reading out loud a line or word or two from a work in progress if I thought there was something really wrong with it. Or if there were two good ways of saying the same thing and I wanted to know which one this person thought was best. You've done that for me," and she said "A number of times," and he said "And you were always right."

He drove into Augusta with the kids and Gwen and got gas at the first service station along the main street. After he filled up, he said "Well, people, I'm going to use the restroom here and pay for the gas. Anyone else have to go?" and they all said they could wait. He went inside, paid, peed, and bought a *New York Times*—something to read with his drink later—and a bag of cornnuts for himself and a bag of roasted sunflower seeds for Gwen. Back in the van, before he started up, he said "You kids must be hungry by now. Pizza okay? It's quick and it's just a few stores down." He parked in front of the pizza shop he saw from the service station, gave them money for pizza and chips or a cookie and a drink—"Even soda, if that's what you want," and they went inside. "Oh, I forgot; I wasn't thinking," he said to Gwen. "You want something besides the sunflower seeds? I doubt you'd go for the pizza here, but you do like the veggie subs at Subway. There's one on this side of the street on the way out of town." She said "I'm happy. Maybe you want one. You like them too," and he said "I do, but I'll wait till Kennebunkport till I get anything. And those things can get messy when you're driving." "I'll take over," and he said "No, you said you were tired before, so you sleep." They held hands and looked out the windows and every so often smiled at each other till the kids came back. "No mess, please," he said. "Napkins on the lap; all that. And drinks, when you're not drinking them, in the cup holders and with the lids on," and he drove to the I-95 entrance about a mile away. "There's the Subway," he said to Gwen. "Last chance," and she said "Thanks, but I'll be all right."

Their first trip to Maine together took the entire day. Long delays on the Cross Bronx Expressway and on the highway through Hartford and then Worcester, and getting through the New Hampshire tollbooth on 95 took another half-hour. And before they got on the road they stopped at her parents' apartment for their Siamese cats, mother and same-litter brother of the two females Gwen owned, and the male was hiding and it took an hour to find him. They'd picked up the rental car in Yonkers the day before and loaded it with their belongings and parked it in a garage overnight near Gwen's apartment. One back window was missing and the other couldn't be opened, so they were able to get it at a reduced rate. She'd wanted to get to the cottage while it was still light out so he could see it from the outside when they got there. "Most people are bowled over by it. I'm just hoping you'll like it," and he said "I know I will. Everything you described. And Maine for two months? And out of the sweltering New York heat? And of course, being with you. As my dad used to say—I've told you, though I think he was referring to making money—'What's not to like?'" The front door was unlocked. "There are keys of an ancient kind," she said, "but I'm not even sure if they still work. Whenever I asked Stan, the caretaker, for them, he stalled me, making me think he'd been given instructions by my eccentric landladies to withhold them. He'll be here tomorrow morning around six with a container of souring crabmeat he'll say his wife just picked. Always does, I always throw it out or bury it, and that'll be the last we see of him, except by chance at the Brooklin general store, till the day we leave, when we'll drop by his shack on our way out to say goodbye and tip him." "It's safe, though, to go to bed with the doors unlocked?" and she said "Break-ins around here only occur in winter. Antique thieves, who spend the summer selling their booty at flea markets in the area. The cottage has lost two precious wind-up clocks and most of its rare books." They brought in the cats, put out food and water for them, set up the litter box and a wicker basket piled high with old towels for them to sleep together. Then they emptied the car of the rest of their things. She took him for a quick tour of the cottage and said "So be honest. What do you think?" "It's beautiful," he said. "The wood, stone fireplace, whatever those little diamond-shaped window panes are called, cathedral ceiling, the what looks like Shaker and Adirondack-style of just Maine-lodge-like furniture. Even the ceramic plates and bowls, I see. Nothing tawdry. Everything elegant. And you said a great view of the bay from the upstairs bedroom window? What a treat. Thanks for inviting me," and she said "Thanks for coming and paying half the rent," and she kissed him. "Now, lots of work to do before dinner and, for you, a pre-dinner drink, unless you want to fall asleep smelling mouse droppings and winter nests." She swept the entire cottage. He wanted to help her, but there was only one broom. "Next summer," she said, "if we're still together, we'll make sure there are two. You can strip the newspapers from the furniture and beds and burn them in the fireplace. And I guess you can hang up and put away our clothes upstairs and make our bed with the linens and pillows we brought up. But first clean out the mothballs and mouse droppings, if there are any, from the dresser and desk drawers. And as long as you're up there, set up your work space. Mine will be the living room desk, where I always work. The table's a bit wobbly upstairs, but maybe you can fix it. Do I sound too bossy? I don't like it when I act like that, but I want to get everything out of the way tonight so I can get back to my writing tomorrow morning," and he said "That's how I am about my work too, and I'm glad for whatever I get here." After they finished, she showered and he prepared dinner. Opened a bottle of Chianti from the case they brought from New York, poured himself a glass, put water on for green fettuccine, made an *ajo e ojo* sauce for it, salad, dressing, grated fresh Parmesan into a dish, sliced bread, got out the butter, put some cookies and grapes on a plate, set the dinner table. "Ready to eat?" he yelled upstairs, where she went after her shower. "Starving," she said. "Be right down." She put two candles in silver candlesticks on the table and lit them. "I know you don't like them—'dangerous' and 'mawkishly romantic' and they smell and eat up the oxygen and give off heat you don't want—but just for tonight and when we have guests?" They sat next to each other, ate and drank. "Oh, I forgot to toast to a great summer," he said, and she said "It goes without saying. Though tomorrow night we should make more room for us at this table. Too cozy, and my elbow keeps bumping yours. I love you but I like to eat apart." Vivaldi's *Winter* was on the Bangor public radio station. "This'd be more appropriate music for the morning," she said. "You'll see. You'll have to wear your flannel shirt and, if you're the first one downstairs, light the kindling in the cold stove to warm up the kitchen." "Is that what that big old cast-iron thing is called?" and she said "I think so. Remember, I'm from the Bronx. Maybe I heard it wrong and it's 'coal.' No, couldn't be. Only takes wood. Probably 'cold.' It can get hot enough to bake bread." They washed the dishes and put them away. She showed him how to get a fire started in the cold stove and made sure the cats were in their sleeping basket. "You going to shower?" and he said "If you want me to," and she said "Not if you think you're okay. The shower—well, you've been to the toilet, unless you just peed in the grass, so you know they're both in the cabinet off the porch. That can be a problem when it's raining. And never shower during an electric storm. The floor's metal and it's not grounded well," and he said "Then I'll call in an electrician to fix it and pay for it myself if the landladies don't cough up," and she said "They won't, so we'll share." They went to bed. "Good, no mosquitoes yet," she said. "The one drawback of a cottage by the water. In a week they'll be keeping us awake unless we plug up the window screen holes that have materialized since last year, though they also come down the fireplace." "There are kits to stitch up those holes or I'll just staple new screens on, but leave it to me. As for the fireplace, let's get a glass shield or screen that completely seals the opening. It'd be worth it, not to lose even one night's sleep, and again, I'll pay for it out of my own pocket. After all, we've got more than two months here." "You're full of good ideas tonight and so generous," and he said "Are you being sarcastic? That'd be so unlike you," and she said "Not at all. Fact is, I feel remiss I didn't think of taking care of the fireplace that way before." "Nah, come on. You think of things that I don't and I think of things that you don't and we also both add to the other's ideas. We're what's called a couple." Stan came around six in the morning with the crabmeat. "Find everything in order? I left a lawnmower and can with enough gas in it in the woodshed, in case one of you feels inclined to cut the grass. I wanted to, but got busy opening a half-dozen houses." They went back to bed and stayed in it till seven. "Gets light here so early," he said. "What was it, five?" This is the routine they fell into. They each made their own breakfast, read a little—he, the *Times* from the previous day—and worked at their desks till around one, when they stopped for lunch. She: a soup and bread and dessert or a sandwich and salad; he: a few carrots and celery stalks and a piece of cheese and more coffee. They'd eat lunch at the small wood table in the kitchen or sitting on the porch and talk about the work they'd done that day. That's how it went for a week. Nobody she knew was up yet, so they were just by themselves and he loved it. After lunch: walks on the road, or along the shore with three of the cats. Kitya, the mother, liked to stay home. Or a drive to Naskeag Point to look for sea-polished or unusually shaped stones and to watch the lobster and other boats come in or leave. Or a drive to the library in town or the general store there for essentials they were out of. Their big shop they'd do in Ellsworth next week, and have lunch there, and one of these days, she said, they should go to Acadia National Park and have popovers and tea at the Jordan Pond House. She didn't know it had burned down the previous winter. Before or after dinner, they drove several times to an ice-cream stand about ten miles away on Deer Isle. After they finished their cones, he hugged her from behind—it was already getting chilly—as they watched the sunset. "This is already my favorite thing to do up here," he said. "The sky, delicious ice cream, cone's good too, holding you, and of course gushing about it." "I knew you'd like this particular spot. Ice cream's local, I want you to know. Made in Ellsworth, where we'll be going to," and he said "I'm looking forward to it." "A friend here calls it

Asphalt Acres," and he said "Then maybe it isn't too great." Then something happened to spoil the good mood for a while. It was a couple of weeks before he got into an argument with her mother, when she was visiting, so maybe this also contributed to her breaking up with him the day they got back to New York. Just thought of that but now doesn't see how it couldn't have. He wanted to mow the grass around the cottage before the caretaker took the lawnmower back. "He said we could have it for a few days and it's been way more than a week." "He might leave it in our woodshed all summer. That'd be just like Stan," and he said "Still, I'd like to get it done at least once. It really needs it, and it'll give the mosquitoes less place to hide." She said "Before you do, let me point out the places I don't want mowed because of the flowers." She had driven somewhere for something. He thought he'd surprise her by mowing the grass before she got home. He was finished, putting away the lawnmower, when she drove down the driveway and got out of the car. "I could smell you mowed, all the way from the road. Looks nice, but I asked you to wait till I showed you what I didn't want mowed," and he said "I was very careful to stay at least a few inches away from all the flowers." She looked around. "Well, you didn't get the peonies, thank goodness." Walked around the woodshed; he followed. "Oh, no," she said. "You destroyed every one of them." "Where? What?" and she said "My foxgloves." She pointed to an area about ten by fifteen feet, and he said "There were foxgloves there? I don't know what they look like, but I saw no flowers. Just weeds." "They were just coming up, were going to flower in a few weeks. Damn, that was so willful of you. You don't listen. You do what you want. Not just willful. Pigheaded. Stupid. Stupid." "*I'm* stupid?" he said. "I'm not saying you are, but I'm not. That's what my father used to call me when he got mad at me, and I hated it," and she said "Maybe he was right. For look what you've done. You cut them clear to the ground. They'll never come up again. They took so much doing to get them started two summers ago, and when a few appeared last summer, I knew they'd taken. I planted them from seeds, did all sorts of things to make them work." "So we'll do it again this summer so they come up next. Or you'll tell me how and I'll do it alone," and she said "I don't want to wait two more summers to see a big patch of them. If you knew what they looked like and how hard they are to grow and to keep coming back, you'd understand." "What I don't understand is why you're going so crazy hell over it. In the end, beautiful as they might be, they're just flowers; flowers." "I can't believe you sometimes," and she went to the car, got a big paper bag of something off the front seat, started crying and headed toward the house. "Are you crying over the flowers?" and she said "Shut up." "Listen, Gwen, I'm sorry, truly sorry, which I forgot to tell you, but I truly am." She went inside without looking back at him. So maybe this was the first time he saw her cry, or over something he said or did. She was cool to him for a few days. They ate dinner together and slept in the same bed, but she kept as far away from him on it as she could, and when he touched her shoulder once from behind, she flinched. "Don't worry; I'm not in the mood either. It was just my way of saying goodnight." Her mother called every night—her father would get on when her mother was through—and probably asked how things were, because he overheard Gwen say "Not that great," and another time: "Same as before. No, it isn't my health or work. I'll explain when you get here." "Funny," he said, when she seemed to be feeling better to him, "how fast things change." "The foxgloves?" and he said "Yes, and I'm not saying it was because of nothing," and she said "Please don't remind me of them or I'll get angry and sad all over again. It won't be easy to forget what you did." "It'd be best for both of us if you did, but okay. And they might come up again next year without our replanting them. But we got pretty close to ending things, didn't we?" and she said "Martin; I asked you; please."

There were two other incidents similar to that, maybe three, but little to no crying. One took place just a few months after they met. Seventy-nine; February, or March. It was on the park side of Riverside Drive, right across from her apartment building. In fact, there was even another incident outside, much like this one, but he already went over it. It had snowed, was still snowing. Maybe ten inches. He watched it from her living room window and said "What do you say we go out and walk in the snow? I've always wanted to do that with the woman I loved and kiss her with snow on our noses." "That's sweet," she said. "I don't know about the snowy nose part, but I'd love to," and they started to get dressed for the outside. "Boots, too," he said, "so your feet don't freeze. I'll just put on two pairs of socks, if you loan me one of yours." They didn't walk far, maybe a block and back. Then at the wall separating the Drive from the park, she turned to look at the snow coming down over the river. He made a snowball and threw it at a tree. "Missed," he said. "What?" and he said "The tree. Snowball." She still hadn't turned around. She was wearing a cap, gloves, her coat buttoned up to her neck. He had a cap on but had left his gloves in his apartment and his hands were getting cold. Time to go in, he thought. But first a little fun. He made a much smaller snowball, one not so compact as the one he threw at the tree, and lobbed it underhand at her. He'd aimed at her backside but it hit her just above her coat collar and got down her neck. "What are you doing?" she said, brushing herself off. "That's cold and I can't get it out. And I wasn't prepared for it and could have slipped. I could break a leg here." "I didn't think I was doing anything bad, and hitting you so far up wasn't where I was aiming. So, sorry once again," and she said "What other time were you sorry for something with me?" and he said "Then this is the first. Here, let me help you," because she had taken her gloves off and was trying to dig out the snow from in back, and he put his hand down her coat and got out what snow he could find. "Enough, already," she said. "Your hand's as cold as the snow. Thank you, but I'll get out what's left when we get home." "Now, instead of that snowball, if I had grabbed you—that would have been something else," and he pretended to cackle and put his arms around her and bent her back as if he were going to drop her into the snow. "What's with you?" she said. "Let me up. You could slip, and my coat's new," and he lifted her back up and let go of her. She picked up a glove that had fallen and said "We better go inside." "You're angry," and she said "Yes. I don't like being bullied or scared or treated roughly or falling on my back. I didn't think you were being funny, no matter what you might have thought," and she stepped carefully over the snow—he put his hand out to help and she said "Don't give me your hand; I don't want it"—and waited for some cars to pass before she crossed the street to her building. In the elevator going up, he said "I'm sorry again, and this time it is again," and she said "You should be. You acted like an immature kid." "I know," he said, "and also like a dope. But that's not the first time I heard that in my life. Am I forgiven?" "I'll think about it." "Can I get the kiss I didn't outside?" and she said "If you want. But do it before the door opens."

He's not sure where the second one was. Either a railway station in London or one in Paris. Waterloo? Gare de Lyon? He's just pulling names out of the air. Says to himself: Let me think. The name of the station he might never come up with. It was the end of May, 1985. Gwen was five months pregnant with Maureen. She and Rosalind and he had been to several countries the past month—Germany (really only Munich), Czechoslovakia, Poland, Austria—and were either heading to London, after a week in Paris, or to the QE2, after four days in London. He remembers wanting to buy a book at the railway station. Faulkner's *Collected Stories*, Penguin edition. So it almost had to be the London railway station, where they were waiting to board a boat train to the QE2. He thought it might have been at the French railway station because he complained to her there how she was always running late and they could have missed the hydrofoil to Dover, which they had unrefundable tickets for, if they'd missed the train to it.

They did get there late, but the train wasn't there yet and they were told the hydrofoil would wait for it or another one would honor their tickets. "Saved by a tardy train," he said, "but I'll take anything," and they each had a sandwich and Gwen and he shared a beer and they checked out the magazines at a newsstand and souvenirs at a gift shop and bought Rosalind a Mickey Mouse doll and got on the train. No anger or crying and in their passenger car Gwen rested her head against his shoulder and slept all the way to the dock. The argument at the London railway station was much worse. They were running late again because of her. "I'm heavy and slow and lack my old energy, what can I say?" she said. He ran to the train station from the cab, carrying Rosalind in one arm and with the other their larger bag. "Come on, come on, hurry; we'll miss it," he said to Gwen. She was walking as fast as she could behind him and pulling a bag on wheels. He was afraid they'd miss the boat train and the QE2 would sail without them. It turned out she got the train departure time wrong and they had more than two hours to kill. "I can't believe you sometimes," he said. "What am I going to do the next two hours? You know I hate waiting for anything very long, and we've already stuffed ourselves at lunch." "I don't know what you're going to do, but I'm happy just to sit here. I'm tired and I can use the rest. Walk around, have another cup of tea," and he said "I don't want to walk around. Where would I go?" "Then buy a *Herald Tribune* and sit beside me and read me the news. Or take Rosalind outside and get her some sweet tea. But whatever you do, don't start with me again. I've had my fill of your blaming me." "Don't blame Mommy," Rosalind said. "Be nice," and he said "Okay, I won't. I'll blame you. Only kidding, my little putchky. How's Mickey today? Better?" and she waved the doll in the air and said "All better," and he patted Mickey on the head and said "Good." And to Gwen: "If only you'd gotten the train schedule straight. I ran so hard from the cab, my shirt's soaked." "Look," she said, "you might have been the one to get our visas in New York and who's done most of the heavy carrying, but I've done practically everything else to make this trip work. Hotels, reservations, itinerary, planes and trains, the QE2 standby fares, and all the confirmations and translating and who knows what else. So give me a little credit, will you?" and he said "I do. I'm just saying—" and she said "I know what you're saying, so stop it." "I will when I'm sure it's registered with you, because I don't know how many times we almost missed a train or plane." "But we never did, did we?" and he said "But it got too close—you could even say with that hydrofoil—and it makes me nervous and I don't want it to happen again. Prague, for instance, giving the cab driver the name of the wrong train station. And the plane out of Kraków and forgetting our passports at the hotel there for a few minutes and we had to go back." "That was you as well as me, right?" and he said "Right. You were in charge of the passports, but I should have been covering for you. And I know I can be a bit obsessive in getting to places on time, but you could be a lot more careful." "Oh, screw you and your anxieties and taking part of the blame only when you're forced to. Why do you always have to act this way and then make me act as bad as you?" and he said "I wouldn't if you got things right and prepared your departures from the hotels better." "You want to win the argument? All right, you won. But I can't stand this. I told you, I'm tired, I'm pregnant, but look at you. You're always complaining about me," and he said "No, I'm not," but she started crying. Rosalind took her hand and said "Don't cry, Mommy," and he said "It's the baby that's making her cry," and Gwen said "It's not; it's you. You can be so awful. I wish I weren't married to you." He remembers again the time they were driving to Maine and she was six months pregnant with Rosalind and she took the wrong turn to get onto the Mass Pike so that they headed toward Springfield instead of Boston and he complained and, he thinks, cursed her with something like "Damn you," and she cursed him back with something like "Fuck you," and brought up that she was pregnant and look at the way he's treating her when they're supposed to be happy with her carrying their first child, but he doesn't think she cried. Maybe she did. He thinks she said something about how her tears were affecting her vision, or they would if she cried. Now she was crying. Not heavy sobs and, really, no sounds. A few tears, which she wiped. And that crying look. Her nose got red. It always did when she cried, even at movies, if there was enough light to see her nose, or when she heard a particularly sad piece of music. The Tchaikovsky *String Sextet*, he thinks it is, at a Kneisel Hall concert in a church in Blue Hill. Other chamber music at the Hall. And once while they listened to Bach's *St. John Passion* on a record or CD at home. They had it on both. He said "I'm sorry. Very sorry." Rosalind still held her hand and said to him "You shouldn't be mean to Mommy," and he said "I know. —I'm glad I'm married to you," he said to Gwen. "Please don't think what you said." "It's the truth," she said. "Maybe we're not suited for each other. This happens too often." "When, often?" and she said "We should think seriously about it. Now leave me alone. We have plenty of time before they let us on the train, so why don't you take the walk you don't want to? It'd be good for Rosalind and me." "Do what Mommy says," Rosalind said. He got up and said "I won't go far," and walked around outside and got a beer at a pub and thought "Why do I say those things? Why do I do those things? Idiot. Asshole. Moron. Fool," and went back inside the station and stopped at the bookshop there and saw the Faulkner collection, which he'd never seen in the States and he thinks he would have if it were there, and wanted to buy it but it cost too much, he thought, so he put it back on the shelf. He went back to where they were sitting and said to Gwen "I saw a book I wanted to buy—Faulkner's *Collected Stories*. It had stuff in it I'd never seen before, but it was very expensive. Maybe I should buy it anyway. It's a big book and it might only be sold in England, and we have a five-day voyage ahead of us," and she said "Do what you want. What do I care? But don't talk to me again till after we board the ship." "Don't be mean to Daddy," Rosalind said. "Be nice," and Gwen said "All right. Your father deserves it, but all right. And don't worry, my darling. Everything will turn out okay." "You're not going to go away from Daddy?" and she said "No." He tried to talk to her on the train. She said "Please"—Rosalind was asleep in his lap—"I don't want to speak to you now." "I just want to say how relieved I was at what you said to Rosalind," and she said "Good for you." It was her birthday that day. He'd said "Happy birthday" when they woke up in the morning and kissed her, "but I'm afraid I don't have a present for you," and she said "There's no room in our bags to cram anything more in them anyway." He ordered a bottle of champagne at dinner on the ship and she said "I don't want any, and I'm in no mood to celebrate." "The champagne will go to waste, then, because I'm not going to drink the whole bottle and you know it doesn't keep. Here," and he held the bottle over her glass and she said "Okay, a little, but no toast," and he poured and wanted to pour her another, but she said "It's good, but no more. The baby." He drank the rest of the bottle with dinner and got high and said what he thought were funny things and she laughed at some of them and said "If only you were always this way; not giddy from drink, but sweet and nice." "Well, you can't expect everything," and she said "I found that out." They walked around the ship and sat down on one of the decks and looked at the water and she pointed out some constellations to Rosalind and said "The amazing thing is, we'll see the same ones in Maine. Am I right, Martin?" and he said "Beats me. You know that subject much better than I." After they got back to the cabin and washed up for bed—they had individual bunks across from each other and Rosalind was in a large crib between them—he said "Are you feeling a teensy bit better toward me?" and she said "I'm all right. What's the sense of carrying a grudge? We're stuck with one another for five nights in this pint-sized room." "You think I can climb into your bunk when we turn off the lights?"—Rosalind was already asleep—and she said "There isn't room enough for two," and he said "Sure there is, if that's all that's stopping you. We've cuddled in narrower spaces. And I won't stay there all night. Just for a little while, to hug you from behind and whisper loving things to your neck." "Don't tell me; I know what you want. You have a hard-on and you want relief." "No, no, it's not that. And I don't, or didn't, till you brought it up. It's that I feel so horrible how I acted to you today, and on your birthday, no less, which makes it even worse. We're on this great ship together with our sleeping cutie. We should be having a great time. And I promise never to be such a bastard to you again," and she said "I've heard that before. Okay, I guess you can try." "My getting in your bunk with you?" and she said "Yes, but let's get it over with now. It's been a long strenuous day for me and I feel emotionally and physically drained."

The third time he doesn't remember at all. He was driving Maureen to her first day at college. Gwen had a lot of school work to do and asked Maureen if it'd be all right if she stayed home. She could use the time. Maureen said "Daddy's just going to leave me there anyway, once we get my things into the dorm, since I don't want anyone hanging around." "And you?" and he said "It'd be nice having Maureen all to my own for a few hours. And much as I love your company, I don't mind driving back alone. Plenty of classical music stations between Connecticut and here." "Dear God," she said, starting to cry just before they left, "this'll be the first time since they went off sailing in Maine for a week, when they were what?— nine and twelve—when one of our daughters wouldn't be home." "It'll be sad," he said, "but we'll survive," and he thought what he's going to tell her when he gets back is now they can run around the house naked again as much as they like and make love with their bedroom door unlatched and open. During the drive, Maureen said "Something just came to me which we never talked about. But it was the most frightening experience in my life. Maybe you don't want to hear it," and he said "No, tell me," and she said "It was when Mom said she was going to leave you." "Do you mean permanently?" and she said "Yes." "When she say that? She might have said once or twice that we need a break from each other for a day or two—every couple, married as long as we've been, goes through that—but she never wanted to leave me permanently." "That's what she said. You had a big fight that not even my being there could stop. And one as bad the previous day too. I was nine, same age I was for that sailboat trip Rosalind and I took, which is maybe why it came to me now, but about a half year earlier. Rosalind wasn't in the house. I heard yelling and cursing from both of you and ran into the kitchen just when you called her a bitch." "I never called her a bitch even once," and she said "You did that night. 'A rotten bitch.'" "No, I've never used that expression for anyone," and she said "Believe me, you did. That's when Mom said that was the last time she was going to take that kind of crap from you. That's the word she used, or 'shit.' She said she wanted to move back to our apartment in New York and that she wanted to take us kids with her if we didn't feel it'd be too much a disruption in our lives." "But I would have remembered something like that if she'd said it," he said. "It's not something you forget." "I remember it distinctly," she said. "In the kitchen. It was dark out, around six. I think you were both cooking dinner, or Mom was—fish and a polenta dish, which went to waste that night—nobody wanted to eat—and you were making salad. At least that's what you had on the counter in front of you, lettuce and things. Mom said she wouldn't care giving up her teaching job, since it was a skimpy-paying adjunct position your school had only given her because they wanted to keep you. This was before she got a more regular position there. Worse comes to worst, she said, if the kids wanted to stay in their schools till the end of the school year and live with you, she'd go alone to New York with the cat, and Rosalind and I could move in with her sometime before the new school year began. Of course, she said, we could do what we want: stay with you permanently or live with her." "No, it couldn't have happened. You have to be imagining it," and she said "It happened, Daddy. You just don't want to admit it to yourself or it was such a bad experience for you that you pushed it out of your head. Mom even called Nona that night and told her of her plans to leave you. Later, Rosalind and I asked her what Nona had said, and Mom said she fully supported her and if it was a question of money, she'll back Mom till she was able to look after herself, though you'd be contributing to her living expenses too." "Did you ever speak about this with Mommy? Particularly about how it frightened you so much?" "Once, a few years later, and she said the same thing as you. That things like that can happen in even the best of marriages and that they're usually worked out, with or without professional help, or blown over. With you two, I guess you eventually came to some kind of understanding." "I don't remember that either," and she said "I'm sure if you think some more about it, it'll come back. Mom also asked me if I ever spoke about it with you, and I told her no. Then she advised me not to bring it up with you. That you'd feel very hurt about it. That some things between two people, after they're worked out, are better left alone. And Rosalind was so upset when I told her what I witnessed, she never wanted to talk about it." "So maybe it did happen," he said, "but I've still no recollection of any of it. Let me ask your mother," and she said "I'd say don't. From what I could make out, I don't think she wants to go over the experience again, and I doubt she'd appreciate that you completely forgot about it." "Then let me ask you, and this is going to sound awfully silly to you, but did Mommy leave me and go live in New York, even for a few days? If it was more I'm sure I would have remembered it," and she said "No." "How'd it get resolved, then?" and she said "First you took a long walk around the neighborhood that night—anyway, you were away from the house for hours, and you didn't take the car." "Where could I have gone? No bars or anything like that around there, and all the stores would be closed. Was it cold out?" and she said "It was winter, a little before or after Christmas," and he said "Then I couldn't have stayed out too long or gone very far unless it was an unusually mild night. I don't know." "When you came home, Mom had already gone to bed in your room. You went up to her closed door—I think I even remember hearing her bolt it when you were out—and asked if she ate and she said no. She wasn't hungry. Then you said 'You want me to prepare something for you, because you've got to eat?' and she said she didn't want anything. 'Make something for the kids, not me,' she said. 'Because you upset them so much, they didn't eat either.'" "This isn't coming back," he said. "I don't see how it couldn't, but it isn't. What happened next?" and she said "You said you'd sleep on the couch that night, and she said 'The girls can sleep together and you can have one of their rooms,' and you said you didn't want to make it worse for them than you have. You asked her if she was still planning to go to New York, and she said 'No more questions; no more talk.' For you to leave her alone. 'If you're going to do anything,' she said, 'fix things up with the kids,' but you didn't. You seemed to want to stay away from us, so we also kept our distance from you. I remember you had a drink or two. We didn't see it, and Rosalind was afraid you'd get drunk that night, but we heard the ice clink when you took it from the freezer and dropped it into a glass. You made the couch up for sleeping or maybe you just slept with a blanket over you and a couch pillow. Then you sat in your Morris chair and read and drank and had a CD on to some choral music—" "Hildegard von Bingen, probably. She was my favorite for when I wanted quiet spiritual music and was feeling low," and she said "I think I remember you playing her other times and wanting us to listen to her with you. Anyway, it was late by then and Rosalind and I were hungry—we really hadn't had dinner. We cooked up a box of Annie's or Whole Foods shells and cheese, which we'd been making for ourselves for years, and still do when we want something filling and quick, and then went to bed. Next day, while we were in school—and you had to have driven Rosalind to hers. I always took the school bus. Or it could have been the weekend by now or the first day of our Christmas vacation and we went to be with our friends—anyplace, to be out of the house. What I'm getting at is Mommy and you must have worked it out while we were gone, or started to, because the previous night was the last time I heard her say she was leaving you or wanted to leave you or you should leave her." "Where'd I sleep the second night?" and she said "I'm not sure. I think on the couch again. Or Rosalind and I may have had a sleepover that night—I'm sure we would have tried to—and you slept in one of our beds. I don't think things were good enough between you and Mom yet for you to sleep in your bedroom." "Oh, by the way," he said, "since you remember so much, do you remember what the argument was about?" and she said "That I don't know. Not because I can't remember, but because I didn't hear what started it; just the yelling and cursing." "I still can't believe it," he said. "I mean, I believe you, but I just can't understand how I could have forgotten such a singular and disturbing event," and she said "I'm surprised too. Well, now that we've finally talked it over, I won't bring it up again. I think I even feel I shouldn't have brought it up now." "I'm still going to speak to your mother to find out what she knows about it," and she said "I wouldn't, but that's up to you." But when he got back home he forgot to talk about it with her, or something kept him from talking about it, and this is the first time he's thought of it since.

That bolt on their bedroom door. Doesn't know what its original purpose could have been. The elderly couple they bought the house from and whom they'd never met were the only previous owners, so they had to have put it on. Maybe they feared burglars—they might even have been burglarized before they got the bolt—and used it when they went to bed. They had no children, the real-estate agent said. The kids' bedrooms had been this couple's studies and Gwen's study had been their TV room. Gwen and he only used the bolt when they were about to make love, or knew sometime beforehand they were going to make love, and the kids were home. Didn't want one of them suddenly opening the door on them in bed, which Maureen did once and saw Gwen on top of him. She was seven or eight, and she said "Oh," and ran out. "What was that?" Gwen said, still on top of him but no longer moving, and he said "Maureen; she's gone." "Good God," she said, getting off, "what she must have thought," and he said "That's what I was thinking. We can tell her you were massaging me for something that aches…a sore muscle," and she said "Massaging the front?"

"The shoulders, or you'd fallen asleep reading on my side of the bed and were climbing over me to get to yours. That's why the light was on," and she said "But why would I have no clothes on? Do you think she was sick? That's why she came in? One of us should check. And no, we'll say nothing about what happened, unless she asks. If she does, we'll say…we'll come up with something by morning. If she saw your erection, then I don't know what, but it makes it even worse. I don't want her not only confused but frightened." "She didn't. I was inside you the two seconds she was in the room," and she said "Not all the time. All the way in, half out; that's how it works," and he said "I think this time I was all the way in when I saw her. And your hair was spread out and covering a lot of me, so she might not have seen anything." "From now on," she said, "we should use the door bolt every time we go to bed, or when we know there's a good chance we're going to make love. And if we don't know, but start to make love, one of us will get up and very quietly slide the bolt in." He was going to say, but didn't. Too stupid a joke. "Should I bolt it now?" and she said "Her seeing us has taken whatever there was out of me." "I'll be extremely quiet and go on top; make it as easy for you as can be," and she said "Tomorrow. Will you see if she's all right?" and he put on his bathrobe and went into Maureen's room and she was sleeping or pretending to.

They were in bed, watching *Key Largo* on Maryland Public Television for the second time that year. She was laughing and said "The dialog really kills me. 'All right, you guys, I'm Johnny Rocco, see? See?'" and he said "I think the 'see' part of your impersonation is from another Edward G. Robinson movie. And the 'All right, you guys,' is James Cagney, if he ever said it in a movie. But let me watch it, will ya? It's a good picture, good acting, and some of the lines are classic." She sat up against the headboard and made as if she were chomping on a big cigar and then holding it and flicking its ashes to the floor and said "Listen, wise guy, nobody tells Johnny Rocco what to do, see? You think you're a big war hero, but you're nobody compared to me. I'm Johnny Rocco, king of the rackets, once. That's who I am. And after my deal goes through I'm gonna be on top again, you wait and see." "Okay, Johnny, but the movie—" and she said "Okay, nothing, wise guy. Mess with Johnny Rocco and his boys and you'll get what's coming to you, or what's coming out of you, your last breath, see? See?" when the phone rang. "Late," he said, and got out of bed, lowered the television sound and picked up the receiver. "I'm sorry for calling at this hour," their real-estate agent said, "but I have good news. The Hendricksons have taken your offer"—he raised his fist above his head and said to Gwen "They've taken our offer" and she yelled "Hurray"—"and if there are no unexpected setbacks," the agent said, "—mortgage, financing, deed; you know—the house is yours." "Oh, that's wonderful," he said. "Call anytime you want with such great news. My wife and I are very happy," and she said "Have a good weekend." He hung up and said "That was Mrs. Blinkova, of course. They actually took our low offer. We're in," and she pretended to puff on a cigar and blow smoke out of her mouth and said "Know how we got the house, wise guy? Hey? Because Johnny Rocco told them to. Nobody says no to Johnny Rocco and lives to tell it. Nobody, you hear?, or they're dead meat." "Okay," he said, "we can see the movie anytime," and turned it off. He sat on the bed and put his arms out and they hugged. "You can be very funny sometimes," he said, "did you know that?" "Well, as my mother likes to remind me—" and he said "You've told me, you've told me, but it just ain't true. You were always clever and had a great sense of humor and flair for mimicry. I had nothing to do with it. It's just, once you got rid of your suspicions about me—" and she said "And what were they?" "That I was a bit of an oddball or strange. Just the way I approached you the first night we met. 'You probably won't want to speak to me—'" and she said "You keep saying you said that. I forgot what you did say when you first spoke to me, but it wasn't that. I admit I was a little leery of you. First of all, the shirt you wore to the party," and he said "I've told you. I didn't know it was going to be a party. I thought— " and she said "I know, but it was such an ugly shirt. And the way you stared at me every chance you could, without coming over and introducing yourself. Or just coming over and standing there and saying nothing would have been better. And that you waited to speak to me till I was at the elevator. Strange, really; as you said, odd behavior. I'm surprised I didn't think you were a little creepy." "Then I'm lucky you even consented to meet me the first time," and she said "Oh, you were nice looking, and when you finally did speak, you spoke well. Those were pluses, and you seemed smart. Besides, it was only an hour out of my time—on my way home from my therapist—and if it didn't work out, no great loss for either of us. But after our first date—or after the second. No, the first, for coffee, the Ansonia, I was no longer leery of you and thought you were just fine." "That's what I meant. You relaxed. And you were funny, showed a terrific sense of humor, or one I certainly appreciated, from the second or third date on. But what are we talking about this for? The new house, Gwen. Baltimore County. More land and trees around us and the nearest neighbor a few hundred feet away. A carport. A garden shed. Cheaper real-estate taxes and auto insurance than in the city, I hear, and better schools for the kids.

A screen painting on the front door. And a complete house, not semidetached, so windows on all sides and everything on one floor and no more going up and down stairs." "A ranch house," she said. "An unfinished basement we'll have to pour several thousand dollars into it to make it habitable." "As my father would probably have said: 'You own a ranch house, you could buy a horse.' But this is great. We got what we wanted, and at a steal. Let's open a good bottle of wine to celebrate. I'd say champagne, but we haven't got one that's cold." "No wine for me—too late for it—but you have," and he said "I don't mind if I do," kissed her and went downstairs and got an expensive bottle of wine from the wine rack in the dining room, opened it and poured himself a glass. He should bring up a glass for her too, he thought. He drank his glass, poured himself another and one for her, sipped at his because he'd filled it to the brim and he didn't want to spill any carrying it, and brought the glasses upstairs. "Do you want to go back to the movie?" she said. "It still has a long ways to go. The hurricane; the two dead Indians; Bogart knocking off the whole gang in the boat," and he said "I've had enough. How about you?" and held out a glass for her and she said in her Johnny Rocco voice "Johnny Rocco told you he didn't want a drink, din't he? Din't he? Why you always got to do what Johnny Rocco says he don't want you to? But okay, he don't want to ruin your fun, so he'll let you get away with it today," and she took the glass.

This was at the cottage in Maine they rented together for two to three months every summer for seven years. Nothing much; the last summer they were there before Maureen was born. It was on what they called "A Maine day": mild, sunny, low humidity, little puffs of white clouds, blue skies, temperature around 72. If they were lucky: a light breeze coming up from the water. They loved the cottage—she started renting it three summers before she met him—and would have bought it if they had the money when it was being sold. He was in the kitchen, taking the forty or so diapers out of the washing machine and dropping them into the laundry basket on the floor. They bought this huge used washing machine the summer after Rosalind was born. They had no dryer. At the time, they couldn't find a cheap used one and didn't think it worth buying a new dryer for just a few months every summer, especially when the cottage could be sold out from under them, and eventually decided they could do without one. They'd hang their wash out in the sun, and if there were repeated days of rain or cloudiness, they'd drive to Blue Hill about twenty miles away and make a day out of it by shopping for groceries and having lunch in one of a number of good simple places while the diapers and other wash were being dried in the coin laundry there. He brought the basket of diapers to the porch. They had a couple of clotheslines strung out on poles he'd cemented into the ground in an open space near the cottage. But he needed clothespins for that, which took lots of time to use for so many diapers, and after a few minutes of hanging them up, his arms hurt. Instead, he now hung them and things like socks and shorts and, when the sun was very strong, towels and jeans over the porch railings. "Need any help?" Gwen said. She was lying on a chaise longue, reading; wide-brimmed straw gardener's hat shading her face. There were a few moth holes in the brim and he could see a spot of light from one of them on her cheek. He said "No, no, you rest; I don't want you to get up. Besides, you want to deprive me of my next to most favorite domestic chore?" "And what's your most favorite? I remember what your favorite day of the year always is, but this one I forget," and he said "Stacking them after they've dried." "You'll get no fight from me on that score. It's so tedious, hanging an endless number of diapers out to dry. And maybe equally as tedious to stack them, so the job's all yours," and she went back to her reading. She was in a bikini top and Bermuda shorts. Prescription sunglasses; sandals off. Probably they were special shorts with an elasticized waistband, she was so pregnant. Half-filled glass of something in arm's reach of her on the floor. By the color of it, iced coffee, with milk in it, and where the ice had melted. The four Siamese cats sleeping or resting under the chaise longue, their eyes closed. "You're not going to burn?" and she said "Sun block. I've slathered myself silly with it." "Still, you're so fair; but it's your body." He started draping the diapers over the railings. The last few, when he ran out of room on the railings, he hung over the rim of the laundry basket and spread one out inside it. He used to also hang them over the porch's staircase railings, but when they were done they often slid off. In an hour, if the sun didn't disappear, they'd be dry. Then, on a small metal table out there, he'd very neatly stack them one on top of the other in two to three piles and bring them inside and take one pile to their bedroom upstairs where Rosalind's crib was. At times, when he stacked them, he'd press a diaper to his cheek to feel its softness and warmth. He could see why she might not like hanging the diapers out to dry, but how could she not like stacking them? Not that she needed one with him, but it was probably just an excuse to get out of doing both because, unlike him, she liked reading more.

His favorite day of the year. Didn't he go over that? Even if he did, maybe something will come out of it that he hadn't thought of before. He'd begin talking about it with her and the kids days before they left New York for Kennebunkport. "Guess what? We're getting close to my favorite day of the year. I can hardly wait." Or "Two days till my favorite day of the year. Everybody thinking about what they want to pack? I know, it's crazy, but I so much look forward to it." Gwen and he would share the driving, even the times she was pregnant—"No; my stomach doesn't get in the way"—so that part of it wasn't difficult. Six, seven hours. If they left on a Friday, which he liked to avoid, maybe eight. He'd sleep for about an hour in the front passenger seat. "Where are we?" he'd say when he woke up. "God, we've made great time." Lunch at a family restaurant they always stopped at in Connecticut right off the highway—81? 94?—about ten miles from the Mass Pike. The kids loved its homemade pies with two scoops of ice cream on top. "Can we get two flavors?" He'd start singing moment after they crossed the Pisca-something bridge into Maine and the kids would join in—Gwen never did: "It's too silly a ditty": "We're here because we're here because we're here because we're here-e-e-e," their voices rising on the last "here," and then a repeat of the line without a rise at the end. It was something—not a song, really—his busload of summer campers when he was a kid used to sing when the bus pulled into camp, also for two months. Bringing into the motel room their briefcases of manuscripts and one of his two typewriters—hers and then her computer and printer were too heavy for someone to steal, though he covered them and his other typewriter with blankets—and a suitcase for them and knapsacks for the kids and stuff for the cats. And a shopping bag of cotton sheets and pillowcases for them to replace the linen already on their bed. The kids didn't mind the hotel linen and didn't understand why they did. "They all feel the same." "That's because your body isn't supersensitive yet," he said, and when she started crying—he forgets which one—he said "I'm sorry, I didn't mean it that way. You're sensitive; I know. Please, darling, don't spoil a great day." Running around the beach with the kids—being chased and then chasing them—three of them jumping into the water together at least once. "Br-r-r-r, it's cold, our annual membership renewal in the Polar Bear Club." The kids able to tolerate the cold water much better than he—even swimming in it a few minutes—all while Gwen read or napped or both in the room. "If you can swing it, I'd love to have two hours alone. Even to see what's on cable," since they didn't have it at home. Showering. "You too, kids. If you want to sleep without scratching your feet all night, you have to wash the sand out of your toes." He'd get cheese from the little cooler they brought from New York and put it on crackers and pass the plate around and then just leave it on the night table. Vodka over rocks but probably two before heading off for dinner. He always offered her a beer or glass of wine in the motel, but she'd hold off drinking till he ordered a bottle of wine at the restaurant. "A half bottle or wine by the glass won't do? After all, it's just the two of us drinking." "What we don't drink, I'll cork and bring back to the room and we'll finish it tomorrow night. But you know me. It's the one evening I don't mind getting a bit lightheaded, and we're not driving." Delicious food. He thinks he ordered the summer's first New England clam chowder as a starter every year and then scallops as an entrée. Sunset from the glass-enclosed porch they always tried to sit in. He'd call the restaurant before, sometimes from New York a week ahead, but if he didn't he'd stop by the reservation desk on his way to or back from the beach with the kids to see if he could reserve a table by the porch window around seven. Because they always ate at the Breakwater Inn: just a short walk from their motel. After dinner, the kids usually ran ahead. "Give us the key." "It's dark, and there are no street-lights, so watch out for cars when you cross the road." Gwen and he either held hands when they walked back or he put his arm around her waist or shoulders. Because of the wine and food and that they were feeling so good with each other and everything had gone smoothly that day and this was the first day of their long stay in Maine, with no classes to prepare till the end of summer, and maybe something to do with the sea smells and air, he could almost say they always made love that night, but only when they were sure the kids were asleep in the next bed. When Rosalind got older—fourteen? fifteen?—which would make Maureen eleven to twelve—the girls got their own room in the motel. "Come on, kids; it's getting late. Time to turn off the TV." "Ten minutes?" "Okay. Sounds fair."

He was in his study in their Baltimore apartment. They also used it as a storage room. It had no door, just a door-sized space to walk through. He's not being clear because it's not easy to picture. To get in and out of this small room, which once could have been the maid's room in this big apartment—three bedrooms, separate living and dining rooms, large kitchen leading to his study—you walked through an opening the size and shape of a door. There was probably once a real door there—in fact, he knows it, since the marks where its hinges and screws had been were still on the jamb—but there wasn't one now to open and close; just an open space. Oh, he gives up. Why can't he come even close to describing it? Maybe not enough sleep. Gwen knocked on the wall outside his room, or maybe the jamb. He was typing, his back to her, and was startled by the noise. "I'm sorry," she said; "didn't mean to scare you. I have some good news that I don't think you'll entirely like. I just got a call—" "The phone rang?" he said. "I was so absorbed in my work I didn't even hear it." "Am I disturbing you then? I can tell you later," and he said "No, go on. You got a call from whom?" "Someone at the NEA. She said I got a fellowship in translation." "Oh, my goodness," he said, "that's great," and stood up, almost knocking over his chair as he did, and went over to her and hugged her. "Jesus, you really did it. I'm so happy for you. But why would you think—" "Because you didn't get the one you applied for." "How do you know?" and she said "I asked the person who called me—an official there—if my husband, who also applied for one this year, got it in fiction. She checked the list of this year's winners in everything, said she didn't think she was supposed to be doing this—revealing other names—and your name wasn't on it." "So what?" he said. "I love it that you got one. You deserve it." "You deserve one to. And you've applied five years straight, or something, while I only applied this once and mostly because you urged me to. I'm sure I got it because so few translators apply. And it could be they don't give it the same year to husband and wife applicants, even if they're in different fields, and if I hadn't got mine, you would have got one," and he said "Nonsense. How would they even know we're married? We've different surnames." "But the same address and apartment number." "I'm sure they don't look at the addresses very carefully," and she said "They do. What state the applicant's from and what city. I heard they try to spread the fellowships around the country so no state or city seems favored." "Please," he said, "you got it because you earned it, and the panel of judges for translations was probably the most selective one, since they really had to know what they were doing." "I wanted you to get it more than I," and he said "Same for me with you. But I get lots of things. Nothing as big as an NEA yet, but I'm in a field where more things are given for it than for translation. I'll just apply again, that's all. My sweetheart, I'm so proud of you, and it's so much money. Baby asleep?" and she said "Yes." "Let's get her up and tell her." "No, let her sleep." "You're so modest." "And you can be so silly sometimes." "Should we celebrate with a glass of wine?" and she said "Too early. I'm still working." "The news of the fellowship doesn't stop you for even a few hours?" and she said "This is for school." "Then dinner tonight at a good restaurant and with good wine." "No, I've already prepared dinner. You're being very nice about it, Martin." "You still don't know how happy I am for you?" "You're not even a little bit jealous or bitter?" and he said "What a thing to say."

Then there was the time—he might even have put it in one of his fictions—when he and Gwen and the kids and his in-laws were walking on the south side of 72nd Street toward Broadway. He was carrying Maureen, so she must have been one or two. Gwen was pushing Rosalind in the stroller. If Maureen wanted to be in the stroller, or he got tired carrying her, then Rosalind would have to walk. They'd just had an early dinner at a Jewish restaurant-deli a little ways up the street. Moscowitz and Lupkowitz, he thinks it was called. No, that was the restaurant-deli his father used to speak about going to, on the Lower East Side, he thinks. He knows Moscowitz was the first name but he's not sure if Lupkowitz was the second. Fine and Shapiro. That's what the name of the restaurant they went to was. Had been in the same location for about forty years, and for all he knows, is still there. "They bought the building they're in," his father-in-law once told him, "which means they'll never have to go out of business because of the landlord tripling the rent." When a car pulled up and double-parked in front of a grocery they were passing. Two men jumped out, the driver stayed, and ran into the store. It was owned by Koreans. They sold mostly produce. Before he moved to Baltimore, he bought some fruit and vegetables there a few times. They were more expensive than the Korean grocery on Columbus and 73rd, but both stores had some of the best produce in the neighborhood and were convenient because they were so small. The store was completely open to the street, its glass front folding all the way in to both sides. In winter, thick plastic sheets covered the outside of the store. One man had a gun—maybe the other did too, but wasn't showing his—and said something to a Korean man sitting on a milk crate, who'd been taking green peppers out of a cardboard box and arranging them on a display stand. The Korean man went to the cash register, opened it and began filling a brown paper bag with cash. "Robbery," Gwen's father had already said. "Let's get out of here," and pulled the stroller with one hand and grabbed his wife by the arm with the other, and said "Martin; quick what're you looking at? Come with us," and they all walked quickly toward Broadway, Gwen pushing the stroller. "Wait a minute," he said to Gwen. "They can't do this on the street, in broad daylight." He handed Maureen to her and started back. "Martin; don't," she said. He didn't know how far he'd go or what he was going to do, but he'd at least get the license-plate number. The rear plate was covered with mud, or something brown—even the state it was from, and he didn't want to go around to the front because the driver would see him. A Korean woman was filling a second paper bag with money from a metal box under the cash register. The gunman was making motions with his hand for the woman and man to go faster. Nobody else on the street seemed to notice what was going on. They walked past without looking at the store, or if they did look, didn't think anything was unusual.

The gun was now hidden by the man's leg. His father-in-law grabbed his shoulder. "Are you crazy? It's not your business. You're a family man now; with responsibilities. I know all about your past heroics, but this time you'll get us both killed." Gwen and the rest were at the corner. His mother-in-law was waving frantically for them to come. Just then the two men walked out of the store to the car, the gunman carrying a plastic shopping bag, and they drove off. The Korean man ran to the sidewalk and screamed "Police. Please, police, police." "Don't even say you'll be a witness," his father-in-law said. "They'll never catch the thieves. And if they do, you'll have to come back to New York at your own expense and identify them and later testify against them, and that could take days out of your time. Your place is with your wife and children and job. Let's get home. Do you have the doggy bag?" and he said "It's hanging on the back of the stroller." They went to the corner. "This the newsstand where you once stopped a robbery?" his father-in-law said, and he said "They just wanted to steal a few magazines, and I sided with the newsstand owner." "You got a cracked head from it, no?" and he said "The city's Board of Estimate gave me a Good Samaritan citation, which meant the city reimbursed me for all my medical expenses." Gwen handed him Maureen and said "What were you thinking?" and he said "I'm not sure. To yell at the robbers and then get out of the way." "I don't know what you're going to think of me for saying this, but I can guess what my father told you and I agree with him a hundred percent." His mother-in-law said "Grisha just told me what you wanted to do, Martin. You're very brave and normally quite smart, but you can also be incredibly foolish. You have to think of the consequences more." "Okay, okay," he said, "I've been outnumbered. You kids have anything to say about it?" and Maureen rested her head on his shoulder and Rosalind said "About what, Daddy?" There was a commotion now in front of the grocery. A police or ambulance siren could be heard getting closer. Maybe it was for this. "Come," his father-in-law said, "before we get in even more trouble," and they waited for the light and crossed Broadway and went to his in-laws' apartment.

They were in the car going to New York for a long weekend. While they were crossing the Delaware Memorial Bridge he said to Gwen "I have to make a quick decision. Should we take 295, which is right off the bridge, to the Jersey Turnpike, or get on the turnpike about a mile from here? We've never gone that way before, and judging by the map I looked at yesterday, it doesn't seem any longer. And there might be better scenery on it than the Turnpike, and, if we want to stop, a better place to eat." "Anything you want," she said. "We can pick up the Turnpike around Fort Dix, the map said—we'll see signs for it. This'll also break up the monotony of the hundred-plus miles of the Turnpike," and she said "Fine." Half an hour later the kids said they were hungry and had to make. He said "Nothing so far on this road, after the public rest area when we first got on it, so maybe there's nothing any farther." And to Gwen: "Think we should get off and look around?" and she said "If that's what you think. You decide." "Okay, we'll get off at the next exit. They come quick enough. Maybe taking 295 wasn't a good idea, and it's only a bit more interesting than the Turnpike. I don't know what I was expecting. I didn't take it to save on the toll, I want you to understand," and she said "It never entered my mind." They got off, there were no signs for the Turnpike, saw a diner soon after—"Looks all right from the outside," he said—and parked in front of it. "Going to come in?" he said to her, and she said "I'm not hungry." "Don't have to use the restroom?" and she said "No." "I can bring you back something," and she said "I said I'm not hungry." "French fries? Ice cream? Something to drink?" and she said "Thanks, but will you stop?" "You didn't say you weren't thirsty, but okay, I won't nudzh you anymore." The kids and he went inside, used the restrooms, sat at the counter. The place was neat and clean but smelled of cigarette smoke. There were a few other customers, at the counter and three at a table, and most were smoking. No one was behind the counter. In fact, nobody working at the diner seemed to be around. There was an ashtray on the shelf behind the counter with lots of butts in it. "Maybe we'll just get something to go," he said to the kids. "I don't like it here," Rosalind said. "It's too smoky." "Neither do I," he said. "All right, we'll find another diner. Or we'll just wait till we get on the Turnpike and go to one of those big rest areas we know there," and they left. On the way back to the car he saw Gwen looking at him through her open window. Her expression was pretty blank. He smiled and waved to her but she didn't smile or wave back. Just stared at him. Why does he bring all this up? Because she was acting in a way he'd never seen before. That true? Well, it was very unusual and it stands out. The kids got in the car—he thinks it was the first minivan they had, the one that gave them so much trouble—and he went up to her window and said "You're not smiling or waving at me anymore?" She said "Why would you think that?" and faked a smile and flapped her hand at him. "That's not a real smile," and she said "So? That's what I'm like. I can't put one on." "You unhappy?" and she said "I don't want to talk about it." "You don't love me anymore?" he said, smiling, because he was kidding, and she said "Don't be an idiot. I was thinking about something else, not you or the kids or my parents. That's why I didn't smile or wave, but must I explain?" and he said "Not if you don't want to," and she said "Good," and turned to the windshield and stared at it. He got in beside her, slapped her left thigh gently, wanted to rub it as he often did in the car, even when he was driving, but knew she wouldn't want him to, and started the car. "You know, your not smiling at me is taking away one of the great pleasures of my life, and even your waving back to me with a real wave gives me a big kick," and she said "Oh, knock it off." "God, you're in a pissy mood," and she said "I told you. It's not about you, but it's becoming you. Why can't you accept that?" "Now I definitely won't ask you what it is," and she said "Don't," and he said "Jesus," and she said "Too bad." "What's wrong daddy?" Rosalind said. "Why aren't we driving?" "It's nothing, sweetheart. Everything's fine, and we'll find another place to eat at soon. Now, which way should I go? Dumb of me not to have asked inside, but I just wanted to get out of there. Probably, right. That's where the Turnpike should be or the signs to it," and he drove.

He never told her this. Thought to, then thought how she would have taken it. She would have got very angry. Screamed terrible things at him. Or maybe not. Not like her, the screaming, though there were times. She would have said "Who gave you the right to do that? And for what? Some stupid sex?" That is, if he had also told her why he did it. Since she would have asked, he probably would have. He would have said "I didn't want him in the room while we were making love, or scratching at our bedroom door to be let in. Plain and simple, I didn't want to be interrupted." She would have said "After what you just told me, I don't know if I can ever trust what you say again. What a despicable thing to do. And look what it cost us. Between the two vets and medications, more than a thousand. If you had done the right thing—let him in when he wanted to—all of that would have been avoided. You knew there were foxes out there at night. We've seen them a few times during the day. But it's night, under cover, when they're mostly hunting, and squirrels and mice and cats are what they like to attack and eat the most. Poor Sleek. What he went through. He lay around the house for two days, not eating or drinking or doing anything but crawling to the litter box and usually missing, till you took him to the vet here. I wanted you to take him right away, not that it would have helped him with that vet, but you said that cats have a way of healing themselves. Since when had you become the expert? The first set of antibiotics weren't working. The vet had no doubt given him the wrong one. But you said to give them time, and I like a fool agreed. It was only after he continued to get worse, or just didn't improve, that you did the right thing: before we left for Maine you made an appointment with the Blue Hill vet for the afternoon we arrived. They saved his life. And now you tell me you've this confession to make, something you never told me and wanted to get off your chest—that Sleek didn't get attacked the morning you let him out, but the evening before, when he wanted to come in. From now on, when I say, as I probably did that night, 'Is Sleek in?' don't lie to me that he is. I'm so upset. Part of me wishes you hadn't told me. Some things are better left a lie. But tell me, did you learn from your mistake? Have you kept him out some nights since then? If you have"—he had, once, and after they'd made love he'd planned to let him in but fell asleep and didn't wake up till around four in the morning, when he whispered to her he was getting a glass of water and went to the kitchen to open the door for Sleek—"You'll probably lie to me that you haven't, so what's the sense of asking the question?" "I haven't," he would have said. "Not even for an hour. I realized my mistake and was glad we were able to save Sleek, and I regret what I put him through and also the distress I caused you. I'll never do anything like that again. You have my word, for whatever you think it's worth. If, some nights, I don't want him in our room or scratching at the door to be let in, I'll put him on the porch, leave some water for him there and maybe his litter box, though he's good at holding it in, and shut the porch door. That is, if it's all right with you. And then let him out when I get up or if he starts whining or crying before, or if you want me to. But I really don't mind him sleeping on our bed when we're just sleeping. I actually like it, except when he tries to squeeze his way in between us or gets under the covers. But don't I get some credit for finally telling the truth? It wasn't easy, you know. I had a good idea how you'd react and what you'd say." "No, no credit," she would have said. "It's not going to go away as easily as that." So he never told her. What use would it have been? Getting it off his chest? He never put much stock in that, and the consequences from it all would have been too great.

　　Just about every time they were at her parents' apartment after one or two in the afternoon or at night, but not when they only came to say goodbye before they drove to Baltimore, her father would say "Like me to make you a Bloody Mary, Martin?" If it was five or six or later, he almost always said "Sure, I'd love one; thanks. But please not too strong." If it was earlier, he'd say "Much as I like your Bloody Marys, it's a bit early for me to drink, but thanks." "I make it with V8 juice," her father would often say. "And no Tabasco pepper sauce in it for you. I know you don't like hot foods, and I won't make it too strong." "Still too early for me. You have one," and her father would usually say something like "I'll wait till later, when I have my one drink for the night. But you, you're a young man, and can take one now and one later." Gwen would sometimes say "A little drink won't hurt you," and he'd say "Sweetheart, you know I don't like anything alcoholic to drink till around six or seven. Not even a glass of wine if we're having lunch at a restaurant. Though I will make an exception for one of your father's Bloody Marys after five." "Be a good husband and listen to your wife," her father would say. "She knows I make a good drink." "Grisha," her mother said a couple of times, "if he doesn't want one, don't force him. He knows what he's doing." "Who's forcing him? I know what I'm doing too. Stay out of it," and she said something like "Grisha, please don't talk that way. You're with the children. It doesn't sound nice." "Okay," he'd say, "but a short one. And half the vodka you put in your evening Bloody Marys." "Not half; that's not a drink," and he'd say "Half," and her father would smile impishly and say "Good, I've got a customer. One Bloody Mary coming up. Gwendolyn, can I get you anything?" and she'd say "Nothing, Poppa." "I can open an excellent bottle of red wine a client gave me. He's a wine expert. Said it was top-notch. I don't drink it and your mother never touches a drop." "It'll go to waste if you only open it for me," and her father would say "It won't go to waste. Maybe you'll have two glasses. And then you'll take whatever's left home with you. I'll recork it real tight." "All right, then, but like Martin's, a small one. I'll open the bottle for you," and her father would say "Let me do it all myself. It's a great pleasure for your mother and me to see you here and you both so happy," and if the kids were with them, "and my darling grandchildren so pretty and healthy." Because of a problem her father had with both ankles for years, he'd shuffle instead of walk, his feet, in orthopedic boots he only wore at home, barely lifting off the floor. Still, he insisted on getting the drinks himself. "Sit; sit; it's good exercise for me. I haven't been on my feet all day." Smiling, he'd shuffle to the kitchen, and a few minutes later, shuffle back to the living room holding a small tray in both hands with the Bloody Mary on it. "No; again, it's good exercise for me. Let me get the wine too." Then he'd sit and say "So how is it, Martin? The wine I know is very good." "A little strong, but a terrific drink. As I said, you make a great Blood Mary. And I'm not just saying that. You know I was a bartender before I met Gwen, and yours is vastly superior to the ones I used to make, and I had the best ingredients to work with." "It's the V8 juice. Much better than regular tomato. And no Tabasco sauce. A few drops would have made it even better, but you didn't want. And I know you don't like salt—with my ankles, I shouldn't either—but I sprinkled a little in out of habit. Gwen, your wine? What I gave you couldn't have been enough," and she'd say "It was plenty. Your client certainly knows his wine." "Seeing you kids enjoy your drinks so much," he said a few times, "I think I'll have a Bloody Mary myself. I was going to wait, but what for? It'll still be my only drink of the day." He'd get up—"Let me, Poppa," Gwen would say. He'd say "No. Yours would never be as good as mine." "*Grisha*," her mother would say, and he'd say "Well, you're always telling me to be honest, so I'm being honest. I know how to make a Bloody Mary that I like to drink. If I'm only going to have one, why not the best? Gwendolyn doesn't mind." He'd shuffle to the kitchen. Few minutes later, he'd shuffle back carrying his Bloody Mary on a tray. He'd sit and push the ice down with a finger and drink. At least once he said "Oh, I forgot. *L'chayim*," and they raised their glasses and her mother said "I wish I had a glass of water." Gwen said "I'll get it, Momma," and she said "It's all right, darling I was only saying that to have something to toast. Drink," and she held up her hand as if she had a glass in it and said "*L'chayim*, everyone," and the others said *L'chayim*," and drank. One of those times after they left, he said to Gwen "How come the only time you encourage me to drink is at your folks' apartment?" She said "You know how much it means to my father to do something for you. He wants to buy you a raincoat, he wants to go downtown with you to buy you a suit. He wants to take you out for lunch, just the two of you, and you always refuse. It's as if you don't want anything from anybody, and he might think it's especially to him, so it's good I push you. And you like to drink, and you had two when you could have stopped at one, so why are you complaining?" "I'm not complaining. And I already have a raincoat and suit. But if my drinking his Bloody Marys makes him happy, and making him happy makes you happy, then I'm happy. If only we could make your mother happy, and I'm not saying that has anything to do with getting her to drink." "That's sweet of you. But just our being there and also acting as a buffer between my dad and her, makes her happy. They really love you." "Me? It's you, the kids, they love seeing." "You see? You always refuse. Boy, I married a character," and he said "Kiss me, kiss me, kiss me."

When both girls were in college, and before that, when one was and the other had the little Echo to drive to high school and didn't need one of them to pick her up anymore, Gwen and he would teach and hold office hours at the same time on the same days in the same building on campus. After school, they liked to stop off at a bagel shop on the way home to buy a half-dozen bagels. Then, as one of them drove, they'd each eat a bagel with nothing on it, he usually an everything bagel and she a sesame. Then she went on a gluten-free diet—he forgets why, but she stuck to it—and they'd stop off at the same store after school and he'd eat a bagel as they drove and she'd finger around the bottom of the bag for the seeds of the poppy and sesame bagels and the garlic and onion bits from the everything bagels and eat those. "We should ask the people at Sam's Bagels if they could make a gluten-free bagel," he said once when they were driving home. "There's got to be a market for it, just as there seems to be for banana and blueberry and chocolate and Old Bay seasoning bagels and, around St. Patrick's Day, green bagels, all of which we hate. It isn't fair that I get to eat a whole bagel, when we're so hungry, and you only get what's fallen off in the bag." She said "I doubt I'd want to eat a gluten-free bagel. Amaranth? Millet? Brown rice or quinoa? I'm sure they'd all be tasteless and difficult to chew. These dregs will hold me till we get home."

How could he have not thought of this one till now? The examining nurse, if that's what she's called, sent them back home from the hospital, which they'd gone to that morning, because Gwen hadn't dilated near enough to think she was going to give birth anytime soon. "Your baby's coming, don't worry about that, but probably not till late this afternoon or tonight. You don't want to hang around here, do you? We have no place for you to lie down." At home, about two hours later, while she was resting in bed and he was in the kitchen reading because he couldn't stand the music the radio was playing in the bedroom—an entire morning devoted to Dvorak, they said—she started screaming. He ran in. "It's the contractions," she said. "I think the baby's coming out. Check." He lifted her nightgown; didn't see anything. Spread her labia wide and saw the baby's head two to three inches in and for a moment slowly moving forward. "Oh, shit," he said. "What are we going to do? We'll never make it to the hospital in time." She yelled "The baby's going to die. She's going to die. The cord will strangle her." "Shhh," he said, "let me think. Worse comes to worst, I'll pull her out myself and cut the cord with scissors, so don't worry. Of course!" He dialed 911. The dispatcher took his name and address and asked a lot of medical questions. He said "But when will they be here?" and she said "An emergency team is already in the truck and on the way. Keep your front door open; also the door leading into the building." "I can't. The cats will run out. Tell the team both doors will be unlocked and just walk in." "They're on the way," he told Gwen. "Feeling any better?" "Feeling better. Not as much pain. Thank you about the cats." "Just stay calm. It'll be all right. The damn Dvorak. It's making me crazy," and he shut it off. "Leave it on," she said. It's one of the *Slavonic Dances*, or *Rhapsodies*—I suddenly don't remember—but the one I love most," and she laid her head back on the pillows and closed her eyes and hummed the rhapsody or dance. He turned on the radio, unlocked the front door, went downstairs one flight with a plant and put it up against the building's entrance door to keep it open, ran back and said "I won't leave you again," and stroked her forehead, which was wet, and kissed her fingers. "Thanks," she said. "I'm so glad you're my husband. Could you wipe my face?" and he wiped it with his handkerchief. "It's clean; never used." "And the baby's alive?" and he said "I'm sure it is. Don't worry." Five minutes after he dialed 911, a woman yelled "We're here. EMU. Which way do we go?" and he yelled "Through the kitchen and then to the right. The woman and two men came in with what seemed like valises and a duffel bag and folded-up gurney. They quickly examined her, plugged something into the wall and attached some wires to her. The vagina was dilated all the way and the baby's skull was almost sticking out of it. "This'll be easy," the woman said. They delivered her on the bed, Gwen gritting her teeth and he holding her hand through it. The radio was still on and he shut it off. "Fastest delivery we ever had," the woman who pulled out the baby and now held her said. "It's a girl," and he said "We know." "Most parents don't with the first one," and he said "They told us earlier by accident at the obstetrician's office. The baby looks healthy. Be honest; is she?" and she said "She looks good to me. Lots of color; breathing's okay. Nothing clogging her and strong healthy cry. But they'll give her a full exam in the hospital and tell you. How do you feel, Gwen? And congratulations," and the other two, detaching wires from her and the wall and putting things back in the valises and duffel bag, said "Yeah, congratulations, ma'am." "I hurt and I'm tired and I know I don't look ecstatic, but I am," Gwen said. "Thank you all so much. Are you going to cut the umbilical cord?" and the woman, cleaning the baby with what looked like Handi Wipes, said "We've been advised, since it isn't necessary to do it right away, to let the doctors cut it in the hospital. Less chance of infection. Now we got to get you there," and they opened the gurney. "What's that?" Gwen said. "Something else feels like it's about to come out of me," and the woman said "I was hoping we could avoid this. Probably the placenta. Most times it takes longer to come out. Now we have to cut the cord, but it won't hurt you or the baby," and she cut it and pinned or tied it up and said "Do you have a clean bucket or big bowl you wouldn't mind it being in?" Some more liquid came out and then the placenta in one piece. She picked it up and put it into the salad bowl he'd rushed into the kitchen to get. "If you don't mind, we'll have to take the bowl with us in case they want to look at it for anything—that part of it I'm not too knowledgeable about. You know about the fontanel?" and he said "I've been warned." She handed him the baby wrapped in a towel. Then she and the men lifted Gwen onto the gurney, put a blanket over her and strapped her in. She took the baby from him and set her beside Gwen and covered them with a sheet she took out of a sealed plastic bag. One of the men said to Gwen "Keep your arm around her but not too tight. We'll go very slow and careful." They carried the gurney downstairs to the first floor and wheeled it to the street. Some tenants from the building were on the sidewalk and waved to Gwen and said "Good luck." She said "See my baby?" and pulled the sheet down to the baby's chin. He kissed Gwen and said "See you in the hospital," and the gurney was slid into the back of the truck. "Can I come along?" he said, and the woman said "You don't have a car? By city law you should ride up front and it'll be crowded back there with two of us and your wife." "I'd rather not leave them." He sat in the seat next to the driver's. The driver turned the siren on and they drove to the hospital he and Gwen were at a few hours before. "Siren on because you think something might be wrong with the baby?" and the driver said "No; just gets us there faster and we don't have to stop for lights." "It was a close one, though, wasn't it?" and the driver said "Your baby? No, they usually turn out all right. Those little things are tougher than you think. You got a name for it?" "Rosalind. My wife's choice. Sort of a family name." "Everyone will call her Roz," and he said "I hope not, but if they do, we'll still call her Rosalind at home." "And if it was a boy?" and he said "We knew it wasn't, so never chose one." "And sorry about the mess we made at your place. Couldn't be helped. You're going to have a lot to clean up when you get home." "Doesn't bother me. Right now everything's just fine." He looked through the little window behind him to the back. The woman and man were seated and Gwen and they had their eyes closed. He couldn't see the baby. "Is there enough air back there? They all seem to be sleeping," and the driver said "Probably everyone's tired. Been a long day for all of us. It also shows there's no problem with your wife and kid. If there was, the monitor alarm would be sounding and my co-workers would be up and working on them. You should get some sleep too. You look exhausted." "I've got a long wait till then. I want to make sure everything's okay with them first." "They'll be all right. Go home early. Take advantage of the hospital. We're lucky, living in this city. It's got a rating for being the best medical center in the country, maybe the world. I don't know about obstetrics, but I know for just about everything else, so obstetrics has to be right up there on top too." "Good; good. I'm still worried—that's my nature—but I'll be okay."

He dropped in on his mother the day after he introduced her to Gwen. They sat in the breakfast room, each with a drink he'd made them: Jack Daniels on the rocks with a splash of water and for her with a lemon peel in it. "Cheers," he said, and she said "Cheers," and they drank. "So, Mom, tell me what you think of her," and she said "What do I think? I think she's wonderful and perfect for you and you for her. She's charming, precious, elegant, very intelligent, and with such a sweet face and voice. I always wished I had a voice and complexion like hers." "You have a nice voice. What's wrong with your voice? And your complexion? It's still smooth and you hardly have a line." "Thank you. And you seem to like her parents. That's a good sign," and he said "Oh, what they went through. Before they came here they lost everyone in World War II but her mother's father. To tell you the truth, her coming from people like that I find very attractive about her too." "So you like that she's Jewish? Because before you only went out and got serious with Gentile girls, or since you were in college," and he said "There's been a Jewish girl or two in there, but it's fine." "What I hope she doesn't end up thinking is that you're too old for her. More than ten years. That's a lot." "You and Dad were nine years apart," and she said "And when I met him, and I was much younger than Gwen, I already thought of him as a middle-aged man. Something else could work against you. That you don't have a profession but writing, which is a wonderful thing to do but it so far barely pays you enough to live on for one. If those don't bother her, then everything should go well between you. I've got my fingers crossed. I already foresee myself feeling toward her as if she were my own daughter. I was that impressed by her at our lunch and saw immediately what sort of person she was—the best sort. So I'm warning you," and he said "Oy, I knew this was coming." "Listen to me. Don't do anything stupid to lose her. You're reaching an age where it won't be so easy finding another girl like her, especially one with so many child-bearing years left. You want to have a family, don't you? You've spoken of it enough, so I assume you still do. You'd be reducing your chances by getting a woman your own age or one a few years younger. You're not going to get married right away. That could take a year or two and a child a year more, and two children—well, you figure it. So you're fortunate she fell for you, or is starting to, and I can only hope and pray it gets even better and lasts." "Come on, Mom, it can't be that bad for me. There are plenty of terrific women out there," and she said "If there are, then how come you always choose the wrong one? Maybe with the exception of Diana, who I liked, but that relationship was bound to fail—she was simply too capricious, which this one doesn't seem to be. I like it that she gives you a look that she adores you. That can also stop, with a few mistakes by you, so anything you can do to help make it work, do." "I knew you'd like her. I don't know if she adores me, like you say, or what she really thinks of me, although she is showing some very nice feelings and seems to like being with me." "Does she call you if you don't call her?" and he said "What does that have to do with it? We speak to each other every day on the phone, even if we see each other that day. So yes, she does. And it's not a case of if I call, then she makes the next call, and then I make the one after that, and so on. We call when we want to, which is a lot. Anyway, I'll try not to screw it up, I promise." "It's for your benefit, you know. Mine too, of course, that I want you to finally be settled with someone so nice, but mostly yours."

He went to his mother's apartment the day after he got back from Maine the first time. He brought a bottle of Jack Daniels with him because she might be running low—it was the only liquor she drank—and he knew he was going to have two drinks, and then she'd want a second too. It was a hot day, around six, and they sat in the shaded L-shaped backyard that bordered what they called the breakfast room. "Cheers," she said, and they drank. She asked if he got a lot of work done this summer, and he said "Yes." "How was it with her parents for a week?" and he said "Fine. Her father only stayed two days. He hates mosquitoes. Reminds him too much of Uzbekistan, where he was in a Soviet internment camp. But they were very easy guests, as you were." "I'd like to meet them again. I know I'd get to like them, short time I was with them and their having such a wonderful daughter. I could invite them for lunch," and he said "We'll see." "You get along with them, though, don't you?" and he said "Her mother can be a little overprotective of her, but yes." "How is Gwen?" and he said "Fine." "She teaching at Columbia this year?" and he said "Yes. Second year of her post-doc fellowship. Humanities again. I think she starts in a week." "And you start your own teaching at NYU in a few weeks," and he said "It's nothing compared to hers. Continuing ed. Two fiction-writing classes that meet ten times a semester, at five hundred dollars a course. Slave wages, but it's a start and it'll get me out of the house." "You need money? I can spare some," and he said "I have enough, thanks." "Enough might not be enough," and he said "I'm fine." "You don't seem yourself, Martin. I thought you'd come in all chipper, but you seem down. Anything bothering you you want to talk about?" and he said "No." "You don't want to talk about it?" and he said "Nothing's wrong." "Don't tell me. You know you can't pull the wool over my eyes. It has to be something to do with Gwen." "All right. She dumped me."

"She broke it off? I can't believe it. When I was in Maine, you two were so close. When did this happen?" and he said "When she dropped me off at my building yesterday." "You had no inkling?" and he said "There was some trouble between us this summer, but I thought we'd worked everything out. So a big shock." "Is it another guy?" and he said "No. I'd rather not talk about it anymore, Mom," and she said "What a pity. I was hoping, when you said you were coming over, for so much better news. You're going to have to look hard for another girl like her," and he said "I really don't want to hear it. I feel lousy enough." "I understand. Of course there's nothing I can do or that you'd let me try to do to fix things," and he said "What an idea. I can just see you calling her up and saying what a perfect match you thought we were." "Well, it's true; you were. I wasn't the only one who thought so. But at least you still have your sense of humor about it. You didn't do anything bad to make her change her mind about you?" and he said "No. I just think that in the long run she thought I wasn't the ideal mate for her. She eventually wants marriage and children, which is what I want too and with her if I could, but she thinks I'd make a very poor provider because my writing would always come first." "So tell her you'll put aside most of your writing for the time being to get a good job and work hard at keeping it," and he said "She'd see that as a desperate and insincere move on my part to get back with her. She knows me. And it's not that I can't write and hold down a full-time job at the same time. I've done it—I mean serious jobs; news work, technical writing, editing magazines—but all that's way in the past. I've managed to arrange my life the last ten years where I'm basically unemployable for any other work but jobs like bartending and waiting on tables and driving a cab and teaching in continuing ed at fifty bucks a class, and that isn't going to do it. I've tried to get appointments in writing departments that pay fairly well and have benefits and everything else, but nobody's interested. I have four books and a hundred published stories and a couple of good fellowships, but they all say, when they answer me—only two have but it must be what the other fifty are thinking—that I need an M.F.A." "You know what? I think she's going to call you in two weeks and say she misses you and wants you two to meet to talk things over." "She won't call. I've been in this situation before. Once they say they're though, at least with me, they're through," and she said "That wasn't so with Diana. She broke it off with you so many times and then came running back, you stopped telling me." "I should have stayed broken up with her the first time, which isn't how I feel about Gwen. But it's over with, really," and she said "It's not. Take it from me, Martin. She'll call, maybe even sooner than two weeks, and you'll talk and get back together and be married in a year and have children, or just one child, but you'll be happy again and a wonderful couple. I could see this summer how much in love with you she was, and that was just a month ago and it doesn't stop so fast," and he said "I'm now beginning to believe she wasn't that much in love with me at all. I now don't even know why she even started with me." "Don't say that. She started with you because you're a great catch." "Oh yeah, great catch. No dough, no prospects, just my writing, which doesn't pay off much. Hair going, in my forties. Sure, great catch," and she said "You are. Stop belittling yourself. You're handsome, you're polite, you're nice, built like a circus strongman, creative and smart, and you're tall. Who wouldn't want you? So let's try and put our heads together to see what we can do to make things better for you. Here," and she gave him her empty glass. "Have another drink and refill mine." "Didn't Dr. Gelfand say—I know he did; I was there—that for you to stop from falling and to get sufficient sleep, one per day should be your limit?" and she said "Listen to me, not him. One more won't kill me and it'll keep you here longer and I don't drink this much every day." They had another drink and talked about other things and then he left.

Whenever he brought her flowers. So why didn't he bring them to her more? He was so cheap at times…. Their wedding in her apartment. Forty, maybe forty-five people there. The rabbi said they had to start on time—they were waiting for some guests to arrive—because he had a funeral upstate to officiate at and it took an hour to drive there, "and to a funeral you don't want to be late." Gwen's piano teacher played Bach on Gwen's piano before the ceremony began. His brother was his best man. The rabbi said "No glass to smash? What kind of Jewish wedding is this? Okay, you're man and wife." The ring bearer, the son of the pianist, said just before Gwen and he kissed, "Why is Marty crying?" and started giggling. His mother said "Martin, I want to talk to you in private," and took him off to the side. She handed him an envelope. "What is this, my bar mitzvah?" he said. "Thanks, but I'm not taking anything from you," and she said "To help defray the cost of the honeymoon." "We've defrayed it already. It's just Connecticut, an hour and half away and for three days," and he gave her back the envelope. "Truly, Mom, it's enough for us that you're here." "I can't begin to tell you how happy I am for you both. And such gorgeous food and your bride is beautiful. But crying at your own wedding?" and he said "You know it wasn't because I was sad." "Of course it wasn't. It shows how sensitive you are and how much she means to you. I'm only saying I never saw or heard of any groom doing it before, and I've been to plenty of weddings. I can just imagine how you'll react when your first baby comes out and you're in the room," and he said "Gwen say something to you?" and she said "No, what? If you say you think she's pregnant, that's too much excitement for me in one day, so don't tell me till it's officially confirmed." They'd made half the food the past two days and got the rest from Zabar's. The wedding cake—a huge untiered Black Forest cake—was from Grossinger's, the same bakery that made his bar mitzvah cake, shaped like a Holy Ark, so maybe that's why he said what he did to his mother when she handed him the envelope. Gwen chose the beverages—champagne and cognac Winston Churchill favored and wine from the French region where she worked for a week harvesting grapes. Temperature was below zero by the time the wedding ended, so he drove his mother and several other people home on the West Side. When he got back to the apartment, there was an elderly couple who needed to be driven home across town. "We had no luck calling a private car service," Gwen said. "And you know cabs never cruise the Drive, and it's too cold and steep a walk to go to Broadway for one." They cleaned up the apartment for about an hour and then went to bed. Gwen said "I'm too tired to make love," when he started to. "But if you feel you have to fulfill some wedding night rite, and think you can, go ahead, but don't expect a lot from me." He tried and then said after a few minutes "We'll wait till morning or after we get to the inn. I'm obviously too much of a flop now." They were still so tired the next morning and a bit hungover that he called the inn to say they'd be a day late, "but not to worry: we'll pay for the entire three days." "Since it's your honeymoon," the innkeeper said, "and we'd like to think you'll return here each year to celebrate your anniversary, we'll waive the third day," and he said "No, we want to pay. It'd only be fair. Maybe, in exchange, you could provide our cottage with a bottle of red wine and two wineglasses, but you don't have to and I'm now embarrassed I asked. In fact, don't." Later he said to Gwen "What do you think? Should I call my mother and say I married a virgin? That's what she said my father did with his mother the day after they got married." The cottage had a Franklin stove and firewood and a comforter they knew would be too warm to sleep under, so he asked the innkeeper for two ordinary blankets. He thought, even though in the end he told the guy not to, there'd be a bottle of wine or champagne in the room, but there wasn't. First thing they did after they unpacked was open the early pregnancy kit they brought with them and follow the directions. Then they took a drive, had lunch in town nearby, went to a small private modern art museum, but it was only open Friday through Sunday, bought a pair of heavy woolen socks for him because his feet were cold, came back and checked the results of the test. "Oh my goodness," he said, hugging her, "you're pregnant. Look at it: we're gonna have a doughnut."

She liked thin slices of prosciutto wrapped around a thin slice of honeydew melon. He didn't like the combination. "Melon and ham, and all that fat? Doesn't do it for me." If they had prosciutto but no honeydew melon, she'd say "I can use the cantaloupe we have. It's not nearly as good with prosciutto as honeydew, but it's still quite good if you slice it real thin." If they had prosciutto but no honeydew or any other melon, she'd sometimes say "Know what I'd love with this?" and he'd say "I do, and if you want I'll go to the market and pick up one. If they don't have honeydew, then a cantaloupe, and if they don't have that either, which I'd be very surprised at, then a ripe melon of some kind." If they had honeydew at home but no prosciutto and she said she'd love to have some with melon—she never said it if they just had cantaloupe or some other kind of melon—he'd say "I'll get some at the Italian market in Belvedere Square," and if they were in Maine, "the gourmet market in Blue hill. If they don't have it, then I'm willing to go all the way to Rooster Brothers in Ellsworth, who always carry it and sometimes two or three versions of it." "Since I'm the only one here who's going to have it," she said, "you don't have to go just for me," and he said "But I want to and I could use the break." And if the kids were home: "And I'll take the kids with me, if they want, and get them a treat there too." "If you do get prosciutto," she reminded him a couple of times, "make sure you first ask for the Parma kind and sliced paper thin. It's twice as expensive as the American prosciutto—to cut the cost you can even ask for a little less than a quarter of a pound—but it's more than worth it."

He bumped into the daughter of Gwen's Ph.D. advisor on Broadway. It was near where her family owned a brownstone off Riverside Drive and about ten blocks south from where he and Gwen had their apartment. They got to talking—the usual stuff: "How's Gwen?" "How's the family?" "How's your writing going?" "How's school?"—and then she said she wanted to tell him something she never told him or Gwen but had her parents. "I once saw you and Gwen not far from here in front of the Cuban restaurant on a Hundred-ninth on this side of Broadway. That's probably why I'm now recalling it. This took place soon after she brought you to our house for dinner and we first met you, so long before you were married and had kids. I didn't reveal myself to you and Gwen on the street because, corny as this must sound, you only seemed to have eyes for each other, which I think is also why you didn't notice me, and I didn't want to spoil it by saying hello. I was young but I at least knew that. You were standing on the sidewalk, each holding one of those corrugated paper cups of what I guess you'd call Cuban ice. I'd got some of it there myself a few times. You fed Gwen a plastic spoonful of it out of your cup—you must have had different flavors—and she in turn gave you a spoonful from hers. You did this a few times, then kissed. Then you each finished your own ices and you dumped your cup and spoon into a trash can at the corner—I think you even took Gwen's cup and spoon to dump with yours—and grabbed each other's hand and walked up Broadway, I assume towards home. I'd never seen a couple so happy, is what I'm saying. I thought, watching you walk, when I fall in love with someone, that's the way I want it to be." "You know, we've had our bad moments too," he said, "and once even stopped seeing each other for a while, maybe even around that time," and she said "Of course; every couple goes through that, and sometimes more than once. But then, it was pure joy between you two, and what a wonderful thing to witness. It really seemed rare." When he got back to the apartment he told Gwen who he'd met on the street and what she'd told him. She seemed to think about it a few seconds and then said "I don't remember that day but I'm sure it happened. I do remember the ices at the Cuban restaurant that they used to scoop into paper cups. We should go there and get some one of these days, or their bolitas, I think they call that fruit drink. I love them."

Another scene he thinks he already thought about tonight. Once? More? Twice? It was about a month after they started sleeping together. They were in bed, it was night, lights were off. Her back was to him. He moved his hand down the side of her body to her underpants, to get inside them and eventually to pull them off, and felt her two cats there, lying against her thigh. His hand jumped. The cats didn't move. She laughed and said "I forgot to tell you. They occasionally like to sneak under the covers with me. Do you mind?" and he said "At the moment, yes. I'd rather not have them there." "Gee," she said, "I don't know how to stop them, or if I want to. They're used to my letting them stay there. It's the cold." "Please," he said, "could you try? Or I could do it." She picked up the cats one at a time and set them down on the floor. They jumped back up and crawled under the covers again. He leaned over her, pulled back the covers and pushed the cats off the bed. "Be nice," she said. "Remember, they were here first and you're taking their place and they might feel squeezed out." "Do you think I did it too roughly? I'm sorry. —I'm sorry, cats," he said. "Try to understand." He pulled the covers back over her, waited about a minute, stroked her thighs and pulled her panties off and tried tugging her nightshirt over her head and she said "Let me keep it on. I'm also cold."

She'd come into the kitchen in their New York apartment, where he'd be working at the typewriter table by the window, and say "Like to take a break?" She'd come into the bedroom of the cottage in Maine they rented and say "Are you deeply involved in something that can't be immediately interfered with or in the next few minutes?" She'd come halfway down the basement stairs of the first house they had in Baltimore, or just yell down the stairs from the top "Martin, think you can tear yourself away from your typewriter for a brief intermission?" She'd come into the narrow storage room where he worked in their Baltimore apartment for six years, or else knock on the door frame of it, and say "Care to take a short rest?" She'd come upstairs to the spare bedroom he'd turned into his study in the farmhouse in Maine they rented and say "Would you have strenuous objections to being interrupted awhile? I hope not, and it'd be a nice way to break up the day." She'd meet him at the front door after he'd just come back from town in Maine and pretend to stifle a yawn with her hand and say "I'm a little tired. Are you, or do you need to get right to work?" She'd say to him after he'd come back from driving the kids to day camp in Maine or to school in Baltimore or after walking them to school in New York when he was on sabbatical for a year: "I know it's early and you probably want to get to your writing, but would you like to take a pre-work break?" She'd come in to whatever room he was writing in, from behind put her hands over his eyes or arms around his chest or cheek against his cheek or chin on his shoulder and say "Don't jump. It's only me. Like to take a breather?" or "Recess time. Think you'd like to join me?" or "What do you say, my dearie? Kids are out of the house. Not expected back for hours. We've already put in a good morning's work. Want to have some fun? I know I feel like it." Of course he did this lots of times to her too. He thinks he never refused her, or at most said "Just let me finish what I'm doing—it shouldn't take more than a few minutes—and then, if you're in bed, I'll meet you there." While she said a number of times something like "If you're suggesting what I think it is, don't I wish I could. We'll have other opportunities."

Here's another one he doesn't know why it keeps coming back. Strange thing is, the woman in it was Gwen's best friend since college and he suddenly now can't think of her name. He tries to come up with it again. Runs through the alphabet. Still can't. Okay. But that evening. This woman and her husband, Vincent, and their two kids and his family had dinner in Chinatown at a restaurant Vincent recommended. Vincent and his wife had been there several times and he ordered for all of them, even the kids. "No," Vincent said, "you have to eat what we eat—I promise you won't regret it, and there'll be plenty to choose from—although you don't have to have squid." As usual, Vincent ordered too much. After Gwen and he had thought all of them were done eating, Vincent said "I still want to get their very special scallops and mussels in garlic sauce. What we don't devour, you'll take home with you and have it for lunch tomorrow or for dinner in Baltimore tomorrow night, along with the rest of the doggy-bagged food I want you to have. But you can't leave here without tasting the dish fresh out of the kitchen." "No, no, we're stuffed," they said, and Vincent said "Yes, yes, there's always room for a pinch of something more." Gwen's best friend said to them "Don't argue; there's no stopping him when it comes to good food and drink. And because he over-ordered and there'll be plenty left over, you're going home with it, so it's your treat." "Then we'll buy the pastries, later," Martin said, and Vincent said "Not on your life. When you're in our part of the city, you're our guests." They lived on Broome Street in SoHo. They walked from Chinatown through Little Italy to get there. Vincent and his son went into an Italian bakery and came out with two large white boxes each tied with string and full of cookies and cannoli and other Italian pastries. Then they went to their loft and plates of dried and fresh fruit were put out and Vincent opened a bottle of fifty-year-old Armagnac and one of a rare Port and they ate and drank and the adults reminisced once more about how each couple had first met and how soon they knew they were in love—"With me, it was my first sight of Gwen," and she said "I've heard that from him before and I don't see how it could be possible. As for me, though I found him immediately attractive, falling in love took a while longer." The kids made up a play for four lead roles and wrote it down and spent fifteen minutes rehearsing it in another room and then in costume performed it. The adults clapped and cheered and booed at the right moments and then finished the evening with Irish coffees, though he had his coffee straight because he was driving. And as the two families went downstairs in what used to be this former commercial building's freight elevator, which Vincent let his son run, and then outside in front of the building where the car was parked, they kissed and hugged one another and said what a great evening it had been. "We always have good times together," Gwen said. "I don't think I've heard Martin laugh like that since the last time we were here. The doggy bags. Did we take them?" and their kids held them up. "Goodbye, goodbye," their friends and their kids said to them, waving and blowing kisses as they drove off, and they all waved and blew kisses back. "Steer me to the West Side Highway once we get to Houston Street," he said to Gwen. "I always get lost," and she said "You don't go to Houston Street. But I'll get you there." When they were on the highway and heading uptown to their apartment, he said "That was terrific tonight. What wonderful people, children and adults. I'm so glad you know them. And the kids get along so well together. —Did you have a good time, kids?" and one said "I did, Daddy," and the other said "It was great. I had so much fun. We should do it again soon. Can't we live in New York always?" "It would be nice. We could also see your grandparents more. But what can we do? We're sort of stuck." And to Gwen: "It's probably dumb of me to ask, but you had a good time too, didn't you?" and she said "It was delightful. I'm so glad we all like each other." "I love your friends," he said, and she said "And they love you." "And they'd give the world for you, of course, and our darling children, which makes me happy in case anything happened to me," and she said "Don't think of it. You're going to live forever, but I know what you mean." He still can't remember her best friend's name. First time he thinks he forgot it. It'll come. It's not Natalie. It's not Naomi. It's not Ronnie. But it's something close. This happens. Maybe more now than before. Don't worry about it.

It was a few months after they first met. He was having two wisdom teeth extracted under gas at a specialist's office on West 57th Street. "I just don't want to hear the bones again, or whatever they are, crunch when the teeth are being pulled out." She asked if he wanted her to come along with him. "Thanks, but I'll be all right." "You always say you'll be all right," and he said "Believe me, I'll be fine, once the teeth are out." She came anyway. He was in the recovery room when a dental assistant said "There's someone here for you. Good thing, too, as we were worried how you'd get home." "Why? I'm not driving. And I know who it is." He was escorted out of the room. Gwen was sitting in the waiting room, reading a magazine. She said "Oh, my poor darling," and was about to kiss him and he said "Don't. That's my bad side. Actually, both sides are bad, but that one's beginning to hurt. It's so nice of you to come here. Am I talking funny? I seem to sound it. And I now see I can use your help. You're so considerate. So nice. So nice. We'll get a cab to my building and then you can continue in it to yours." "No, you're coming home with me and staying the night. You're a bit shaky and I want to make sure you'll be okay." As they were walking to the elevator, she holding his arm and saying "Lean on me if you need," he said "This is real service. Did I ever tell you what Diana did when I was in the hospital after an operation on my leg?" "What she didn't do, you mean. You were living with her in the Village then." "East Tenth. I don't mean to bad-mouth her, but she never came to visit me. I was there for two days. Memorial, so just a bus ride up First or Second. I didn't have insurance then—I still don't—and it was costing me plenty out of pocket, but they wouldn't discharge me till I was able to walk out of the hospital—at least to the elevator on my floor—on my own. And she also didn't come to the hospital to help me get home, and I could barely walk. I went in there with them thinking it was cancer—neurofibromatosis; one of the things my father had but didn't die of. But after they cut me open and sent a piece of me to the pathologist, it turned out to be a Baker's cyst, which all they needed to do was drain. To top it off, it was Diana's former father-in-law I went to, whom she got to examine me gratis, and he diagnosed me and sent me to this surgeon. A double doctor screw-up. So what am I saying? I forgot." "I think it was about my picking you up here. Diana. That I acted differently." "That is what I'm saying. You're everything I ever wanted. I'm so glad it took me this long." "What a nice thing for you to say. I'll remember it if we ever have an argument and you say about me what a mistake you made."

They were in a mall in Baltimore. Maureen, a few months old, was in a baby carrier on Gwen's chest. Gwen said she wanted to look around a little. "In stores that would bore you and make you irritable. Could you look after Rosalind? I know you'd prefer sitting on a bench here and reading, or having a coffee, but the two of them will be too much for me to deal with. Meet you back here in an hour? It's almost two, so say, three?" He walked around with Rosalind. Went into a store and bought a short-sleeved T-shirt because the two he had were starting to have holes in the collar. Went to a different floor and looked in a bookstore window. "I know what," he said. "Let's go to the food court and get something." He turned around. She wasn't behind him where she was just before. He looked around. How the hell could she have gotten away so fast? The bookstore. That's what he should have suggested to her. She loves picture books and they've been in it before. He looked around inside. Went to all the stores nearby. Ran in, looked, ran out, quickly said to a salesperson "Have you seen a little girl here alone? She's three, but tall for her age. Blond. Very pretty." All the time looking around him for her. "Wearing…wearing what? I don't know what she's wearing. Name's Rosalind." "So she's lost?" one saleswoman said. "Want me to call Security?" "Call. Give my description. Tall, blond, three. Very pretty. Name's Rosalind. Tell them I'm worried." She called. "Missing child. A girl. Blond. —Very blond?" and he said "Very." "Three. Tall for her age. Name's Rosalind. Can you send someone up here? The father—you're the father?" and he said "Yes." "Is frightened something's happened to her." "I'll look around in the meantime; leave my things here," and he put the bag with the shirt in it and a book on a counter and ran out of the store and looked in all the stores he hadn't been in yet on the floor, running down one side of the mall, then the other. The department stores at each end of the floor. Looked in, but they were much too large. "What am I going to do?" he said. "What am I going to do?" Gwen. Ran to the escalator well and yelled "Gwen, come quick. It's me, Martin. Second floor. By the escalator. Rosalind's lost." Repeated it. Then yelled "Rosalind, it's Daddy. If you can hear me, come to my voice. Come to Daddy. Go to the escalator so I can see you. Ask people where the escalator is." People stopped. Some of them asked what it was and if they could help. "Yes," he said. "Look for my daughter. She's lost. She's three. Alone. Tall for her age. Pretty. Very blond. Name's Rosalind." "What's she wearing?" someone said. "That would help." "I don't know. That's right. Red and white striped long-sleeved shirt and blue overalls. Look in all the stores above and below. I'll go to the food court. Security's also looking. If you find her, tell Security." Several of them went in different directions. One said "I can't help. I have to be home. But don't worry, it'll be all right. I'm sure they never lost a child here. Just looks that way to the parents while it's happening." "Good. Excuse me." He was about to get on the up escalator to the food court when he saw Rosalind going down the escalator to the main floor. He didn't want to yell her name because she might get startled and fall. She was holding the railing with one hand as he and Gwen had instructed her to. She stumbled a little getting off. Then he yelled from the top of the escalator "Rosalind. Rosalind. Stay where you are." She looked around and then up at him. She didn't move. He went down the escalator. When he got to her, she smiled and he took her hand, got them out of the way of people, dropped to one knee, held her with his eyes shut and then looked up at her and said "What were you doing? I thought you were lost. Daddy was so worried. I should hit your hand, just slap it lightly, something I've never done, so you'd remember never to run away from me like that again, but I won't. Please, dear, never do it again. Do you hear? Do you understand?" and she started crying. "Oh, I'm so sorry," and he held her closer. Then he saw Gwen coming down the escalator. From halfway up, she said "Was that you shouting out my name?" He nodded and she said "What were you saying? I couldn't make it out. And why's Rosalind crying?" Rosalind squirmed out of his hold and ran to her and hugged her waist. He stood up and said "She disappeared for a few minutes and I panicked. I got the whole mall looking for her. It's all right now. I didn't hit her. I suppose I looked angry for a few seconds, though I didn't feel my face forming an expression in that way, so she's just afraid.

I'm still a little unsettled. But how'd it go with you? Get what you want?" and she said "I did. Perfume. Jessica McClintock, my favorite. A terrific sale on it. It'll last me ten years. And for some reason, with each purchase they give you a small stuffed animal—mine's a rabbit—which the kids will like." "Then let's get out of here. But let me get my package and book first. I left them in a store upstairs." "Oh, you bought something?" and he said "A T-shirt. Not on sale but reasonably priced. I needed it. I also have to tell Security everything's okay. Wait here. People might stop and ask you—they were very kind and went out looking for Rosalind—if this is the girl who was lost. If they do, thank them for me." "I wasn't lost," Rosalind said. "Okay, we'll talk about that later," and he brushed her hair back with his hand and took the escalator up.

He drove to Brooklyn to a friend of Gwen's who had a very good crib to give them. "And you can keep it," she said, when he called for directions to her building. "Or after you're through with it, give it to someone you like. We've definitely maxed out at two, so we won't be needing it anymore." Gwen was in her eighth month with Rosalind. He left at six in the morning and hoped to be back by midafternoon, avoiding heavy traffic both ways. "You'll be all right, won't you?" he said, just before he left, and she said "I'll be fine. It's you. I don't want you getting tired on the road with so much driving." "I've driven a lot more by myself than eight hours in a day, and without an hour's break, which I promise I'll take—even a nap—when I get there, so don't worry. Go back to sleep." He was approaching the Holland Tunnel on the Jersey Turnpike when he heard a piece of music on the radio for chorus, soloists and orchestra. He loved it. It was still playing when he parked near the woman's building, so he sat in the car listening to it till it was over. He wanted to know the name of it and the composer so he could buy the record soon after he got back to Baltimore. It was an oratorio: *A Child of Our Time*, by Michael Tippett. And "Sir," so he assumed he was English, and because it's a modern piece, maybe still living. Never heard of him, and what a coincidence: the title of the piece and all those sweet children's voices in it, as he drives in to pick up a crib for his own child. He wrote it down—also the conductor and orchestra—in his memobook; had a Danish and coffee with the woman, got the crib into his car's trunk and a bag of baby and toddler clothes and a long padded bumper to go around inside the crib and drove back. He told Gwen about the music. "One of the most stirring pieces for voice and orchestra I've ever heard, and I don't think I missed much of it, though I won't be able to tell till I hear it again. It was the highlight of my trip." "So let's buy it," she said. "From everything you said, I want to hear it, and it doesn't seem like something the Baltimore Symphony will ever play." "It might be an expensive recording," and she said "What of it? Once the baby's born, think of all the money we won't be spending on restaurants and concerts and so forth by staying home. And just the coincidence, as you said, that it was about a child." "I'm not sure what it was about," he said. "Though it was in English, I was able to make out very few words. I do know there were parts in it with children's voices, and there's the title. Okay, I'll get it, or maybe have to order it at the record store." He bought the record the next day and played it that night. He didn't like the first side of it. It didn't seem the same piece, though he recognized some parts and it was the recording he'd heard in the car and their record player had much better sound than the car radio. He thought he must have been in some other state of mind when he first heard it, or it was because of the small enclosed space of the car, or something, but he just couldn't explain it. "So what do you think so far?" he said, when he turned the record over to the second side but didn't put the needle down on it yet. "Oh, it's pretty good," and he said "Once again, you're just being nice. Don't worry about my feelings. You didn't like it, say so." "It's true. It wasn't as stirring and beautiful as you made it out to be. It could be I just don't like twentieth-century English music." "Ralph Vaughan Williams? *The Lark Ascending*? His *Fantasia on a Theme by Thomas Tallis*? You love those." "I thought, because of the way his first name is pronounced, he was Scottish or Welsh," and he said "No, English. And Britten's *Simple Symphony* and *Variations on a Theme of Frank Bridge*? And some stuff by Frank Bridge too?" "I'm unfamiliar with him. And maybe I'm only talking about twentieth-century English music for voices," and he said "Britten again. *Les Illuminations* and his *Serenade for Tenor, Horn* and something else. *Strings*. But why am I giving you a hard time and acting like a pedant? I'm sorry. I felt the same way about the piece. A disappointment. It had its moments when the kids sang. I love children's voices—Bernstein's *Chichester Psalms* and at the end of the first act of *Tosca* when the boys choir from the church comes in. But it didn't seem the same music I heard driving on the Turnpike, which was then blanked out in the Holland Tunnel, and then going across Manhattan to Brooklyn and sitting in the car near Penny's building till it was over. I was overwhelmed by all of it. Not a bad part. What could it be that changed it for me?" and she said "I can't help you on that." "Let's put it away for now and listen to the rest some other time, or only I'll listen to it and from the beginning. What'll really make me screwy is if I find I love it again. And I should probably set up the crib," and she said "There's no hurry. The baby's going to sleep in the pram in our room the first three or four months." "Then just to do something and get it out of the way. I hate things unassembled and in lots of parts and leaning against the wall or taking up too much room on the floor and the chance of it falling down or our tripping on it," and she said "Okay. I'll help."

Her miscarriage. Odd that he hadn't thought about it till now, or had he? Gwen was in for her annual gynecological exam. It was about two years after Maureen was born. The doctor asked for a urine sample. She sat on the toilet there for half an hour, she said, and couldn't pee a drop, so the nurse practitioner, he thinks she was, catheterized her and botched up the procedure. She poked the fetus with the catheter. Something like that. Or touched something in the vagina with the catheter that started the miscarriage. He knows they're two distinctive holes, but that's what he thinks Gwen told him. It was so long ago; he forgets most of it. And Gwen came home and was never clear about what happened, and he knew it upset her so much that she didn't like talking about it, so he didn't ask her about it much after that day to get the details straight. He remembers her saying that night "All I can tell you is that the woman did a lousy-ass job—I actually think she wasn't adequately trained for it and had her eyes closed when she inserted the catheter—and she and the doctor weren't very apologetic about it either. Afraid of a suit, you think? They knew we didn't want another child"—"You mean you didn't want another," he said—and she said "All right, I didn't, so they may have thought they'd done us a favor. But they still could have shown some remorse." She hadn't known she was pregnant. So it was very early on; maybe the first or second month. "Did you see it?" and she said "It was almost too small to see—certainly too early to tell what sex it was, and technically not even a fetus yet. And after they scooped it all out and I got off the table, I think they flushed it down the toilet. No, I'm sure they have a special disposal bag for that." He got sad. Some tears too. "Oh, what's wrong, my darling? I'm being too cold and clinical about it, I know." "This was probably our last chance to have another child," he said. "If it hadn't been aborted and you had come home and said you'd found out you were pregnant, I would have asked you to have the baby." "I've told you," she said. "I never wanted to get pregnant again. I want to get on with my life other than just being a mother and part-time teacher. And two's ideal for me and them, and should be for you too, and affordable." He would have begged her to have the baby and he thinks she would have gone through with it because it meant so much to him. That so? He's almost sure of it. He'd have three kids now. The third might be in his first year of college. She did say

"We have to be more careful with my diaphragm. I take full blame for what happened because I'm the one who put it in. But I have a bit of arthritis in my left hand. Also, in that hand, this bony knob or swelling below the thumb near the wrist that's painful sometimes and which I'll get checked out, but in the meantime get a brace for it at night, so I'll need to teach you how to put the diaphragm in when I don't feel a hundred percent able to." "Glad to, but who's to say I'll do it correctly? It'd seem it'd take a lot of practice," and she said "I can feel when it's in right. It doesn't slip or hurt. This time I must have just let it go, or your penis knocked it awry." "It can do that?" and she said "Sure, although I think I would have felt that too, so I don't know."

He often walked the forty blocks from his apartment building to hers. He doesn't think she ever walked from her building to his. The ten or so times she was in his apartment, and two or three times she stayed the night in the almost two years they saw each other before he got the job in Baltimore, she came by taxi or subway or bus. Or walked up from West End Avenue and 74th Street after her therapy session, or she was with him after they went to a restaurant or movie or dinner party that was a lot closer to his apartment than hers, so they ended up there. Usually, though, if she was in his neighborhood with him at night, she said she'd like to go home to take care of her cats, or some other reason—she didn't have her diaphragm or medication with her; she wanted to get an early start in the morning; she still had some work to do that night—and he almost always went with her. Times he didn't, he put her in a cab. To get to her building, he walked down 75th Street from his building to Columbus Avenue or Amsterdam Avenue or Broadway. Sometimes he went north on Columbus to 96th Street—farther than that, the neighborhood could get a little dangerous—and then go to Broadway and head north to her building from there. More times, he took Amsterdam to 96th Street, and a couple of times to a Hundred-third—Amsterdam seemed safer than Columbus around there—and then go to Broadway and walk to a Hundred-fourteenth and then down to Riverside Drive and her building. Most times—nine out of ten, he'd say—he walked north from Broadway and 75th Street all the way to a Hundred-fourteenth, and almost always on the west side of the street because it was more interesting—more pedestrians, it seemed, and restaurants, markets, bookstores, coffee shops, sidewalk vendors—than the east side of the street, at least once he got past 79th. Also, on Broadway, he liked that he occasionally bumped into people he knew, something he doesn't ever remember doing on Columbus or Amsterdam. For some reason this seemed to happen a lot more above 96th Street than below. Did he know more people up there? Doesn't think so. Although from about a Hundred-sixth Street on he would see people from her apartment building she'd introduced him to or he'd met at gatherings she was invited to there or just recognized from the elevator or lobby or standing in front of the building or had started up conversations with in the elevator or lobby, or at the annual pre-Christmas party and used-book sale on the ground floor and once at a party in the lobby for a much-loved doorman who was retiring after working there for thirty years. He also has to consider that her building was much closer to Broadway than his. He never walked to her building from Central Park West or West End Avenue. They'd be dull walks, and going up to Central Park West would be taking him a little out of the way. He doesn't know why he never walked to her building even part of the way on Riverside Drive. He now sees it could have been an interesting walk, with the view of this park and river from various spots, and if the sun was setting, beautiful. He did, a couple of times, walk inside Riverside Park from 79th Street and Riverside Drive to a Hundred-tenth. And he once jogged from his building to Riverside Park and then all the way in it to a Hundred-tenth and Riverside Drive, walking the last two blocks to her building so he wouldn't come into the lobby panting and sweating. He walked a few times to her building when it was snowing, even heavily, because he always dressed for it—warm coat, wool cap, boots, gloves—and he had a complete change of clothing at her place, which she didn't have at his, if any of his got wet. He never, though, walked there when it was raining hard. Then, with an umbrella and raincoat, he'd take the subway or bus. If the weather was sticky and hot, he'd still walk to her building, but more slowly, and about half the times stopped around 86th or 90th Street and Broadway and took the bus the rest of the way. He also never—or maybe he did this once and found out it was a mistake—walked to her place with a heavy package or two or a briefcase loaded down with books. Sometimes he stopped for coffee on these walks. Or he'd pick up food for them for dinner that night, Chinese or Indian takeout or from the market right up the block from her building, or bread or pastries or both from one of the bakeries or gourmet food stores on Broadway. Then he would reach her building, say hello to the doorman, take the elevator up and ring her bell, even after he had a key to her apartment for more than a year, just to have her open the door and smile at him, and often she'd already be smiling, and say something like "Hiya, lovie" or "I'm so happy to see you" and he'd say something like "I'm so happy to see you too," and they'd kiss, a lot of those times even before one of them shut the door.

She thought of and arranged so many of the things for them. The one big exception that he can think of now might be the apartment in Baltimore they moved into five weeks before Rosalind was born. He was at a dinner party about six months before and a woman there, an art history professor at his school, mentioned she had a year's sabbatical in New York the next academic year and was looking for a sublet there. "That's a coincidence," he said. "My wife and I will have to find a nice apartment here. Maybe we could swap for a year." He looked at hers, liked it, she said she liked theirs sight unseen—"Doorman? Columbia area? Overlooking the river? And at that rent? Let's shake on it"—and when the year was up they stayed on because the woman got a teaching position somewhere else. He was also the one who suggested they add a porch to their house, but she got the builders for it and designed it herself. They were sitting on the porch of the farmhouse they rented in Maine. Maybe ten years ago. Having a drink and watching the sky light up in different colors from the sunset, and out of nowhere he said "I just had a brilliant idea. The sky inspired it. You might not go for it, but it's so pleasant out here, why don't we have a porch like this one built onto our house?" "Not go for it?" she said. "I love the idea and have thought of it myself several times but never brought it up because I was sure you'd say it would be too expensive." "Hang money for once," he said. "I've been thrifty for too long. Save, save, save, and for what? For something like this. And what could it cost? Oh, maybe a lot. But the house is paid up and the expenses and taxes for it aren't too bad. A porch would raise the value of it a little, so also the assessment of the house the next time around. But we both have good jobs—mine I can't be fired from—and where we get a small raise every year. And we'll keep it simple. Interchangeable glass and screens. Raw wood. No fancy furniture or embellishments. When we want something to sit on, we'll bring out the chairs from inside. Okay, that's going too far. Buy two chairs. Buy a little table. I figure the best spot for it would be off the living room, since we have that door to the outside there we never use and all that space it opens to. Though we won't be able to see the sky like this from it and the occasional rainbow, we'll still have a nice view of our woods and the road. We'll watch joggers jogging past. Cyclists. The mail deliverers in their electric trucks. But you tell me." "I can't believe you're saying this," and he said "I know. Because I've also been so cheap." She took his free hand and squeezed it. "That clinches the deal," he said. Maureen came out and said "Why's Mommy crying?" "Is she? Over something as silly as a porch." The VCR. Rosalind was a few months old. Gwen said "That poor French poet I'm translating wrote that he bought a VCR in Paris and watched *Fanny and Alexander* on it. If he can afford one, we can too. I want to be able, when I don't feel like reading while I'm breastfeeding or just listening to the radio, to have something to watch other than mindless morning and afternoon TV. And it's Bergman, and that one we missed and some people say it's his best." "I don't mean to sound stupid, but what exactly is a VCR and what do the initials stand for?" and then asked what she thought one would cost. She said "The *Sun's* running ads with VCRs being much cheaper than they were last year, which means they're probably half of what they go for in France. And the video cassettes—I've looked into it at the record store in the Rotunda Mall, which has a whole wall of them— are only three dollars to rent for the new releases and two dollars for the oldies, and the new ones you can keep for two days and the old ones for a week." "Sounds good to me. It should be fun." They bought a VCR player that week and rented *Fanny and Alexander* at the Rotunda record store. She read the instruction manual how to hook up the VCR player to the television set and how to play the cassette, and they watched the movie. "That was terrific," he said. "Not the film as much as I thought it'd be but to be able to see it in your own home, and you put everything together so easily. Next time teach me how to use it." "It's all in the manual. Read it," and he said "Me? Learn from an instruction manual? Just imagine what would have happened if I were the one who had to set up the VCR player. It would have ended with me kicking it across the room. Better, you show me how to put the cassette in and play it next time we rent one, because I don't want to have to keep relying on you so much." Getting things done in the house like new drapes and their bedroom carpet cleaned. She said "I want to explain why we need new drapes in all the rooms we have them in so you don't think I'm putting us through an unnecessary large expense. They're old, soiled beyond cleaning, torn in places, and came with the house when it had different colored walls." He said "Our bedroom drapes, maybe, since we use them almost every night. But we've never drawn the drapes closed in the dining and living rooms, so can't we just take them down and not replace them?" "No. If we did that, the sides of those windows would look bare." "I don't want to get into an argument about it," he said, "but it never would have crossed my mind to change any of them, bedroom drapes included. They all look fine to me. I also don't like the idea of more workmen in the house, measuring, fitting, choosing the right colors, and then installing them." "Don't worry; you won't have to deal with any of it. I don't mind taking care of it. I like doing it. I like making the house look nice." And he said "So do I, but okay. You want? Do. I can see you're determined and that you don't think I know much of what I'm talking about." After the drapes were hung, he said "I have to hand it to you. The rooms look much nicer with the new drapes," and she said "I thought you'd appreciate the difference once they were up. And these are washable, while the old ones would have run." She said their bedroom carpet was stained in a dozen places because the cat had vomited on it so many times and from the coffee he's spilled carrying it to his desk. He went in to look and she followed him. "I don't think it's so bad," and she said "Of course not. And look at the carpet in the hallway outside here," and he looked and said "That too. I'll get some carpet cleaner and do it myself." "Like for how many years you promised to scrape and paint the register grill in our bathroom because it was so rusty, till I finally had to do it for you. No, the carpet is in such sad shape, it has to be done professionally. If it's all right with you—well, really; even if it isn't; give me this, please?—I've made an appointment for a carpet-cleaning company to come. They're offering a special price for an introductory one-room cleaning, and they'll throw in the hallway. Unfortunately, the carpet will be wet for an entire day, so you'll have to bring your typewriter to the dining-room table and work there." "How much is this introductory offer?" and she told him and he said "For one fifteen-by-twenty-foot room, or even twenty-by-twenty-four? Okay, I won't object. If I do, you'll say I always object to these things," and she said "I probably would, because you do." After the carpet was cleaned and he'd removed the little square pieces of paper from underneath all the furniture legs in the bedroom, he said "Want to know what?" and she said "You're about to say the carpet looks pretty good." "They really did a job. It looks as new as when it was first put down. But one question. Why'd we ever get such a light color that shows all the stains?" and she said "We both agreed to it, don't you remember?" "I think you gave me three to four swatches of almost the same gray color, each one slightly lighter than the next, but let's not go into it. Your decision to get the carpet cleaned turned out to be a great success." Taxes. Before he knew her, he always did the short form. "Why?" he told her. "Because it's quick, easy, I'm used to it, and I never made much money." She urged him to do the 1040. "The section C form was made for you. You're a writer so you have a little profit from your writing but lots of losses. Once you know how to do it—and what would it take you? A few hours? And your earnings are bound to increase over the years—it'll begin to pay off." "You know me by now. I hate change. All that time learning something new interferes with what I really like doing. If, by some accident, I make a bundle from one of my writings, I'll be able to pay for a tax accountant." She offered to do his taxes that year. "Then, the next tax year, just copy out what I've done." "No, you've got your own things to do—taxes, teaching, writing, reading," and she said "But I love you. So I like doing things for you. And this is some-thing, because of my father, I've learned how to do well. If you happen to get back much more from the IRS than you usually do, or you have to pay it much less, you can treat me to an expensive dinner at a place of my choosing, or at least a relatively modest dinner with an expensive wine." This was for the '78 returns, so around March '79, a few months after they'd met. She did his taxes the next two or three years—let's see: '79's, '80's and '81's, so three. Then they got married and they filed a joint return. She'd call her father for advice every night she was doing the taxes. "You don't have more gifts to charity than that in Schedule A?" "Martin's taking too large a loss for his writing, when you compare it to what he earned from it, and five years straight? You'll be flagged." "By now," she said he told her, "you do it so well I could hire you as my assistant and pay you good wages, but stick to your teaching. Less stress and longer vacations and more time with your husband and darling little angels." Then she'd fax him the completed 1040 form, he'd go over it for errors and what she might have missed and mail it back with his new corrections, and she'd fill out the entire form again but in ink this time. She never once finished the returns before the last day. "Done yet?" he'd say around eight that night. "We don't want to be penalized for filing late or draw suspicion from the IRS," and she'd say "I need another half an hour" or "hour." Two hours later or so—one time it was 11:30— she'd say "Hurray. I'm done. All I need now is your signature," and he'd sign the second page of the federal and state forms above her signature, stick them into their envelopes, which he'd already put stamps on, and drive to the main post office in downtown Baltimore—trip took about twenty minutes at that hour—and drop them in their respective baskets postal workers held up to his car window or the one on the passenger side. He said one time after he got back "I wish we didn't always have to wait till the last minute to get our income taxes in," and she said "I'm sorry, but that seems to be what it takes." "Couldn't you start doing them a week or two earlier?" and she said "Because you think I'd get them done sooner? It doesn't work like that. Listen, though. Have we ever been audited? Ever wonder why? But if it's too much for you, we can get a tax specialist to do them from now on. That'd also mean less work for my father. He works too hard as it is during tax season, and I'd love for him to cut back," and he said "Nah, it's okay. We've never been late, and I can handle the pressure. And it's kind of fun down there the last night, with all the tax protesters and their banners and chants. You should come with me next time. A kind of excitement you never see in Baltimore except, I guess, at Ravens games." Bookcases in their house. She said "I can't stand our books all over the place and in different bookcases, but not enough of them and each in worse condition than the others and half of them about to collapse from the weight. Let's get floor-to-ceiling bookcases built into three of the living room walls." "Hold off a second," he said. "You're talking about a job only a master carpenter can do, which'll cost us your arm and my leg," and she said "Probably, because I'd want them to look good. But I'd think they'd increase the value of the house by as much as we spent to build them, so in the long run it'd be as if we got them for practically nothing." He said "Where are we going? I like our house and want to live in it for many more years. And most people don't give a damn about bookcases or even want them for the ten or so books they own. Especially built-in ones that'd cost plenty to have removed and then to repair the damage to the walls they made." "Would you object to my getting an estimate?" and he said "Go ahead. Doesn't cost anything. Get two." After they were built—"I know you'll eventually come around to think 'How did we ever do without them?'"—he said "There was a lot of noise around here for a while and the house was a mess longer than I thought I could take, but the bookcases are beautiful. Matthew was expensive but he did a great job." "Now we just have one small additional expense," she said. "I want to hire a graduate student from my department to help me shelve all our books by category and in alphabetical order." "I can do it with you," and she said "You have your own work to do, and I don't know of any grad student who couldn't use the money." "How much you thinking of paying them?" and she said "fifteen an hour." "That's a lot. Why not get an undergrad?" and she said "Graduate students seem to appreciate books more and don't handle them as roughly. So, my dear, no more looking all day for a book. You want a particular Bernhard novel, and you haven't left it in the car, you go to 'B-E' on the fiction shelves. You want his memoir, then 'B-E' in the bio section. Poetry, its own section. Philosophy, art and travel books, literary criticism, etcetera—maybe even the classics—each separate. My French books, literature and criticism, in both languages, will take up one entire wall and probably continue into my study. For your published books, a row of their own on the top shelf there, with room for more." He said "I'd rather not show them off like that in such a prominent place. Better, I keep my work in the old bookcase in our bedroom." A video camera. She wanted them to buy one about twenty years ago and he didn't want to and now regrets not having any videos of her other than a short part of one a friend gave them that's around someplace, and of the kids when they were growing up. "You're being unreasonable again," she said, and he said "When was the last time? All right. But I just don't see the point to them. We'll never watch them after the first couple of times, and to me they're so self...self... self-something. 'Look at the mundane things I'm doing.' 'Watch me leaving the house holding Maureen by the hand.' 'See Martin and Gwen smile for the birdie and kiss for the camera?' That kind of stuff." "Even if my parents want to buy us one?" and he said "Like the microwave oven they also offered to buy us. It was generous of them, but I don't want either gift or think we need them. We have enough things as it is." "I won't fight it," she said. "It isn't important enough to. Besides, I don't like to be on camera myself." "Same here, so what are we arguing about?" "The kids, perhaps. Years from now they might want to know why we don't have any videos of them and us." "We have photographs," he said. "Envelopes and envelopes of them, we also don't look at. But they take the place of videos, I'd think." "I still feel you're making a mistake. We'd use the camera sparingly. Birthdays. Once a summer the two kids in front of The Bubbles at Jordon Pond House. Like that. You don't ever have to pose for it. Maybe you'll change your mind on getting one." Their first minivan. She thought they needed a bigger car for the family and all the things they take to Maine that they don't send UPS. He said "Doesn't seem like a bad idea. But I don't want to own two cars. After we buy the van, we'll sell the Citation." "But this way each of us would have a car," and he said "Insurance for both? Repairs? Getting them tested for emissions every other year? We'll manage with one." She looked into buying the van. Visited auto showrooms. Spoke to people they knew who had vans. *Consumer Reports* and other magazines. Even stopped people at shopping centers who were getting in or out of their vans and asked them what they thought of this particular model. "How is it on gas? Is the middle row as easy as they say to take out?" "This is what I've come up with," she said to him. "The Plymouth Voyager seems to be the one we should buy. It's been making them the longest, handles like a smaller vehicle, and is the most fuel-efficient and trouble-free. And I know the dealership in the area that offers the lowest price and best warranty. If you'd like, we can buy one this weekend. Any particular color? Though I've been warned, for reasons not entirely clear to me—something to do with day and night and other drivers' visibility—to stay away from the very dark and very light." "You choose," he said. "I'll go along with anything you say." "God, you're being so agreeable about it, and have been from the start," and he said "Well, while I sat on my fat ass, you did all the research and legwork, so it's the least

I can be. Maybe it's the new me, though don't bet on it." The first house they bought. She said "I think the ideal place for us to live is Mount Washington. It has lots of trees and hills and open spaces and is just a fifteen-minute drive to work. It's considered liberal politically, has almost an even mix of Jew and Gentile, and many educators and arts and crafts people have homes there. But what's most important, and no doubt this is so because of some of the things I mentioned, it has the best elementary school in the city. The two disadvantages are that the middle and high school that serve that community aren't very good. If they stay as bad as the test scores and graduation rates and some people I've spoken to say they are, then when Rosalind's about six months away from entering middle school, we'll put the house on the market and look for one in this very attractive area I've got my eye on in Baltimore County, a few miles north of Mount Washington. It's less populated and more rustic, is close to 83 so takes only five minutes more to get to work, doesn't have the same comfortable mix of Jew and Gentile and is almost uniformly white, which I don't like, so it's not as liberal politically. But the middle and high schools for it are supposed to be as good as any in the state, and it has a more than adequate elementary school for Maureen's last three years in one and I hear it's improving every year, so by the time we move there it could be as good as Mount Washington's." His teaching. She encouraged him to apply for a college teaching job that had opened up in Baltimore. He was interviewed, was offered the job but reluctant to give up his apartment and move down there without her. She said he had to have a full-time job if he eventually wanted to get married and have children, not that she was proposing to him, and there were very few well-paying creative writing teaching jobs in New York for writers with little recognition and no advanced degrees, no matter how many books and stories they've published. "Take the job. You don't know how lucky you are they made you the offer. It's a three-year contract, you can always leave in a year or two, but I wouldn't advise you to unless it's for a much better position. You don't want to get a reputation in academia of breaking a contract for nothing else or something less. And I've checked the train schedules between Baltimore and New York. They run almost every hour and the fares aren't that expensive because they're subsidized by the government, so we can still be together every weekend. If you can arrange to hold only afternoon classes and none on Friday, we'll have even longer weekends together, and from time to time I'll drive or train down to you." "All right, you convinced me, but what am I going to do not seeing you those four other days?" and she said "You'll get your teaching work done, to free up your weekends with me, and write more." St. John. She said at dinner—it was soon after his fall semester began—"When's your spring break?" He said he didn't know and she looked at the school calendar on the refrigerator and said "Good; March. Let's spend a week of it on St. John." "Where's that?" and she said "The Caribbean; the Virgin Islands. I read a travel article in the *Times* about it. Rosalind will be a year and a half then, old enough to fly. For not too much money we can stay in a cabin at a campground on Cinnamon Bay. I'll show you; the photos of it are gorgeous. But you have to promise you'll try snorkeling. It's one of my main reasons to go there; for me to get back to it and for you to start doing it, and I know you'll love it." "Sounds okay to me. Late winter in paradise? Seeing a place I've never been and learning something new? What could be better?" She arranged everything: flights, ferries, living arrangements. Morning after they got there she rented snorkeling equipment for herself, wanted to rent for him, but he said "Don't; it'll be a waste of money. I know I'll never be able to breathe underwater through that tube." "Practice in shallow water," and he said "No. I'll swallow water even there and choke." Last day they were there she said "I'm going to make a threat I know I can't carry out. We're not leaving this island till you try to snorkel at least once." He used her mask and tube, caught on to it quickly, snorkeled for about two hours and didn't want to come out of the water. "All those little fishies; they really do swim in front and alongside of you. What a dope I was not to do it the first day." "Oh, I'm so pleased you like it. To be honest with you, your sitting on the beach with Rosalind for five days and taking her back to the cabin for naps, gave me more time to snorkel and that made the vacation for me. But you should listen to me more. Sometimes I know better than you what will make you happy." "From now on," he said. "Just watch me." The QE2. "Are you kidding? Who's got that kind of money?" and she said "You're not listening. I said we'd only go if we get standby. That's half the regular fair and practically nothing for Rosalind but the crib rental and all-day nursery. All day, Martin. Think of the time we'd have to loll and laze around and even get some work in. We'll know a few weeks before the Queen sails if we got it. They told me that at that time of the sailing season, east to west standby is almost a sure thing. By chance we don't get it, we'll fly British Airways, which I'll also make reservations for. They're run by the same company, so the deal is we won't lose our deposit for whichever one we don't use." Or maybe she said there was some agreement between the two companies and they only had to pay for their plane tickets once they learned they didn't get on the QE2. He knows she arranged it some way where it wouldn't cost them any extra money.

Anyway, they got it and loved the trip home. Great weather, smooth crossing, they both got work done—she, the galleys of a book she translated;
he, the first and second drafts of a short story he wrote by hand in one of
the ship's quieter lounges and which turned into an enormous novel that
took four years to write—lots of reading of books from the ship's library,
movies, wine was cheap, good food, and once they worked things out after
a furious argument they came on board with—"You made me cry," she said,
"and hate you"; "Funny," he said, "but I could never say that about you, but
I know why you could to me"—more daytime lovemaking than usual. And
every morning she was delighted and amused that they got an hour added
to the day. Converting the cellar of their second house to a playroom.
"You're planning to break through the walls to make windows? Cover the
dirt floor with cement and linoleum? You're talking big money for something that isn't necessary. Leave it as it is, just for storage. Each kid already
has her own bedroom. What more do they need?" "Don't worry. I'll take
care of it all," she said. "Contractor; builders. You won't have to do anything
but make sure we've enough money in the checking account to cover it. I'm
also having the room heated and soundproofed. That way, if the kids want
to have sleepovers for ten friends or play loud music downstairs, they can."
"Wouldn't it be cheaper and simpler for us to limit their sleepovers to three
to four girls in their bedrooms, and tell them that as a common courtesy,
and also for them a lesson in civility, to keep the music volume relatively
low?" and she said "No." Rosalind's baby photos. Gwen wanted a professional
photographer to take them when Rosalind was around six months old. Six
months seems right. She has little hair in the photos and by the time of her
first birthday party, which Gwen and he took pictures of, she had hair
halfway down her neck. A photography studio must have got their name
and address from the hospital Rosalind was born in and mailed them the ad.
"We get two large prints of the photo we like best, and six wallet-sized ones,
all for forty dollars, and get to keep the contact sheet for ten dollars more.
My folks would love to have one of the large prints and we'll frame the
other." "I hate those professionally done photographs," he said. "They
always look fake, too perfect, with their phony backdrops and lighting, and
the babies never look real. And you know they'll give you the big sales pitch
to buy more, and that you won't be able to fight them off," and she said
"I promise I'll hold the line to the least expensive package we sign up for. I'm
not a patsy, you know. And it'll be fun watching her interact with the
camera." It *was* fun. Rosalind loved the attention and became something of
a ham. The photographer got expressions out of her—wily, funny,

charming, coquettish, serious, pensive, playful, and others—they never saw
before, or not all at one sitting. They hung the framed photo on the walls of
their three bedrooms—Baltimore apartment and both houses—and her
folks loved the one they gave them. "We should have ordered three large
prints," he said, "for how much more would it have cost us? The third one
for my mother, which I also would have got framed, as we did for your parents."
He doesn't know why they didn't get a professional photographer for
Maureen when she was that age. Money again, probably, but he never
suggested it to Gwen and she must just never have thought of it. The osteopath.
He had painful back spasms that went on for two weeks. "I don't want to
see our doctor about it. He'll recommend a specialist, who'll send me
through all sorts of tests. It'll go away by itself." She told him about the
osteopath who cured a friend's Bell's palsy in two visits, while her regular
doctor said there wasn't much he could do and her paralysis wouldn't start
to go away for three months and a complete cure could take a year, and he
said "I'm glad for her, but it's not for me. Acupuncturists, chiropractors,
osteopaths, vitamin therapists, Chinese herbalists, macrobiotic dieticians.
You name it and I or one of the women I've known has done it, and they're
all quacks." "You're being stubborn and ridiculous again and saying what
you know you don't believe. But all right; suffer." After another week of it,
but now where he couldn't even stand or sit up straight, she said "You either
go to the osteopath or I drag you to the doctor. I've gone online about it.
Most people with your problem claim much better and faster success with
it than any kind of traditional medicine. And no surgery or medication's
involved, so what do you have to lose? Try it just once?" The osteopath
wanted to put him on a couple of machines in his office. "I don't want
anything like that. They'll take too long and they look like remedial artifacts
from a century ago that in no way can help me. I'll be frank with you. I
didn't want to see you but my wife insisted I come. She did some research
on it and what she came up with is that just your working your hands on
me like a massage therapist does is the treatment that gets the best results."
The osteopath had him sit on an exam table, got behind him and grabbed
his head firmly with both hands—"Don't be alarmed if you hear a couple of
loud cracks"—and gave it two quick twists. "Miracle," he said to Gwen
when he got back to the waiting room. "I can stand up straight and walk
normally again and pain's all gone. And look; I can wrap my arms around
you without any part of me hurting," and he wrapped his arms around her.
"How come you know how to fix everything up?" First time they went to
France together. It was his idea—he'd wanted to go there with her the June

after they first met, but didn't have the money to. As with the week's vacation on St. John they had with Rosalind more than two years later, she took care of everything: travel, lodging, itinerary. Big cities like Nice and Marseilles but also small towns and chapels and museums in the south he'd never heard of. Day after they got to France, she took him to an outdoor food stand in Paris that was famous for its onion soup, she said. "The workers and farmers used to warm themselves up at night when the old wholesale food market was here. Now it's strictly for tourists like us in the day, but it's still supposed to be the best in the city." She translated the sign for him. The soup had two prices: one for sitting at a table under a tent and the other for standing at a counter. "Let's get it standing up," he said. "It's the same-sized bowl, you say, for half the price." "It gets too sloppy, eating it that way," she said. "And we're in no rush, and I want to sit after all our walking this morning." "We can sit on a park bench, after. —All right. But maybe we should get one bowl between us, sitting down, because it seems awfully high for a small bowl of onion soup in not the fanciest surroundings, no matter how good it might be. Then, if we don't particularly like it, or I don't, we wouldn't have ordered two." "What am I going to do with you?" she said. "If you're to enjoy our month in France, and I'm to enjoy it with you, you'll have to be much freer with your cash. Face it; things are more expensive here and the dollar's down." "Okay, two soups standing," and she said "No. You stand and I'll sit." "Okay," he said, "we both sit, but I hope they give us a roll or slice of bread or two with it, because this is our lunch." "You have to be kidding if you think this is our lunch. What we'll do, to compromise, though I wish you hadn't forced me to, is get two bowls at the counter. Then, in about an hour, we'll go to a sit-down bistro or bar for lunch." She ordered two soups. "No bread?" and she said "If you'd look you'd see it's in the soup, so please don't ask for it." After two spoonfuls and a chunk of grated cheese on top, he said "I'm being honest here; I really don't think it's very good. The cheese, yes. But I've tasted much better French onion soup in New York and at places that weren't even famous for it." "You're lying," she said. "To win the argument or prove me wrong or spoil any pleasure I might have in eating the soup. Or I don't know why, but there it is. You and I have the same soup from the same tureen and oven. And I've had onion soup *gratinée* about a half-dozen times here—once, when it was still in the old market—and its quality has always been the same: great. You're just ticked off about the price. Admit this one little thing to me and you'll make me think I haven't made a mistake coming to France with you." "All right," he said. "Maybe it is good. Maybe it is the price. I'm not completely sure, but it sounds right. You didn't make a mistake coming to France with me and I'll try from now on not to be so cheap or penny-pinching or money conscious, or whatever I'm being: tight! But you know, I've only had my teaching job a year. Before that—I'm giving you my excuse—it was more than ten years of not having much dough. You can say I haven't quite adjusted yet to a full-time decent-paying job, and with a two-thousand-plus raise for the next academic year, no less." "I guess there's something to what you say," she said. "Let me think about it. Meanwhile, please, no more chintziness. Trust me, my sweetheart, I'm doing my best, as I did with our airfares and hotels, to keep our expenses down. But I'm not, for both of us, going to do it to the point of ruining our trip." "Got ya," he said, "completely. And as you saw, I had some more soup. It's actually quite good. And the top layer—must be some kind of Swiss—is the best I've ever had." "I'm not going to say anything to that. Let's just enjoy ourselves." The farmhouse. The cottage she started renting in Maine ten years ago was up for sale. They wanted to buy it, but that would mean not buying a house in Baltimore. "So what are we going to do next summer?" he said. "I'll come up with something," she said. She tried all the rental agents in the area. There were very few houses available for an entire summer and what was available they couldn't afford. "We're really screwed," he said. "I've come to love it here and would hate not coming back." "Don't worry," she said. "We still have two weeks left and I haven't tried everything." She placed an ad in the local weekly—checked the wording with him first—that said "Writer and translator, husband a university professor and wife trained to be one, with a small child, another baby on the way, four well-behaved scratchless cats of the same Siamese family (mother and brood), would like to rent house in quiet, appealing surroundings in Blue Hill Bay area next summer for two to three months, and, if it's a good fit for both parties, for as many summers after that." "Perfect," he said. "Every word and comma. And honest, intelligent, personable and informative. Add that we're long-time summer residents here, and the responses should pour in. I know I'd be interested." They got one call. She was out. "You should probably speak to my wife," he said. "She handles everything like this," and the woman said "Why? I've got you, and you can tell her what I've said. My husband and I thought we were done with all the problems of renting the farmhouse and would use it only when we needed to get away from each other. But your notice intrigued us. For one thing, we feel that intellectuals make the most responsible and congenial tenants. For another, we do a smattering of writing ourselves. Topical articles for the *Weekly Packet* and the Sedgwick

Historical Society, nothing academic or of literary value that could gain us a Pulitzer Prize. Tell me what you two do." He told her. "Talking to you and hearing your adoring description of your wife, I like you both already and my husband will too. The farmhouse sits atop a hill, is nice and isolated, old, somewhat run-down, has sloping floors you'll at first have trouble maneuvering, and there's a bit of a mouse problem, which your cats will take care of in days. But so we don't get too many complaints about the condition of the house and the noise the wild turkeys make as they strut through the property at dawn, we keep the rent cheap. Come and take a peek, and while you're here, we'll all have tea." Second summer they rented it, Gwen bought a new double bed for them, had all the rooms painted and new screens put in, and a heating stove installed in the living room for the chillier days. "We might as well have rented a luxury house for what all this is costing us," and she said "Everything we're adding will make the place cozier for us, even the paint job, which will cover all the smutched mosquitoes on the ceilings and walls." A few summers later, while Emma and Tom, their landlords, were over for dinner, she asked them if it'd be possible to have a screened-in porch built for next year. "I didn't talk this over with Martin—you're about to see his surprise—but we'd go in for half of it. If we stop renting here, and I don't know when that could ever be. We love the place and the house is now in such great shape, other than for the floors— the porch, like the heating stove and washer and dryer, will be yours." Emma looked at Tom, he nodded, and she said "It's all right with us, dear. We'd do anything to keep you on as tenants, and of course you're talking of a very simple porch." "What were you thinking of?" he said to Gwen later. "Wasn't putting in new appliances and stuff enough? Suppose we can't come back here anymore, for some reason?" and she said "And what could that be? One of us dying? The other, I'd hope, would continue to rent the house with the children till they were grown up. I realize it was unfair of me to spring it on you like that. It just came, and I'm usually not that impulsive. But just picture those magnificent sunsets and far-off storms and rainbows we'd see from the porch without being bothered by bugs. 'Pre-dinner drinks and hummus and cheese on the porch, anybody?' Come on; it'd be a terrific addition. And we've gotten away all these years with rent that's half what a comparable place would be, not that we'd ever find another spot so beautiful and private." Their fifteenth or sixteenth summer there, five years after Tom died, Emma told them that after they leave at the end of August she was going to renovate and winterize the house. New kitchen and bathroom and windows and floors. A furnace to replace the one that conked out thirty years ago. The foundation jacked up to make the house level. "Been think-ing of doing it a long time so I can turn it into a year-rental and maybe even get a tax break out of it. I may even live there myself awhile and rent my house for the summer. Would you be interested?" and he said "Afraid not; too close to the road. Do you agree, Gwen?" and she said "Unfortunately, yes." Later he said to her "What are we going to do now?" and she said "Same thing we did last time. Speak to friends and rental agents. Tack up notices in libraries and bookstores and wherever there's a bulletin board. And place an ad in the two local weeklies, the *Packet* and the one that's for Deer Isle." I wish we still had the old ad," he said. "We only have a few weeks, and look how fast it worked," and she said "One call. But a good one. And what would we use of it: 'small child and a second on the way'?" She checked the wording with him again. "As usual, it's perfect," he said. "though this time maybe add we've been dependable renters up here for nearly thirty years and will provide references." They got a few leads and phone calls. All the houses rented for three to four times what they were paying Emma. "Who knew it's become the in-place to summer?" he said. "I understand people even see celebrities dining in Blue Hill and sailing in at the yacht club there. Nobody we'd recognize, but celebrities nevertheless. Maybe we should think of a coastal area farther north in Maine or even renting in another state. Vermont," and she said "Never. This will always be our summer destination. You feel that too, don't you?" They got a house on Cape Rosier they could afford to rent for five weeks. "What do you want," he said, "July or August?" and she said "Which month is hotter? But then I'd hate to return home a month before school begins, if we choose July." During their two summers there—the second for six weeks: last half of July and almost all of August—she spent a lot of time looking for a house to buy or a small piece of land to build a house on. "You know, I hate to be so cold-blooded about it," she said. "But with the real-estate market crashing, this could be our best chance." She even got architectural plans for a guest-house a friend of hers had built on Mount Desert Island and which she said wouldn't be that expensive. "Like our first cottage, it's just wood; no insula-tion or fireplace or cathedral ceiling or cellar or even a crawlspace. It'd be ideal for us, now that the kids are out and who'll probably only visit us for a week or two, though of course more if they want to. One bedroom and a sleeping loft; bathroom, combined kitchen and dining and living room. And a deck with a shower on it to spray your tootsies before you come in, though we could save on that because I guess it's for sand and we'll never be able to afford a place near the shore." She also got the plans for a shed in the back for one of them to write in. The other can use the bedroom, she said. "It'd be what we like: simple and compact and attractive, and it'd be fun bumping into each other ten times a day. We could even get the same kind of heating stove for it we had in the farmhouse. It worked beautifully. Or I should email Emma, and if she's not using it in the renovated house and didn't throw it out, get it and store it in the barn here." She looked at the houses and land by herself. Maybe twice he went with her. "I know how you hate looking at property," she said; "it can be a bore. But if something looks promising—and I'm serious about finding a house or land this or next summer—you'll have to see it," and he said "When that time comes and the price seems fair to you and you think we should buy it—well, you've been right on just about everything else in our lives and I've been too cautious, so I'll go along with anything you say. I'll even put that in writing." "Don't talk silly. And I won't make any decision like that unless you agree to it." "In the meantime," he said, "we have a nice place here for five weeks, and if we like, six weeks next summer, and possibly the summer after that, another week more. And if it ever comes up for sale—they've given hints—it won't come cheap. But by then we might have enough money to buy it, or we'd put up most and maybe your dad could loan us the rest." Doctors. She got her Baltimore obstetrician through her New York obstetrician. Their Baltimore general practitioner through her Baltimore obstetrician. Their Baltimore dentist and ophthalmologist and optician and the kids' pediatrician through their Baltimore general practitioner. So what's he saying? That though he'd been living in Baltimore for two years before she moved down there, she got them all. "I asked Dr. Vogel who does he go to for his teeth? We'll need a dentist here unless we want to go to my regular one in New York for a checkup and cleaning twice a year and every time a tooth hurts." "You're right. I haven't had my teeth looked at and cleaned for almost two years. And it's stupid of me, because I now have insurance for it through the school." "How'd I get Dr. Vogel?" she said. "I asked Dr. Nancy for the G.P. she goes to. I figured, one doctor taking care of another and her husband, who's also a doctor; he'd have to be good. We need one if we'll be living mainly in Baltimore for at least the next few years. And you should get a complete physical. When was your last?" and he said "Probably not since I was a kid and my mother took me to Dr. Baselitch in Brooklyn once a year. But I don't need one. I'm healthy; I'm fine. If I ever do get that sick where I need to see a doctor, I'll go to yours." "It's not as easy as that. He'd never take you if you weren't his patient. Listen, I don't want you to argue with me on this. Vogel says he has room for you if you come in for a checkup now.

So I've made an appointment for you on a day I know you don't have office hours or teach. Wouldn't you feel stupid if something terrible happened to your health that could have been averted with an annual checkup?" "Sure, but nothing bad's going to happen to me for the next thirty years, although I promise to see a doctor before that time's up." "I know you're healthy," she said, "and you take good care of yourself. But I want to keep you that way, just as you should feel the same about me," and he said "I do; what do you think? Okay, you're looking out for me. I appreciate it. Maybe, for the physical after this one, we can have ours on the same day and take Rosalind with us and have lunch out after. Or you and Rosalind can come with me for this one and we'll have lunch after. What time did you make it for?" *Twenty Stories.* When she was pregnant with Maureen in Maine, she said "I've got the time and I'm not working on anything right now, so I'd like to assemble your next collection from stories that have never been in book form. You can give me as many as you want, but I get to select them and what order they fall in. It has to be my collection. Not the dedication—that should go to Rosalind and whatever we name the new one—but in things like signing off on the cover and even the print. Do you agree to the terms?" and he said "For another book that previously wasn't there? Sure." She chose twenty stories from about sixty he gave her to read, most of which had been in magazines or were coming out in them, and also the title: *Twenty Stories by Martin Samuels.* "There were five others I liked as much as the ones I picked and I would have included them. But twenty's a better number and more memorable title for a collection; not too many, not too few, and no hyphen." He couldn't get a literary agent or publisher interested in the collection for more than three years. "I don't know why," he said. "It's my best and also my favorite, and not just because you put it together, though that helped." "I don't feel I chose wrong," and he said "You didn't. You also made it my most diverse collection." Then a small university press accepted it but wanted to cut it down to fifteen stories. She said "Hold out for twenty. They'll agree to it. Tell them your wife, a professor of literature whose principle concentration is the contemporary short story—you don't have to say it's French and that I'm an adjunct assistant professor—worked hard at compiling the collection—use that word. I know I'm being maddeningly dictatorial about all this—not only giving you orders and no say but telling you what to tell them—but this collection's special to me, so say your marriage is in jeopardy if you remove any of the stories or change the order they're in. They'll know you're being facetious, but it might help persuade them. Also, that you want to see the book cover they have in mind and the design of the book and have the first right of approval of them. I think that's the legal term." "That isn't done ever unless you're a big-shot literary agent with tremendous clout or a writer making millions for them." In Maine again, at the farmhouse a few weeks before the book's publication date, she said a woman she knew in the French department at grad school gave up trying to find a tenure-track teaching position in New York and became a cultural affairs writer for *Newsweek* and also does occasional book reviews for it. "Evelyne's specialty, of course, is all things French, as a writer and reviewer. But I saw some time back that she reviewed a new British novel. I want to send her a copy of *Twenty Stories*. I won't tell her my part in it. I'm sure she'll like it—our tastes were remarkably similar—and it might inspire her to review it, but without my suggesting she do it. I think it's best when they come up with the idea themselves." "*Newsweek* magazine? A review of a story collection by an almost complete literary unknown from a small university press in Baton Rouge? No chance," and she said "What do we have to lose?" "One of my ten author copies, and I'm already down to three," and she said "So we'll buy more. Or you'll ask the press to send it. No, she might not connect the name and will disregard the book. Chances are better if it comes directly from me with a personal note. That I'm teaching, living in Baltimore but still have my old apartment in New York, married to the writer, two children, and okay, this is our newest offspring… something, but I'll work it out. I'll send it off today." The woman called a week later, thanking her for the book, saying it was a fast read and several of the stories were funny, the rape story and what seemed like an AIDS story very disturbing, and that she liked the collection enough to see what she could do to review it for the magazine. "No promises, but keep your fingers crossed. When you're in New York next and hubby will look after your daughters, let's you and I get together for a long overdue lunch. I have a lot to tell you and you were always an interested and broad-minded listener." It was a week later. He'd just come back from the Blue Hill library with his mother. Gwen was on the second floor of the farmhouse. She must have heard the car and went to the room he worked in and raised the window screen and stuck her head outside and shouted "Martin, Martin, I have the most wonderful news. It's in. We did it. *Newsweek*—not Evelyne, so even better, for less possible taint of cronyism, but a regular book reviewer—is doing the review. They're sending up a photographer from Portland this week to photograph you. Oh my darling, I'm so happy for you. I'll be right down to hug you." His mother said "*Newsweek* magazine. You're really getting up in the world. Your father would have liked that." The photographer wanted some ideas where to photograph him. "Somehow, backdrops of stunted trees and blueberry fields with rocks sticking out of them don't do it for me, and to be honest, the house is kind of shabby." Gwen suggested the shore. "People always look good with the ocean and a beautiful sky behind them." They drove to it. The photo that ran with the review showed him sitting on a big boulder about ten feet out in the water. "Is there some way you can get out there without soaking your sneakers and socks?" the photographer asked him. "I'll carry them," he said, "or just photograph me barefoot. That'd look more normal, surrounded by water," and Gwen said "No bare feet, sweetheart. You'll hate me for saying this, but it isn't dignified for an author's photo in a major newsweekly." The photograph made him look good. Thinner, no stomach bulge showing, his hair thicker and darker. He remembers sucking in his stomach when the photographer was snapping pictures, and stiffening his upper arms so they'd look muscular in the short-sleeved polo shirt. "What a fake I am," he later told Gwen. "Why can't I let myself look like I look?" "You did fine. And who knows if the photo they use won't be one where he caught you off-guard, so you'll get your wish." That was a while ago. Fifteen years. He does the math in his head. Eighteen. He supposes it could be called a good review. At least positive. Nothing bad said but nothing laudatory. "Fast pace and dialog," he remembers. And the word "quirky." Either for several of the stories or some of the writing or maybe even some of the main characters. An appealing and clearly written mix, the reviewer said, of eros, thanatos, deep feeling and snippets of humor. And that this book of interrelated stories could have been called an unchronological novel of self-contained chapters, a form, the reviewer said, that had become prevalent the last ten years. The first printing of fifteen hundred copies sold out in a week because of the review, the editor said. The book went into a second printing, the only book of his that had, of a thousand copies, and is still in print. New Year's Eves. He thinks it was four years ago near the end of December that she asked him "What do we have planned for New Year's Eve?" and he said "Nothing; you?" "For a change, let's go to a really good restaurant. Will you let me take care of it? The kids are probably going to their own parties, but we can eat early if they want to come too." She made reservations for the two of them at an expensive restaurant. "I don't know," he said, looking at the menu. "Why don't you choose both entrées? Whatever you pick, I know I'll like. And you know more about wine than I, so you choose that too." The next year she asked him again and he said "Nothing. You know me, I'd be very content to stay home and uncork a terrific bottle of champagne. And maybe get fancy take-out from Graul's or Eddie's or that Persian restaurant you like so much and a movie we both want to see." She said "Those we can do anytime. How about this year we go to a concert or play? But good seats—I'm sure the kids, like last year, will have their own things to do—and dinner in a restaurant after. We'll have a glass of champagne there and of course a good red wine. I won't drink that much, though. I want you to have a really good time, so I'll drive us home." "Suits me," he said. "Then when we get home we can have some more champagne." Year after that she said "Got any ideas for New Year's Eve? There are no parties we've been invited to, and I doubt I'd want to go to one anyway. They're always such drags," and he said "You've done such a great job making plans for us the last few years, why don't you decide? Although, think you'll be feeling up to going out?" "Right now I do. We'll see at the time. It's not always necessary to make reservations. Even at the last minute I'll find us a place if we don't stay home," and he said "No, let's go out. Let's have fun." She chose the restaurant. He sat beside her at the table so he could help feed her. "You don't have to," she said. "I can manage," and he said "I know you can, but I want to." She studied the menu and said "Food's a bit pricey. You don't mind?" and he said "Why would I mind? It's New Year's Eve." "Since you're the one who's going to drink," she said, "you choose the wine. I'll just have water and maybe tea, and what you don't drink, we'll take home. But don't drink too much, okay? Because you no longer have a fill-in driver." "If I order the least expensive bottle of red, will you think I'm being cheap?" and she said "I'm sure all the wine is good here, and I never would anyway." The kids were out of town, though had been with them a few days before and after Christmas. Babies. A month before they married, she said "It's my optimal fertile period, so let's try conceiving a baby now." "So you're actually going through with the marriage?" and she said "If we're successful, late September or early October are ideal times for having a child—not too hot—and then for lots of years later, birthday parties." But he already went into that. She on her shins with her rear end to him and telling him to stay in as long as he can after. Same thing with Maureen? Same. Last two weeks of December. This time Bach. The procreative *Partita Number 2 for Unaccompanied Violin*. Nursery. She did some research and visited several nurseries in New York and chose one Rosalind would go to for three hours every weekday morning while Gwen was on fellowship and he was on leave for a year. "That'll give us enough time to get something done," and he said "Plenty, and then later, to enjoy ourselves and maybe work some more." Rosalind's first movie. Gwen said "There's a movie at the Charles I want to see," and he said "So go. I'll stay

home with Baby." She said "Let's all go together," and told him how they'd
do it. The theater was the only foreign film house in Baltimore. It was still a
single-screen then. Rosalind was in a padded baby carrier that was like a
small duffel bag with two cloth handles. She was only a few months old and
slept through the entire movie. If she woke up, or even stirred but wasn't
going back to sleep immediately, he'd already designated himself as the one to
take her to the lobby till she was asleep again, and Gwen would later tell him
what he'd missed. The seat next to hers was too narrow to put the carrier
lengthwise against the back, so she set it on the floor. "Not too dirty and
cold down there?" and she said "I checked. She'll be all right. And she's
covered." They bought a medium-sized bag of popcorn, with no butter on
it because it made their fingers greasy, and she held it while they watched
the movie. "I'll take that off your hands if you're tired of holding it," and she
said "It's okay. You're always doing things for me. Have some more." The
movie was Brazilian or Argentinean or Chilean—anyway, South American—
had the word "case" in its title—*A Special Case? An Official Case?*—and was
a contemporary historical political drama of people—opponents of the
government—being picked off the streets by party thugs, shoved into cars
and never seen again. He thinks he has that right. The police state finally
ends and some of those who disappeared are released, or something good at
the end happens. He knows they both thought the movie powerful. Why'd
he bring all that up and in such detail? To show them some more together
and how she handled so many things for them—well, he already said that,
and he for her sometimes too, and the two of them also just having a good
time. So what else? All those languages she knew. French she became fluent
in as an undergraduate, Italian and German and a little Spanish she studied
while going for her Ph.D. Russian and Polish she learned from her parents.
He loved hearing her speak one foreign language or another, but usually
French, when she was on the phone. When they went to Germany with
Rosalind in '85, he didn't know that she knew German and he was the one
who ordered the food for them in the restaurants and asked directions on
the street. He had two years of German in college and brushed up on it
before they left for Europe and he also knew some Yiddish from hearing his
folks speak a little of it at home. But she corrected his German once when
they were in a café in Munich, or maybe it was when he was buying tickets
at the modern art museum there, and he said "Wait a minute. You speak
German too?" and she said "I had to pass a test in it to get my doctorate—
that or Italian, and for some unaccountable reason I was better in German—
but my proficiency in it is mostly in reading." "How come I never knew?"

he said. "Now, if it's possible, I'm even more impressed by you." Anything else? Someone knocked on his classroom door. He was standing at one end of the long seminar table, about to write some proofreader's marks on the blackboard and explain what they mean. He said to his students "Now who could that be?" or "Now what can that be?" and he indicated to the student nearest the door to open it, and then said "No, sit; I can do it," and said loudly in the direction of the door "Come in."

He reaches over to the night table for his watch and presses the button on it to light its face. But he's holding the back side of it up and turns it over and presses the button again. Five after seven. Thought so—seven-ten, quarter after—because of the light outside. It was like that early yesterday morning when he looked at his watch. Doesn't want to try sleeping some more and is bored with just lying in bed. Read? No. Time to get up, he supposes. Later he'll take a long nap when the kids are out. Reaches over to the other night table on what used to be his side of the bed and turns the radio on to the Baltimore classical music station. The dial's always set to it; he hasn't moved it since Gwen died. At night, if they were preparing for bed, or he was going to bed before her, he'd turn on the radio to the music. He'd listen to it no matter what it was. Low, though, if it was something he didn't like. If she didn't like what was playing she'd say something like "Do we have to listen to that?" or "Oh, no, not another Strauss waltz" or "Sousa march." In the morning, if they were getting up at the same time—if she was still sleeping or even just resting in bed, he wouldn't turn the radio on—she'd ask him to switch to the public radio station for the news. She didn't read newspapers anymore. Maybe the Book Review in the Sunday *Times*, but that's about it. "I'm tired of turning the pages and seeing the same stories or daily continuations of them, but mostly ads." For the last three years she got all her news from the radio and her computer and what he'd tell her he read in the paper that day and she might find interesting. "You're not missing much," he told her a number of times. A Beethoven piano sonata was on. The volume's low because he doesn't want to wake the kids. He sits on the edge of the bed and listens to it for about two minutes while he does some stretching exercises. It's a late sonata, but not one of the last three. Those he's heard so many times on records and CDs and the radio, he knows them almost by heart. Or at least knows when it's not one of them. Maybe the "Hammerklavier," the 26th or 29th, or whatever number it is. Why's he so sure it's opus 106, when he couldn't give one of the other opuses? The "Appassionata"? Knows it's not "Les Adieux." Liked that one a lot once but hasn't for years and doubts he ever will again. Too schmaltzy. No, definitely the "Appassionata." He'd say to her now, even though he knows she didn't, "You played this once, the 'Appassionata,' didn't you?" And she'd say something like, which she said for another piece he once asked her about, "Never. Much too hard. The only Beethoven I learned to play, or let's say, practiced, was several of the *Bagatelles*. Those were what my piano teacher thought I was ready for after Brahms's *Intermezzo*, not that they were simple. But I never gave enough time to them, so played them quite badly." "I'd still like to hear you play them," he'd say, "and also the *Intermezzo* again. I loved it. More than anything you played. Would you do that for me one day?" and he could see her saying something like "The piano isn't what it was. I have to get it tuned and one of the keys replaced. And I haven't practiced those for years. I'd embarrass myself, even if the piano was in good shape. But maybe." He turns the radio off, Not because the kids might hear. Well, that too. Beautiful as the piece is, or gets to be, he doesn't want to listen to any music; wouldn't care what was on, and doesn't know when he will. He does some stretching exercises on the bed. Oh, what the hell am I exercising for? he thinks. If I hurt, I hurt, and I'll take a couple of aspirins to relieve it. Meaning? He stretches so he won't hurt later, after he exercises, but it's boring and isn't what he wants to do now. Who knows about later. He's been going, before Gwen died, to the Y just about every other day for an hour for years, but isn't sure if he'll ever go back. Just doesn't see himself there anymore. And some people he knows there will ask, and he'll tell them and break down, and he doesn't want that. He gets off the bed, pees, makes the bed—that, he's always done, even before he met Gwen; can't stand an unmade bed—brushes his teeth, flosses out a few irritating pieces, sits on the toilet. While he's sitting, kicks one leg up twenty times—counts as he does—then the other leg twenty times, then each leg twenty times again. Why? To do something while he's sitting here and also maybe it'll get something started. Then he rubs his scalp briskly for about a minute, digs in deeply at the end as he rubs, scratches the back of his head so hard he draws blood. Well, so what? Finds the rubbing and scratching, which he does every morning on the toilet, but not scratching as hard as he did today, make him more wide awake faster. That what he wants? Sure; why not? Sits some more. Nothing comes or even seems to be there, but he thought, as he does every morning, he'd try. Likes to shit first thing in the morning, but should give up trying so hard to. Should try not to obsess over it and to just let it come naturally. Doesn't, then there's the next day, and not that day, the day after. But don't force it. It'll come. If it doesn't by the end of the third day, take some milk of magnesia or mineral oil—there's still some of Gwen's in the refrigerator. Or mix together water and orange or grapefruit juice—she preferred cranberry—with the psyllium husk fiber she used to use once or twice a day. There's almost a whole container of it in one of the kitchen cupboards. He was planning to throw it out, but now he won't. Her medications, she said, made her constipated, and constipation gave her a bellyache. "I don't like talking about it," she once said—oh, not so long ago. Months. "Why not?" he said. "It happens to everybody, or every adult, and you and I have been through everything. I'll do what I can to help you with it, though I don't know what that could be. Shaking up the fiber drink for you till it's absolutely smooth. Anything you ask me to do to make things easier and more comfortable for you." "I still don't like talking about it," she said. "While I'm still able to, I'd like to deal with it myself quietly." "My baby," he said, "I love you, shit and all," and she said "Please don't talk like that, and it's not because it's not a joking matter. It makes me feel worse. And I'm not your baby," and he said "I meant 'my darling, my sweetheart.'" "Did I ever tell you about one incident with my father?" he said to her that time or another, but when they were on the same subject. "When I was living up the block from my folks? I used to make sure every night, around eleven or twelve, that he was all right in his hospital bed in their apartment." "You told me," she said. "I told you that if I came into his room and he'd had a bowel movement since my mother had put him to bed, and you'd know it before you got there, I'd clean him and it up?" "Yes," she said. "I suppose most children couldn't have done it. I doubt I could have." "That's okay. But did I tell you it almost always made me gag and want to throw up? But then I told myself 'You have to get used to it. If you're going to do it, you can't be put off by it. It's just shit. So stick your fingers in it once and that'll cure you of your squeamishness,' and I did and it worked. Didn't gag again, neither coming into the room or taking care of him. Did it like a pro. So don't be concerned about it with me. I'm used to it. I've done it. I can handle it." And she said "I don't want to hear anymore. If it happens, do what you have to, or what I can't do, but please don't talk about it," and he said "I just thought you'd feel easier, knowing." Feels the back of his head. Blood seems to have dried. Should remember to wipe the back of his head with a wet towel in case there's any blood there. Doesn't want to scare the kids. And give up. Nothing's going to come, and he stands up and flushes the toilet. Why did he even flush? For a little pee? They get their water from a well, so he's always trying to conserve water though they've never run dry except when there was an electrical outage.

And look at him, still with the "we" and present tense, and he does mean Gwen and he and not his daughters. That'll change, but he bets not for a year or more. After a number of these outages—most of them short, an hour or two, but one for four days, where he had to get their water from a neighbor—he had a generator installed that automatically turns the electricity on a few seconds after the outage. So what's he saying? Lost track. That he didn't want to be without water with her the last two years, that's why he got the generator. Before, except for that four-day outage—or five, or six; he forgets, but it was unbelievably long and very hard for them—they would use candles and the fireplace and gas stove. It would even be romantic and then joyous or at least cause for cheers when the lights came back on. Because sometimes—and this is the main reason he needed the well working—after almost a week of her being constipated, she would shit several times in an hour, and even after that, most of them normal bowel movements but some so large that they stopped up the toilet when he flushed it and poured over the rim with the water and he then had to use the plunger for he doesn't know how long to unclog it and wipe up the shit and paper and about an inch of water on the floor and give it and the toilet a good cleaning. "I'm so sorry and ashamed," she said the first time, and he said "Don't be. Didn't I tell you that once? It's not a job I like, and I for sure know it's not one you wanted to happen, but what can we do?" The second time, after he flushed the toilet and saw the shit and paper rising to the top, he cried "Oh no-o-o-o," and then screamed when they spilled over the rim, "I can't stand it, I can't stand it," and banged his fists against the wall. She started crying. He thought "Good God, what am I doing? I'm making things worse. She could have another stroke." He said "Okay, I'm better; I got it all out," and told her to kick off her slippers—"Let's try not to track up the rest of the house—and after I finish here I'll wash them or throw them out." Later he said he was sorry. "I swear, I swear; deeply sorry. I obviously wasn't as adjusted to it yet as I thought. But, cleaning it up, I figured out how to avoid the toilet overflowing again when your bowel movements are that large. And I'm not blaming you for them, just saying. First of all, no paper in the toilet. After I wipe you, or you wipe yourself, we'll put the paper into a plastic shopping bag and get rid of it in the garbage. Then I'll get half the feces out with a kitty litter scoop into a pail of some kind with a little water in it and flush it down the other toilet. Or even less than half, but get it down to the size of a normal bowel movement, and do that a couple of times. That should do it," and she said "I hope it works." "It'll work. Why shouldn't it?" and she said "You know, with our luck."

Lets the sink water run hot. Sometimes he gets the hot water in a large plastic container from the kitchen faucet. It comes there faster, so there's less waste. Then swishes around his wet shaving brush inside the shaving soap dish—the same cat-food tin he's used for about the last ten years—and lathers his face and neck. New blade? The last few mornings he's asked himself that and then thought "Tomorrow. I don't want to bother." And today he thinks the shave doesn't have to be that close, for where's he going? The lather's disintegrating, so he starts shaving. Shaves every day. Maybe he should change that. Skip a day now and then, or maybe grow a beard. If he did, it'd come in gray. Finishes the neck and starts on the cheeks, always the right one first. Doesn't think he'd like having a gray beard. It'd just make him look older than he looks already. Mentioned to Gwen about possibly growing one a year ago and she said "How big a beard?" and he said "Full. A goatee or anything like that wouldn't be for me. Too foppish, and they look pasted on," and she said "I don't like kissing a man with a full beard. I don't even like touching it with my hand." "I know; it scratches your face. Lots of women say that. And it probably doesn't feel good when I'm going down on you," and she said "Maybe. But that was so long ago I don't even remember if my bearded man did that to me." "I shouldn't have brought it up," and she said "It's true. It wasn't necessary." Does the chin and above the lip and is finished. He always did a quick shave, with very few cuts. Once did have a beard. Twice. Before he met her. Witch hazel? Don't bother. Once in the summer and his face sweated so much from it, that he shaved it off after a few weeks. Another time, before or after the other one, it itched and he kept scratching it and pulling on the beard, something he doesn't like to see other men do, and every so often he had to tweeze a hair that had got ingrown and hurt. That beard he kept longer. It was almost the same color and texture of his head hair—the only difference was that it had a little red in it—and he felt it made him look artistic. One person even said he looked like van Gogh, which he liked, and another like a young Pissarro, which he didn't know what to make of, and the woman he was seeing at the time said it made him look rugged. But then he felt he was hiding behind it—he wasn't showing his real face; this was around the same time he stopped for good combing his hair over his bald spots—and shaved it off. Shaves every day because he doesn't want to look even slightly like a bum, which is what his father said about men who looked as if they hadn't shaved for two or three days, and he doesn't want to look artistic or rugged either. His father also shaved every day, even when he wasn't going anywhere, till he got sick with a couple of diseases and couldn't shave himself, so he'd shave him almost every morning with an electric razor. Doesn't think he would have been able to do it with—do they still call it this?—a safety razor. His mother said, watching him once, "You can do it better than me because you're a man and you know a man's face. I'd be afraid." She did, last few years of his father's life, give him haircuts and shave the back of his neck with a special attachment on the electric razor. Sits on the bed and starts to dress. Socks from the floor. Doesn't usually start with them, but does today. Then thinks Maybe get a fresh pair. Smells the one in his hand. No smell, but the bottom's dirty and he must have sweated a lot in them yesterday, and he takes off the one he put on and opens the top dresser drawer. Black or white, that's his choice. Both are all cotton, but the white's more an athletic sock and never as tight, and takes out a pair and puts them on. Smells yesterday's shirt at one armpit. Stinks, and he opens the bottom dresser drawer where all his shirts are. Actually, the tank tops are in the top. There are several long-sleeve T-shirts, black and navy blue and all of them cotton, and he takes out a black one because the material's lighter and smoother than the blue, and puts it on. Opens the three middle drawers, which her things are still in, and quickly closes them. Why'd he open them? Doesn't know. Impulse. Wasn't looking for anything. Got a whiff of her perfume in the most middle drawer, but that wasn't why he opened it. That'll always be her smell, more than anything. Thought of something like that last night. Can't imagine what he'd do if he started up with a new woman sometime and she wore that same perfume. That's a scene for a short story. He'd say to her next time not to and tell her why. Anybody would understand. Or he wouldn't say. He'd just fantasize. Might be nice. If he'd be seeing that woman he thinks he'd eventually be sleeping with her, that's how it's always been, and if she had on that perfume in bed? What's he going into? That he'd make love with another woman? Sure, one day, he'd want to, but a long ways from today. Not a long ways from wanting to but from doing it. Hard to imagine, too. Actually, not hard at all. Naked, feeling each other, kissing, hugging, sucking, breasts, cunt, pubic hair, going down on each other, or just him on her—anything to get him excited—sticking it in? How do you first get to bed, though? You're at either of your places and drinking and kissing and maybe feeling and one of you, as Gwen did to him, says "Think we should go to bed?" That's all it took. After that it gets much easier, or used to. But it might never happen again with him. Not just because of the way he is now, his depression, if that's what it is. And his predisposition to solitude—well, he was always like that a little—that might last and even, longer he cuts himself off from people, get worse. But his age, primarily, and what he'd call his wariness or even his fright at getting involved enough with someone new to make love with, and so on. "And so on" what? Other things he hasn't thought of, and maybe not so much the ones he gave. So then what? Just jerking off for the rest of his life? Buying girlie magazines, raunchier the better? Those vacant faces in them, those beautiful bodies? Going into a convenience store—parking in front just to buy the magazine—and taking one off the rack and paying for it and getting back change? Doesn't see himself doing that. Did before he met Gwen, once or twice a year when he wasn't living with a woman, but never felt comfortable doing it, and now? But he'll have to, won't he? What other way? Subscribe? How do you, and he'd just want one issue, not one mailed to him every month. He'd keep it under some shirts in his dresser drawer, wouldn't use it all the time, because how many times could he do it to the same nudes before he gets tired of them? But maybe the photos are so graphic now, and there are so many different nudes in each issue and a wide variety of poses, that one issue would be good for a year or so and almost every time. Because how often would he jerk off? Once a week? More likely, every other week? Has seen them in those stores. Band around them or shrink-wrapped, so you couldn't open them at the stand. Lingerie issue. Back-to-College issue. Summer Girls. They have to be a lot more revealing than they were thirty years ago. Has a hard-on but not a full one. Not the first he's had since she died but the first that's come while he was awake and thinking about sex. Plays with it a little but with no thought of ejaculating. Just curious. Doesn't get harder or larger and he didn't think it would, and stops. Not while his daughters are still here. Think of something else. Finish getting dressed. He's thirsty and a little hungry too. Did he eat yesterday? Knows he drank. He ate. Little. Baby carrots. A cracker. Piece of cheese. Some celery sticks. He's not starving. And less he eats, less he'll need to shit. Should suggest to them they take whatever they want of hers from the dresser and closets. And dishes and pots and pans and cookbooks and cutlery they might be able to use and artwork she owned before she knew him and stuff she bought after they married. Antique goose decoy on the fireplace mantel and several smaller ones of ducks around the house. Miniature Russian icon triptych her parents gave her and her first husband when they got married, but maybe that's too valuable. Also on the mantel: two tiny porcelain figurines in a bell jar she got at a silent auction in Maine. He likes that piece. "The old couple seems so happily married and physically right for each other," he once said to her, "I can't think of looking at them without thinking of us," so maybe he'll keep that one too, and the kids move around a lot and the bell jar would be too fragile to travel. Binoculars she observed birds with from her study here and apartment they had on Riverside Drive and desk in Maine. Victorian candlestick he gave her for her birthday a half year after they met. So many things. Too many for one person living alone. Wants to clear out half the house. Furniture and linen if they need some in their cities. But senses it's too soon for them. They even said so, so why harp on it? He knows how they feel. They feel the way he does. And he's sure they have enough reminders of her for now. Fresh boxer shorts. The old ones he didn't have to smell. Thinks it's been two days, and after he zips up or just pulls up his pants if he's been sitting on the toilet he frequently pisses or drips a little into the shorts. Pants off the chair. Nah, get your sweatpants. Be comfortable, and no pants are more comfortable, and he hangs these up on a hook in the closet and gets the sweats out and puts them on. Sneakers. Fresh handkerchief. Two ballpoint pens in one side pants pocket and memobook in the other. Doesn't need his watch because he knows he's not going anywhere today. Starts out of the room with his dirty clothes. His glasses. How could he have forgotten? And goes back and puts them on and goes into the kitchen and drops the clothes into the washing machine. Some of the kids' clothes are in it and a tablecloth and dish towels. Tablecloths they should also take. Doesn't know why Gwen had so many, because they almost always, when they had guests for dinner, used the same green and yellow one from India with matching cloth napkins. On the dryer next to the washing machine's a note from Maureen. "Hi Daddy. We hope you slept well. We'll be sleeping late unless you need us for anything. We've been meaning to tell you. We have Mommy's cell phone if you want to start using it. It's part of a group plan. You must know that. You've been paying for it for years. It allowed the three of us, when Mommy was alive, to call each other anytime of the day for free. The phone's being recharged now in Roz's room. But we have to warn you. It has Mommy's voice on it. Just her saying her name when the automated voice says she's not available and your message has been forwarded to an automated voice message machine. If you do want her phone, and we hope so because that would mean Roz and I would be able to talk to you more, we'd like to keep Mommy's voice on it. Do you mind? We think it would be nice to hear Mommy every time we call you and the message system picks up. Love from Roz and me. Maureen." He writes under her note "Dear Maureen. I would like to take over Mommy's phone. I wasn't aware of the cell phone message—I suppose I should've assumed so—but if you both want to keep it on, fine with me. I'd get upset hearing her speak myself. But there's no reason that should happen unless I call the cell phone just to hear her voice, which I don't see myself ever doing. Love, Dad." Then thinks But what's with this note business? He'll tell them all this when he sees them, and tears up the note and sticks the pieces into the recycle bag next to the trash can. It's almost full. Later he'll stuff all the paper down in it so they won't blow around when he brings it outside to the carport, and open up another bag by the can. Looks through the kitchen door. Could have just looked at the inside light switch by the door. Outside lights have been turned off. Now he remembers. Her mother kept giving her tablecloths, ones she brought with her from Russia and others she bought here for Gwen, and she said she didn't have the heart to tell her she already had more than she could use. "The kids will take them," and he said "Don't count on it. Most are a little dowdy." Her cameras. Two very good ones. She liked taking pictures of birds, especially hummingbirds at the various feeders if she could get her camera quick enough, and flowers and the star magnolia in bloom and their cats. Those he thinks the kids will want to take when they leave. They're not as personal as most of the other things he mentioned, and a number of times they needed a good camera to take pictures a photo lab would turn into slides of their work. Doubts he'll be taking pictures anymore. Took a lot of them of the kids and her, in Maine, mostly with cheap throwaway cameras. Plenty of her alone too, even though she never wanted him to, when she was still healthy. How could he not? She always looked so great in them. And those Polaroid nude shots of her—how'd he ever get her to let him?—when she was seven months pregnant with Rosalind, ones he ended up with only one good one of and she said she tore up. Maybe she didn't and only threatened to and then forgot about it. One day he'll look for it and the two or three others he took that time and which were too dark and blurry to see anything and would probably, if they survived, be worse now. Go through all the boxes and file drawers in her study she kept most of their photos in. They're certainly not in any of the albums. Didn't he think this last night? Yes, but not that they might still be around. Wishes he'd taken a few of her nude when she wasn't pregnant. Standing facing him. Sitting in a chair like an artist model—that's how he could have worded it to her. Lying on the bed or couch with her back or front to him. But he knows she wouldn't have let him if he'd asked. But he should have asked. What a dope that he didn't. "They're Polaroids," he would have said. "Nobody will see them but me." "What do you want them for?" she might have said. "You have me," and he would have said "For when I'm away." Well, he didn't know things would turn out like this. Her feeling, he thinks, was that her body in the pregnant photos no way resembled hers, which is why she went along with the two or three she let him take. He thinks she even said something like that. "I'm unrecognizable. Look at my breasts and stomach and from what I can see of my buttocks. Even my face is a bit bloated and my thighs seem fatter too, though I suppose everything but my breasts will go back to the way they were before." Anyway, he doesn't know how to use either of her cameras, or even load them. She showed him once, but he's long forgot. I'll never remember," he said. "I like simple cameras." So he'll insist the kids take them. "They're wasted here," he'll say. "And you each can use one, and it won't take you anything to learn how. I'm sure you have friends who'll show you. If there's film still in the cameras, just develop them and send me the ones you think I might find interesting. I'm sure there's none of Mom. And while we're at it," he'll say, "maybe you can take back with you a lot of the photographs too. Help me to start getting rid of things." Opens the dishwasher. Nothing in it. All the dishes and such from yesterday have been washed and put away. Good. They did everything right. Countertops even look cleaned. Not a crumb. Opens the refrigerator. Plenty of food in it in plastic containers and bowls covered by saucers and plates. He never had plastic wrap—the environment—and Gwen agreed they didn't need it. And then the stuff that's always in there. So, plenty for them, and if there isn't there what they want for breakfast and lunch they can take his car and get it. He'll give them money or say "Use the credit card you have of mine." They'll probably want to go for coffee at the nearby Starbucks on North Charles as they do almost every morning when they're here together, and ask him if he wants to join them, and he'll say "Not today and maybe not tomorrow. I don't know when. But enjoy yourselves and use the credit card I gave you for anything you want there," and they might say they have their own credit cards. The one they have of his is only for plane and train fares and taxis late at night and emergencies, and he'll say "While you're here, everything should be on me. That's what Mommy would want for you too." Or maybe not the last. Sleek seems to have been taken care of before they went to bed. Still plenty of kibble in his food bowl and water bowl's full almost to the top. All the cat food on the saucer's been eaten. They may have even given him some sliced turkey and other deli meat that was out there. He gets the saucer off the floor and washes it with the scrub side of the sponge and puts it in the dish rack by the sink. Only thing in the dish rack; not even a spoon. That's how thorough they were, and dish rack mat's been cleaned too. He'll open a can of cat food—didn't see an opened one in the refrigerator, but he might have missed it it was so crowded in there—and spoon half a can of it onto the saucer next time he sees Sleek. If the wet food's been out there too long—a half-hour, an hour—he won't eat it. Thinks he hasn't seen him since yesterday, and then not much. Could he be outside? The girls wouldn't have let him out at night intentionally. But he has a way of scooting out the door when you open it without you seeing him. And some days he lets him in and out so much he doesn't know if he's out or in. Gwen used to ask him "You see Sleek?" and he'd say "Cat makes me dizzy. I don't know if the last time I saw him was when I let him in the house or let him out, I have to do both for him so much." Maybe he's sleeping somewhere or just keeping to himself. Sleek loved Gwen—he could say that about a cat? He swears it sometimes seemed he was looking adoringly at her—and it's possible he knows she's dead and misses her deeply. Sleek came into the room when she was being lifted onto the gurney by the Emergency people that last time—the door was closed till then—and sniffed at all their shoes and the wheels of the gurney and then ran out of the room and hid somewhere in the house till that evening. When she was sick in bed with the flu or a bad cold or worse or was just reading or resting, he'd lie beside her and raise a front paw with the claws out and hiss at anyone who came near her but the kids. Even him. Scratched him a few times when he got too close. "Sleek, *n-o-o*" she'd say, and then to him once, "Don't worry. He loves you as much as he loves me. It's just he thinks you can take care of yourself and I need protection. He has such old-fashioned notions about females." One hears of dogs suffering when their owners die, but cats? Wasn't it Gwen who told him that her dissertation advisor's dog, a corgi, hours after the man died of pancreatic cancer in his summer home in Maine, walked out of the house and down to the shore that bordered the property and swam out into the ocean and drowned? It *was* Gwen, this happened the summer before they met, and it was another type of cancer, one also very quick and with a small chance of curing, and the dog kept swimming farther and farther out—the man's children on shore were calling her back and then went after her in a rowboat—till the waves went over her and she disappeared. "Was she found?" he remembers asking, and she said "Days later, a couple of coves away." He'd never heard anything like that with cats. Devoted, but dying? He'd have to ask someone who knows much more about them than he, but he won't; he'll forget. Or something. Gwen said she took her advisor's death very badly. He and his wife by this time had become close friends of hers. He unlocks and opens the kitchen door and goes outside. Maybe he is out. "Sleek? Sleek?" he says. Walks to both ends of the carport and a few feet along the driveway. "Sleek, you out here?" We don't want to lose you.

That would be too much," and he starts crying and wipes his eyes with his sleeve. "Oh, shit, what the hell is happening to me?" he says. "This whole fucking thing is making me crazy. Please, Sleek, if you're out here, listen to me. You have to come home." He whistles for him and makes tsking sounds with his mouth, something he does to get him back into the house when it's getting dark outside or into the kitchen from another room when he puts fresh food on the floor. But what's he thinking? Cat's got to be inside. It's what he previously thought: the kids would have made sure he was in before they locked the outside doors and shut off all the lights and went to their rooms. He's probably with one of them. If he is, they'd keep the door partially open, and he goes in to look and both their doors are closed. He's still sure Sleek's with one of them. Just, whoever he's with forgot to leave her door open so he could get water or food in the kitchen or use the litter box in the hallway bathroom. But they both know if he wants to get out of a room and the door's shut, he'd stand on his back paws and scratch the door till they opened it. Everything's all right. Again, he's making something out of nothing. Well, he's fragile; has become so; look at it that way, what can he do? He's grieving, let's face it, grieving, and that might go on for he doesn't know how long, so cry all you want. Cry when you feel like crying. Cry when the feeling swoops over you for you don't know what reason, but don't go batty, that's all. And if you can, try to keep it to when you're alone. If the kids happen to witness it, and it wasn't that their crying precipitated it, that'd be okay, too. Is he making sense? He thinks so. As he said before, everything's okay, at least for now. Though maybe Sleek heard him calling his name before and only just came back. He looks outside though the kitchen door and then goes outside to look. No, Sleek's inside. And while he's out here, should he get today's newspapers by the mailbox? It'll only take a few seconds. But a neighbor might drive down the hill on his way to work or the gym and stop to ask him how he is and he'd have to speak, if he couldn't wave him off, and then what? He's not ready. And he doesn't want to read the news. Knows that much about himself. Doesn't want to hear it on the radio either. Doesn't want to look at the papers for anything that might be in them. He won't cancel his subscriptions, but he doesn't know when he might want to look at them again. If he thinks it's going to be a while—more than two weeks—he'll cancel. But now he doesn't see himself sitting in his Morris chair with his mug of coffee on the chair's arm, as he's done with the *Sun* just about every morning for around the last twenty years. Or the *Times* at night before dinner for probably the same number of years, with a drink on the chair's arm. First reading the headlines of each paper and then the beginnings of two or three of the articles underneath them. Then turning to page two of the first section of the *Times* to see what section and page the obituaries of noteworthy people are in. If it's of someone who might interest him—a writer, a war hero, a baseball player or movie actor or actress or entertainer like that who was prominent when he was a kid or till he was around sixteen or eighteen—he usually reads it. The ones of fiction writers and poets and literary critics he always reads. The *Sun's* obituaries he's less interested in unless it's someone he knows or is familiar with personally or the obituary headline says he went through some war experience or something like that, and they're always in the same place in the paper, right after the op-ed page at the end of the first section. Then reading the various sections of the papers in no regular order. And today's weather, tonight's, tomorrow's, sometimes the box that has the national forecast, and on the same weather report page, what the temperatures are in Fargo and Phoenix and Los Angeles and Des Moines. Old friends of his now live in the last two cities, or the friend in Iowa in a small city forty miles from Des Moines, and he liked to see what the weather was like for them there. Fargo and Phoenix because it gets so cold in one and hot in the other and it sort of was a game he played with himself comparing the two temperature extremes on the same day. He also checked almost every day what the temperature and forecast were in Paris. Gwen and he had lived there by themselves at different times in their lives and stayed there three times together for up to two weeks, once with Rosalind and the last time with both kids, and talked about renting an apartment there for a couple of months on his next sabbatical. Could they have done that? Doesn't think so. Not after her first stroke, or definitely her second. Of course, New York too, and he also would have liked to see what the weather was like every day in the area they summered at in Maine for so many years, but the closest city listed, Portland, is more than a hundred-fifty miles away. Just realized: he exchanges letters with those two friends every month or so, and next time he writes them, and he doesn't know when he'll feel like doing that again, he'll have to tell them about Gwen. "I have very bad news. My dear Gwen…" But very short. If he first gets a letter from them—he forgets who owes whom—they'll ask about her and hope she's well, as they always do, and for him to give her their best or love. If he doesn't write them for months after that, they'll sense—probably even before—something's wrong because of her two previous strokes, and call, and he'll have to tell them then. "I want to make this quick. It's been months, but I still have trouble talking about it. Our dear Gwen…" Maybe he'd be better off writing them a brief note in the next week. In almost one sentence, that she suffered another stroke at home and died in the hospital and when—the exact date—and that he's unable to write any more about it now. And if they call to offer their condolences and find out how he is? "As you got from my note, it's impossible for me to talk about it. Maybe down the line sometime. I'm sorry for being so abrupt—you know that's not the typical me—but I'll have to say goodbye." No, they'll worry. Just say it's been a terrific blow, but he's all right and for them not to worry about him and he'll call sometime soon, which he won't. What's he doing? There is no way; he can see that. Maybe if he gets the kids to write his two friends about Gwen and anybody else who doesn't know she died but probably should, though he can't think of anyone else right now. In her address book and computer she has a number of names of friends and scholars in her field and home-care providers—women who looked after her while she was recovering and he was at work—they say they didn't contact about her death or for the memorial, but he assumes they knew what they were doing. Didn't mean anything to him who came to the memorial or not. They can say to his two friends that their father asked them to write. But they shouldn't say anything more about him except, if they want, that he's all right. Ah, let them write what they want. They're bright, tactful, sensitive to other people's feelings; they'll write good letters. The important thing is to get it out of the way. They can even use the same letter for both his friends and anyone else they might want to write to about Gwen. So that's what he'll do. As he said, his friends and whoever else will just have to understand why it's not coming from him. So where was he? Thinking about something, but what? The papers. News. What he read in them every day and in what order. Important? Doubts it. But he was thinking about it for some reason, so maybe he'll find out why by finishing the thought. Reviews after what was the last thing he said he read. And that was? Forgets. *Sun* didn't have many of them. Maybe a Baltimore Symphony concert during the week and a new TV show or two and a play once a month and always movies—lots of them—every Friday. *Times*, of course, had them all the time. He rarely read the *Times'* reviews of dance or popular music or architecture or Broadway musicals, and in the *Sun* he doesn't think he read a single review of a musical that came to Baltimore. Didn't read TV reviews in either paper, except of *Masterpiece Theatre* and a few other PBS specials, but only so he could tell Gwen about them. She watched and he sometimes did to have a couple of glasses of wine during them, but mainly to keep her company in the bedroom so she wouldn't watch them alone, especially the weeks after she returned home from the hospital. He thinks that's the second time since last night he mentioned that, maybe the third. Why? Pictures her sitting in a chair in front of the television, not looking well but a lot better than when she was in the hospital, and…what? Shudders. Sees her sick. Weak. Everything an effort. Closes his eyes, opens them. She's gone. She'd look at him from the chair, smile. He'd say "Program's pretty good. I'm enjoying it," and she'd smile again, glad he was there, and look back at the television. Did she believe him? Probably not. "Can I get you something?" he'd say several times while they watched the program. "I don't mind missing a little," and she'd shake her head or say no. She must have known he was going into the kitchen to fill up his glass. Did she think "He needs to drink to be with me?" No. "Are you comfortable? Do you want a pillow for your back? You've been in that position for so long," and sometimes she'd say yes and he'd get it for her, or something to cover her legs. Oh, if only he could have had her illness for her. He means that. Easy to think it, though, right? But he would have. And then, if that was the deal, she could get whatever was coming to him later on. But she was almost eleven years younger than he, so she'd have those extra pretty healthy years, at least. And then who knows how he'll go. Maybe in his sleep overnight. Maybe a stroke in his sleep that'd kill him the first time. Stupid thoughts. Why think them? They don't make sense and what do they bring? Not comfort, that's for sure. Dreams of her do. The ones on which she's healthy and not angry at him. The best are when they're embracing and deeply kissing, better than the ones with sex. Why? They feel real, the two or so he's had. After he woke up from them, for a few seconds, he still felt her on his lips. Crazy, he knows, but it made him feel good, as if she'd forgiven him. The sex dreams he's had always ended before he came, and he woke up frustrated. No, in one he came. But the papers. Get to the end of your thought. Which reviews did he also read? Never of video games, something new in reviews and which hasn't come to the *Sun* yet. It will. The games have become too popular not to. Also, never of movies listed as having strong violence or were for children or seemed geared to adolescents or even to people in their twenties. *Times'* review he usually read first of the many it'd have of different things on just an ordinary weekday—not Friday—was the book one if it seemed like an interesting subject to get some quick knowledge of or a book he might want to buy and read. Always looking for them, or used to. Couldn't imagine not having a book to read. Not reading anything now. Looks at the first page of a book he took out of one of the bookcases or the page he last left off at of the novel he was reading before she died and can't concentrate, reads the first sentence or paragraph over and over again and still can't quite make sense of it no matter how simply it's written, and puts the book down or back. *Demons*, a new translation, was more than halfway through it. Liked it? Kept his interest. Lots of good characters and dialog and he liked that some of what they said was in French with translations at the bottom of the page. Read a much earlier translation of the book under a different title more than fifty years ago when he was eighteen, nineteen, and he read almost straight through everything of his he could find in the Donnell Library on 53rd Street. Seemed the best place to get them. He's saying it had shelves and shelves of Dostoevsky. He remembers where they were: in back, on the extreme right, first floor. He'll go back to the book or start another. When, he doesn't know, but he has to. What else is there for him to do? Make soup, a salad, clean the house, launder his clothes once a week and his linens every other, resume his workouts at the Towson Y three–four times a week when he's ready to? Maybe, once the kids leave, he'll go every day, just to be around people and lots of noisy activity for an hour and use the showers there, which are much better than his. And watch one of the cable news shows while he's on the exercise bike, after he's done with the resistance machines and weights, or switch around from one news station to the other or movie channel if it's a good film. In other words, to get out of the house to do something other than shop or take a short walk in the neighborhood around dusk and maybe once or twice during it say "Hello" or "Good evening" to someone he passes. He might even start using the Y's pool if the water's warm enough. But he's a ways from doing any of that yet. Will he go back to teaching? Doesn't think so, at least not for a while. He can't see himself seeing any-body who knew Gwen, without breaking down. Did he ever go to the ballet with Gwen? Just thinking. The opera, of course, many times in Baltimore and New York, but the ballet? Once, in Baltimore, with the kids about ten years ago. Forgets the name of the company—it was from France and they sat in the orchestra because the balcony was sold out. One of the dances was to a recording that sounded like a full orchestra in the pit and a singer off to the side of the stage of Strauss' *Four Last Songs*, a piece Gwen and he loved before they even knew each other and which was why they thought they had to go. Oh, yeah. Another time, just the two of them, more than twenty years ago at the State Theater he thinks it was still called then in Lincoln Center. Her mother bought them the tickets and looked after Rosalind that night. He thinks they went to a Japanese Restaurant for dinner after—Ozu. No, that's the one they liked in the Eighties on Amsterdam or Columbus. Dan, on Broadway and 68th. Their first time there. Funny how things come back. Remembers during an intermission looking down to the lobby from one of the top floors and wondering if anyone in all the years this place has been here had jumped from it. And then the hospital she was brought to after her first stroke. There was a walkway—a bridge over a huge atrium, really—to her intensive care unit, overlooking some other part of the hospital three to four floors below. Maternity, the waiting area, and he thought when he stopped on it if anyone…not "if anyone." He thought if she dies he might come here and check that nobody's directly below him and throw himself off. Why? Thought it several times when he walked over the bridge and stopped and rested his forearms on the railing and looked down, but not the second time she had a stroke and was brought to the same ICU. Because he didn't think he could live without her. Well, can he? Has to. The kids. Their mother dying so suddenly? Gwen's mother, whom they also loved very much, committing suicide six years before? Then their father going the same way? That's just what they needed. And he'll find other good reasons not to, but that one stands out. Anyway—get off that subject— since Gwen and he liked ballet and modern dance and most of the music for them, how come they didn't go more? And both girls were in dance classes for years, as was Gwen when she was young and her mother took her to see lots of ballet, so why didn't they take them? Doesn't know. No, not that excuse again. Maybe it never came up. But he's making himself less observant than he is. He read the *Sun* every day. He always knew what was playing in town—movies, plays, music, museum shows—since there wasn't that much. What's true is that very few dance companies came through Baltimore, and like the one they finally went to, usually for just one perfor- mance and at night. And so they might have wanted to take them to other dance concerts but it was a school night, let's say, or in some other way the timing wasn't right. Also, the Garry Trudeau comic strip on the op-ed page of the *Sun*. That, he read first when he turned to that page. And in both papers, he'd say about half the letters to the editor. Although in the *Times*, all of them if they were on a subject he was deeply interested in and wanted to read other opinions of or get reinforcement of his own—the war in Iraq, for instance; torture there; tax laws that so one-sidedly favored the very rich; the current president. He wrote a few letters to the *Times* but always tore them up, two or three in the envelopes he'd already addressed, sealed and stamped. Other people were able to write these letters on the same subjects so much more articulately and succinctly and informatively than he and get their outrage across without, like him, sounding a bit crazy. And some of the papers' op-ed articles and editorials and, in the baseball season, the sports pages. He never opened the Styles section of the *Times* or that other section in it the same Thursday, rarely looked at its Tuesday science section or the *Sun*'s health section unless there was an article on strokes or caregiving or something that might relate to his own health or talked about the aging process or memory loss or drinking too much or the vitamin supplements he takes or should be taking at his age. Starts every morning with one of several different pills, but he can take them later today or wait till tomorrow. No hurry. What's a day or two? And what do they do for him anyhow? Forgets why he started taking them years ago. Gwen encouraged him to. But what's folic acid and Vitamin E and B-50 for, and so on? Why not a different B, and why the E 400 pill and not another number? Gwen knew. Maybe he'll stop taking them altogether or just take C and the baby aspirin once a day? Didn't open the business section in the papers either unless, as in the *Times*, it was where the sports pages, and again only during baseball season, or obituaries were that day. He's back in the house. Doesn't remember walking to it or even opening the kitchen door to get inside and doesn't know how long he's been here. Few seconds? More than a minute? What else has he missed? Later he'll ask one of the girls to get the newspapers from the driveway. He'll say he doesn't want to read them but they can if they want. They also might want to see what movies are playing. If they feel like it, they should go to one tonight. Might be a nice distraction, he'll say, and he'll be fine alone. Or just take the papers out of their plastic bags and put them in the recycle bag by the trash can. He empties Sleek's water bowl into one of Gwen's Christmas cactuses on the dining room windowsill. They're so pretty when they bloom. There must be six or seven of them and they all started from pieces of a plant that had broken off, and the first one from a broken-off piece someone had given her when they lived in their first house, and they all always start flowering about the same time of the year. She fed them plant food a couple of times a year, and if he can't find it—it came in a box with a little plastic scoop—he'll ask the girls to go to a garden store and get the right one. Feels inside the water bowl. It's not slimy, which it can get if it's not washed with detergent every three or four times. He fills the bowl with fresh water and puts it back on the kitchen floor. Thinks: Didn't he already do that this morning? Knows he thought of opening a new can of cat food and emptying half of it onto Sleek's plate and putting the plate on the floor next to the water bowl, but only when he comes out from wherever he is. Cat's gotten so picky. Won't eat the canned food if it's been sitting around on the floor for more than half an hour. What next? To do. Coffee he definitely wants and can use. What mug today? Big decisions he's left with. Looks at the six mugs hanging on pegs attached to the bottom of the spice rack on the wall. Most of the spices are way past their "best by" date and should be thrown out. Will he replace them? Doubts it. Probably just the curry powder and cumin for soups and maybe the red pepper flakes. Last couple of years he really only cooked for her and for a few small dinner parties they gave, but otherwise he didn't care what he ate. Didn't he already think that too? Something like it. Nothing new to say. But he doesn't think he'll get interested in cooking again, unless it's for the kids when they're here. And all those special German knives and French pots and pans she had before they met. More things to give to the kids. For himself, if he wants something more than a sandwich or salad or quick soup he'll make, he'll rely mostly on restaurant take-out and prepared and ready-to-cook foods from the local food market. He has more mugs in a kitchen cupboard, no two alike, and he never uses the one he drank from the morning before. Any reason why? Seems silly. He should break the habit. All right, he'll break it, but some other day. The ceramic one's his favorite. There were two—a friend's wife in Maine made them—but he broke one, or Gwen did, just a few months ago. The mugs were given to them as a good-bye gift the last time they saw the couple there. Gwen and he gave them that same day a copy of a book each of them wrote. "I never know what to inscribe," he said to her, and she said "Just say 'with love.' You mean it." "Is that what you're going to say?" and she said yes and he said "Well, we can't say the same thing. I'll think of something," but he forgets what. The couple—they're both around eighty—lives year-round in the woods there, about three hours north of the cottage they last rented, painting and potting, and also don't know about Gwen. He should make a list. The ceramic mug, and Gwen felt the same way, is not only nice to look at but to put his hands around, so smooth because of the special glaze, which might have been why it slipped out of whoever's hands were holding it. Odd he can't remember whose. But the black mug keeps the coffee hot longer; what he wants today before the kids get up: to just sit down in a quiet place and drink slowly. Its better heat containment—now that's a fancy term for it and possibly a wrong one—might have something to do with what it's made of, the thickness of it, maybe also the color; something, and the handle's large enough for him to get his three fingers in, the only mug he has where he can do that. Gwen could do that with most of their mugs; he's even seen her get four fingers in some, her fingers were so thin. Takes the black mug off its peg and puts it beside the coffeemaker on the other side of the sink from the dish drainer and rubber mat. Some heated-up soy milk with it, maybe half? Easier on the stomach. Too much bother, and then the saucepan to wash. Really has to scrub hard with the sponge to get all the soymilk off the bottom of it. But again, much better for the stomach so early. Nah, a quicker pick-me-up if it's all black. Turns the coffeemaker on and goes into the living room, where he'll wait till the coffee's made. He'll hear it, after all the water's gone through: the hissing and steaming and a sound that's almost like someone gargling. He sits in the Morris chair. No need to turn the floor lamp on. Most times before, when he sat like this waiting for the morning coffee to be made, he did it with something to read. Did he buy this chair or the Maillol print in his bedroom with some of the money from the first story he sold to a major magazine? Whichever it was, the other he bought with just about all the money he got from the first sale of a story to any magazine. Someone suggested he do that. His mother, he thinks: "This way you'll always have a tangible reminder of your first acceptance" or "sale." He got both so cheap. Chair in a used furniture store at the Columbus Avenue corner of the block he lived on, and the print—actually, a woodcut of a clothed peasant woman sleeping on her back in a field—at Brentano's bookstore on Fifth. Suddenly he thinks of a dream he had between Gwen's first and second strokes, but when she seemed fully recovered. Now where the hell did that come from? he thinks. He wrote it down when he woke up from it. Gwen pushed herself up on her elbows— she'd been sleeping on her back, so the peasant woman? Gwen?—and said "Why's the light on? It's still dark out. You feeling okay?" and he said "Sorry. Dream I had. I want to write it down or I'll lose it. It's so interesting, I'll tell you about it later," and he finished writing it in the notebook he kept on his night table and shut the light and probably turned to her—she was already asleep on her side—and held her from behind and went back to sleep. It was one of several dreams he wrote down around that time and he must have read it when he woke up later or sometime after, and maybe a number of times. It seemed pretty clear what it meant then, but you never know. He remembers thinking it was one of the more vivid dreams he'd had with her in it. They were on Broadway, walking north on the west side of the street, between 115th and 116th Streets, which was a block away from where they had their Riverside Drive apartment till a few years ago. They were on their way to a restaurant on 117th Street and Broadway for lunch. There is no restaurant there; no side street, either; none till about a Hundred-twentieth. Just Barnard: a college dormitory or school building, he forgets which. He'd passed it many times on his way to or back from a garage farther north on Broadway. About twenty young doctors, male and female, all in lab coats, he thinks they're called, or just white coats, the kind they wear when they make their hospital rounds.

The doctors stopped at the 116th Street corner and waited for the light to turn green. They stood behind the doctors. Then he said "Let's go around them. I'm sure they're going to the same restaurant, and if they get there before us we won't be able to get a table." He put his hand on her back and guided her into the street and they started to cross a Hundred-sixteenth against the light. Cars going both ways had to stop so they could get to the other side. A couple of cars honked at them, and she looked alarmed. "Don't be worried," he said. "You're with me. You're safe." They got across the street and he looked back. The light hadn't changed yet and the doctors were still standing on the corner. Most of them gave Gwen and him dirty looks, as if they shouldn't have gone in front of them and then crossed the street against the light. She said "They look angry. I don't like people to be angry because of me or something I did. Maybe we should wait for them here and apologize." He said "And let them get in front of us and to the restaurant first? You're okay. It was nothing you did." He took her hand and said "I love you." She looked lovingly at him and said "I love you too." "Good, we're in love," he said, "so nothing should really bother us," and they continued walking, holding hands. When they were a few feet from the restaurant, he said "I know what I'm going to have. Their chicken salad platter, if they're not all out of it," and she said "And I'm going to have their fried oysters." "Less chance they'll have those left than my chicken salad," he said, "but maybe you'll be lucky. I hope so. I know how much you love them." She smiled and said "You bet." That he especially remembers from the dream. It was something he used to say a lot and she never did. But she adopted it the last few years and he, for the most part, stopped saying it because he felt the expression had become more hers than his, and he knew how much she liked saying it. No, that's not quite it. Then what is? She used so few colloquialisms in her speech that he didn't want to make her self-conscious of sort of stealing this one from him and stop saying it. No, that's not quite it, either. He opened the door of the restaurant and stepped aside so she could get past him. The place was crowded. He took her hand again and led her to the one free table. The dream ended. Oh, there was a little more—they looked at the luncheon specials on a blackboard as they made their way to the table—but that was basically it. A nice dream. Long. Nothing bad happened. The doctors never caught up with them. The day was sunny and mild and the restaurant was brightly lit inside only by daylight coming through the windows. She was well, happy through most of it, and looked so pretty. They were hungry and about to eat. They held hands. They loved each other. But why didn't they kiss? Would have been a nice way to end the dream or to happen right after they said they loved each other. But what he dreamt was good enough. He doesn't know if he told her the dream when they woke up later that morning or after they got out of bed. If he ever told her. He told her just about all his dreams she was in except those where she died or was dead or very sick. Or if she was in one where one of the kids died. What's that smell? Electric? As if a short, or something like that, and coming from the kitchen, it seems, and he gets up and goes into it. Coffeemaker's sputtering, making almost hiccupping sounds. Thinks he knows what it is; same thing's happened to him once or twice. Shuts off the coffeemaker, takes the carafe off the warming plate, shakes it, and nothing's inside. Opens the water tank cover and looks inside. It's what he thought. Dummy; dummy. He didn't put water in the tank or a paper filter into the filter basket, so of course also no coffee grounds in the paper. He usually does all this the night before—sometimes even the afternoon before, when he knows he has enough coffee in his thermos for the rest of the day—so he won't have to do it the same morning he's going to make the coffee. It doesn't make for better coffee. It might even make it worse, with the water staying in the tank so long, and who knows if the coffee grounds aren't weakened or marred or something a little by being in the same closed compartment with the water all night. But he likes the idea of just walking into the kitchen the next morning and, without any preparations, pressing the on switch to get the coffee started. He fills the carafe with water up to the four-cup level inside. Waits another fifteen seconds to make sure the heating coils, or whatever they are, aren't still too hot to pour the water in, which might harm the machine, and empties the carafe into the tank. He puts a paper filter into the filter basket, flattens the seams of the paper so none of the dripping water goes down the outside of it, chooses the bag of Colombia Supremo coffee grounds over the Kona—it's lighter, so more a morning coffee, and smells and tastes better; he's never going to get the Kona again but will use up what he has—and puts three tablespoons of it into the paper and turns the coffeemaker on. Go back to the living room chair while the coffee's being made? Why? It'll take no more than four minutes. He can even pour some coffee in mid-brew by taking the carafe off the warming plate, which stops the flow for up to thirty seconds, so maybe he'll do that. But then the coffee will be too strong for so early in the morning, unless he adds soymilk. He opens the refrigerator and takes the soymilk out. But he wants his coffee hot and black—that's what he feels like this morning—so better wait till it's done, and he puts the soymilk back. No, he'll have some now and sit with it, and he pulls the carafe out and pours the little that's in it into the mug.

Fantagraphics Books
7563 Lake City Way NE
Seattle, Washington 98115

Editorial: Gary Groth
Proofreader: Paul Maliszewski
Designer: Jacob Covey
Editorial Assistants: Tom Graham and Janice Lee
Associate Publisher: Eric Reynolds
Publishers: Gary Groth and Kim Thompson

Excerpts from *His Wife Leaves Him* have been published in the following
publications: *Boulevard, Fifth Wednesday, J&L Illustrated, Johns Hopkins
Magazine, Per Contra,* The *Doctor T.J. Eckleburg Review,* The *Hopkins Review,*
and *Three Quarters Review.*

To receive a free full-color catalog of comics, graphic novels, prose novels, artist
monographs, and other fine works of high artistry, call 1-800-657-1100, or visit
www.fantagraphics.com. You may order books at our web site or by phone.

ISBN: 978-1-60699-604-1

First Fantagraphics Books printing: June, 2013